TROUBLED TIMES

Kurt Ahrens' eyes raced over the graceful, flowing script.

> Kurt dear, this note is to keep a promise and to give you sad news. Abigail slipped away from me in the night. She must have been more conscious of the Indians than ever I guessed, for she faded rapidly from that day on. She hardly slept, she no longer knew me. Yesterday she fell into a troubled sleep. I was outside the wagon when I heard her shriek: "Father! Joel!" Joel, you know, was her husband. I ran to her, but she was unconscious and never moved or spoke again. We buried her under the big oak at the edge of the hollow . . . Now I shall push on to Albany. It would help so much if I could see you. But I haven't the courage to say, "Come to me." We may meet again, but we live in a tangled world that seems to have little pity on individuals. If we do not meet—then the thought of you will be a very precious thing to me. Oh, my love, do look to yourself in the hard days to come.
>
> JUDITH

Almost mechanically he slipped the letter into his inner pocket. "Good God! How shall I ever find her now. She's off for Albany and may get there before we do. Where will she go?"

Kurt pulled on his boots and scrambled out of the shelter. He was very young and it was his very first war . . .

Other Pinnacle Books by Bruce Lancaster:

THE SECRET ROAD
PHANTOM FORTRESS
BLIND JOURNEY
GUNS OF BURGOYNE

GUNS OF BURGOYNE
by Bruce Lancaster

PINNACLE BOOKS   NEW YORK CITY

GUNS OF BURGOYNE

Copyright 1939 by Frederic A. Stokes Company
Copyright © renewed 1967 by Mrs. Bruce Lancaster

A Pinnacle Books edition, published by special arrangement with J. B. Lippincott Company

ISBN: 0-523-00986-0

First printing, January 1977

Cover illustration by Bruce Minney

Printed in the United States of America

PINNACLE BOOKS, INC.
275 Madison Avenue
New York, N. Y. 10016

FOR
MY WIFE
JESSIE PAYNE LANCASTER

CONTENTS

Guns of Burgoyne

While minor chronological liberties have been taken with the movements of some of the lesser historical characters, the general course of events as recorded in contemporary documents has been followed.

In the Cambridge scenes, nomenclatures which post-date the Revolution have been applied to certain localities and districts. This has been done to facilitate identification.

The Inn

I

The Inn

KURT AHRENS paused by the broad door of Der Rosenstrauch and watched the long-tongued flames that
leaped and darted from the big bonfire in the Altstader
Marktplatz. They traced a scurry of dancing light on the
timbered front of the old Town Hall and along the steep
pointed gables of the houses that crowded close. The
wavering glow, ebbing and mounting under a steady
rain, made of the crowd in the wet twilight a shifting,
unreal, amorphous mass. Faces blurred drunkenly under
sodden woolen caps, were swept into the deep shadow
of cocked hats, were thrown into sudden, startling relief
beneath the peakless brass plates of the grenadiers' towering helmets. Here and there flickering random light
touched for an instant on gaiter-buttons, on brass gor-
gets, on a bayonet's tapering blade, then fled to glow on
a sullen peasant mouth, the tines of a clumsy pitchfork,
the soft liquid eyes of a patient ox.

The knot of peasants who huddled dully within the
ring of bayonets blinked and shifted uneasily, their eyes
flicking furtively from the crowd, which pressed as close
as it dared to the steel points, to the hard faces of the
sergeants who stood in a stiff group on the streaming
cobbles of the Platz. The evening hush was unbroken,
save for the persistent hissing of the rain and the dull
rumble of heavy carts somewhere off by the Frankfort
gate. Suddenly a woman's voice shrilled piercingly:

3

"Heinrich! Heinrich!" A head lifted within the ring behind the grenadiers, the sergeants glared angrily at the crowd, waving the people back with wide sweeps of their canes.

One hand on the latch of the heavy door, Ahrens looked at the slow shift of the silent mass away from the bayonets. Under the jutting peak of his cocked hat his eyes softened, grew troubled. He shook his head. Then he shrugged wide shoulders and with an easy heave swung open the door. Its slant cut him off from the world of dripping peasants and the brass mitres of the grenadiers. The broad passage before him was dim and warm, reeking pleasantly of fat roasts and mellow beer. He hailed a scurrying maid.

"The room of Colonel von Kleist, liebchen?"

The girl, arms full of folded blankets, stopped, then came slowly toward him, eyes sparkling behind fluttering lids. "The Colonel is in the great room that looks on the Platz. A sergeant guards the door." Plump and demure, she stood close to him. Then she raised her eyes to his. "There is to be a room prepared for the Lieutenant?" she asked softly. The shoulder-knot beneath the flung-back cape had not been lost on her.

Ahrens smiled down at her for a moment. Then he laughed. "That we must leave to the Colonel. It may be that he will send me to the Mill Barracks where the chambermaids are stumbling farm-boys, not plump pixies like—what is your name? ... Ah—like this Nelchen who is going to show me the Colonel's room." Hands lightly on her shoulders, he spun her about and urged her ahead of him with a gentle slap on her generous plumpness. Nelchen giggled, squeaked: "Ach! Lieutenant!" in hushed protest. Then she sighed and trotted on down the corridor, stopping before the blue-and-red sergeant who stood stiffly to attention by a broad threshold.

Eyes on the opposite wall, waxed mustaches stabbing

4

upward, the sergeant saluted. "Sergeant Pruss, Crown Prince Regiment. At the Lieutenant's service."

Ahrens named himself. The sergeant swung open the door, shouted in a parade-ground voice. "Lieutenant Ahrens!"

Ahrens saluted the stout German who goggled bloodshot eyes at him over a paper-littered table, then the tall Englishman in artillery blue and red who lounged negligently by the fireplace.

Colonel von Kleist turned his flushed face to the Englishman and said in a wheezy voice: "Here, Major Charteris. Here's the Saxon I promised you. We've accepted him. He'll take the recruits for Pausch's guns." He held out a pen to Ahrens. "Sign here, young man. Here, where it says, 'At the City of Hanau, twelfth day of March, 1777.'"

Major Charteris rose slowly from his deep chair, stepped to the table. "Just a moment, von Kleist. Like to ask a few questions. His papers?" His German was excellent, though blurred by a strong accent. He took the flimsy sheets, then looked with lazy eyes at the newcomer.

He saw well-kept brown hair, ending in a neat queue, keen gray eyes set wide under a good forehead, well-modeled nose, firm mouth that tended to quirk at the corners, square-cut chin. The Major's eyes lost something of their languor, as he thought to himself: "Six feet and a shade over. Must strip at close to two hundred, but he's not slow. Look well in the ring." Nor could he find fault with the set of the blue jacket with its red plastrons, the white breeches or the shining black boots. Particularly the boots. The Major was a connoisseur of boots. He veiled his eyes again, ruffled the papers.

"Saxon, are you? H'm yes. Born at Dresden, 1750, son of Freiherr Wolfgang Ahrens and so forth and so on. Hello—what's this? Educated at *Harrow*? Harrow?" He raised his eyebrows.

5

"My father was attached to the court of the second George. It was a family office. I spent my early years in England."

Charteris nodded. "More German than English in London in those days. But—educated at Harrow! Why, blast me, so was I!" He slipped into English. "Here, here! Sit down! No need to stand to attention. Harrow! Well, damn my eyes! Know Tommy Tileston of the 45th? Sister married a cousin of his just after Tommy was sent down from Harrow. Well, well." He turned back to his papers. "Now about your service. Never thought much of the Saxon gunnery myself. Waste too many ranging shots. Won't do, you know. Makes the gunners careless. Damned if I wouldn't make each gunner pay for his wasted rounds and have him bloody well flogged into the bargain. Sharpen his eyes for him. How do you handle your galloperwagons? What load for your tumbrils?"

Ahrens sat easily in his deep chair by the fire and answered Charteris' interminable questions on gunnery. From time to time, as he defended some view of his own, points of light showed in his gray eyes, points like sunlight striking on steel.

In the middle of an involved reply dealing with the handling of howitzers in swampy country, the Englishman's clipped tones broke in.

"That's enough, Lieutenant. He'll do, von Kleist. Sorry to have used so much English. Wanted to test him in that, too. Sound man, I say. But look here, Lieutenant, there's one flaw in you. You're too soft with the men in your theories. Work 'em, damn it. Use the cane. Men are cheaper than horses. If you served under me you'd soon learn a thing or two about discipline. Too bloody much pampering in your ideas, just pampering. Old Frederick of Prussia has the right idea. Counts his regiments by the number of canes—five men to a cane and a good sergeant to use it. Your gunnery's good, though, very good."

6

Von Kleist worried at the tight black stock which rose from his yellow collar. "You're prepared to swear him in, then? Never heard so many questions in my life! I've always said that if a man understands a horse and a sword, he's a gentleman. Thank God I'm a dragoon. Can't understand why anyone should want to fuss about with wagons and charges and elevations. Like a teamster or a navvy!"

Charteris flicked up the blue tails of his jacket and sprawled with lazy grace in the chair opposite Ahrens. His gaze on the Colonel was gently quizzical. "I'll not undertake to enlighten you on that point. Doubtless you found my questions interminable. Pitched it in strong to this fellow because you've tried to fob off so many tinkers and merchant tailors as gunners. But he'll do, I say."

Ahrens felt a glow of satisfaction steal over him. His years of study and application at which so many of his Saxon fellows had laughed had borne good fruit. He stretched his long legs toward the fire, flicked a bit of dust from the red cuff of his jacket. Perhaps he would be dismissed now. Well, there was plenty of time, plenty of time. He smiled quietly to himself. The Englishman spoke again.

"These papers, Lieutenant." His dark eyes lost something of their languid superciliousness. "Look here. This says that you are qualified for infantry command as well as artillery." He leaned forward in his chair, his gaze narrow and piercing. "Damn it all! Competent in two branches of the service! Speak English and German equally well. An Harrovian into the bargain and your father a Freiherr. Why the devil do you come to *us*?"

Ahrens met Charteris' gaze steadily. Then he smiled. "My father *was* Freiherr, Major. He died not long ago. There are estates. Also debts. Also entails. And a question about the title. Have you investigated the Saxon service of today? Could you face an eternity of rigid drills, dusty parade-grounds, gunnery limited to firing salutes whenever one of the Elector's mistresses gives birth to another titled bastard? Your whole soul devoted to the exact angle of a gunner's cockade or the precise number of buttons on his gaiters? A palace revolution over the color of jacket-facings? And no advancement?"

Charteris sat back in his chair, laughing. "Damned if I don't think you're right! Dashed good bargain for us, though, and for the whole Hesse-Hanau contingent. You know," he turned a lazy head toward the red-faced Colonel, "you know, von Kleist, there's hardly a man in your lot who can do more than make German grunts. This fellow's English is better than mine. Important thing. Well, give him a pen and he can sign the oath. No need to gabble through it all."

Under the eyes of the Colonel, which bulged as though his tight stock was trying to force them from their sockets, Ahrens signed interminable army forms. He laid down his pen with a sigh. "Are there more formalities, Colonel?"

Von Kleist shook his head. "All is in order," he wheezed. "Unless Major Charteris—" He tilted his head toward the Englishman.

The Major waved a languid hand. "Lieutenant Ahrens has completed another cycle. He has two languages, two branches of the service. Now he has two sovereigns—the Elector of Hesse-Cassel and His Majesty, George the Third, by grace of God King of England and so forth. He will presently set forth by order of the former to do battle for the latter. Let us, von Kleist, call in that black-eyed baggage I saw in the corridor. She shall bring us brandy which we shall drink to the Lieutenant's fortunes in those battles."

Von Kleist flushed with pleasure. "Sergeant Pruss!" he yelled. "Tell the serving wench—brandy for three, large glasses of brandy!"

Three rims clinked by the deep fireplace. Then von Kleist retired behind his table, where he grumbled among his scattered papers between long pulls at his brandy. Charteris lolled in his chair again, attention divided between a long pipe and his rapidly emptying glass. Ahrens sipped slowly, smiling to himself. When Nelchen had served him, her eyes had suddenly sought his, then dropped as she smiled softly. And there was surely no accident in the way her full skirts had brushed against him as she swept out of the room. "Very likely, very likely," he thought. "A pity I have other plans." Covertly he looked at his watch. Just past six. There was plenty of time. He crossed his knees, watched the firelight flick on the shank of his bright spur. He hoped that he might be given leave to go soon.

Charteris rose, set his glass on the mantel with a thud. "Now, Colonel—about those recruits. Why not have your sergeant call them in?"

Von Kleist frowned over his sheets, nodded. "Ready if you are, Major." Then he bellowed: "Pruss! Step to the Platz and tell Sergeant Pirsch to bring in the recruits. Remember—by the rear door of the inn, and one at a time, under guard. No, Lieutenant, you'd best stay. Some of these men may serve under you."

Charteris nodded as the door banged on the retreating Pruss. "Good idea. Ahrens shall see 'em in the raw. *Ab ovo*, I might say. How long will this take, von Kleist?"

The Colonel hitched his heavy chin. "That rests with you, Major. There are twenty-five recruits in this lot, which is the last. If you would only waive the formality of looking at their stupid faces, I'd give you their papers in two minutes."

Charteris laughed. "You know damn well why I insist on feasting my eyes on them. The military commissioner in Anspach foisted off some old men and a few crippled boys as able-bodied grenadiers last month. Colonel Fawcitt blew up like a grenade when he saw them on the ships at Nimwegen. Now his agents must pass each man."

Von Kleist gave a thick grin. "I heard a whisper of that." He wagged his big head. "But was that any worse than the trick your people played on the Brunswick regiments last year? Riedesel bought boots for his men and for the Rhetz regiment in England. The cases were opened at sea. What was in them?" He looked severely at Charteris. "Ladies' slippers, and second-hand at that."

"Honors even, then," chuckled Charteris. "I only hope that your people have wit enough to inspect purchases in advance as we now do. Ha! There's a din outside. Must be your eager volunteers. Here, Ahrens. Will you take this form? It's filled out in advance, one line for each recruit. Note each man, and be sure that everything tallies. See, here. Right! Now, Colonel, I'm ready."

The Englishman was tall, but the grenadier sergeant who saluted from the threshold topped him by half a head. He stooped slightly as he entered, his brass-fronted helmet with its tuft of red wool at the tip tucked under his left arm. Ahrens stared at his scarred face, his abnormally long arms and speculated on the sergeant's reach with saber or bayoneted musket.

"The men have been quiet, Sergeant?" asked Von Kleist.

A hint of a smile flickered between the sergeant's beak-like nose and upturned mustaches. "*I* have been in charge of them, Colonel." His heavy jaws snapped shut on the last word.

"Question answered—and fully," murmured Charteris. "How long have you held them on the Platz?"

"Since three o'clock, Major."

Ahrens looked up from his papers, startled. Since three o'clock—in this rain? Couldn't they—

Von Kleist rasped out Ahrens' unspoken question. "Since three o'clock? In this rain?" He rose, flushing angrily. "What sort of business is this, Sergeant? I've had men broken for less. Over three hours in the rain!" He turned to Ahrens. "What would they say of that in the Saxon service?"

Ahrens frowned. "In any service it's bad soldiering. Why, the recruits will be drenched."

10

"O God!" Von Kleist threw up his hands. "Who said anything about the recruits! Damn the recruits! What about the guard? What about the guard? Keeping *them* in the rain! Don't you know, Sergeant, that their uniforms and equipment are the property of their Colonel, the Count of Hanau? You do? Of course you do! What will the inspector say when he sees their trappings ruined by all this drenching? What did you say about flogging, Major? By God, you were right! Excuses, Sergeant?" He glared at the cloaked giant before him.

"Begging the Colonel's pardon, I know my duty." The sergeant's broad face did not show the slightest emotion. "My men mounted guard by reliefs. Those in the Platz were cloaked. As they were relieved, they gave their cloaks to the new guard, and then waited in the taproom of the Krug. The equipment is dry."

Von Kleist choked. "Cloaks! Cloaks! Since when have the grenadiers of the Crown Prince Regiment been given cloaks, as though they were—were *Colonels*!" He glared at Pirsch.

"The regiment is not given cloaks. But when that line-regiment passed through Hanau last week, I made free to borrow several from them. I serve them out to my men in dirty weather."

"Is it your opinion, Sergeant, that the line-regiment will ask for the return of their cloaks?" drawled Charteris.

Pirsch's eyes swiveled toward the Major. "No, sir, that is not my opinion. They were borrowed beyond the limits of Hanau."

Von Kleist roared with laughter. "By God, Sergeant, you're a soldier, a real soldier! I'll drop a word to your colonel. Let that be a lesson, young Ahrens. Never—er, borrow from your own regiment, and never borrow so that yours may be suspected. Very good indeed, Sergeant. Now for the recruits!"

Ahrens rubbed his chin and remarked dryly that he hoped the recruits were duly consoled for their wetting

11

by being guarded by so expert a soldier as Pirsch. Charteris chuckled. The literal von Kleist nodded violently. "Fine example for them, fine example. Come, come, Sergeant, the first man."

The wet countryman between the tall grenadiers shook back tangled hair from his eyes, looked timidly at von Kleist.

"Name?" snapped the Colonel.

The peasant gulped, his mouth worked feebly.

"Speak!" shouted Pirsch.

"Wilhelm Gold," mumbled the peasant.

" 'Excellency'!" rasped Pirsch.

"Wilhelm Gold, Excellency."

"Age and trade?"

"Twenty-two, Excellency. I work fields by the Kinzig, the left bank."

"Married or betrothed?"

"Betrothed, Excellency." The man's eyes sought von Kleist's. "To Gretel, daughter of Klotz, the miller. We—we wed in May. She was frightened when she saw me with the soldiers. Excellency, I want—I want—"

Von Kleist cut in. "Who the devil cares what *you* want. Let her wait for you. Now, where did you—oh, blast him! Pirsch, you answer for him! Now, where was this man Gold when he volunteered for service?"

"He was in his fields, Colonel."

"And in his fields, he expressed to you his wish to serve in the armed forces of the Elector?"

"That is so, Colonel."

Von Kleist looked over at Ahrens. "This agrees with your papers, Lieutenant?"

"All in order, Colonel." Was all in order, he wondered. He felt a little sick as he stared at the wet man who crouched half dazed between the grenadiers. Nothing to be done, he told himself. Such things had to be. Von Kleist's hard voice recalled him to his list.

"You're sure? Good. Pirsch, have this man Gold wait in the far corner of the room. These two grenadiers will

12

guard him and the others who are brought in. The rest of your command will wait outside and within call. Come, come, animal! Move!" Von Kleist's finger pointed across the room. Uncomprehending, Gold stared at him. Then the butt of a musket jarred on his ribs, forcing him away from the table. Ahrens' eyes followed him, frowning, puzzled. Then a lighter look came into them. Charteris, in his careless drawl, had told the guards to let the man stand near the fire.

Name after name Ahrens checked off. One man had been a silversmith's apprentice in the new quarter of the city, another a boatman on the Main. Here was a farmer, then a tapster, followed by a cooper. Pirsch's testimony never varied, save as to place. All had volunteered for service, he said, one in a rye-field, ten in a church, several more from their homes. Two, who required support from their guards, had come from a tavern, others from glades in the Spessart. Pirsch's patrols had been far-flung.

Ahrens looked up from his list at a new note in von Kleist's voice. "You suspect his papers are forged, Sergeant?"

"Yes, Colonel. I have compared them with the records of the Carters' Guild."

"He made some difficulty about—volunteering?"

The sergeant pointed. There was a fresh cut on the man's cheek-bone, a bruise on his chin.

Von Kleist's congested face turned a deeper shade. "You still say your name is Johann Schmidt?"

The man nodded sulkily.

"Schmidt, Schmidt?" Ahrens saw the Colonel's eyes narrow, studying the man, then heard him bark: "Attention!"

As though a cord had been pulled, the man stiffened. His peasant slouch vanished and his arms snapped to his sides.

Von Kleist sprang to his feet. "By God! I knew it, I knew it!" His voice was husky with excitement. "A deserter from the Prussian army—the Prussian army, as God lives! Look, Charteris, look! The palms of his hands turn outward when he stands to attention." He strode to the man, clamped thumb and finger on an ear half covered with hair. "A deserter! Sneaking south to the French borders, eh? Thought you'd hoodwink us, eh? A carter, eh?" With each exclamation he shook the man's uncropped head. The deserter looked sullenly before him.

Von Kleist drew a long breath, then burst out again. "A carter, eh? Back you go to the arms of His Majesty, King Frederick of Prussia. A warm welcome there, eh? And you know it, you know it! Pirsch! Have this man held in the wagon-shed till further orders! Double guard! Ha! By God! Twenty-five thalers reward into the bargain!"

Charteris' slow drawl seemed to envelope the Colonel's thick tones. "Quite so, quite so, von Kleist. Twenty-five and old Fritz pays on the nail. He must go back, this carter."

Ahrens coughed. "If you don't mind, Colonel—?"

Von Kleist stared. "What is it?"

"A simple question of arithmetic. The man is worth twenty-five thalers as a deserter. But as a volunteer, he is worth thirty to the Elector, if I understand the treaty."

Von Kleist frowned, plucking at his thick underlip. "You mean—"

Charteris stretched himself before the fire. "He means, Colonel, that you had better accept his somewhat headstrong offer to enlist. The difference of five thalers saves him a not too pleasant return journey to Prussia and, no doubt, a firing-squad. Am I right, Lieutenant?"

"Quite, Major," said Ahrens.

Charteris turned to the deserter. "That satisfies you? Loud cries of 'Hear, hear!' from the House. I quote from the Parliamentary Record. Next man, I think."

Ahrens settled himself in his chair again. "Better a live grenadier in Hanau than a deserter before one of Fred-

14

erick's firing-squads," he thought. "Hello, hello! What's this?"

He saw a strongly built man in his early twenties who faced the Colonel with tossed-back head and blazing eyes. His arms were bound behind him. "Good-looking boy," he thought. "Good spirit in those eyes. Pity to see him tied up like a sheep for slaughter. Wonder what—"

Von Kleist's voice rumbled. "You talk for him, Pirsch! We can't be all night! What is the obstinate swine's name?"

"Gustav Rentner." Pirsch glared at the straining man. "Trade?"

"Apprentice to Marx, the wheelwright."

"Married or betrothed?"

"Married."

"Now, Sergeant, where was the man Rentner when *he* volunteered for service?"

Rentner suddenly lunged forward, bound as he was. His guards clamped heavy arms about him, pulled him back from the table panting and struggling.

Von Kleist glared. "Call in one more grenadier! Pass a ramrod through those ropes! Twist it tight! If he struggles again, spread-eagle him."

Ahrens started in his chair, but the sight of von Kleist's furious face killed the protest that was forming on his lips. He shrugged and sat back.

Von Kleist rasped: "Now, Sergeant, my question. *Where* was he?"

Sergeant Pirsch cleared his throat, then bent delicately and whispered in the Colonel's ear. Von Kleist's eyes bulged, his face crimsoned, then his voice whooped in a choking laugh.

"No, damn it! Was it? Ho-ho-ho-ho-ho! The very *night*? And in his cottage? Oh, Sergeant! Rot my blood! No, no! Was she? Oh, damn it, this is too rich!" He wheezed and choked. "Slap my back, Sergeant. Thanks. Oh-oh-oh! Listen to this, Charteris, and you, Ahrens. It was his wedding night! Pirsch and his men visited the

15

cottage to inquire about this man's wishes for service. Ho-ho-ho-ho!" He wiped his streaming eyes, then pointed a trembling finger at Rentner, held helpless by his ropes. "They entered the cottage and there was this man about to tumble his lovely bride. They bound him up, threw a blanket over him and marched him away, leaving the sweet sacrifice unconsummated. Eh? What's that, Sergeant? Oh, God's golden throne! Charteris! The little bride in her shift—or mostly without it—flew at Pirsch's corporal with a knife. He had to trip her up and there she was, rolling in the floor with her shift about her pretty little chin, naked as Mother Eve. Ho-ho-ho! Then he tied her feet and dove out the door, glad to be alive. No one harmed her, beyond the tripping. But she's been wailing like a poltergeist outside the barracks where the volunteers were confined." He wiped his eyes again.

Charteris, shouting with laughter, leaned against the mantel. "Damned if I won't try to get Fawcitt to add another five thalers to the price of this man. Here, here! Guards! Can't you hold that man?"

Rentner was lunging and heaving among the grenadiers. His body shot out across the table, eyes savage and teeth bared. Pirsch sprang forward and forced back Rentner's head with a powerful hand. "The guardroom, Colonel?" he snapped.

"No, no. To the barrack-yard. Peg him out, hands and feet. Six men to stand over him!"

Wrestling and struggling, the knot of men rocked and swayed, then moved slowly toward the door, lunged through it.

Von Kleist wiped his eyes again. "Damned if I would have cared if he'd bit me. Worth it! What a story!"

"Still, pegging out is a bit drastic." Charteris smoothed his dark hair. "Can't blame the lad, goaded like that. He'll be a good man for someone, once his spirit's broken. Fire in him. How do you peg out? As we do?"

The Colonel nodded. "Like a figure 'X.' Pegs in the

16

ground and hands and feet lashed to the pegs. Can't be helped. He'd no right to lunge at me."

"Discipline, von Kleist, discipline. You were right. Note that, Ahrens. Your soft theories would rot a battery in a week. Take the Colonel as a pattern. No shillyshallying there. Next?"

Ahrens' mouth set in a hard line, his eyes glinted. There had been flogging in the Saxon service, prompt punishment for minor infractions, death for desertion or insubordination. But peacetime had eased rigidity a little and the Prussian model had not been so slavishly copied there as in other countries. "Damn it," he thought. "Discipline or no discipline, that man was baited beyond endurance. Can't von Kleist see that a man is a better soldier if he's treated like a human being? A little less luck, a little less money at birth and von Kleist might stand in that man's place. Pegged out on a night like this! Well, nothing that I can do." Then he stared. "Good God, what's this?"

A bright-eyed young man stood jauntily between grenadiers and laughed in von Kleist's teeth as he waved the sergeant aside. "My name is Rudolph Meister, Colonel. Student at the University of Bonn. There was a student joke to which the Provost objected, so I came up the Rhine to the Main and here I am, your very humble servant, begging admission to the armies of the Elector." He bowed with a flourish.

Von Kleist smiled wryly. "You may wish yourself back at Bonn," he observed.

"Not I," Meister laughed. "Your sergeants can be no worse than the combination of my guardian and my tutors. Ho! for glory and a free life!" He bowed again.

Von Kleist turned to Pirsch. "This is true?"

"The papers prove it," said Pirsch. "He ran after Corporal Diehl's squad, begging them to take him. Never heard the like in twenty years' service."

"A little too gay, Sergeant? You'd relish having him in your platoon?" Von Kleist raised heavy eyebrows.

Pirsch's mouth set in a thin line. "I'd give a month's pay," he growled.

From the fireplace Charteris yawned and stretched. "I'd doubt that, my good Pirsch. He'd lead you a merry chase. Well, well. Step aside, lad. Join your new classmates and let the next eager schoolboy face appear."

The rest were unexceptional. Frightened men from farm and workshop, from road and river, ending with an unfathomably stupid young man named Heinz who, through a thick veil of bewilderment, exuded simple-hearted friendship on all the world and tried to chat with the scandalized Colonel about the yield of his land.

Ahrens folded up his list. The tally of recruits was complete. He slipped out his watch. Half-past seven. Still early. It would never do to rush matters. Then he realized that the Colonel was making a speech to the huddle of men in the low room, Charteris affecting to applaud at places he thought to be appropriate.

"—and formally inducted by your own wish into the army of the Elector of Hesse-Cassel and of the Count of Hesse-Hanau. By your agreement, you will now say 'Yes' as sign of assent that you further bind yourselves to serve under the orders of His Majesty, George the Third of England." He turned to Charteris. "You heard their assent?"

Charteris bowed gravely. "It was deafening," he said.

Von Kleist swung back to the crowd. "Under your oath to the Elector *and* to the King of England, you will shortly sail to join that part of the Elector's army which is now serving with the British forces in North America, where they conduct a just and lawful war to wipe out the rebel colonists. Success will attend you."

A low sound, half wail, half moan, rose from the men. A stunned voice muttered, "North America!" Then, with heads bowed and feet dragging, the new soldiers of the Elector shuffled out of the room, von Kleist yelling after them: "Sergeant Pirsch! Make sure that every man knows that desertion, real or attempted, brings the death penalty!"

"Last of the lot, Colonel?" Charteris yawned.

"The last. Tomorrow I go back to regimental duty, God willing. Ouf! What cattle! Did you see the troops that sailed last year? What men! Pausch and his gunners, von Gall and the Crown Prince Regiment!"

Charteris nodded. "Saw 'em at Spithead in the transports. Also Riedesel's men, and Specht's and Baum's and the rest, the Brunswickers. These tonight weren't so bad. Don't forget that last year's lot must have looked like these at some stage in their existence. They're all the same, once a rebel bullet finds 'em. Tell me those louts shoot like devils. Dirty business all around. Might be over there myself, but I've an uncle in Parliament who sees that I stay here. Don't fancy fighting against my own flesh and blood. Cousins in Boston. Dirty business, too, buying your farm-boys and sending 'em over."

Von Kleist spread out his hands. "The Elector so wills it. He has made a bargain with your King, who needs troops. As for tonight—well, if people *won't* enlist, how else is the Elector to keep his promise? *Answer me that.*"

Charteris shook his head. "The Gargantuan Pirsch has answered you in his own inimitable fashion. I'd not venture to improve on that. Well, I'm off for the palace at Philippsruhe. Turn a card or two. See you before you sail, Ahrens. Must look over the Army List and see what old Harrovians are in Canada now. Give you a letter or two. 'Night, Colonel von Kleist." He strolled languidly from the room.

The Colonel looked after him enviously. "He won a hundred crowns at cards last night at the palace." He pursed his lips. "Now as for you, Lieutenant, you'd better report at the Mill Barracks. The Barrack-master will tell you where to bed down. But you're free of duty till nine tomorrow morning. Then report to at my quarters." He goggled his eyes, settled his thick neck in his stock and clumped out of the room, bawling for Pruss and his horse.

Left alone, Ahrens stared into the fire. The procession of dazed men had depressed him, taken some of the edge from the thrill he had felt at the prospect of active service and possible advancement. Active service—with men like that, men dragged from home, from farm, from shop, the only consideration being "Are they strong and healthy?" He sighed, shrugged, told himself again there was nothing he could do about it. He had left the artificial daintiness, the brittle polish of Dresden life and cast himself in with the Hessians, cast himself, he supposed, with his eyes open. The extra pay and allowances would be welcome at the little schloss by the Elbe. No telling what advancement might result, too. A campaign with the British and his sword would be something to sell. Russia? The Turks? He settled his belt about his slim waist. Here he was and he mustn't be too nice about the tools given him.

Then he smiled to himself. Not yet eight, and the Mill Barracks were close by, huddled along the Main. He rubbed his hands in growing contentment, depression vanishing. Not yet eight. He shouted down the broad corridor. Another brandy would banish the last ghosts of the sodden men, quicken his own sense of anticipation. Also he wondered how Nelchen with her plump sparkle would behave now that the others had gone. The prospect was stimulating. With quick fingers he settled the frill of crisp linen that peered from between the buttons of his long white waistcoat, looking down with an expression of indifference. The door swung open and he grunted in disgust as a hard-faced elderly woman appeared.

With an inward laugh at himself he tossed off the brandy. It would hardly do to ask about Nelchen. She was superfluous in any event. Sheer curiosity and time wasted, he thought.

20

The bridge over the Kinzig rang to the hooves of the bay which Ahrens had managed to wheedle from the black-bearded Swabian at the Mill Barracks. "Hope that sergeant won't sit up, waiting for this mount to be brought back," he thought. He patted the bay's neck. "Don't mind being out in a good cause, do you?" he chuckled. The horse whinnied, tossed his head. Ahrens looked at the dark hills, tree covered, that hunched steeply to the night sky. There was a spatter of lights in a half-seen gap, then the hills closed in again.

He found his mind swinging back and back to the men at Der Rosenstrauch. War was hard on poor people, hideously hard. To what would those men return, if ever they did return? Very likely they would be unfitted for their old civilian life, would drift about Europe in the professional armies. One or two might rise to be sergeants. The rest would stagger on till they were worn out, with a license to beg as the only fruits of their years. Hard, damned hard. But—here Ahrens shrugged— for hundreds of years it had been the same story. Why, he himself would much rather work with chemicals and acids, long mathematical equations, the blind forces of nature, than teach country boys the workings of a field-piece. The officers? He never ceased to be amazed at the heavy weather that the professionals made of such really simple chemical and physical phenomena as were involved in gunnery. What other course had been open to him? He must be a gunner, his fate was sealed as were the fates of the drenched men at the inn. The rasonable man adjusted himself to things as they were—and survived.

He marked a crossroads inn at his left, windows shining yellow under the lifting clouds. He stood in his stirrups.

"The road to the right must be the one that turns off to Schollkrippen. There should be a ruined chapel, then a set of iron gates just beyond. Ah—the chapel—the gates!"

Dismounting beyond the pseudo-French tracery of a gate, he slipped the bit from the bay's mouth and tethered him to a tree. "Graze away," he said, slapping the horse gently on his sleek neck. "Don't be afraid if a stranger rides you back to Mill Barracks. Graze and wish me luck!"

The small wicket set into the arching grille gave easily at his touch, then gravel crunched under his light boots as he followed the drive which seemed to curve away into infinity.

"The Count does himself well," muttered Ahrens. "I'll bet a year's pay that when I top this rise I'll see a flat-chested sham Versailles, with a mock Orangerie below. There it is! I knew it!" A huddle of roofs, long windows and balconies loomed ahead in the darkness. A blur of light marked a vast entrance and terraces.

"Now along to the left, till I see a balcony of white marble. This must be it. Yes—second floor, but low, as the ground slopes up steeply."

He halted, peering up at the soft light which filtered through heavy curtains. The bits of gravel he tossed snapped crisply against the panes. Light flared. A figure slipped through partly opened casements. "Lisa!" Ahrens' voice was low, but full.

The woman leaned out, staring into the darkness. "It is you, Kurt? Ah! I am glad. It is *so* long since I saw you in Dresden. I keep your letter telling me that you were coming in my little rosewood casket. You are glad to see me?"

Ahrens laughed in the night. "Here I am, my Countess. Your note described my route perfectly. A staff couldn't have done better. May I inquire as to the health of the Count?"

There was a shrug. "As well as his seventy-two years allow."

"And he is?—"

The light from the window showed a slow smile on her full lips. "He is still in Dresden, Kurt."

"I enter by the main door?"

Lisa drew back slightly. "No, no, Kurt. It is late. I—I could not admit you."

Something heavy seemed to strike and settle about Ahrens' heart. "You set the hour yourself." His voice was impatient. "Lisa, is this to be a repetition of our Dresden meetings? You said then—"

"Hush, Kurt, hush!" Her white arm flashed in the night and something light patted on the ground at his feet. "There—a knot from my gown. You may wear it for a cockade. Now—tell me you've been lonely for me." She leaned on the broad rail, smiling down at him.

Ahrens picked up the silk trifle, crumping it in his hand. "Dresden again, Lisa? When we first met at a palace ball, you told me to forget your title. We should meet again, you said. There was a moment in a carriage—you gave me your lips. What else did you promise, Lisa? Your lips you gave me again. The rest—always excuses. The time was wrong, the place was wrong, we were watched."

"Kurt, Kurt! Be still! Yes, I said what I said. I—I meant it. But you are so much in a hurry. Now go back quietly. I'll send you a note soon, soon. No-no-no! Kurt, you must go!"

With a powerful leap he had swung himself onto the balcony, where he perched lightly on the broad marble rail. "So!" he said. "There is room for two here." Smiling, he looked into her round face topped by masses of straw-blond hair. "The hour is late: eh, Lisa? But—" He swept the tall woman into his arms, pressed his mouth against her full lips. , She gasped, her lips parted, one hand stole to his cheek as she sighed gently. Then she pushed him away, stepped swiftly back by the casement.

"You must go," she said with difficulty.

Ahrens did not move. "Charming, Lisa, charming in that light."

"Go, go, Kurt. We may be seen."

"Who is in the château?"

"Only the servants. My maid is with me, in this wing."

"You trust her?"

"Marie? Oh, yes."

"Then send her to bed—and tell me to cross the sill of that most inviting window."

Lisa shook her head. "No, no, Kurt." She spoke rapidly, nervously. "You may stay—but just where you are—for another minute. Oh, Kurt!"

With firm hands he drew her out of the halo of light, gently tipped back her head. She twisted her neck, straining away from him, shaking her blond curls. "No, no! Kurt, be a good boy. Can't you—can't you forget about Dresden?"

He smiled down on her. "No, Lisa. Nor can you. Do you remember what you said to me? Shall I tell you? You pressed against me in the carriage that time. You said your love answered mine, that you wanted to be mine, that you wanted me as I wanted you. Often after that you said it. Lisa—here I am!"

Suddenly she kissed him, an arm flung over his shoulder. "I *did* say that. I still say it, Kurt. See. I kiss you so, and so and so! Ahhh! Kurt, give me your hand. See how my heart beats—for you."

There was firm flesh beneath his palm. Slowly his hand stole upward, slipping the covering from her soft shoulder. "Lisa! Lisa!" he whispered.

With a wrench she freed herself, one hand rearranging her disordered dress, her face pale. "There is a bell-pull just inside the window!" Her voice was tense. "If I ring it, the major-domo will answer. He is devoted to the Count. Now—go!"

Ahrens stepped back, eyes narrowed. "Yes—you would pull that bell, too," he said slowly. "Damn you for a cheating cat!"

Lisa's eyes blazed. "Once more—" Her round arm reached inside the room.

He stared at her. Then suddenly and uncontrollably he began to laugh. He bowed mockingly, and said between peals of laughter, "My dear Lisa. Really, you are superb. Magnificent! Ho-ho-ho-ho! My compliments!"

He slipped easily over the rail, dropped to the soft earth. Hand pressed to her cheek, Lisa stared after him. Her lips began to quiver. She threw her hands over her eyes and stumbled into the room.

Still laughing, Ahrens rode back toward the bridge over the Kinzig. "Damned if she wasn't right," he thought. "I trotted after her, panting, like a green boy. H'm, she'd better not miss many more opportunities. Begins to show her age. What a figure, though—and what a skin! She was perfectly shameless in her love-making in Dresden. I wonder if she knew that von Seeckt woman, who used to strip before her husband's pages, and then have them flogged for attempting liberties which she seemed to offer?"

The Swabian sergeant at the Mill Barracks blinked in the lantern-light. He had seen countless young officers ride off into the night. Rarely did he hear their hoof-beats until the sun had cleared the spires of the Walloon church in the Neustadt. Ahrens laughed at his amazement, tossed him a coin, then walked slowly away. What should he do now? He drew out his watch, held the dial up to a flickering lantern set in the barrack wall. A little after ten? He snapped his fingers and strode off.

"This room will suit the Lieutenant?" The old porter of Der Rosenstrauch bowed before the open door.

"Perfectly." Ahrens stepped over the threshold, barely glancing about him. "I'll ring if I need anything."

The porter bowed over the coin and shuffled away. Ahrens closed his door, then opened it gently. Brisk feet were tapping along the passageway.

"The Colonel was kind to me. See, I am to pass the night here." His outflung arm had halted Nelchen in mid-flight.

"Lieutenant! I was so frightened!" She put her hands

25

to her cheeks, eyes wide. Then she smiled. "I am sure the Lieutenant will sleep well." She moved off, slowly.

Ahrens chuckled, stepped up beside her. "But I sleep badly. I grow frightened in the dark—alone."

"There are candles in the Lieutenant's room," said Nelchen. She caught her underlip in her white teeth, swinging her shoulders slightly.

"And they will keep me company?" Gently Ahrens tilted her round chin upward. Her eyes dropped. An almost imperceptible step brought her closer to him.

"The English major sent word that he wished to speak to me. What will he say if I stop to talk with a lieutenant?" Her eyes were round and solemn, then they wrinkled in a sudden light laugh.

Ahrens frowned in mock solemnity. Hands on the girl's shoulders he looked gravely at her. "Major? Lieutenant? Nelchen, what is rank? A shoulder-knot on a coat. The Major's coat is hung in a press. Mine will be shortly. Then, Nelchen, where is rank?" With a sudden motion he picked her up in his long arms. "Damn the Major! I'm commanding officer now." He carried her into his room and kicked shut the door. Then he kissed Nelchen soundly. She turned away her head, giggled, suddenly pressed her lips to his almost fiercely, arms tight about his neck.

Gently he set her on her feet, hurled his cocked hat deftly at the wavering candle.

"Lieutenant!" Nelchen's low laugh rippled out. Her hands were busy about her bodice.

Pale spring sunlight splashed through the slanting windows set high in the roof of the gun-shed, touched on brass barrels and was thrown back on the ceiling in shimmering aqueous pools. Ahrens sat on the shafts of a field-forge, counting the vehicles and checking them off on a long list. He might have turned this purely routine work over to a sergeant, but some of the items seemed to differ from those he had known in the Saxon service and he felt it would be a good way to familiarize himself with them. Two more galloper-wagons? Where were they? He walked along the shed, eyes roving. Through the big doors that led into the stables he could see Sergeant Zimmer's men breaking open bales of dusty hay, washing down the stone floors. There were the gallopers—there by the big door. He checked them off, started on the tumbrils. In his mind's eye he saw Nelchen slipping from his room in the most fragmentary attire in the grayest of gray dawns, heavy-eyed but smiling. He pulled himself back to reality and in a moment was frowning over the pintle catch which seemed to him better than those he had known in Dresden. He looked up.

Heavy hands thudded against a little door set in the wall at the far end of the shed. He rose, frowning, and walked toward it along the echoing floor. The frame shook, then burst in and a bleeding tattered man tore into the shed, wild-eyed. From outside angry voices stormed: "Stop him! Stop that man!" Hooves thudded and clattered, there was a hurried jingle of dismounting men. The fugitive glared over his shoulder, then rushed to the nearest brass muzzle, throwing his arms about it.

Ahrens drew a deep breath. "What the devil—" he began, his voice rattling among the rafters. Through the flung-back door poured a knot of black-coated infantry, an undersized officer in their rear. "There he is! There he is! Take him, you swine!" The black jackets hesitated, then poised their short carbines and advanced on the man who crouched by the twelve-pounder, gripping it fast. His lungs were working like bellows. His voice crackled: "Sanctuary! I claim sanctuary! Military law! Sanctuary!"

The guards dropped their carbines, nodding wearily. "Three days only," said the sergeant, scowling. "We know your name."

Like a whirlwind their officer was among them, striking right and left with a light cane. "You scum! You swine! Take him! To hell with sanctuary. Eight men to one! Take him!"

The men skipped away from the swinging cane. Two of them laid down their carbines and threw themselves on the ragged man, who raved and struck at them. The officer's voice rose to a shrill yell. "Take him! By God, I'll flog his stinking hide off with my own hands! I'll—"

With cat-like quickness Ahrens stepped to the shouting man. "Call your pack off!" His voice was hard. "Don't you know military law? Bringing your catch-polls into a gun-park! Call them off, I say!" He looked down into shifty cold eyes, a wry nose, an abnormally broad upper lip, all contorted with rage. "Do you hear me?" Ahrens snapped out the words, his eyes steely, narrow. "Your name and regiment—at once! Bringing dirty provost-guards into a *gun-park*! Have you never heard of the rights of the artillery?"

"That man is a deserter! He escaped last night when he was about to be pegged out. I'm taking him with me, or, by God, someone will fry in hell!"

Ahrens turned to the guards. "Release that man! At once! By God, it's Rentner! Sergeant! You heard me. Stand clear!" He pointed to the officer. "Your name and regiment!"

"My name? You'll learn it soon enough. Lieutenant Donohoe of the Provost's staff. That man goes with me."

"Military law! If a soldier of any arm, pursued by the provost, can reach the artillery-park and lay his hand on a gun, he thereby gains sanctuary for three full days. Correct me if I misquote. No? Then—march!"

Donohoe fell back a pace. "Sergeant! Take the prisoner! You other men—cover this officer with your carbines." The men shifted uneasily, then looked up as a voice, rising almost to a screech cut through the air.

"What in the name of ten thousand devils are those stinking guards doing in *my* gun-park?" From a balcony set high on the wall the savage face of Major Zapfel glared down. "You—artillery lieutenant—what's the meaning of this? In my park!"

Ahrens faced the balcony, saluted. "Lieutenant Ahrens, sir. The guard tried to seize this man after he had laid hands on a gun. Their officer says he will use force to remove him. He does not appear to know the law."

Zapfel reared back as though struck. "Take a man from *my* park—after he has touched a *gun*! You! I've seen you before! Donohoe, that's your name. Your father served with me in Claire's brigade. He'd turn in his grave to see his son, an *infantryman* and a provost, enter a gun-park! March those men out!"

Donohoe's broad lip quivered with anger. He started to speak, but a yell from the balcony and a sweep of the old Major's arm cut him off. With a sullen glare at Ahrens, he filed his men out, muttering.

"See to the fugitive, Lieutenant. Don't know what he's done. Don't want to know. Turn him over to the barrack-master. Provost in *my* gun-park! Gaaahh!" The Major stumped away through the narrow door at the rear of the balcony.

Ahrens looked at the man who still clung to the twelve-pounder, panting. "You're in a tight corner, my friend," he said.

Rentner's sunken eyes stared wildly at him. "I've three days, three days!" he muttered.

"And then?"

As though violently pushed by an unseen hand, the man collapsed over the barrel of the gun, head buried in his arms. His shoulders heaved. "I don't know. They can't take me. Seven years I've served as 'prentice. Next month I should be journeyman. I—I married yesterday."

"Too bad. Too bad." Ahrens' hand fell gently on the man's shoulder. "But the Elector must have men. You know that. He must keep his promises."

Rentner's head slowly lifted from his arms. "Promises! That is easy to say. But his promise to me? My name was drawn a week ago. According to law I bought a substitute. Fifteen thalers I paid—all my savings and my brother's. They took the substitute. Then they took me, although I had paid."

"You wander from the point, man." Ahrens shrugged. "The Elector *must* have men. Do you forget that you, that all peasants and townsfolk, owe allegiance to him for his protection? Who keeps your fields, your shops from being ravaged? The Elector. Now you make return to him for his benevolence."

"Protection!" Rentner's head rocked on his crossed arms. "From bandits, marauders—yes. But I had rather have them than the Elector's bailiffs and tax-men. The bandits I can fight. The others—they suck our blood. It is death to resist." He pushed himself erect. "My master, the wright, sometimes builds fine coaches for the court. Does he profit? The bailiffs see to that. Look, Lieutenant! The Colonel was angry last night because none of the men knew firearms. Why didn't they? Because the peasant is forbidden them. My father works his fields. The birds eat his crops. He can't drive them off, he can't shoot them. He may not own a musket. Why? Because it might frighten off the birds that the lords from the court love to hunt. Mustn't spoil their game. So, as a reward for killing taxes and ruined crops, I am cheated of the substitute I hired for the army. I am seized, to be sent I don't know where."

"Damnably hard, damnably hard." Ahrens was thoughtful. "But there is no help for it."

The man muttered on. "And if I return? My trade will be gone, my skill forgotten. My wife—who will feed her?" He slammed a big fist on the smooth brass of the barrel.

"There is no answering him," Ahrens thought. "Nor for that matter can *he* answer me. The Elector holds the power. Struggling is no solution. Here—what the devil am I doing? Chatting with a recruit, a runaway one at that!" His eyes flashed. Last night at the inn he had pit-

30

ied the man, but realized himself helpless to do anything. Now the mazes of military law showed him a way. He slapped his hand on the broad rim of the wheel.

"Look up, man, look up." Rentner raised heavy eyes to his. "You have three days' grace. At the end of that time, that Irish ape will take you. You'll probably be shot."

"No—no. Not that! I'll slip over the border!"

"Have you thought just how? There are tight cordons about Hanau for just such emergencies. No, no. You mend nothing by struggling. But I can do this for you. I will have the barrackmaster place your name on the list of artillery recruits. No provost may touch a gunner— only his own officers may. Major Zapfel will never move against you—he's too furious at Donohoe's intrusion. The custom of sanctuary and other artillery privileges are silly but—it's the way things are. Might as well take advantage of them. I guarantee, once you're a gunner, that you've heard the last of your pursuers."

Hope flickered in Rentner's eyes. He plucked at the torn sleeve of his coarse linen shirt. Then the light died again. "But I still lose Hedwig."

"By no means! A girl who has the heart to fly at Pirsch's men is too good to leave behind. We sail with nearly as many women as men. The artillery complement is not filled yet. Tell your Hedwig to pack a bundle and be ready to join you. She'll draw the same rations as you do. Matter of law. You'll berth in the married quarters on the transport. Very comfortable, I'm told. Three couples to a berth and no single men allowed beyond the doors."

"Sail? Sail?" repeated Rentner unsteadily.

"Sail—yes. We join the British in North America, help them against the rebels there. Come, man. Head up! There will be an easy victory. After that—who knows? I've heard rumors of free lands for the asking. The Americas are big. Better than starving as a wright. Lord of your own acres, perhaps!"

31

Rentner straightened up. "*You* will do this for me? You, an officer? Free of the provost! Hedwig may go! Lands, lands of my own—perhaps." He swayed, still frozen to the brass throat of the gun. Suddenly he sank to the floor, racked by dry sobs.

Ahrens turned away. Almost irritably he said, "On your feet, man. This is no way to begin as a gunner. Here—help me with the tally of the park. Your first work. You'll learn something, too. Now, in this tumbril there should be a full set of pioneer's tools. Twelve picks—twelve long-handled shovels. Count them, then we'll go on to the other tools."

Rentner's wide shoulders bent over the thrown-back lid of the wagon, strong hands rattling among the tools. "Twelve picks, Lieutenant. Shovels—shovels?" His voice suddenly exploded. "Thieves! Thieves! Look, Lieutenant. Two are missing. *Someone has been stealing from us!*"

Ahrens grinned as he studied his list.

"Major Charteris, will you be good enough to explain the embarkation orders to the Lieutenant?" Colonel von Kleist set his stein on the table with a gurgling thud, wheezed slightly as he brushed stray crumbs of tobacco from the yellow facings of his coat. "He was on special duty yesterday and missed the discussion."

"Please, Colonel." Charteris' muscular hands unfolded a mass of heavy sheets. "Now look here, young Ahrens. Recruits form here, infantry on the right. March from the barrack-yard to the river-front. Boats moored here. Follow?"

Ahrens nodded. "The first boat is about by the old sawmill, according to the map."

"Right. Now, you are in charge of boat Number Three. Forty men, eighteen women. Don't get the single men mixed with the married. Elector doesn't get paid if there are deaths from brawls. Provisions stored here. If they run short, clap the head cook in irons. Means he's been pilfering. Boats lie-to each night."

"Lie-to each night?" Ahrens looked at the map. "May I billet my men ashore, then? Much more comfortable for them. I can smell those river-boats a mile from the banks."

"Now, now, Lieutenant. Your humanitarian instincts run away with you. This war is *not* being fought to make the men comfortable. See these crosses marked on the river? Ships anchor in midstream, proceed at daybreak. See the logic?"

Ahrens smiled dryly. "In his address to the troops, the Elector stressed the blasting enormity of the sin of desertion. Few of the men can swim. You lead them not into temptation, which might come their way if they were billeted ashore."

"Exactly. You see, no payment is made the Elector for deserters. Therefore, dreadful crime. Now, for communication between boats on the river." He explained arrangements, touched on possible difficulties in passing the frontier of Rhenish Prussia, of Holland. Ahrens jotted down notes. Von Kleist grunted and puffed at his pipe.

At last Charteris folded his papers. "That's all. You cross the Dutch border at Nimwegen, drop along to Dortrecht, where you will be packed on transports. Sail to Spithead, meet other transports, some with British troops, some with Brunswickers, an Anspach unit or two, probably men from Anhalt-Zerbst and Waldeck. The fleet assembles, you'll be reviewed. Then ho! for the bounding main or something of the sort. Take plenty of books. You may be ninety days or more at sea. What do you think of your men?"

Von Kleist leaned forward in his chair, twisting his mustaches till their sharp points seemed to threaten his congested eyes. "I'll tell you what he thinks of them. He thinks they're all young counts and barons. Listen to me. One hundred and seventy-eight recruits, counting those who volunteered the same night that he joined us. Twenty-seven assigned to the artillery. How many floggings has the Lieutenant ordered? I've seen the books. Three, Major—three in nearly three weeks." He thrust out his heavy chin. "Three—and twenty-seven recruits. Pampering. Just as you said. And worse—he stole that man—you remember him, the one whom Pirsch took hot from the marriage bed, the one who tried to assault *me*. Stole him, he did, from the provost and had him enrolled in the artillery. Old Zapfel yells like a fiend in the pit when I talk of seizing him. Stole him, sir."

Charteris laughed, slapped his thigh. "Did you, by Gad!"

Ahrens nodded. "A misshapen ape of an Irishman who has somehow drifted into this service, tried to drag him from the gun-park where he had taken refuge. Major Zapfel was furious."

Charteris gaped in amazement. "From—from the gun-park?"

Von Kleist worried at his stock. "Oh, the Lieutenant was within his rights, even if the custom, a damn silly one, ought to have been dead these fifty years."

"In a *gun-park*!" Charteris shook his head. "As to those floggings. Have to mend that, young man. Doesn't matter if the men don't deserve it. Flog 'em anyway. Keeps 'em alert, I tell you."

Von Kleist rose, belching slightly. "Well, that's your responsibility now, Major. He's under your flag. Gentlemen, I wish you good-afternoon." He swept from the room in a cloud of beer and tobacco fumes.

"Fine old fellow," smiled Charteris. "One of the old school. Not many left. Real soldier, you know. Well, duties clear to you?"

"Thanks to you, Major. May I suggest a libation?"

"Excellent idea. Here—no need to go out. Let's take advantage of the Colonel's good brandy." He coolly opened a cupboard whose shelves glowed dully with squat bottles. "Brandy—yes, brandy." He filled two glasses. "Your health."

"Yours, Major." He drank deeply. "Why are Mars and Bacchus so inseparable? I made a call last night on some

34

infantry officers. They were still opening bottles when I left a little before sunrise. Thank God I've a good head.'"

"If it weren't for Bacchus—*and* Venus, Mars would starve. Give me a hogshead of rum, a competent number of wenches—oh, yes, and a band—and I'll recruit your brigade in a Quaker meeting-house. You'll need your head, serving under Burgoyne. In Portugal we used to call him 'Bed-and-bottle Johnny.' Great man for a drink or a wench. Now I hear the men call him 'Gentleman Johnny.'"

"How do you, know that? That Burgoyne has a command and that we are to serve under him?" Ahrens stared. "I thought our destination was secret."

Charteris filled the glasses again. "So it is. That's how I happen to know. A secret expedition, my young friend, is *always* cloaked in deep mystery—to those most concerned. The rest of the world knows every detail. Gentleman Johnny is an old Westminster boy. Parenthetically, Harrow will impress him. From a friend, also Westminster, I learned all that Gentleman Johnny knows about the expedition—and more, a good deal more."

"Then he will replace Howe at New York? I've heard that there's damn good artillery country about there."

"Devil a bit. Look here. I'm communicating treasonable matter to you. No one else, save all London and the Cinque Ports, knows of this—not to mention all Canada and probably Mr. Washington." On the back of a paper-bound book he sketched rapidly. "Canada. Here's the St. Lawrence River, cutting in—*so*. Here's a long lake, Champlain, driving south, deep into the heart of the rebel country and draining into the St. Lawrence by this little river, the Richelieu. Now—south again, the lake narrows. Forts here and here—east and west bank. Montcalm defended the west forts against Abercromby in '58 and scuppered most of the Black Watch. Name is—is Ticonderoga. Now these forts cut off all travel up and down the lake if the right party holds them. Clear?"

Ahrens studied the sketch. "The forts are where the

lake narrows. Yes. Can't be more than a cannon-shot across if you've drawn them to scale."

"I have, pretty nearly. Well, last fall we destroyed the rebel fleet on the lake. Early this summer Burgoyne will move south by water and attack the forts. Then the the big set-piece. He takes the forts, moves south. Here's Lake George, really an arm of Champlain. Here's the Hudson, just a short jump from the south end of either lake." His pencil moved back and forth. "You see? Water communications from Quebec, which is the base, clear to the Hudson, barring the short neck between lakes and river. Now—Gentleman Johnny moves south, south again, down the Hudson, driving the rebels before him."

"If they permit, I suppose," murmured Ahrens.

Charteris waved the rebels away carelessly. "No choice. Because, according to plan, when Burgoyne reaches—reaches—oh, yes, Albany—here—he will join hands with Howe, who will have pushed north along the Hudson from New York at the mouth of the river. A third column also joins them, having marched east along the Mohawk River, which joins the Hudson at this same Albany, or just above it. Follow? We hold a water-line nearly unbroken, from New York clear to the St. Lawrence. The rebellion is cut in two." He threw down his pencil.

"Magnificent! Magnificent!" Ahrens struck his hand on the table. "Clear—lucid. Works out like a mathematical equation. And a summer campaign in that country! I've talked with French officers who served there in the old wars. Fish, game, fine trees, country like a king's park. Gad! Wish I were there now. And the rebels will soon be beaten! Major, I'll write you from New York in September at the latest. Only wish I had more time to train my gunners. They've barely learned to wear a uniform and hook their drag-ropes onto a piece."

Charteris laughed, clapped him on the shoulder. "Almost make me wish I were going with you. Don't trouble about your recruits, though. Most likely they'll join

36

the garrison at Quebec for more drill. May never smell powder. If you meet the right people, you'll be sent along to join old Pausch and his guns in the march south. If not, you'll at least have a pleasant summer and autumn in Quebec or Trois Rivières. I've written a letter or two that may help you. Now I'm off for Philippsruhe to give zu Haugwitz his revenge. That's all. Be at Number Three boat at seven tomorrow night, ready for your men when they march down."

"Good-night, Major, and thank you. I'll write you from New York, as I said, after we've met Howe's men at Albany."

A light rain began to fall as Ahrens reached the riverfront close by the fragrant lumber-stacks of the old sawmill. He watched the drops trace an intricate, endless pattern of circles on the leaden ruffle of the Main.

"Poor devils!" he thought. "They'll embark tonight in the wet. Many of them will sleep on bare decks. I noticed that the standards of the garrison troops had oilcloth cases. Why not for the men? Cloaks for *all* ranks! Pampering, Charteris would call it. Sensible idea, though. Waterproofing for a square yard of silk, but nothing for six feet of bone and muscle. I wonder—Ah! Here they come."

Fifes shrieked and raved above a thick mutter of drums somewhere in the city, swelling in volume, then dying away only to sweep up again into shrill levels. "They're coming by the Street of the Goldsmiths," thought Ahrens. "I swear I can follow each twist and bend. There—the music grows faint. They're passing that house with the carved head on the gable. Now they're by the fountain in the little square. Here come the provost's men."

A column of black-jacketed men, cocked hats shining in the wet, filed from a steep street, spread along the quays and halted, blocking all approaches to the landings.

"Is the wry-necked Donohoe with them?" wondered Ahrens. He peered through the rain at the officers, but they were all heavy-set men, obviously German.

The fifes drew nearer. Ahrens' feet tapped in time to the swinging march. A clatter of feet sounded through the snap and bang of the drums. In the dark throat of the sloping street he caught a glint of brass as the tall helmets of the grenadiers swung into sight, followed by rank after rank of cocked hats. They filed onto the quay, lined the walls facing the gently swaying ships. Back of a platoon of mincing cavalry came the white-bound hats of the gunners.

Ahrens walked between the opened ranks of the gunners as they stood stiffly by the wall. In a low tone he spoke to this man or that. "Take up the straps of your pack when you get on board. Hangs too low." . . . "Trim your hair before the ship passes Koblenz. May be paraded ashore there for inspection." . . . "Hat too small? Change with Wolf. His is too large." . . . "Shorten your bayonet-sling." Inwardly, the men relaxed. Inspections by other officers had often meant floggings for a strap too lose, a button missing. This was different.

By Meister, the runaway student from Bonn, Ahrens paused. "Where the devil is your stock?"

"Pocket, sir."

"Why didn't you put it on?"

"Late for parade, sir. No time."

"No one noticed it?"

"Only you, sir."

"Put it on the instant you get on board. And if I ever see you without it again, I'll have you shot by dragoons and buried by sappers without benefit of clergy. Understand?" He passed on. The stupid farmer, Heinz, who had tried to chat with von Kleist, grinned in a neighborly manner, in no way abashed by the savage glare that Ahrens gave him. "Have to speak to that fellow. He'll try to pass the time of day with a general and ask him how his old woman is. God!"

The ranks closed, the line wheeled, broke into column and marched off toward the gang-plank. Now for the women. He broke the line of guards at the mouth of a side-street and found nearly a score of women waiting patiently in the rain. They sat on awkward bundles on the cobbles while their guard of grenadiers leaned on thick muskets and exchanged a steady flow of coarse banter with them.

"What do you go off with that green lot for?"

"At least they're *men*. Going to the wars, not swilling in Hanau taverns!"

"*We're* not men? Who said that? Slip up this alley, pretty, and I'll show you I'm a better man than any yokel on the ships."

"Know what the girls in town call your lot? The Poxy Fusiliers."

"Poxy?"

"Yes, Poxy. That's why you're left behind. They won't send pox-ridden men to the wars."

"Damned trollop! Where— Beg the Lieutenant's pardon. Didn't see him in the dark."

"You in charge? Rank? Can't see your uniform in this light. Corporal? Too damned much loose talk here. Fall in your men. On your feet, girls. Off you go!"

In a chattering mass they surged past him, young girls and mature women, some pretty, some coarse, some reeling a little. Bringing up the rear a tall blond girl stepped briskly along, head held high and carrying lightly a great bundle. As she came abreast of Ahrens she hesitated, then said in a low, clear voice, "The Lieutenant was good." He walked slowly after them.

Hoof-beats sounded on the empty quay and Ahrens found himself admiring the English seat for the hundredth time as Charteris rode down through the rain, accompanied by several officers of the garrison.

"All in order, Lieutenant?" the Major called, recognizing Ahrens' tall form in the murk.

"All in order on Number Three boat, sir."

39

There was a chuckle in the darkness. "Right. Never commit yourself about others. See you at Dortrecht." He clattered off toward the first river-boat.

A last look along the quays. Something white waved under the elbow of a guard at the street mouth. Ahrens stepped to the provost's line, which parted to let him through. From the depths of a capacious hood a tilted nose and round cheeks, ruddy with the light rain, peeped out.

"A letter for the Lieutenant. The bearer—a lackey—waits. I did not tell him the Lieutenant would not return."

He sniffed the heavy reek of the paper with distaste, then held a coroneted sheet to the light of a lamp that guttered in a niche in the wall.

"*Kurt, my love. I am sorry. I will be on the balcony tomorrow night. L.*"

He crumpled the note, pitched it into the streaming gutter which carried it off to the Main.

"There is an answer? The lackey waits."

"No answer fit for *your* ears, little Nelchen." He stooped and kissed her lips, fresh and cool with the rain. "Now run along to the inn. I'll bring you an Indian slave and a pocketful of gold from America."

Nelchen giggled. "Bring me another kiss like this." She clung to him for a moment. Then her wooden shoes clacked away through the wet darkness.

Ahrens ran to the gang-plank, up its swaying length. "Guard! No one else is to land."

The guard saluted. Ahrens started along the deck. Then he turned. "And, guard!" he snapped. "Remember—no single men in the women's quarters!"

Day by day the little flotilla dropped down the Main, the Rhine. Each night they anchored in midstream off Frankfort, off Caub, off Ober Winter, Koln, Zons whose distant lights glowed and twinkled across the river-ripples. Ahrens, lonely on his crowded ship, wondered what lay at the end of that watery track stretching west from the blunt bow.

A war in a wilderness, armies maneuvering over an empty continent. He saw himself moving his guns deftly, swiftly, across endless level plains saw swarming uniforms, red for the English, blue for his people, pushing on along the smooth banks of a mighty river. Of the enemy he seldom thought. His gunner's mind shaped them as "targets," went no farther than that. His own men? Charteris seemed faintly contemptuous of the foreign troops his King had hired. Why? Well, after all, such troops *were* mercenaries; that took away from their stature a little. Had to be, though, even if not quite admirable. With a sudden shock he realized that *he*, himself, was mercenary. He had sold his sword to the Elector, knowing that the latter would in turn sell it to the English. A mercenary, as were the various Dutch, Danish, Swedish officers he found in the Hanau contingent. Well—it was the way things were.

The blunt bows drove on down the Rhine. Ahrens watched the high banks slip by. By day the men and women crowded the deck, staring. By night they huddled in their quarters. Often they sang. "Psalms," thought Ahrens. "How Charteris sneered at that! Fighting men singing psalms! Why not? The English don't. Therefore Charteris waves it away." He cocked his head. Rich tones welled up through the planks of the deck:

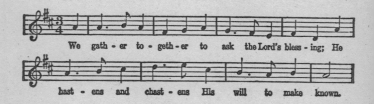

We gath-er to-geth-er to ask the Lord's bless-ing; He hast-ens and chast-ens His will to make known.

Ahrens sang softly with them:

> "The wicked oppressing
> Cease them from distressing.
> Sing praises to His name, He forgets not His
> own."

The river current hissed and slapped about the bows.
The boats slipped on as the men sang.

The Lake

BURGOYNE embarked his army in a vast flotilla and moved easily down Lake Champlain. He landed at Crown Point, a few miles above Ticonderoga, and slowly hushed his advance corps under Fraser south along the west bank toward the neck of land which jutted out into the narrow throat of the lake.

In the blue-stone forts of Ticonderoga, General Arthur St. Clair counted his scanty, ill-trained force, his slender stock of supplies, and looked across the strong bridge that linked him with the works on the east bank which had been christened Mount Independence. That bridge secured his retreat, if necessary, to the country at the head of the lake where he could join his garrison to the forces of General Schuyler commanding the Northern Army. In the meantime, he wondered just where Burgoyne was and what he planned to do.

II

The Lake

LATE June sunrise flicked the crests of the Green Mountains, threw a dull glow over the flats below, turned the waters of Champlain from a dead steel to a molten gold, then skirted the tops of the pines that ran endlessly north and south and lay full on the peaks of the Adirondacks. Along the west bank of the lake, pine and hardwood presented an unbroken front of lifting trunks and jutting branches save where some rare cabin, huddled in a clearing, clung close to the water's edge, and where, in a jagged belt of sand and stumps, seven thousand Englishmen and Germans had spread their white city of canvas about the stone barracks of Crown Point.

There the lake-front began to dot with the life of a new day. Smoke, blue and twisting, coiled into the fresh air, axes rang with a hollow "pock-pock." Over a slight rise, eager horses stamped and snorted, tugging at their halters as they dragged sleepy-eyed men in white breeches down to the crisp waves that slapped and hissed on the shore. Tousle-headed figures, singly and in pairs, trotted heavily to the lake with buckets and fat-bellied camp-kettles. By a stream in a grove, half-naked men shaved in cold water, washed shapeless garments, flogged at dangling white breeches to rid them of dust and dried mud.

From the mouth of an alder-hung stream a long canoe, snake-like in its deftness, shot out into the lake,

45

thirty paddles rising and falling in unison, copper arms catching the oblique rays of the sun. Feathers, braided into stiff scalp-locks, quivered in the steady breeze from the shore. Thirty heads turned to the north, beady eyes fixed on a spatter of white sails working up the lake. The Indian in the bow grunted, "English." Thirty paddles dipped again.

On the deck of the leading sloop Ahrens stood by the bow-sprit, one foot on the low rail, his right hand clutching a halyard. Head thrown back, bright eyes fixed on the glowing surface of the lake, he laughed aloud as he drew into his powerful lungs great gusts of early morning air, heavy with the scent of wet moss, pine-needles, rocky brooks and all the exhalations which the wind brought with it in its easterly career over a thousand miles of untouched country.

For sixty-three days he had pitched in a foul transport, released from the Guinea slave-trade and the hot swamps about the mouth of the Niger to bring Hessian peasants to fight for an English king in the echoing New World. His brother-officers had been quarrelsome, there was always trouble in the married quarters, and the fresh food had spoiled at the end of the second week.

Then there had been the St. Lawrence, the high bastions of Quebec and a sudden plunge into seemingly hopeless routine at the Army base among English officers who looked down on him because he was not English. There had been an almost unbelievable rescue when a tall man in red lounged up to him, said abruptly: "See here. Tell me you were at Harrow. Like to see a bit of the country?" In an hour he was on his way, rocketing over vile roads whose sides seemed studded with crosses, before each of which the driver of his calèche must rein in, leap to the ground and kneel. "Une petite prière, mon officer, une toute petite prière!" A sloop followed the calèche, a canoe the sloop, till he had finally passed the castellated stone walls of the old

French fort at Chambly and pushed up the Richelieu to the teeming base at St. John, where, in the dusk, he had swarmed aboard the present craft just as she was slipping into the current.

Disconsolate on the deck he had found Rentner and his wife, the student Meister and the incurably grinning Heinz, who chattered in low German to a half-breed Canadian who spoke a bastard French tacked onto some Abenaki dialect. He had taken command of the Hanauers, forlorn and forgotten, quickly settled a question of priority as to space with an old sergeant of Brunswick dragoons who was bringing a half-company of men released from hospital to join the army again. Then he made friends with the master of the chartered craft, a villainous-looking French-Canadian who surprisingly produced excellent brandy in his hutch of a cabin and poured with a lavish hand.

Now in the new morning he turned a freshly shaved cheek to the wind and laughed again, staring ahead as night lifted from the lake like a slow curtain. Steely points shone in his eyes. He spun round, caught the master of the sloop in a powerful grip. "Look there!" he shouted.

The master peered forward. "Nothing there, m'sieu. Unless you mean Crown Point, where we anchor!"

"Nothing? Nothing, Maître Chabot?" Ahrens' voice rose in his excitement. "Look—Indians in the big canoe. Twenty, thirty of them! Indians—painted!"

Chabot snorted. "Fi, fi, donc. You cry out over that? One day I take you to the big lakes—not puddles like this. There you see true Indians, fifty, one hundred in a canoe and red and black with their killing-paints!" He shrugged and slouched away.

Ahrens turned back to the lake again. The canoe was slipping easily toward the east shore, then was lost behind a pine-clad point. Two sailors pattered up to the bow, busied themselves coiling a heavy cable. As their hands skilfully paid out and looped the thick strands, they sang:

O Ca - ril - lon, je te re - vois en - core,

Non plus, hé - las, comme en ces jours bé - nis.

Où, dans tes murs la trom-pette so - nore—

"That song again!" thought Ahrens. "Heard nothing but that since I left Quebec. Haunting air, though." He turned to the sailors. "What's that you sing, lads?"

One sailor looked up with a flash of white teeth in a deep-tanned face. The other still bent over the coils, singing. "Ah, the song, m'sieu? It's the lament for Fort Carillon, what you call now Fort Ticonderoga, a lament for the fort and the days of Montcalm." He bent to his work again. The song went on.

"Oui, près de toi, venant chercher ma tombe,
Pour mon drapeau, je viens ici mourir."

"Cheerful," Ahrens smiled. "Every verse ends with dying at Ticonderoga. There it goes again. 'Je viens ici mourir.' Must get that tune, though." He hummed to himself.

In a burst of high spirits Ahrens laughed into the wind that washed about him like a cool stream. He wanted to sing at the top of his lungs, to shout, to share this wakening world with some fellow-being. He looked along the deck where thirty-odd sleepers huddled. "Men

48

and women together," he thought. "Just tangles of cloaks and blankets in all this glory. Funny how all the women in their hour or so ashore at Quebec or Trois Rivières managed to buy themselves that red cloak that seems to be a sort of uniform in Canada. At least, I hope they bought them. Some light fingers among the girls. Well, well. They earn what they get, one hundred times over. It's a long stride from the Main to Champlain."

Yellow light flooded the deck as the sun inched higher. The sprawling forms began to assume individuality. Ahrens eyed them.

"So that's where they bedded down last night! And Hedwig sharing the knapsack for a pillow. There's a soldier's wife." He shouted: "Rentner!"

Cloak and blanket stirred violently. Rentner struggled to his feet, stood to attention with half-closed eyes.

"At ease." Ahrens laughed. "And for your first duty of the day, you might repair a bit of that charming disarray." With his stick he pointed to Hedwig, who, all unconsciously, was offering a quite Hellenic display of her person to the morning. Rentner folded the blanket, adjusted the cloak. Hedwig smiled in her sleep, nuzzling her cheek against the hard knapsack.

"You'll take charge of the unattached men when we land, Rentner, as we arranged last night. The Brunswickers below deck can look after themselves. You are ready?"

"Ready, sir." Rentner's tight jaws snapped, dark eyes on Ahrens.

"The tally?"

"Seventeen men, eight women, sir."

Ahrens drew a list from his pocket, held it to the growing light. "Seventeen and eight. Right. Twelve grenadiers of the Rhetz regiments, two from Specht's and you three Hanau men. We land first, then the women. Heavy baggage the crew will look after. Let the men sleep five minutes more, then wake them."

He turned back to the bow. "Hello, hello!" he muttered. "Begins to look like a war. Two big vessels, almost frigates, anchored off there. Union Jack at the peak and that means Royal Navy. Looks from here as though the shore was paved with barges and bateaux. Gentleman Johnny, you seem to be doing yourself quite well." The breeze stiffened, whipping Ahrens' cloak back from his shoulders. He bared his head, letting the fingers of the wind play through his unpowdered hair.

He became aware of Rentner standing by the rail, eyes glued to the shore. "Wonderful country, Rentner," he said.

The man's gaze narrowed as the unbroken belt of giant trees slipped past. He nodded. "Yes, sir. It's the kind of country that every peasant sees in his dreams. In places the soil is sandy. In others it's black loam. Anything would grow, almost of itself." He sighed. "No doubt some lord keeps it close for his game."

Ahrens laughed. "Open to all, man, open to all. That, is, to all who can fight Indians and bears and wolves."

"You mean, sir, that I, Gustav Rentner, could forget about being a wright and clear me a space by the lake? No count or baron would ride over my fields, send his bailiffs to take my crops—or me?" He laughed. "Indians! Wolves! Those you can fight!" Then he recalled himself. "Any further orders, sir?"

A few moments later Ahrens looked aft. In the stern, Hedwig leaned close to her husband's dark hair as he pointed to the shore. Ahrens chuckled. "God help the bears and Indians!"

Ahrens stood on the swarming sands of Crown Point and watched Rentner scrambling from the bow of a heavy boat. "Land your men and line them up by that beached bateau, Rentner. Women behind them," he called. He saw a puzzled look in the man's eyes, then laughed to himself. There were literally hundreds of bateaux beached on the smooth sand and beyond them some fifty long war-canoes whose coppery owners squat-

50

ted beside them, intent on repairs. "Right, then. The nearest bateau. Then mark a safe place for my baggage when it comes ashore. Stand fast until I send for you."

He walked up the beach. "Now if I ask where Headquarters are, I'll stumble onto some practical joker and end up in a regimental latrine. Lord! It's like Bedlam." He blinked as the swirl of the living camp swallowed him up. Bateaux shuttled back and forth on the lake, laden with men, supplies, horses. Sweating details staggered away from the water carrying heavy buckets on long poles. On a wide, clear space squads of red-coated English and blue-coated Brunswickers drilled, the voices of the sergeants barking sharply in the warming air. Beyond them the city of tents began, with tall barracks of bluish stone looming over them. "Startling, those stone buildings," he thought. "They don't—don't belong here. The trees look as if they were trying to swallow up the walls. It's like finding Versailles at the North Pole."

He skipped past the head of a column of Canadian rangers, vermilion facings on their green jackets, halted abruptly to stare at a file of Indians who drifted past him at a quick, noiseless trot, incurious eyes on the ground. They left in their wake a rank sweetish odor that hung in the nostrils. In the shadow of a fir tree a young bear-cub, chained to a stake, snuffled and grunted as he licked the inside of a tin pail. Above him in the branches, a raccoon clutched a huge turnip in black velvet hands and eyed the passing world through bright, suspicious eyes.

Hooves padded on the ground. Ahrens gave a sudden leap, barely avoided the shoulder of a fine black horse that an English officer was trotting up and down the sands. The black swung on his haunches, a lazy voice said: "Number Three boat still in order, I perceive."

Ahrens gasped, saluted. "Major Charteris!"

The rider slipped to the ground, held out his hand. "I'll be damned, too. Dashed glad to see you. Afraid you got bogged down in Quebec."

"But I thought I saw you row away in a gig after the convoy was reviewed at Spithead!" stammered Ahrens.

"So you may have. But when I reached London, I found that in my absence my uncle had lost his seat in Parliament, and I'd lost my protector. Some people at the War Office who had always wished me out of London, whooped with delight and ordered me to sail at once. I boarded the *Pallas* as she was weighing anchor. Reached Quebec a week before you did—you know how the convoy scattered—and Carlton sent me down here at once. I'm acting A.D.C. to Gentleman Johnny Burgoyne, who appears to be conducting this war according to the noblest traditions of the British stage. Gad, it's good to be on land again! I'll never drink another drop of water so long as I live." He threw back his head, neat queue quivering with his deep laughter. "Not another drop, so help me. And you—you landed from one of those sloops lying offshore?"

"This moment. I was looking for Headquarters. Must report myself and seventeen replacements to the adjutant, then make a dutiful bow to the general."

Charteris pulled out a fat gold watch. "Just lacking eight. Look here, my lad. Rule one: Never disturb Gentleman Johnny before ten unless he sends for you—and then be an hour late. I'll take you to him later. How was your passage over?"

Ahrens smiled ruefully. "There have been worse, I suppose. We were crammed into a Guinea slaver."

"Considering the cargo, I detect a flash of sardonic humor on the part of the Royal Navy. Not bad for a lot of bilgers. Still, that cargo will be damnably welcome. Need men badly, especially gunners. Don't want to be technical, but it strikes me that we are over-artilleried. Fifty-odd guns, and horses very hard to come by. Roads abominable—where there are any."

"What did your ship bring?" asked Ahrens. "Replacements? There were thirty-nine sail in the convoy. Ought to satisfy all needs."

"Ah, but a lot of them swung south to New York. Men for Howe and Clinton. My craft was a merchantman, but she brought the equivalent of, roughly, four brigades of Highlanders."

"*Four* brigades?"

"Their equivalent. No less."

"You mean gold and silver bullets?"

But Charteris was shading his eyes and looking out to the lake. "By gad! Here are the reinforcements now! I couldn't be wrong! 'Pon my soul, it must be! Come along. It should be worth seeing." He strode off toward the beach, hands in his tight pockets, the black clumping obediently in his wake. Ahrens followed, wondering.

By the water's edge Charteris halted. A dozen yards out on the lake, the frailest of birch-bark canoes canted dizzily, then righted itself. The buckskinned Canadian paddling in the bow raised his arms to the sky. In the waist a hooded figure shook a finger at him, clutched at a child who leaned perilously over the side, then turned and harangued the dejected paddler in the stern.

Charteris whooped with laughter. "I knew it! I knew it!" Then he shouted: "My dear Baroness! Welcome to Crown Point and the aegis of His Majesty's Army! I say—look out! She'll be over in a minute!"

The figure in the waist had turned suddenly, causing the canoe to gyrate and the bow-paddler to bury his face in his hands. With a despairing gesture the man in the stern gave a last mighty heave. The craft shot inshore, its bow grating lightly on the sand. Ahrens looked down onto a brown hood which framed a face that seemed to consist principally of a pair of remarkably deep blue eyes and a small, well-shaped mouth that smiled bewitchingly on Charteris.

"Major Charteris, I declare. Take my hand and help me out. What a trip!" Her mouth puckered into a red bud of vexation. "François! Don't drip your silly paddles on my bundles. Gustava! Take your hands out of the

53

water and sit in the middle until Mother gets out. Thank you, Major." She seized Charteris' strong hand, bounced from the canoe, a tiny, vibrant figure. Her mouth puckered again. "Friedericka von Riedesel! Your feet! Your shoes! Soaked, I declare!" She dove into the canoe, lifted out two little girls, who stood solemnly beside her, looking appraisingly at the camp out of eyes as big and blue as their mother's. The Baroness squeaked: "Gaspard! Your feet are resting *squarely* on Caroline and I think you've asked altogether too much for the journey. Major Charteris, isn't ten thalers too much just to bring the four of us from Chambly? And where is my husband? Now, girls, don't you dare move till I get Caroline. No, no! Gaspard! You might drop her." She lifted from the depths of the canoe a bundle of blankets out of which peeped unbelievably a fourth pair of deep blue eyes. "There, Major, you hold Caroline. She's just been changed. What a trip! Who is this young man?"

Ahrens repressed a smile as he answered Charteris' grave presentation. He bowed to the little woman who seemed hardly older than her solemn-faced daughters. "I had the honor of meeting the Baroness' father, Herr von Massow, years ago in Dresden."

"Ahrens?" The Baroness' eyebrows went up. "Son of Freiherr Ahrens of Dresden? Oh, I know all about *you*. Major, his family is *very* nice and I've stayed with his cousins, the von Ahlefelds, near Spandau. The Baron will be *so* interested. And you haven't yet told me where I'm to find the Baron, Major. Perhaps Lieutenant Ahrens knows."

"Unfortunately, Baroness, I only arrived a few moments before you did." His eyes rested admiringly on the upturned face.

"Then *you* know where he is." Her round eyes fixed themselves sternly on the Englishman.

" 'Pon my honor, Baroness, I—"

"Fritschen? Fri-i-i-i-itschen!" A full voice boomed over the water. A canoe swept inshore and a florid, heavily built man catapulted onto the sand, waving his arms from which the broad sleeves of his hooded white blanket-coat flapped and fluttered. "Fritschen, you didn't get my letter telling you to stay in Quebec?"

The Baroness' wide skirts seemed to skim over the sand toward the hooded man. "Friederich! We're here! Such a trip! Where is your uniform? Oh—I'm so happy!" Arms about his neck, she swung her little feet clear of the ground.

"My darling Fritschen! And the girls!" The florid man laughed and swept down on the startled pair. "Gustava! Friedericka!" He held his arms wide, then seized up Gustava. "Kiss your papa, Gustava!"

She wrinkled her face, then suddenly burst into tears, beating little fists against her father's ruddy cheeks. "No! No! You aren't my papa! You're a nasty papa! My papa was pretty. Go away!" She wriggled out of his arms, and hid herself behind her mother's wide skirts.

The Baron looked ruefully at her, then burst out laughing. "Fritschen, Fritschen, she remembers only my portrait in court uniform. Look, Gustava!" Quickly he pulled the blue-edged jacket over his head, stood revealed in a blue coat faced with yellow, immaculate stock and linen, gold edging on his waistcoat. Gustava peered timidly from her refuge, emerged in a noncommittal manner, gave a little hop and squeal of pleasure and was swept aloft in strong arms. Over a gold shoulder-knot she eyed Ahrens. "*Now* this is my papa. Pretty."

"So!" laughed the Baron. "See what gold lace will do to the female heart, Fritschen. And I thought my blue-edged hood so smart! I've had a bout of camp-fever. It seemed to lay one out for three days, no more, no less. Schellen, the surgeon, prescribed this for me to fight off morning chills. But my letter to Quebec, Fritschen?"

Fritschen's eyes grew worried. "Do be careful of Gustava! And you must let me present this nice young

55

man in the artillery uniform. He's an Ahrens from Dresden and a cousin of the von Ahlefelds."

Even with two squirming girls in his arms, the Baron managed to look military as he acknowledged Ahrens' salute. "Any recruits with you? Send them to Sergeant Behr for assignment. He'll look to the women too. Their lines are beyond the barracks. Now, Fritschen, I wrote to Quebec, telling you to stay there. The campaign opens in—oh, almost any day. How ever did you get here?"

"Oh, such a trip! We slept last night on an island. The bushes were full of rattlings and hissings all night long. In the morning we found the place was alive with rattlesnakes. I killed one with a stick and Gustava threw a stone at another and hit one of our boatmen. And there was no place to wash Caroline's clothes. Our quarters are in the barracks? I must unpack at once. Lena and Rockel are coming down by sloop. Oh, and tell General Burgoyne that I *must* have a calèche and a good horse to follow the army." She gently took the Baron's arm, urging him away from the shore. "And you must send a man down to pay my boatmen. The Paymaster at Quebec was horrid. He wouldn't even advance me a thaler and I've no money at all. And give the men two thalers more than they ask."

The General carefully set the girls on the sand, laughing. "To our quarters, then." He bowed, the Baroness bowed. Followed by the two little girls they marched off toward the barracks.

Charteris looked down on Caroline, sleeping peacefully in his arms. "I'll be damned!" he exclaimed.

The Baroness scurried back, snatched up the bundle of blankets, beamed on Charteris and raced back after her husband. Ahrens and the Major heard the Baron's deep voice. "But, Fritschen—my letter to Quebec?" The Baroness' reply was obviously all grave innocence. The Baron's voice rose. "Yes. I wrote, telling you to stop there until the campaign was over."

56

"To stop *there?*" The Baroness' tone was a study in surprise. "The letter must have been delayed. And anyhow, my place is here. Don't scowl, Friederich. I'm twenty-one, after all. Now smile and tell me you're glad that I—that I didn't get that letter." Her voice trailed away across the sands.

Ahrens and Charteris looked at each other, then burst out laughing. "You said the equivalent of *four* brigades, Major? Ten, ten—and a commanding officer of rare talent."

Charteris nodded. "If I were in command, I'd let Mr. Washington know of her arrival. He'd see the point. End the war at once. Better see to your men now. Join me at the barracks at ten. Don't let your men get too settled. Move any day, now."

"Move?" The swarming men, the wide barracks seemed so dwarfed by the primeval stillness of lake and forest that the idea of lunging bayonets and thudding guns seemed almost ludicrous.

"South," said Charteris. "South against the forts at Ticonderoga. Fraser's advance corps must be almost within sight of the works. Just a few miles down the lake from here. Ha! Listen!"

Far down the lake a muffled roar spread over the surface of the water, echoed harshly among the pines. The guns of Burgoyne were speaking. Ahrens' eyes snapped. The thick wrapping of peace fell away from him. "Twelve-pounders," he said. "The light infantry must have pushed up close to the works. Where are *my* guns?"

Morning sunlight, filtered through ten fathoms of pine-boughs, fell like a halo about Gentleman Johnny Burgoyne as he stood, immaculate in scarlet and white, in the deep embrasure of a window that looked out through scattered trees on the sea of swarming canvas and the blue lake beyond. A light step sounded behind him. He turned, smiled on the handsome, full-bosomed

57

and full-lipped woman who looked lazily at him from a little door set in the stone wall of the room.

"Ah, my dear. Charming! That riding-habit becomes you famously, famously. The color—just off gray—and the touch of scarlet at throat and cuff." He crossed to her, bowed, kissed her hand.

Her drooping lids flickered, a smile trembled at the corner of her red mouth. In a low voice she said, "You're not always as ceremonious as this." She moved closer to him, eyes veiled, provocative.

He laughed richly, head back. "Never can tell when some damned aide or other will burst in. Usually they knock. They might forget." He glanced toward the door. "*What* would they say if they saw their General—thus!" His arms folded about her, drew her to him. She gave a low laugh, kissed him full on the mouth. She leaned against him, fingers toying with the gold braid of his long waistcoat. Then she moved back her head, eyes half closed. "I know what *I* say."

"What's that?"

Her voice was low again. "Tell you later."

He pinched her round cheek. Their eyes met in a look of secret understanding. Both smiled. Then he stepped away. "Still, damned awkward if some young prig did dash in. My commissary's wife, you know."

She swung a light glove idly, shrugging. "They all know that Lewis is back at St. John and that Mrs. Lewis is here at Crown Point."

Gentleman Johnny frowned. "Appearances, my dear. Appearances. Good fellow. Lewis. Useful."

The full lips curled scornfully. "He's a sheep." She dismissed the subject. "I've champagne cooling in the well-room. You'll join me soon?" He nodded. Together they strolled to the embrasure, looked on pine-trunks that shone red in the sun. She lifted her chin, stared out. "Dear, dear, dear! Who is *this?* Blue and red, nice white breeches. How well he carries himself! Taller than you—" she laid a white hand on the General's gold-laced

58

cuff, "and what a slim waist! You've not told me of him!"

"Oh, damn his slim waist! After all, I'm fifty-five." Burgoyne laughed a little stiffly.

Mrs. Lewis slipped her hand under his arm. "I know *some*one who'd never guess those fifty-five years." She smiled slowly. "Now tell me who the young man is."

"Blue, with red facings. That's a gunner. No—he's Hessian. See the cut of the hat? They're all blue and red. No—gunner by the boots. Ought to be cavalry. Flat leg-muscles, good length. Here—he must be the gunner Charteris' note spoke of. Was going to bring him himself, but had to send him on alone." He smiled. "I'll join you as soon as I may, my dear."

She pouted a little. "I'm not to meet him, then?"

Gentleman Johnny's eyes widened. "By all means, by all means. But I'll have to put a mess of dull questions to him. Military matters, then pack him off."

She sighed, then smiled, tapped Burgoyne on his red cuff and walked with languid grace from the room.

Gentleman Johnny smiled on Ahrens from slightly pouched eyes, settled the beautifully cut scarlet of his coat. "Just one more point, Lieutenant." He wagged his neatly powdered head. "Charteris is under the impression that your ideas on discipline are not sound. You don't like flogging. Too gentle with your men. Don't damn and curse and rave enough. Now I'll tell you that many commanders would hold that against you. What do you say to that?"

Ahrens stiffened. Then he raised a muscular hand, swayed his broad shoulders toward the General across the paper-littered table, his camp-chair creaking under him. "Men are not cattle, General. If my men fail, I try to show them how they may avoid failure another time. Why confuse a peasant who is learning a hard trade by screaming at him? Why kill his spirit by telling a sergeant to break a cane over his back? I work with my men, share their quarters, their rations if it seems wise to me. My men follow me because they want to, not because they dare not hold back. Hope my theories don't displease you. There they are, and nothing can shake my belief in them." He threw up his firm chin, eyes steady on the big, flushed man before him.

There was an earnest respect written on Gentleman Johnny's pleasure-worn face. Surprisingly he reached across the table, clasped Ahrens' hand in a firm grip. Then he sat back in his flimsy chair, nodding.

"By gad, sir, I honor you for your opinions. When I was appointed to raise a regiment of light dragoons in '59—first regiment of its kind in the history of the British Army, sir—I issued orders forbidding flogging, I broke any officer who cursed his men. The result? One of the finest regiments in the service. Served under me in Portugal. Given the name of The Queen's Light Dragoons. His Majesty, George the Third, reviewed it repeatedly on Wimbledon Common or Hounslow Heath. 'Damn smart troops, Burgoyne,' he said to me more than once. Yes, those were his very words, sir. 'Damn smart troops.' 'Not a lash or an oath laid on those men since I raised 'em, Your Majesty,' I told him. Gad, he praised me properly in the Gazettes. No, Lieutenant. Keep your course. I will stand back of you." He fixed his fine eyes on Ahrens.

Ahrens felt a thrill of pleasure. This was a man under whom one could serve, really serve. He obviously meant what he said about the men. A sound man, despite occasional pompous, almost bombastic outbursts which made Ahrens feel like an audience of one, a sounding-board for the General's rolling periods.

"Then, on taking my leave of you, General, I may report to Captain Pausch of the Hanau artillery? I'm anxious for work."

Burgoyne leaned back in his chair, pursed his full lips. "Pausch—Pausch. Now, by rights I should pack you off to him, after thanking you politely for reporting to me. But I rather think I shall need you here—at least for the time being. Can't tell what sort of a campaign this will be till we've taken the forts at Ticonderoga. May end the campaign at one blow, taking them. You've seen the maps?"

Ahrens nodded. "Major Charteris showed me this morning, sir."

The General unfolded a wide sheet of heavy paper. "Might look again. Dashed good piece of work Twiss did on this map. Now—in confidence, this is how we shall move. You see how narrow the lake is by the forts. The Yankees, under St. Clair, hold the old French works on the west shore, as well as Mount Hope. Latter commands the entrance into Lake George. On the east shore they hold Mount Independence. Bridge of boats connects the two banks. I'm sending Riedesel with all the Brunswick infantry to circle behind Independence and cut off the retreat while we attack the works on this shore, the west. You'll stay here at Headquarters. Act as a link between us and Riedesel. You speak both English and German. Riedesel likes you. Told me so himself not an hour ago. You're from Harrow. That will answer all questions with my people." He beamed on Ahrens. "Of course, I'm from Westminster. So's Acland of the grenadiers. The Earl of Balcarres—did you know we had a title or two along?—is Harrow. Anstruther and Hill are Rugby. You'll be the solvent of all troubles arising from differences of language and customs. Damned good idea, now that I think it over. Position clear?"

Ahrens studied the wavy lines of the map. "Perfectly, sir. Here we are—Crown Point on the west bank. Seven, say, eight miles to the French works. You've got Fraser and the advance corps south of us. They must be able to see the Yankee lines."

Burgoyne nodded. "Fraser tells me that they've some kind of a flag—all red and white stripes and a blue canton—flying over the works. Promised it to Lady Harriet Acland when we take the forts." He chuckled. "By rights it ought to belong to the regiment that takes it. But she wheedled it out of me. The ladies, the ladies!" He sighed and made little clucking noises to himself.

"Then, after the fall of the forts, I'll report back to the guns? Don't want my practice to get rusty."

"We'll see, we'll see." Gentleman Johnny smiled affably. "How d'you like it here? Hunt? Play cards? Confound it, I sat up with Balcares playing loo till nearly sunrise. Killed I blush to think how many bottles. My man used a gallon of lotion after he shaved me, trying to make me look like a schoolboy again. Took ten pounds from Balcarres, though. What d'you think of the camp?"

Ahrens sorted out the stream of questions, smiled. "The camp? Amazing! These barracks. Might be outside London. So might the tents. Then you look at the forest, the lake."

The General slapped the table. "You found it so, too? Amazing! What a contrast! British regiments which have fought all over Europe, camping in the heart of a world fresh from the hands of its Maker." A red arm swept in a great flourish to indicate the unspoiled immensity and Ahrens again had the impression that he was a public, an audience for the big man in scarlet and white. "The lake flows untroubled and unheeding past our—our pigmy rumblings. Its calm surface mirrors His Majesty's colors with the same unconcern that it will later mirror the flaming crimson and gold of the oaks and the maples, blushing under the sharp-fingered touch of autumn!" He threw back his fine head and stared past Ahrens as though listening to fluttering applause.

"Exactly, sir." Ahrens nodded. "The contrast, wherever you look. I saw a platoon of the 21st—your oldest regiment, I believe—halt to allow a file of Indians, painted red and black, to trot by."

"Gad, sir!" Burgoyne shook his head. "*You* see it. But I tried to show it all to Lady Acland. Red skins mingle with red coats. The pavements of London rub elbows with the trackless forest. Rifle and tomahawk, field-piece and arrow, old regiments and old tribes, all crowded about this—this Elysian body of water. Pointed it all out to her. What did she say?" His voice rose to a mincing treble. " 'Oh, General, how nasty the Indians smell!' " He buried his head in his hands, a thwarted artist. "Never mind. One day, Lieutenant, I'll put it all on paper, all on paper. Another child of my fancy to keep these company." He tapped a thick volume on whose cover Ahrens read: *Dramatic Works of J. Burgoyne, Esq.*," over the name of a distinguished West End publisher.

Ahrens nodded respectfully. Then he asked: "What brings the Indians to camp? There seemed so many of them."

Burgoyne's eyes widened. "What brings them? My dear sir, don't you know they're our allies? The eyes of the army, sir! They so screened our advance down the lake that to this day the Scotch-Yankee St. Clair doesn't know just where or how many we are! In-valuable!"

"And later—they will be employed against white men?"

"To be sure, to be sure. Most necessary. In a primitive world, natural man must lead the civilized—up to a certain point, of course."

"But the stories we hear in Europe? Scalping, torturing, killing of women and children?"

Gentleman Johnny's jovial face clouded. "There it is, there it is," he said, half to himself. "What will happen when we push south into the rebel country?" Then aloud he said: "La Corne St. Luc, savage old man of Auvergne, keeps shouting: 'Il faut brutalizer les affaires—il faut les brutalizer!' " He shook his head. Then he brightened. "But I'm sure I can hold them in check." He dove into a mass of papers, selected a couple of sheets. "Listen to this. My address at the Bouquet River last week, my address to the tribes. They tell me it produced an excellent effect."

He cleared his throat, squared his elbows. "I begin by welcoming them—but that wouldn't interest you. Here we are—I flatter them, then admonish them. Let me see—

63

where are we?" He frowned at the sheets while Ahrens' imagination supplied the rustling of a curtain, the flare of footlights.

"Yes, yes. Here it is. 'Persuaded by your magnanimity of character joined to your principles of affection to the King' and so on 'I enjoin your most serious attention to the rules which I hereby proclaim for your invariable observation during the campaign.' At this point, Lieutenant, there were loud cries of 'Etow! Etow!' Like our crying 'Hear, hear!'—a sound which I may say I have often heard during my speeches at Parliament." Then he grinned boyishly. "You know, I felt like an older fellow explaining house-rules to a group of new boys. First day of the new term. Then here are the rules. Pitched it in strong to them, I did.

" 'I positively forbid bloodshed when you are not opposed in arms. Aged men, women, children and prisoners must be held sacred from the knife or hatchet, even in time of actual conflict. Base, lurking assassins, incendiaries, ravagers, plunderers of the country, to whatever army they may belong, shall be treated with less reserve, but the latitude must be given you by order, and I must be the judge of the occasion.' " He raised his eyes, grinning. "Here again they cried 'Etow! Etow!' Then one of their chiefs replied and swore obedience on behalf of the tribes. Or so the interpreters told me. So I shook hands with the old chief and shouted 'Etow!' Really! Just like that! 'Etow!' Should have heard 'em yell! Then I had rum served and they staged a war-dance. Gad, Ahrens! What a sight! Hundreds, thousands of the red beggars. Painted red and black and blue and yellow! Some of them stark naked, leaping and crouching! One of 'em—ho-ho-ho-ho! Never saw such a thing. One of 'em, stripped naked he was, but to preserve decencies, he'd tied a dead blackbird about his privities! Ridiculous! Magnificent! And the others—some wore helmets made of buffalo heads, horns and all. And our men standing about in a great circle. Should have seen it,

64

really. Bearskin caps, brass helmets, red coats, blue coats, with the mass of savages whooping and tossing in the center. And the falls roaring beyond and the pines high over everything! It was— Come in, Charteris. Something for me?"

Charteris, languor gone, stepped quickly through the door. "Word from General Fraser, sir. Runner reports that he has pushed down. Indians are in contact with the forts. Light infantry will be, in an hour or so. Some gun-fire but no damage."

"Contact?" Burgoyne sprang from his chair. "We'll move the main body down the lake at sunrise tomorrow. Land above the forts. Send out the orders to all units, Charteris. At once!" Rapidly he ran over the prearranged schedule of attack, his flamboyancy, his foppishness completely gone. He was hard, keen, competent. "See that they all understand. Translations are here. Ahrens, you'd better take 'em to Riedesel. He'll issue 'em to his commanders. And here's a set for you in English in case there's any question. Lord, I hope Breymann and Baum will forget their eternal squabbling!"

"Then I'll stay with the Baron?" asked Ahrens.

"No, no. Report back to me. Wait, though. I've written a general order for the whole army. You can put it into German for me later. Read it to all units tonight. Listen to this, Charteris."

He selected a small sheet of paper from his table, then faced his two officers, hand thrust in the front of his waistcoat, head thrown back.

"The army embarks tomorrow to approach the enemy. We are to contend for the King and the Constitution of Great Britain, to vindicate Law and to relieve the oppressed—a cause in which His Majesty's troops and those of the Princes, his allies, will feel equal excitement." He fixed Ahrens with his magnetic eye. "The services required of this particular expedition are critical and conspicuous. During our progress occasions may occur in which, nor difficulty, nor labor, nor life are to be regarded." His voice swelled to a rising crash. *"This army must not retreat!"*

Ahrens felt himself carried away by the sweep and swing of Burgoyne's delivery. Even Charteris murmured: "Bravo, General! That will fetch 'em!"

Burgoyne smiled calmly. "Short, soldierly and stirring! By gad, I don't believe you can better it! And the peroration—'This army must not retreat!' Thuds out like drum-beats. We'll sweep the rebels out of their forts and down the Hudson. Untrained rabble, gentleman, cannot stand before His Majesty's fighting regiments. We'll be in Albany in a fortnight! Sooner! Join hands there with Howe and the rebellion is as good as over. Now off with you!"

"What the devil?" Ahrens looked back over his shoulder as he walked with Charteris from the wide door of the barracks, sun-dappled under the pines. Two men were nearing the entrance. The foremost was short, bull-necked and with extraordinarily long arms and thick shoulders which strained at a white coat, almost effeminately laced and braided. But it was his companion who drew the exclamation from Ahrens and even widened the bored eyes of the Englishman.

Six feet four inches in height, naked except for a breech-clout and long Indian leggings, the second man seemed to float rather than walk over the soft carpet of pine-needles. From his shaven head a stiff scalp-lock of pure white jutted up, an eagle feather bound into it. A long white beard fanned out over his muscular chest. His eyes were fierce, blue, staring, his nose a beak, his mouth a steel trap, his whole face like some savage pagan god from the earliest dawn of history, a face of terror, yet of strange beauty.

Charteris rubbed his square chin, eyes narrowed. "God's teeth! If you'd told me of it, I'd have given you the lie. Look at the tomahawk and scalping-knife at his belt!"

"But who *is* he?" asked Ahrens.

"Take a long look, young fellow." There was almost awe in Charteris' voice. "Heard of him, now I see him. That is, that *must* be, La Corne St. Luc. The other, the fop in the white coat is Langlade. Don't be misled by the coat. They are the most famous Indian leaders in America. Both Frenchmen. Langlade sprang the trap that did for my father's old friend, Braddock. But St. Luc! Old Auvergne family. Speaks the primest court French and every known Indian dialect. Can out-run, out-fight, out-think, out-last any Indian on the continent. Going on seventy. Knight of St. Louis. Fought against us in the Seven Years' War. Tried to go back to France after the peace. Shipwrecked. Both sons drowned before his eyes. Led the survivors through fifteen hundred miles of wilderness in the dead of winter. Never heard of pity or mercy. Scalps women and children like any savage. If he takes a strong captive he'll give him a knife, and, unarmed, fight him to the death. The Indians worship him. Has a nice taste in wines and silks, too. Dashed glad he came over to us."

Ahrens' eyes followed the Auvergnat through the gaping entrance. "Women and *children*! A chevalier de St. Louis! And with *us*! What do you think of it, Major? The Indians with us, I mean?"

"Indians? Haven't enough. Bring in ten thousand! Give old St. Luc a free hand!"

"But look here, Major. We aren't fighting savages; we're fighting Europeans, or people who used to be. You'd give that man a free hand against them?"

Charteris gave a wry smile. "Never heard of a tender heart being part of the equipment of a good soldier. These people are rebels, and that's all there is to it. They've asked for it. Give it to 'em. Never forget this, young man. In war your enemy is always a filthy scoundrel. The next turn of the wheel, of course, may make him your ally, in which case you endow him with virtues to which the gods themselves never aspired. But while he's your enemy, you'll never thrash him unless you feel in your heart that he's a son of a bitch. For the duration of the war, of course."

Ahrens shrugged his shoulders. "I suppose you're right. After all, what are we here for? To end the rebellion. Have to do it as best we may. We must accept the Indians, I suppose. Matter of getting accustomed to things."

They crossed a wide clearing where hundreds of red-coated men were going through embarkation drill, the ground being staked off in oblongs the size and shape of bateaux. Ahrens eyed them keenly. "Thought all your light infantry was ahead with Fraser. What are these fellows?"

Charteris shaded his eyes. "Light infantry? Oh, I see what you mean. Skull-caps and short jackets? They are just ordinary infantry. Usually wear tail coats and cocked hats. No new uniforms in over a year. Someone forgot. Cut up the tails for patches. Hats wore out. Trimmed down the cocks, tacked brass plates on front like the L.I."

"Better than tails or cocked hats for this sort of country, I'd say, with its undergrowth, brambles and so on."

Charteris shook his head. "Not regulation. Should be in tails. We'll give them new coats in Albany."

"When do you think that will be, Major? The General said a fortnight. Sounds too soon to me."

"Never predict on professional subjects. Tell you a few things, though. In addition to too much artillery, we've too much baggage, too few horses. When Burgoyne got to Quebec, he found Carlton had done nothing about carts or animals. Gentleman Johnny didn't do much either. Too busy with—well, you'll see her. Need double the number of beasts we have, treble. Seen our wagons? A few heavy ones, from England and the Continent. The rest, little two-wheeled carts pieced together here in Canada. Green wood. Tell me they fell to pieces by the hundred on the march down from Chambly. And we've got fifty miles of wild country before we reach

Fort Edward at the headwaters of the Hudson. Need cavalry, too. What have we got? Two or three hundred Brunswick dragoons and never a sign of a troop-horse. Laughing-stock of the army, plunging along in their great boots and spurs."

"You paint a cheerful picture," said Ahrens grimly.

"That's not all. Bad feeling. St. Luc frothed at the General's speech to the Indians. If he walks off, they'll go trooping after him. We look down on the Brunswickers and Hessians. They don't like us. *Our* fellows get along after a fashion, but on your side Breymann and Baum are at each other's throat half the time. Hard to keep their swords in their scabbards. Albany in a fortnight? The way needs smoothing."

"But there's another side of the picture," said Ahrens. "We've got, by all accounts, a first-rate commander."

"Agreed. And the men worship him."

"Also, you've some of the finest regiments in the British Army here along the lake. Ours aren't far behind. The General tells me we've Canadian rangers and Tories as well as Indians for irregular troops."

"Yes, yes. There's that," said Charteris abstractedly.

Ahrens laughed. "Wouldn't the General fume if when we reached Albany we found Howe sitting waiting for us?"

There was a dry cough. "Look here. I imparted treasonble matter to you in Hanau about the plan of campaign. I'm going farther now. When we get to the Hudson and start down toward Albany, don't get eye-strain looking for Howe's bayonets coming north. Can't tell you more than that, and keep it to yourself. Now—follow that path to the left. Take you to Riedesel. He holds court in a marquee to be nearer his troops. My respects to the Baroness. Put her in command and we'll be in New York in a fortnight, not Albany."

Fourteen war-canoes, long, slim, deadly, rocked and bobbed under the sunrise breeze that swept gently from the tree-packed shore across the mile-wide surface of the lake. Ahrens, squinting in the strong light that had just begun to flood over the crests of the distant Green Mountains, gaped in amazement. In the leading canoe he could make out the towering form of La Corne St. Luc, white beard fanning across a chest hideously painted with black and white stripes. Langlade, foppish coat discarded, rested his hand on the thwart of his canoe and seemed to be calling over his shoulder to his twenty-five paddlers, daubed like himself with red and ochre. Eagle feathers and oiled scalp-locks swayed and ducked with the motion of the canoes. Black, green, red, yellow bodies, naked to the waist, gleamed in the sunlight.

Ahrens looked back along the deck of Burgoyne's pinnace. It was almost a comfort to see Gentleman Johnny's full, smiling face, his immaculate scarlet and white uniform, his air of London clubs and theaters, after the overpowering burst of savage splendor in the canoes ahead. Now the General bent over a light table set at the foot of a bare mast and laughed as he studied a map with his Tory adviser, the tall Skene, one-time major in His Majesty's armies. Behind him, solid and alert, stood the Chief of staff, Kingston, and nearby, Charteris, muffling a polite yawn.

A-port lay Riesdesel's pinnace. On her neat deck, blue-coated men bent deferentially about a short, slim woman in summery skirts who appeared to be asking questions eagerly about the blunt-nosed guns jutting from the pinnace's flanks. Her head nodded vigorously and in the morning hush Ahrens could hear a light ripple of laughter.

Starboard was a third pinnace, from whose deck welled a rumbling, rasping voice. General Phillips, just promoted to command all the English units and the expedition's artillery, was shaking his fist and storming at a dejected-looking officer in red and blue. Ahrens grinned. Burgoyne smiling and placid, the Baroness laughing,

Phillips storming and cursing—the keynote of the expedition was struck.

His eyes narrowed. He looked toward the west shore astern of the pinnaces. It was suddenly thick with orderly lines of red and blue along the great gash of the clearing. Red lines and blue moved forward into the long fringe of blunt-nosed bateaux which lay dark on the yellow sands. Oars glinted in the sun, the bateaux nosed heavily out in a dancing line in the deep blue of the lake.

Ahrens shaded his eyes and watched the wallowing boats. "Powell's brigade," he thought. "Yellow facings—the 9th. White—the 47th, and red for the 53rd. Hamilton's next down the line. Blue—21st. Can't see any more than that." Then he thrilled with pride. In the thickening mass he caught sight of solid phalanxes of blue coats and towering brass helmets, behind them, cocked hats, then more helmets winking just within eyeshot.

Slowly but deftly the long mass edged out to midlake, then swung in a wide wheel, square bows pointing south. Ahrens drew a deep breath. "The picked strength of Europe!" he muttered. He snapped his fingers at Charteris' foreboding.

There was a dead hush over the floating army. It was broken by the Cockney whine of an orderly, crouched in the bows. "St'y 'ere? Not me. W'en the war's over, back ter Lunnon for me." An unseen man rumbled in a voice reeking of some green shire: "Ah! But a body c'd farm here. Wouldn't you stay if you got land?" The Cockney whined again. "St'y! Me? Nao. Too bloody lonely. An' I can't abide the beer!" The hush settled again. Ahead, the blaze of canoes rocked and dipped.

Gentleman Johnny's rich voice rolled along the deck. "Now then, Mr. Kingston. *If* you please—"

The Chief of staff raised his arm, then cut it to his side with a sweep. A sailor touched a linstock to the breech of a small brass cannon. There was a shattering roar which crashed and thudded among the hills. From the leading

71

canoe a white arm, black-smeared, raised a glistening paddle to the sun. A forest of dripping blades flashed an answer. Then the lake boiled as the canoes drove slowly forward, the wild voice of the old Auvergnat leading a whooping, screaming chorus.

The pinnaces moved gently after the Indians. Astern over the water, Ahrens saw the yellow arms of the drum-major of the 9th raised high in the air. They fell. Drums pounded and rattled, fifes of two brigades stabbed the soft air, swept up in the opening bars of *The White Cockade*. Oars churned the water and the dense mass of red and blue ploughed on in the wake of the General.

Charteris leaped to the low stern rail, steadying himself on the slanting flagpole. His long arm swept over his head and his voice crashed out to the bateaux: "Up, the Infantry! Three cheers for Gentleman Johnny Burgoyne!"

Surprised, Ahrens found his throat swelling as he joined in the staccato roar; surprised, too, to find that he was trembling, that his hands were moist. Then he smiled. Burgoyne, magnificent in scarlet, white and gold, stepped to the stern beside Charteris. Head thrown back, his chest out, he flourished his hat in gracious salute to his cheering troops. "Curtain on the first act," thought Ahrens.

The Forts

THE MAIN ARMY *of Burgoyne landed a short distance above the Ticonderoga neck, across whose base Fraser's corps stretched its lines. The Brunswick infantry under Riedesel, were sent to the east shore, where they floundered through thick forest and swamp, hoping to get astride the road that led south from Independence, St. Clair's only possible escape. Burgoyne studied the works of Ticonderoga, noted their natural strength. Red-faced General Phillips, commanding the allied artillery, stared at the ragged crest of Mount Defiance below Ticonderoga, saw it was not occupied by the Americans, believed that guns, once on its summit, could command all the forts and the lake-throat.*

St. Clair saw the force slowly closing about him, hoped that Burgoyne would be rash enough to repeat the tactics of Bunker Hill and assault his men, who were at least good marksmen, across the open slopes that led from the west to his lines. It was St. Clair's only hope.

III

The Forts

It was hot in the green tunnel that curved up the west slope of Mount Defiance, hot and deafening as the axes smacked wetly into green trunks and pine and maple crashed and ripped onto the rocky soil. Kurt Ahrens reined in the shambling cart horse that Headquarters had given him for a mount and tossed the lines to Rentner, who sat rigid on a strange honey-colored beast whose ears stood out at right angles to its head.

"Too steep for comfort," he said. "Wait here with the horses. I'm going to the crest to find General Phillips."

He pushed ahead past groups of sweating, coatless men who dragged heavy trunks out of the way, hacked at obstinate stumps, rolled massive boulders from the climbing track that inched up the steep incline. Farther on, feet sinking into moist soil, he saw daylight through the trees whose tops swayed and rocked as quick axes bit into living wood.

He shouted at a red-faced sergeant: "General Phillips?" The crash of a tree drowned him out. "Where is General Phillips, Sergeant?" he yelled again.

The sergeant wiped a streaming face. "At the summit, sir. Listen and you'll find him." He turned back to his straining squad.

Ahrens scrambled over the side of a mossy boulder, ducked past a detail of streaming sappers who tugged at a rope lashed to a thick trunk and then felt fresh air on his forehead. He looked back down the long clearing which boiled with dripping men, wiped his face with a damp handkerchief, and swung himself up a steep rock, rasping his hands on a pitchy pinebranch.

"To the summit and listen!" he growled to himself. "How can you hear in a din like this? Damn these flies! Sting like bayonets." He lashed at a buzzing wisp of black that hovered about him. "Listen for what—in God's name?" Then he nodded to himself. "Clever man, that sergeant."

A deep voice roared and rumbled among the pines by the crest. "God damn it, sir! Where a goat can go, a man can go! And where a man can go he can drag a cannon! Use the horses till they give out, I tell you. Then cannoneers on the drag-ropes, cannoneers on the wheels! Bring 'em on—and don't run. Fly, by God!"

A blue-coated gunner officer pelted down the slope past Ahrens, face crimson and eyes staring. "Bombardier! Bombardier Phelps!" His voice cracked. "Bring up the guns, Bombardier!"

Ahrens grinned. "Listen and you'll find him," he said softly, and struggled on over the broken ground till he caught a flash of blue, red and gold between the last trunks. Then he straightened up as hard blue eyes fixed themselves on him, glancing from a flushed face.

"Well?" The question was barked out.

"Compliments of General Burgoyne, sir. He is particularly anxious that the summit be kept clear as possible. He is afraid that the rebels may see the works here too soon."

"O God!" Phillips' voice rattled his throat. "A cavalry man to teach me my business!" He swallowed hard, then spoke with painful preciseness. "My compliments to the General. He may rest assured that no God-damned rebel is going to see so much as a dirty shirt-tail of those lazy swine he sent to cut the trail. My gunners will have sense enough to keep under cover without being told." He snorted again. "Have you brains enough to tell the

General what this site is like when you get back to him?
What arm of the service?"

Ahrens flushed. "Hesse-Hanau artillery, sir. On duty
with Headquarters."

Phillips stared. "Gunner? Why didn't you say so?
Can't expect me to know every rag-tag and bobtail uniform in the army. Why didn't he send Charteris? Sending a bloody Hessian with orders for *me!*"

"Major Charteris is surveying the old French lines below, sir."

"Well, you're a gunner, at least. Come with me."

He followed the snarling Phillips through thinning
trees where a long, flat space stretched north and south.

"What d'you think of *this* for a gun-position?" growled
the General.

Ahrens dug the toe of his boot into the spongy
ground. "Flat enough, sir. Too soft though. You've
twenty-four-pounders waiting at the foot of the hill.
They'd mire here."

"Too soft, eh?" Phillips stared. "What does your active
brain suggest?"

"Platforms, spiked to those flat rocks. Run the guns up
on them."

Phillips smiled grimly. "Just what I'm going to do.
Sent for Twiss and his engineers. Don't mind my barking. Just trying you out. Know your trade. Now look
here and keep low."

Ahrens carefully parted the bushes that grew thick
along the east edge of the summit. Then his eyes
widened. The slope fell away sheer in front of him. Below lay Champlain like a thin ribbon stretching away to
the south on the last dozen miles of its course and across
the narrow throat the white cliffs of Mount Independence peeped out through a tangle of pine. Beyond the
trees at the summit he could see trim lines of stone-
faced earth-works, a matted jungle of fallen tree-trunks
in front of them, wooden barracks and a trail leading to

a bridge of boats which linked the Mount with the forts of Ticonderoga.

"What range?" snapped Phillips.

"H'm. Difference in elevation—allow for slope—h'm, say sixteen hundred yards."

"Close enough," growled Phillips. "I'd say fifteen. How about eighteen-pounders here? What could you do to that garrison over there?"

"Garrison? Garrison?" Ahrens frowned. "Sorry, General. Can't make out a single soldier in the works. Crowds of country-people wandering about. Curious, I suppose. But no uniforms." He looked up. "D'you think that St. Clair can have slipped out in the night? Ah—there's one uniform. See—by the stone powder-house? Blue coat, buff facings."

"Damn my soul!" said Phillips. "Aren't we fine, we Europeans! Have to have a Potsdam parade to recognize a soldier? *Look* at 'em! Every man a soldier—smocks, shirtsleeves, bibs, round hats, no hats, cocked hats! Rebel soldiers—such as they are. D'you expect the Yankees in a frontier fort to look like the guards at Versailles? Wait—here come a few men in uniform marching round the end of that long cabin. Does that satisfy you? Now—what could you do to them from here?"

Ahrens shook his head. "Not much, directly. Raw troops, though. It would shake 'em just to know that there were guns here." He peered out again. His breath hissed in a sharp intake. "Here's what I *could* do, General. See those boats lining the banks? Must be two hundred or more. I could give anyone who tried to load them a lively time."

"And you're kept at Headquarters!" snorted Phillips. "I had to point that out to all my officers. None of 'em saw it. Now let's look to the north."

Even closer than Independence lay the sloping peninsula with the star-shaped fort of blue stone that was the legacy of Montcalm and his French sappers. To the west stretched the waterway that led to Lake George and the

78

still-hot ruins of the rebel buildings on Mount Hope. Little dots of red, of green, moved in the thinning trees at the top of the neck where Fraser slowly pushed his advance corps toward the earthworks which lay west of the glacis and bastions of the main fort. North on the lake, pinnaces and light frigates rocked gently in quiet menace.

"Well?" Phillips' voice cut in. "Comments? Or does this cursed sun make your brains stew as it does mine?"

Ahrens straightened up, brushing scraps of bark and moss from the knees of his white breeches. "Same as the other side, General. Could make anyone on that bridge pretty uncomfortable and do a good deal of damage in the works themselves."

"Right. Now go back and explain that to the General. Here—take this map. See this hill? Mount Defiance, where we are. Road has been cut up the northwest slope, hidden from Ticonderoga and Independence. St. Clair can't see us. We'll keep the guns masked until Riedesel gets round to the south of Independence. Then we shall proceed to make ourselves *most* objectionable." His jaws snaped on the words, making them far more deadly than his most flaming oaths. "The red-headed St. Clair will have to retreat. He'll find he can't. He'll surrender."

Ahrens nodded. "When did we take this hill, General? I was across the lake with the Brunswickers."

"Take it? We didn't. Those damn fools below us in the forts thought it was too steep to bother about. I didn't. Here we are. Give a year's pay to see St. Clair's face when he learns we've guns up here. Be sure and explain at Headquarters just what our barkers can do. And say we must have all the ammunition that can be spared."

"No worry about that, sir. Orders say you're to have every round you can drag up here."

A smile spread over Phillips' grim face. "Am I, though! Good old Gentleman Johnny!" He threw back his head. "Well done, the cannoneers! Here come the guns!"

The last trees along the northwest rim had gone down before the hacking steel, and the brown-floored chute, stump-studded, echoed with thudding hooves while the oaths of the drivers snapped and popped like rifle-fire. Beyond the edge of a huge boulder which masked the trail from Ahrens and the General, a horse's head suddenly jutted, a long straining neck, lurching shoulders and stabbing hooves. A bow-legged sergeant ran by the heaving flanks. Another head, staring eyes and bared teeth, laboring haunches; another, while far behind the heavy piece they dragged clanked and jolted.

"Don't let 'em slow up!" The sergeant danced with excitement. "Cannoneers on the wheels! You drivers! Give 'em the whip, damn it! Shoulders into it! By God!" His voice rose to a scream. "You've done it! You've done it!" The leading horse, his driver spurring and thrashing, drove his hooves onto level ground. One by one the twenty animals of the long hitch struggled after him, while a confused knot of soldiers, dust-streaked and dripping with sweat, grappled with the spokes, kept the heavy wheels turning and rolling, shoved and pushed and butted wherever a hand or shoulder could find purchase.

Ahrens ran down the trail, stumbling over stumps and roots. By a shoulder of rock he stopped to let a heaving line of men inch slowly past him. Weaker horses or less skilful drivers had bogged down the rumbling wheels of the heavy piece and the cannoneers with their drag-ropes had been substituted. Then he cut past the swaying muzzle as the piece slowly rocked and heaved up the slope. Fifty yards below he could see the extended head and cracking nostrils of the lead horse of another gun. "By God!" thought Ahrens. "That Phillips is a gunner! Every man and horse is on this!" Then he caught sight of Rentner among the trees. He had slipped the bits from the horses' mouths and was letting them graze on the tufts of pulpy wood-grass that sprouted between the heavy boles of the trees. The two saddles were neatly stacked out of reach of random hooves.

"All quiet while I was gone?"

"Quiet, sir. Two English gunners tried to take the horses."

"I'll be damned! What did you do?"

"Took your pistols from the holsters, sir."

Ahrens chuckled. "You did? What did they do?"

"They went away, sir." Rentner's voice was gentle.

He looked at Rentner's tight jaws, solid neck. "They showed damned good judgment. How is the pretty Hedwig enjoying the war?"

"Well enough, sir. She's back with the other women at Crown Point. Won't move until General Burgoyne orders the rebels out of the forts." Ahrens smiled to himself over his conception of grand strategy. Rentner went on. "Some of the women that follow the army aren't what she's used to. But she gets along. Likes the forest, sir. Says the sun on the trees makes her think of the cathedral at Koln. She's a Koln girl, sir."

They mounted, thudded heavily down the rough trail, the horses shaking their heads in sharp jerks as vicious, black-bodied flies swarmed from every bush.

"You've seen Phillips?"

"Yes, sir. He sent you this map. Three pieces were at or near the top when I left."

"This the map?" Burgoyne rose from his chair under the shade of a huge pine. "Guns are where? Oh, I see. Command both east and west banks *and* the bridge. Good. Now those guns must hold their fire until Riedesel has worked south of Independence. The Yankees mustn't even *imagine* they are there or could be there. South of Independence. Gad! What ghastly names the Yankees choose! Independence! You were across with Riedesel. How long d'you think it will take him to close in?"

Ahrens was thoughtful. There came into his mind a

picture of a grenadier he had seen on the east bank, a grenadier loaded down with a high brass helmet, cumbersome knapsack whose straps cut his shoulders, the blue and red of his coat staring in the forest light, long tails catching on every bush, useless sword tripping him at every step, white breeches a pulpy mass of sweat, moss and dirt. The man's face had been streaming, his eyes congested and wild as he thrashed through the undergrowth trying pathetically to preserve his bit of the traditional order of march learned on smooth treeless drill-grounds in Europe.

Somehow that grenadier typified Riedesel's whole force—mind, body and equipment in an alien setting where every influence of nature was hostile, from the close-packed giant trees to the almost invisible black-flies that fed on swollen wrists and hot, wet necks. He considered the picture, then looked at the cool man in scarlet and white who stood so smiling and confident before him. Then he said slowly. "Heavy troops, sir, his infantry. Line, grenadiers, even the light infantry. They may take some time."

Gentleman Johnny spread out his hands. "But they landed on the east shore yesterday. What can stop them? Question only of miles."

Ahrens hesitated.

"Well, what can?" urged Burgoyne.

"They landed on the other side of that creek that flows into the lake on the east side of Independence, sir. The banks are very swampy. The road is a mere sketch. The Baron may have to move a long way inland before he has a chance to swing west."

"Damn it, that's so. Bad, eh? Swamps, I mean. Man can't walk and he can't swim." He frowned, delicately nibbled his thumb. Then he smiled suddenly, slapped Ahrens on the shoulder. "But I'm *sure* they'll close in very soon. Thing's a certainty. Why, they're as good as there now. Then we have Mr. St. Claire on toast! He'd like us to assault over open ground, but we'll not oblige. Damned rebels are the best marksmen I ever saw. Read about Bunker Hill? I saw it. Appalling! Every shot was aimed. Our men went down in swatches. Luckily the Yankees ran out of ammunition. Don't want that sort of thing here. Let Riedesel slip round to the south while we hold on the west. Then unmask those guns up there. What can St. Clair do? Surrender! . . . Ah—my dear!" He turned with a flourish to the marquee under the big pine. "I didn't see you. May I—Lieutenant Ahrens of the Hesse-Hanau artillery."

Ahrens bowed. There was something in the lush figure of the woman who smiled at him out of veiled eyes that disturbed him, revolted him a little and yet left a sort of piquant fascination. Her eyes were on him, weighing, appraising. She nodded slowly, full lips moving a little. Then she turned on the General. "Is that whipper-snapper Money in command of the army, or are you? He tells me that *I* can't bring more than one box of clothes! Why, I'll need a dozen in Albany and twenty in New York!" Her over-red lips tightened. "If it's a case of my going south in rags and tatters, I'll pack now and thank you for your pinnace to take me back to Quebec. How dare he talk to *me* like that? *One* box!"

Gentleman Johnny raised a soothing hand. "There, there. Orders have been issued. Have to march light, you know. We're all sending our extra trappings back. But I'll have a word with Money, my dear. Arrange something, I'm sure."

"*I'm* sure, too. Or back I go to Quebec!" She smiled dazzlingly on Ahrens, then swept away into the marquee, well-cut riding-habit billowing about her.

Gentleman Johnny coughed behind his hand. "Wife of Commissary Lewis who supplies the army. Sister married to a Tory in Fraser's Corps. Most important that Lewis be kept in good humor. Must have our supplies, must have our supplies." He coughed again.

The following noon, high on the summit of Mount Defiance, Heinz, the Hanau farmer, set down his heavy buckets of water with an explosive sigh. Then he wiped his broad, good-natured face and beamed in naive friendliness on the masked battery and its guards. "Ha! These punkies!" He flapped a moist hand at the swarm of black-flies that darted about his inflamed neck and wrists. "These punkies! Never did I see the like!" The hard-faced English sergeant in charge of the crew of gunners busy about one of the platforms stared uncomprehendingly at him, then turned his attention back to his men. Unabashed, Heinz wiped his hands on his draggled white breeches which were generously spattered with moss and pine-needles. He addressed himself to a fierce-mustached Brunswick dragoon who, with a dozen others, had been sent from Headquarters to insure the sanctity of the precious position and to dream about the horses for which they pined and prayed. Heinz' voice was confiding. "Never in my life did I see the like! How'd you like to plough a field with these punkies chewing at your neck?"

The dragoon, magnificent in gigantic boots to mid-thigh, light-blue coat with yellow facings and a huge cocked hat with a towering plume, only glared in reply and rattled his heavy saber against a rock.

"No, but how'd *you* like it?" persisted Heinz.

The dragoon snorted. "Me? *Farm?* I've been a dragoon for five years. What would I know about farming?"

Heinz sat on a flat rock and smiled up at him. "Just think! A dragoon! Where's your horse?"

"My horse?" He reddened with anger. His squadron had been the target of endless jibes in the march south from Chambly as they lumbered along horseless, in their heavy boots.

Heinz' china-blue eyes only showed kindly interest. "Yes. Your horse. You always see pictures of dragoons galloping about on horses. There was one in Emil Klein's

84

pork-shop in the Darmstadtstrasse in Dietzenbach, near Hanau. Ever been there?"

"Klipfel!" He called to another trooper who was watching the British gunners with an air of stupid solemnity. "Klipfel! Here's a lousy recruit, a damned Hanau gunner, who needs to be taught respect for the dragoons."

Klipfel walked slowly over, tugging at his pointed mustaches. "What did he say?" He stared at Heinz out of small, mean-looking eyes set too close to a long nose.

"He asked—" The dragoon's voice trembled. "He asked me where my *horse* was?"

Klipfel's eyes narrowed. "He asked that? Ha! Stand up!" A gauntleted hand seized Heinz by the red facings of his jacket, jerked him onto his feet.

Heinz' broad mouth trembled, a look of bewilderment spread over his face. He grinned nervously. "Hard—sitting on the ground. Sun bakes it, sort of. It's not soft—like sitting in your saddles."

Klipfel ground his teeth. "God in heaven! Do you hear him? Horses! Saddles! I've not seen a proper horse since we left Wolfenbüttel." He shouted: "Fürst! Come here! This Hanauer! Talks about horses and saddles!"

Fürst, long-armed and spare, slowly stripped off his elbow-high gauntlets. His voice was soft, almost purring. "Tell the swing what we did with the Canadian who laughed at our spurs."

Klipfel's mouth tightened. "We took off his shoes. We made him run barefoot through a briar-patch." He shook the staring Heinz. "Through a briar-patch between a double row of dragoons. They made a fine mess of his back with their belts."

The English gunners picked up their tools and moved away toward the path that led down the slope. Fürst threw his gloves on the ground. "Now, by God, we're alone! Let's put this Hanau monkey through his tricks. If he doesn't know his drill, he'll run the gauntlet. There's enough of us here. Recruit! Do you know how to fire one of those damn things?" He pointed to a twenty-four pounder that stood silent and heavy on its platform.

Heinz looked up at the dragoons. Why were they so angry, so rough with him? He wiped his hands on his breeches, gulped; "Oh, yes. Do you?"

Fürst roared. "Do *we*? A dragoon know about those stinking things! Where did *you* learn?"

"In—in the gun-park at Hanau. Lieutenant Ahrens taught us all. He's a fine gentleman. Do you know him? He told us—"

Klipfel made a threatening gesture. "Show us, then, and less of your God-damn chatter. Move!"

Heinz blinked and nodded, then ran to the piece with shaking knees. "There's powder here." He laid a sweating hand on the breech. "Then you take long stick likea this." He picked a linstock from its rack while the dragoons looked sullenly at him. "You wave it in the air like this. If it was real, there would be a spark on the end; it would glow." His eyes jumped from one tormentor to another. "I don't—don't know why. Lieutenant Ahrens knows. Then you do like this—"

There was an ear-splitting screech from Fürst. "God in heaven! Stop him! There *is* a spark!"

But Heinz, his lower lip quivering, touched the linstock to the vent of the gun. There was a shattering roar, a flash, a cloud of smoke. A round-shot sang wickedly and crashed through the deck of a galley moored far below at the foot of Mount Independence.

Heinz blinked. "There must have been a real spark," he announced. Then he saw the expressions of the dragoons, frozen in attitudes of horror. Other troopers from farther down the position were recovering from their first shock and clumping heavily toward him. Then Klipfel screeched: "Grab him! By God, he'll sweat for this! Wait till Colonel Breymann gets his hands on him!"

With a leap and a bound, Heinz crossed the clearing and plunged into the woods, easily outdistancing the dragoons in their crippling boots. As he thudded over the broken ground that paralleled the trail he thought, "I must have done something wrong."

The splintering roar from Mount Defiance seemed to quiver among the tree-tops which loomed high over the camp-table. Gentleman Johnny Burgoyne shot up, erect and staring. "Hell and death! What was that?" Pale and shaken, he clutched the shoulder of the tall, handsome man by his side. "Skene! Do you hear that? Some screaming fool has loosed off a gun from the Mount! St. Clair will be warned!"

Mouth set, Skene stared south at the rugged crest of Defiance. His eyes narrowed. He muttered: "That's done it! The plan is ruined!"

Slowly Burgoyne loosed his hold on Skene's collar. Through pale lips he stammered: "Fatal! Fatal!" He sagged back into his chair, shoulders drooping. Dully he shook his head.

Suddenly he brightened. "Buck up, Skene! Even so, St. Clair is in a devilish tight place. How *can* he slip away? Tomorrow Riedesel will be south of Independence, if he isn't there now! By Gad, I believe he is! I swear I do. Pushing fellow, the Baron."

The General's burst of optimism lifted a little the mask that the thunder from the Mount had stamped on the Tory's keen face. He even forced a smile. "Damned if I don't believe you, sir!" he said, smiling grimly. "What is your next move?"

Gentleman Johnny sat erect in his chair, luminous eyes fixed on Skene. "Do? Back to my headquarters on the pinnace! We'll watch St. Clair like a hawk. We'll follow up any move he makes by land and water. Riedesel's on the east now. St. Clair will have to fall back across his bridge to Independence and either make a stand there or retreat over that one road to Hubbardton and Castleton. He'll march straight into the Baron's arms, while we send Fraser across that same bridge, hard on his heels. The nut in the pincers. Then we'll move our main army straight down the lake and disembark in your own dooryard at Skenesboro, having first polished off the Yankee boats. See? Riedesel and Fraser will crush St. Clair, then they will circle west through Castleton and join us at the head of the lake at this same Skenesboro where you may play host to the victors."

Skene looked at the map. "Sound, sound. We drive straight down, the others loop around to my lands and join us."

"You're sure, Skene, that that is the best way?" Burgoyne rested his full chin in his hand. "That way—to the end of this lake, then overland along Wood Creek to Fort Edward on the Hudson? Wouldn't go by Lake George? Ferry our men by water all the way? Might be much quicker. Hear there's heavy going over the other route."

Skene shook his head. His imagination showed him the army ploughing south through his own lands, building roads in the dense tangle of forest, roads that would link the estates he had held since his retirement from the army with the Hudson, roads built at the King's expense. He saw himself a rich man with the coming of peace. So he tapped the wide map with a thick forefinger. "Distance, General, distance. Float your guns, your heaviest luggage down Lake George, by all means. But—" The finger tapped again. "But your main body straight south—overland."

White fingers pinching his full lower lip, Burgoyne pondered. "You know the country, Skene, you know the country. We pass over your own holdings and you must know them. You say that the Loyalists will flock to us? Good." He suddenly smiled, clapped Skene on the shoulder. "South we go!" He gathered up his papers, sighing. This move back to the pinnace—there were a dozen bottles of champagne in an ice-cold spring nearby and he had thought himself sure of an afternoon's seclusion. Well, well. He could send a note to Mrs. Lewis. Damn that fellow on the Mount, though. Most annoying. He brightened. Why, Mrs. Lewis could be installed on the ship! He hummed an air from *The Beggar's Opera.*

In the shade of an improvised shelter of canvas, Kurt Ahrens tossed his jacket over a pine-bough and set himself to render Gentleman Johnny's somewhat pompous periods into terse, military German for Riedesel's consumption. "How the devil—" He frowned. "'Animated by these considerations; at the head of troops in full power of health, discipline and valor—' Gentleman Johnny seems to have written a book about the war. The Baron doesn't want all that. He wants to know where to go and what to do when he gets there. Hello—what's that?" There was a rustling in the swaying leaves where the canvas was pegged to the ground. "Snakes?" He picked up a loaded stick, listening for the warning hiss or rattle. The rustle and crackle continued. Something bulged against the canvas, bellied it out at the bottom. A dirt-streaked face suddenly thrust up among the grasses.

Ahrens dropped his stick. His voice rapped. "Get on your feet. Heinz! That's no way to approach an officer."

The thick body slowly wormed through the space between canvas and ground. Heinz scrambled to his feet. "No, sir. The Lieutenant has often told me. But the dragoons were angry."

Ahrens wiped his forehead with a despairing gesture. Time and again he had rescued Heinz from blasting punishment which the fat farmer's invincible good-natured stupidity had brought on him. Wearily he asked: "What have dragoons to do with you?"

China-eyed and innocent, Heinz expatiated on the unreasonable fury of the troopers. Ahrens' head sank lower and lower on his chest. So the blast from the Mount was not a signal! St. Clair in his bluestone fort was warned. He said in a dull voice: "Do you know what you've done, Heinz? You've shown the rebels our trump card. God knows what will happen now. St. Clair may be able to slip away. Why, the campaign might have ended right on this lake! Now we'll have his men in front of us all the way to Albany. Damn it, man. This is serious. If I turn you over to Baum or Breymann, they—well, there's no telling what they may do to you." He sat scowling, drumming his fingers on his knees. "Ought to do just that. Or let General Burgoyne know."

"Yes, Lieutenant."

"Well—" Ahrens sighed. Then he swore under his breath, crumpled a bit of paper and hurled it through the opening of his shelter. The dejected Heinz, streaked with dirt and sweat, looking trustfully at him, destroyed his sense of discipline for the dozenth time.

"Look here, Heinz. Do the dragoons know your name?"

"I didn't tell them, sir."

"Thank God for that!" grumbled Ahrens. "What were you doing up there, in the first place?"

"I had been cutting trees with Corporal Bittner. An Englishman gave me two buckets of water and pointed up the hill."

"Did he say anything more?"

"Yes. He said, 'Dutch bugger.' Very loud, sir."

Ahrens snorted, then composed himself. "There were other men of ours working up there?"

"Yes, Lieutenant. Recruits like me, but from the grenadier regiments. Men who are too green yet to go with their companies. Oh—and there were two gunners—men who had been sick."

"There's just a chance, just a chance," mused Ahrens. "You see, your name will be on no roster of men working up there. That's where they'll look. Never think of a wood-cutting detail. Now, Heinz. Keep your teeth on this! You were on Bittner's detail, halfway up the mountain. You've never seen the summit. You don't want to see it. You don't know how to get there. That's your only hope. Now get along! Wash the moss and bark and pine-needles off your face and give your uniform a good beating."

Heinz' smile was beatific. "Yes, Lieutenant. Thank you, sir. And wasn't it funny that there *was* a spark on that stick?"

Ahrens leaped to his feet. "Heinz! Forget it! Forget all about it! The linstock and the gun. You were never near them!"

"Of course not, Lieutenant. But it was funny, just the same." He saluted deplorably and edged clumsily away. Ahrens, stony-eyed, stared at the canvas wall.

The Pursuit

AFTER MOON-SET, ST. CLAIR *quietly slipped the Ticonderoga men across the bridge of boats to Mount Independence, consolidated the two garrisons. He packed what stores he could in his great flotilla of flat-boats and bateaux, and sent them south to Skenesboro at the head of the lake. He had lost his forts, much of his stores, but he had saved his army, which he hurried overland by the road that led through the wilderness in a great arc by Hubbardton and Castleton to Skenesboro.*

When early morning showed empty works on the west shore, Burgoyne sent Fraser over the same bridge of boats, hard on St. Clair's trail, while he himself, with the main body, pushed south by water. On the Hubbardton road Fraser met Riedesel and his Germans, exhausted by their bloodless battle with the wilderness, and far too late to cut off St. Clair's retreat. Fraser pushed on, leaving Riedesel to follow as soon as possible. Over the curving route there struggled three straining forces—Americans, English and Brunswickers.

IV

The Pursuit

A PARTRIDGE scurried across the rough wagon-track. Birds began to waken in the thick undergrowth and something solid plumped into the waters of a swampy patch that shimmered in the woods to the left. Ahrens sniffed the heavy, earthy, damp smell that he had come to associate with early morning in the New World forests and was grateful for the faint, luminous tinge of green that began to filter down through the upper leaves of the giant trees. "Nothing like war to interfere with sleep," he thought. "This is July—July seventh. Nearly four o'clock. The fifth—yes, I slept a little on the fifth." His horse, a better mount this time, beat heavily along the rutted dirt road that snaked through the woods. He turned in his saddle, peering back at the bobbing shape of Rentner. "All right?" he called.

"Right, sir." The reply was bitten off crisply. Ahrens was relieved. Rentner's clumsy mount had stumbled two hours earlier as the pair rode through the littered lines of Independence some time after Fraser's troops had crossed the solid bridge and plunged off in quest of St. Clair's retreating men. No wonder the animal had stumbled. What a state the Yankee lines had been in! Sick left behind, stores abandoned, strewn everywhere, a few horses wandering about. Then the Indians who should have led Fraser's advance had stayed behind to loot and to drink and whoop about the captured rum-stores, had staggered in knots and groups, whooping and yelling. And the Yankees away, clear away. Well, it was lucky about Rentner's horse. Must have worked out any lameness resulting from the stumble. Lucky, too, about Rentner. Ahrens had persuaded Riedesel to assign the man to him as part orderly, part aide, for such time as the staff assignment might last. Consent had not been too difficult, as all the guns were going by water over Lake George to rejoin the column on the Hudson by Fort Edward and a recruit like Rentner would have little to do on the water-passage.

Ahrens rode on, wondering what the rebels were like, what they thought of the heavy troops who marched against them with the English. So far he had not seen an enemy, except for those tiny figures who moved about on Independence and in the Ticonderoga works and at whom he had stared with the choleric Phillips. A few prisoners had been taken before the flight, but he had not seen them. The young Earl of Balcarres had described them to him as old farmers in big wigs and boys no higher than a cricket stump. They didn't sound very formidable. If the army pushed hard on the retreat, the line of the Hudson should open like a ripe peach.

Autumn in New York. Perhaps a winter crossing. Then Dresden. Might be some interesting new faces in the Ballet. There had been talk of a new Italian troupe that ought to be interesting. Would the wanton-chaste Lisa be about the court? He chuckled at the thought of her. Then he sighed. Lord above! What a long time it had been since he had as much as talked with a woman, except for the little Baroness and the sulphurous Mrs. Lewis. Mrs. Lewis—he felt his neck flush as he thought of her. Eyes always on him. Might be awkward if the General noticed. Give Headquarters as wide a berth as possible.

The horse plodded on. Fresh scents rose from the thick woods on either side. Some bird, a lark perhaps, suddenly flooded the early air with its song, a glad, lifting song that threw back Ahrens' head, a smile on his firm lips. That was it. Enjoy this country in its fine summer. Let cold fall and Europe look after themselves. These deep woods, the wine-like air. He laughed and slapped his thigh. A hundred paces down the road a doe shot out from the trees, halted in a patter of sharp hooves and stared at the two horsemen, brittle, slender legs poised. Then she tossed her head, snorted and broke into graceful flight. "Europe!" said Ahrens aloud. Then he called over his shoulder: "Come on, Rentner. Light enough for a gallop!"

The horses pounded along the soft dirt on which a few dim shadows had begun to show, traced by the climbing sun. Something glimmered by the roadside and Ahrens recognized a tall grenadier helmet, brass fronted. Beyond it was an odd-looking haversack, doubtless rebel, and a broken-stocked musket pitched onto a bed of moss beside a British water-bottle. Three bodies of men had passed this way, each leaving its own peculiar sign-manual to mark its passage. Riedesel could not be too far ahead. Ahrens could deliver his message, perhaps, take one in return and be back at Independence in time to catch a canoe up the lake and be in at the death of the rebel flotilla.

The road suddenly climbed sharply, vanishing among the tree-tops up the side of a steep ridge. Ahrens leaned forward in the saddle, staring along the brown track. Something long and solid inched its way up the grade far ahead. Then he caught a flash of brass, a hint of blue and red, saw the rhythmic drive of a hundred legs, black gaitered, the swing of a hundred blue arms, red cuffed. "Grenadiers—the Specht grenadiers," grunted Ahrens and spurred his laboring horse up the slope.

Drawn faces, caked with sweat and dirt, looked dully up at him through sunken eyes as he shouted: "General Riedesel! Where is General Riedesel?"

One man pointed stiffly ahead, then dropped his arm as though all his strength must be centered on moving his draggled white-breeched thighs. The mare struggled and blew on the long slope. Once she skipped across the road as a grenadier abruptly jerked his hands in the air, reeled out of the column and fell, bayoneted musket thudding in the dirt beside him, clashing against his light sword.

The column was left behind. Another, equally racked and spent, overtaken and passed. There were more figures in the road, sprawling grotesquely, more men slumped over against the rough tree-trunks as heat and fatigue took their toll. Still the hill stretched out endlessly.

Then at the crest he rode suddenly into the clear morning, the sun full in his face, and found a company halted, men and officers sprawled about the long grass of a field. He looked at the white facings of their dust-covered blue coats and their gilt buttons, knew them for a company of the Rhetz regiment. A haggard lieutenant, his face a drawn mask of sweat and mud, panted as he leaned on his stick and pointed ahead down the road.

"The Baron left us long ago. We made a late camp." The lieutenant gulped between sentences. "We marched at three this morning. An English messenger came up. The Baron took the Jaeger company and eighty of the best marchers of the grenadiers. He pushed on, telling us to follow as quickly as we could."

"How far is the Baron by now?"

The officer shook his head. "He is like a madman. He believed that the English Fraser would soon be in contact with the rebels, so he took the swiftest and drove them on. He is like a young ensign of cavalry, rather than a stout general of forty. I hope there will be no action. The men are done for. Heat, heavy marching, stinging flies, little food."

Close by, a grenadier sat up in the long grass, tried to shift his heavy pack, then vomited agonizingly. His squatting comrades, heedless, breathed heavily through open lips, dull eyes on the ground.

Ahrens nodded, signaled to Rentner, whose slower mount had just breasted the rise, and cantered on. The trees were thinner here. Then they closed in, opened, closed. Ahrens was suddenly reminded of a strip of road—was it toward Chemnitz?—where he had cantered years ago, his father on an easy-gaited bay, himself on a fat little tub of a pony with his chubby legs sticking nearly straight out from a deep saddle. The picture faded, its last image torn to shreds. On the right of the road was a gutted cabin, forlorn and smoldering. Tumbled heaps of clothing, scarlet-topped, lay in the rough dooryard. Ahrens choked back a wave of nausea and spurred his mare. One of the sprawled bundles had once been a child. Now it lay, one hand stretched toward the body of a naked woman, its pate glistening stickily. Not all the Indians had been too drunk to push on.

There was movement up front where the trees met overhead, movement and a sudden bray of field music as fifes squealed and drums slammed. Full-throated, the crash of voices swept back:

A might-y fort-ress is our God, A bul-wark nev-er fail-ing.

Ahrens pushed the mare to a gallop. He wanted to put leagues between himself and that ghastly dooryard. A bulwark never failing? To the people who had called that dooryard home? The singing faces under the high, pointed helmets were sunken-eyed, dirt-caked, but the stride of the company was smooth and cadenced, the muskets slanted evenly over aching shoulders. Ahrens overtook the rear files, shouting: "The General! Where is the General?" The singing men drove on, careless of the sweat that dripped from neck and chin onto the red facings of their heavy coats. Leaning from his saddle,

Ahrens caught the collar of a stocky lieutenant. "Can't you hear?" he yelled. "Where is the Baron?"

Through cracked lips the officer mumbled something inaudible, pointed forward along the line of sweating blue. Then his eyes bulged. Ahrens straightened in his saddle.

Far away, muffled by the tangle of trees, there came a drumming, crackling rattle. Sporadic, it grew and swelled to a steady roar.

"They're at it!" croaked the lieutenant. He stared off toward the head of his column at a lumbering trot, sword banging at his knees. His voice broke as he yelled above the deep notes of the hymn: "Pick up the step! They're at it! They've caught up with the damn rebels! Pick up the step!"

"Rentner!" Ahrens' strong voice rang above the tumult. He heard the thudding of the man's horse behind him as he galloped past the head of the straining column.

The country seemed to open up before them as they raced on. There were more frequent clearings, larger clearings, then a steep rise up which the horses labored, and beyond it a green, sunny world which snapped and roared with a hidden fury. They topped the rise and Ahrens reined in to stare at the tumble of round hills dotted with open fields which spread out before him in the flooding sunlight, and at the point where the road dipped into a deep-scooped valley with scattered roofs and a rough-spired church.

"Look, sir!" The exclamation seemed to be wrenched from Rentner's tight jaws. His eyes were staring, wondering.

The jutting hill to the southeast, just above the roofs, threw off dull blossoms of gray-white smoke, stabbed with flame. A few puppet figures in red moved slowly across an open patch toward a ragged line of puppets in gray, in brown. Other red figures moved into the patch. There was more smoke and an incessant, tearing din.

100

Redcoats stumbled, scrambled up again, stumbled, fell and were blotches on the green. The drab line spread, began to lap around the red forms, spilled through some woods, lapped farther and farther around a prolongation of the red lines. In the center of a clearing, a man in red sprang onto a high rock, faced about, waved a bearskin cap in wide circles to other red figures. There was a whitish puff from the branches of a high maple. The red figure spun about. The bearskin sailed away in a wide arc.

Ahrens watched, incredulous. The red lines slowly sagged and sagged. The drab arc spread wider. He shook his head. It couldn't be. That was Fraser's advanced corps, picked companies of picked regiments. Yet—yet—they *were* falling back.

Thin and clear, fifes shrieked above the banging and slamming of muskets. "What the devil!" muttered Ahrens. On the left of the red line, a wave of steady green appeared, a stout figure in blue and buff at their head. The green line halted, fired a crashing volley that rolled a thick pall across the sunlit grass. Ramrods flashed. The green line moved again, the blue and buff leader waving a bright sword, drawing his men on toward the right tip of the drab line of brown and gray. Ahrens narrowed his eyes, then laughed explosively. "Run you to earth at last, Baron, run you to earth at last!" The green wave crept on. Ahrens stood in his stirrups.

"Watch, Rentner, watch! Now—now! They'll close with the bayonet. Now they'll break those damned rebels! Watch!"

The space between the green line and the drab narrowed, narrowed. The red lines began to move steadily on. Ahrens stared, rubbed his eyes. Where were the men in gray and brown? "I'll be damned!" he muttered. The fields were empty, save for the men in green and red, save for the tumbled patches of every color strewn about on the bright grass. The rebels had melted away through the woods, loosing off occasional shots.

When Ahrens reached the top of the next rise, the firing had died away entirely. The red and green lines had joined in a wide semicircle. He dismounted, tossed the reins to Rentner. "Wait here," he said, and set off across the clearing.

The grass in the sloping field was deep, and Ahrens started violently at the first red-jacketed body that lay so heavily among the roots. There were more beyond it, three privates and a fresh-faced ensign who lay across a lean man in a blue coat, bone buttoned, then more men in homespun, in red. Ahrens sheered off toward a patch of woods where English officers directed a search for wounded. He must find the Baron before the pursuit of the Yankees got out of hand. Burgoyne's orders had been positive.

"General Riedesel?" A grenadier lieutenant looked up from the dead sergeant by the maples. "Straight on. Talking with General Fraser in the next clearing. Here—lend a hand with the wounded."

Ahrens shook his head. "Have to find the Baron. Orders from General Burgoyne."

The grenadier slipped off his low bearskin cap, wiped his damp forehead. He looked queerly at Ahrens. "He'll wait. No hurry."

"Must get to him before his troops are committed to the pursuit."

There was a queer, choking noise in the officer's throat. "Pursuit? Oh, my God!"

"What do you mean?"

"You'll see." The grenadier smiled grimly, moved off toward a thick-set private of light infantry who rocked to and fro, cursing monotonously and clutching a knee where raw, shattered flesh showed through a sodden crimson rent in white breeches.

The red-coated private in the next clearing wiped grimy hands on his jacket and stared sullenly at Ahrens.

102

"Red Hazel? Ain't seen him—sir." The "sir" was grudging, reluctant.

"*General* Riedesel, and not so slow with that 'sir'!"

The man's eyes bulged. "Beggin' your pardon: sir. I thought—I mean to say as how—that coat, sir. Thought you was a bloody Dutchman."

"So I am a bloody Dutchman. See that you keep a civil tongue in your head, or the fifers will be tricing you up for a flogging!" He snorted and walked on. "Bloody Dutchman! Looks to me as though all Fraser's men might be dead or on their way to Boston if Riedesel hadn't brought his 'bloody Dutchmen' up in time! Next clearing—next clearing! Which *is* the next clearing?"

Long grasses flicked across his boots. He stumbled on over hummocky ground. The sun was beating down from an intense blue sky across which clean masses of white sailed lazily. He stopped to stare, amazed, at a tall, white-haired man who lay quietly on his back, looking peacefully at the clouds through glazed eyes. His clean-shaven lips were set in a firm line and his cold musket lay strangely across his decent black coat with its buttons of dull silver. Ahrens shook his head. "What was *he* doing on a battlefield?" There was something unsettling in the calm of the old face, the long white hair. If *such* people were turning out from their chimney-corners! . . .

From a nearby thicket where panting grenadiers sprawled, he heard a high, Cockney whine. "W'it! Just w'it! That's all! W'it, I s'y! Red-bloody-'Ayzel'll be s'yin' as 'ow 'e won the bloody battle. Bringin' 'is lousy Dutchmen onto the field after we'd blasted the Yankees!"

"The sacred ties between gallant allies!" muttered Ahrens. "And over on the left I'll bet that some Jaeger is bellowing that the British will claim all credit." Then he saw blue and buff under a wide apple tree where the florid Baron, cocked-hat fanning desperately, talked with a heavy man in red and white.

103

"I agree. They will surely re-form, attack. We'll fortify that rise on the left, join up my breastworks with yours."

The man in red and white rumbled. "Can't feel safe in the open. Lord, what shooting! I wouldn't have believed it. They even sent men up into the trees to pick off the officers. Last shot drilled Major Acland through the legs. Ensigns, lieutenants, captains—went down like carpetbowls!"

"Mine, too. Ten men down on the first volley. They— Ah! Here's Lieutenant Ahrens. Tell me you were sent with guns! Two six-pounders, two only, and I'll sing like an angel above!"

"Sorry, sir." Ahrens couldn't help staring at the sweating, disheveled Baron, powder-blackened and hatless. "I was only sent with orders from General Burgoyne. I was afraid I'd not reach you before the pursuit got under way. The General's orders are that you push on west through Castleton and from there to Skenesboro at the head of Champlain."

Riedesel whistled. "Push on? My men are dead beat. No sleep, no rations and a hot action. Do you know that there are a hundred and fifty dead, British and Brunswickers, in these fields? The rebels are sure to attack again. General Fraser, here, agrees with me."

Fraser looked at Ahrens sourly, nodded. "Dig in. Try and get some rations. Heard that there are cattle wandering about. Suicide to advance."

Ahrens turned to the perspiring Baron. "The orders were positive. 'Push on to Skenesboro,'" he ventured.

"Damn it, so are the Yankee bullets positive!" cried the Baron. Fraser nodded glumly. "No, I'll stay here till we see better how things stand. You saw the Baroness?"

"Just as I left. She was on your pinnace with the children, following up the main body. I heard that they caught up with the rebel flotilla in the narrow end of the lane. Sure to blow it into the woods. Burgoyne will make his headquarters at Skenesboro and wants to push south from there as fast as he can. Sent all the artillery

104

by water down Lake George. He's very eager to reach Albany before Howe."

The Baron's blue eyes narrowed. "Ought to do it, ought to do it. But—" he pointed to crumpled bodies scattered through the field—"but, there are some of our best troops. What did they meet? A long line of farmers with rifles, officers mostly in smocks. The rebels broke at first, then rallied among the trees. They only gave way when the Jaegers outflanked them. They've scattered. They'll form again. We'll break them again. They'll vanish and reappear. Every man is a marksman. Few of ours can hit at thirty yards. Bewilders our troops. It's— it's new. We form a line, we charge. There is nothing to charge. Well, well. Of course, we've collared about four hundred prisoners, but—"

Fraser's growling voice said, "It was a damn close-run thing. Let's start the men digging and felling logs for a breastwork."

"The sooner the better," said Riedesel. "If you'd only brought two six-pounders, young man, just two." He sighed, shook his head. "You'd best stay by me now."

Ahrens shook his head. "I think I'll hit across country to Skenesboro. There's work for me at Headquarters."

"Across country! My dear Ahrens! We don't know *where* the rebels are. Off there in the woods somewhere." He waved a vague hand. "I've told you of their shooting. Your six feet on top of a horse! If you ran into them—" He shrugged expressively.

"You say yourself, Baron, that the rebels may strike again here. They can hit me in a redoubt as easily as on the open road. No rule against shooting a sitting officer so far as I know. I think I'll trust to flight. I've seen the route on the map. Along that road to Castleton, then on to Skenesboro. That is, if those houses over there are Hubbardton."

"Hubbardton—such as it is." Fraser smiled, pushed his cocked hat back on his forehead. "Our first captured city. Let him go, Baron. He can give the General a verbal account of our position and plans. I'll send that Tory lieutenant, David Jones, with him."

The Baron threw out a hand. "So be it! At your own risk, though. Mind, I warn against it. I don't order it!"

Fraser roared: "Lieutenant Jones!"

The young man in Tory green was grave-faced, steady of eye. He listened respectfully to Fraser. "To Skenesboro? I know the road."

"You'll accompany Lieutenant Ahrens to Headquarters. You will wait there yourself for further orders."

Jones looked dubious. "It's a rough road, General."

Fraser glared. "Afraid of it? Afraid of a rebel or two?"

"Of course." Jones looked at Fraser with frank eyes. "I'll risk all that, though. I mean—better if I go alone? Some of the regular officers, sir—new to this sort of thing—"

Fraser flushed. "New—are they? Well, good time for them to learn—if *you* can teach them anything. This officer will go with you."

Ahrens felt uneasy as serious appraising eyes played over him. Then Jones suddenly smiled. "Where is my horse, sir?"

Freshly mounted, they jogged off the field of Hubbardton and started down the six-mile slope that led west to Castleton, Rentner plodding stolidly in the rear on a heavy black. Jones looked over his shoulder at Ahrens.

"Hope you aren't offended by what I said about regular officers."

"Not I." Ahrens laughed. "Probably deserved it."

"You don't look like most of them. They frighten me."

"Frighten you?"

"Can't learn. When we pushed out toward Ticonderoga, I guided a detail of light infantry. They wanted to reconnoiter the Yankee outposts. The officer in charge marched the men through waist-high scrub in parade formation. I could almost hear the rebels licking their lips. Dropped five of the men. Did that officer learn a

106

lesson? No, sir! That was the way British infantry always advanced, he said. Said he wouldn't have *his* men wriggling on their bellies like Indians. Must have comforted the five men to know that they were winged when in perfect formation. There may be wild riding ahead of us and I didn't want to squire anyone like that over *this* road."

"You know this part of the country?"

Jones nodded. "My home," he said tersely.

"Home? I thought your corps was Canadian."

"Tories? No. We're all from south of the border. My home is at the mouth of Moses Kill on the Hudson. Just below Fort Edward."

"A soldier by profession?"

"Not I. I was a student at the College of New Jersey at Princeton. When the trouble came, I chose for the King."

Ahrens raised his eyebrows. "Isn't that unusual? I heard Carlton, up in Quebec, cursing the American colleges for rebel hotbeds. He mentioned Harvard and Yale as well as yours."

"Why—perhaps it was." Jones' eyes were on the horizon. "I quarreled with another Princeton College man— John McCrae, a colonel in the rebel militia. He's a neighbor of mine down Moses Kill way."

"Seems an odd reason, a personal quarrel."

"Not so odd. The quarrel was about his sister, Jane. She was outspoken for the King."

"And so—I am still puzzled."

"And so—as we expect to be married, Jane and I—why, you see I took the green coat. And I'll be able to look after her when the army moves down the Hudson. Look— lot of men crossed the road here."

Ahrens reined in, peered at the soft dirt track. "How can you tell that?"

Jones pointed to bent and broken bushes on either side. "Twenty or thirty men. May be stragglers. They were going south. Better be careful now."

107

"Careful be damned!" Ahrens looked down the long funnel of green that stretched away before him. "Fast on the straightaway, slow around curves, wide and slow. That's good practice in any kind of warfare. Come on. Ride for it!"

The horses pounded down the long slope, bushes snapping at legs and flanks, light branches lashing their riders. In the thick woods a rifle cracked, something whined between Ahrens' chest and the straining neck of his mount. "Faster, faster!" he yelled. Two shirtsleeved figures, trailing long muskets, scuttered out into the road, stared in astonishment at the onrushing horsemen, fumbled with their pieces. Ahrens drew his pistol. "Don't swerve!" he roared. "Hard at 'em!" His pistol slammed, there was a crash behind him as Rentner fired. Then the shoulder of Ahrens' horse caught one of the men, knocked him spinning into the bushes. The other dove out of sight into the underbrush. The horses crashed on, riders low in their saddles.

After a mile or so of frantic galloping, Ahrens crooked his hand across his forehead, the old signal to decrease gait. The horses slowed down to a jerky trot, then a puffing walk.

"All right?" he called, turning in his saddle.

"Right enough." Jones grinned at him, eyes bright. "Think your orderly's touched, though."

"Just touched, sir." Rentner's voice was hard and clear. "Man fired from the woods just as I raised my pistol. Scraped the skin on my forehead. Stopped bleeding already."

"Lucky enough." Jones laughed. "Must have been a dozen stragglers in the woods. The two we rode down were the laggards. Hi! Look there!"

The trees fell away to the left, exposing a broad vista of eastern hills. A road showed plainly across a shoulder, lost itself in a valley, then reappeared on higher ground. Along this road trailed scattered groups of men, moving east, men in homespun, men in uniforms.

"There they go!" cried Jones. "Look, there's a line of regulars—the ones in blue. Continentals, the rebels call 'em. Mile—two miles away. All going east. That means that there'll be no more attacks on Fraser. Means the country is clear ahead of us, which is more important so far as we're concerned."

Ahrens strained his eyes after the vanishing lines. "Sure they won't rally and go back to Hubbardton?"

Jones shook his head. "No organization. They're willing enough if someone would only give 'em the lead. Now all they think of is getting back to their crops. Local farmers, most of them, except the regulars of course. Thank God we're safe now. Lord, how this horse is blowing! See that water ahead on the right? South end of Lake Bomoseen. Let our horses gulp a little there, get their wind. I could use a little myself."

Through the long hot day they followed the road. Ahrens found that he was nearly reeling in the saddle with fatigue. Through his tired brain there whirled a medley of confused impressions. Those fields by Hubbardton, the sprawling forms. That old man with his long white hair, his firm mouth—what *had* brought him onto a battlefield, what business had he there? Yet— there he lay in his decent black coat. Looked like a country preacher, a school-teacher. Other bodies had been young, almost boys, just a few hours before. Should have been tending cattle, stalking deer, angling for trout—not lying in heaps in the sun, their homespun blood-spattered, their bodies torn. It wasn't like war, fighting an army that drew all ages into its ranks.

Good shots. What targets the grenadiers and the light infantry must have given them! Red coats, white breeches, brass-fronted helmets, green coats faced with red, those colors against the green fields and the neutral tint of the thick tree-trunks. Long lines halting, dressing, firing, moving on, halting, dressing, firing. Albany in a fortnight? Light points began to dance in his eyes. Why not—why not strip down the equipment, dull

109

the brass, break up those solid, mechanical formations; meet the rebels with light, loose lines whose dull colors would melt into the countryside; make the men as agile as those farmers. No more polish on musket-barrels to catch the sun and show a target to a skilled marksman. No more time wasted on drill suited for European battlefields. The force must be light, mobile, like rangers, supported by the tried organization of the old armies. He'd talk to the Baron about it when the army reassembled at Skenesboro.

It was late in the afternoon when the first roofs and a glimmer of lake-front showed over the tree-tops. The horses plodded wearily along. The roofs grew clearer, a great sweep of white on a sandy plain, a sweep of white cones where Burgoyne's thousands had suddenly thrown up a canvas city.

The three horsemen began to meet small parties of men in red jackets, in blue. Ahrens shook himself, told Rentner to straighten his stock and sit up in his saddle. The army was closing in about them. In knee-deep grass, long lines of picketed horses tossed their heads, whinnied, bit and kicked at each other, at the men who groomed them. Ahrens turned in his saddle to thank Jones for his company. He started to speak. Then his eyes narrowed. He shook his head, listened, shook his head again, held up his hand, reining in his horse. Jones looked at him in surprise.

"What is it?" he asked, brushing dust from the green sleeve of his coat.

"Listen!" Ahrens bent his head.

"Can't hear anything," said Jones.

"I don't quite make it out, yet it's distinct," said Ahrens. He took off his cocked hat, held the crown back of his ear.

The breeze freshened, sweeping through the big elms behind them. Far to the south they caught, faint but unmistakable, the pock-pock-pock of a hundred axes driven into hard wood. Pock-pock-pock, pock-pock-pock. It was

110

slow, monotonous, continuous, almost menacing. Now and then the steady, distant beat was punctuated by a muffled crash. Pock-pock-pock.

Low sunlight slanted through the maple leaves and stamped a dappled pattern on Kurt Ahrens' sleeping face, traced shifting smudges on the white waistcoat and breeches which were revealed as an unconscious arm flicked back the light blanket. A fly lit on his forehead, zigzagged with quivering steps across his high-bridged nose. Ahrens' hand, futile as a baby's, brushed indefinitely at the fly. The motion awakened him. He blinked upward through the spreading cloud of leaves under which he had slept. Where was he? His face went vacant in the effort of returning consciousness. Had he been asleep in the park of the great Kentish house where he once spent a long holiday? Or in some orchard close by the sharp hill of Harrow? The edge of the playing fields? Slowly he decided that that must be it. The playing fields—for dimly there came to him a sound which must be that of a broad-bladed cricket-bat, several batsmen facing sweating bowlers, for the smack of the wood was steady and continuous.

Lazily his eyes swung about him, widened in something approaching terror. A tall form, smeared with black and white, stepped into his range of vision, gliding through the long grass with a noiseless step, toes swinging inward. Other shapes followed, black and white streaked, naked save for loin-cloth and moccasins. Between them a handful of white men walked dully, eyes on the ground, their country clothes tattered, their empty hands swinging heavily by their sides.

Ahrens sat up abruptly. The vision of peaceful Harrow and its spire-topped hill was snuffed out like a guttering candle. He stared after the thick-muscled legs in their stockings of heavy wool that tramped between the coppery calves of their captors. But the sound of the bats? Even the ghastly reddish forms that stalked away

111

with their rebel prisoners could not dispel that. He shook his head. The sound was still in his ears, rapping, rapping, rapping with a maddening insistence. His eyes cleared. That was it! The sound of distant axes that he had heard, riding down the wood road into Skenesboro.

He sprang to his feet, snatching up the crumpled blue coat which had served as pillow. Suppose that the army had pushed on while he slept! When he had ridden into camp with the news that the rebels had been driven from the field at Hubbardton, he had sensed the feverish tensity, the hectic drive of victory, in the stone house of Colonel Skene where Gentleman Johnny had set up his headquarters. The rebel flotilla smashed, St. Clair's men scattered, the garrison at Fort Anne, just a few miles south down Wood Creek, driven away. Albany in a fortnight! Move any minute! A lightning drive forward—twenty miles to the Hudson, forty to Albany, with the wreck of St. Clair's men flying before them!

Infected by this temper, Ahrens had not bothered about pitching a tent for himself. He had rolled up in his blanket under the big maple, haversack and sword close by him. What had happened while he slept? He slipped back the straps of his haversack, burrowed in among the neatly folded shirts and stockings, hunting his case of English razors, a bar of French soap. He would squat by the little brook that flowed into Wood Creek, remove a three-day beard, and then see what could be learned at Headquarters.

He knelt by the grassy edge of the brook and splashed cold water about happily. He had sent Rentner to the bateaux by the lake-front to retrieve the heavier pieces of his baggage. There was a lighter uniform coat in a valise that he particularly wanted, if the weather were to keep so blistering. He lathered his face, listening to the endless din beyond the cabin-like houses that fringed the south end of Champlain where a ceaseless rumbling and stamping arose as the Canadian teamsters screamed curses at their scrawny horses and the little two-wheeled baggage carts rocked and skidded among the tree-stumps. Men in green, in red, in blue, shuttled among the forest of dingy white tents, along the water-front and in and out of the wide door of Skene's house under the round mountain of rock.

The cool wet edge of the razor bit cleanly into his beard. He screwed up his eyes as he scraped carefully down one lean cheek. Then he opened them wide. The shuffling hum of a marching column drifted to his ears, a column of red trudging painfully west along the road from Castleton. He stared. The setting sun in their faces, the men who had fought at Hubbardton slowly and stiffly filtered out of the semi-gloom of the forest road onto the cleared plain that was Skenesboro.

He recognized the heavy figure of General Fraser, the tall young Earl of Balcarres, his clothes riddled with shot. Then came limping the green-fronted coats of the 24th infantry, the light infantry and the grenadiers. Glassy-eyed and stumbling with fatigue the column moved on, white breeches soaked and stained from wading creeks and pushing through swamps, faces still blackened with powder, jackets torn and soiled, hatless heads, bandaged heads, heads topped with bullet-pierced hats and caps. They halted jerkily, the men leaned heavily on their muskets and looked dully at the ground with heavy-lidded eyes. A grenadier of the 9th infantry, yellow facings stained with powder, moss and pitch, took off his low bearskin cap with trembling hands, wiped his steaming forehead. Ahrens heard him say in a low tone: "It ayn't 'uman, that's all. It ayn't 'uman. Bloody roads through trees and never a sound you don't myke yourself. Damn rebels shootin' at you, and nothing' to charge. S' 'elp me, I seed a thousand of 'em, and ayn't used my b'yonet once. No village what you could rightly call a village, no towns." Another voice answered: "Just bloody woods and rebels back of trees shootin' at you. Call this a war! I'd sell my soul to hear an honest cannon rumbling over Christian pavements or

113

see a tidy stone village like we used to see in the Low Countries. But these trees an' the silence an' the rebels back of the trees." The first voice repeated: "It ayn't 'uman, just ayn't 'uman."

The column moved on. Ahrens looked after it, frowning. He remembered the faces of the men who had come back the day before from the skirmish at Fort Anne, their haunted eyes, their staring, staring at the endless surge of tree-trunks about them, the spasmodic, nervous glance over the shoulder at the slightest sound. With meticulous care he finished shaving, his mind still full of the men he had seen, men not cowed, but bewildered, ready to strike but not sure of what they could strike at. He dashed running water over his face and neck. The stinging of his fresh-shaven chin cleared away his slight depression. He saw a solid figure dumping a heavy bundle on the grass where he had slept. "Rentner!" he called. "You'll find a light coat near the top of that valise! Lay it out on the grass. And find me a fresh fillet for my queue!"

He ran up the gentle slope that led to Skene's house, settling the collar of his new coat, sword banging against his knees. He returned the salute of the Brunswick dragoon, whose unit had been formed into a headquarters-guard pending the securing of horses for them, and stepped onto the ringing boards of the wide porch. He turned and looked south into the living sweep of crowded pines that seemed to have no beginning and no end, that dwarfed the sandy plain with its dingy white tents, that shrank an armed city into the merest speck in an ocean of tumbling green. Something of the look of the spent infantry came into his gray eyes. Over the tree-tops there came to him that steady, insistent rapping far away, the distant crashes. He stared. "God in heaven!" he muttered. "Does that go on forever? Worse than the blasted mosquitoes!" He shook himself. "Let's see about this war!"

The Forest

BURGOYNE massed his main army about Skenesboro at the head of the road which ran south by Wood Creek to Fort Anne, Fort Edward and the Hudson. Most of his artillery, his heavy baggage, he sent by water up Lake George to be landed at Fort George and dragged overland to meet the army at Fort Edward.

The men were poised, tense, as they camped at the head of Champlain, eager to follow up the victories they had won over the Americans. But Burgoyne waited. Only the Indians were active, shuttled back and forth on the far flanks of the army, under the savage leadership of St. Luc, while screaming men and women died in isolated clearings under the heavy pall of their burning cabins.

The army chafed, began to lose its keen edge. No one thought to send out light troops to inferfere with the thousands of axe-men whom Schuyler had sent into the woods in the path of the eventual advance. The army chafed, with the eternal pock-pock of distant axes ringing in their ears.

V

The Forest

"THEY issue fresh beef tomorrow, Gustav."

"How do you know?"

"I heard Sergeant Zacher's wife say so." Hedwig settled the broad kerchief which fell across her shoulders and breast, frowned at a tiny gold-washed brooch that pinned the ends.

"Thank God for the news." Rentner squinted along the lake at the distant bateaux that were still unloading at the Skenesboro landings. "Salt-pork for four days and nothing to drink with it except this stuff the natives call spruce-beer." He made a wry face.

"Fresh meat," said Hedwig again. "I've saved a lot of cornmeal. We'll boil it with the beef. It will make a good thick stock, and I've found some onions to put in it. It's pretty here." The tents of the Skenesboro camp were dull blotches in the distance. Sounds came faintly through the hot afternoon air to the grove on the rocky point where she sat with her solid husband. Birds twittered among the springy branches of the white birches and a gray squirrel raced through the soft grass in a series of jerky runs and sudden halts. Out in the lake a fish streaked out of the water, fell back with a dull plop.

Hedwig leaned back against her husband's shoulder, settled herself on her rocky seat, looking out over the tumbling blue of the lake, flooded with slanting sunshine. He gently ran his thick fingers through her hair.

117

She twisted her head, looked up at him. "Say it's pretty," she said.

"I like the Odenwald better."

"Yes, but this is pretty, too."

"I didn't ask to come."

She plucked at the coarse red cloth of his cuff. "We're lucky to be here. If it hadn't been for the Lieutenant—" She shuddered a little.

He nodded. "That's so. He just says: 'It's the way things are; make the best of them.' I'd have gone before a firing-squad if it hadn't been for him. He's a good man."

"He has the funniest way of looking—as if he were laughing at himself and at everything—kind laugh, though. Does he know when the army moves?"

"Every day he says: 'This is the day.' He won't let me unpack his things. But it's been nearly ten days now, and when we rode in from Hubbardton that night, he thought the army might have gone without waiting for him. He doesn't know why we wait. Nobody knows. Just waiting—and that noise going all the time." He raised his head. The incessant sharp thudding still drifted up from the south. He made an impatient gesture. "Can't get it out of my ears."

"It's dreadful." Hedwig shook herself, settled her head back again. "What is it?"

"The Lieutenant says it's the rebels, chopping down trees across the road we've got to follow—if we ever follow. Across the road and across the creek. I talked with a grenadier yesterday. He's with the rest of the infantry that the Baron keeps off at Castleton and came into camp to bring a message. He says the men at Castleton don't hear a thing from one day to another. Just their own voices and that sound. He told me that the men say the ghosts of all who have been killed by Indians in the old wars and this one are swinging axes against the trees, trying to build safe places for themselves."

"There are always wars and always ghosts, aren't

there, Gustav?" She spread well-shaped fingers on his white knee. "You haven't said much about the battle you saw. What was it like—being in a battle?"

"I wasn't in it. Only saw it from a hill."

"No, but what was it *like?*"

"Not much of anything. Just men in a field, moving about in smoke. Then some of them went away."

"Did you see any of the rebels—afterward, I mean?"

He nodded, lips compressed. "A lot."

"What were *they* like?"

He wrinkled up his forehead. "Like—like anyone else, except hardly any had uniforms. Our men looked better. The rebels looked like—oh, I don't know. Just decent folk. Some looked like schoolmasters or preachers. I saw one colonel who looked like the Count—the one who lives in the big stone house on the old road to Offenbach."

"Corporal Zimmer's wife says the rebels eat their prisoners."

"I don't believe it." Rentner shook his grave head. "They're wrong to rebel. But they don't eat people."

"Are they wrong to rebel?"

"The Lieutenant says they are—they are fighting against the way things are, and the things are too strong for them. They were decent-looking folk."

"Were you frightened, Gustav?"

"Too far away. I felt sick on the field, though. And when we passed that cabin where the Indians had been. That naked woman with no top to her head and—"

Hedwig placed a hand across his mouth. "You told me about that. You've talked about it in your sleep. There was a child, too?"

Rentner's jaw tightened. He nodded. "I think the Lieutenant felt sick, too. He galloped away like the devil."

"And when the rebel fired at you?" Her finger touched lightly a fading red streak on his forehead. "It's nearly gone, now. Were you frightened then?"

"Too excited. It happened too quick. I felt weak afterward, my knees wobbled against the stirrup leather."

They fell silent. He took her hand, gently stroked its back. She stared across the lake. "I hate being in a tent with other people."

He smiled. "It's not so bad. There are four other couples in our tent—the whole squad is married. Think of Muller's wife—the only woman and four men, not counting her husband."

Hedwig wrinkled her nose. "I'm not Mrs. Muller. Besides she'd hate to be in a tent with other *married* people. The day I washed your white breeches in the creek, she was there. She sleeps under different blankets every night."

"She told you that? Does she like it?"

"No. She said the tent was too small. I wish that we had a tent to ourselves or could sleep in the open—away from the others."

He slipped his arm closer over her shoulders. "We do—most every night."

"But most every night it rains and we have to go back into the tent. You know there's been thunder so often. And then when we come back, everyone holds his breath and listens—or doesn't. That's almost worse."

"Never mind, Hedwig. When the march starts, we'll be moving all the time and camping in the open."

A drum rustled and rattled far away at the edge of the camp. Hedwig sighed. "That's the four-o'clock drum. When do you have to go back?"

"I don't have to. The Lieutenant is dining at Headquarters and then riding over to Castleton. Said he wouldn't need me till tomorrow."

"And you never told *me*?"

He stirred uncomfortably. "I—I've been trying to think how to tell you. I—"

She stretched her round arms up and drew his head down to hers. "You're such a silly goose, Gustav. You're just as bashful as when we were courting. If that rebel

120

had only known it, he would have taken your horse away from you and made you walk to Skenesboro." Her white teeth nipped delicately at the lobe of his ear. He slipped his palm under her round chin, turned her face to his. She laughed, ducked her head, then moved her lips to his.

After a moment he said in a low voice, "I saw a place today when I was walking with the Lieutenant. It's back of us—not very far. There's a little waterfall, like the ones in the Spessart, and little trees." He stod up, held out his hands to her. She laughed up at him, then rose, brushing pine-needles from her wide skirts. Her eyes were suddenly demure. "Do you think you could find it again, Gustav?"

He threw an arm about her. They walked away under the pines.

Gentleman Johnny Burgoyne's infectious laugh rolled jovially through the cool, raftered rooms of the Skene house. "Just a moment, Lieutenant. I'm writing a note to the Baron over there at Castleton. Sending him the last two dozen of this lot of Madeira. Lost it to him on a bet."

Mrs. Lewis leaned back in a deep chair. Her loose gown did ample justice to her remarkably white and full breasts. She pouted, said in a sulky voice: "It was *my* favorite, next to the champagne." Her eyes were on Ahrens.

He shuffled his feet a little, toyed with a horn-handled carving-knife that lay by the cold roast on the broad plank table. "What was the bet, sir, if I may ask?"

"The bet?" Gentleman Johnny chuckled. "Why, I wagered the Baron that my family was older than his. He was obstinate about it. You heard him, Mrs. Lewis. Obstinate as a mule. I thought I'd floor him, so I quoted the original grant made my ancestor by 'Time-honored Lancaster,' as the Immortal Bard calls him. The grant was made in thirteen hundred and eighty-seven. Really, it's worth repeating." He narrowed his eyes in thought. Mrs. Lewis yawned behind a small fan. "Had it letter-perfect last night. Oh, yes—the grant goes:

> *'I, John o' Gaunt,*
> *Do give and graunt*
> *Unto Roger Burgoyne*
> *And the heirs of his loyne*
> *All Sutton and Potton*
> *Until the world's rotten.'*

"Delightful, isn't it? But damn him—the Baron, I mean—he had me. Seems *his* family goes back to eleven hundred and something. So he won the Madeira and may he enjoy it." He turned to include Mrs. Lewis in his beam, saw her eyes lazily on Ahrens. He coughed. "My dear Mrs. Lewis—ah—military details of no interest to you. Perhaps you'd be bored? Besides, it's two o'clock. Time for me to be official." He rose with a bow. Mrs. Lewis slipped from the room, her mouth curling a little at the corners.

Gentleman Johnny rubbed his hands. "H'm, h'm. Yes, yes. Ladies best out of the way in such discussions. Mustn't let Mars and Venus quarrel, eh? H'm, h'm. Well, how've you been spending your time at Skenesboro? 'Fraid I haven't had much for you to do."

"I've taken the opportunity to drill the Hanau gunners who march with the column. They're not more than a dozen. General Phillips gave me permission to use his six-pounders. It keeps the men alert and gets me back into practice."

Burgoyne beamed. "Good boy! The men take to it?"

"I've kept the drill simple and they get on well enough. Just advancing with drag-ropes and a little simulated fire."

"Splendid, splendid. Recruits good?"

"Good—barring one man. He's Heinz, a farmer, who'll

122

never do as a gunner. Good man around horses, perhaps."

"Send a note to the adjutant about him. Must make proper use of our material. Now, Lieutenant, I didn't send for you to discuss recruit-drill. I've heard you frothing a bit because there wasn't enough for you to do. See this report? A ranger tells us that there are a lot of stray horses in the woods to the west; knows just where they are. Now, I want you to take twelve men—Hessians or Brunswickers—and round up as many beasts as possible. Most of your people are over at Castleton with the Baron, so you'll have to take what men there are to be found on details and so on about the landing. See that fellow Strachwitz—he'll look after you. Then report to Captain Fraser—*Captain* Fraser, not the General. He'll produce the ranger to act as guide. You'll draw halters from army stores. One man to four horses—that'll make forty-eight, even if you and the ranger don't bring any. Whew! Forty-eight to fifty horses! What a difference they'd make! Can you picture the Baron, being given fifty horses for his dragoons? He'd have you canonized!"

"Infantry men, gunners, chasing wild horses, sir?"

"In the forest—in the forest! There their matchless speed will be fettered by the luxuriance of nature. Small clearings, thick trees! Simple, my boy, simple. Now off with you and see Strachwitz about the men. Plan to leave just after daybreak tomorrow and have the ranger ferry you back by sundown."

Ahrens held up his hand. The straggling file behind him halted gratefully on the forest trail where hot, damp air hung like a palpable cloud, wrapping about arms and legs, forcing into gasping lungs, lying like a dank, humid bundle between sweating shoulders.

"Sergeant Barkopp!"

The big sergeant, flushed face streaming, trotted heavily up from the rear, grounded his piece and swung his hand in salute.

"No sign of that ranger?"

"No sign, sir."

Ahrens frowned. This was damned annoying. "Fall out the detail. Twenty-minute halt. Let the men eat their rations, but keep on the alert. Can't tell where the Yankees may wander and I've heard that Indians sometimes don't pay attention to uniforms. A scalp's a scalp in their reckoning. If the ranger doesn't come up, we'll have to push on without him."

The men sank panting onto the damp trail. They sat with their shoulders hunched, eyes haunted by the silence about them, by the towering menace of the giant trees that shut out the daylight. Ahrens scrambled up onto a broad-topped rock and ran his eye over the detail as he drew fried bacon and hard bread from his haversack. "What a collection! Should have been all Jaegers or light infantry, troops drilled and dressed for this sort of thing."

He munched at the hard bread, eying the four grenadiers with their mass of equipment, the four dragoons in their appalling boots and heavy sabers. Rentner and the other gunner were well stripped down and the two Jaegers sitting just beyond them were alert, hard, competent-looking. Sergeant Barkopp at the far end of the line was loaded down like the other grenadiers. He looked very sulky, Ahrens thought, had been sulky since the early morning start when he, taking advantage of the material offered by a burned cabin, had ordered the entire detail to blacken their musket-barrels with soot, then forced the almost tearful grenadiers and dragoons to smear the scabbards of their sabers. The grenadiers had nearly mutinied when they heard the order to dull the high brass plates of their helmets. Well, their sullen looks were worth the absence of bright metal on the forest trails.

Ahrens stretched out on the rock. Below him the men fumbled awkwardly in their haversacks, began to eat.

124

Something of the bewildered terror of the forest ebbed away. Scraps of conversation drifted up to him.

"Sergeant says them as wants it gets free land when the rebels are beaten."

"I wouldn't mind. Land's good hereabouts. Look at the color of this."

"Black as my woman's teeth. This is rich loam. Now, along the Kinzig, you have to manure all the time."

"Lot's of work to clear this, though."

"Who said clear it? They take the land away from the rebels, the farms, houses, horses, cows, and give 'em to us."

"Fool! That's a shave you heard at Headquarters!"

"I swear. The captains and colonels get big houses in the towns. Sergeants gets houses in the villages. We take the farms."

"Ever seen a rebel?"

"Too many. Up in the hills. They hid in trees and shot at us. Ten of the lads fell in less than a minute. Dead, too."

"Well, I've never seen a rebel. We *hear* 'em, though. Their damn axes. Hummel went mad, listening to 'em, and they brought Francke in from Castleton yesterday, raving. Why don't the General or the Baron send Jaegers to drive 'em away? The swine are felling trees across the road we've got to follow; trees, like this one here. Look at the time we'd save, if they sent Jaegers. Might be on our own farms now."

"*I* don't know why. Look—why do the rebels fight? What *for*, I mean?"

Someone sucked his teeth noisily, spat. "They don't fight. We come along and they go away." There was a snicker.

"No, but why *do* they fight? We fight for our Duke. You fight for your Elector and the English for their King. Who makes the rebels fight?"

There was a silence. Several men started to speak at

125

once, broke off. Ahrens listened, interested. Rentner's voice cut through the murmur. "Land," he said.

Surprised grunts echoed against the rock. "Land? How can land make a man fight?"

The familiar tight voice answered, "It's *their* land. They fight for that."

"You mean their landlords make them fight?"

"They have no landlords. It's *their* land, their own."

There was a mutter of laughter. The heavy voice of an older man rumbled. "Look here. You're still a recruit. A corporal tells a private what to do, a sergeant tells a corporal and so on. Now—" a hand smacked the ground—"a landlord tells a peasant to plant cabbages or rye or lentils. How can you have a private without a corporal or a peasant without a landlord?" There was a ring of triumph in his thick voice.

Ahrens looked at his watch. Past noon. Where the devil was their ranger guide? An hour ago he had said that he was suspicious of the surrounding forest and would make a short detour, rejoining them within fifteen minutes. There had been no shots in the woods. How could he have come to harm? A growing suspicion hardened in Ahrens' mind. The stray horses had not materialized, nor any sign of them. He swore under his breath. "The Canadian son of a bitch! He's used this as a pretext to get out of camp. He's either made his way to the rebels or he's headed back to Canada by one of the old Indian trails. Blast his soul to hell!"

A chill settled over him. In what direction did Skenesboro lie? He had trusted implicitly to the guidance of the ranger. Now the camp might be half a mile away or ten.

Again he looked at his party. They were all old soldiers, except Rentner, perfectly at home on known battlefields or cruising through the close-packed towns of Europe. Not a man under six feet, not a man who was not thoroughly skilled in his trade. But in the virgin forest? Helpless as babies! He squinted up at the sky.

126

The interlaced branches of the trees that welled up so thickly on all sides from the damp, clayey soil cut off any view. "No help from the sun? Well, mustn't let the men see that there's trouble." He shouted: "Fall in the detail, Sergeant!"

The trail dipped away and the heavy men slipped and slithered on the greasy slope. As they approached a spot where it wriggled away between two colossal boulders, he fanned his men out to cover the flanks. "Perfect place for an ambush," he told himself. "Pinned between those rocks we'd be wiped out." The detail reassembled on the trail beyond and dug their heavy boots into the treacherous clay of a steep upgrade.

Light showed through the pines ahead of them. Ahrens' hand went up and the thin column halted jerkily, the men puffing and blowing, flapping futilely at the swarms of black-flies that fed on their necks and wrists. He sent a Jaeger and Rentner ahead while the rest of the party waited in dull misery. The Jaeger trotted back. "Open fields, sir. No one in sight."

"Where's Rentner?"

"Stayed at the edge to watch, sir."

Ahrens nodded. He had noticed the way the Jaegers and Rentner had made use of cover when the detail had fanned out by the boulders. The others had simply blundered ahead.

From the last trees, Ahrens looked up at a round hill. a hill whose steep slopes had been cleared at some earlier time and now was covered with a light growth of brush. "I'll get a look at the sun!" he thought. But a hot gray haze hung in the sky like a dull bowl, not a shadow showed on the grass. "North, north—where the devil is north?" He bit his lip. Then his face brightened. The rebel axes! For once they might be useful. He heard their pock-pock through the hot air, beating like a faint pulse. Where were they? They should mark the south for him. He listened intently. Then he swore savagely. The hollow beats seemed to come from all points of the compass. He

127

gave a command. The column deployed into line and started up the hill.

The grade was steep and Ahrens found himself drenched with sweat as he pushed through clinging brambles and jabbing thorns. Locusts rose from the ground and droned away, whining like spent bullets. White butterflies danced against the gray-green of the shrubs and somewhere in a little grove to the left a tree-toad chirped its forewarning of rain. He stumbled over a flat stone, saw charred wood about. Cabins had been here once, several cabins. His foot turned up a bit of polished wood, now weathered and charred on one end, then a book, its leaves gnawed and blackened by fire. He picked it up, riffled swollen pages. On the scorched title-page he read: *The History of Tom Jones, a Foundling. By Henry Fielding, Esquire.* Books, polished wood? In the wilderness? He looked back at his men. They were panting and struggling, stopping to gasp out exclamations at what they saw in the rank growth, struggling on again. One man tripped, fell heavily. He rose to his knees, holding a half-burned snathe. Another waved a moldly leather box.

At the tree-fringed crest he paused to let the straggling line close up. Below him lay the bare slope up which he had scrambled, then a solid floor of green, unbroken, a solid waving floor of tree-tops. There was something menacing in the limitless expanse, some sinister force within it which seemed to close in slowly on the pigmies in red and blue who swarmed somewhere off to the north by the head of the rippling lake. He had a strange illusion that all the tree-trunks, all the heavy boles, were moving slowly and purposefully on the invaders, moving to smother them under their tons of leaves, crush them under their myriad branches. He rubbed his eyes. The trees were motionless, save for the waving, tossing plumes of the tops. He shook his head angrily. "Hurry them up, Sergeant," he called and went on.

The pines at the crest were big and old, but beyond them was soft grass, low tangled bushes. He passed under the straight masts of the trunks, stepped out onto the turf. Then he halted abruptly. Before him was a blackened chimney, gaunt and naked, and at its foot sat a bright-haired woman, gently rocking a cradle.

Ahrens held up his hand, motioned to Barkopp to keep the men out of sight beyond the trees. He moved across the waving grass. There was no sign of a house, just the blackened stones of the old chimney. Gray sky and grass and the woman bending low over the gently rocking cradle.

Ahrens swept off his hat, bowed. "I trust I do not disturb you, madame. May I inquire the way—"

A strikingly pretty face turned to him. Then something cold settled over his heart. The brown eyes were vacant, unseeing. The cradle which rocked so gently was empty. Ahrens stammered: "Your pardon, madame. I—" But the face bent over the cradle again, crooning low:

> "One for the blackbird,.
> One for the crow,
> One for the cutworm
> And two to let grow."

Frozen to the spot. Ahrens fumbled with his cocked hat. Then from behind a nearby tree something cracked viciously, a bullet spatted into the ground close by his foot.

Sergeant Barkopp shouted, musket-locks clacked among the trees as Ahrens stared into deep blue eyes that blazed in the shade of a faded sunbonnet. A slim girl in homespun pointed the muzzle of a long, heavy rifle unwaveringly at him. A second piece leaned, still smoking, against the tree. Then the girl spoke, using the stilted German of the universities. Her voice was low and tense. "Take your men and go."

Ahrens turned on his heel, swept his arm toward the

129

trees where his men rustled and crackled among the dry twigs. "Uncock the pieces! Not a man is to move!" Then he swung round and walked toward the slight figure. The level barrel did not waver. He spoke crisply. "Are you aware that your bullet struck within an inch of my foot?"

"That was precisely where I aimed it. Will you take your men and go?" The eyes still flamed over the sights of the long rifle, whose muzzle was steady.

He came a pace nearer, eyes on hers. "I shall give no order until you lower you piece." There was no reply. He stepped forward again. "Must I take it from you?" His voice was low.

She shivered a little, straightened. Slowly the barrel dropped. "Please go," she said in a low, choked voice. "Go—the way you came."

"My men are tired, madame. They have come a long way. They will do no harm."

"They must *not* cross this clearing."

"Would you have me drive them back through the briars?"

The blue eyes dropped for an instant. "There is a path that skirts the clearing, just below the crest. It begins by the split oak. Now take them and go—go!"

In admiration, Ahrens looked her full in the eyes. Then he bowed, turned and walked away. "Bear to the left, Sergeant, by the big oak. No one is to enter the clearing."

The air was baking in the belt of trees that straggled away on the other slope of the hill. The men staggered along, gaudy uniforms sweat-blackened, helmets and cocked hats shoved far off streaming foreheads. There was a dull crash. Ahrens looked back. The tallest of the grenadiers pitched to the ground, rolled over and lay breathing heavily through purple lips. Coming to his aid a dragoon caught his ridiculous spurs among gnarled roots and sprawled headlong, where he lay sobbing with rage, heat, exhaustion and the incessant torment of black-flies.

Ahrens groaned. "Oh, the devil! Lost—and now this oaf must collapse! How can we ever carry him?" He wiped the sweat from his face and doubled back to the prostrate man. The dragoon had struggled to his knees and was fumbling hysterically at the buttons of the grenadier's long vest. As Ahrens knelt beside him, Rentner stooped, deftly loosened the man's choking stock. Barkopp leaned on his musket, scowling.

Puzzled, Ahrens studied the gasping infantryman. "Ever seen a man taken like this before?" he asked.

Rentner nodded. "Just like this. It was the hot sun. The rays burned through his hat and made his blood boil. But there's no sun here."

Ahrens got to his feet. "Well, keep fanning him with his hat. We'll make some kind of a stretcher and carry him." Then he looked at the spent men. His eyes clouded. The grenadier was a six-footer, heavily built. "Hard—but we've got to do *something*," he thought. He called: "Come on, Barkopp—have your men hack down— Eh? What's that?"

Gray showed between the thick boles of the trees, a voice cried: "What's this? Here—don't you know what to do for him? It's heat, of course, nothing but heat."

The girl from the clearing knelt beside the grenadier. The men fell back, gaping as she pillowed his hot, damp head in her lap, staring as they heard her stilted German. "Where's his hat?" she asked.

Rentner handed her the tall, brass-fronted miter with its back of heavy red cloth. She surveyed it with disgust. "What a thing to wear in the summer woods!" She slipped a slim, sunburned hand into the crown. "Like an oven!" She turned to one of the Jaegers. "Go get me a handful of those leaves in the little clearing there—yes, those big leaves." The Jaeger trotted off obediently. She said to Rentner, "Now take this—this thing—" She held out the tall helmet. "There's a cold spring just below

131

those rocks. Fill this and bring it to me. Don't drink any yourself; you're too hot." She looked down at the grenadier, a tiny crease showing between her eyebrows.

Ahrens looked on amazed. "This *can't* be true! The heat has touched me as well as Schnabel, there. Yes—it's the same girl. Only saw her eyes back there, eyes and the rifle. White feet in Indian moccasins! The voice of a lady, frontier clothes, speaks bookish German in a forest clearing and—that rifle!"

He watched her almost incredulously as she took the broad mullein-leaves from the Jaeger, deftly made a wet pack for the grenadier's head. Then she looked up at the sergeant. "Here—take his stock off. It's choking him. I want it to bind these leaves around his head."

Barkopp's sullen mouth tightened. "Not the stock. Colonel Breymann would have him flogged and me broke if he came back to camp without that stock. It's uniform!"

The girl's eyes widened. "Flogged? Because this ridiculous thing is round his head instead of round his neck? Well, loosen it, anyway, and give me a cloth of some kind."

The dragoon produced a broad handkerchief and the girl set to work. Soon the flushed eyelids began to quiver, congested whites showed. She nodded to herself, lips compressed. "That's better now?" she asked. Her voice was suddenly gentle, soft.

Schnabel blinked, squinted, trying to focus his eyes. Then his jaw dropped as he found himself staring up into a smiling face. "Lord Jesus!" he muttered thickly. "Lord Jesus! What in the name of ten thousand devils!" He closed his eyes, opened them slowly. "A lady—a lady in the forest!" He struggled to rise. A firm hand on his forehead held him down. The girl turned her head slightly. "Sergeant—strip that heavy coat off him. Now slip it under his shoulders. No—higher. Thank you."

For the first time she addressed herself to Ahrens, superbly unconscious of the stares of the sweating men.

132

"Let him lie there a little. When he gets up of his own accord, he'll be able to walk. And you'd best throw that ridiculous helmet away." She walked easily to a nearby tree, picked up her long rifle.

Ahrens followed her, hat in hand. In English he said: "I—I am greatly indebted to you, madame. But for you—"

She turned grave eyes on him. "You speak English well. But don't thank me for what I did. Any child could have done as much."

"That doesn't lessen my debt to you. May I present myself? I am Kurt Ahrens, Lieutenant in the Hesse-Hanau artillery. Our—the guide deserted this detail on the trail. There is some question about the proper road back to camp. Would you be kind enough to set us right?"

She gave him a level glance. "Where do you wish to go?"

"To Skenesboro." He felt nettled that she had coolly passed over his introduction.

"Skenesboro?" The corners of her rather full lips twitched. "You've taken an odd— There! Your man's on his feet." Schnabel leaned dizzily against a thick oak while his comrades brushed bark and moss from his dank clothes. "He'll be all right," she went on. "Someone else had better carry his musket and don't let him march too fast."

Ahrens nodded. "And the trail to Skenesboro? I'll be doubly in your debt."

"You're far afield," she said. "You've no map? No compass? And they sent *you* in command in— Yes, I'll set you on your way."

She led the way along the trail, the little column moving painfully after her.

Ahrens shook his head in bewilderment. Presently he ventured: "Your home is in Skenesboro, madame?"

Without looking back she replied: "Not in Skenesboro."

"Perhaps we take you out of your way."

"Not at all."

"Damn the girl!" he thought. "Why won't she talk? She can smile—I saw her waste an incomparable flash on that Brunswick oaf with his head in her lap." He eyed her narrowly as she swung along under the heavy trees, stepping with sure grace. Where *did* she come from? Where did she learn German? And that rifle!

The trail, well marked now, wound away through the huge boles, twisting now to skirt the base of a great rock, now slipping painfully around a deadfall. The girl, deft and silent, pressed on steadily. The men behind her puffed and clumped in the dank forest gloom, stiff branches and twigs tangling in their deep cuffs, catching at swinging straps and chains. When they spoke it was in the hushed pitch that was gradually enveloping the whole army, a low tone that would not echo and bring some nameless terror out of the crowding trees.

By a low waterfall which hummed and rumbled among ferns and sleek black rocks, a wide trail crossed theirs at a right angle. The girl halted, half turned and said in her rich voice: "This will lead you to the lake. There is no other crossing it." Ahrens drew a sigh of relief, then disappointment surged over him as the girl, without another glance, started off at her swinging step.

"But, madame! You—you surely won't go on alone! Through the forest! We—my men will escort you. It's the least we can do."

The soft lips curved in a half-mocking smile. "You're afraid I might lose my way?" Her eyes softened for an instant as though regretting the advantage she had taken of a man who seemed so helpless to her. She shook her head. "Thank you. I know my way. And here is my escort." A slim brown finger touched the barrel of her rifle.

"May I not know to whom I am indebted?" Ahrens' full voice carried a hint of exasperation. But the girl was moving away along the trail without a backward glance. He looked after her until her homespun skirts vanished around the face of a gray boulder. Suddenly he drew his sword, cut a deep, wide gash in the bark of a young maple that grew by the trails' crossing. His men, leaning on their weapons, exchanged glances. Lieutenant was touched, eh? That fetched him. Heads wagged, forgetful for the moment of the endless battle with black-flies. Then heavy muskets were heaved onto aching shoulders and the column moved off, still adjusting its pace to that of the recently stricken grenadier whose musket Rentner carried.

"Now to what point of the compass are we moving?" wondered Ahrens. "Damn it, was I a fool to trust that girl? *She* might be a rebel. We may be heading straight for Schuyler's lines—or whoever's in command now. A trap? No, not with those eyes." He shook his head, recalling their level gravity. What else had been in them? Bitterness, yes, and scorn. What else? Something untouchable, a sure serenity. He hitched at his sword-belt. How much more of this trail? How those men behind him must suffer in their heavier equipment! His own legs ached dully, his wrists, swollen into clumsy blocks by the bites of black-flies and mosquitoes, throbbed and itched maddeningly. He felt dizzy with fatigue.

By a small stream he halted the column, and while the men drank sparingly he strained his eyes for some sign that would show him the points of the compass. But the sky, where scraps of it could be seen through the branches, wore its uniform haze of gray. He shrugged, gave it up and looked at the men sprawled by the stream. He smiled grimly as he noticed the rope halters wound about each man's waist—to bring in the ranger's horses!

His eyes caught Rentner's. "What is it?"

"My grandfather was gamekeeper in the Hartz Mountains. I mind his saying that bark always grew roughest on the north side of a tree." His rather sullen blue eyes were fixed on Ahrens. "Does the Lieutenant think that might be true here in America?"

Ahrens nodded coolly. "Very likely." To himself he chuckled. "Smart man, Rentner. I won't forget that." Then he signaled to Barkopp. The halt was over.

"Heading north," he said to himself. "Bless old Rentner for remembering that about the bark. Now, that means we've made a great circle west and then south. We went east after we met the girl and now—" He sniffed the air. It was heavy with a cool tang. "And now we're heading slap for the lake. We're getting close." He lengthened his stride. Blue and red, blue and yellow, green and red, splashed white breeches and splashed black boots, the weary men trailed after him under the sweeping branches of the trees.

Magnificent in scarlet and white, Gentleman Johnny Burgoyne rose from his baronial chair at the head of the long table. The wine in his glass glinted, his voice rolled richly in the raftered gloom of the Skene house.

"Gentlemen—the King!"

Chairs scraped and twenty voices muttered: "The King!"

The General's eye followed the uniformed waiters, gauged the exact moment when the last glass had been filled.

"Gentlemen—the Duke of Brunswick!"

The response rumbled along the rafters. Ahrens, swaying on his feet from fatigue, shuddered as he added up the number of allied princes whom the General would unfailingly toast. One by one they were named, the rulers of Hesse-Cassel, Hesse-Hanau, Anspach, Bayreuth, Waldeck.

Across the table Ahrens caught the sardonic eye of Colonel Peters, commander of the small Tory regiment which marched with the advance corps. Peters coughed, observed in a low, dry tone: "After the seventh or eighth potentate has been toasted, I seem to detect that the responses grow tolerably blurred and the emptying of the glasses notably accelerated. Let us praise the Lord that

136

the General did not bring Russians as well." He pursed his thin lips, turned bright eyes on Burgoyne as he waited for the next health. Ahrens grinned. It was the first sentence he had ever heard Peters utter at table. He leaned forward, hoping for further muttered comments, but the thin lips remained primly pursed.

Chairs scraped again. Ahrens leaned back, his head swimming as a fat decanter of port started its slow way round the candle-lit table. If only he could leave decently! The day in the steaming forest had spent him. He envied those of the junior officers whose duties took them away and who were bawling for their orderlies and their horses under the wide porch outside.

He looked at the remaining guests who inched their chairs toward the head of the table. The three brigade commanders, Simon Fraser, Hamilton and Powell. Then Acland, who commanded the grenadiers, still pale and weak from his Hubbardton wounds, the young Earl of Balcarres, gay and reckless, a string of officers, anxious-eyed majors and graying captains, then Colonel Peters. On his own side sat Specht, fair and red-faced in the absent Riedesel's place, then Gall, Breymann with his hard, brutal chin and keen, fanatic's eyes and, as far away from him as etiquette would allow, Breymann's arch enemy, Baum, the commander of the Riedesel dragoons. Red jackets and blue, yellow facings, green facings, blue facings, they began to swim and dance before his aching eyes. He passed the decanter to his right-hand neighbor, Geismar of the Baron's staff, being careful that the bottom did not touch the cloth. Gentleman Johnny was particular about such things. Then he reached for a bottle of brandy. Port was too mild for him after such a day. He drained a small glass and the room cleared. He poured again and was aware of his name rumbling in the air.

"So, Colonel Breymann, you'll have to tell the Baron that we've still no horses for his dragoons." Burgoyne shook his head sadly. "The rascal of a ranger deserted the party in the forest. As I say, young Ahrens here was

137

in command and it's only by the grace of God that he got back to us."

"Grace of God?" thought Ahrens. He closed his eyes to conjure up a vision of grave blue eyes under a faded sunbonnet, a long rifle in the crook of a slim arm. *Who* the devil was that girl? She haunted his brain like the sound of the axes, now far distant.

Breymann scowled down the table at him. "You, was it? I hear that you forced the grenadiers to smear soot on their helmets. You're not under my command, but by God if you were, you'd sweat for it! Cowardice, that's what it is! Turning grenadiers into Indians—into stinking rebels! For fear that some one might fire a musket at you in the woods!" He sneered, drained his glass and went on. "This country's no good. Nothing but trees, trees, trees. There's—there's—" he waved a vague arm— "there's no *order* to it. And the war's no good. Wish I were in the Jerseys with Knyphausen. *That's* war. Towns and villages and don't our lads loot! My cousin, Dessau, wrote me. If it's a Tory house they loot it because the Tory ought to be glad to help. If it's a rebel house, they loot it because he's a rebel. Half the grenadiers are sleeping on Yankee feather-beds. And silver!" His face flushed at the thought.

Baum's voice was purring, soft. He leaned toward Breymann. "Oh, yes. In the Jerseys. Your cousin was with Rall's brigade. At Trenton, wasn't it? Yes, yes. All killed or captured. And by that farmer Washington. Surprised in their beds, weren't they? Yes, yes, Colonel Breymann, it's a pity *you* weren't there. *All* killed or captured!"

Gentleman Johnny looked bewildered at the thick flood of rapid German. Then he half rose in his chair as Breymann rapped out an oath, reaching for the hilt of his sword. "Gentlemen, gentlemen—" He paused, eyebrows lifted, admonitory finger poised. Breymann growled in his thick mustache, compressed his lips. Burgoyne went on. "Gentlemen. I was about to ask young

138

Ahrens here to tell us something of his adventure. I'm sure we'd all benefit." He smiled down the table. "Young man, we're listening."

Wearily Ahrens told of the precautions he had taken to make his little group less glaring in the forest, more mobile. He felt fatigue slipping away from him as he reviewed the lessons of the march, became absorbed in plans for doing away with at least some of the hardships. He concluded: "If I go out again I'd like to have all the men wear skull-caps with the brass taken off. I'd like to give 'em short jackets, light haversacks, leather overalls like the rangers'. Nothing shiny, nothing heavy, nothing dangling. Sir, if you'd seen us on the trail! Staring blue and red, long tails, brass everywhere, swords which they never use tripping 'em up, clumsy haversacks and cartouche boxes swinging and flapping. The cuffs ought to come off the jackets, too. They catch in the underbrush." He drank more brandy, aware of the puzzled frown on Breymann's face as he tried to follow the English words.

Gentleman Johnny nodded. "Idea does you credit. Must look into the matter. Eh? What's that?"

A storm of protest rumbled about the table, then burst out. "I say, sir, the regimentals! Can't alter them!" ... "The uniform of the 21st is the oldest in the army, sir. Colors go back to James the First!" ... "What does this young scatter-brain want to do? Turn line troops into skulking backwoodsmen?" ... "Won't do with the 9th, sir! By God, the men would *mutiny*!" ... "Now, see here, young man, I've fought all over Europe and let me tell you that the uniform is like a flag to the men! They—" ... "A grenadier is a grenadier. Gad! He'll be saying that we ought to paint ourselves like stinking Indians!" ... "Young man, troops are for *battle*, not crawling through woods on their bellies. Battles are fought when two lines of infantry, advancing on each other in perfect order, arrive within mutual range. Then they fire by command. *That*, sir, is a battle."

139

"Suppose your enemy won't fight that way?" ventured Ahrens, turning to the last speaker, a gray-haired captain with a long, stupid face.

"Then, by God, sir, I say—I say he's *no soldier.*"

"Bravo, Captain!" . . . "Listen to *that,* young man. The Captain has put it in a nutshell!" . . . "Well done, Captain! 'Then he's no soldier!' " . . . "As for you, young man . . ."

A soothing hand was lifted at the end of the table. Gentleman Johnny's voice rolled out. "There is a good deal in what Ahrens says. *And,* in what you say, gentlemen." He smiled impartially along the board. "The solution, if I may use the word, must lie in employing light troops for such work. Then let the grenadier, the infantry of the line be saved for the more suitable tasks to which he has been so capably trained. Let them—" The deep tones boomed on. A slim ensign whispered in Ahrens' ear: "Bloody well thinks he's back in Parliament!" Ahrens nodded dully. "Suitable tasks!" he thought. "Where can he find 'suitable tasks' in the swamps and forests?" The brandy was clearing his head and he tried to recapture once more the image of a graceful form in homespun moving softly across a grassy clearing. He opened his eyes again. Gentleman Johnny was still declaiming, glass in hand:

"But I am happy to say that I view the question as largely academic." He pursed his lips and nodded. "Academic. I have felt so for some time. I venture to express my opinion—unofficially, of course—that the rebellion is broken. Skene assures me that the Loyalists, a great majority of the colonists, he says, will rally to us in thousands with each step we take to the south. Over four hundred have come into this camp so far. They are merely the earnest-money, if I may say so, of vast numbers to come."

A murmur rippled along the table. The door at the General's scarlet back opened and the long form of Charteris glided into the room, tiptoed over the wide

140

planks and sank into a chair opposite Ahrens. "What has he been saying?" he whispered. Ahrens raised a finger. "Listen," he said. The Major poured a glass of brandy and turned sleepy eyes on his general.

"The rebels have fled before us. In ten days they have not drawn a trigger. They have tried to block our way with their axes, but tonight's reports show me that Twiss and his sappers have cleared most of the road and the creek. St. Clair's army is scattered. Schuyler lurks helpless south of Fort Edward. At this very moment, Colonel St. Leger is close to Fort Stanwix at the head-waters of the Mohawk, ready to swoop east. Tomorrow, gentlemen, I shall give the orders to advance!" He slapped his hands on the table. "We'll move the day following, straight down Wood Creek to Fort Edward—well, as far as Fort Anne, anyway—then, ho! for the broad Hudson and the bayonets of Howe's men moving north up the river!"

An electric shock seemed to jar the listening officers to their feet. Ahrens found himself shouting with them. "Advance at last! On to Albany! To Albany!" A short captain of infantry threw his arms about Ahrens, shouting: "Then the cursed war's almost over! Oh, damn me, almost over! Hurrah for Albany and Howe's men!" Ahrens pounded the captain's broad back, cut a wild caper that made the boards ring under his feet. The whole room seemed to whirl and echo. Gentleman Johnny beamed benignly on his yelling, stamping staff. Ahrens snatched up his glass from the table, filled his lungs for a great shout. Albany and Howe's men! Then he caught Charteris' quizzical eye on him. Elation emptied out of him like quicksilver. He sank into his chair, swallowed his brandy at a gulp. God above, but he was tired!

Early that morning, the head of Fraser's red column had plunged into the woods, the men stepping out eagerly. Now, in the hot glare of late afternoon, the tail

141

end of the last Brunswick unit had just been drawn into the green funnel of trees as though by some slow, irresistible suction. The suction had not been steady. The long columns had plunged ahead, halted, plunged. Ahrens remembered the descriptions of the country that Lieutenant Twiss of the British Engineers had given him: hundreds, thousands of giant trees stacked, heaped, interlaced over a poor road, the creek filled with them; swamps drained to flood low-lying land, bridges wrecked beyond repair; he remembered as he sat his rather mangy roan by the edge of the woods and watched the constant step, halt, step, halt, gradually dull the spring of the legs, white-gaitered, black-gaitered, that passed into the forest.

They were gone now, anyway, and he could start the long line of carts and wagons that waited, a tumbling welter of tossing horses' heads and bristling ox-horns, far away by the end of the lake. He'd have to watch them carefully, for the General's orders about loading, about cutting down equipment, had been stringent. He raised his arm. Whips popped and snapped, shrill Canadian voices cursed and the first of the two-wheeled carts, a crawling dot on the plain, began its bumpy progress toward the wood road. From the dark pines back of Skene's house another whip cracked sharply, two ill-matched horses lunged into sight and a deep calèche rolled and rocked after them.

Ahrens bit his lip, frowning, as the high-wheeled vehicle careened crazily across the level. Nothing had been said about a calèche! He gathered up his reins, trotted to meet it. Then he saw that the man on the tiny box wore green and red. Brunswicker! He'd soon see to that! He flung up his arm. The driver brought his pair to a sweeping halt. From the depths of the carriage a solemn young face peered out, mouth puckered into a bud. The bud melted into a smile.

"Oh, it's Lieutenant Ahrens. I was *so* afraid it might be someone nasty and oh! how many thalers I had to pay for this calèche! Of course, it's not strictly regulation, but it was the best I could do." Two bundles on either side of the Baroness stirred, lifted blond heads and stared with round blue eyes.

Ahrens sighed. "The Baron said nothing to *me* about your marching with the troops."

The round face became grave. "No. You see, he *couldn't*. He didn't know."

"Didn't know?" Ahrens' voice rose. "But how can I send you along the trail? The Baron will be furious. I've a complete list of every carriage here, but there is no mention of yours."

The Baroness smiled and leaned forward in her seat. "See what a splendid traveling basket I've made for Caroline. Rockel drives so carefully that she sleeps sounder than in her cradle." She gently rocked a deep basket slung just back of the box. Caroline, eyes screwed shut, slept on.

Ahrens smiled in spite of himself, then returned to the attack. "The base remains here, Baroness. You'd be far more comfortable at the base than on the march. So would the children. Camp fare, you know."

"Oh, but while we waited at Ticonderoga, you've no idea how we ate. Geese, capons, all kinds of meats, partridge, all sorts of vegetables. They were *so* good. And beaver-tails. Rockel learned how to cook them. But we had no cauliflower or lentils. We shan't mind camp rations, shall we, children?" The little girls shook solemn heads. "And I've been growing fat as a Baden dowager." She swelled her petite form, blew out her cheeks. "Really, it will do me good, the march!"

"But the Baron—" persisted Ahrens.

The Baroness' round chin tightened. "You leave the Baron to *me*, young man."

"General Burgoyne will—"

The little figure leaned forward. "I saw a calèche containing Mrs. Lewis and a scandalous number of boxes and bottles, drive off two hours ago. And, besides, she

143

was brazen enough to offer *me*, the wife of General Baron Riedesel, a place in it!" The chin set in a tight mold.

Ahrens backed his horse away from the calèche. "You know the trail is narrow? Once in it, there will be no turning round?"

The blue eyes suddenly twinkled. "Yes—isn't it nice! Then the Baron *can't* send me back! Oh, Rockel! Hurry, hurry! Those nasty little carts will be entering the trail ahead of us! We *must* get in front of them! Hurry, hurry, hurry! Thank you, Lieutenant Ahrens!" There was a smile, a wave of a round arm and the calèche reeled away, Rockel clutching his cocked hat with a free hand.

By the first trees Ahrens dismounted and watched the long line of carts defile across the sandy plain and into the woods. His eyes widened as he counted. "Twenty-seven, twenty-eight—thirty carts, by God! Loaded with the possessions of one J. Burgoyne, Esquire, and nothing else! A big mouthful to swallow, Gentleman Johnny, after your pleas to cut down baggage. Why, I can live out of my haversack and saddlebags for a week if I have to."

The carts bumped on. "How far will they get? Look worse then the Brunswickers' shoes. Tacked together and falling apart already. That axle will split again in a mile. Hello—what's this?" He stared at an approaching cart, then shouted: "Wagoner! Cut that cart out of line! Cut it out, I say! Loaded against regulation. Pull out and halt by those broken carts under the birches."

The nervous little French-Canadian halted his dejected horse, fumbled at his jacket. "I have *petit papier*, mon officier. Zis cart, she all right." He produced a sheet of stiff, folded paper. Ahrens grunted. To himself he read: "The loading of carts 43–57 (inclusive) has my personal approval. J. Burgoyne." He shoved the paper back at the grinning wagoner. "What's loaded on there?" he growled.

The Frenchman's eyes rolled upward. "Ah, m'sieu. Zey were brought by ze men of ze General. But I nevaire see

a General who wear stays. One beeg box, she broke open.
I see stays, bonnets. I sink—" he held up an arch finger,
"I sink zey are ze boxes of Madame la Commissaire."
Ahrens waved him on. The wagoner flung his arms in
the air, screamed: "Fi, fi, donc, sacré animal!" The horse
leaned into its crude collar and the cart heaved on into
the wood. "Good example to set the army," thought
Ahrens. "Still, she's a neat bit. Damned if I wouldn't
break a regulation or two myself—if I were a general."

The carts rolled slowly by till they became a meaningless blur. Ahrens welcomed the occasional splashes of
color when the red coats of the strung-out wagon guard
passed by, trudging sullenly beside the shifting wheels.
Every now and then the stream halted—a broken axle, a
spilled load somewhere up ahead. Then the wheels
creaked forward and the sun picked up scattered moving
bayonets again. A thickening fringe of broken carts lined
the edge of the woods, where the wagoners tinkered with
hub or axle and the horses snatched at leaves, gnawed
bark, shifted, turned in equine perversity that reduced
their drivers to hysterical screeches.

Ahrens settled his cocked hat on his damp forehead,
thinking for the hundredth time how much more sensible it would be to turn the brim out flat and shield eyes
and nape from the sun; how much more sensible and
how utterly damning to hide-bound army minds.

Almost the end of the carts. Next would come the
relatively few heavy wagons which had not been sent by
boat up Lake George, then the women, the sutlers and
their carts, followed by two companies of the 21st as rearguard. He watched the rocking wagons start across the
sand, head toward the mouth of the road. He suddenly
slapped his boot with his crop; the green-coated rider
sitting a bony horse by the nearest wagon looked
vaguely familiar. He seemed more so as he trotted up to
the road, elbows flopping and knees jerking against awkward saddle-bags. Ahrens stared hard. Yes, there was no
mistake. Small, stoop-shouldered, snub-nose and abnor-

mally broad upper lip. Then he saw the close-set eyes and was sure of his man.

"You're a long way from Hanau, Donohoe," he said coldly.

Donohoe squinted down from his perch, staring. He hesitated, then said, "You seem to know me."

"I had the somewhat dubious pleasure of meeting you. It was in Major Zapfel's gun-park."

Donohoe scrambled down from his horse, mouth twisted in a smile. "You don't hold *that* against me, I hope. I had to get that runaway bastard."

"So I recall. You were a little insistent. About to set your men on *me*, I recall, when Zapfel appeared."

Donohoe guffawed. "Now, Lieutenant! You know the army. You're no fool. Of course, I was going to get that man, if I could. Had to. But I wouldn't have interfered with *you*. You know that."

"No?" Ahrens was noncommittal. "What brought you here?"

"That same God-damned runaway bastard. Zapfel reported me to von Kleist and what did that whore's bastard do but have me transferred from garrison duty and shipped off to England. Must have come here in the same convoy with you. Held me at Quebec, Jee*sus*! The women there! I'm bled white. Then I came to Ticonderoga, was ordered here yesterday. I'm in charge of the Hanau wagons."

Ahrens gave a dry cough. "Anything to keep out of gun-parks, I suppose."

Donohoe laughed hoarsely. "Grin all you like! That would have been all right if that bastard Zapfel hadn't poked his nose in." Then he scowled. "All the same, he hasn't heard the last of *me*! I know the army. I bought into the service with the understanding that I was only to do garrison duty. They can't ship me off here like this."

"Can't they? They seem to have approximated it."

"I know, but they haven't heard the last of me, I tell

146

you. Look here, you know the army. Did you ever see anything so God-damned funny as those two old sons of bitches, Kleist and Zapfel, trying to run a *garrison!*" The grotesqueness of such an idea seemed to double the little man up. He slapped his thigh. "Jeeesus! Nearly as bad as the people over here. Did you ever see such a lot of ignorant bastards?"

Ahrens shrugged impatiently. "Well, you'll have to wait till *this* war is over before you start the other one against von Kleist and the rest. This is the last of the English wagons. Better bring yours on now."

Donohoe raised his arm, shouting. The first of the German wagons rumbled out. Ahrens watched their heavy wheels and thought of the two-mile causeway over a deep swamp that the engineers had built, of the forty-odd bridges across gullies and ravines. "God help those wagons if the bridges give way!" he thought.

Donohoe's voice, thick and confidential, buzzed in his ear. "You've been in camp a long time. Anything good in the lines?"

"What do you mean—'lines'?" asked Ahrens.

"Oh, you know what I mean. Women's lines. By God, if I'd been round camp as long as you have, *I'd* know. It was easy enough in Quebec, ought to be here. What have you found? Don't keep it to yourself!"

Ahrens wondered if it wouldn't be simple to pick the man up by the seat of his breeches, throw him across his saddle and cut at the horse with a switch. That might keep his mind occupied. He said, "Give an Indian a handful of buttons. He'll pimp for you among the squaws. I imagine they'd be more to your taste and they're not particular."

Donohoe roared with laughter. "By Jesus! That's good! Give an Indian—what was it, now?—a handful of buttons! Jeeesus! Well, here come the last of my wagons." He scrambled into the saddle. "See you again. Keep your buttons on! Jeeesus!" He trotted awkwardly off in the wake of his crawling wagons.

Ahrens drew a deep breath. "Officer and gentleman!" he snorted. "Five hours' staring at those blasted carts! At least, I'll ride into camp with a thirst I wouldn't trade for a colonelcy and there'll be cold champagne, ice-cold, wherever Gentleman Johnny is. Hope Baum and Breymann don't fight all evening. Now for the last act. Here come the women and that's all except for the sutlers and the rearguard and those last are no responsibility of mine."

Along the little plain they trudged, bent under heavy loads or walking easily, small bundles slung on sticks. English women, German women, Canadians and half-breeds. Fresh gowns, tattered gowns, leather shoes, wooden shoes and bare feet, sunbonnets and bare heads. Some laughed and chattered, others marched with lowered eyes and set mouths, or breathed heavily through half-opened lips. Ragged children scampered along the fringes of the mass, wild with excitement, and there was frequent evidence of more to join them before long.

The head of the column halted, the rear closed up jerkily. Another of the countless obstructions on the road ahead, Ahrens supposed: a wrecked cart, a bridge down. The women leaned on their sticks, cut from the hardwood forests along Champlain. There was an unshatterable atmosphere of patience about them.

He rode his horse slowly along the column. The women looked at him, some curiously, some wearily and without interest. One slim girl, black hair bound in a band of scarlet cloth, turned snapping dark eyes on him, lips curved in a challenging smile. He felt a tightening in his breast, stared back. Her gaze did not waver. She planted herself, arms akimbo, watching him. He shook his head, touched his horse with his crop. The girl tossed her chin, swung her elbow in an easy gesture. The blue and red shawl drew apart as by accident, exposing an expanse of white, white skin, the swelling of a firm breast. Ahrens heard a laugh as he rode away.

Then he saw the face that he sought, a thrown-back

head, a strong throat tanned by weeks in the open. He raised the handle of his crop. "How goes it, Hedwig?"

Steady blue eyes lifted to his, white teeth flashed in a smile. "Thank you, Lieutenant. It goes well."

"The life is not hard?"

The firm, round chin lifted. "I am with my man, Lieutenant."

He smiled. "A good answer—and he's a good man, Hedwig. You don't fear the campaign?"

"Not while I am with my man."

"After the campaign?"

She threw out her hands in a wide gesture. "After? Oh, to own a corner of this land. To be free to hold it, work it, build a home on it. No bailiffs, no conscription. Just work, work, work. There—there may be another with us one day, Lieutenant." For an instant her pretty face was touched by beauty.

Ahrens threw back his head. "Another? My blessings on you both. And if I'm not godfather, I'll see the pair of you court-martialed. There! Off you go! I'll see your man when we make camp and tell him I spoke with you."

The column moved slowly on. Ahrens touched spurs to his horse. Ahead of him he saw the girl with the flaming head-dress. She had her arm over the shoulder of an older woman who was limping badly. As Ahrens passed, the black and flame head was tossed back and a strong voice sang:

> *"Cet étendard qu'au grand jour de bataille,*
> *Noble Montcalm, tu plaças dans ma main—"*

"Lord! That song again. Haunts me. All the ghosts of Carillon. Singing together." He started humming. The voice followed him:

> *"Et dans ma tombe, emportant ta mémoire,*
> *Pour mon drapeau, je viens ici mourir."*

Sergeant Barkopp dismissed the detail. Ahrens watched the men trot away in their round skull-caps and short, cuffless jackets through the orderly welter of dingy white tents that sprouted like some lush fungus growth along the ravaged banks of Wood Creek. He nodded in deep satisfaction, then turned up the path that wound through a hopeless tangle of giant, fallen trunks and splintery stumps to the marquee that Gentleman Johnny had pitched close by the charred walls of Fort Anne. From a tangle of broken branches and searing leaves a voice hailed him. "Turned ranger, have you?"

In spotless blue and red, Charteris smiled with lazy amusement from a comfortable seat on a smooth birch-trunk.

Ahrens laughed. "For the day only. I went out on a tour for Gentleman Johnny and he let me rig up the men and myself according to my own ideas. It was a great success—from my standpoint at least."

"Tour? What were you doing? Trying to capture a rebel or two?"

"Hardly. He wanted to know if any of the tributary streams that flow into Wood Creek are navigable and if they are, had those damned Yankee axe-men blocked them."

"Tributaries? That would be useful. Can't float a thing on Wood Creek farther than Fort Anne. Were they any good?"

"Not a bit. You couldn't float a haversack, and they all flow in the wrong direction, anyway."

"Call that a success?" Charteris flapped an indolent hand at a bit of cobweb that dangled from a branch above him.

"Oh—that? No. But you should have seen the men. They even seemed to think more easily in their light gear. As for mobility! They moved like Indians."

"All of 'em?" Charteris yawned behind his hand.

"Well, all except the three oldest. They seemed lost. They missed their damned packs and sabers and coat-

150

tails. Seemed to miss being in a tight, heavy column, too. Anything new?"

"Usual lot of shaves. We're going to meet the fleet on the Hudson, sail down to Florida and start harrying the Spanish colonies. We're going to Quebec to put down a French uprising. Washington has challenged Howe to a duel. Howe has captured Washington and hanged him on a liberty-pole on the Battery in New York. Gentleman Johnny's been made an earl. Breymann and Baum have ended their squabbling and spend all their time singing hymns together. Take your choice. All I *know* is that every gun—except those here at Fort Anne—is afloat on Lake George and will join us when we reach the Hudson at Fort Edward. And I also know that Fraser is within hailing-distance of that fort with all the advance corps."

"In sight of it? Hello! That means we ought to move down. Anything else?"

"No, but I imagine that St. Leger must be moving down the Mohawk toward Albany. We'll move in a couple of days, I expect. Look in at my tent tomorrow night. I've a bit of rum that needs drinking badly."

"Rum? Oh Lord! I'm dining with the Baron tomorrow. I'd like to look in later, though, if I may."

"Save a trickle for you, but don't wear that blasted backwoods rig. Scandalize my orderly. He's most correct."

Ahrens made his way to the marquee, where he found Gentleman Johnny bending over a beautifully drawn map. He looked up.

"Ah, there you are. Come see this map that Twiss of the Engineers made for me. A marvel. I'll have it framed and presented to His Majesty after the campaign. I swear I never saw a finer. See—here's Wood Creek so real I've been trying to dabble my fingers in the water. This dark square is Fort Anne. Now—match this with the other map he made. See the waterline. From Quebec to Champlain to Wood Creek. We can float every last

151

crumb of supplies as far as this point by Fort Anne. The umbilical cord of the army, if I may use the expression. Here's Fort Edward down here. Gad! You've no idea what a mess the Yankee axe-men made of all this. Trees felled and crisscrossed over the creek and the road, streams dammed, good ground turned into the foulest swamps you ever saw. I've a thousand Canadian axemen out clearing the way." He sighed. "Just a few miles to the Hudson on the map, but an eternity until the road's cleared. And they've done the same thing from Fort George to Fort Edward. Ah—let me see. Why did I send for you?"

"About those streams flowing into Wood Creek. I'm sorry to report they're no possible use to us."

"Oh, the streams. Yes. It's a pity. But I fancy it hardly matters. You've heard about Fraser? He'll probably take Fort Edward tomorrow or the next day. Won't have to fire a shot, I'll bet. Well—thank you, Lieutenant." Then as Ahrens hesitated, he raised his eyebrows. "Anything else?"

"About the men, sir. I equipped them like rangers."

"Oh, yes, yes, yes. I remember now. You'd talked about it at mess one night at Skenesboro."

Ahrens grinned. "Some of the older officers wanted to burn me for a witch."

"Professional feeling, sir, professional feeling. Backbone of the army. H'm, h'm. Well, how'd the men do?"

"Very well. I gave them a hard march through heat, broken country and several corps of black-flies. They ate frontier rations and came in just now heel and toe, looking very fresh. They looked well on the trails, sir."

Burgoyne nodded. "On the trail. Yes, yes. Very likely. But my dear sir, did you see them in camp? I saw them march past a file of Specht's men. The contrast! Shocking!"

"I don't want to press the point, sir, but on the trail the contrast would have been shocking the other way."

"Oh, no doubt, no doubt. But most unsoldierly. However, your idea does you credit, my boy, does you credit!"

Ahrens' face fell. "Then, sir, you want to give up the idea of adapting the troops to the country?"

Burgoyne's hands went up. "By no means, by no means! I wish—I wish that you'd write me a report on your expedition. That's it—a report. We'll press the matter on a more suitable occasion. Have to work slowly on some of the old sticklers. In the meantime, if you have any fresh ideas, bring 'em to me, bring 'em to me." He rose smiling. "In two days' time, the tide will flow again. Flow south. Then our eyes shall see no more of the forest! The broad river, the plains about Albany, and bayonets, Howe's bayonets, moving north along the Hudson!"

Ahrens ran down the slope from the marquee. "Really, I ought to have applauded! And 'write me a report.' By God, I'll do it in blank verse and he'll make me a colonel. Well, the day wasn't a total waste. I found the trail, I found the blaze I put on that tree with my sword! I could find it again. I bet I could find it in the dark. Wonder what that girl is up to now. Those eyes! She's not pretty, exactly. But— Is there a house there on the round hill? What about the other girl by the cradle?"

The Baroness beamed at her husband over the guttering candles as the servant Rockel set a steaming platter in front of him.

"Bear's paws!" she announced. "Lady Acland told me at Ticonderoga how good they were, so I sent Rockel over to Colonel Peters to learn how to do them." Her eyes were on the Baron, magnificent in light blue and buff, as he carved.

"And the paws?" asked Ahrens. "Did Rockel find an obliging bear on the way?"

"Oh, no." Her glance was wide and innocent. "The Colonel sent such a nice Tory boy from Yale College to ask me if the bear was black or brown. I told him there

153

was no bear and the Colonel sent me eight paws with the most graceful note. Wasn't he nice?"

Handsome and florid, the Baron smiled. "My dear Fritschen, you should have been the wife of a marauding baron of the fourteenth century, not soberly married to a peaceful cavalryman of these prosaic days."

Gravely she considered the notion. "I think I might have liked it. A big stone castle on a hill and a militant bishop for a neighbor. Why *is* beef so scarce now?"

"Only five hundred head of cattle in the army herd back at Skenesboro," said Ahrens.

"And more are hard to come by," nodded the Baron. "That man Schuyler ordered all the farmers to drive their herds away. If they didn't obey, they were denounced as Tories and the cattle taken, anyway. Delicious, Fritschen!" He bowed to the Baroness. "We must take this recipe back to Wolfenbüttel when the war is over. Astonish the Duke."

"Oh, yes!" cried the Baroness. "And we'll serve it to him just as we have it here. Planks laid on barrels for a table, a sheet of canvas stretched from the calèche as roof and more of this Madeira in thick glasses."

"Schuyler—that's a good Dutch name, by the way—he must have a depot where all these cattle are herded," observed Ahrens. "Anyone know where?"

"Skene says he has thousands—and horses, too—in what he calls the Hampshire Grants. There is a great river valley there, the Connecticut." The Baron made heavy weather of the word.

"Guarded?" asked Ahrens.

Riedesel smiled. "After a fashion. I have submitted a plan to the General, a plan for plucking the nosegay that Schuyler has so carefully gathered for us. The Tory Skene tells me that when the first column crosses over into the Grants, the people will come over to us in thousands."

"But he said that at Ticonderoga," said the Baroness. "Don't you remember? As soon as the forts fell, he said,

154

the Loyalists would take heart and come to us in regiments and brigades."

"Well, well, Fritschen. These Loyalists in the Grants may have been the ones he meant. At any rate, the General is considering my plan. Horses! I'd give ten cows for every horse brought in. Think of Baum's poor dragoons! Best heavy cavalry in Europe and forced to waddle along like conscripted infantry. The ridicule is breaking their spirit. Doing duty as Headquarters guard for lack of better employment. Disgraceful!" He sipped his Madeira.

"A raid, eh?" Ahrens was interested. "Light troops, a quick march and so on, I suppose."

"Oh, some light troops, certainly. But—light troops *only* serve to precede your regular line infantry. They can't be your sole reliance in actual battle."

"But what if the enemy is stubborn and won't suit his tactics to yours?"

The Baron frowned. "That's true. Now, at Hubbardton we lost far more than we should have. They feinted and sparred and each rebel was his own commander. But—that is not scientific war."

"What do you think, Baroness?" Ahrens turned to his hostess.

She compressed her lips judicially. "Everyone says that the Yankees do shoot well. But I do *not* think that they are justified in deliberately aiming at our *officers* with rifled muskets. It seems contrary to military custom as I used to hear it discussed at my father's house. But it won't frighten *us*, I'm sure." Her chin set firmly. Then she spoiled her dramatic effect by calling to Rockel in a loud whisper: "You have saved some of the bear's meat for the children?"

Ahrens laughed. "Where *are* the girls? I've a deer and a bear carved out of wood by an old Indian that I brought them."

The Baroness rolled up her eyes. "They strayed off into the woods and found the prettiest black and white cat. Or so they thought. Friedericka tried to pat it. They've been in exile ever since and I've burned their clothes. Such a waste."

The baron wagged his head. "I warned them, I warned them about black and white animals in the woods. Anburey, a gentleman-volunteer in the 53rd, had the same experience last fall near Trois Rivières. He seemed impressed." The Baron smiled. "But you're right about the rebels, Fritschen. If you deliberately wipe out the officers, who will lead the men? And then—where's your battle? Men won't fight by themselves. Suppose *both* sides did it? Well, we've seen nearly the last of it, I'm sure. Some of the youngsters growled at the delay at Skenesboro and here. But it was worth it. Skene says just our presence has heartened the Tories and will bring them streaming to us. The rebels will have to give up."

Ahrens looked doubtful. "Isn't it a military axiom that all time not turned to account serves the defense?"

"Ah, young man, that applies to proper war, formal war. Not a war like this where your enemies are not soldiers. I do hear, though, that in the south Mr. Washington is creating something like a proper army. More pleasure in *that* theater of operations, I should think. Dangerous man, Washington. Too bad Howe can't take him."

Ahrens studied his glass. "If I were Howe, I should be inclined to offer handsome subsidies to Mr. Washington."

Riedesel's head jerked back. "Subsidies? Why, in God's name?"

"Mr. Washington is, to my way of thinking, one of our most valuable assets. At the outset of the war he had the finest irregular troops in the world and a leavening of drill-ground fellows. What has he done? He's done his best to change his irregulars, the only kind of troops really adapted to this kind of war, into rather shabby copies of European troops. He seems to be planning to fight just the sort of campaign that Howe wants him to

156

fight. He maneuvers in the plains, near such cities as there are, just as though he were in the area of Minden—in a small country with a network of roads and chains of fortresses. He must know that the war won't end until his army is destroyed and he obliges us by making it as easy as possible for Howe to do just that."

"What would you do in his place?" The Baron stared.

"In his place I'd break every officer who had ever served in formal warfare. I'd send a boatload of the foreign advisers of whom we hear into the open sea with no rudder. I'd concentrate on developing a system of supply for strong, mobile columns and keep to the forests and mountains. Let Howe hold the cities. What good do they do him? I'd—"

Riedesel held up his hand. "You are very like your maternal uncle who was chancelor at the court of Baden. The most radical-headed man I ever knew. For God's sake, don't air views like that before Breymann or Baum. They'd be howling for your scalp like St. Luc's Indians. Not that I mind. Shows that you think about your profession. But the plan is unsoldierly."

Ahrens narrowed his eyes. Perhaps this was his chance. "I may have been too long away from troops," he said with a laugh. "Except for my two expeditions, I've hardly given an order, or marched with more than three men at a time. Glorified messenger for Headquarters. A clerk could have done as much."

The Baron shook his head. "No, no. There have been many matters that your knowledge has smoothed out. But perhaps you're right. Headquarters is a dull place for one of your age. I beg your pardon, Fritschen?"

Demure and innocent, she smiled down the table. "Isn't Lieutenant Bache a *little* young to be in charge of the Hanau gunners with the column? Of course, there are only a few of them and there won't be any guns till we reach Fort Edward, but—"

"Upon my soul, you give me an idea. Now, young man, if I can get the General to release you from staff,

I'll give you those gunners. How would that suit you? But no ranger tricks with them, mind now!"

Ahrens walked happily away from the grove at the west of the old fort where the Riedesels had established themselves. That would be a relief. Back to service with troops! He filled his lungs with cool pine-scented air. Staff work had been interesting, but there was always an undercurrent of politics, of feverish activity with no end save self-advancement, that irritated him. Back to real duty again; and when the guns came across from Lake George there would be work in which he could lose himself.

As he passed Headquarters he noticed something vaguely familiar about the dragoon who stood guard by the outer line. He peered through the dark. Then he was sure. "Good God, Heinz! What the devil are you doing in dragoons' kit?"

The square man drew himself up, saluted proudly. "I *am* a dragoon, sir. The dragoons needed more men. They saw I was too good for a gunner and took me."

Ahrens swallowed this bit of news. The adjutant had lost no time in acting. Heinz a dragoon! Then he recalled a hot afternoon back of Mount Defiance. "But look here, Heinz—the dragoons. Don't they remember you?"

Heinz smiled broadly. "Oh, yes. They remember me. They took me aside and swore to kill me if I breathed a word about the gun. They were to blame, for they were on guard. They couldn't catch me, so when questions were asked, they swore the gun had gone off by itself, and it was the sun shining on the vent that did it. Now, whenever I drink three of them sit close to me for fear I'll let my tongue trip. They are hard men, Lieutenant."

Ahrens felt a little weak. He looked at the smiling man. "Heinz, let me give you one word of advice. Tread *very* carefully. In this matter of the gun you've used up

158

all the good luck you'll ever have in the army. Used it up at one stroke. Understand?"

Heinz nodded, his foolish smile gone. "Yes, yes, Lieutenant. I was lucky to become a dragoon. An officer asked my trade and I told him I was a farmer. He asked if I understood horses. Then he took me to a tent and they gave me this uniform. And the officer said: 'Now you're a dragoon. See that you act like one.' And just then a Jaeger shouted: "Where's your horse?' and I knocked him down and rubbed his face in the pine-needles. The officer laughed and called me a good dragoon. Gave me a half-thaler to drink, but the sergeant took it away from me."

"Good God!" Ahrens ran his fingers around the rim of his stock. "Well, and you like being a dragoon?"

"Oh, yes!" Heinz was vociferous. "But I would rather be a farmer. When we march I make the miles pass by pretending I own each field I see and then I decide what I'll plant in it. It's hard, sometimes, deciding. And at the big clearing by the lake, there were men cutting hay and I joined them. They gave me a scythe. It was like being at home again. It was good. All farms are good." He sighed deeply.

The camp in the woods was very black as Ahrens walked on, black and slashed here and there with orange and red where fires flared and lanterns glowed, lighting up an outthrust face, a cocked hat slanted down over a forehead, a broad back bent over a rude table. By a tent close to the stream, a voice hailed him: "That young Ahrens out there in the dark? Come in and have a drink. Thought I recognized your martial strut as you passed that fire."

Ahrens ducked his head and stooped under the entrance of Charteris' tent, where a smoky lantern flared on a pine-board table. "A seat. A mug! And drink! Let me introduce Ensign O'Callaghan of the Royal Artillery, just down from Ticonderoga." The ensign, a smiling, black-browed young giant, bowed ponderously from the rude bench which creaked and groaned with his every move, then buried his face in a mug of rum and water.

"The Ensign doesn't talk much till he's had his fifth mug," explained Charteris. "He was commended to me by my friend Strathcona of the Dublin garrison. I found him wandering about the forest asking every drunken Indian he met where the fighting was. I told him there wasn't any. Brought him here for a drink and found he had a letter to me."

"Quiet at Ticonderoga?" asked Ahrens politely.

"But I'm from beyond Ticonderoga," the giant explained earnestly in a soft brogue. "By rights I'd be sailing now down Lake George with Hadden and Duncombe and the rest of the boys, for I was here last year and made the campaign by Valcour Island. Were you gentlemen present?"

Charteris raised his hand. "Now, Ensign, that's a dangerous question. Every soul I meet says: 'Were you here last year? Should have been,' and then expatiates on the extent which my knowledge, morals and manners have suffered through having been elsewhere. I am sure our Hanau friend has had the same experience."

Ahrens nodded. "If I say that it is hot or cold or rainy or dull or lively, a voice pipes up from the wings and murmurs: 'Ah, but you should have been here *last* year.' I'd been hoping, Ensign, that you were a newer arrival in America than I. Then I'd have pushed out my chest and said: 'Ah, but you should have been here last week!' I've been looking forward to the chance."

"And I," Charteris nodded. "What kept you in Quebec, Ensign? Staff work? We're short on gunners, you know."

"Devil a bit of staff work. A misbegotten son of hell in the shape of a provost took exception to me in Quebec and I landed in quod. The army sailed without me."

"Provost?" asked Charteris, raising languid eyebrows.

"No less." The ensign looked mournfully into his mug,

which Charteris at once refilled. "A slip of an officer found me in bed with a French girl."

"No harm there," Charteris grinned. "Have the whole army in quod if that were an offense."

O'Callaghan shook his head sadly. "It was *his* girl. He was objectionable. I'm kindly by nature, so I said to myself: 'Now Shawn, you'll not be killing him.' Accordingly I took the little man and threw him into the big river."

Ahrens choked on his rum and water. "Could he swim?"

"Now that's just what I was asking myself, Mister Ahrens." The black head leaned earnestly across the table. "So in a minute I said to myself: 'Shawn, you'll be after hauling him out of the big river.' Then the devil's whelp of a provost came by with his patrol and me with the limp thing in my arms. They were for calling me a hero, thinking I'd rescued the little man. They took him to the guardroom and stood him up before a fire." He drank deeply. "As he dried out, they saw he was a captain!" Mournfully he drank again.

Ahrens roared with laughter. The Major wiped his eyes, shoulders quaking. "By Gad, sir! The Duke of Marlborough would have had him broke. Instead, the provost quods *you*! *O tempora, O mores!*"

Ahrens emptied his mug. He found himself wondering where the girl of the clearing might be at that moment, what she might be doing. He must tell Charteris and the young Irishman about his two meetings. No—on second thought decidedly no. He could see the lazy lift that Charteris' eyebrows would give. He started. Charteris was addressing him.

"Tell the Ensign about your stealing the runaway conscript from the provost at Hanau. He'd— Oh! Come in, come in! Been expecting you." The lantern flooded harsh light on the grave, open face of the young Tory who had ridden with Ahrens from Hubbardton. "Take a seat, Lieutenant Jones. See you know our Hanau friend already. From Hubbardton? Stout bit of riding. The

161

black-browed Celt opposite you is Ensign Shawn O'Callaghan. Uniform will tell you the rest about him."

The bottle tipped, gurgled, was emptied and replaced. Jones showed himself as competent with the Major's thick mug as he had been with a horse on the forest road. The humming of the camp gradually died away about them as Jones told a long story of rebel raids on Tory homesteads before the army moved down Champlain, Charteris' clipped comments punctuating the tale, while O'Callaghan listened, black-eyebrows knotted, and Ahrens sipped his rum and wondered about the girl in the clearing.

A harsh voice sounded out in the darkness, speaking German. "Where? By the big tree? Well, answer smarter next time or you'll find out more about *me*, by God!" There was a sound of a blow, then footsteps coming toward the Major's tent. The voice shouted again: "Lieutenant Ahrens!"

"Oh, the devil!" growled Ahrens. "Who wants me now?"

"The majesty of the staff," Charteris explained. "All hours of the day and night they lay siege to our mighty minds. Ask him in and give him a drink, Ahrens." He shouted. "Come in and have a drink, whoever you are!"

A shape blurred outside, grew more distinct. Ahrens swore disgustedly as he recognized the broad upper lip and little eyes of Donohoe. Wearily he introduced him, the Major gave him a brimming mug while O'Callaghan stared at his fellow-Celt in undisguised amazement.

"Sorry to intrude, Major." Donohoe's manner was heavily deferential. "I wanted to ask Lieutenant Ahrens a question about tomorrow's loading. Captain Spitz said he would know. You'll excuse me?" The question which followed was trivial. Ahrens answered shortly, suspecting that Donohoe had had wind of his presence in the Major's tent and had followed him in the hope of basking in such an exalted spot, not to mention the probability of being given a few drinks.

"Ready to move tomorrow?" asked the Major affably.

"I'm always ready to move!" Donohoe set his mouth in a thin line, thumped the table with a freckled fist.

"Hanau wagons?" asked Jones. "Why, my company escorts them. We've had so much outpost work lately that we were assigned to baggage-guard for this move. The road will be quiet, I imagine."

"Quiet?" Donohoe laughed. "March a conventful of nuns along it and *they'd* be safe. Won't say what the *nuns* would do, though." He guffawed, drank noisily. "Maybe *they'd* be giving out buttons, eh, Ahrens? Giving out buttons? Jee*esus*! That was good!" He doubled over the table, guffawing. Charteris raised his eyebrows in mild surprise, the ensign wrinkled his nose and Jones looked quietly bored.

"Well," said Ahrens, picking up his mug. "Tomorrow at this time we'll be looking out over the Hudson from Fort Edward." He looked at the young Tory. "To your happiness, Lieutenant Jones."

Jones smiled quietly. "Thanks," he said.

"Fort Edward!" Donohoe doubled up again. "Jee*esus*! Saw the God-damnedest thing down there. Went ahead to old Fraser's headquarters. While I was there, three Indians brought in an old bitch they'd captured farther down, somewhere near the fort. Christ! Wish you could have seen her! They'd stripped her from her arse to her feet and back all the way up to her chin. God, what a sight! Thought I'd die laughing. Stood there in front of old Fraser, tits hanging down to her belly and her belly hanging down to her knees. Then she flew at him, at the old bastard. Christ, you ought to have heard the way she pulled him apart! He just stood there gaping at her. Didn't say a word, and his face as long as a whore's dream!" He bent over the table again, choking. "God! It seems the old bitch is a cousin of his and a red-hot *Tory*! Finally they gave her a cloak of Fraser's. Nothing else in camp big enough to cover her fat arse!" He slapped his knee, wiped his eyes. "Then the richest part—had to go outside and lie down, I laughed so hard. She was huddling the cloak around her and laying into the General when more Indians came in with a scalp. She let out a screech! Oh God, oh God! Her face! She recognized the scalp. Tremendous long hair. Belonged to a trull down the river who was trying to slip up here to sleep with some Tory bastard who's keeping her. Name's McCrae—the girl's. She—what's the matter?"

Ahrens had swung suddenly round in his seat. Like lightning he jabbed a short pistol into Jones' ribs. "If you so much as stir, so help me I'll shoot!"

Jones, his jaw sagging, made an animal noise in his throat and gathered his body as though to throw himself at Donohoe.

"What is it, Ahrens? Are you mad?" Charteris' voice bit hard through the night air. O'Callaghan stared.

Jones stirred convulsively. Ahrens clamped a powerful arm around his neck, forced his chin back. "Major, for God's sake, put him under arrest at once. There'll be murder in the camp if you don't. You've the power! There!" Jones suddenly collapsed and lay back, his head on Ahrens' shoulder, his breath coming thick and heavy. Donohoe, pale and staring, edged to the door of the tent.

"For God's sake, Major, will you act!" Ahrens' voice was hard. "Under arrest at once! Don't you understand? The McCrae girl was his sweetheart. They were to have been married when the army reached the Hudson."

Charteris shot up from his chair. "O'Callaghan! Pitch that bit of filth as far from my tent as you can. Then run to Headquarters—"

The ensign lunged toward the door, but Donohoe's white, scared face stared, then vanished into the darkness. There was a bitter Irish curse and O'Callaghan stood, half sobbing with rage, glaring. Ahrens relaxed his grip on the Tory. The head still lay heavy on his shoulder, face the color of chalk.

"Betrothed, eh?" Charteris moved along the tent wall.

"What a stinking little swine that was! Good fellow, Jones. Know some of his people in Surrey." His voice was a little choked. "Here, Ahrens. You know the camp. Leave him to O'Callaghan and me. Fetch the guard yourself. Sergeant Timms and ten men, to make it look official. Hurry. This man will be raging when he comes to. I'll talk to him while you're gone. Leave him to me—leave him to me!"

Ahrens ran to the great guard tent, brushed aside the dragoon who would have stopped him and shook the snoring sergeant of the English detail. Twice he repeated his orders. Then the sergeant tramped about in the gloom, rousing his men. Ahrens tapped his food on the dirt floor and waited.

Fully awake and accoutered, the file started down the slope toward the creek, Ahrens leading. A heavy bulk loomed ahead of him. "That you? That you, Ahrens? O'Callaghan here. Send back the guard."

The column came to a heavy halt, musket-butts thumped on the ground. "Send them back?" Ahrens cried. "What's the Major thinking of?"

"Talked to Jones, he did. God! What a five minutes! It's in purgatory I've been, listening and sweating and the Major gentle as a woman with the poor lad. Jones will put himself under arrest with his own people. 'Twas the Major who talked him round. He'll go to Colonel Peters and the Major with him. I'm thinking he's a little touched and it's God's own mercy that he is. Look!" He pointed to a glaring fire. Two figures, one tall and slim in blue, the other shorter and in green, walked slowly past it. The tall man's arm was over his companion's shoulder, which he gently patted from time to time. Occasionally the shorter man seemed to stumble as he walked. Then the long arm about him closed tighter. They vanished beyond the glow of the fire. "God!" said the ensign.

Ahrens stared after them. Then he dismissed the

guard. The men plodded gratefully away, the sergeant yawning behind an enormous fist.

" 'Nother drink?" asked the ensign. "I'll be seeing that face when I'm buried on the banks of the Liffey. That and the thing that calls itself Irish. The whelp! Dragging the fine name of Donohoe after him!"

Ahrens shook his head. "I'll look in at Headquarters and then get some sleep. 'Night, Ensign." The big man turned away toward Charteris' tent.

Ahrens went up the slope to Headquarters. A voice hailed him. In the darkness he recognized Plesse, a young Bavarian of Breymann's staff. "You missed an exhibition, Ahrens. There was a Tory girl murdered this morning down by the fort. The General was furious. He demanded that the Indians give up the man who did it. Said he'd hang him. Then old St. Luc broke in and said if he did the Indians would all go home, looting, burning and scalping as they went, all the way back to the Abenaki country.

Ahrens whistled. "He said that, did he? Hope the General told him to go to the devil. Ought to hang the murdering swine."

"Well, no." Plesse coughed. "The General reserved decision. I think he'll yield. After all, we need those Indians. Fraser said we had to remember that we were in invaded country and we'd have to wink at a lot of things like this. Accidents of war, you know."

"I suppose so," Ahrens sighed. He couldn't get Jones' distorted face from his mind. Another accident of war? "No orders in?"

"Nothing new since you went off duty. Well, I'm going to take a little walk along the lines. Will you join me? No?" He walked off toward the ragged tents and flimsy huts that stretched along Wood Creek beyond the baggage lines.

"Must have some Canadian wench hidden away there," thought Ahrens, looking after him. "Well, there are some pretty ones there. That girl with the scarlet band about her black hair—" He thought a moment. "No. Too tired. I'll roll up in my blankets." He stretched his long arms over his head, flexing the ropey muscles of his shoulders. He felt spent, yet nervously alert. Donohoe's hideous laughter over the misery of others, Jones' mad rage and collapse, had shaken him. He drew a deep breath and started slowly toward the tree under which his tent was pitched. Then he stopped abruptly, spine tingling.

Far away toward the east a hideous whooping arose, a hollow, unearthly hooting. "Indians! There it is again!" Closer this time, as though in answer to the first, it rose, swelled, died away. Then an old musket crashed. There was more whooping. A cold hand seemed to pass over his whole body. He shook himself, laughed. "The rum issue. Indians are drunk and letting off their muskets along Wood Creek." He walked on carefully along the path. It would be good to sleep.

Another Indian whooped, away to the south. Ahrens halted again. St. Luc's threat? Back to Canada, looting and scalping as they went? He saw the dark trails filled with gliding throngs, saw painted bodies filtering through clearings, felt in his nostrils the sour stench of red torsos smeared with rank bears' grease, yellow, white, black, livid clay. Through clearings, muskets poised, keen tomahawks gripped, eyes a-glitter in the faint light of the stars. He saw gutted cabins, sprawled corpses with a halo of flies dancing about sticky reddish heads. Through clearings. Something cold, some formless dread seemed to steal slowly over him. He found himself walking rapidly back toward Headquarters. His walk broke into a trot, his trot into a run. Who was on night duty in the big tent under the trees?

Among the cleft rocks that capped the southern lip of the round hill, a girl crouched on a pile of bracken, blue eyes looking steadily at the trees that dipped and tossed beyond, black against a black sky. One arm rested lightly on a long rifle that lay across her knees. Under the other she could feel a second rifle, the smooth cheek of a powder-horn, the bulge of a bullet-pouch bedded among the yielding twigs. Occasionally she raised her head with a quick, fawn-like motion, listening. Once she delicately moistened a finger-tip and passed it over her nostrils, then sniffed the night air that flooded over her.

Toward midnight she yawned, shook her head violently, then looked over her shoulder to a broad grassy hollow beyond the rocks where her keen eyes could make out the rough boards of a cabin roof, jutting like splintered teeth against the night sky. Again she shook her head. Mustn't sleep. She turned her gaze toward the blackness of the rocks behind her, nodded as she heard the sound of regular, gentle breathing. Then she resumed her vigil, staring over the sky-line where the stump of the cold chimney jutted nakedly.

It had been bound to happen, white men egging Indians on against white men. The grunting, filthy Oneida, last link with the outside world, had slipped into the clearing that afternoon and told her of the McCrae girl. Then he had spoken at length—for him—of the fury of the Wyandots at the white chief's stinging rebuke, of his threat to hang the man who took the scalp. The Oneida thought that the Indians would break with the white men entirely, would start back for Canada, picking up scalps and loot on the way. Then he had slipped off into the woods again, a lost man, cast off by his own tribe and so scorned by the Wyandots and others that they did not think his scalp worth taking. She was sure that he had filched that bit of salt pork from the cabin before he left. She shrugged. Welcome to it. And he knew that he was welcome to it, but had been too proud and too shy to ask for it. There was plenty more, the corn patch flourished and the game had been little disturbed if you went west a few miles.

Would the Wyandots follow the hidden trail that skirted the clearing on their way north? She started.

There were faint whoops, a shot or two in the east. Settling back she told herself that the sounds were far beyond Wood Creek, beyond the swarming camp of clumsy men in uniform. She shivered. The wind was damp, chilling. Her eyelids drooped. She threw her head back, breathing deeply. Then she set her mind to count the books that she remembered in a pine-paneled study, books that reached from broad planked floor to smooth ceiling. The narrow case by the left of the fireplace— Thucydides, Homer, three different editions of Homer, Virgil, Xenophon; then—then, oh yes, "Gulliver" followed by Spinoza. That ended the shelf. Below? First came Hobbes, then Smollett, the fat leather back of Rabelais, two volumes of Montesquieu and a thin Tasso. Next shelf. She shook herself. Montaigne, Lessing— She suddenly froze into her bed of bracken. Out in the darkness the long grasses stirred violently, a light twig snapped with the faintest of pops. She relaxed. Just a rabbit, hopping along on some absorbing business of his own. Crickets chirped and rustled in the grasses and a whippoorwill poured its liquid whistle into the night somewhere down the hill. She took up her count of the solid volumes which rested so safely in a far-away past, her eyebrows lifting as she heard a pair of owls hooting in the woods to the west.

With a start she pressed her hand against her firm breasts. *Those* were no imaginary noises. Where did they come from? By the trail, surely; faint cracklings, a clink of something hard striking against a rock. Slowly her hand closed over the lock of her rifle. She shook her head impatiently, puzzled. The noises were faint because they were distant. She was sure of that. Indians? Impossible! No Indian, even a drunken one, would make that much noise. Again she moistened her fine nostrils, sniffed. The air was soft, pure—no taint of rancid bears' grease.

A deep furrow formed between her sensitive eyebrows. Slowly and carefully she rose, stepped like a gliding shadow out into the night, her figure merging with the

169

black rocks behind her. The noise on the trail increased, the cracklings were louder. Could cattle have strayed from the army? She was unable to imagine a human being making so much din in a night forest. Whatever it was, it must have strayed from the trail, for the crashings in the underbrush were continuous. She crept forward a little, leaving a clear retreat to her old place among the rocks. The light was treacherous, but she was sure that she could make out a distinct shape under some tall elderberry bushes not fifty yards away. She crept closer, then with steady hands she raised her piece. "Up with your hands! Up—so I can see them! Now—move ten paces to your right, away from your musket. No—sideways!"

Something white glimmered by the bushes. There was a flourish like a bow in the dark and a laughing voice said: "It seems my fate always to be an unwilling target for you, madame."

She gave a quick intake of surprise. "The Hessian! Why are you here in the night? I thought my welcome the other day was definite enough. No—stand where you are! And keep those hands high—high, where I can see them. An officer! Skulking in the bushes, looking for two lone women!"

"My dear madame, my intentions were and are beyond reproach. With your permission I should be glad to lower my hands. I find the posture not only humiliating but fatiguing."

"Keep them where they are!" Her voice was low, firm. "Again, why did you come here?"

Far away, but clear and chilling, the hollow whooping of an Indian soared up through the tree-tops. "Perhaps that may answer your question," said Ahrens. "Now, about my hands."

The girl's voice cut. "You keep watch to be sure that the work of your hired savages is thorough?"

"On the contrary. There were rumors in camp that there might be—misbehavior."

There was a silence. Then the girl said: "One man—to

insure court manners on the part of drunken Wyandots?"

"By no means. There are ten others ambushed along the trail below."

"Ambushed?" There was a faint trace of amusement in the girl's voice. Then more seriously: "I did not expect such consideration. The General sent out parties tonight?"

"N—not exactly. He authorized them, perhaps unconsciously. I had to take a few liberties with the orderly-book, but the expedition stands duly blessed."

"You brought a *party* here? There are no others out?"

"None."

"So you callously broke the sleep of tired men, marched them through the forest at night to—to bring them here?"

"Oh, not callously. I did wake them in their various lairs. When I told them what was afoot, they volunteered. You see—they remembered you. Now—about my hands."

There was silence from the rocks. He began again. "How can I convince you of my good faith? I have explained my presence, *foi d'officier*. Here—will *this* convince you? There is my carbine—a good ten paces away. My back is toward you. Now come forward, with the eye of that blasted rifle of yours drilling a line through me."

She hesitated, then came closer. "More," he said. "That's it. Press the muzzle of that thing against the small of my back. Ouch! A little less enthusiasm! Now you will see that this jacket of mine is fitted with tails, in which there are pockets. The one at the right is empty as you can see. In the left—ah, you've found it? Such weapons seem to be rare on the frontier. You would do well to recall their existence should you ever find yourself in a similar situation."

She lowered the muzzle of the rifle, staring at the short, heavy pistol. She stepped back a few paces. "You may lower your hands," she said.

"And turn around? Thank you. Ouf! You've no idea what a racking pose that is to hold. Eh? Oh, thanks once

171

more." He took the pistol she held out to him, dropped it in the pocket of his jacket.

She stood looking intently at him. At last, she said: "You really came over the trail in the night to guard this clearing?"

"No less. And I greatly regret that you were disturbed. It was my intention to lie along the trail till daybreak and then slip back to camp. I had no idea that you would detect us."

She stared. "*Detect?*" Then surprisingly her laughter rippled softly in the night. "I heard you, I think, when you were not less than a half-mile down the trail."

Ahrens shook his head sadly. "I thought our woodcraft was rather fine. We slipped along as quietly as any Indians, though we did have trouble finding the mouth of the trail in the darkness. It's masked by rocks and ferns."

"Your men came alone—over the trail? And you really did that for—because you thought the Indians might come by here?" Her voice was puzzled.

"Why, of course it was good practice for the men. We hardly expected to find you wandering about under the sky. They *might* have come, you know. The Indians, I mean. They may still. What brought you out?"

"I had word of a—of a terrible crime. I learned that the Wyandots were angry. I have watched all night."

"It was the same news that brought me out. I heard it in a rather horrible manner. Then there were whoopings and shots in the dark. I picked my men and came."

She sat on a broad-topped rock, hands resting on her rifle. "There were no orders, no other troops sent out?"

"None."

She raised grave eyes to him. Then her throat tightened. There was something inexpressibly pathetic to her in the thought of this big man, glaring in white breeches, floundering about in the crashing woods with his clumsy men at his heels, signaling every move with a din fearsome according to forest standards, wearing clothes that would act as a magnet to any hostile eye.

172

She said: "I believe you. I am grateful. Your action was—was unusual. If I seemed hard to convince, please forgive me."

He bowed. "There is no need for forgiveness. In any event I had intended to come and go without your knowing."

Again an Indian whooped. The girl listened intently. Then she drew a deep breath. "Earlier in the night there were shouts on this side of the creek. Since then they have been all on the east. The Wyandots have either decided to settle down in camp or are going north by the eastern trails. There is no more danger—at least for tonight. Now—my thanks once more for a generous act. You can take your men back to their tents."

Ahrens laughed and shook his head. "If you could see the orderly-book! We shall all be in hot water. I in the hottest of all, if we appear before sunrise, which is still some hours away. Forgery is the least of my military crimes tonight. No, no. The men must lie along the trail. At least, I'll let them sleep. They are scattered at intervals at what I took to be strategic spots. I'll have word passed down." He trotted off, calling: "Rentner!" The girl heard low tones in the darkness. Then white breeches twinkled in the gloom again. Ahrens' laugh echoed under the trees. "They seem disappointed. They hate the Indians and would have relished a brush with them." He sat on the rock beside her, fanning himself with his hat. Overhead a few stars began to wink through a thin haze that covered the sky. He turned to her. "How did you hear of the trouble, buried on this hilltop?" Inwardly he marveled at the piled masses of soft hair which had been confined by a deep sunbonnet on their previous meeting.

"I was told."

"Told? Do people pass this way?"

She moved a little farther along the rock, turned slightly so that she faced him. She seemed to be weighing his question, studying him with grave eyes. Then she

173

raised her chin, leaned back against a tree-trunk. "There is an old Oneida who sometimes comes here. His people have been friendly to the whites. His own tribe disowned him because he failed to pass one of those ridiculous tests of courage that men seem to love to invent for their own torment. The other tribes look on him as a weakling and will not harm him. He told me today about—about Jane McCrae. It was a dreadful shock. I knew her, once."

Ahrens nodded. "Terrible business. Appalling. If I had my way I'd drive every Indian back to Canada. This is a filthy war."

Almost abruptly she asked: "Why are you here? Most officers would shrug and say it's too bad about the Indians, but they *are* useful. Or they did in the old wars. You are the first I ever heard speak against them. What brought you here?"

Ahrens shrugged. "The usual reasons. I must rise in my profession. I had served in Saxony, but there was peace and no advancement, so I came to Hanau and offered my services. My family is old, but poor. There are debts, entailed estates. I should prefer to be a physicist. Mathematics and the forces of nature fascinate me. In a limited way I may employ them as a gunner, and, as things are, it's the only way." He paused, rather astonished that he should be speaking about himself so freely and to a stranger. Almost against his will he went on: "Perhaps when my soldiering days are over, I'll be able to follow in the steps of Boyle, von Guericke or your own Franklin. But for the moment, here I am." He smiled, raised his eyes to hers. It came to him as a slight shock that he had been totally oblivious of the fact that he was talking to a girl, talking about himself—which was not odd—but in a very sober way.

"And after the moment? The war will not last your lifetime—unless of course, it exceeds it."

Ahrens laughed. "There is always that latter possibility. Failing that—why, I don't know. I think that there

174

may be chance for action with the Russians in the Caucasus. Then, there is no telling when Europe may flare up again. There are a lot of fools sitting about in the various chanceries, smoking among open powder-barrels."

"And these same fools might provide employment for you? What do you think of that?" The gloom about her hid an expression of something akin to pity as she studied his clear-cut profile, faintly outlined against the sky.

"Of that? Why, I really think there is some hope. Then I might have a chance to see the theories of this Frenchman, Gribeauval, his new ideas on artillery, put into actual practice."

"And your men? Will they say, 'I really think there is some hope'?"

He laughed shortly. "Afraid not. Some of them grow to like the life, but most had rather stay by farm or shop. But then—I can't follow my wishes any more than they can. It's—it's the way things are."

"What is their life?"

"Hard, hard, I'm afraid. My seniors think me too lenient because I try to make things as easy as I can—which isn't much. The men—" he paused almost diffidently—"the men seem to trust me."

"And you still think there is hope in Europe?" Her question was rather a statement.

"Oh, a fine chance! And that's much better artillery country than this. You can maneuver; good roads; good targets; a chance for initiative. Why, do you know that Phillips, who commands all our artillery down there, was the very first man ever to bring guns into action at a—" his voice dropped—"at a *gallop!* Fact. In the Seven Years' War. They tell me he broke fifteen canes over the backs of his horses bringing up the guns."

She clasped her hands across the muzzle of her rifle, rested a smooth cheek on them. She spoke softly. "You're very young, aren't you?"

He started violently. "Young? Young? Why, I've spent nearly eight years with the guns! I've been in most of the countries of Europe! I—" His eye caught a shimmer of white in the grass, a bare foot in an Indian moccasin. Almost wildly he looked about. "Dear God! Who *are* you? I see you in this clearing on a cloudy day. You nearly blow my foot off with a rifle that most of our men would commit murder to own. You speak text-book German. You revive one of my grenadiers better than a doctor could and you know all the trails about here. You ordered me about like a sergeant-major that day. Tonight you stalked me like an Indian. I give you my word I didn't know that you were about till you spoke. Now you ask questions like a—like a man about Europe and end up by telling *me* I'm young. God above! You wear homespun, live in a clearing, have moccasins on your feet like an Indian and speak a purer English than any lady at Bath! Who *are* you?"

Cheek still pillowed on her clasped hands, she shook her head. "Does it matter? I'm sorry that I puzzle you. But I liked what you said about your men, Kurt Ahrens."

"I was rude. Forgive me." Fascinated, he looked long at the soft mouth, the round cheek faintly lit up by the stars, at the eyes gravely surveying him. Then he said: "You know my name. How?"

The dark head raised slightly, the mouth curved a little. "You presented yourself like a court chamberlain the day you were lost, so lost."

He had an uneasy sensation that this slim girl was sorry for him, deeply sorry. He twirled his cocked hat between his forefingers. She spoke again. "Tell me about your men." Her eyes were soft and luminous in the dark.

Ahrens found himself suffering again over the agony of Rentner at Der Rosenstrauch, at the heartbreaking scenes at the barrack gates. He showed her the terror of the men in the vile quarters on shipboard; the nameless dread that settled over them as they plunged into the wilderness of the New World lived in him as he spoke, the haunted eyes of the men who fought so desperately at Hubbardton but who felt the clutch of the wilderness about their shoulders, the wilderness which spewed raging men at them, only to swallow up its uncounted hosts when the frantic strangers tried to strike back. He suffered again with clumsy recruits who shrieked under the lash for some tiny infraction of rules, for some minute slip at drill. He brought out for her the men in barrack uniforms who stumbled over miry trails, unharmed, but with the unseen axes biting into their very brains as well as into the distant trees. He smiled ruefully over Heinz, chuckled as he told of his transformation into a dragoon. He showed her the women, trooping along in the wake of the army, honest women, trulls, thieves, drunkards and the great ruck of stupid good intent. He spoke of Hedwig, striding on like some personification of the Rhine, blond, blue-eyed and fearless. The girl listened, eyes closed, heard of the savage Breymann, of Baum, Fraser who feared his own soft heart and was harder than hard in consequence. At last he was silent, fearing he had said too much. After all, those men were his superior officers.

The girl drew a deep breath. "And that is the army that lies along the creek." There was an odd finality to her tone.

He nodded. "That is the army. No worse than others, better than some. Why, in Russsia—"

As if she had not heard him, her soft voice went on: "And in that army there are men who are better by the accident of your marching with it."

"Oh, well, well!" He hadn't thought of it in that light. Odd that he should feel embarrassed. He went on: "Of course, there are some who can't be helped. At the hospital at Skenesboro I saw a Brunswick grenadier, a magnificent fellow. Fully six feet four. He's sung his last psalm on the march. He lies on his back, helpless as a child. His big hands brush feebly across his face, his

177

only motion. Driven mad by the black-flies and mosqui-toes in the hot woods. A pity."

There was a catch in her gentle voice. "And he—he was dragged from some home in the Duchy to be driven mad by flies in an American swamp."

"They tell me he was a very gifted metal-worker of Hildesheim. Well, the Duke *had* to have men. No help for it. It's the way things are."

There was a silence. Then the girl said: "No help for it? That's the voice of defeat." Suddenly she turned to him, laid a light hand on his arm. "Not all men accept—what is that hateful shibboleth of yours?—'the way things are.' You asked me who I was. Several times, in fact. I'll have to answer, because I want to tell you of one man who would not accept. My great-grandfather came from England and settled in Boston. His exile was refusal to accept. In Boston he did well. So did his son, my grandfather. There was no struggle, because life ran along about as they felt it should. As my father grew up, he saw the colony, all the colonies, growing into replicas of the old countries. He saw money and privilege killing merit. Why should the blacksmith's son with the healer's touch be turned into an itinerant quack, while the stupid boy whose father's house faced Boston Common frit-tered away his time in Leyden, in London, in Edinbor-ough, because it pleased the father to say, 'My son, the surgeon'? He thought and thought, did my father. Then he began to talk. He was, when he married my mother, a tutor at Harvard College. She joined in the discussions that grew as a salon sprang up about them, the oddest salon. There were sea-captains, blacksmiths, cobblers, an English colonel, preachers, farmers, merchants, printers."

She paused, rested her cheek again on her crossed hands over the muzzle of the long rifle. Crickets chirped madly in the grass and somewhere in a swamp below a bob-white flooded its two notes into the night.

"Word got about Cambridge of the salon. There were whispers. A petition was sent to the Overseers of the college, denouncing my father as a dangerous man. The Overseers answered in the public prints saying that as a teacher of Greek my father was unsurpassed. For the rest, they were not interested." She laughed softly. "That was so like them. As time passed, more and more people came to the house. It was in Cambridge and the study windows looked out over the marshes to the Charles. Meddlesome people talked and talked, complained to the Governor. One fall night my father gathered most of the group about him. I can see their faces now: Eliphalet Tucket, the sea-captain, Lionel Freyern, the colonel, Asa Rudge, the printer, Seth Carter, the cobbler, and the others. My father smiled and looked at them. In effect he said: 'We don't like the way things are. People don't seem to like us. Let's pool our resources, go west and found a community where merit is the only currency. Those who have special gifts or knowledge will teach those who want to learn. We've all tilled the soil. Let's go where land is rich and free. Go, with our families and our goods.' They went the next spring. That was five years ago."

"One moment." Ahrens was bewildered. "You're telling me colonels and merchants and tutors and ship-masters sat down with peasants, with artisans? Way things ought to be, perhaps, but—"

"Those were the people. Not peasants, though. There are no peasants in this country. Not yet. But it was the fear that there might be—would be—that brought those men together. They made a pact, some thirty families, and started out through the little towns of Massachusetts. Some dropped out, but others joined. People from Sudbury, from Marlboro, from Worcester and Petersham. The wagons went on into the Berkshires and one man rode at the head of the train—Josiah Hunnewell, my father."

Ahrens shook his head. "I don't see it. I mean, I see the wagon train and the long marches. But the colonel! And a blacksmith! Don't tell me there was a tinker!"

179

"Three," said the girl. "And a wheelwright. Not to mention a butcher and two horse-traders."

"Gad!" said Ahrens.

"The country was peaceful, had been since the end of the French Wars. We camped by streams and lakes. The young men hunted. We danced in the evening to our own music. There were several really gifted musicians. Sometimes my father read Homer aloud or two of the preachers set theological discussions going. We crossed the Green Mountains—they're over there to the east in the Hampshire Grants—and saw Champlain below us with the Adirondacks beyond. Our wagons came down into the valley, we crossed Wood Creek and settled on this hill. We were off the beaten track. No Indian raiders had been seen in years. They took the easier course by Lake George on straight down from Champlain. Their trails aren't far, but they miss this section completely. Cabins were built, farms laid out, shops and schools set up."

"Cabins? Cabins?" Ahrens remembered the charred wood, the gutted book his foot had turned up climbing that hill. "And then?" he said.

Her voice sank lower. "Even here, rumors of trouble reached us. Chipmunk, the old Oneida, was our link with the outside world. Some of our people had befriended him and he never forget, never has forgotten. But at last his news was bad for the settlement. He told of the troubles with the troops. Some on the hill declared for the King, others for the colonies. They fought. Some drifted off to the armies, others fled to the towns. Only three families stayed on. Then last fall your General Carlton came down the Lake. He went back, but Indians and whites worse than Indians swept over the country. They came to the three families on the hill. My sister and her husband—a doctor from Springfield—and their baby. Then there were the Doanes, Cape Cod people, my father and myself. We saw empty cabins on the west slope burning one morning, early. The men

180

went to see, thinking a spark from one of our chimneys had started a blaze. We heard shots, then saw my father carrying Doane. Doane's head was bloody. Luckily the Indians were hurried and heavily loaded. They drove off some of our cattle and went northwest into the mountains. The next day rebels came, with Stockbridge Indians. They burned more cabins and took more of the herd. We were prey for both sides."

Ahrens wiped his forehead. "Why didn't you go to the towns, the forts?"

"Both sides plundered us. We wanted no sight of either. More rebels came and my father, as he had done before, tried to persuade them to leave us in peace. We had no quarrel with either side, he said. He was stunned by a blow from a musket-butt and lay senseless for three days. Then Indians and whites came from the north again. I don't remember much about it. There were painted faces at the window, and whoops and shots. I remember a sudden glare, then something struck me as I ran outside. Whatever it was, it stunned me and I must have rolled out of sight. When I was conscious again it was sunset, but of what day I don't know. There was smoke coming out of the ground and a blackened mass against the sky. I crawled to my feet and stumbled over the body of my father. I thought he had a red cap on. He'd been scalped. The doctor lay a little way off, scalped. By the chimney Abigail, my sister, sat, rocking her cradle and crooning to it. I thought at least the baby was safe. Then I saw the baby. Its little head was crushed and the rocks were dreadfully stained where some Indian had swung it."

"Then—your sister?" Ahrens had difficulty in speaking.

The girl nodded. "Her mind must have gone when the first Indian snatched her baby. That protected her, because they won't harm anyone—anyone like that. She hasn't spoken since, except to the empty cradle. She smiles at me, takes the food I give her. The rest of her waking hours she sits, rocking the cradle and crooning to it."

"And you stayed?" Ahrens' voice was shaken.

"Where else could I go? The winter was unusually mild. Some of the herd was left, and two families came back. Chipmunk came by from time to time. We planted. It grew peaceful here and I thought I saw signs of recovery in Abigail. Then we heard the war-whoops again. Your army came down the valley. The two families fled. They've gone back to the Mohawk Valley. I've not left my sister alone since then, unless I go after a deer, leaving Chipmunk with Abigail." She fell silent.

Slowly Ahrens straightened up. "How *could* your father have stayed on here, kept women and children here, after the first Indians came? Or if he must stay, a word would have given him the protection of one side or the other."

She turned on him. "But he was right, right, right!" She hammered on the rock with little fists. "Don't you *see*? If he had gone back, if he had taken a false oath to a party that meant nothing to him, it would have been a compromise with things as they are. It is those very 'things as they are' that I blame for the deaths and the burned cabin and Abigail with her empty cradle, not Father. The colony compromised, went back. He stayed—and won!"

"Won?"

"Yes, won! When there is peace again, if I am alive, I am going to go back to Boston. I'm going back to gather up more people to live here, live as Father planned that men should live."

"I think," said Ahrens slowly, "that I should like to have known your father."

She turned thoughtful eyes on him. "Father would have liked what you try to do for your men. He would have hated your acceptance of what you know to be wrong. Are you too weak to fight? Why waste your time with gunpowder and brass tubes? You feel that some-

182

thing stronger than yourself keeps you from doing what you were meant to do. You accept these wheeled toys, your mind grows fat, playing with gunnery—it's child's arithmetic."

"But suppose everyone acted on your theory? Suppose—well, suppose that the Hanau peasants to a man had refused to answer the summons?"

"Well—suppose?"

"Don't you understand? They would have been shot."

"Again—well? Shot in a Hanau Platz, shot in an American forest—or going mad like the Brunswicker."

"Why—why, there would have been no army!" He stared at her. "No army at all."

"You see tragedy in that?"

"In heaven's name, how could you have a war with no army? There must be *someone* to be led!"

"Must there?"

Ahrens started to speak. Then with almost feverish clarity he recalled Riedesel's words: suppose each side shot the other's officers—where would your battle be? Well, where—and what of it? He hesitated and said. "You think, then, that we should bow gracefully and leave the field to the rebels? That would bring your thought down to the present moment."

"You could do worse. Perhaps you could do better. I don't know. I don't know that what the rebels will create if they win will be better than what you force upon them. You'll admit that on this hill there is little to choose between the two sides. It's hard not to cry, 'A pest on both your houses!' Men are men. You speak movingly of your soldiers, of your sympathy with them. But yet you will stand quietly by and watch the next confused peasant who is flogged for what is very likely another's stupidity. The men in Boston, in Philadelphia, shout about freedom, the equality of men. But they will wink when, in the name of that freedom, their own people plunder and kill in peaceful settlements like this, which only asks to be allowed to live in quiet. In the name of the King—in the name of the people—in the name of the Duke or the Elector, the result is much the same. You yourself would raid this hill if you were ordered to—" Ahrens started in vehement protest. She held up a small hand. "Yes, you would. Your heart would bleed properly, I'm sure, but you would obey. It would be the way things are."

Over the shoulder of the hill waking birds started a great twittering. Ahrens looked up in surprise. There was a faint glow in the east and the tree-tops glimmered vaguely, isolated giants began to detach themselves from the stirring black loom of the forest. The girl slowly got up, looked at the pan of her rifle. "I must see to my sister," she said. "When night came I put her to bed in a cave not far from the cabin. It would have been safer if the Indians had come. They would have burned the cabin, of course—it's the last one standing on the hill—but they couldn't have tracked us to the cave in the dark."

"Where did you learn your woodcraft?" asked Ahrens. "From your father, perhaps?"

"We all learned. We had to. Chipmunk was my teacher, though Father taught me how to use this." She patted the rifle.

"Thoroughly." Ahrens smiled wryly. "There is not a man in the army who could have placed a bullet so nicely by my foot as you did. He'd have shattered my ankle or knee, more likely."

She stood looking at him in the growing light. "A fine face," she thought. She was suddenly conscious of a warmth stealing over her, a quickening of her pulse. "Is this the man I talked to in the dark? Alone?" Then she was aware that he was smiling down on her. Hurriedly she said: "You'd best gather up your men. You've five miles to cover before you reach the creek. Thank you again."

Still smiling he said, "I don't yet know your name." His eyes were full upon her.

184

"Is it necessary?" Then she thought: "After all, he did try to protect us and asks nothing." Her eyes met his. "I am Judith Hunnewell."

In the softly growing light he could make out the simple lines of the cabin, the long bulk of a Conestoga wagon. Far away by dim trees, the blackened chimney jutted cold and hard.

He spoke slowly. "I shan't forget this night. Perhaps—another time—?"

She shook her head. "It's not likely."

"Not likely?" His voice fell.

"No." Suddenly she smiled, an almost impish gleam shining from her blue eyes. "You see—it's the way things are. Now I must see to Abigail." Her feet twinkled across the grass. He stood looking after her.

The men, yawning and stiff, tramped along the trail in his wake. His thoughts ran on. "Idealistic, that father—not a reasonable man. Ideas may be right but—what right had he to kill off a settlement to prove them? Sometimes you have to compromise. That girl—so loyal to him that she doesn't see that side. One day she'll wake up, begin to wonder. And—why, damn it all, I sat there in the dark through a whole night and vapored like a Heidelberg student. I sat there and talked about the Rights of Man. She's—she's nothing but a *bas bleu*. Rights of Man! There are rights that a man has when he's alone with a pretty girl. No—she's not pretty, really. There's something else when she smiles—and when she doesn't. A—a serenity. And at the same time she's *piquante*. Nice figure in that clumsy homespun. Hands are sunburned, but they're slim. Not frontier hands or feet. I almost lost track of what she was saying to me when she leaned her cheek on her hands and looked sidewise. Oh—but men and women don't talk together that way for a whole night! This *would* astound—well, some people. Shall I see her again? What a hideous story—and it all took place up there on the round hill. You never think that such things happen to people you

185

know. And the settlement! Actually trying to live like that. Who said, 'I'm tired of people who govern from garrets'? Oh—Voltaire, the Frenchman. But her father was no talker. He took people and founded a state. How long could it have lasted? People ought to live like that—but they can't. Silly to try. And yet—and yet—" The distant snarl and grumble of the reveille drums somewhere off among the trees broke in on his thoughts. He called the column to attention, straightened his belts. "Not really pretty. And yet—"

Like a slow, broken-backed snake, the army started moving through the forest to Fort Edward. Morning passed and noon. The afternoon wore on and still Ahrens led his men through air that was dead and still, a deep tank in which dances of flies and midges swam erratically. The road from Fort Anne to Fort Edward climbed and dipped, twisted and bent in crazy curves. At times he could look far ahead from a slight rise to see a crawling column flowing sluggishly along among the shattered trees that marked the line of march. Again he could look to his right or his left and see the red jackets of the English marching due north as their way swerved sharply to avoid a hill, a mass of boulders or a patch of swamp. Then he himself would be threading along that very trail with nothing but the light blue of the dragoons ahead of him and the English red far out of sight and heading south again.

He sweated heavily in his wool uniform, his stock chafed a raw red line about his neck into which stinging perspiration rolled in great drops. His sword banged against his legs and his lumpy haversack thumped and thumped on his hip. He wondered how others were standing this sunless oven of hot air. He shook his head irritably, then sniffed. Was there a touch of freshness in the air? He sniffed again. There was.

Unconsciously his body reacted to it, his shoulders straightened, his stride grew crisp, sure. The long lines of giant trunks which had been rolled heavily to the side of the road now flowed past instead of hitching along with leaden heaviness. He looked back at his toiling men. They noticed it too, eh? They were beginning to quarrel, to complain about their rations. With stiff lips Ahrens grinned, then realized that even the heavy heels of the dragoons seemed to thump less wearily in the broken dirt. Below him and to his left he saw a struggling column of blue strung along a sweeping S curve as Barner's light infantry followed the tortuous track over which he himself had passed nearly fifteen minutes before. From the blue coats a clear tenor voice soared suddenly up through the trees:

"We gather together to ask the Lord's blessing."

A full-throated volume picked up the burden:

> *"He hastens and chastens His will to make known.*
> *The wicked oppressing*
> *Cease them from distressing,*
> *Sing praises to His name, He forgets not His own."*

The deep notes died away among the heavy boles. The tenor took up the next verse, a hundred voices roaring in his wake. Ahrens nodded. "Not my imagination. That's the first psalm I've heard today. Hallo! What's that?"

The road bent again. The blue dragoons were trailing away to the north, then bending sharply south. Through wide-spaced trees, Ahrens saw scarlet and white flashing on rising ground ahead, saw horses stamping among long grass and riders in blue and red staring south. From some hidden English troops out of sight down the slope came a shout: "Good ol' Gentleman Johnny. 'E'll see us through!" A ragged cheer swept up. Burgoyne's hand flew up in salute. His rich voice rang out: "Thank you, lads!" There were more cheers. Then the General

187

turned to his staff, swept off his hat in a wide gesture, pointing south. There was a solemn ring to his voice. "Gentlemen! The Hudson!"

Ahrens quickened his pace. "It *is* getting fresher. Brighter, too. Wonder what I can see from this rise where the staff pulled up. Wonder—" He gasped, stopped short.

The brown road fell away in front of him and lost itself in a sweep of open meadow land that stretched away to the right and left, sparsely dotted with trees. There was a flash of blue, silver-tinged, off in the west, a blue ribbon that flowed gently east past three little cabins and a palisade, then turned due south and swept away through broad fields until it lost itself in a pearly haze of mist far away.

He pushed on, blinking, filling his lungs with the cool breeze that swept out of the west. The road ahead of him bristled with troops. The meadows by the river were stained red with the coats of Fraser's corps whose pygmy forms shuttled about in seeming aimlessness in their green setting. He rubbed his eyes. There was something wrong, an indefinable strangeness that troubled him. Then light came to him on a murmur from the tramping ranks behind him, a hushed voice that almost whispered: "No trees!"

He tossed back his head. By God, that was it! For the first time since he had plunged into the forest back of Mount Independence, he could stare and stare at will, without the insistent boles of the ancient forest blocking his view, parting to allow a brief vista, then closing in again inexorably. His spirit seemed to step out of the fog of his deep fatigue as his body had physically broken away from the overwhelming immensity of the forest. He suddenly felt gay, wanted to shout, to sing, to toss his absurd cocked hat into the air. A few hours' sleep among the rich grasses of the fields below, during which time the guns would roll down from Lake George to meet the column, then swift marches down those soft banks to Albany. Good old Gentleman Johnny! He'd push hard, now. A bare forty-five miles to Albany and through open country. Five days—a week at the most. He looked back up the slope. The head of Barner's column was just emerging from the trees. The same tenor voice threw its clear tones into the sunset air:

"*A mighty fortress is our God.*"

The trees behind him roared in a great organ-swell:

"*A bulwark never failing.*"

Albany! And Howe's men, likely as not, marching north at the very moment somewhere in the heart of that pearly haze down the river. And St. Leger storming down the Mohawk! The hymn rolled and rumbled out of the woods into the sweet air of the meadows.

The River

THE ARMY *lay in the broad meadows of the Hudson, eyes straining down the river. Burgoyne settled himself in the Smythe house, built of the heavy timbers of the first Fort Edward and listened to Skene's whispered tales of the thousands of Loyalists who would soon flock to his colors. Riedesel fretted about transports, about his fine cavalry which rotted away, horseless, and proposed an expedition into the Hampshire Grants, to seize the great reservoir of animals and wagons of which Skene had spoken.*

The American forces, out of sight of the invaders since the skirmish at Fort Anne, fell back, back down the river. They fell back past Moses Kill, past the Batten Kill, crossed the Hudson and dropped south again to the Mohawk.

VI

The River

AHRENS saw huge bare feet protruding from the slanting door of his tent. "I'll be damned!" he muttered. "This is a cool proceeding." A very tall, very thin officer lolled in inexpressible comfort on a sort of divan, ingeniously and fearsomely contrived of packing-boxes, blankets and a saddle. A pair of long black boots with broad splay feet stood by him. A violently colored handkerchief covered his face. At slow, regular intervals it fluttered slightly in answer to the blast of air from the very obvious Roman nose which it covered.

Ahrens coughed, moved into the tent. A long-fingered hand slowly rose, flicked off the handkerchief, revealing a dark, strong-featured face marked with deep lines. Large rather sad eyes looked up at him.

"Haven't you made a mistake?" Ahrens began politely.

The mournful lines grew more pronounced. "A great many. To which do you refer?"

"Why—this is my tent."

"That was my impression." The lean man raised himself slightly on one elbow.

"You perhaps prefer it to your own?"

"Not at all. My own is rather roomier than this. And the canvas is whiter."

"Then may I suggest that you remove that most luxurious bit of furniture to—"

"To my own tent?" There was a deep sigh. "Unfortunately it is now on its way to Canada. I came down Lake George with the guns, and old Pausch, when we landed, insisted that we lighten baggage. So we sent back a great deal of personal equipment, including tents. He said that we could double up with the officers already at Fort Edward. I made inquiries and chose you."

"But Captain Pausch said nothing to me about it. I was talking with him just a moment ago. We were watching the eighteen-pounders come over the road from Fort George."

"Why should he say anything to you? It involved no activity on your part. Only on mine."

"Still—"

A long arm waved. "Oh, I see your point. It really must be very disturbing to seek the quiet of your tent and find six feet four inches of Spangenberg preempting a good part of it. But it is war-time. We must steel our souls."

Ahrens began to chuckle, his first flush of irritation fading. "That, I take it, is by way of formal introduction. Well, the niceties are observed. So you were with the flotilla?"

"As I said. I brought in the twenty-four-pounders this morning. Then I made inquiries and sought out your tent. Had the devil's own time getting the guns overland."

"You'll have more, once we move again. What's the point of bringing all that heavy stuff, eighteens and twenty-fours and so on?"

"Sieges, of course."

"Sieges where?"

"Here. Wherever the rebels build forts."

Ahrens laughed. "Have you seen any?"

"Ticonderoga."

"Don't judge by that. You've seen the fort here? You could blow down the walls with a coehorn, or even a musket. And Fort Anne was worse. Ticonderoga is unique—and even that we took without bringing guns into play. No—if we'd only lighten our loads, strip down the column and push ahead, I believe we'd reach Albany without using anything heavier than a musket, if that."

Spangenberg shook his head. "Ah, but you weren't here last year."

Ahrens threw up his hands. "So everyone tells me," he grinned. "Whether they're talking about fish or game or women or liquor."

"Well, you should have been here," Spangenberg laughed. "You'd have a different idea of the rebels. That fight on Champlain off Valcour Island! Colossal! Don't know how many ships we had. Carlton built a huge raft, a hundred paces long and fifty square. Pausch put all our guns on it and the ships tried to tow it right in among the rebel fleet. But the wind took us and carried the raft way down the lake. Fellow named Arnold commanded the rebel fleet. He was a soldier but the fight was open to anyone. Two small frigates, any number of sloops and our big raft. Called it the radeau."

"A hot fight?" asked Ahrens.

"Hot?" Spangenberg crossed one long leg over the other with a flourish. "The next day Arnold fought his ship so long that it almost burned under him. Fact is, they say he couldn't save his wounded—no time. The English could hear them scream as the flames reached them. And eight-pounders crashing shot into Arnold's hull. Interesting, I tell you."

"Then you think we'll see more action?"

Spangenberg looked gravely at him. "All that the worst fire-eater could hope for."

"You differ from most people about here. They seem to feel that the rebels won't dare stand again."

"You've been too long around the staff. Talk to the people who were at Valcour last year. Can't kill a spirit like that just be taking a lot of stone walls on a point. I fish a lot. By the way, got some fine salmon in Lake George. Well, few of our people care much about sport, so I had to choose my fishing friends from among the

195

English. Learned to speak English a little—mostly fish-talk. Before I curled up in my little corner here, I saw some of my fishing friends. Most of them were at Hubbardton or Fort Anne. They feel that they were lucky to come out alive. It's my humble opinion that when the Yankees recover from the loss of material they'll be at us again. What do you think of our troops? You ought to have a good vantage-point for judgment."

A frown grew, deepened over Ahrens' wide-set eyes. "The men? Hard to know what to say."

Spangenberg rose jerkily from his boxes, elbows twitching one way, knees another. Then he looked at Ahrens. "I was puzzled when I came into camp today." He rumpled his dark hair, scratched a mosquito bite on his long, thin neck. "When I left the main army at Ticonderoga, the men looked to me to be pawing the ground and arching their tails. Something is lacking now?" He seated himself on his saddle, an odd figure with his shirt open on his bony chest, breeches unbuckled at the knee and gaunt toes scrabbling in the short grass.

"Yee-es." Ahrens stroked his square chin. "You notice it more than I, because I've been in the atmosphere. Yet you lack my perspective. The army came storming down the Lake after the Yankees pulled out. The Yankee fleet was smashed; there was an official victory, at least, at Hubbardton and Fort Anne. When I rode down onto the plain at Skenesboro, I could feel a tension, a drive forward. Then they waited, waited for days. I think that spirits recovered entirely on the march to Fort Anne, a matter of twelve miles or so. But—again there was a wait. Nothing to do, mind you, and no hostile action except for the sound of the rebel axes felling trees across the road. Incidentally, no one interfered with the axemen. It would have been so easy. I tell you, that constant dull thud began to get under our skulls. There was no relief, day or night. At last we left Fort Anne and pushed down here to Fort Edward. We had taken twenty days to cover the twenty miles from the Lake to the river! But you should have seen the change in the men. Clear of the forest! Out in the plains and the Hudson in front of them! They'd beaten the rebels and the wilderness. It was amazing."

Spangenberg nodded. "I can imagine. All checks removed. A straight road to Albany."

"Exactly! Why, I've seen big Englishmen throw themselves on the grass and roll in a sort of voluptuous delight. Open country, no more damn forest with a rebel back of every tree. Every moment of their spare time Germans and English swam in the Fort Edward Creek. They built crazy little coracles and pushed out into the Hudson itself. Boatloads of naked men from Brunswick and Surrey and Hesse—Cassel and Lincolnshire, whooping and yelling like a crowd of schoolboys! But— we wait. We came here on July 28th: This is August 3rd and the guns and barges are still being hauled overland from the head of Lake George. The English seem to be puzzled but eager. Our people just go into a sort of daze; they bathe in a deep lethargy instead of the Hudson."

"I thought so." Spangenberg's face was long and mournful as a bloodhound's. "If you'd been here last year—"

"Not again!—" Ahrens threw up his hands.

Spangenberg smiled slowly. "Well, all the same, last year we drove the rebels off Champlain, had a clear road to Ticonderoga and then went back to Trois Rivières for winter quarters, The men ebbed. They picked up when we began the movement down the lake this summer. Now they seem to be losing the fine edge again. Well, well. We'll just drag the guns after them and hope for the best. You know, I always wanted to be a grenadier, but when I applied for admission to that body, the inspectors seemed to be of the unanimous opinion that my figure was not suited to the martial array of which they are so proud. They recommended the artillery to me, adding that if worst came to worst, the commander could always use me to measure off ranges." He sighed, "Oh, I don't know if this interests you, but one's of General Burgoyne's orderlies was sniffing around here."

"An orderly? What did he want?"

"You."

"Good God! And you're just telling me now?"

"Well, *he* didn't really want you. The General did. 'At your pleasure' was the phrase."

Ahrens fumbled in his haversack, drew out a soft rag and scrubbed at his boots. "And you—you've let me wait about like this? Gentleman Johnny is probably boiling a kettle of oil for me at this moment."

Spangenberg looked aggrieved. "He said, 'At your pleasure.' I supposed you would rather talk with me than with a general. They're bad people. I'd rather talk with you than with a field marshal—and then you turn on me."

In spite of himself Ahrens laughed. "Well, at least I hope that you will preside at my courtmartial. Hell and death! Past six! No sense in going up to Headquarters till after dinner. Well, get your uniform on. I'll have my man Rentner—or rather his wife—do something to the issue of salt pork. No fresh meat here in days."

Spangenberg shook his head. "Under this middle box there are two fat Lake George salmon, packed in wet moss." He moved about with high, bent-kneed steps, kicked over a box. "Here—fresh as when they were caught. No—no! They're to be cooked first. Call your man and tell him to throw the salt pork into the river."

Ahrens walked slowly up the hill to the old Smythe house where Burgoyne was quartered. He topped the crest and looked west to the road from Fort George beyond the close-packed whitish peaks where the city of British tents spread over the level meadows. As usual the road was choked with slow-moving traffic flowing east; lines of sweating horses tugging at clumsy guns and after them endless strings of slow oxen, twenty-four and even thirty in one hitch, dragging great wheeled cradles where rested the flat-boats which would later bridge the Hudson and then the Mohawk, or follow the army downriver as floating storehouses. He shrugged. They were all right, those barges and bateaux, but why the endless artillery? It seemed to him that the army dragged enough ordnance in its wake to reduce the best fortress that Vauban ever built. Fort Anne? Fort Edward? He had heard, too, that Fort George was as flimsy as the others.

The Smythe house loomed ahead of him in the half-light. He would go across the soft grass in back of the house and save himself a few steps. He saw a light burning in the window of the one room where the Riedesel family lived an animated and joyous, if somewhat crowded existence. A little voice sounded: "And I caught a frog and he's in a big bucket on Papa's campbed." Ahrens grinned. The little Riedesels, at least, had pushed their reconnaissances briskly.

There was no light in Gentleman Johnny's big room as Ahrens turned the corner of the house. "That's funny," he thought. "No lights? I'll go round in front and see what the officer of the day can tell me." Then he stopped short. The dark window was open. Something inside clinked and a low, rather thick voice muttered: "Damn him! Wrecked everything! That's what he's done." Another clink. "Beaten. Floored, b'God. And whose fault will it be? Answer: Mine! Go on? Fall back? By God, I c'n hear him, see him, too. Put on that pious look, mimp up his lips. 'Why did you do what you did?' Won't matter *what* I did. *Wrong!*" Another clink. "Here's damnation to him. Wrong whatever I do. He—he holds trumps. An'—an' here I am." The voice grew thicker. "An' here I am an' there's Howe. An' *where's* Howe?" A chair scraped, glass crashed on the floor. "B'God, I don' *need* him. Do it alone! I'll—I'll win through yet! Bring it off and throw his triumph in his teeth. *He'd* rather score over me than beat Mister-bloody-Washington. I'll do it m'self!"

Surprisingly another voice broke in, low, rich, soothing, its words indistinguishable. Then the first voice went on: "Yes, m'dear. Still got you. *You'll* stand by me, eh?" The tones strengthened, cleared a little. "Still got you, still got the army. Did you hear 'em cheer me? Called me 'Gentleman Johnny.' I'm their friend. Know it, they do. I've got you, got them. Got good ol' Riedesel. Know what the men call *him*? 'Red Hazel.' 'Pon my word. 'Red Hazel.' He'll stand by." The words trailed off again.

Ahrens shook himself. "Here, this is pretty! Eavesdropping on the commander!"

He walked softly and rapidly away, heading for the meadows below the bend of the river where the Hesse-Hanau artillery had pitched its bell-tents by the slowly filling gun-park. The Brunswick infantry lay to its left, and far beyond the last of the grenadier tents, little lights winked where the dwindling Indians held the outermost line.

"What shall I do now?" he thought. "Wonder what Judith"—the name slipped easily into his mind—"is doing back there on that round hill. Fifteen, call it twenty miles by road from here. Got a mind to ask old Pausch for leave and ride back there one day. Would she shoot? Damned if I won't try! Pausch—he was pleased with the recruits I've been training. Rentner and Meister are the best. Rentner can't do more than read and write, but his mind is sounder than Meister's. What if Rentner had studied at Bonn and Meister lived as a peasant? Damn! There I go on the rights of man again."

He crossed the road below the ruinous stockade of the fort and skirted the shimmering line of old tents and flimsy huts where the women of the British regiments were camped. A clear voice suddenly swelled in the night. By a fire in front of a hemlock shelter Ahrens saw flashing eyes, white teeth and black hair bound with

scarlet, a generous sweep of white skin below a strong
throat which poured out the naïve pathos of *O Carillon!*
The voice followed him over the heads of the two red-
jacketed men who squatted by the fire and nodded in
clumsy time?

> *"Vous, qui dormez dans votre froide bière,*
> *Vous, qui j'emplore à mon dernier soupir,*
> *Réveillez-vous! Apportant ma bannière,*
> *Sur vos tombeaux, je viens ici mourir!"*

"Haunting thing," thought Ahrens. "Damn it, that girl
saw me. Was there—was there a slight emphasis on that
'vous'?" He remembered how she had stared at him as
the column left Skenesboro. Once or twice since then
she had seemed deliberately to put herself in his way.
"Flaming bit," he thought. "Well, some of the girls have
changed from the lines to more august protection. But—
good God! I'd have to *talk* to her."

Footsteps beat on the road behind him, a flushed man
in semi-military dress padded along, panting. "Beggin'
your pardon, sir. Major Charteris would be pleased if
you'd step to his tent. I'm to show you where it is."
Ahrens turned and followed the servant. A few drinks,
Charteris' spicy talk, would break the depression that
had deepened since those half-understood words had
floated from the General's window on the knoll.

The tent stood high and isolated on a little rise among
granite boulders and a few young firs. Charteris rose
from his campstool with an exaggerated bow, waved
Ahrens into a seat built into a curiously shaped rock.

"Seat of honor," said the Major. "Pollock!" The servant
"pointed" like a well-trained bird-dog. "Pollock, you've
set out plenty of gin? And plenty of cold water for the
throat of Dives? Good. Then kindly go to—to Albany. Or
better yet, New York. Inform Lord Howe that I wish to
speak to him. Clear, Pollock? New York, and Lord
Howe. You may then immerse yourself in the river, or
experiment with Indian wenches or cuckold a sergeant.

You're your own man until an hour after sunrise tomorrow, when you shall wake me, bringing three bottles of cold water for every empty gin-bottle you see on the grass here."

The man smirked, bowed and went away. Charteris swayed in his seat, pushed a mug of gin and water to Ahrens. The latter stared. Was he the only sober officer in camp? With an abrupt motion, Charteris emptied his mug, refilled it eagerly. Then his lazy drawl slipped out into the night.

"Imprimis—thought you'd like to know that Jones is on his way to Canada with a party. Official business. Saw to it myself. Keep his mind busy."

"May I say that you were admirable with the poor lad?"

"Jones is a gentleman. Glad to do what I could. Damn little. Can't say I take to your brother-in-Hanau. If my horse ever develops an eye like his, I'll shoot the beast."

Ahrens drank. "Then, Major," he said, wiping his firm, clean-shaven lips, "then you must have revised your opinion about old St. Luc. At Crown Point you were all for giving him a free hand. But after this shocking McCrae business—"

"Change?" Charteris waved a vague hand. "Not I. The scalping is beside the point. What upset me was a little lout like Donohoe being able to torture a gentleman, which Jones is and Donohoe isn't. McCrae—why, damn it, we're in invaded territory. Got to wink at such things. Get more Indians. But I didn't ask you here to talk about Indians." He drank again, fell silent, staring out over the plain below him where the endless fires of the Brunswick camp swept away in a senseless pattern of gold against soft black. Somewhere in the darkness a dog barked sharply. The lazy voice began again.

"You behold, my lad, the wreck of a calm philosopher. Total wreck. A badly shaken man who thought nothing could shake him. You have before you a singed soul who must talk to a man of sympathy, a man of good-will. I

202

speak to you as a brother officer, as an old Harrovian but chiefly as a man of good-will."

Ahrens stirred uncomfortably in his rustic seat. "May I ask if your trouble arises from—from leanness of the exchequer? In that case, I'm delighted, so far as I may—"

A hand was lifted in the gloom. "Thanks. Not that. Nothing personal. Though in a way it is. Concerns me. Concerns you. Concerns every bloody rifleman and gunner out there." He swept an arm toward the meadows in front of him. "But *that's* not what I'm talking about. It's about—about a *worm*!" He leaned forward in his chair.

"Good God!" thought Ahrens. "He's farther gone than I thought." Aloud, he said politely, "A worm, Major?"

Charteris slapped his own broad chest. "This is not gin. This is man—as God gives it me to be a man. A worm, I say, a worm and its slimy track is very likely to trip up a very gallant, if somewhat pompous, gentleman who happens to be a damned competent soldier and who commands my admiration. And affection. About the worm—" He leaned back in his chair. "Knew something about the worm and its track months ago. Knew it might happen. *Has* happened, and by God I'm floored, floored as though I'd had no warning. Wrecked me. Don't know how many bottles of wine I've put away. No bite to it. Changed to gin. Not much better. Drink up."

Gin splashed into Ahrens' mug, a water-bottle gurgled. The Major went on: " 'Member our talk at Crown Point?"

"Crown Point?" The man's evident distress puzzled Ahrens. "Yes, I remember. You told me not to watch too hard for Howe's bayonets coming north along the Hudson. You've reminded me of it, directly or indirectly, several times since."

"Do again." The Major hiccoughed slightly. "Want to tell a story first. Go back to 1759. Battle of Minden. French retreating before the Allies. Duke Brunswick, commanding the Allies, sends a courier to the commander of the English cavalry. Heard the message with my own ears: *'Voici le beou moment pour la cavalerie;*

courez-y! The commander did—nothing! In fact he was in a complete state of funk. Cavalry didn't charge; the French got off quite decently. Commander brought back to England. Courtmartialed at the Horse Guards. Broken. Sentence read out to every unit of the army! 'Judged unfit to serve His Majesty in any military capacity.' Damning?"

"Swine!" said Ahrens over the top of his mug. "I heard from my father about the cavalry not moving, but I never knew why. Who was the commander?"

Charteris' voice was tired and flat. "His name? Lord George Sackville."

Ahrens started. "Sackville? But—but Sackville is Lord George Germaine, Minister for the Colonies. He's directing the whole war!"

The Major nodded dully. "The whole war. From London." He shuddered slightly. "The *whole war.* I go on with my story. He had family, friends. Became a symbol. Catapulted by influence from black disgrace into the office you name." He tilted up his mug, set it back on the table with a sharp rap. "Well. Gentleman Johnny came to Boston in '75. Saw Bunker Hill. Saw what Gage didn't. War—not a matter of policing a province. War, in which *he'll* never make a frontal attack against intrenched rebels. Went back to London. Drew up a plan. Got it to the King, to Germaine. You know. Main body goes up the Hudson, meets smaller body coming down from north and another from the west, and the rebellion is neatly cut in two. The King approves, delighted. Burgoyne is put over Carlton and given command of the northern army of which we have the honor to be a part. He's given full, exact and precise orders that allow *no* deviation."

"Well?" Ahrens lifted his eyebrows. "That was the plan as you told it to me in old von Kleist's quarters."

"Patience, patience." The Major waved a hand. "One day, in the Colonial Office, my old friend Billy Knox, after deep thought, ventured to suggest to Germaine that, as Howe was to form the main part of this great move, it might be well to let him know of it. My Lord George condescended to bless a set of instructions for Howe, told Billy to draw them up. Oh, yes, he'd sign 'em, would Lord George. Now—picture the Colonial Office. It is Friday afternoon. My Lord George drives up to the door. There are papers for him to sign. Majestically he seats himself at his desk. The instructions for Howe? Not quite ready? My lord fidgets. There are his horses, standing in the raw March air. He is due to spend the week-end in Sussex. 'Blast the papers!' says my lord. 'Keep my horses standing out-of-doors? Be late for a week-end?' And away he goes. The papers are tucked into a pigeon-hole in the Colonial Office." Charteris laughed harshly. "Admire my lord's solicitude for his horses, damned if I don't!"

Ahrens stared at him. The meaning of the mumbled words in the house on the hill began to grow clear. "Then—then Howe may not start till too late?"

"Too late?" Charteris almost cackled. "I knew about the pigeon-hole when I talked with you at Crown Point. But today I learned the whole story. Those papers are *still* in their pigeonhole in London. They were never sent to Howe, and he—he, the bulwark of the whole plan, has gone morrising off to Philadelphia with his whole God-damned army! To Philadelphia, trying to lead Washington into a trap, and it will take a cleverer man than Billy Howe to do that!" He filled his mug with a shaking hand.

Ahrens sat frozen. "God in heaven, man! Then you mean that we are marooned, alone, in the middle of this howling wilderness?"

"Oh, that!" Charteris snapped unsteady fingers. "Won't affect us very much, except to make the work harder. Get to Albany all right and St. Leger will come down the Mohawk. Don't y' see? Rebels aren't *soldiers*. *But*— being in Albany—just *us*, won't cut the rebellion in two, won't come near to ending it. We'll just be in a city.

March on down to New York. Well? Could have done it much simpler by sailing the army from Quebec. Quicker, too. Will Germaine admit *his* error?" He pointed a wavering finger at Ahrens. "Will he? Gad, sir, never! But the swine will bloody well break Gentleman Johnny, for *obeying orders! He* will. That cowardly swine who funked at Minden!" He leaned his head in his hand, then jerked upright, staring into his mug. "Is this bloody thing always empty?" He splashed a good deal of gin over the rough table.

"Who knows this?" asked Ahrens. His throat felt dry, his hands clammy.

Again the finger pointed through the darkness. "You, your very humble servant, and the General. Runner came through this afternoon. First word we've had from the south. Letter from Howe. He's off for Philadelphia with most of his army. Wishes Gentleman Johnny well with whatever plans he may have afoot. Not a word about Albany. Told *me*, the General did. But even Riedesel doesn't know. Won't know. Bad effect on the army."

"Why didn't you warn the General?" asked Ahrens.

"Warn him? What good? Always a chance that the orders *would* come through to Howe, even if they were late. Better than nothing. If so, all right. But in any event, Burgoyne had *his* orders, even if Howe didn't. Orders from the King. 'Go to Albany. Howe will meet you.' D'you see? 'Go to Albany'—only part that concerns Burgoyne. No turning back from that."

Ahrens' fingers drummed on the table. "This is going to be hard on the men—if the rebels *do* stand. Now—if Howe were coming up from New York *and* St. Leger from the west at the same time, why, that's one thing. But now we'll have every rebel thrown against us. They can forget about the south. Rush their best men, their best leaders, against a force that was supposed to be secondary even by Germaine. We're far from our base. And—note this, Major—with each step we take we grow fewer. We have to garrison our line of supply. We've left men at Ticonderoga. There are guards at Skenesboro, at Fort Anne and Fort George. When we move on from here, we'll leave more men. Difficult for us, the officers. But it means that each grenadier, each gunner, fights against heavier odds."

Charteris stirred impatiently in his seat. "The *men*! Now what do *they* care? Killed by one rebel, killed by fifty. What's the difference? Forget about 'em. But Gen'leman Johnny—he'll be killed by one blasted little worm in London. Killed—but he'll live on. Grenadier catches a musket-ball in the heart. Right. He's done, finished. But ol' Burgoyne, he'll be tortured, then killed—an' he won't be *allowed* to die. That's the horror."

Ahrens picked up his untouched mug, then set it down again. Darkness hid the steely points that began to fleck his gray eyes. "Bad, I agree. But you've *got* to think about the men. The difference between a corporal and a colonel is only relative. A drummer can suffer as much as a general."

Something of its natural smoothness came back to Charteris' voice. "Now, now. Don't preach, m'lad. You talk like those fellows the French court is said to be gaping over—Rousseau and that lot. Amusing, I grant you. But"—he rapped on the table with strong fingers—"damn it all, they aren't *gentlemen*. Like *your* idea of pushing yourself ahead through *experience*. Look at Gentleman Johnny. Passed over for promotion once, years ago. What did he do? Did *he* write the War Office, bragging about his successful campaign in Portugal? Not he. He wrote them that he would blush to ask for promotion on grounds of service. Just mentioned his family and connections. Got the promotion, too. That's the way. No damn nonsense about *merit*." His voice trailed away. Presently he began to snore gently. Ahrens rose, tiptoed off through the long grasses that were alive with the steady, vibrant chirp of crickets. The river shimmered across the meadows. He looked south. "What are the rebels up to, off there in the dark?" he wondered. "They must be somewhere below us, but no one seems to know. Or care. There's something eerie about it. Have they had enough, broken up their army?" He stretched his tall frame, then walked carefully through the meadow-grasses that whipped and hissed about his boots.

The next morning Gentleman Johnny rode through the camp, shining in scarlet and white, barbered, groomed and polished, exuding confidence. Even the Brunswickers cheered him. He smiled, swept off his hat in a conqueror's gesture. But still the army lay at Fort Edward.

A frown deepened over Ahrens' gray eyes as the days limped by, days of boiling heat, of splitting, ripping thunderstorms, deepened as he watched the men. The creek was deserted except for groups who gathered there after the reveille drum to shave in silence, to beat their white breeches with willow wands, to grunt in dull monosyllables with the women washing clothes by shallow pools. Even the long lines which filed by the various quartermasters to draw the usual four-day rations had stopped grumbling, although the fairly fresh and varied diet of Skenesboro had given way to a monotonous stream of salt pork and moldy flour. Silent were the groups about the squad-kettles at the end of company streets, silent save for mechanical conversation or occasional wild bursts of joyless laughter.

Through still August air that lay like a damp blanket over the flats, Ahrens walked by the slow-flowing river. He had formed the habit in his leisure hours of exploring the country about the great bend by Fort Edward, marking down possible gun-positions which might be utilized if a rebel force suddenly appeared from the east or south. Today's reconnaissance had taken him scrambling among some low, rocky hills a short distance below the orderly park and neat rows of conical tents which marked the camp of the Hanau artillerymen. He squinted across the river at the steep bluffs which rose beyond the meadows of the west bank. "Still early," he thought. "I'll cross the road and see what the ground is like north of the fort. Wonder if those masses of clouds mean a thunderstorm. Hello! Who's the fisherman? Of course—those long legs." Aloud he cried, "What luck?"

The thin man who squatted on the grassy end of the point looked slowly round, then swung his eyes back to the alder pole which jutted out over the water. A long arm detached itself from the rod, held up a string of white perch, dropped them, clutched the rod again. Ahrens walked softly out to the end of the point, eyed the catch appreciatively. "Eight? Fat ones, too."

Spangenberg nodded, then squatted lower, his sharp knees jutting about his ears. His eyes were on the bit of wood which he had tied to his line by way of float. The wood suddenly wabbled, dipped. Spangenberg's wrist flicked with surprising delicacy and a ninth perch struggled in the grass beside him. As though a ritual had been completed, he became voluble. "Nine, and in less than an hour. You know, I've fished all the streams of the Black Forest and the Hartz Mountains, not to mention the Odenwald, but I've never seen such waters as there are here in America. Hope the war lasts fifty years. When we reach Albany, one of the Indian chiefs has promised to take me back into the hills south of the town. Alive with trout, those hill-streams, he says." He held up the withe and deftly threaded the last fish with its fellows. "Well, this is enough for today. I'll send a couple to old Pausch and turn the rest over to your man Rentner's pretty wife to cook for us."

"Well, don't wait for me," said Ahrens. "I'm playing at war all by myself. Picking out gun positions in the face of an imaginary rebel advance."

Spangenberg's mournful head nodded. "Good thing, professionally. Pausch has heard and is pleased. He'll mark you out for something really hard, if the campaign ever starts."

"I'm glad he approves. Some of the English seem to think it's bad form, taking interest in a profession." He slapped a particularly fat perch. "Why don't the men do something of this sort? Help out their salt meat and spoiled flour."

"The men?" Spangenberg sighed. "Wish they would. You weren't here last—"

"So I've been told," murmured Ahrens.

"Hence you didn't see the way men act under strain. The English grow sullen and murderous. Ours mope. Wish I knew what you do to *your* men. Out of all our force, they're the only one who *do* anything. They sing, play cards, fight, steal from other regiments, get drunk when they can. The others just sit and stare at the ground."

"I try to get the men interested in their work. Show 'em what I'm trying to do when I bark orders at 'em. Why do I make 'em hitch the drag-ropes on and move a gun? Why, for this reason or that. Seem to like it. Let one of 'em play officer, then let the others criticize. But I wouldn't worry about the others moping. Cure that once action starts."

"What time is it?" Spangenberg asked. "Going on four? I *ought* to be able to show you something that will add light to my remarks. Wait till I hide my pole under these rocks. No one will take it, but it is a fisherman's prerogative to be suspicious of non-fishermen. Read the Englishman, Walton? My bible. There—hidden. I'll take the catch along with me. Perhaps we can see something of true melancholy."

He led the way toward the pointed tops of the tents of the Hesse-Hanau infantry, skirting the ends of the company streets with their charred spots where the men boiled their kettles, then cut inland toward a slight rise in the meadows. Ahrens followed, wondering what on earth this long-legged man could have to show him. Suddenly Spangenberg slackened his long stride, held up his hand. He whispered: "This is one of the places. Look down through those bushes."

Ahrens parted the fronds of birch that topped the rise and looked down into a cup-like depression some thirty feet deep, with sloping sides. Sprinkled through the grasses clear to the bottom were huddled heaps of blue, of green. By the foot of a clump of white birches, a big grenadier of the Rhetz regiment sat, hands locked about his knees, broad, fat face staring dully before him. Ahrens thought he had never seen so hopeless, so miserable an expression. It would have been almost pathetically funny save for its blank inertness, an inertness so profound as to be far deeper than mere resignation, a look of surrender in the eyes that denied that use of the word "despair" with its implication of attempted struggle. The other faces grouped about had drawn the same mask over them.

Endlessly the Rhetz grenadier shook his head. Then he spoke. There were no tears in his voice. There was only—what was it? Ahrens struggled to define it. A horrible nullity, a negation of the existence of hope, now or at any time. The head rolled on broad shoulders, the voice droned on. "I shall never see Halberstadt again." Then like some devilish litany, responses echoed flatly from the grassy amphitheater.

"We shall never go home." ... "We'll never see our parents again." ... "Never again shall I hold 'Trudschen in my arms." ... "My farm shall never know me again." ... "Who will bury my old mother?" ... "We shall all die here." ... "I shall never see the banks of the Aller again." ... "There is no hope."

Silence fell. A sudden breeze rocked the grasses and the tops of the white birches, bright in the strong sun. A Jaeger, tears falling on his red facings, said in a heavy voice: "There was a little dog I loved. I shall never walk through the fields by Clausthal with Pommers at my heels. He would fetch sticks for me."

The response wailed from the banks: "My children will never know me." ... "Our bones will whiten the forests." ... "The savages will fall on us." ... "The peace of the Odenwald—I shall never know it again." ... "We are lost." ... "There is no hope."

Ahrens shuddered, backed away from his leafy screen. "In God's name, Spangenberg, what is that?"

"Melancholy, my friend. Those are strong men. But when sadness strikes them, they gather in twenties and thirties. They talk as you heard them, but their gloom increases in a neat, geometrical progression. Sometimes the women join them."

"It should be stopped!" Ahrens jaw snapped. "Bad for morale."

"Baron Riedesel will be greatly obliged if you are able to suggest a means of stopping it. It goes deeper than morale."

"What is deeper than morale?"

"Death," said Spangenberg.

"Death?" Ahrens stared at the thin man.

"Death. Those men die of their melancholy. Not all, of course. But gradually some pine away. The doctors are helpless. Last winter at Quebec, at Trois Rivières, they died by the score, men like those in the hollow. They crept to the hospitals and lay down. They never got up again."

"And the English?" asked Ahrens.

"No. It seems to be a national trait of ours. It has been noted before. Homesickness among us can be fatal. You never heard of it?"

"Never. You see, I spent my growing years in England, then came to Dresden, where my father was a court functionary. There may be despair, madness in a country, but it is never allowed to show itself at court."

They walked back toward the park where the brass guns sat hunched between their high wheels, their brightness canvas-shrouded. Ahrens was deep in thought. "What an appalling thing!" he said at last. "Yet

212

I *saw*, in the woods of Hubbardton, Jaegers—perhaps some of the same back there in the grass—advance in perfect order against a fire which seemed to me to be of hellish intensity, not to say accuracy."

Spangenberg flipped his long legs across a little brook. "No doubt they were the same Jaegers. They will advance again. But the offensive spark dies and dies. When they have time to think—or not to think, just as you like—they will begin to mope. One man will moan to another, a third will join. If it goes on long enough, they will sicken and die. A sort of involuntary, or rather unconscious mass suicide. I wonder why. Interesting, isn't it?"

"Interesting!" cried Ahrens. "God!"

Captain Georg Pausch of the Hesse-Hanau artillery blinked heavy-lidded eyes in the early sun and shook his tough old head at the tall officer who pleaded with him. "No, no and no, Lieutenant Ahrens. It's Bache's turn for duty."

Ahrens tried to hide his disappointment under a thick layer of respect. "But you told me, Captain, that I'd have the first chance for active service—not having been here last year."

Pausch smiled slowly. "Active service? This is just an excursion into the country. Active!" He laughed. "I don't know why Colonel Baum is taking guns at all. Just a pair of three-pounders. He'll never need them. He's taking most of the dragoons and a few men from other regiments. Skene has had word of a big depot of Yankee horses and supplies off in the Hampshire Grants. Baum is going after 'em. Wants horses for the dragoons. They'll come back with two thousand horses, a lot of carts, supplies, food and—so I hear—most of the population of the Grants, who are really Tories. Guns! Why, they might just as well carry wig-powder in the ammunition wagons! It will be a march, that's all. Bache needs work with the men. You don't. I can use you far better

213

drilling the recruits than in following two light pieces through the Hampshire Grants and back. Now, if it were a question of gunnery—"

Ahrens saluted and walked away. He felt bitterly disappointed. He had learned of the expedition the night before on his return to the artillery lines from an unauthorized ride over the miserable road to Fort Anne. Of course, there had been no time to swing off in the direction of the round hill, but riding back he had fallen in with a ranger who told him of a shaky Conestoga wagon lurching south, a wagon driven by a girl in a faded sunbonnet. The ranger's news had elated him. He felt sure that he could track down the wagon, which must necessarily adapt its pace to that of the army, halting and moving with the main body. She would hang well off to the right flank but he would get news of her one way or another. Then Rentner had told him of the expedition to a place called Manchester in the Hampshire Grants and at sun-up he had gone to Pausch, feeling that the old veteran must give him command of the two accompanying guns. Two days, three days on the march and then he would come back to find Judith settled. As it was—he shrugged.

With a sudden fierceness he loathed the thought of standing in the blazing sun by the river, shouting at staring recruits: "Now, when the pieces are advanced by hand, numbers one and two hook their drag-ropes to the right axle, three and four to the right trunion, five and six—" That—while he was laying plans to find Judith, not daring to make a premature move that might frighten her into some unknown hinterland. Let her get accustomed to the new setting, the idea that thousands of troops were nearby. Then—a little later he would discover her.

He stepped out of the rutted track as slouchy Canadian drivers trotted the gun-teams past him on the way to the park, four chunky horses in single file to each hitch. He watched Bache marching the cannoneers past

214

the big twenty-four-pounders, the sixteens, the twelves, saw red cuffs flash as the canvas covers were flicked off the stumpy threes that were to follow Colonel Baum and his column. His jaw tightened. "Damnation!" he muttered. "Why can't I go with them?"

A long shadow fell across the grass beside him.

"We had prime fish again last night. I waited for you as long as I dared." Spangenberg stroked his lean jaws. "And was it necessary to hang your coat and hat on my feet when you came in at last?"

Ahrens smiled quietly. "You've no idea how inviting they looked, sticking out there in the moonlight."

Spangengerg shook his head mournfully. "Off bibbling again. Four nights ago you drank with low characters at Headquarters. Last night you were somewhere off in the hills and came back skipping and singing. Is that right when the man whom you invited to share your tent has tasted nothing but spruce-beer for a week? Not to speak of using his feet for a clothes-horse?"

"Now, as to that invitation—" began Ahrens.

Spangenberg raised a slow hand. "I know, I know. But you *would* have extended it. I merely saved you the trouble. And how do you repay it?"

"I give you my word that I had nothing stronger than water," said Ahrens. He smiled to himself as he thought of the ranger's news. Already it was dulling his disappointment.

The thin man contemplated nameless calamities down the river. "You must have found the Fountain of Youth." He turned his eyes to the busy park. "Wish I were going with that column. Very hilly country off there. I'd lash my rods to one of the pieces and watch for trout-brooks. The country must fairly itch with them." His eyes looked less mournful.

"I tried to talk old Pausch into letting me go," said Ahrens, shrugging. "He's set on young Bache."

"I know, I know. Dead set." Spangenberg was a picture of woe. "I used the strongest arguments I had to get him to take me. I pointed out to him that I'd probably never have another chance at such streams. Two weeks of it, at the very least. He was adamant."

"Was he?" Ahrens laughed. "Unreasonable—eh? What's that? What did you say about two *weeks*? Why, they're only going out to round up a few horses."

"Two weeks. Kolster of the dragoons told me. Quiet, though. Everyone knows it. No possible chance of action. All my friends say there's no one there to fight. All Tories. What fishing I'd have!"

"Two *weeks*!" Ahrens said again. He felt suddenly relieved. In two weeks' time there would be no telling where two decrepit horses might not drag a blue-eyed girl in a faded sunbonnet.

Fifes screamed away on the right. Ahrens pointed to a gap in the tents past which flowed a steady line of red coats and bearskin caps. "Look there! Fraser's whole corps must be moving."

Spangenberg nodded. "If you hadn't gone to bed at sunrise this morning you would have heard the orders. They move south and the rest of the army will follow in a day or two. Baum's column follows Fraser now, but instead of halting by Fort Miller down below there, they'll swing off into the Grants. May even get down into Massachusetts. Those mountain streams!"

"Off at last! And you never told me! That's gratitude for covering your feet last night," said Ahrens. "Hi! There go the dragoons' drums. They're sounding off. Let's cut across and watch them march off."

With Spangenberg he stood by the edge of the road and stared as the light blue coats of the dragoons moved sluggishly past. "Look here, they're sending *those* men on a two-week tour into enemy country?" he asked.

Spangenberg laughed. "Enemy? In name only. There have been no enemies since Fort Anne. They could send children just as well."

"Better. Look at those dragoons! Do you know how much those boots weigh? Twelve pounds a pair. Their

216

carbines are far too heavy and what could they do with those ghastly swords, dismounted. That's the last file. One hundred sixty, one hundred seventy-five dragoons. Might as well have the same number of oxen. Those rebels move like ghosts. And look—the rest of the column. Like Noah's Ark."

Twenty grenadiers of the advance corps followed the dragoons. Then came two unexplained men from the Rhetz regiment, seventeen from Riedesel's, sixteen from Specht's. The little column moved slowly along, the twenty brass hats of the grenadiers jutting up from the mass of flat cocked hats. Pounding hooves and a rumble of wheels brought on the little three-pounders, Bache's men marching stiffly in thin files on either side of them.

"Safe enough, I suppose," said Ahrens. "But if—if they should fall into a trap? Spangenberg, can you imagine it? Can you see those dragoons trying to sift through wooded country? Every man carries at least eighty pounds on his back and the weather is stifling."

"Suppose and suppose!" Spangenberg chuckled. "Suppose they suddenly met Swedish infantry off there in the Grants! Just as likely. Everyone *knows* how safe it is. Talk to the staff. See—off there in the meadows. Three ammunition wagons waiting to fall in behind the guns. Two transport wagons back of them. Would they take as little as that if the country wasn't quiet? The General knows! Personally, I'd rather relish a brush with the Yankees. Those dragoons—they're terrible fighters."

Ahrens shrugged. He had seen the broad face of Heinz, the proud dragoon, marching among the light blue and yellow of the lumbering men. "Well, there are three hundred rangers out ahead and Indians covering the rangers." He looked gravely at the little three-pounders that jumped and jolted over the ruts. "It may be all right. Now for my recruits."

All day he worked with his men in the hot sun. That evening he prowled fruitlessly among the low hills to the

217

north of the Fort George road. He could find no trace of a charred wagon and two decrepit horses.

The main army moved heavily down the east bank of the Hudson, leaving behind it a trail of red and blue, lengthening the string that already stretched from Ticonderoga to Skenesboro, Fort Anne, Fort George and Fort Edward. Again the meadows about Fort Miller bristled with whitish peaks as the regiments pitched camp by the river. Burgoyne's scarlet and white flashed on the deep porch of the Duer house, from whose windows the bright eyes of Mrs. Lewis peeped out on the Hudson.

In the shade of the porch, Gentleman Johnny felt a deep sense of well-being. A letter had come in from Baum, saying that the march went well and that he had already secured a number of horses. Too bad, of course, that the Indians shot so many of the cattle for the sake of the cow-bells they prized so highly. Left the bodies to rot in the sun, Baum reported. Well, well. No doubt Baum would find some way of curbing the Indians. Skene could help, too. It had been a good idea, sending him with the column. In the meantime, everything showed that his own last-minute inspiration which had disturbed Riedesel so much—that order he had given after the column had started, changing the destination from Manchester to Bennington—had been wise. Gentleman Johnny stepped from the porch and looked toward the Hudson. Flat bateaux packed with the red coats of Fraser's men were moving slowly across to the west bank. Well, he'd follow with the rest of the army in a few days and then ho! for Albany! Now about that champagne that the last wagons had brought in. He entered the house and tapped on Mrs. Lewis' door.

Ahrens leaned against the charred side of the battered Conestoga wagon. A soft voice said: "I knew you'd come, Kurt Ahrens!" a light hand touched his shoulder. "Kurt Ahrens! Kurt Ahrens!" Strangely the voice seemed

218

to deepen, the hand on his shoulder grew heavier and heavier. Now the words were a rumble, the hand shook him violently. "Lieutenant Ahrens! Lieutenant Ahrens!" With a jerk Ahrens sat up in his blankets, rubbing his eyes, staring through the dark at Captain Pausch's old orderly, who still tugged at him. "Lieutenant Ahrens! Captain's compliments. Please report to him at once!"

Ahrens blinked again. It was pitch-dark outside. A thin drilling rain hissed in the long grass about his tent. "Right, right," he growled. With stiff hands he fumbled for his boots.

Spangenberg's long nose appeared over the edge of a thin blanket. "Here! What's up? What are you doing? Where are you going?"

Ahrens shrugged himself into his jacket. "Don't know. Orders to report to Pausch at once."

Long arms and legs suddenly waved violently on the camp-cot by the opposite wall of the tent. "Here! I know! Where are my boots? Bache has been taken sick! Want someone to replace him! You don't want to go. Tell Pausch that I'll go! Damnation! That's the wrong sleeve! Go tell him! I'll take an ammunition cart. Lash my rods to the side. Bache can come back in it. Tell—" But Ahrens was already out of the tent and squashing through wet grass to the Captain's tent.

He found Pausch, a weird figure in cotton nightcap and wildly figured dressing-gown, staring at papers in his tent by the light of a dancing candle. "So! Now you've got your chance!" growled the veteran. "Colonel Breymann's whole corps moves at once. I'm sending two six-pounders with him. You'll command them. Take Spangenberg. Sergeant Pertz is routing out the men now. You'd best join them at the gun-park."

The cool wet air cleared sleep from Ahrens' brain. His gray eyes began to spark as he controlled a wild impulse to whoop like an Indian. "Active service, Captain? Any special orders?"

Pausch shook his head, the tassel of his nightcap

brushing across his beaky nose. "Don't know. Breymann is being sent out to reinforce Baum. Seem to be a few rebels about. But Baum is pushing right on to the depot at Bennington. You'll probably join him there. This is all the orders say: 'In consequence of the good news received from Colonel Baum.' Probably he's rounded up so many horses and cattle, carts and supplies that he has to use his whole force to look after them. Baum's a cautious man and Skene is with him. Probably the only use for your guns will be to tie strings of horses to them. Look out for a good black for me and a couple of bays."

For two rain-drenched hours, Ahrens and Spangenberg stood in the sodden gun-park, fretting and fidgeting. Their oilskin coats kept them fairly dry, but the fourteen men who marched with the guns could only hunch their soaked shoulders, pour cascades of water from their pulpy cocked hats, shift their leaking boots from one wet spot to another. The horses shook themselves with an unearthly jingle of toggles and chains, stamped broad hooves in puddles. For the rest, a dead silence hung over the park. Once Spangenberg stirred uneasily, squinted up at the dull gray piles of rolling clouds. "Fish won't bite in this weather," he mumbled, trying to draw his long thin neck deeper into the collar of his oilskin.

At last drums snarled and rattled far off on the left, fifes took up their reedy screech. A dark column moved out from the distant tents of the advance corps, started over the soaking ground toward the road to the south. Music raved at the column's head, drumsticks flying and drums swaying rhythmically to the cadenced step. After the drums came the thick ranks of Barner's light infantry, the men stepping briskly, free hands swinging in unison. In the dull light behind them glowed the shining helmets of the grenadier companies.

"Thank God! At last!" growled Ahrens. "Stand by, Spangenberg. I'm going to call the men to attention as soon as that Jaeger column back of Barner's men reaches the road. What the hell delayed them? They could have recruited an army in the time we've been standing here."

"Hope they got as wet as we did!" Spangenberg glowered at the green coats of the Jaegers. "Listen to them sing. Not much volume to it."

"Don't blame the men, myself," said Ahrens. "Probably afraid that if they don't sing, Breymann will have one man in every ten flogged the way he did on the march to Fort Anne. There go the last of the Jaegers. Now we'll start and just swing in behind the grenadier companies." He filled his lungs. His voice rolled out through the gun-park. "Atten-*tion!*" Then traces hissed, harness creaked, the wheels of the guns cut through the mud and grass with a sucking noise, hooves clopped and the two guns slowly swung across the wet ground onto the road, ammunition carts and baggage wagons rolling heavily after them.

They lurched on along the road, Ahrens and Spangenberg splashing in the interval between the two pieces, grateful that the shortage of horses decreed that they must walk, pitying the drivers glued to their saddles, motionless in the cold rain.

Five times in the first hour, seven in the second, the column halted. Ahrens, heedless of mud, leaned against the wheel of the first piece and fumed to Spangenberg. "Halt, halt, halt! I've not taken a free stride since we left camp! What the devil is the matter up there?" Hooves splashed in the mud as a mounted officer rode down the column.

Spangenberg hailed him. "What's the delay, Lieutenant?"

The dripping man reined in, staring. "Delay? No delay. But in this damnable mud the men keep losing their alignment. *Have* to stop and dress the ranks. But there's no delay." He urged his horse on through the rain.

"But there's no delay." Spangenberg gritted his teeth.

"Halting to dress the ranks! Is this a parade? I thought we were pushing ahead to join Baum."

"More likely to meet him coming back," growled Ahrens. "Here we go again."

Once more the lead horse leaned into his collar and the guns slithered on through the mud. Ahrens strode along, watching the white breeches of the grenadiers ahead of him splashing through the shallow ford of the Batten Kill, mounting the higher ground beyond. Across the ford, the ground rose, then dipped again. The horses lowered their thick necks, set their shoulders into the collars, hind feet digging and straining. The pieces lumbered and wallowed through the current, then bit their wheels into the miry slope. Ahrens stood on the high ground, watched the gun teams toiling on. Not too bad, this bit of road. The gunners, without being ordered, had sprung to the wheels, heaved on the spokes at the slightest sign of bogging.

The last of the wagons was clear and rolling fairly easily on. Ahrens ran back to his place between the pieces, looked out on rolling country, slashed with slanting rain. He frowned, called Spangenberg's attention to the road, a thick rope of mud which stretched away to the southeast as it made for higher ground which showed through the storm. And beyond each rise, another showed higher than the last. It would be hard going, even for the infantry. Spangenberg pursed his lips. "What d'you think of your horses?"

"Passable. Wouldn't say more. Hope I don't have to say less. That road is going to be a test. Got good men, though. Sergeant Pertz, some old-timers and the recruits, Meister and Rentner. Lord, how that rain comes down!"

The march became a nightmare. The storm drove down, turning thick mud into a viscous river in which the heavy wheels bit deep. On a twisting slope the second piece shivered, lifted one wheel in the air, poised, then overturned with a crash, terrified horses backing and stamping. Dripping men righted it, wrestled it back on the road, their sodden boots slipping in the slime, their sleeves masses of cold mud.

There was a long halt, during which a rumor slithered down the column that their Tory guide had lost the way. Ahrens' gunners, hats pulled over their eyes, leaned heavily against gun and limber wheels, dreading the command to march which would set their cracked hands on the wet, gritty spokes again, shoving and pushing until the driving hooves could start the wheels turning freely.

The day wore on. Cold rations and the wet spurred on the dysentery which had seized the army, and the road was lined with squatting men. The mud-splashed ranks ahead of the guns were halted and halted again, on the level, on up-grades and on headlong slopes, while swearing officers pushed and shoved their men into drill-ground alignment which was lost with the first step forward. The gunners jammed rocks under their wheels, cursed and waited, then threw themselves on the spokes again.

On an S curve an ammunition cart side-slipped, one wheel axle-deep in mud. Ahrens splashed back, jammed his hands against the backboard, feet braced and back straining. A tall gunner beside him, encased from head to foot in mud, drove against the nigh wheel, slapped down into the mud, scrambled to his feet, drove again. The cart rocked, then moved, the drivers lashed and cursed their horses. The wheels stirred, rolled onto the road again.

Ahrens turned to the muddy gunner. "Good spirit, lad. You had your heart in that."

From the depths of a mud-caked face, a dismal voice spoke. "But one of my rods broke. It was lashed to the nigh side."

Ahrens laughed. "Good God, Spangenberg. Didn't know you. First laugh I've had since the march started. Horrible, isn't it?"

223

"And this is supposed to be a forced march! How far away is Baum?"

"Not over twenty-five miles from camp. But do you know our rate? One mile an hour, if that. And more hills ahead. Come on, let's catch up with the guns." They splashed on, then stopped and cursed. A long-drawn "Haaaalt!" sounded from the rain-drenched distance. "How the devil will we ever get the wheels rolling again on this grade?" mourned Spangenberg.

Ahrens smiled grimly. "Usual artillery solution to all problems: 'Cannoneers on the wheels!' Keep your piece rolling, and don't forget it's a courtmartial offense for an officer to work with the men." He wiped his hands on his oilskin, whose mud-plastered skirt hung in tatters.

Spangenberg turned sad eyes on him. "I'll never testify against you."

"Thanks. Take a look at the horses, will you? They pull well, but I don't like the way they breathe. Looks bad for the hills to come. No fodder on the carts. We're supposed to graze them, but when and on what, no one has had the courtesy to tell me."

"I've been watching them. They don't look promising, but the gunners are all right."

A guffaw reached them from a group of cannoneers huddled under a dripping fir tree. Ahrens recognized Rentner's voice.

"No, I'm telling you he was smart."

"Ulrich Ritter—smart?"

"Smartest man in the army." Rentner was positive. "He joined up in Hanau because the police were after him. Then the Elector wanted to send men to America for the English. Well, Ritter said he'd never go. We laughed at him. Remember he could make his eyes do this?" There was a snicker at some invisible grimace of Rentner's. "Well, we got to calling him 'Bent-eye.' Now, when we heard about America, some of the men tried to buy off, some tried to desert, but not Bent-eye. When that Englishman came to look at the grenadiers he stopped in front of Bent-eye, and Bent-eye looked like this. The Englishman yelled, 'What the devil are you giving me?' and old von Kleist said, 'That's a fine grenadier.' The Englishman said, 'But look at his *eyes*.' There was Bent-eye looking three ways at once and the Englishman yelled again, 'I'll not have him!' The doctors took him, but he kept slewing his eyes around. Then— then, by God, they discharged him, gave him a few crowns and when *we* sailed for America, Bent-eye Ritter was driving a mail-coach between Hanau and Frankfort. Good old Bent-eye! *You* were saying he was a fool because he couldn't read or write. But *he's* in Hanau and where are *we*? Smart man, Bent-eye."

There was a hush almost reverent in its intensity. The men began to chuckle. "Good old Bent-eye!"

A drum thudded hollowly in the road ahead. Ahrens shouted: "Cannoneers on the wheels!" Horses stamped and snorted, the men wrestled and strained on the spokes. A man sprawled in the mud, cursed savagely, then shouted: "Good old Bent-eye!" Slowly the wheels turned and the march began again.

In the wet dark of early evening, camp was pitched among the trees. Ahrens watched his men trying to coax wet wood to burn under their little kettles. From the gloom a hoarse voice shouted: "Good old Bent-eye! *He* was smart!" In the shelter of an improvised tent, Ahrens shared a mug of rum and water with Spangenberg, who had scraped most of the mud from his face. Horses splashed by in the dark. Breymann's snarl cut through the air: "I've sent a messenger ahead to Baum and that's enough. D'you think I'm going to march all night just to please that swine? Let him wait!" the hooves died away. Ahrens raised his eyebrows. Spangenberg looked at him over the top of his mug. "Good old Bent-eye!" he murmured.

The sun broke through ragged clouds a little before noon and beat on the column as mercilessly as yesterday's rain. The stiff men and the unfed horses moved on through a steaming countryside of wide fields and woodland, halted, moved, halted again. The air was heavy, still, like a summer Sunday in Dresden, Ahrens thought. In the village of Cambridge they met Colonel Skene, who had ridden in from Baum's column with a string of captured horses and carts and with the news that Baum was doing well and had only a small force of rebels before him, rebels who did not dare attack.

Ahrens plodded along the miry road on a bony sorrel farm horse, hoping that it wouldn't be necessary to force his gun-teams. The animals looked worse and worse as the day wore on. They had not been fed since they left the camp by Fort Miller, for there had been no forage in the camp in the woods. If he could only find *something* for them.

The column had halted again. Ahrens looked ahead down a gentle slope to a mill by a narrow bridge where Skene and Breymann talked with a knot of men by the mill door. He turned to Spangenberg, who bestrode a short, clay-colored horse, his heels nearly dragging on the ground. "I'm going to ride ahead. There may be a ford by the bridge. If there is, I'll signal; then have the drivers lead out to water."

He trotted his sorrel along the resting column, noting how the heat was telling on the heavy grenadiers. He found a ford close by the mill, rode back into the road to signal Spangenberg. Then he cursed under his breath. Breymann and Skene had remounted by the mill and he could hear the heavy Colonel's saddle creak as he settled himself, heard him wheeze as he snarled to an aide: "The command is forward!"

"Oh, the devil!" growled Ahrens. "A dozen halts in three miles and then when we get near water—'The command is forward.' How does he expect the horses to keep up?" Then he recognized a grenadier officer with whom he had once talked by the lake at Skenesboro. "Lieutenant Zweig—any news?"

226

The big man looked up. "Hello." His face was sweat-streaked and haggard. "News? Isn't any."

"Then why so short a halt? I wanted to water my horses."

Zweig shrugged. "There were four men from Baum's column at the mill, here. No two of them told the same story. A Tory captain and Baum was cut off—surrounded. A dragoon said he was in danger. An Englishman said he was doing very nicely, though all the Indians had run away. A lieutenant from Specht's regiment said there had been no fighting and no signs of rebels, beyond a scattering few who ran away into the woods."

"Wide range of choice," commented Ahrens. "What were the men doing at the mill?"

"That's what I can't understand. *Something* has happened. They were separated from their units. That doesn't happen unless there's a reason. Skene believed the Englishman—thinks the rebels may have attacked and been driven off. So the column is moving on." The grenadiers started off across the bridge, useless swords knocking against their legs.

Ahrens rode back to Spangenberg and the guns, told him Zweig's report. "Odd, damned odd," he concluded. "Those men were stragglers."

"But Baum can't be more than four miles away, unless the maps are wrong," objected Spangenberg. "So far, they've been right. This is Owl Kill, the mill is San Coick and that must be the Hoosic off there. Now, if there had been trouble, we'd have heard firing. It's peaceful as a convent garden."

Ahrens looked dubious. "Can't tell by that. A ridge or a line of hills *can* blanket sound. The range outside Dresden was like that. A quarter of a mile to the southeast you couldn't hear a shot. Wonder if— Well, Skene thinks everything is satisfactory."

"Isn't that enough? He knows the country and the people."

"But he's always talking about Tories swarming to join

us. How many have you seen? A few hundred came to Skenesboro, and most of them deserted as soon as they were given a meal and a musket. Skene believes what he wants to."

The guns rumbled slowly along, hooves rang on the bridge across Owl Kill, timbers shook hissing dust into the smooth water below. Spangenberg leaned from his saddle, peered down into the cool depths of the kill. "Now if there aren't fish in that water, I'll, I'll—" He wagged his head. "I'll guarantee to reconcile Breymann and Baum."

Ahrens smiled. "I'll hold you to that. Wonder how Baum *is* doing—and the dragoon Heinz. Particularly the dragoon Heinz."

At that very moment the dragoon Heinz stood near the end of a long line of blue and yellow that sheltered itself behind a loose breastwork of logs and earth and fired his musket down a steep slope covered with sparse timber. It was very easy. You fired, then dropped your piece, reloaded, primed, raised it to your shoulder till it was almost on a level with your collar-bone, then you pulled the trigger and did it all over again. You always waited until the little three-pounder in the middle of the line had slammed, because the concussion made you wince, but otherwise, the whole thing was very easy.

As he raised his carbine he saw the slope was swarming with farmers. That's what they were, farmers. All except the huge man in blue and buff who kept calling to them. What were farmers doing in a battle? They might get hurt. He closed his eyes, squeezed the trigger again, blinked rapidly and dropped the butt to the ground to reload. The farmers were behind trees, they were creeping among piles of rocks. There was a dreadful sound of firing somewhere behind him, more firing down the hill, but the slope was so steep that he couldn't see the base where the Tories and the British sharpshooters had been stationed. His lieutenant kept screaming commands. Foolish. *Heinz* knew how to load, take time from the

228

man at his left, fire. No need to shout at *him*! The farmers were coming closer. Something thudded close to Heinz and the man beside him slipped quietly to the ground, knees bent, head sagging forward. Heinz wondered why he didn't get up. The crashing muskets, the shouting, the clouds of smoke made him a little dizzy. Then he realized that he was shouting too, that the farmers—who were very close now—were shouting. The farmers had rifles, muskets. They were attacking *dragoons,* shooting at them. Country-people! Something buzzed viciously past Heinz' cheek. Why, they were shooting at him, at Heinz, the dragoon!

The firing died away for an instant. Heinz looked around. The lieutenant was no longer shouting foolish orders. Instead, he was lying on his back, arms over his head, mouth open as though stretching after a long sleep. And the sergeant, that hard man from Bremen—he was rolling back and forth slowly, clutching at his belly while black blood spouted from between his fingers. Beyond him were two dragoons, three dragoons, a dozen, on their faces, their backs, lying quietly, writhing. Klipfel, whom he had first seen among the hot rocks of Mount Defiance, pawed the ground with hands and elbows, dragging useless legs behind him and staring through bulging, sightless eyes.

Heinz' mouth quivered. His throat grew dry, and it was hard to swallow. His hands seemed absurdly light, and when he moved them they flew up to his face like feathers. Then a quiet voice behind him said: "Close up, close up!" Heinz grinned nervously, his wide mouth twitching. He sidestepped to the left until he closed with another dragoon. "Quite right, Captain," he thought. "Good idea, closing up." Odd. The Captain's voice had been so low, almost gentle all day. In camp and on the march he roared like a crazed bull. Why was it?

Muskets glazed again. There were shirtsleeved farmers inside the breastworks. Heinz couldn't understand it. They should have been frightened away. Out of the corner of his eye he saw a yellow-haired man in a smock kneel behind a rock far down the line and take aim at him, at Heinz! Heinz chuckled. That showed how stupid these farmers were. Taking all that time just to aim! Red suddenly crawled down the blond man's temple, his head jerked back. Slowly he crumpled over the rock. It was a lesson, Heinz told himself. Taking all that time to aim! He raised his own piece slowly. When it was nearly level with his shoulder, he fired. Much simpler. He fumbled in his cartridge box. Empty! He turned to the man on his left. There was no man on his left. Nor on his right. Nothing but swarming country-people and that big man in blue and buff and a handful of dragoons running down the hill. Heinz dropped his heavy carbine. With a start he realized that he had been running, that he was among a knot of dragoons, all running headlong down the hill, boots clumping and spurs rattling among hidden stones and mad things hissing in the air about them.

Then he found himself scrambling over a rail fence to join a stout man who stood on a rock and yelled: "To me, dragoons, to me!" as he waved his sword over his head. Others joined Heinz in his rush and he was shocked to find that the stout man was his colonel, the dreaded man Baum. Heinz found himself in a solid knot of nearly thirty dragoons rallying about the Colonel, who yelled that they should throw away their carbines, draw their sabers and cut their way out. Steel flashed about him and the knot moved on, Heinz stumping docilely along with them. Then more shirtsleeved men appeared. The Colonel yelled again: "They have no bayonets! At 'em with the saber!" Muskets blazed and the Colonel doubled up suddenly with a dreadful noise in his throat. The dragoons left him sprawled on the ground and Heinz ran with them.

It was nearly dark. Heinz found himself alone in a field. He was aware of a hideous din far away down the road along which he had marched with his fellows the day the Colonel had ordered them to climb the steep hill and throw up earthworks. Why, that was only yesterday. Building breastworks in the rain, a wet camp, more rain and then the sun and the fields around the hill full of farmers in smocks and shirtsleeves.

He stopped and shook his head. He couldn't understand it. The dragoons had fired and fired, but still the country-people had come on, while more and more dragoons pitched headlong over their carbines. Why didn't the farmers fall, too? And where were the other men, the English sharpshooters, the grenadiers, the Tories, the Indians? He shook his head again. It was too much for him. Dragoons! Their own colonel had said that they were the finest troops in the army, and there they lay, huddled over their carbines or dragging useless legs after them like Klipfel, shot by farmers who were so stupid that they aimed their shots. Why, they didn't even have uniforms!

His throat felt parched, his eyes ached violently. Water! Where could he find water? His own gallon canteen that had cut so cruelly into his shoulder on the march, was empty, pierced by a bullet. Some farmer had shot a hole in it and now it was useless. But there must be water nearby. Perhaps if he had a long drink, a drenching drink of clear, cold water, he could understand about dragoons huddled over silent carbines. There *must* be water! Why, in soil like this— He dug the toe of his crippling boot into the ground. Then he made little grunting noises, squatted to look at the dent. He prodded the loose earth with his finger. Ah, this was loam, this was *earth*! He clucked to himself, picked up a handful, kneaded it in his palms. "Now here," he thought, "here I should plant wheat, good wheat!"

He lifted his head with a jerk. A tall man in gray smock and black knee-breeches was covering him with a wicked-looking rifle. The English words fell uncomprehended on his ears, but he understood the muzzle. "Hands up, Dutchy!" Two other men, one smocked and

231

the other shirtsleeved, came into the field from a belt of trees. They were both tall and lean like his captor and spoke in slow, measured sentences. One of them leaned his musket against a tree, took the dragoon sword from the farmer Heinz, the sword he had found such a trouble to keep bright, felt of his pockets. Again slow voices spoke: "Come on, Dutchy!"

Heinz brightened. They talked so like the English. He dropped his hands, thought of words he had heard when on guard at Headquarters. He grinned. "Ja, ja! I—gome!" Then his eyes fell on an English canteen slung about the shoulders of the shortest of the men. The word—the word he had heard the English general use so often. Ah—almost like German. "A—a trink!" The men looked startled. Then the eldest spoke. "Dutchy allows he'd admire a pull at your canteen, Bije."

Blessed water slid down Heinz' throat like silk. He handed the canteen back, bowed awkwardly. The men handled their rifles, looked up at the darkening sky. "Cap'n Blake'll be waitin' us. 'Tain't suitable to keep *him* tarryin'. Come along, Dutchy!"

Ahrens shifted uncomfortably in his backwoods saddle, wishing that an easier-gaited horse had been sent back for him. Then he grinned as he saw Spangenberg hitching up his long legs to keep his heels free of the ground. It was a mercy that he was mounted at all, now that the weather had turned so hot. Skene's carts had helped, too, although they only just offset that ammunition cart which he had had to abandon a mile back with its axle broken and a squad working at it. It would catch up in the course of time and then he would really have a surplus of vehicles. Horses, though—they looked about finished. Nothing but grazing and rest would bring them back into condition. He called to Spangenberg: "When we reach Baum, I'm going to talk to Breymann about cutting out these horses and leaving them to graze. No sense in knocking them to pieces."

"Good idea." Spangenberg nodded. "Only Breymann hates his men so much that he'll probably make us all drill in the dark till we drop. How much farther to Baum, do you think?"

"No telling. I'm taking a bearing over my horse's ears. Keep your eyes ahead of you and you'll see Baum before too long."

The road twisted ahead of them, bearing due east along a stream that must be the Walloomsac. Far ahead Ahrens could see the dark mass of the advance guard, some three companies of light infantry, then a knot of horsemen, Breymann and Skene riding at their head. Rising ground hid the rest of the light infantry, but he knew that they were in the blind space between Breymann's staff and the head of the grenadier column that stretched straight along in front of him. He shook his head. "Lord, how they drag! Long sleep tonight is what they need. Spangenberg, I'll bet you're right. Breymann will give everyone two hours of stiff drill when we get in tonight, just to show he's still master. He'll—" His arm shot out, caught Spangenberg by a bony shoulder. "Look, look!"

A rocky hill on the left of the road, nearly opposite the advance guard, was suddenly swarming with drab figures, with light-stepping men who ran easily, carrying long rifles. Spangenberg stared. "But—but they aren't uniformed! They're just farmers, peasants. Shouldn't be allowed muskets. What are they doing?"

"Farmers be damned! Look like the Hubbardton men to me. They're rebels, rebel militia! Don't you see, don't you see? *They're between us and Baum!* God above, what's happened? Look, they're taking cover behind that rail fence on the crest." He swung in his saddle, roared: "Prepare for action!" He smiled grimly as the men stripped tompions from muzzles, loosened the covers of the tumbrils, cleared rammer-staffs and worms, shifted their coiled drag-ropes from waist to shoulder. His recruits moved as deftly as the oldest soldier.

"Better stand by the second piece, Spangenberg. What? What's that?"

A long arm pointed to the hill whose low-running occupants were now sunk behind the rail fence, muskets bristling toward the road. "Sorry to take your rebels away from you," said Spangenberg. "Those are Tories, the Loyalists that Skene has been promising us. Look—there he goes to meet them." A single horseman had broken away from the staff group and was urging his mount across the fields. There was a dead hush along the halted column. Faint but clear Skene's voice ripped the still air. "Are you King George's men?"

"There!" said Spangenberg triumphantly. "Tories, See—Skene waves to them. He's— Lord *God*!"

Smoke suddenly billowed from the rails with a splintering crash. Skene's horse reared, lashed out viciously with its forefeet, then pitched sideways in a sprawl of waving legs and curved neck. The rider rolled clear, scrambled to his feet and ran back to the column. Spangenberg spun his mount about, galloped to the second piece. There was shouting up ahead, Breymann's bitter voice blurring all other sounds. The column moved on.

"We don't reply?" fretted Ahrens. Then he stood in his stirrups. The light infantry left the road, formed into line and started slowly up the slope, company after company. The rail fence still blazed. Here and there bluecoated men spun, doubled up, dropped, white-clad legs stumbled, tripped, but still the dark lines went on. A distant voice roared: "One volley, then at 'em with the bayonet!" The blue lines halted, dressed, fired, then broke into a clumsy trot, steel slanting before them. Ahrens pounded the pommel of his saddle. "They're closing, they're closing!" he shouted. "Ten yards more and they'll be among 'em with steel!"

The fence blazed again, more blue coats tossed heavily to the ground. Like a cloud of wild-fowl, the drab figures rose, scattered and sifted away through the thin woods beyond the fence. Ahrens cursed. Like Hubbard-

234

ton. Ran before there could be any real action. He was now abreast of the slope down which the light infantry were trotting. An excited young ensign shouted to him: "They've black fellows with 'em! Saw 'em myself, two, three of 'em, black as the pit! Why didn't they wait? They're not soldiers!" He moved on down the road at a double, his men clumping after him.

Ahrens looked back up the slope. A few blue and white patches showed starkly in the lush grass. The ground back of the rail fence was bare. Beyond the woods he could see rebels emerging from the trees, moving at their light, quick pace. From the north another group moved easily along, joining the men from the fence and seeming to flow along toward some still higher ground to the left of the road.

Trees were denser now. Occasional shots cracked from under low boughs. A grenadier a few ranks ahead of the guns stumbled, fell heavily, his brass helmet rolling crazily into the long grass. Ahrens ducked his head as something snarled in the air above him. Then he saw four lean men loping away across the fields parallel to the road.

Another hill, more figures in smocks and shirts by another fence, among gray rocks. More lines of blue and white moving heavily on them. Smoke and fire from the crest, blue and white on the grass, then brass shining in the green as the grenadiers swung out to support the light infantry. Another shout of, "To the bayonet! Give 'em steel!" Another covey of drab men rising from the ground, melting away like ghosts just before the heavy-stepping men could lunge among them with the bayonet.

The columns re-formed, went on, leaving another trail of still shapes in the grass. The grenadiers returning to the road cursed and raved, calling the Yankees cowards.

"Cowards?" thought Ahrens. "Why should they wait to be butchered?" He called back to Spangenberg: "If they stand long enough to let us come into action, try to get a

235

shot on the uprights of the fences. Strip the whole line bare."

The thin man nodded, then shouted: "Bad soldiers, the rebels. They should have waited after that last volley and received our charge. Read any authority you like. They'll all say the same thing."

"Without bayonets? I've not seen a rebel yet with a bayoneted musket."

"They *should* have bayonets." Spangenberg was severe. "And see!" He pointed to a high fringe of woods that overhung the road. "They're firing on the column. The fields must be full of 'em. I'd planned to look at a couple of brooks back there as soon as we made camp. May have to wait till tomorrow."

"Tomorrow?" Ahrens laughed shortly. "I've only seen two or three rebels fall yet. And these are only scattered groups, come from God knows where. How'd you like to see a thousand, shooting like that? And what *can* have happened to Baum?"

He watched the grenadiers ahead, saw their lagging pace, wondered how, even if fresh, they could manage to come to grips with the rebels where their magnificent discipline and training with the bayonet would count. Even if fresh—and some of the men ahead were staggering.

Rifles and muskets cracked from time to time on the high ground to the left, isolated shots which occasionally left a light infantryman or grenadier sprawled beside the road, or kneeling in the mud clutching arm or knee and swearing through white lips.

Musketry crashed somewhere up ahead, crashed and rolled in heavy volleys. Ahrens felt a tingling along his spine, an empty feeling in his stomach, moisture in his palms. He felt as though he were riding into a gathering storm. The rebels must have halted, and in force. Hooves drummed along the road and Skene rode down the column on a fresh horse, face crimson.

"God damn it, Lieutenant, why aren't your guns

ready? They're needed!" Skene's voice blared like a trumpet.

"In order for action, sir," Ahrens snapped.

"Then why in hell don't you bring them on?" the Englishman snarled.

"Is that an order?"

"From Colonel Breymann. The whole column will be engaged in a minute. Now, move, move!"

Ahrens' right hand stabbed the air with short jerks. He heard the quickened beat of hooves behind him as he set spurs to his horse. The grenadiers were already running, slanting off in long lines into the wide sweep of open fields at the left. At the edge of the road, Ahrens tossed his reins to a driver, ran over the slippery grass to the knot of men who stood behind Breymann. As he ran he saw that there were sloping woods at the distant edge of the field, woods which suddenly flamed hideously in a ripping crash. Light infantry and grenadiers in long lines marched steadily but sluggishly toward the trees, halting every now and then to dress their ranks. The air was full of hissing, wailing noises.

Breymann glanced over his shoulder, snapped: "Bring your guns into action! I want solid-shot among those trees at the left—see, by those piles of rocks. The rebels are trying to work around to that flank." He swung his head to the front again. There were more whining noises in the air. Breymann drew his sword. Without looking around he said through set lips: "I shall personally cut down any officer who flinches."

Ahrens ran back toward the guns, spread his arms wide. The cannoneers unlimbered the pieces, hooked on their drag-ropes and slowly trundled the guns over the bumpy ground. "First piece here!" he shouted. "Second at twenty paces to the left!" Something hot flicked past his face. He hoped the men didn't notice the start he gave. He covered himself by crying: "Hurry up those ammunition carts! Drive right onto the field!"

The first round crashed among the trees. A swarm of

men in gray and brown scattered, loped away out of sight. The gunners cheered. Ahrens ordered three more rounds. The men seemed to be working the pieces coolly enough. The guns thudded and flashed. A mass of men in column loomed among the trees, began flowing out into the open, heading toward the open flank of Barner's light infantry. Ahrens sprang forward, pushed away the two gunners who stood by the trail. He seized the hand-spike in his powerful hands, swung the trail until the brass muzzle bore full on the Yankees. Then the trail thudded on the ground. "Fire, bombardier!" yelled Ahrens. The linstock fell on the vent. The gun roared and rocked in a welter of smoke. When it cleared, Ahrens saw shattered forms on the grass, the rest of the column plunging back into the cover of the woods, while Barner's men, undisturbed, loosed a volley at the shifting lines in front of them.

More rebels appeared, working round on the left. The two pieces were slewed around and again the drab men fell back; sifted away like wraiths. "Not getting away quite scot-free," muttered Ahrens grimly. Aloud he shouted: "Less water on the swab, first piece. Damp is all you need."

The musketry died away. Ahrens realized with a start that he felt very weak, that his hands were shaking. There was a stir in the distant woods and he felt fear-fully conspicuous, standing there back of his gun. He turned his head wondering if there were some more sheltered place for the pieces. Then the musketry swelled to a sudden roar. He saw that the lines were no longer advancing, that the light infantry and the grena-diers were standing their ground, firing into the woods. Some Jaegers slipped up on the left of the light infantry, began firing.

Ahrens started violently, mouth suddenly dry, eyes hot. Something whacked the ground at his side. "Was it my imagination, or did that shot come from the left rear?" He tried to think coolly, precisely, to cover up the feeling of near-nausea that flooded him. A bullet rapped sharply on the axle of the first piece. By Spangenberg's gun a cannoneer collapsed over the hot breech, another suddenly clapped hands to his head and ran jerkily in short circles, then pitched to the ground. Ahrens' heart pounded, his throat felt actually shriveled. The fire *was* from the left and rear. Masses of men, not mere straggling trickles, were filtering through the trees just out of range. He screamed a command. His voice sounded thin, reedy to him. The men sprang to the drag-ropes and the piece bumped away to the left, Spangenberg's leading it at twenty paces.

There was no need to indicate the target. The trails thudded to the ground, the guns banged. Men leaped to the muzzles with rammers. Again there were hot hissings in the air. The bombardier of Spangenberg's piece staggered back, tripped over a rock, fell heavily, his linstock flying in the air. Another gunner snatched it up, again the piece slammed. Spangenberg waved his long arms, raved at his men.

There was a flat slam from the woods, Spangenberg turned a wild face to Ahrens, shouted: "Look!" Brass gleamed among the trees, there was another crash. Two solid-shot sang through the air, ploughed at the ground at the left of the Jaegers. "They've brought guns of their own!" Spangenberg's voice cracked.

Ahrens bellowed: "Drag-ropes! We'll take 'em in the flank!" The volume of his voice startled him. He still felt weak and a little dizzy. The clamps of the drag-ropes snapped crisply, the pieces rocked ahead over the matted grass. "There! By that rock, Sergeant Pertz. That'll take 'em." Then his shout pealed over the ground. "Spangenberg! *Those are Bache's guns!* Where in hell did the Yankees get 'em? Where in hell is Baum? Sergeant Pertz! How many rounds left?"

"Only two cartridges, sir. Plenty of ball."

"Two only? Good God! Send a man back at the double to hurry up that ammunition cart. They must have mended the axle by now. Hurry!"

A cannoneer started for the road, running desperately. A snarling voice whipped through the air. "Bring that man back!"

Ahrens swore under his breath. "After more ammunition, Colonel."

"Send that skulker back to his piece! Keep your men at their posts till the carts come up!"

"But, Colonel—"

Breymann screamed: "Are you trying to argue with *me*? Shut your mouth and give us more fire on the left!" He waved his arms, then screamed again: "Hell and death! Hold those men firm!"

A thin trickle of infantry began to flow back across the field, then the wavering lines sagged, broke and plunged heavily in the direction of the road. Yells echoed among the trees, the rebels broke cover and moved forward cautiously, firing as they came. Ahrens ran back to the limbers, shouting. One horse, then another slumped down in its harness. The rebel guns slammed again, furrowed the earth by the waiting teams. He cried above the din: "Cut those dead horses loose! Move on with what are left! My God, we'll lose the guns!" A driver toppled from his saddle, another leaped to the ground, ran off down the road. Muskets and rifles cracked nearer and nearer. Ahrens shouted again: "Cannoneers on the drag-ropes! Pieces to the rear by hand! Lieutenant Spangenberg! Bring 'em off!"

He sprang into the saddle of the lead horse, but even as he leaped, there was a dull smack. The horse tossed its head in the air, screamed, then lunged forward, collapsed in a kicking tangle. Ahrens cleared himself from the stirrups, unhooked the traces with frantic hands, shouting to the drivers to help, but found that he was calling to empty saddles. Then a torrent of staring infantrymen engulfed him, carried him away down the road. He fought his way clear, struggled back to the field, where he saw his two pieces moving slowly along, cannoneers straining at the drag-ropes as though on parade. Beyond them a knot of grenadiers stood firm, exchanging shots with the rebels as they fell back, step by step. Breymann had rallied a mass of light infantry and some grenadiers and was moving off the field with them. The rebels, lacking bayonets, did not dare close on the remnants of the force, but hung in clouds on the flanks, firing.

Ahrens battled his way to his piece through a crowd of staring men who wanted only to get away from that distant belt of trees at the top of the slope which had spit death at them. He seized a trailing drag-rope and heaved with his men. The air about them was stinging and sharp with flying lead. The rebels had marked their prize. The man on the next rope threw out his hands and lunged forward, his face a streaming mask of red. There was a curse and Rentner went down, clutching at his shoulder, then struggled to his feet. He had not let go of his drag-rope. Sergeant Pertz sprang into the air, spun and thudded to the ground.

There were shouts close behind. A hard voice called in English: "Clean out the gunners! Swing your butts if you've no more shot!" The rolling wheels checked, stopped, the carriage was buried under a swarm of sweating men in homespun. A musket-butt fell with a sickening whack on the head of the man beside Ahrens. He went down like a log, lay heavily, arms twitching. Ahrens seized a rammer staff from the ground, turned to face the men who swarmed over the piece. He felt a queer exaltation, a high, cold rage at these country-men who dared lay hands on his piece. Above the dreadful tumult he yelled: "Abandon the piece! Rally on the road! Do you hear me, Spangenberg?" Then he slammed viciously with the metal end of the rammer. It was struck from his hands by the heavy down-swing of a rifle. A short, broad-shouldered man sprang at him, weaponless, shouting: "I've got an officer! I've got an officer!" Ahrens grappled him. Their bodies locked. Slowly Ahrens swung the man's feet off the ground, tightened his grip about the barrel-like chest, pitched him head-long into the oncoming mass.

He fell back, brushing against two Jaegers who trotted doggedly along, shoulder to shoulder. He saw the second piece engulfed in a silent flood of rebels. He shouted again: "Spangenberg! Abandon your piece! The men are to rally in the road! It's an order!" Even as he spoke the thin man wrenched a musket from the hands of a gray-haired Yankee, leaped astride the trail of his gun, swing-ing in wide sweeps. The rebels fell back, then a power-ful man, sleeves torn off at the elbow, rushed at him, parried his swing with a strong guard. A butt whirled in the air, cracked against Spangenberg's head. Ahrens saw long arms fly up in the air, saw white legs sag at the knees as Spangenberg slipped heavily down on the trail of the piece he would not abandon. "Spangenberg!" Ahrens yelled again. But the long form was still and two Yankees were lifting it clear of the trail with a sort of rough reverence.

Then he found himself near the edge of the road, a choking sensation in his breast. He wanted to stop each grenadier who jostled past him, explain that he was too late to save Spangenberg, that he *had* shouted to him to abandon his piece. He stumbled on blindly, seeing with every beat of his pulse the dread sag of those long white legs, the helpless clutch in the air as the Yankee swung his musket. What would his men think of him, of Kurt Ahrens? Lost his pieces, lost his horses and lost the tall man with the sad eyes! He could never face them again. Pertz was dead and Slagle and Heim and the tall man who loved clean rocks and running water was dead, dead across the trail of his gun.

It was dark on the road whose wooded sides occasion-ally blazed stabs of flame into the fugitive mass. Jostled by Jaegers and light infantrymen, Ahrens swept on with the ruck. Then in the darkness a voice spoke: "Now we're all right. Here's Lieutenant Ahrens." "Where? Where do you see him?" "Where is he?" The questions popped in the night. To his amazement Ahrens heard himself saying crisply: "That you, Rentner, Meister? Who's that beyond, Meyer? Good. How many in all? Eight? Got your carbines? Fall back with me to the rear of the column."

They drew out of the press, formed and worked their way to the rear. Meyer, the oldest soldier, explained: "We tried to wait for you on the road, but got carried along. Then Rentner made us pick up all the cartridge boxes that were thrown away and we've got a few rounds apiece."

"Good!" said Ahrens mechanically. "Now fall in here at the end of the column. There'll be no more coming now."

The pursuit was not close. Random shots cracked out from the gloom, occasionally men staggered and fell, but there was no concerted effort to round up the broken, nearly defenseless mass. Waves of panic swept over the retreat. Ahrens saw unwounded grenadiers scream with terror and break into the woods where merciless branches caught their trailing swords, knocked off their tall helmets, ripped at their heavy packs until swift-moving rebels nonchalantly disarmed them and took them to the rear. Unwounded men suddenly turned, knelt in the mud, arms raised in supplication and waited for the stealthy advance that would engulf them. The rest staggered on, heads down and shoulders hunched as though they were breasting a heavy rain.

From time to time Ahrens faced his men about, ordered a volley fired into the crackling woods from which fire still spurted in rare jets. The blackness deepened and the column swayed on, a limping figure bringing up the rear where Breymann, last of his command, his temper sharpened by a flesh wound in the leg, cursed Ahrens and his gunners for not having more ammunition. The dark woods on either side of the road still rustled as silent shapes flitted between the trees, keeping pace with the column. Then little by little the ghostly forms dropped behind and the stillness of night fell over the road through the trees.

Captain Thaddeus Blake leaned on his long rifle and looked at the three men lounging by the wide elm. Their prisoner, the dragoon Heinz, sat awkwardly on the ground, resting his back against the great bole of the tree. "So you boys are resolved to return to your farms?" the Captain asked, drawing a bony hand over the stubble of his lean jaws. He frowned, turned toward the tallest of the three, who wore Heinz' broad saber. "You, Ephraim Hicks, you don't see your way clear to tarrying a little?"

Hicks held his powder-horn to his ear, shook it. "No, Cap'n, I 'lows to how I don't. Powder don't even rattle in the horn and they ain't any more this side Bennington. 'Sides, I got to git the hay in. Might set in to rain 'most any time. The woman'll be lookin' for me. Parlin and Joslin, they aim to move, too."

Both men nodded slowly. "Best be movin'," said Joslin, squinting up at the darkening sky.

Blake shook his head. "You were very late at the rendezvous. I sent Nehemiah Sherwood and his squad off with their prisoners as General Stark ordered. Had you come earlier, your man could have gone with them. It is out of the question for me to remain longer. I have my school, my sermons to consider. Tomorrow is the Sabbath."

Parlin drew a long knife, began slowly to whittle a dry stick which he had picked up. "Best be movin', as Bije says," he remarked. The blade rolled thin shavings from the stick.

Blake sighed. "Well, boys, something must be done. I consider that it would be most unfitting to release the man. He might do us considerable harm. These mercenary troops, you know. Now I, propose that one of you

244

escort him to Bennington. I hold that it would be quite proper for you to draw lots. Of course, it is after sundown and the Sabbath has technically begun, but as an ordained minister I authorize you to overlook that point this once. It is not like drawing in a game of chance."

Heinz spread his tired legs in their gigantic boots and fanned himself with his heavy hat. The conversation was far beyond the fragmentary English he had picked up in his service. Dully he wondered where these strange men might take him, and if there would be food for him. He felt dreadfully empty.

Parlin shifted the rifle to the crook of his left arm, snapped shut the blade of his knife and threw away his bit of wood. "Now, Cap'n." He spoke respectfully but firmly. "Johnny Stark called us boys out to fight Dutchies. We've fit two lots of 'em and them as could has gone home. So we're goin' home, too, like the Dutchies. Johnny Stark ain't no king to keep me fiddlin' round these woods while my hay spoils. *I* ain't got time to trail clear to Bennington." His companions nodded in silence."

Blake's eyes fell on Heinz, who stared uncomprehendingly at his captors. "I repeat that I feel it would be *most* unwise to release him," he observed.

Joslin plucked a long blade of grass and chewed at its white, pulpy stem. "You ain't partial to freein' him, Cap'n. We ain't partial to totin' him over the trail to Bennington, not none of us." He picked another spear of grass, eyed the root reflectively. "He ain't worth a haycrop. Maybe we better shoot him."

Thaddeus Blake gravely considered the thought. "I can foresee no reasonable objection to such a course," he said at length. Then he slung his piece under his arm and moved lightly off through the woods.

Joslin threw away his spear of grass. "Might take a bite, first," he said. He began gathering dry twigs. Hicks got out flint and steel. Parlin dug into his deep haversack. "I'm plum worried 'bout my hay. Been on my mind. Spoilt my aim twice today. Shot at a gunner and only hit him on the shoulder. 'Twa'n't more 'n a hundred yards. I'd have let Johnny Stark holler like a hootowl if I hadn't heard 'bout that McCrae girl. Made me downright uneasy. Ain't been a mean redskin in these parts nigh on ten year."

Hicks eyed him. "That dried venison looks prime, Ez. Go good with the cornbread. Yes, I talked to my woman. She 'lowed I'd better go. Story didn't seem to set easy on her mind. What you think, Bije?"

Joslin dumped a heap of crackling twigs on the bare ground. "I been bundlin' with neighbor Brigham's girl nigh two year come hayin'. Any Injun that wants her scalp had better talk to me. I'm peaceable-natured, but I'm kind o' partial to that girl. What a tone she can get from a spinnin'-wheel!" He sighed.

A small fire snapped and glowed in the dusk under the great elm. Heinz drew up his knees and squatted on his haunches like a clumsy bear, nose quivering as the venison on the ramrods hissed and sizzled. Hicks shook the hot meat from his rod. "'Bout done." He sniffed. "Prime, prime!" Then his eye caught Heinz' hungry stare, which seemed to stab out from under his battered hat. His knife neatly divided the chunk of meat. Half he tossed to Heinz. "Have some, Dutchy," he said. Parlin and Joslin nodded approvingly. "That were kindly in you, Eeph," said Parlin. He went on in food-muffled tone: "Too bad we got to shoot him. Don't look like a bad Dutchy."

The sense of the words was lost on Heinz, who was tearing at his venison. He pointed at the blackened lump of meat and mumbled: "Gut! Gut!"

His captors laughed and repeated: "Goot! Goot!" Heinz beamed and gnawed away.

Between bites Joslin said, "Wonder what he does at home? Hey, Dutchy, what you do at home, huh? Work—what work, huh?"

Heinz' face twisted in an exquisite agony of thought.

Then he grinned. "Ach! Vork! Me? I vos—I vos Bauer!"
He made vague motions of digging and reaping.

Hicks looked up. "Bower, bower? Look—look at him!
He means he worked a piece of land. Like this, Dutchy?
Farm, huh?" With his knife he mowed tall grasses close
by the fire's edge.

The dragoon nodded frantically. "Ja, ja! Pfarm,
pfarm!" He swept his arms as though they held an invisible scythe.

"Damned if he *ain't* a farmer!" said Hicks. " 'Pears like
he don't hold a scythe same as we do. Snathe too close
to his body. I'd admire to see them thick legs of his followin' a furrow in my north forty, I would I vum!" He
plunged his rammer into the soft ground to cleanse it
of venison grease. "Well, who's goin' to do him in? I
ain't. I got to move. Joe Bagby's ailin' and can't help me
with this lot of hay. You boys draw lots." He rose slowly.

Parlin picked two spears of grass and palmed them expertly. Joslin drew the shorter blade. "Looks like your
chore, Ez," he said. "I'll go 'long the trail a piece with
Eeph." Parlin sighed and looked at the priming of his
rifle, then at Heinz, who still gnawed at his last fragment in deep unconcern and content.

Hicks started along the trail, then stopped short. His
voice boomed through the clearing. "Hey, Dutchy! You
like farm? Goot, huh?" He waved his arms like a man
pitching hay. "Goot? You like, huh?"

Heinz looked up, nodding and grinning. "Ja, gut!
Pfarm iss gut!"

Parlin changed the priming of his rifle. Hicks slouched
over to the dying fire. "Stand up, Dutchy!" he said.

Heinz struggled to his feet, long spurs rasping against
the jutting roots of the elm. He stretched himself, repeating: "Stand op! Stand op!"

With quick hands Hicks slapped the dragoon's arms
and chest. Then he nodded. "You'll do. The woman'll
feed you when we get in. Hay needs tendin' bad." He
turned on his heel and started off. Heinz stared after

247

him, mouth open. Parlin rammed a fresh charge into his piece, sighing. From the darkness Hick's voice called: "Ain't you comin', Dutchy?"

"Ja! Ja! I gome, I gome! To der pfarm!" The heavy dragoon boots clumped and crashed in the wake of Hicks' light tread. Parlin grinned and drew the charge from his piece.

The woods were silent but the broken column still thrashed along the dark tunnel of the road. Occasionally Ahrens stumbled over a musket, a pack, thrown away by some fugitive up ahead, still in the grip of panic. Every now and then he checked his step to listen, but there was no sound save the wind in the trees, the irregular champing of heavy feet in the road, the dry rattle of equipment and the creaking of belts. His own men seemed to huddle closer together, looking back over their shoulders from time to time as though more fearful of the hush of the woods than they had been of the orange flashes which had spat so viciously from between the trunks. Their pace lagged, their shoulders drooped. With an effort he straightened his back, took a deep breath. "What's the matter up ahead? Haven't you got a song left in you?"

Heads turned in the gloom, there was a low murmur in which he seemed to detect surprise and resentment. Suddenly a strong voice burst out:

"We gather together to ask the Lord's blessing;
He hastens and chastens His will to make known."

Others joined in, the psalm rose, gathered strength, stole up and up along the creeping column, was picked up by grenadier, light infantryman and gunner.

"The wicked oppressing
Cease them from distressing.
Sing praises to His name, He forgets not His own."

Gradually the faltering tread of the column grew solid, crisp, broke into a swinging, cadenced stride. Somewhere far up ahead a drum tapped sharply, caught up the step. Others sounded in unexpected spots along the column, rattled and muttered in the sticky darkness. Muskets shifted to trim angles on aching shoulders, swinging hands made light blotches in the night, blotches that cut back and forth in unison. The last notes of the hymn died away, but the tread of the column stayed sure and marked. The drums rolled and snapped. From the darkness behind him, Ahrens heard Breymann's bitter snarl: "Not bad for a damned gunner."

The column wound on over the miserable road. Beyond the mill of San Coick there was a halt. The men dropped in their tracks, sprawling in the wet grass or in the mud of the road itself. Breymann hobbled up to the head of the column, units were sorted and assembled, thin companies of Barner's light infantry were sent back as rearguard. Then drums beat again. The column moved grudgingly toward the killing grades that the dark in front of it masked. Ahrens looked at his watch. "Not more than two minutes' halt," he grumbled. "What does Breymann think the men are made of? Rawhide? Ten, fifteen minutes would have done no harm." Stifled curses from marching men showed that his opinion was shared by many. Suddenly he grinned to himself. From the dark mass of his own men, he heard a muffled voice: "Good old Bent-eye! He's driving the Frankfort mail!" There were stifled chuckles, a chorus of, "Good old Bent-eye! He fooled 'em all!"

Ahrens moved stiffly over the broken road, conscious that the furrowed surface rose and rose under his feet. His men moved as mechanically as he, the sullen flow of the column seeming to drag them along. Fatigue settled over him like a powerful drug, numbing his mind while his body drove on of its own volition. Dimly he thought of the great wide bed in his quarters in Dresden, of the unearthly softness of its feathers, the crisp, cool whiteness of its linen. If he had that ahead of him at the end of this march! He would throw away his torn, dirty uniform, plunge to his ears in a tub of boiling water. Dry, he would put one knee on the yielding surface of that bed, slip his legs between the cool whiteness of the sheets. He could almost savor the softness, the soothing touch of the pillows on his aching neck. He shook his head, then relived the scene in his mind, his muscles actually shivering at the thought of hot, clear water wrapping about them.

The miles dragged slowly past. His eyes began to play tricks on him. He started once as he saw a neat row of galloper-wagons drawn up in a clearing at the left of the road, but the wheels and shafts melted away at his approach. Piles of twelve-pounder balls were stacked in the heart of a swamp, neat white tents in long rows behind them. They vanished as he rubbed his eyes briskly, vanished as did the squadron of heavy cuirassiers who looked so solid and real among a tangle of wild rocks and brushwood. Then the song of the French-Canadians began to beat through his brain, inescapable, maddening. Still marching, he began to doze, eyes open, feet moving in time to the soaring sweep of *O Carillon*. Over and over two lines slipped across his brain, etched themselves on his drugged consciousness.

> *"Cet étandard qu'au grand jour de bataille,*
> *Noble Montcalm, tu plaças dans ma main."*

"Noble Montcalm, Noble Montcalm!" The phrase whirled and whirled about. Montcalm. He would have a high-nosed, patrician face, powdered hair, gorgeous uniform of white. The figure materialized, white and gold, a slim tapering hand holding out the French standard of white with its gold lilies. It became more real than the thick column of dirty, exhausted men trudging at his side. His hand twitched, half stretched out to take the standard from the tall Frenchman. The jerking muscle roused him, brought him back to the dark, sticky road, the sweating stumbling men who were turning off into a wide clearing, swinging from column into line.

"Halt for one hour?" he fumed to himself. "What's the good of that? Just enough to stiffen the men. Delays our getting back to the camp just that much. At least we're making better time than on the march out. No one gives a damn about dressing the column and we've lost all our wagons." He watched his men stack their carbines, then kicked away broken branches from a hollow under a great elm. "Just lie here and stretch a bit. No good trying to catch a nap. Ground's too hard. Just stretch out." In the very act of stretching, he was sound asleep.

The day promised to be hot as the column wearily topped the last high ground and stared with bloodshot eyes at the Batten Kill far below and the Hudson winking in the distance, then stumbled down the long slope, the sun at their backs. Ahrens kicked his feet ahead of him, maddeningly aware of a paper-thin spot in the sole of his right boot under which sharp stones jabbed viciously. The morning air was fresh and fragrant on his hot face, which still stung with the sweat of the long climb that lay behind him. He closed his eyes, stumbled, letting the momentum of the column beside him drag him along.

Then he looked up with a start. Music crashed and blared ahead, the road was lined with a double rank of men in red jackets, faced with white, men who presented arms stiffly. Mechanically he looked at the facings, muttered: "The 47th." Dully he wondered what brought them out on this road, why fifes should be squealing out *The World Turned Upside Down*. He heard the soft clop of hooves, heard a familiar, rich voice. Shining in scarlet and white, Gentleman Johnny Burgoyne rode slowly down the weary column. By the grenadiers he reined in his glossy horse, swept off his hat. His full voice swelled in the still air. "Gentlemen! I thank you. Let me assure you that the rebels have felt your very pretty little success severely, most severely." A German aide by his side shouted a careful translation. Startled heads lifted along the column, wide eyes stared.

Ahrens banged his hands together. "All together, lads! A cheer for General Burgoyne!" He was astonished at the deep-voiced "Hurrah!" which roared out from the spent files, astonished to find himself joining in. The men stepped out more briskly, seemed to find hidden reserves of energy. A warm smile glowed on Ahrens from the big man in scarlet and white, sitting his faultless horse so easily. "There you are, my boy. Glad to see you safe and sound. My compliments on your men. They're marching splendidly. Soldiers, my boy, soldiers."

Gentleman Johnny Burgoyne bent over his desk in the big room of the Duer house, his pen scratching and hissing over foolscap sheets. As his eyes followed the nib from line to swift line, a frown deepened in his forehead, the corners of his mouth contracted more and more. Mrs. Lewis lolled on a rough divan and watched him with heavy-lidded eyes.

"What on earth are you writing there, Johnny?" she asked.

Burgoyne put down his pen, the frown and the drooping lines about his mouth vanished. "Do you know, my dear, that yours is a voice that should never be heard outside the confines of, well, of a boudoir, let us say. There is a timbre to it that suggests infinite depths of—of *volupté,* to quote our French friends. But your question—I'm writing a despatch to Germaine and a plaguy thing it is. Got to include that little affair at Bennington. Got to tell him that Langlade and St. Luc have taken most of their Indians and gone home to Canada. Got to tell him—oh, a nasty mess of things that I won't bore you with." He bent over his papers again. His forehead creased, his mouth drooped and drooped. At last

252

he threw down his pen, picked up the final sheet, settled back in his chair and reread what he had written, frowning heavily. As his eye ran along his finely penned lines, the frown slowly lifted. His full lips began to quirk at the corners, his eye sparkled. He chuckled under his breath, then aloud. "Listen to this, my dear. By Gad, I don't know of another general in His Majesty's forces who can turn a phrase to equal this. In my final summing up I say: 'Wherever the King's forces point, militia to the amount of three or four thousand assemble in twenty-four hours; they bring with them their subsistence, etc., and, the alarm over, they return to their farms.' Now—just attend to this: 'The Hampshire Grants in particular, a country unpeopled and almost unknown in the last war, now abounds in the most active and rebellious race on the continent and hangs like a gathering storm upon my left.' What d'you think of that? 'Hangs like a gathering storm upon my left.'" He slapped his thigh, rolling the sonorous words out into the pine-paneled room.

She smiled with the brilliance of utter non-comprehension. "I think it's beautiful." She nodded vigorously.

His face fell. "I really did hope you'd like that. There is a sweep and swing to it."

She rose, crossed the room and stood by him, arms about his neck. "But it *is* beautiful. And everyone says your proclamation to the rebels—you know, the Putnam Creek one, is the finest thing that's ever been written in America."

He smiled up at her. "Do they? Well, there were some passages that struck me as fine, and I'm my own most bitter critic, you know, most bitter critic. Now you'd best run along. I expect Colonel Kingston in a few minutes."

"And after that?"

He pinched her cheek, laughing. "You're thinking of that Madeira that just came down, eh?"

She stooped, kissed him. "Well, partly," she whispered.

"Now, this is all clear, Kingston? We stay here at Fort Miller, collect twenty-five days' supplies, then cross the Hudson and advance till we meet this new man Gates who's commanding the rebels."

Kingston nodded, his ruddy handsome face serious. "We leave a garrison at Ticonderoga, at Fort George and one at Thirty-mile Island in Lake George. In effect, that cuts us adrift from Canada."

Burgoyne looked out of the window at the broad river-meadows. "Have to. Haven't enough men to garrison a string of posts clear down the river. Wouldn't have men enough to fight. We cross on the bridge of boats, then break up the bridge and use the boats to float our provisions."

"Dangerous, isn't it?" ventured Kingston.

Burgoyne slapped his hand on the table. "What else can we do? Retreat? Not while I command! What we know, *entre nous,* about Howe mustn't stop us. After all, he left Clinton in New York. Perhaps he'll do something for us. And we know that St. Leger beat one rebel army up the Mohawk. It's not too desperate."

Kingston's heavy fingers worried at the gold buttons on his cuff. "*If* Clinton does something," he said. "A raid up the Highlands beyond West Point."

Burgoyne rose, walked slowly to the window. "If, if, if. I've sent six young officers south, hoping that they'd work through the rebel lines, see Clinton and bring me word. None of them has ever come back. Good boys, too. Young Hallam and Bennett and the rest." He drummed on the wavery glass of the pane. "What are the last returns from that Bennington affair?"

Kingston shook his head. "Nothing new. Of Baum's column, only nine men, six of them dragoon privates, ever came back. Breymann lost nearly a third of *his*

254

command and every last stick of equipment he took with him."

Gentleman Johnny sighed. "Bad business, bad business." Then his eyes began to sparkle. "And yet you know, Kingston, I can't help taking a sort of pride in that affair. Why, damn it, after all what was it? A thousand or so English freemen, who happen to be in revolt against the Crown, turn out from their farms and their towns and thrash a lot of stiff military pedants from the Continent. Our own flesh and blood, Kingston, even if they are wrong-headed, our own flesh and blood, and what do they do? Rally in their villages, just as if they were in some shire in England. Damn it all, when I think of old Stark and that fellow Warner standing up to these European troops, it makes me proud to be an Englishman. It's the spirit of Runnymede all over again."

Kingston coughed discreetly. "Heard the same thought about camp from more than one officer, sir. I'll grab any rebel I see and thrash him within an inch of his life. But when I hear of these same rebels chasing those stiff-necked Brunswickers through the forest, I—why—why, I have some difficulty in keeping a sober face when I warn a young officer that on no account must Riedesel and his men guess how we feel."

Burgoyne nodded. "Well, that's easy enough, so long as he's up at Fort Anne with the Rhetz and the Hesse-Hanau infantry, keeping the lines of communication open. We'll call him in when we're ready to start across the Hudson. By the way, he's sent a request that the Baroness be allowed to accompany the army when we move. See any reason why not?"

Kingston shrugged. "None. Especially since I pleaded so successfully to have Lady Acland granted permission."

"Sets a precedent, sets a precedent," laughed Burgoyne. "Though in Lady Acland's case, I could hardly refuse. She's so dreadfully pregnant. If I sent her back to Canada, there might be an accouchement in the middle

255

of Champlain with painted Indians for midwives. I'll write Riedesel a letter, giving permission for the Baroness and the children to come with us. Might as well for Major Harnage's wife and Lieutenant Reynal's. Look. Here's an idea. As soon as we reach Albany, we'll give a grand ball. Have the four ladies—if Lady Harriet is able—to give it tone. Let the Loyalists bring all their rustic beauties. Do a lot for us and the King's cause there. We'll hold it in the Schuyler mansion. They tell me that it's the finest house in the town."

"Must say I admire the pluck of those ladies. It may not be an easy trip," said Kingston.

"Easy?" Gentleman Johnny raised his eyebrows. "Now that we've decided what to do, it will be childishly simple. We *must* move, and that's the only considerable town till we come to New York. We can refit, re-equip there, gather supplies, spend a pleasant winter even if Clinton and Howe do nothing. We'll travel very, very light. Everyone must send back heavy equipment, surplus trappings, to Ticonderoga."

"Everyone?" asked Kingston.

"Everyone." Burgoyne's lips set in a firm line. "Limit each officer to one of those two-wheeled carts, the men to what they carry on their backs."

"Good. I'll issue the orders." Kingston scratched hasty notes on a sheet of paper. "Send all the stores of wines back to Ti, eh? That'll release carts to carry provisions."

"Wines? Wines? Eh? Why, damn it, have to have the wines!" Burgoyne paced about the room, jangling the heavy seals that hung from his fob. "Wines—why, Kingston, you know as well as I do that the men *expect* a commander to keep up a certain amount of style. Lose confidence in him if he doesn't. And see, Kingston—if we *did* leave the wine behind, what difference would that make to our five thousand odd men? The space the bottles take up wouldn't feed a quarter of 'em for a day. There's gin, too, that we'll have to take along. No telling what we'll find in Albany. Nothing but spruce-beer, like as not."

Kingston sighed, nodded. "I had hoped we'd get those carts. Each cart we have means the less we're tied to the barges that follow us down the river."

Burgoyne looked out the window. Without turning, he said, "And, Kingston." He coughed, fumbled with his seals, then went on: "Each time we've moved, there's been a group of carts that—you know about 'em. Write the same order for me to sign. You know—to the effect that the loading has my personal approval—and so forth and so on."

Kingston, face impassive, scratched another note.

For the men who swarmed among the forest of crowded tents that filled the flat meadows where the Batten Kill flows into the Hudson, life traced the same monotonous pattern as at Skenesboro, Fort Anne and Fort Edward. The days were blazing, dripping, under a metallic sky that every now and then clouded sullenly, ripped itself apart with crashing, blasting thunderstorms, then cleared to let a pitiless sun draw steaming clouds from the spongy meadows. Every four days the men stood in long lines, shuffling and grumbling as they drew rations that were always salt-pork and flour, brought down by barge and cart from the depot at Ticonderoga. The country about them was stripped bare and there was little hope of the most expert shot slipping off by himself and bringing in fresh meat, of the most skilful marauders finding a stray cow, an abandoned truck-garden. In the heat and the reek of the camp, dysentery flourished like a rank weed and the hospital tents were crowded with pale, emaciated men who staggered about, weak-kneed and watery of eye. Then a strange fever crept into the canvas city, striking among the lines of British tents close by the Hudson and among the Germans along the frontage of the Batten Kill, a fever that gripped suddenly, raged for three days and then went

257

away as mysteriously as it had come. It left its victims alive but weak, so that for another two days they had to lie in their stuffy tents flapping feebly at the mosquitoes who reigned supreme now that the black-fly period was past.

The English chafed and cursed, but always looked hopefully up at the Duer house on the high ground, upriver, thinking of the day when the man in scarlet and white whom they loved would lead them on again.

The Germans poked dully about their dusty company streets, sweltered in their heavy uniforms, were increasingly a prey to melancholy which sent its dozens to the hospital tents to lie passively and hopelessly among the dysentery and fever victims and the rapidly-healing casualties whose wounds had been light enough to allow them to escape from the crackling fields of Bennington. As they moped about they noticed that each day there seemed fewer and fewer men in the Canadian and Tory camp across the river covering the British, that the Indians on their own front had dwindled to less than a hundred. Occasionally they heard that in a company of Barner's light infantry, of the Riedesel regiment or the Specht, such and such a man had not answered roll-call, had slipped away into the green of the countryside.

They woke at night remembering the hideous beat of the axes that had sung and echoed under their skulls in the dense woods about Skenesboro, remembered—and heard faint cracks and crashes to the east, to the south. Each night they heard them, and nearly every morning one of the pickets thrown out to make up for the thinning ranks of the Indians brought into camp the body of a light infantryman, a Jaeger or a grenadier, neatly drilled through the head or the heart, never wounded. To the jacket of a Jaeger corporal, who had strayed too far from his picket, his men found pinned a scrap of paper, covered with writing. It was clumsy German script and read "For Jane McCrae." Sweating through perfunctory drills, panting on work-a-day details, their heads carried the echoes of these scattered reports; they wondered what made the rebels so bold and why so much importance seemed to be attached to the death of one girl in invaded territory. They grew to listen for the distant shots as they lay in their breathless tents, to hold themselves tense waiting for the faint crack that the night wind was sure to bring them. Those on patrol huddled together in rocky hollows strengthened by logs and sandbags, ears straining, well content to let the wilderness noises go uninvestigated, hoping for the first streak of dawn that would show over the rising ground to the east.

Through a breathless noon, Hedwig and Rentner jolted north along the Hudson, perched on the rear of an empty cart which was making for Fort Edward and the Wood Creek road. When the wheels rattled the loose planks that bridged Moses Kill, they slipped off, Hedwig with a springy hop, Rentner more gingerly, one hand to his right shoulder where bandages bulged under his worn blue jacket. They followed the road a few yards beyond the bridge, then scrambled down the river-bank. Barefoot, their shoes hung about their necks, they waded into the river, following a ford whose sandy streak showed white under the greenish ripples. Midway in the stream, Hedwig turned, her skirts gathered above her knees and started wading cautiously toward a small bushy island topped by a tall pine.

"See, Gustav. The water is low now and we can wade along this spit that juts out from the island. An Indian woman showed me while you were away with the guns." She splashed on through the sun-warmed water. "And by that pine there's a little pool that the river scrapes out when the water is high. It faces the west bank and is quite screened by the bushes." She dug her feet into the undercut sides of the island, pulled herself up by a tough alder shoot.

Sun beat down through the wide branches of the pine,

dappling the sandy soil, dancing on the pool whose water gurgled and slapped as the river swept in and out of the deep elbow. Rentner, still pale from his wound, sat by the foot of the pine while Hedwig stood on the brink. She slipped off the vivid kerchief, shook out her masses of blond hair that tumbled to her waist, sunlight sparkling in its waves. Then she smiled over her shoulder at her husband, slowly unlaced her bodice, stepped out of her gray dress, gave a shake of her white shoulders that dropped her shift about her feet. Deep-chested, full-bosomed, she balanced on the edge of the pool, arms above her head. Rentner laughed deep in his throat, scrambled to his feet. She smiled again, held out a hand to him, then plunged into the pool. Her body was old ivory, tinged with pink, as she swam about in the clear water. Her laugh rippled out as she called: "Poor boy! Your shoulder will soon be well." She stood on a sunken rock, the water lapping about her waist and held out her arms to him.

He smiled his slow, tight-jawed smile, eyes eager. "You're like a Rhine-maiden, like the Lorelei."

From her rock she laughed again. "I'll have a golden harp and sing to you, and you'll have a ship that will be dashed to bits on this rock. And then, and then I'll catch you up in my arms."

"And then?"

Slowly she stepped from the rock, swam a stroke and waded to the shore, hands stretched out before her, water racing from her firm shoulders, her fine breasts. She was smiling to him.

Hedwig turned her head from its pillow on Rentner's sound shoulder, smiled sleepily at him as she patted his flat cheek. Then her eyes grew grave.

"What did that man say to you yesterday? You were funny about it when I asked you."

Rentner settled his head more comfortably on his rolled-up jacket, spread out Hedwig's shift to cover the spot on her back where the sun fell full. "Didn't know I was funny. Corporal Miedbrodt was around. I hate to talk when he's near."

"Well, what did he say? I saw you talking together under that twelve-pounder limber. Is he a Loyalist, a Tory? How did he come to know German?"

Rentner's eyes were on the patch of dense blue sky above the pine. "No, he wasn't a Tory. He was a rebel."

Hedwig started. "A rebel? A prisoner? What was he doing in the gun-park?"

"Everyone thought he was a Tory. It's hard to tell the difference."

"What did he want? Could he really talk to you?"

"Talk to me? Of course he could. Don't think he could speak much English."

"A *German* rebel? I never heard of such a thing!"

"He's a rebel and he's German. At least, his father was. His father came from Zweibrücken in the Palatinate. A lot of people came from there and settled along the—the Mohawk River, I think he said. Hundreds of them. His name's Hoffmann."

"A German rebel!" Hedwig's blue eyes were round. "Just think! And from Zweibrücken in the Palatinate! Why, that can't be two days' journey from Frankfort or Hanau! Just think, Gustav—why, you might have killed him in battle and it would have been like killing a neighbor!"

Rentner shook his head. "I never thought of the rebels like that. He said there are people from Holland and Sweden, too, and a lot of English along the Mohawk."

"Do you suppose there were Hanauers with the rebels in that battle?"

"Don't think so. They hollered in English."

"Well, but, Gustav, what did that man *say?*"

"He wanted me to desert to the rebels."

"Desert to the *rebels?*"

"He's been 'round before. So have others. A good many men have deserted."

"But why go to the rebels? They're going to be beaten and the General and the Baron will hang most of them."

"Hofmann didn't think the rebels could be beaten."

"He's crazy. Why did he think *you'd* desert, anyway?"

"He showed me a paper. Some rebel named Benjamin Franklin had signed it, and there were some German names, too. It said all Germans had been sold as slaves by their princes to the English, and that any German who deserted wouldn't have to fight any more. He'd be given land, fifty acres, in places where there were other Germans. *Given*—to work for himself. And, Hedwig—no one's *making* the rebels fight. Hofmann has a big farm and three cows. A rebel general named Harchheimer—no, Herkimer—called for volunteers to come and talk to us in German. Hofmann left his farm. Two of his brothers were killed in a big battle against Indians and English not long ago. They left their farms and marched because—because they were *their* farms."

Hedwig's eyes were wide with astonishment. She raised herself on her elbows, breasts swaying. Her voice was almost a whisper. "Gustav! We'll go! Fifty acres—for our own!"

He was silent. She shook him by the shoulder. "Gustav! We'll go, go, go! When? Will Hofmann come back? Didn't you tell him we'd go?"

His jaw tightened. "We stay."

"But Hofmann was right! We were sold as slaves, all of us. Who cares about us? The rebels shoot us, the English sneer at us. The Elector sold you like a black man." Her eyes snapped. "Do you mean—do you mean to tell me you let him get away, get away with his fifty acres that might be ours?" She straightened up, kneeling, torso erect and head thrown back. "Do you know where to go? Who sees to giving out the land? Oh! Let's get back to camp right away! I'll make up a little bundle. You can take your carbine and some powder." She shook her head violently. "This hair! Will it never dry out? Let's go back now, now!" She picked up her shift and began scrubbing her long hair with it. "My dress will be scratchy, but I've an extra shift in camp. Get up, get up. Gustav! Do hurry!"

Gently he took the shift away from her, threw an arm about her round shoulders and drew her to him. "We stay, Hedwig!"

Her mouth quivered, eyes filled. "Gustav! You make me so angry. Stay? Why do we stay?"

He ran thick fingers through her damp hair, smiling at her. "You're beautiful when you're angry, Hedwig. So—lie quiet. Now think. You remember yesterday that the Riedesel regiment paraded. You know why?"

Still hot and flushed she shook her head.

"You knew Fasselabend?"

"The grenadier—that fat fool with the red face? Yes."

"He deserted on the march back from—from that battle. I can't say the name. Some Indians found him and brought him into camp. Then he had to dig his own grave and stand in front of it before the whole regiment. There were some of his friends in the squad that shot him."

She turned pale. Then she said in a softer voice: "But Fasselabend was such a fool. *You*'re so clever. They'd never catch you."

Rentner's eyes were on the sky again. "Many of the gunners are sick. Those who are well have to work very hard. There are so many guns, so much to do. If I desert, that means someone has to do the work that I leave. It makes it harder for those I desert."

She placed a firm hand over his lips. "Oh, but, Gustav! Don't you see? If you go, others will go and just leave those foolish guns standing along the river, all alone."

"I took an oath, you know, back there in Hanau. An oath to the Elector and to the English."

"Well? Was that oath of your own free will? Was it? Was it?"

"It was an oath."

263

"But you're so silly." She smiled at him, tweaking his thick eyebrows. "When is Hofmann coming back?"

His eyes were grave. "You didn't like thinking about Fasselabend? Well, do you remember that they almost did the same thing to me? Who saved me? Who said you could sail with me?"

Her eyes softened. "I know. I—I hadn't thought of him."

"He was fine in battle. He fought his piece until there were rebels all over us. He picked a rebel up and threw him the length of the gun. In the retreat he was never tired. We were dead, wanted to drop out, curl up by the roadside, but whenever we looked up, there he was, walking along, smiling. He made us sing, he laughed with us. The hills were terrible. He walked up them the same as he'd walk in some platz on a Dresden Sunday. And the English general spoke to him, said something nice. In English of course, but I knew it was nice. And he smiled at us, just at us gunners and waved his hat and said something else, and the Lieutenant said he called us soldiers. If I left him, Colonel Breymann would hear of it and blame him. He hates the Lieutenant because he is good to his men. He tried to blame him to the Baron because he lost his guns, and the Baron wouldn't listen. He knew we served the guns as long as we had ammunition and were the steadiest on the retreat. The Lieutenant would look sad if one morning I didn't answer roll-call."

The blond head pillowed on his shoulder quietly. In a meek voice Hedwig said: "You're right, Gustav. We'd better stay."

He smiled up into the tree above him. "Yes, we stay. Look, Hedwig, the wind is changing. That will bring mosquitoes back onto the island."

She wrinkled her nose, sighed and sat up, struggling into her shift. "I wish we lived here on the island and never had to wear any clothes or go anywhere. When do you go back to duty?"

"One more day. The wound was only flesh, you know. The surgeon says it's closed and healing well. I can throw away the bandage tomorrow and go back to duty. I'm going to build a sort of tumbril for the Baroness. Her calèche broke down and the Lieutenant spoke to her about me. It's regular work, but she'll make the Baron give me a thaler for the building."

Hedwig nodded. "And you give it to me to keep."

He squinted up at the sun. "Don't have to go back to camp for a long time. Don't have to go back till sick-call tomorrow if we don't want to. Look—let's wade over to the west bank. I've never been there. We can walk down as far as the bridge of boats and cross there."

"Wonder where that road goes?" Rentner stared down the faintly marked track that led west from the river road across the meadows to the wooded heights beyond.

Hedwig stood by his elbow, holding the tail of his coat between thumb and finger. Her eyes danced. "Let's follow it."

He nodded silently and started gingerly along the grass-grown ruts, Hedwig walking nimbly beside him. She looked about her, lips parted. "It makes me feel—feel new," she said. "I mean being off here where the army hasn't been."

"It's safe," he said shortly. "Fraser's men are on this bank below the bridge."

"Never mind Fraser's men! I'd like to see a rebel. I'd send him back to his plowing quick enough. There's been no one on this road for a long time. See how the moss grows where the earth is damp in the ruts? Oh— and there's a cabin—two, three cabins, all empty and one hasn't a roof."

Rentner grunted. "Probably belonged to Loyalists. Sacked by the rebels. Or the Indians. They don't care—a scalp's a scalp. Rebels, though, most likely. They've cruel men among 'em."

"But the Loyalists bring Indians among the rebels. So do we. Isn't that cruel?"

"That's different. They're rebels. Besides, we *have* to use Indians. The Lieutenant says so. He doesn't like our doing it, but says there's no other way."

Hedwig sighed. "I suppose not. Stein's wife told me that when the Indians brought in those rebel prisoners at Fort Edward, they only showed a few of them to the General, and kept the others themselves. She said they did awful things to them. Oh—this road leads into another. See—way ahead there. It must run south like the river road!"

There were more trees along the road to the south which skirted the western heights, more trees and scattered boulders which hung out from the steep scarp. "Might follow it," said Rentner. "Easy to get back to the river if this doesn't join up near the bridge. Hi! Look—there's a cart on the road. It's in trouble."

Far down the rough track a long wagon canted at a crazy angle, one wheel leaning outward drunkenly. Hedwig stared at it. "Is it one of ours?" she asked.

"Don't think so. Let's go ahead and see." He lengthened his stride over the broken ground. Hedwig close at his elbow. "Here—there's a woman sitting on that rock beside the road. See her?"

"Yes, yes! On the right-hand side. What can she be doing here? Do you think she's a rebel, trying to get to their lines?"

He smiled grimly. "She'd have a long way to go. They're miles below us. Fraser's men will turn her back, anyway. Look at that wheel. Axle-box is bad. That woman must be waiting for some one. She's—wait a minute! I told you about her."

"About her?"

"Yes. Better stop. She may have that gun. If she—here, we're going back!" He seized Hedwig by the arm. "That's the one! Don't go near her!"

"Gustav! What are you talking about? *Who* is she?"

"I told you. The girl in the clearing. She helped us when we were lost, after she shot at the Lieutenant."

Hedwig stared down the road at the slight figure in gray huddled on the rock by the tilted wagon. "You're sure? But *she's* in trouble now, Gustav. Look the way she's got her sunbonnet all on one side. No woman would wear a bonnet like that if she wasn't sad." Hedwig's chin lifted, her mouth tightened. In a new voice she said, "Come on, Gustav." Without looking behind her she walked rapidly down the road. Rentner shrugged and followed.

Her chin cupped in one grimy hand, the other dangling loosely across her knees, Judith Hunnewell stared mistily at the axe and the light maul that lay in the dusty road beside the listing wheel. Her back and shoulders ached, her palms were red and sore. She had worked for over an hour at the aged axle, and the wheel still tilted drunkenly, mockingly. She did not dare drive on, for the wheel might skid off at any moment and the prospects of a sudden crash on the villainous road were appalling. A wave of hopelessness swept over her, her chin quivered. She tried to draw comfort from the fact that her sister Abigail still slept on peacefully in the wagon, but sooner or later she would wake, and in any event the wagon couldn't stay indefinitely blocking the road. She stared at the black eye of the axle, at her arms, grime streaked to the elbow, at the three-cornered tear in the hem of her dress. Suddenly a voice spoke close by her, spoke in low German. "You're having trouble? Perhaps my man could help you."

Head still averted, Judith dabbed at her eyes with the hem of her sunbonnet, resolutely set her face in a smile and turned to the pretty blond girl who smiled so shyly at her. Then she caught a flash of blue and red in the road behind her, winced inwardly. If this road was used by the troops, then she had been foolish to disregard Chipmunk's advice and push on when she had learned

267

that the main army had gone south from Fort Edward. She forgot the question, asked quickly: "You are marching down this bank?"

Hedwig shook her head. "Just my man and I."

"You are sure?"

"Oh, yes. The English are on this side, some of them, but they're much farther down. You are in trouble?"

Judith looked back at the sagging wheel, her heart heavy. Then she smiled with mechanical brightness. "It's nothing. There's—there's help coming." As she spoke, she wondered from what quarter it might come. Chipmunk would overtake her sooner or later, but she knew him to be strictly limited in things mechanical. Quickly she turned her head away, feeling a tear splashing on her cheek. There was a light touch on her shoulder.

"We'd like to help. My man is deft." Then another voice spoke, a man's voice. "I was apprenticed to a wheelwright for seven years." The sentence ended abruptly as though strong jaws had bitten off the words.

Head still turned away, Judith said: "You know, I'm not a Loyalist."

The male voice said: "The wood in the axle looks old. And the felloes are springing."

Judith controlled herself, faced the pair in the rutted road. There was sympathy in the candid gray-blue eyes of the blond girl, an innate friendliness and courtesy. Then she looked at the blue-and-red man, whose cocked hat was pushed back from a broad forehead. There was something vaguely familiar about him.

He spoke again. "You're the girl—the young lady in the clearing. You sent me to fill a grenadier's helmet with water."

Instant relief swept over Judith. "Then, you're one of the men who came to the hill the night that—that people were afraid there might be Indians about."

He flushed uncomfortably, moved toward the side of the cart. "What's happened here?" he asked. He dropped on his knees, ran practiced fingers over wood and metal,

268

Hedwig beaming down on him. At last he rose, dusting his knees with his left hand. "That's a bad axle-box."

"But you can fix it, Gustav?" cried Hedwig eagerly.

He rubbed his hands on his breeches, looked at Judith, who watched him almost feverishly. "Have you a shim?" he asked.

Judith looked blankly at him. "A shim?"

Hedwig repeated, "A shim?" The two women looked at each other. Then dimples began to appear about the corners of Judith's mouth. Hedwig broke out in a rippling laugh. "Gustav! What a question! You expect two women to know what a shim is?"

He scratched his head. Then his eye lit on the axe. "I can hack one out of the log over there." The chips flew, Rentner explaining that the axe was awkward to use with only one hand.

"He's *so* deft," Hedwig explained to Judith. "Oh, the hand? He was wounded in the battle over in—in the Hampshire Grants. Many were killed, but Gustav, he came back." She looked proudly at the grunting man, squatting over his log.

Judith started. "In the Grants? A lot—you say a lot were—didn't come back?"

"It was bad," said Hedwig. "Corporal Hess' wife said the rebels didn't fight like soldiers, so you can't blame our men. But the gunners were lucky. There were only eighteen who didn't come back. And only four of my man's lot. One of them was a lieutenant."

Judith felt a cold weight settling about her. She traced circles in the dust with her moccasin, eyes on the ground. Her voice seemed thin to her as she asked: "An officer? He was someone the men will miss?"

From a litter of thin chips Rentner spoke. "Yes. He was a good man."

Judith felt the road rock beneath her. She leaned suddenly against the wagon as she told herself that the fate of one Hessian lieutenant or another meant little to her. Rentner's axe split off short, thin slabs from the log. Judith watched the bright blade flashing in choppy strokes as though it were the one vital thing in her world. She barely heard his quick words that seemed to fly out with the chips. "Good man, as officers go. Saw we looked after our feet on the march. Made us keep our rations." Judith numbly thought that a horse or an ox would receive equal thought. "Yes, he was good. But he hadn't been with us long. He came down Lake George with the guns. I think he got his ideas from our other lieutenant." He straightened up, gathered a pile of thin slabs which just covered the palm of his hand. He looked at her, pushing his cocked hat farther back with a sweaty wrist. "You remember the other? He came with us to the clearing."

Judith met his eyes. "Yes. Of course—that is, he was the one who brought you out the night of the Indians. He was in the Grants?" Her breath came freer.

"In the Grants. *He's* all right." The tight jaws closed.

Hedwig clapped her hands. "Now, Gustav, don't start talking about him. You've the wheel to mend."

Rentner crouched by the axle. Judith beside him. Over and over in her mind she was saying: "I don't care. I'm glad, glad, glad. I shan't see him again, of course, but I'm—oh! if he should have been the one. And he made the new man look after the men the way he did." She shook herself, bent low beside the solid man who was hammering a thin, flat piece of wood into a gaping crack near the hub, listened to his abrupt words. "Drive it in like this. See where it holds, now! Wheel will always be wobbly, but it'll stay on. Look at it once in a while. This ought to hold for a hundred miles even over these roads. If it wears, I've cut these extra ones. Just drive one in like this." Hedwig smiled down on the faded bonnet so close to the battered cocked hat.

Judith dropped the flap that closed the back of the covered wagon, gently shot the crude steps into their frame. "She's still asleep," she said.

"Oh—a baby?" cried Hedwig.

Judith shook her head. "My sister."

"I told you about her," said Rentner. "She was by the chimney. She's innocent."

"Ohhh!" The descending inflection of Hedwig's voice fell over Judith like a caress. "And you're alone to see to her?"

Judith nodded. "But she sleeps nearly all the time now. I'm glad for her. It makes the trip easier. It may be that the Albany doctors can cure her. Do you think the army will move soon? I follow behind it."

"Hope so," said Rentner.

"Hope so?" cried Hedwig. "We're nearly crazy waiting. That general likes his good houses and his wines and—and other things. *He's* in no hurry."

Rentner frowned. "The lieutenant says he's collecting provisions. When we've enough we'll move."

"Provisions!" snorted Hedwig. She turned to Judith. "If I could talk to the General, *I'd* make him move. To think that your sister can't get to the doctors because that man is comfortable in the big house! Well, provisions. That means we'd best be moving, Gustav, if *we're* to have any tonight."

Judith was staring down the road, shading her eyes. "Do you have to go back?" she asked.

"Rentner nodded. "If we eat."

"If it's only a question of eating, why don't you stay and have your dinner with me?"

Hedwig's eyes widened. "Stay and eat up *your* rations? You can't carry very much in that wagon. No, no. We'd best go back to camp."

Judith laughed. "But I see my rations, as you call them, coming down the road now. Venison, and much more than two people can eat. What's not eaten will spoil." She waved her hand, called: "Chipmunk!"

A hundred yards down the road, a squat, bent figure halted, leaning on a long musket. Judith waved again. The figure shook its head, dumped a heavy burden from its shoulders and squatted unshakably by the roadside. She turned to Hedwig. "It's Chipmunk, an old Oneida who has appointed himself my guard. I think he is afraid of your husband's uniform. I'll go to him."

Hedwig watched her run off down the road. "Gustav! You didn't tell me she was pretty! She's like one of the ladies who used to drive out the road to Phillipsruhe."

"I did tell you she was pretty—and talked like a great lady."

"You told me about her talking, but you didn't say she was pretty."

"Yes, I did. I said she was all right."

She made a face at him. "Well, I suppose that's praise according to your lights. Here she comes. See how she walks; she'd be even prettier without—without her dress."

Rentner sat up. "Wouldn't she!"

"Eh?" said Hedwig. "I meant—she'd—why, that's an Indian with her! Ugh! Isn't he filthy!"

"Got a good hindquarter of venison over his shoulder. Dear God! Haven't had anything but salt-pork for so long, I'd eat that haunch raw. Look—the Indian's stopping. Won't come any farther."

The Oneida, a dozen paces away, halted suddenly, heaved the hindquarter onto the grass, glared at Rentner from under the brim of an unbelievably greasy round hat, then turned and trotted away down the road, his long leggings and drab shirt shiny with dirt.

"Chipmunk wouldn't come any nearer," said Judith. "He's so suspicious of strangers." She opened a box built under the seat of the wagon, produced two broad skillets, a long knife. "Will you build a fire? I'll get the sacking off the deer and cut it up. Chipmunk flayed it, so there's nothing else to do. The fire would burn well under that rock by the trees and there's a spring close by."

Hedwig twisted a long blade of grass between her fingers. "I don't think it'd be right—" she began.

"Oh, you'll have plenty of time to get back to camp,"

272

said Judith. She knelt by the solid meat, turning back the sacking.

"I mean—it wouldn't be right—" began Hedwig. "I mean—we're both country-folk. You live in the woods, but— It wouldn't be right for you to cook for us. Give me the skillet. You sit where it's cool."

Judith rose, came quickly to Hedwig. "We're both women in a new land," she said. "And besides, it seems to me that I know about you—who you are and how you came to be here. No. We'll work together, and make your husband keep his arm quiet. I've cut a big steak here. You wash it in the spring and see to the fire while I unhitch the horses."

"And then he made Captain Pausch issue you all those linen overalls?" said Judith, as she scoured the skillet with dry sand.

"He did so. The Captain bought them in Montreal before our lot came out. They're loose and they're tough. Wash easy. And mosquitoes don't bother you so much. Better than breeches. But Colonel Breymann said they didn't look military. So the Lieutenant showed Captain Pausch how mosquito-bites got poisoned and laid the men up. Showed him how much quicker we moved in the overalls, so the Captain went to the Baron and the Baron said as we were artillery it didn't matter much how we looked. Now, the Baron—"

Hedwig interrupted. "Tell about the Lieutenant on the retreat." She gently nudged her husband with her knee. Judith listened intently, smiling to herself in the late sunlight that flooded the meadows, secure in the protection of her deep sunbonnet. Rentner talked on, describing the retreat in his tight, sparing way, while the women burned the bark plates on which the meal had been served, set aside a portion against Abigail's awakening. Rentner finished: "And that's how we came back. Don't think we would have, but for him. He was—he was—fine," he ended. He stretched out on the soft grass, flapped at a late fly that buzzed about him. "You know, Hedwig, I don't think these boots are going to last much longer. They—"

"Oh, he'll see you don't go barefoot. Tell about that time he made that nasty little man—you know, the one who was provost in Hanau, pay the Indian fairly for his skins." She explained to Judith: "When the army came down from Canada, they brought a lot of sham rebel money, all paper. It was to make people suspicious of the rebel government. And this man, you see he tried to make an Indian take the sham money. Go on, Gustav, tell how."

The tale spun on. Judith sat at the foot of a big elm, more at peace than she had been in many months. Abigail slept quietly, the wheel was mended and the two horses she could hear cropping the meadow grass. "I wasn't even going to think of him," she told herself. "But this man seems to love talking about him. And besides—oh, what harm will it do? I'll never see him again, just a roving soldier."

When Rentner finished one story, Hedwig reminded him of another, stories of Skenesboro, Crown Point, the filthy slave-ship, Hanau. "We've no parson in the artillery, so the Lieutenant wrote a note to Pausch asking to be appointed chaplain, because of there being so many marriages, and Pausch took it seriously and sent it to the Baron."

"Marriages? In the camp?" Judith's blue eyes were wide.

"Marriages. Lot of men didn't come back from the Grants. Their women—most of 'em had wives—remarried right away."

"Well! That was rapid," said Judith. "They didn't seem to lose time."

"Oh, you see they have to remarry," explained Hedwig. "Otherwise they can't draw rations. Only married women can. Not that I think much of *some* of the marriages." She sniffed.

274

"Remember that Canadian girl who always wore bright red around her hair? Bold, she was. And always singing that song about Montcalm and Carillon."

"I remember her." Hedwig pursed her lips. "Tried to sidle up to every man she saw. Even you."

"Well, you know her husband never came back from the Grants. He was a Canadian ranger. And I think she's trying to make up to the Lieutenant."

Judith lowered her head, the wide bonnet hiding her face. She did not see Hedwig's stout shoes dig viciously at Rentner's ankle.

He looked up in surprise, saw Hedwig's mouth beaming at him, her eyes glaring. "Oh, Gustav, that's not so!" Her voice was careless, a hint of laughter in it. "You know she's to be married today to that little Frenchman who sells rum to the Canadians—when they have money to buy it. The Lieutenant!" She laughed easily, eyes still denying the laugh. With her lips she formed the words: "Say something!"

Rentner stirred uneasily. "Well, I—I only heard it from Schwill. He's always hanging around the women's lines."

"Schwill's a gossiping old midwife. What does *he* know? I don't think the Lieutenant even knows that girl by sight! Or any of the women around there, for that matter!" She glanced at Judith, who was calmly plaiting a fresh raw-hide lace into the mouth of the little bag that hung at her waist. She couldn't see her face. Furtively she jabbed her husband with a long stick, made horrible faces at him.

Mystified, he blinked at her, then said slowly, "No, you're right about Schwill." Hedwig nodded ecstatically. "I wouldn't take stock in anything *he* said," he went on. "I've never seen the Lieutenant notice any of those women."

Hedwig edged over to him, picked up his hand and began patting it. She looked at Judith, who had suddenly begun to hum to herself, smiling softly as she worked the rawhide through the loops of the bag.

275

Rentner was knitting his brows, turning some thought of his own over and over in his mind. He spoke abruptly. "You're Yankee. How can you talk to us in our tongue?"

"Gustav!" Hedwig turned on him. "You're rude!"

Judith smiled. "I think he has a right to ask. It must seem strange—here in the forest."

Rentner sat up. "It *is* strange. And—and where are you going? What were you doing in the clearing?"

"You mustn't ask questions like that, Gustav." Hedwig was stern. "But it is funny. Like our being here, everybody being here. Across the river there are boys from Hanau and Aschaffenberg and Darmstadt and Hildesheim and Wolfenbüttel and I don't know what English cities and towns and they march with dirty Indians through a wilderness to fight people they've never seen or heard of. Isn't it funny? It makes me feel creepy, sometimes, just thinking of it. And here we are, Gustav and I from Hanau and you—where did you say your home was? It can't be the forest. You talk like the Baroness. Where did you say?"

"Do you know, I was just thinking that I've been more content, sitting and talking with you than I've been since—well, for a long time."

Rentner growled something into his stock, flushing. Hedwig said, "I've never really known anyone who talked like you. We're country-folk. At home, I'd be frightened of you. But you don't seem proud and you don't stare at me as if I was something that shouldn't be there. And I know you'll forgive Gustav for asking so many questions."

"But there's nothing to forgive." Briefly and simply she told the story of the settlement on the round hill west of Fort Anne. Hedwig and Rentner listened, eyes wide. "And so," Judith concluded, "I'm going to Albany as fast as your army will let me."

Rentner shook his head. "For thinking of such things—your father's plan—a man in Hanau would be in

276

jail. He'd be executed. And anywhere in Europe. Hedwig, what do you think?"

"I think you and I would have stayed on the round hill. You and I would have liked it."

Judith leaned forward, her eyes shining. "It was a good life. We worked hard, but it was such fun. The forest was kind and so was the land. We had festivals through all the seasons. The last harvest festival—that was nearly two years ago—we danced in the open on a great flat space till the sun came up. There was white frost on the ground and the sunrise seemed to set it on fire."

"The forest was kind," said Rentner slowly. "Kind—and then men came. I think your father should have taken you all away then."

"Oh, no!" cried Judith, flushing.

"He should have taken you away," repeated Rentner. "It is right that you feel he made no mistake. But—" He seemed to fumble for words. "But think of him as a man you've only heard of, not as your father. He felt he couldn't leave, he must prove himself strong. He must be stronger than other men. To prove that to himself, many died. His plan for men to live was wise. I could have lived under that plan and been happy. But—" he tapped his broad red cuff with a hard forefinger—"instead of living, men died. Don't be angry. He would say what I say, if he could have seen you, sitting on that rock beside your broken wagon."

Judith shook her head. "If he'd gone, what he'd hoped to prove would have been gone for himself and for everyone who believed in him—and it was for them, not for himself, that he was concerned."

"No," said Rentner slowly. "I know it's good to plant corn. But not in a thunderstorm. If a storm comes up, I wait till it passes. I don't let the grains get washed away because I'm bound to plant, rain or no rain. Hedwig?"

"It is all over. It's easy to say what would have been best, sitting here full of venison. I only know that I would like to have been on that hill." She leaned her head back against her husband's sound shoulder, looking at Judith. "It must be lonely for you. I wish we were going with you. The camp is so hot and so crowded and we've had nothing to eat except salt-pork for weeks. How ever did you make that leather bag? I've always wanted one. No—no! I wanted to make one myself."

Black head and blond bent over the little bag as Judith's slim fingers ran along the seams and the gathers. Rentner leaned against his tree and watched them. Some sides of war weren't too bad.

Hedwig and Rentner followed the tumbling stream across the meadows in the moonlight. Rentner walked ahead, pondering tenaciously on Judith's story. Finally he said: "It was all right to tell her that about her father. He was selfish without knowing it and she's losing her whole life brooding over his plans because they were *his*. Look, Hedwig, what did you make me tell so many stories about the Lieutenant for?"

Hedwig's strong thumb dug him in the small of his back. "You're a goose, Gustav. Because that's what she wanted to hear. She looked almost sick when you were talking about Lieutenant Spangenberg not coming back from the Grants. Oh! I could have jabbed you with a bayonet when you talked about that nasty Canadian slut. She wears more clothes than any woman in camp, and they cover less of her. Oh, I could see her smiling to herself under that big bonnet of hers when you talked. She told me to call her Judith. It's a hard name to say. Wouldn't the Lieutenant like to know where she is, though! He'd recognize the name even if an Indian said it."

Rentner frowned over his shoulder. "But I promised her I wouldn't tell him where she was, or that we'd seen her."

Hedwig was all innocence. "Gustav! You never did! When?"

"She asked us both. You heard her."

"Did she? I *didn't* hear her. Isn't that funny? Anyway, you may have misunderstood her."

"No, I didn't. She said not to tell him."

"Well, anyway, I'm going to give him some of this, a good big slice." She slapped the slab of venison that Judith had pressed on her at leaving. "She's too young and fine to be tied to a household of two sick horses and a dirty old Indian."

"What's that got to do with venison for the Lieutenant? And besides, you forget about the sister."

"Never you mind about the venison, and I hadn't forgotten the sister. She's part of the household, isn't she? I wonder if he'll be awake when we get to camp."

They tramped over the swaying pontoon bridge that was a bar of black across the wide silver of the river.

Captain Pausch's mouth set in a thin line across his oaken face. "Dear God and all his blasted little cherubs! I've just had one petition, praying that my humble servant be given leave to go back to Ticonderoga to see a wench; then there was another—wanted two weeks' leave to go into the forest and catch a raccoon cub for a pet; and now you—just *what* are you asking for? To be allowed to go on outpost duty? *Out*post duty! A gunner!" He bowed with mock servility. "Is there anything else with which I can oblige you? Oh, Lord Jesus! Outpost duty!"

"Yes," said Ahrens, smiling calmly at the old captain. "And I want to take seven men of my own choosing."

Pausch made gurgling noises in his throat. He spoke with a heavy sarcasm. "Oh, and is that all, Lieutenant? Wouldn't you prefer fifty! Drawn perhaps from the Headquarters guard?"

"Dragoons?" Ahrens threw back his head, laughing. "Not with me! Seen too much of them. I'm serious, Captain. When we came back from the Grants, you gave me the six-pounders and my pick of any twenty men."

Pausch growled: "Well, suppose I did. I wanted them trained by you. You seem to have luck."

"I've trained them, though most of them didn't need it. But in addition to their usual work, I've been taking them out into rough country with a Tory ranger."

"In God's name, what for?"

"From what I saw at Bennington, we're going to need men who can look after themselves if they have to, look after themselves and still be dangerous. We're not having a parade-ground war."

Pausch snorted. "Wish some of those dumb-heads up in the big house could see that. How do they learn?"

"Quickly, most of them. I've weeded out the stupid ones."

"And now you want to patrol with them, with gunners?"

"No less. They've carbines. Thanks to you they've got overalls and not those blasted tight breeches. I've got a few buckskin shirts and light infantry caps. When I see them lined up, they even frighten *me*."

"Where d'you get the caps? No—no. Perhaps I'd better not know, from the grin you're trying to hide. What d'you expect to do on patrol?"

"Experience, mostly. Keep their minds busy. I want to take these men over onto the west bank. The damned rebels are thick there every night. Stole a whole picket of the 9th last night. The night before some of them worked up as far as the bridge itself. Walked off with a lot of tools and left a very courteous receipt for them. Besides, it'll be good for the men. They're rotting. Hard to keep 'em up to the mark with nothing but drill and fatigues."

"So you want to throw a little romance into what's left of their lives?" growled Pausch. "Well, the Elector would smile on you. Wrote me not long ago complaining that we didn't have enough casualites. He needs money and gets thirty thalers for each man killed and another

280

thirty for a recruit to take his place." Pausch snorted. "Any other reasons?"

"You've noticed the men's boots?"

"What about 'em? We're fops compared to the Brunswickers. They're all rags and patches. What about our boots?"

"Captain, their toes flop out like sausages when they walk."

"Hah? Hah? Like sausages?"

"There may be rebel casualties if we go out, and the last reports said that the rebel boots were getting better all the time. I'd like to see if that's so."

Pausch locked his hands behind him and rocked back and forth on his heels. "We-e-e-ll! I'll not put anything in writing, but—see if you can get a pair of boots that'll fit me. Long feet and not too snug about the ankles. Want to go tonight? Suppose you'll take that man Rentner. The order-book returned him to duty today. Tell him the Baron countersigned a warrant for him. He's corporal as of yesterday, pay reckoned from that date. It'll be read in orders tomorrow, but if he goes mosstrooping about the country with you, he may never get back to hear it." He acknowledged Ahrens' salute and walked away toward the gun-park. Ahrens watched him disappear among the high wheels of the pieces. Then he turned and raced toward the street of tents. "Rentner! Rentner! We're going tonight! Have the squad ready by six! Oh, yes, and your warrant came through, Corporal."

In his tent Ahrens stretched out his long arms, admiring the fringe that dangled from the buckskin sleeves. He flexed his knees, slapped the flat muscles of his thighs under the light linen overalls. He whistled to himself as he adjusted a long, leather-sheathed knife in his belt, looked at the lock of a light fusil. Then he began to sing:

> "O Carillon, je te revois encore,
> Non plus, hélas, comme en ces jours bénis—"

281

A light step sounded on the grass outside, a discreet finger scratched on the laced flap of the tent.

"Who's there?" he cried.

The laces rattled through the metal eyelets, a sleek black head bound with flame-colored cloth appeared. Bold black eyes sought his, a red mouth, startling against clear white skin, smiled.

He started. "Look here," he began. "You can't walk in and out of tents like this!"

The girl calmly walked in, sat on the edge of his camp bed. In spite of the damp heat of the early evening, she wore a long cloak of black, edged with flame. The "V" at the throat of the gray dress underneath was wide and deep. "You sing my song?"

"Didn't you hear me? Shall I call the provost? Don't you understand English? Well, then, *fiche-moi le camp!*"

She looked up at him, smiling. "You not call provost."

"How do you know I won't?"

"You sing my song—*La Chanson de Carillon*. An' you know if provost take me, he flog me. He make mark on my skin. It is so white. See?" She shrugged a round shoulder forward, exposing an expanse of ripe flesh.

Ahrens frowned, then laughed in spite of himself. "You're persistent. But listen. There's a war. D'you see? A war. I'm going to it in three minutes. And when I come back I don't want to find a black-eyed minx sitting on my bed. I don't want to see her there at all. Come along!" He held out his hand. "Scamper off, or I'll *have* to call the provost."

She seized his hand. "I stay, eh? My 'osban' he was kill. If I stay wis officer, I not have to marry again. *Je suis sage.* You look at me when I sing by ze big lake, in woods, on river. You like me a little, hein? An' I teach you my song. You no say ze words right now."

Ahrens ran his hand over his neatly clubbed brown hair. The muscles of his lean jaws were flicking, bright points showed in his gray eyes. "Damn it!" he thought. "Why does she have to be so pretty! Just asking for trouble if I don't throw her out." Aloud he said: "The army is full of officers and husbands. Thousands of them—minus me. Hello! What's that?"

"Eh?" she said.

"Thought I heard someone outside. And the canvas front is flapping."

She reached for his hand again. "Come, sit down. No one come in. I good girl. You know my name? Adrienne Moneuse." Her hard little paw clung to his, her eyes sparkled.

"No need to tell me your name. I'm not going to use it." He suddenly gripped her hand, swung her to her feet. "Now out you go." He gently propelled her to the door of the tent, pushed her out with a light slap.

She ran a few feet, then laughed over her shoulder. "If I not find someone else, per'aps I come back."

Ahrens scratched his head, staring after her. "Wouldn't Charteris call me a damn fool! Maybe he'd be right. Oh, blast her! It's past six!" He shook his powder-horn, slapped his bullet-pouch. "All in order." He picked up his fusil and trotted away toward the rendezvous. Beyond the gun-park he met Hedwig, carrying a flat package. "Well, Hedwig! What have you there?"

She met his glance coldly. "A bit of fresh meat, Lieutenant. I'm taking it to one of the men in the hospital."

"Now that's a fine thing to do. Those men need a bit of good meat."

She inclined her head politely. "I'm glad the Lieutenant is pleased." She walked on, nose in the air.

He looked after her, frowning and rubbing his firm chin. Then he tucked his fusil under his arm and quickened his pace. "There are my banditti. Rentner and Meister, Zoll, Pach, Schmidt, Heisse and—yes, there's Ott."

The men looked hard, competent, in their overalls and buckskins. They stiffened to attention at his approach, then followed him across the gently rocking pontoons. The thin column filed away across the meadows in the

283

twilight, Ahrens' tall figure slipping along through the grasses at an easy, swinging gait.

Ahrens peered cautiously over the tangle of rocks into the wooded hollow below, straining his ears. There was a whisper of wind in the trees above him, in the hollow and along the edge of the broad meadows, a wind which flowed gently down from the bluffs at his back, across the flats and on to the river which he could dimly see. He cupped his hand back of his ear. There was something else stirring in the night, stirring gently as the air, a stealthy rustling that gradually filled the rocky bowl like a thin mist. Then he saw a tall figure slip out from among the muttering trees, another, another till twelve dark forms stood below him. Cautiously he reached out, tapped Rentner twice on the shoulder. He vaguely saw a soot-blackened face nod. He watched the group, who seemed to be leaning on long muskets, waiting for something. He set his teeth. "Here's the test of my discipline. If one of my men moves, let alone fires, we'll be wiped out." His throat felt dry, his pulses pounded in his ears till he thought the ghostly men beneath him must hear. There were more stirrings, three new forms glided, cat-like, up to the short broad man who seemed to be the leader. There was a whispered parley, the three took their places. Then the leader spoke in a creaky, nasal voice. "Ammon Craw, he's give himself up, accordin' to plan. A lobster-back took him. He'll tell Burgoyne 'at Gates has fifteen thousand men downriver. Anyone want to say anything."

A tall man leaned on a rifle at the end of the line and said: "My squad rushed a post near the river. Killed four grenadiers. Others came to reinforce the post and I saw fit to withdraw my squad."

The leader laughed a low-pitched laugh. " 'Tain't bad for Massachusetts. Connecticut got anything to say?"

A deep voice rolled low. "Spiked a cannon, captured three flasks of powder. Likewise a keg of rum."

"Where's the rum?"

"Return Meigs has it."

"Trust him?"

"Served on my ship. He's scairt of me. The rum's all right."

"Better call roll and then move. Don't like this spot. Lucky the lobster-backs don't patrol more 'n fifty yards beyond their lines. I'd admire to set an ambush here myself. Ready?" Slowly the names drifted up to Ahrens on his rock. He wondered and listened, listened too to the voices that answered, some uncouth and harsh, some well-modulated.

"Nehemiah Sherwood?"

"Here!"

"Ezekiel Whitney?"

"Huh!"

"Jekiel Burr?"

"Here!"

"Remember Sheldon?"

"H'yo!"

"Shadrick Boswick—Levi Munson—Jehiel Galpin—Abiel Cook—Hezekiah Tuttle—"

At last he was done, leaned on his musket and faced his men. "Back by the same route, and remember we got to dig when we get to the Heights. That Polish feller and General Arnold, they hate to see dirt that ain't been turned. Now scatter and get back any way you like. Amasa Loomis tarried back there to watch the Britishers digging a gun-pit. He'll tell us about it and we'll come back and spike the guns. Amasa'll be 'long 'fore you use up a chaw. Who'll wait for him? Aaron Drake? 'Tain't needful, but it's more seeming."

The men drifted away south through the woods, and the night was still again. The man Aaron Drake sat on a log close under the rock which sheltered Ahrens.

Ahrens squinted down at him. "Hardly six feet away," he thought. "I'll wait a bit longer—" He counted slowly to one hundred, then tapped Rentner once on the shoulder. He could feel the man's muscles stiffen at the signal. Another count of ten and he pressed softly on the end of a long slender sapling that lay at the top of their little moraine. The far end of the fallen tree stirred, spoiled the balance of another which lay across it and thudded a heavy stone into the hollow a good hundred feet from where they lay. Ahrens felt a wild surge of excitement grip him. It was hard to breathe, hard not to laugh at his plan which had worked so well. Aaron Drake had sprung to his feet at the crashing of the stone, facing away from the little knot of gunners. His musket at ready, he backed slowly toward the rock, his heels biting into the sloping ground.

Ahrens tapped Rentner again, laid down his fusil, crouched and sprang. His powerful arms flailed about Drake's neck, forcing his head back in a paralyzing hold. The man struggled, but Ahrens held him as though he were a child.

"Quick—the gag, Rentner! That's it. Now—the others? Cords for his arms. Leave his legs free!" Ott, Zoll, Meister and the rest rose from the spots where Ahrens had posted them when he first laid the ambush. "We'll not wait for Master Amasa Loomis. On, now! Hit for that trail that skirts the top of the bluffs, then we'll double back to the meadows when we're opposite the bridge. Move! Quiet as you can, and don't be rough with our guest." In English he said: "No tricks, now. You're safe unless you make trouble. These are my men, and I'm sure you won't make a row and force me to choose between them and you."

Drake's eyes widened. He was obviously puzzled by men in buckskin who not only ambushed him, but who spoke in a foreign tongue that wasn't French and surely was no Indian dialect. He nodded and fell in between Ott and Heisse.

The woods were thick along the crest of the bluffs and except through rare clearings Ahrens could not see the river off at his right. The party was out of danger of running into stray Yankees by now and the men smoked and talked as they tramped along. The gag had been taken from Drake's mouth and his arms loosed. Ahrens turned and shouted: "Pass the prisoner up to the head of the column."

It was growing light and Ahrens looked at a tall man, rather heavy in the shoulders, who walked with a light step. He wore ragged leather breeches and a woolen hunting-shirt, but his dark hair was neatly clubbed and he had evidently shaved quite recently. His eyes were clear and steady and there was a healthy color under his tan. He raised his eyebrows as he fell easily into step beside his captor.

"I must confess that I eavesdropped a little, so I know something of what your command did tonight. Do you want to add anything?"

Drake ruefully rubbed the back of his neck. "I suppose that I'm due for the cells at Chambly? Well—" he shrugged—"it won't mend matters to complain. No—I've nothing to add to what you heard. It was you, I suppose, who jumped on my back. I thought it was a catamount."

"The hold is painful, but not damaging," said Ahrens.

Drake smiled. "I was counted strong and a good wrestler. I'm afraid I didn't test you much. What are you, anyway? You dress like Morgan's Rifles and you speak—it's German, isn't it?"

Ahrens laughed. "I thought *I* was asking questions. We're from the Hesse-Hanau artillery company, doing a little detached service."

Drake looked astonished. "Mercenaries? I'd heard they were all so fat and heavy that by the time they'd put one foot on the ground, the other had gone to sleep. I had a cousin at Bennington and he wrote me. He was with the Berkshire men."

"We're light and heavy, both. Like all armies, I imagine." He was a little nettled to find that the rebels

287

looked on his people nearly as unfavorably as did the British. "You're a ranger?"

"Captain Wadsworth's company of rangers. We're chosen from men who know the country about here. I came out with Captain Elijah Kellogg's company, and I'll go back to him when—when things change."

"Been here long?" asked Ahrens.

"Only two weeks. You see, I rather favored the King, and most of the people in my town did. Didn't care much one way or the other, so long as we were let alone. I attended Harvard College for a year and then came back to teach in the town school. I didn't want to leave, but we heard that Burgoyne was bringing Indians and mercenaries, and that got our dander up. There haven't been Indians around Barre in thirty years. I've never even seen one. But we all know the old stories of the raids, Haverhill and Deerfield and the other places. And we didn't like the King sicking mercenaries on us worth a continental. Then we heard about that girl up the river here—Ray, McCrae—that was it. The town thought we all ought to go. You don't mind my saying that about mercenaries? I think you'd have felt the same way."

Ahrens waved the matter aside, knitting his brows as he walked on. "You mean that the people decided for themselves whether to turn out or not?"

"Well, I'd hardly say 'decided,'" said Drake. "Their minds seem to have been pretty well made up when they came to the town meeting. I might even say they appeared to be determined."

"How many came from your town?"

"Why, a considerable proportion. Not every one, of course. Bartholomew Peckham, he's eighty-one. He was displeased when they wouldn't take him. And Nahum Fielding's wife was poorly and he had to stay. But the rest of the men came."

"And those men in your company tonight—they all came the same way?"

"Most. Two have been in the Continental Army since '75. Others were with Arnold at Quebec and Valcour. The rest came out like me, some from Connecticut and some from Rhode Island and New Hampshire. As I say, we're chosen for knowing the country. I spent summers near Albany with my uncle, but they don't like New Englanders there."

Ahrens filtered the fringe of his sleeve through his fingers and walked on, eyes on the ground. "What a tale! This is like one of Judith's ideas. A whole village goes to war because it wants to. The people decide for themselves whether or not they'll take down their muskets and go. All the same, there's something about it—this man Drake doesn't stump along like most of our men. He knows why he's come and what he's come to do." He narrowed his eyes, remembering the field at Hubbardton, the body of the old man, his calm face framed with soft white hair. He remembered the swarming men who broke like a tidal wave over his guns and engulfed them He looked at Drake out of the corner of his eye. He could easily picture him in that mad rush of clubbed muskets. "Gentleman Johnny," he thought, "a whirl-wind is gathering against you. Do you realize it? No. You only listen to the Tory Skene." He turned to Drake again. "Have you thought into the future? Do you expect to stop us, and if not—what then?"

"There will be a certain amount of resistance opposed to you," said Drake. "I think we may hope that it will be successful. If not—why, we may try again."

It was much brighter now, with a bar of pale yellow showing in the east through thinning trees. Ahrens sent Drake back to his guard and walked on, chin sunk on his chest and full of forebodings. It was childish to think of Howe's men coming north. They were off for Philadelphia. Now Burgoyne must cut his communications with Canada and plunge down the river when he had enough supplies. Into what would he plunge? A country swarming with rebels, hasty militiamen like

289

Drake, and, according to reports, solid regiments who had been fighting as units for three years. "Can't wave that aside by calling 'em raw troops, farmers and so on. Lord above, those were raw troops at Bennington and see what happened to us. It's unthinkable that our men and some of the best regiments of the British Army won't be able to go where and when we please. We've trained men, experienced men. But Baum was a tried soldier and so was Breymann. They had veteran troops. Are we marching into a trap? The rebels must be massing to the south of us, while we're yawning our way along the river."

From the bluffs he looked down into the still-sleeping camp of the British advance corps, their white tents misty and unreal in the shimmering light of false dawn. He halted his men, looked them over. They leaned on their muskets, tired but still exhilarated with their foray. "Pach, Schmidt, Heisse and Ott, take the prisoner straight across the meadows and turn him over to Lieutenant Standing of the 9th. He speaks German. And be sure to get a receipt for the prisoner." The four men slipped down a steep path, Drake in their midst. "The rest of the detail will follow me. I'm going along the bluffs past the bridgehead. I want each man to look out for paths leading west. We might be able to make a wide circle and get close to the rebel lines—wherever they may be—on our next tour."

Meister saw it first, huddled in a deep hollow between the meadowland and bluffs. He swung the butt of his carbine and jabbed Rentner lightly in the small of the back. The latter looked around, annoyed, then followed the pointing butt to the bowl-like depression that was faintly lit by the first dull shafts of early morning. He stared, jaw protruding, then looked ahead at Ahrens, who walked lightly along, wiping his muscular neck, all unconscious of the interest behind him. Rentner growled: "Forget it. Just camp-followers." Then he swore

290

under his breath. Ahrens had heard the mutter and turned inquiringly. "Camp followers?" At this distance from the army? They can't—" He stopped as though an invisible hand had clutched his collar, stood staring down the bluff at the hollow and the rickety wagon with its charred sides and broken-kneed wheels. Two old horses, heads low, stood motionless, tethered to a tree. One of them slowly raised his head, gave a half-cough, half-whinny, then drooped again.

Eyes fixed on the blackened Conestoga wagon with its patched canvas cover, Ahrens moved a few steps toward the slope of the bluffs as though drawn on by a magnet. "The wagon!" he thought. "And I've made a dozen trips to Fort Edward and the north, looking for it!" Rentner leaned on his carbine, staring straight before him, his face set. Far away across the river a drum muttered. Zoll lifted his beak-like nose, murmured, "Reveille and rations," shifted his feet expectantly. Ahrens cleared his throat. "Detail wait here," he said.

Rentner stared at the butt of his musket, dogged jaw set. "I didn't see it. I'd not want her to think—"

Ahrens paused, wide forehead wrinkled. "Think what?"

Rentner shook his head, eyes on the ground. Meister and Zoll sighed, thinking of the drums across the river and the smoke welling up under camp-kettles.

Ahrens' white teeth flashed in a silent laugh. "Too early in the morning for mysteries. I'm—" He jolted his heels into the slope, cut his hand in a short downward motion and glided behind a tree. The three men slid into the undergrowth as though drawn by the smooth tug of a rope. Three blackened faces looked inquiringly toward Ahrens.

From the shelter of a gnarled root, he was staring into the low land below them, strong nose and chin tense and strained like the jutting figurehead of a ship. His right hand, flat on the ground, began to quiver, then a

291

long forefinger slowly lifted itself, pointed. The men followed its direction.

Among a heap of boulders fifty yards away across the hollow, masked by trailing vines, something moved. Leaves stirred slightly as though ruffled by a breeze and a head appeared, a head hideously daubed with black, its eyes made huge and staring by broad white circles which rayed out over cheek and chin. Another appeared in a clump of bushes close by. The white-circled eyes were staring at the old horses, at the silent wagon. Ahrens felt a horrible tingling along his spine, a quick cramping at his stomach. He set his jaw, moved slightly to the left, aware that his hands were trembling violently. A third painted nightmare, a fourth, were moving up to the pile of rocks, a fifth slid snake-like from behind a tree. They joined their fellows among the vine-grown rocks, cold eyes on the little camp. Ahrens shuddered. He felt an almost uncontrollable impulse to yell, to leap from his cover and make for the high ground behind him. There was something so inhuman, something so utterly alien to the world he knew in those slinking, staring copper men that they seemed to tear away from him his natural weapons and defenses. At the same time he found himself admiring their use of cover, the animal deftness of their movements. "They must be absolutely hidden from the wagon, and they don't care about this high ground because they are behind our lines. Five—five. Is there another?" He bent his wrist, held up his forefinger, sharply crooked. There was a moment's pause. Then something tapped lightly at his heel, once, twice, thrice, four times, five times. That was something—his little squad checked his count.

Slowly he inched back, rolled behind a fold in the ground, knelt and looked for his men, who were working back to him like thick-bodied snakes. He noticed that their eyes were fixed and staring. With an effort he steadied his hand, rubbed his chin with a gesture which he hoped was slow and casual. Then he spoke in a low-pitched voice. "We've got to go by guess-work, but from what the ranger Evans told us, those bastards will wait a bit longer, watching the camp. Then they'll fire, let out a whoop and rush it. Back to your positions and watch me. When I see movement in the leaves, I'll fire. Take your time from me. No volley, just single shots. By the time Zoll has fired, I ought to be loaded again and so on down the line. That's all, only—don't miss."

He slipped away to his crooked root. "Blasted fool that I was to send the other four away with the prisoner! With extra men we could frighten them off. They're deserting and won't mind a shot at us. Just trying to pick up an extra scalp or two on their way to Canada." Cautiously he poked the dulled barrel of his fusil out through a screen of leaves, sighted along it, eyes narrow.

The rock-heap showed no sign of life. Ahrens moistened his dry lips, staring at the carpet of vines. Suddenly a black and white face, staring horribly, took form, another close by it and a dull gleam of metal. In the mass of green behind the faces, a savage rose abruptly, heavy musket held across his chest. Ahrens could see the painted chin draw in, could see the mouth open to breathe in a lungful of air. The sights of the carbine lay full on the smeared chest. He slowly pressed the trigger. The butt kicked smartly against his shoulder, the fusil cracked. Through drifting smoke he heard a swelling whoop checked in mid-voice, saw the Indian jerk erect, toss out his arms, spin and fall, his musket tumbling among the rocks with a dry rattle. Another carbine flashed and cracked behind Ahrens as he frantically whipped the slim rammer down on a fresh charge.

He raised himself on one elbow, looked out. Two Indians had broken cover toward the camp and stood frozen, looking up at the bluffs. Two more shots flashed behind him, dirt spurted between the strange savages. Then they whirled, plunged back into the tangle of vines, the leaves eddying over their greasy leggings. "Even numbers now, at least. Too bad one of the others couldn't have got his man. Ha! By God, he did!" There was a heavy thrashing among the leaves, a copper body writhed into sight, taut and straining, flopped convulsively in the open, stiffened and lay still. Rentner must have caught him among the rocks. Three left. Will they sneak away?"

In answer to his question, there was a roar and a flash in the bushes, a dreadful scream shivered through the air and one of the old horses fell kicking and lashing while its mate danced frantically at the end of its halter, agonized head thrown back.

Ahrens swore. "Spiteful bastards! Take it out on that old horse! No need of caution now!" He called, "Rentner! Can you see them?"

"Gone to ground, sir. Meister and Zoll say the same. They haven't pulled out, though. I can see the back slope of that rock heap."

"Keep watch. They may try for the other horse. We're out of range as far as any Indian shooting goes. That's it. Watch for the other horse—mark the smoke if they fire. They—" He reared back as though struck. "On your feet! Follow me! They may fire on the wagon!" He sprang up, started off on the north slope of a nose of land that jutted out from the bluffs, scrambling over deadfalls, vaulting rocks, his men thudding in his wake. The nose of land blanketed the hollow, but over the crest came the roar of an old musket followed by a sharper, stabbing crack. Ahrens waved his arm. "Faster! They've fired on the wagon! Now—out into the open and draw their fire. It'll be long range for them!" He crashed through low bushes onto level ground, skirted the point of the nose, his gunners close behind.

Something roared in front of him, his fusil jarred from his hands, the lock smashed. Something coppery and black and white was close by him, lunging with a long knife. Ahrens snatched up the broken fusil, side-stepped in full career and drove the butt downward with a vicious lunge. The wood snapped and he saw a lean red man roll at his feet, hands clapped to a streaming skull.

A carbine ripped the air behind him. He heard Rentner's sharp voice yelling: "There they come, more of 'em!" Another carbine cracked.

Ahrens snatched up the musket of the fallen Indian, squinted at the pan and fired point-blank at a hellish painted face that seemed to fly to pieces through the smoke. Meister slipped past his elbow, crouching low and carbine extended, then pitched headlong, rolled over showing a mask of blood. There were more crashes in front, a dull thud which spattered red from Meister's neck. Ahrens dropped the musket, picked up Meister's piece, roared, "Take cover!" and threw himself on the ground. He saw tangled branches in front of him, rolled to them and peered ahead. Two Indians lay in the open space before him, three more were slipping to the shelter of some trees. He could just see a corner of the wagon, silent and seemingly unharmed. The remaining horse grazed quietly by the body of its mate. In the still air he could hear the clop-clop-clop of its loose lips as it snuffed the ground. He whipped a look over his shoulder. Rentner was safe behind a fallen log, curiously white about the eyes and fingering the trigger of his piece. Zoll lay motionless in the shelter of a stump. "God above!" thought Ahrens. "Just two of us left?" Then he saw Zoll's hand fumbling with the latch of his cartridge box. "Well, three, then. Hi! What's that?" Off on the left front, branches waved madly. He called over his shoulder: "Don't shoot! They're trying to draw our fire! Keep an eye to the front."

Smoke welled crashing from the trees, something rapped viciously on a stump to his left. He yelled, "Watch out! Here they come!" Low bushes suddenly boiled, a hideous whoop shot upward and four Indians raced into sight, muskets held before them. Ahrens roared, "Take the leaders! I'll watch the left!" Rentner and Zoll fired. The leading Indian kicked his feet in the air and sprawled on to the ground, another dropped his musket and ran howling into the woods, clutching a shattered arm. The remaining two came on. The trees at the left were still.

Ahrens rose to his knee, fired full at the broad chest of the nearest Indian, not ten paces away. Then he stood up, dug his feet into the ground and drove hard at the other. A musket crashed harmlessly over him as his shoulders thudded against the slippery legs of the savage. They went down in a whirling heap, hands grappling and knees jabbing. The sickly reek of the Indian's body was strong in his nostrils, the bristly hair of the scalp-lock rasped his cheek. He tried to pin an arm back, but the greased wrist slipped from his clutch, a sharp elbow jolted with wicked force into the angle between his ear and jaw.

Sick and dizzy with the pain, Ahrens dropped his chin, masked his jaw with his shoulder and tried to drive his knee into the Indian's groin. The man wriggled away, clamped a long-fingered hand about Ahrens' throat, forcing his head back. Ahrens tightened his neck muscles, smashed his fist in hard, jarring jabs against the tough muscles of his opponent's belly. With a sudden wrench he freed his throat of the choking grip, caught the Indian's head in the crook of his elbow. The man gasped. His breath was hot and sour against Ahrens' face. Twice they rolled over on the rough ground and he was dimly aware of Rentner and Zoll dancing about the writhing pair, carbines clubbed but not daring to swing.

He gave a twist and a lunge, found himself with his chest pressing hard against the Indian's broad, sweaty back, the painted head still locked in his elbow. He threw all his strength against the straining of that powerful neck, forcing the head around and back. Frantic hands tore at his other arm, gained a paralyzing hold on wrist and elbow, twisted and wrenched. Ahrens set his teeth, his whole might thrown against the quivering head. His own arm cracked and gave, the pain was agonizing. A little more and the bone would break. Suddenly the Indian rattled horribly in his throat, there was a sickening snap and the copper body went limp like a taut cord that has been cut.

Panting and dizzy, Ahrens staggered to his feet. The trees and the sky whirled about in a mad dance. Through a mist he saw Rentner and Zoll staring at him. He looked down at the dreadful angle of the shaven head, then at his men. They seemed to be waiting for something. He straightened his belt with weak hands, tried to smile at them. "Not sure Colonel Breymann would approve of this style of war." He felt that his head was shaking a little. "Better have a look at Meister. I'm afraid he's gone."

Rentner still stared. Then he recovered himself, swallowed with obvious effort. "Yes, sir, he's— Look out!" He threw himself in front of Ahrens. Among low trees on the left, a painted body showed, metal flashed dully. Then from the hollow where the lone horse still browsed noisily, a vicious crack rang out, sharp, spitting. The coppery body collapsed among the leaves and roots.

Ahrens rubbed his hands over his sweaty face. His throat was dry and ached a little. "Come on," he croaked. "Let's see about that wagon." He trotted toward the hollow, Zoll and Rentner at his heels. Rentner called hoarsely: "Please remember, sir, I told you nothing." Ahrens made an impatient gesture.

The wagon lay silent under its canvas cover. On its charred sides two splintery holes showed raw and glaring in the new light. Ahrens stared at them, a cold dread shooting through his breast, spreading. He shouted: "Judith! Judith!" He ran on faster, eyes on the heavy curtain that screened the back of the wagon, on the shaky steps that dropped from floor-boards to ground. Rentner suddenly put out a hand, checked Zoll. "He won't want us. Stop here by this clump!" He heard Ahrens' shout again: "Judith! Judith! Are you all right?"

The curtain swayed, parted. Ahrens saw a dead-white face framed in a mass of black hair, eyes that seemed all pupil, a vivid red mouth. Judith put out a trembling

297

hand, passed the other over her forehead. Her soft mouth quivered a little. Her voice was choked. "Kurt! Kurt! Is it you?" With unsteady knees she wavered down the rude steps, all unconscious of the nightgown of cambric that wrapped her from chin to heels, unconscious of the sudden torrent of black hair that escaped from its broad blue ribbon and flooded over her back and shoulders. Her bare feet felt hard ground beneath them; she swayed.

Ahrens caught her in his arms. "You're all right, Judith? You're not hurt?"

She sagged in his arms, recovered herself, rested her head against his buckskin breast, hands feebly patting his long arm. She gasped, said unsteadily. "Oh, Kurt, I couldn't believe it was you. They won't come back, will they? I'm all right, I think. I don't know. I only had a little powder left and they shot a hole through my best kettle. Have they really gone? What were you doing here?" Suddenly her eyes overflowed. She hid her face against him, shaken with nervous sobs.

He gripped her shoulder, smiling down at her. With a grimy cuff he dabbed at a black powder stain that showed on the curve of her soft cheek, saying over and over: "You're all right? We were in time? You're all right?"

She swallowed hard, shivered a little, her hand still patting the bulge of his arm under its stained leather. "You look so big in buckskin," she said. "What *have* you been doing to your face?" Her hand stole up from his arm, gently touched his flat, blackened cheek. Then she sniffed. "Kurt! You smell of Indian. Have you been smearing yourself with paint?" She wrinkled her nose delicately.

He laughed, threading his fingers through the soft torrent of her hair. "You're so pretty, Judith. I've never seen your hair like this in the daylight. You've always worn your deep bonnet. No, I've not painted. I—we got rather close to the Indians, that's all."

298

With an unconscious gesture she moved her head, shaking the black waves to their full length. Then she suddenly stiffened, stared wide-eyed at him. "We? We? Did you say 'we'?"

He smiled. "Judith, I'd love to tell you that I fought a whole tribe single-handed. But Rentner and Zoll are right here to correct me."

"Oh!" The exclamation seemed jarred out of her. She colored, her hands flew to her hair, she became violently aware of her bare feet, of her cambric nightgown, touched with blue at the throat, under which her breasts showed bold and firm. Hands to her flushing cheeks she looked in amazement on Ahrens, lips slightly parted. "And Rentner!" She gave a little cry. Her bare feet drummed on the creaking steps, the curtain flopped behind her with emphatic finality.

With a wild surge of spirits, Ahrens flung his long arms over his head, cut a fantastic caper, snatched off his leather skull-cap and hurled it into the air, the false energy of over-fatigue adding to his exhilaration. He caught the cap deftly, clapped his hands. Then he remembered his remaining men—and the one who was missing. He shouted for Rentner. A distant hail answered him. At the edge of the tangle of branches where he had sheltered, two men crouched. One of them straightened, wiped his forehead and rose slowly. Ahrens trotted to him. "What are you up to?" he asked.

Rentner wiped his hands on his breeches. Zoll, very white about the face, still knelt. Rentner said slowly, "Didn't think you'd mind, sir. Me and Zoll, we've been burying Meister."

Ahrens' face fell. "He's a long way from Bonn and the Rhine," he said. "He was a good man." He frowned. "If I hadn't stopped for this, he'd be with us yet. This was no military duty. I'd no right—"

Rentner spoke shortly. "We'll miss him, sir. But he'd have wished it this way."

Zoll nodded. "We knew him, sir."

"He'd—he'd been badly hit?" asked Ahrens.

Zoll rubbed his hands in the dirt in slow, mechanical circles. "Bad, sir. He fell apart, sort of, when we tried to pick him up. A big slug hit him in the belly. So we rolled him into this little hollow and covered him up as best we could. And his face was torn cruel. It wasn't like burying Meister, in a way of speaking, sir."

Ahrens turned away. "All right, all right. Put up some kind of a marker." He blinked his eyes to free his lids of the picture of Meister's gay, reckless face suddenly turning into a spouting red mask.

"There's Eller, sir, of the Specht regiment. He's a stonecutter. We thought a pfennig or two from the men—I'd like to have Eller make a headstone." Rentner knelt again, hacked up more loose earth with his hatchet.

"Send Eller to me," said Ahrens. "Now you two better get right back to camp. You, Rentner, as corporal, report to Captain Pausch and tell him I'll be along presently. Tell him, too, that I want to report this matter to General Fraser. He's still Director of Indians, to his sorrow."

"And the young lady, sir?" asked Rentner.

"How'd you know there was a young lady? She came through safely. Here she comes from her wagon now."

She walked to meet them, prim and demure in gray homespun and trim shoes which flashed broad silver buckles. The powder smudge was gone from her cheek and her hair was neat under a faded blue sunbonnet. Level-eyed, she walked straight to Zoll and Rentner. She smiled gravely at them, then spoke in her stilted German. "I've so much to thank you for." Her eyes took on a haunted look. "If you hadn't come! I—I can't say anything, but I want you to have these." She drew from her gray belt two long knives, leather sheathed, held them out.

Rentner and Zoll stared at them, then took them almost grudgingly, very red of face. Ahrens raised his eyebrows, recognizing the knives as English steel, very old, with good hardwood handles. Rentner, eyes on the ground, muttered: "That's all very well. But if someone hadn't shot that last Indian over on our left, someone with a rifle, a long rifle—" Without looking up he thrust the knife in the bosom of his shirt.

Judith colored. "Oh, he—he was just where I could see him." She fumbled at her waist, unfastened the leather bag that dangled from it. "Take this to your pretty wife."

Ahrens and Judith watched the pair stride away to the east. Ahrens drew a finger along his jaw. "Now, how did you know that Rentner had a wife—and that she was pretty?"

She smiled up at him. "You told me, for one thing. For another, they dined with me, very formally, a day or two ago—just before I moved down here."

Ahrens shook his fist at Rentner's back. "Blast him! He knew and never told me! If I've ridden north by the old fort once, I've been a dozen times."

She nodded. "I made him promise. Kurt—it seemed wiser."

He looked down at her, standing slim and straight beside him. She seemed very near. His hands opened and closed slowly. "It was nearly fatal."

She shook her head. "Even knowing, what could you have done? It was luck that brought you here this morning. I—I think I'm still frightened. When I heard the shots, I couldn't know what was happening. I could only see the Indians. They might have been fighting with other Indians for the loot. Then I heard your voice and—and—" She turned blindly to him, hands before her. He caught her, held her close. Slowly she lifted her head, eyes tight shut. Gently he covered her lips with his, softly kissed her eyes. "Judith, Judith, I was frantic when I saw that horrible head staring at your wagon. I don't believe I thought much—just fired and rushed down the slope."

She drew a deep quivering sigh, nodded her head.

301

"Kurt, Kurt," she whispered, arms close about his neck. Locked, they swayed as gentle flames lapped over them. His voice was low. "You mustn't hide from me again, Judith, mustn't run off. You've got to be with me. You've—" Her lips cut off his words, the racing of her heart against him seemed to echo the drumming in his ears, her fingers played about his cheeks, his thick hair. Again he said: "You mustn't hide, Judith. You must come to camp with me. The Baroness will see to you. I can't think of you day after day, night after night, alone like this. Say you'll come, my Judith."

Gently she raised her head. "Kurt dear, I'm not alone."

"But she could come. And be seen to by our own doctors. See, Judith, see—how easy it would be, how much it would answer. I *know* the Baroness would look to you."

"I can only see my sister in the midst of an advancing army. It's people that disturb her, not things. She slept all through this morning. But people whom she saw moving about, heard talking, shouting. It was bad enough when those two families came back to the hill, but in the middle of an army— And then, even if that were right—do you truly want me to come and do I truly want to go? You're a long way from home, Kurt, and you're lonely. I—I've been lonely too. And now we're both under the strain of the morning."

He only said: "I love you, Judith."

She rested her head on his shoulder again. "Kurt, I love you. You're so fine. There's a selflessness that your life has done everything to kill and you won't let it be killed." Her clinging arms tightened. He bent his face to hers. Suddenly she gripped his arm, said in a broken voice: "Kurt—please, please take me back to the wagon. God help me, I can't leave you of my own will. Kurt—please."

Silent and with tense faces they walked slowly back toward the covered wagon. At the slope she said

302

mechanically. "Chipmunk will bring me fresh food today. I must have him drag away the dead horse."

He nodded absently. "He can rig up a harness and have the other horse drag the body away. That's what we do." His voice was forced, lifeless.

By the wagon he halted abruptly. "Well, Judith?"

Her eyes met his. "Kurt—I don't know. I must have peace, time to think. I—I don't know."

"In the meantime?"

She hesitated. He leaned forward. "In the meantime, Judith, promise me this: Never move without letting me know. Get word to me somehow. Those Indians were about the last of the Wyandots. Any other deserters will follow the trails up the east bank. I don't think you'll be bothered again. Now—you'll promise to let me know?"

"I promise, Kurt. I'll get word to you somehow. Please, please, Kurt, be content with that—for now."

He took her face in his hands, kissed her gently. "Goodby, my Judith," he said.

She whispered. "Goodby, Kurt. You're very dear to me."

Gentleman Johnny Burgoyne's handsome face looked drawn, his eyes weary, in the bright sun that poured through the broad windows of the Duer house, but his scarlet and white shone immaculate as ever. He smiled broadly, waved Ahrens into a rickety chair. "What's this I hear about you? It's the talk of the camp. Dashed spirited bit of work. Going to incorporate it in orders. With your bare hands, wasn't it?" He chuckled, slapped his thigh. "Gad, I'd like to have been with you." He rubbed his hands over his tired face. "Damned if I don't think a commander's got to put in twenty hours out of twenty-four seeing that his men are fed. Now, that work of yours, that was *real*. You had something to tell me about the rebels?"

Ahrens fingered a carefully mended rent in his worn jacket. "I was lucky enough to hear them talking, sir."

Burgoyne nodded indulgently. "Good boy. What did they say?"

"Why, I gathered, sir, that men are flocking to Gates from all the provinces—not just from the country about here."

"Interesting, interesting." The General examined his well-tended hands in the sunlight. "You know, of course, that they just turn out for what pay there is in it, then scatter to their villages again. Skene, now, Skene says that as soon as we move downriver, Gates' army will melt away."

Ahrens bit his lip. He had his own opinion of the soundness of the Tory Skene. He went on. "They talked as though they had fortifications under way."

Burgoyne sat up, his face serious. "Fortifications? Why wasn't I told of this before?"

"I wrote a report, sir. It had to be addressed to Colonel Breymann. Then for a week I've been trying to get audience with you."

"A week? By Gad, I'll soon put a stop to that—those puppies in the orderly-room take too much on themselves. What did you hear about fortifications?"

"The patrol leader, sir, said the men would have to dig when they got back to camp—wherever that is. He spoke of 'Arnold and that Polish feller.'" Ahrens mimicked the Yankee twang.

Burgoyne rocked in his chair. "Capital, capital! 'Polish feller'!" He grew grave again. "Know Arnold, right enough. He led the rebel fleet at Valcour. Touched with a sort of mad genius, but—he doesn't know his drill." With a wave he relegated Arnold to his place in the unskilled masses. "But Polish, Polish—who the devil could that be? Might be one more foreign adventurer that Congress loves to foist onto its generals. Like La Roche Fermoy at Independence. Orderly! Is Lieutenant Twiss in the staff-room?"

Twiss' keen, gnarled face appeared in the doorway. "Here, Twiss, young Ahrens tells me the rebels have got some sort of a Pole digging trenches for 'em. You engineer fellows all know each other. Who's it apt to be?"

Twiss scraped a thick thumb along his nose. "Pole? Pole? H'm. Can't think of a soul. Yes—wait a bit. Might be young Kosciusko. Very likely to be. Lot of Poles on the wing since the Partition."

"Good?" asked Burgoyne.

"Said to be. Good eye for country."

"Now, look here, Twiss—supposing a man like that was put over a lot who work as fast as these blasted Yankees?"

Twiss blew out his cheeks, studied the ceiling. "He'd build something bloody tough."

Burgoyne nodded. "Thanks, Lieutenant Twiss." He turned to Ahrens. "That's valuable information, very."

Ahrens leaned eagerly forward. "I could take my men, push downriver and locate these works for you, sir."

Gentleman Johnny waved a wide hand. "No need, no need. Wouldn't risk a man. What difference does it make if they've burrowed in the river-bank five miles away or fifteen? But this—this Pole and Arnold—they give us our chance. They may make the Yankees stand and fight. You see? A crazy leader like Arnold and good breastworks for shelter? Some of our people say this army carries far too many guns. But if the rebels stand, our guns will smash 'em. If they scatter—why, we'll just have little groups in front of us downriver to Albany. Hope they stand, because we can't help smashing 'em. These people simply will not face artillery—terrifies 'em. So if they wait back of the Pole's redans and scarpes, our part of the war will be over before I've had a chance to learn his name. Then we'll lie snug in Albany, glutted with supplies, and see what our New York friends will do."

"Then there's St. Leger, coming down the Mohawk, sir."

Burgoyne coughed. "Oh, yes, yes, yes. St. Leger. Mustn't forget St. Leger."

Ahrens walked down the hill from the Duer house

305

toward the tent-packed meadows. He had hoped that action might come of his news, but it had only served to bolster the General's feeling of bland confidence. "That's damned depressing," he thought. "Wish some of the staff had seen Bennington. Face artillery? The rebels couldn't have got any closer to my guns without climbing in the muzzles. Face guns? They faced 'em around and fired on us with 'em."

Hooves clopped behind him, a lazy voice called out: "Thought you'd be wearing an Indian feather at the very least. What are you trying to do? Outshine old St. Luc? Heard about it clear up at Fort Edwards. Best traditions of the Roman arena."

Ahrens turned to see Charteris, cool and unruffled as ever, cantering up on his sleek black. "Afternoon, Major. Where have you been lately?"

"Expending my genius on the lines of communication—which we're about to cut and go drifting down the river." He dismounted and fell into sleep with Ahrens, the black mincing daintily along at his elbow. "Have you heard the news?"

"News?" Ahrens snorted. "Is there any?" He thought of day after sweltering day slipping by with no word from Judith.

Charteris glanced about. "Here, let's shy off this way, off from the tents. This is about Barry St. Leger. Remember him?"

Ahrens nodded. "The fellow who is coming down the Mohawk to join us? Yes. Ought to be getting close."

"Never confuse 'ought' and 'is,' my boy. The Yankees had a cheesebox of a fort at the head of the Mohawk. Fort Stanwix, that's it. St. Leger sat down to besiege it weeks ago. By Gad, he's had to give up. Yes, sir, give up and go back to the St. Lawrence. Lost a lot of his men. As soon as he began his retreat, his Indians, his own Indians, hung on his flanks and butchered his troops. Looted all St. Leger's personal baggage. He had a few

Hesse-Hanau Jaegers with him. Thought you might have heard."

Ahrens whistled. "That means that two-thirds of the original plan are gone. We never were the major part of it—*that* was Howe. Now we've got to dive headlong into all the rebels that Howe and St. Leger might have been fighting."

"The Gods aren't smiling on Gentleman Johnny. Still, there's no cause for alarm." Charteris brushed the thought aside. "We've still got the best regiments in the British Army and your regiments are good. And an extremely competent commander."

Ahrens sadly examined a fresh slit that was starting across the knee of his white breeches. "If it's not treason, I'm tempted to question that last. Look at us. Took Ticonderoga on July fifth. This is September twelfth and where are we? We've barely covered thirty miles. That's a long time and a short distance. Since we reached the Hudson we've made just one move, which the rebels handled with a certain bucolic heartiness which I must say I found impressive, even if the staff remains unmoved."

Charteris yawned. "I'd call that a regrettable incident, no more. Why, our regiments—"

Ahrens fanned himself with his cocked hat. "I know. You're going to tell me again that the 21st fought at Killicrankie, Blenheim and Malplaquet, that the 20th was at Culloden and Fontenoy and Minden. But this is America and Bennington isn't Blenheim and Stark and the others aren't like Marshal Saxe. We're just blundering on, hoping that the rebels will one day fight the way we want them to."

Charteris clapped him on the shoulder. "You'll end your days in a straight-jacket. War's war. I can't see that Gentleman Johnny has made a single military mistake. I'll admit there have been mistakes, but only political ones and they're chargeable solely to a certain blasted Tory gentleman whose estates at the foot of Champlain

307

have been considerably improved by the road-making efforts of the British Army. Skene, as political adviser, has led Gentleman Johnny astray, made him see popular uprisings, great anti-rebel waves. Why shouldn't the General rely on him? Skene's of a good Scotch family, good school. Had a long service in our army. Knows this country, knows the people. I confess I was suspicious of him from the first, but that was only because that cowardly bastard Germaine liked him."

"You put everything on Skene?" asked Ahrens.

"Certainly. Kept Burgoyne thinking that the country was about to turn upside-down for us. That's why we delayed at Skenesboro—that and clearing roads through the Skene estates. That's why we've taken our time all along the line. That's why Baum and Breymann came to grief. Vast overconfidence in the Loyalist feeling. First and last, Skene's the rock we've split on. Now, mind you, if he'd been right our delay would be all to the good. D'you see? Why get your men killed if each day you expect to see Tories flocking to you? But from a military standpoint, could anything have been more smartly and energetically done than the pursuit from Ticonderoga? Gad, the army worked like a fine watch."

"It didn't give the rebel army a knockout, though."

"If you believe in Skene, it *was* knocked out. Well, it just makes the Albany road a little harder, that's all."

"Then, if it hadn't been for Skene, we might be in Albany now." Ahrens shook his head, watching a file of ragged Brunswickers stump dully past. "Well, I never did like Skene. He's a time-server." He began to grin. "Heard this story about him? When he built that big house by the lake, he brought his mother out from Scotland. Then a little while later he gave it out that she had gone back. Well, the rebels used his house a year ago. In the cellar they found the dried-up body of an old woman—just lying on the dirt floor. Seems she enjoyed an annuity whose wording provided that it run on 'so long as her body remained above ground.'"

Charteris slapped his knee. "So he's probably still touching the annuity, eh? Gad, that's good. Must tell Balcarres."

"Oh, I'm sure he knows it. Common talk down here. You ought to be round the camp more, not running off to Ticonderoga."

"Damned if you're not right. I'd my eye on something very choice in the lines. Don't notice 'em often. Infra dig. But this was really choice. French-Canadian and wore a flame-colored thing round her hair. Always singing that damned song, '*Pour mon drapeau je viens ici mourir.*' Sang with her eyes as much as with her voice." He rubbed his hands vigorously, tapped his spurred boot in the dirt. "What a shape! What fire! Heard her man had been killed. That's really what brought me down here, *entre nous.* What did I find? She'd gone and married herself to a sergeant in Breymann's corps. He can't speak French and she can't speak German. How the devil will they talk?"

Ahrens grinned. "Why should they?"

Charteris tilted his hat forward till the peak nearly touched the high bridge of his nose. "You're right, you're right. I'd have taken her if we'd both been deaf-mutes. Would now, only Gentleman Johnny is death on monkeying 'round the married lines once the knot's properly tied."

Ahrens snorted. "It's a comfort to know the army's morals are so well safe-guarded. I gather that such precautions don't extend to non-combatant branches—such as the Commissary Department."

Charteris wagged his head. "Don't forget the most important initials in military life—R.H.I.P.—Rank Hath Its Privileges.

"Not apt to have a chance to forget," laughed Ahrens. "So you begin crossing the river tomorrow?"

"By noon. The whole British contingent. You'll probably follow by the fifteenth, horse, foot and artillery."

"Horse?" asked Ahrens.

309

"Hadn't you heard?" said Charteris. "Somewhere they've laid hands on about thirty of the most lamentable bits of horse-flesh in the Americas, so thirty of the proud dragoons will at last vault into the saddle, probably to have the horses collapse beneath them. As soon as you've joined us on the west bank, we'll start moving south and, Gad, what a relief it will be!"

"Won't it?" said Ahrens mechanically. He was thinking of the deft silent men he had seen slip away through the night to dig for "the Polish feller."

The Clearings

THE red and blue mass of the army finally crossed to the west bank of the Hudson. Burgoyne waited a day, then reviewed the force. With field-music shrilling and thumping, the ragged regiments marched past their commander-in-chief, happy to be on the move once more. As they passed in review, they cheered him. Gentleman Johnny stood in his stirrups and shouted: "Britons never retreat!" Then the army settled back to its snail's pace. Three miles one day to Dovegat, delayed by halts to mend bridges which no one had thought to see to in advance. Three miles another day, with Burgoyne setting up his headquarters and Mrs. Lewis in the house of a rebel named Swords. The English troops lay in the thick woods that capped the bluffs above the river meadows. Their allies lay in the flats by the Hudson, whose current lapped and snuffled about the blunt noses of hundreds of bateaux which held every last shred of the army's supplies. Somewhere below—no one seemed to know just where—Gates lay behind Kosciusko's fortifications. By night and by day the roads to the east swarmed with ragged lines of men from a hundred New England towns. From the south and west the men of New York slipped on to swell Gates' force of Continentals and militia.

VII

The Clearings

"God's teeth, but it's cold!" Ahrens shivered in the woolly mist that rolled up the river valley, drew his single blanket higher about his neck and plumped his haversack in a despairing effort to find a soft spot for his head. He tried to settle himself for sleep again, but his body refused to relax, his mind seemed unnaturally alert. He gave up the struggle and stared wide-eyed at the thick throat of the twelve-pounder under which he had bedded down at the final halt. "What a climate!" he fumed. "Boiling days and now we freeze at night. Why can't I go back to sleep?"

He forced a yawn, stretched in a vain effort to relax his tired muscles. "Hope Mrs. Lewis finds old Swords' house to her liking. Damn her and her twenty carts of trappings! Shouldn't think *she'd* need many clothes. And I've sent all my things back to the base at Ticonderoga and sleep under a gun, just to save baggage space. Oh, yes, I wanted to march light and, anyway, most of my things were worn out, but at least I can preen myself and blast Mrs. Lewis and her carts. Wonder why I don't hear from Judith! Wish we'd get to Albany in a hurry. I'm sure to see her there. We'll have a military governor—Phillips most likely—and there'll be ways of finding out who comes into town and leaves." The thick spokes began to blur before his eyes. He settled his rather tousled brown head on his haversack. "When we get to

313

Albany! Three—five miles tomorrow, five the day after. Bet Burgoyne and Charteris and Breymann and the others are right. There just aren't any rebels—any rebels." He smiled vaguely. Sleep was sweeping over him in gentle waves. Suddenly he sat bolt upright in his blanket.

Away to the south a deep-voiced drum began to throb. The drummer was expert and turned off rolls and double-rolls with an occasional deft flam. Another took up the beat, thudded and muttered. These drums had a new tone, deeper and fuller than those Ahrens knew. Their sound seemed to well up from the thick river mist, from dark wooded tangle of ravines and broken ground to the south, to hang ominously in the dying night-air.

Ahrens rubbed his chin. "Where are they? Can't be more than three—well, four miles away."

The drums rustled on, menacing, sinister. There was a firmness, a disciplined purpose in each roll and flam, a challenge thrown out to the heavy Brunswickers, the Hanauers, the men from English shires who lay silent along this American river. A chill of foreboding began to play up and down Ahrens' spine. There was all the wild freedom of the ragged, surging militia of Bennington in those pulsations that rolled up from the dark south, the wild freedom linked to a grim purpose that meant discipline. The calm face of the old man at Hubbardton suddenly flashed into his mind, the waves of drab men fading through the light woods of the Hampshire Grants like a blown mist, the dark patrol below his rock the night he captured Aaron Drake. The images whirled about, blended, pulsed to the distant rustle of the Yankee drums off there in the narrow, foggy valley. The vision faded, changing to lean drummers, cross-straps straining, drums balanced surely on hard hips, while behind them innumerable lines of swift-moving men in homespun answered a roll-call that was resonant with Old Testament names.

314

He shook himself. "Something eerie in those blasted drums. Those aren't runaway farmers beating them, either. Gentleman Johnny, you'd better whistle up the reserve guns from the artillery-park if your intention's for Albany. It's a long march back to Ticonderoga."

The drums died away as the glow of false dawn turned the Hudson into a broad path of black and silver. Ahrens huddled in his blanket, plunged abruptly into a heavy sleep. Then his shoulder twitched. He grunted, moved his head a little. His shoulder twitched again, then he felt a light, steady pressure under his left ear. He rose slowly through long fathoms of sleep into a wavering consciousness. With an effort he forced his eyes open. A vague figure crouched on the other side of the wheel, something white glimmered in an outstretched hand.

"Oh, God Almighty!" groaned Ahrens. "Orders at this hour?" He took the paper, fumbled in his haversack for flint and steel, an odd candle-end. The vague figure shambled off through the mist. "You, orderly!" Ahrens called thickly. "Hold on! There may be an answer." The figure did not look around. Ahrens rubbed his eyes, staring. It moved away with a curious, floating gait, toeing in. A heavy musket was slung across its back. "Hell and death! That's no soldier! I wonder—" He hammered out a light.

The paper was thick and soft and its fold was secured with a little bead of sealing-wax. A greasy hand had blurred the writing on the outside, but by the flickering candle stub he could still read the broad-lead lines. "Lieutenant Kurt Ahrens, the Hesse-Hanau Company of Artillery." His heart leaped as he snapped off the wax. "Now, why the devil didn't that surly ape, Chipmunk, wait?" With hot fingers he flipped open the folds. His hands shook, his pulses pounded in his ears. "Perhaps she wants me to come to her. Perhaps she'll—" His eyes raced over the graceful, flowing script.

Kurt dear, this note is to keep a promise and to give you sad news. Abigail slipped away from me in the night. She must have been more conscious of the Indians than ever I guessed, for she faded rapidly from that day on. She hardly slept, she no longer knew me. Yesterday she fell into a troubled sleep. I was outside the wagon when I heard her shriek: "Father! Joel!" Joel, you know, was her husband. I ran to her, but she was unconscious and never moved or spoke again. We buried her under the big oak at the edge of the hollow. I keep wondering if there were something more that I could have done. And yet I'm afraid that my hope of the Albany doctor was largely to keep my own courage up. Could he have brought her soul back to life?

Now I shall push on to Albany. There is a wood-road that runs west of the armies and that I shall follow under the guidance of Chipmunk who insists on staying with me. It would help so much if I could see you. But I haven't the courage to say, "Come to me," nor to tell Chipmunk to wait for an answer. We may meet again, but we live in a tangled world that seems to have little pity on individuals. If we do not meet—then the thought of you will be a very precious thing to me. Oh, my love, do look to yourself in the hard days to come.

JUDITH

Ahrens mechanically blew out the candle-end, folded the paper with meticulous care, frowning over the matter of bringing the edges exactly together, taking great pains to follow the original creases. He unrolled his worn jacket, slipped the letter into an inner pocket, then arranged the garment, being very particular about turning back the sleeves. He looked dully out over the lightening meadows where a few blue figures were beginning to move uncertainly about. Over and over he said to himself: "I'd hoped she'd come. Why wouldn't she come?" Then he sat up. "Good God! How shall I

316

ever find her now? She's off for Albany. She may get there before we do—and then where will she go?" He pulled on his boots, scrambled out from under the shelter of the twelve-pounder shrugging into his jacket. He stared about the meadows. "Why don't we get started?" The drums began beating the reveille. Men stumbled from damp tents, stupid and heavy with sleep. By the river-bank he could see the street-mouth of the Hanau tents and Rentner routing laggards from the canvas shelters for the morning roll-call. Ahrens rubbed his chin, staring at the shifting forms. His eyes narrowed. "If we march today, I'll make 'em sling the drag-ropes over their shoulders instead of winding 'em round their waists. Might need 'em in a hurry." He walked rapidly off toward his men.

The column halted again opposite the mouth of a deep ravine which opened in the bluffs, now close to the river's edge. The bottom was scored by a sandy cart-path which strayed away to the northwest through the cleft. Ahrens leaned back against the off-wheel of the leading six-pounder, his elbows resting on the broad iron tire, one heel hooked through the heavy spokes. He pushed back his cocked hat from his damp forehead and watched the leading companies of the Rhetz regiment deploy across the brow of a hill ahead, over which the river-road traced its lazy course. A solitary dragoon cantered after the infantry, reined in his miserable horse on the sky-line and suddenly became an equestrian statue against the deep blue of the fall sky.

The air was warm and still and Ahrens could hear with startling clarity the slight hiss of the rope traces, the uneasy shifting of hooves as the drivers of the pieces dismounted and fussed about the harness. The cannoneers perched on broad trails, leaned on brass barrels idly chatting in the immemorial fashion of their kind on a halt. Their slow talk rippled on. "Wish Albany was just over the hill there." ... "Damn Albany. Wish it was

Hanau. If I was in Hanau now, I'd go down Darm-stadtstrasse to the Wild Man and make old Udo fill me a hundred dozen steins of beer." ... "Clout him with a rammer-staff, someone. Me, my mouth's full of wool right now." ... "I'll buy you a mug of spruce-beer in Albany, spruce-beer in a birch-bark mug." ... "Who said spruce-beer? By God, I'll feed him to the rebels. Spruce-beer, and my throat like a lime-kiln!" ... "I'd give a hogshead of Hanau beer for a pair of shoes. I'm walking on my toe-nails right now!" ... "Patch your shoes with salt-pork. It's too tough to eat. Bet the officers don't eat salt-pork!" ... "It's the commissaries. There's plenty of food, and the swine sell it to the English!" ... "By God, those lousy commissaries are so fat you could use their sweat for frying-grease!"

Away to the west, out of sight behind the high-wooded bluffs, a faint crackling sounded, a crackling like dry twigs in a slow fire. Heads lifted all along the column. "Hi! The English have stuck their foot into something. Listen to that!" There was a general nodding of cocked hats.

Ahrens took the bridle of his horse from the gunner who had been grazing the animal on the grassy strip by the river, slipped the lines under his arm and walked up the column, looking for the tough, gnome-like face of Captain Pausch. He found him in deep converse with Halvorsen, a Swedish officer of the Riedesel regiment whose men sprawled on the soft turf, chewing grass in bovine unconcern.

Pausch turned, his hard face wrinkling in a tight smile. "Come and join us. Captain Halvorsen and I have been expressing our admiration of the General—your friend, the English General, that is."

Ahrens laughed. "Good old Gentleman Johnny! What's the occasion?"

"Occasion? Why—oh, blast your thick head!" Pausch's horse, clumsy muzzle stretching toward an inaccessible tuft of grass, had planted a hoof squarely across the

Captain's instep. He shoved violently at his mount, rubbed his injured foot, swearing. "If our provisions ever run low, I'll take great pleasure in eating that God-damned camel. Why—as to the General—look what he's done!"

"What's he done?" asked Ahrens. "All I know is that we've been hanging along this road for three hours, and that the English have gone frolicking off out of sight up on the bluffs with their fifes playing *The World Turned Upside Down.* That's the advantage of not being on staff. You don't know what's happening and so you don't worry." He reached up to his saddle, tugged at the bulging flap of his pistol holster.

"Hear that?" Pausch cocked his worn head to the west. The crackling and snapping had swelled again. "May be a good choice, that tune they chose. Why, here's what he's done. He's split the army into three columns. Von Fraser's corps and most of Breymann's men are in the woods, three or four miles away across the plateau. Von Burgoyne—" Ahrens grinned at the "von" which the irreconcilable Pausch still insisted on tacking on to all non-Germanic names. "Von Burgoyne has taken most of the British regiments and steered a middle course—through the woods again. And he's left us down here along the river. When he thinks—*thinks*, mind you—that the three columns are abreast, we all start out together and—and—"

"And win the war," suggested Ahrens. Halvorsen smiled wryly.

Pausch nodded. "We win the war. Now—von Burgoyne doesn't know where the rebels are. By this time he is out of touch with his right column, and if he can see us, he's got an eye that can look right through trees and hills. The Baron up ahead there is listening for the three signal guns that will tell him that von Burgoyne has consulted a soothsayer and been told that the three columns are abreast. It's the only way von Burgoyne will know."

"That's not the worst." Halvorsen pointed north along the road. "Look there." Far away by the Swords house the lines of the reserve artillery-park showed black in the strong September sun. By the river the hundreds of laden bateaux shifted and jostled gently in the slow current. "There's all our food and all our ammunition. All of it. See the red coats by the house? A few companies of the 47th to guard them, and the Hesse-Hanau infantry to guard the 47th. Suppose Gates—that's the rebel's name, isn't it—well, suppose Gates just put out a holding-force against the English on the plateau and rushed us on the narrow road. He'd roll us into the river and capture every crumb of our stores. Then where'd the army be?"

Ahrens scraped a bit of caked mud from his horse's nigh forefoot. "Well, they say the Yankee prison-ships are no worse than the stone cells at Chambly where we put *our* prisoners."

Pausch shook his head. "Von Burgoyne's wrong, of course, to split his army. It shows he despises the rebels as soldiers. That's bad in principle, but the rebels haven't got the men to make a move like that, Halvorsen. Raw troops, raw troops."

"Now, Captain," said Ahrens, "that's what everyone said while I was with the staff. *But—*" he slapped the broad rump of his horse—"but also they used to talk about the rebel leaders. Burgoyne and the others knew 'em. Stark, Gates, St. Clair, Schuyler, Arnold—a lot of 'em. They'd served with 'em. Some of the rebel generals have fought in Europe, the rest fought against the French here."

"Well?" Pausch lifted his bushy eyebrows.

"Those men didn't serve alone. They had junior officers under 'em, they had sergeants and corporals and privates who've had long service in just this kind of fighting. They went back to their farms after the French were beaten, but they've come out again against us. I

320

saw a man at Bennington who wore cross-belts of the *Regiment de Rousillon*."

"Logic, logic," said Halvorsen, nodding his great blond head. "But that doesn't—"

From the tree-screened summit of the plateau a distant field-piece slammed once, twice, thrice, its echoes rumbling ominously down to the river-road, across the bright water and dying away among the trees of the flat east bank. Drums snapped and thudded up and down the column, men scrambled to their feet. "See you in Albany!" grinned Halvorsen.

"Albany?" Pausch swung himself into his saddle. "If you believe this young man you'd better ask him to pick you out a nice cell on a rebel prison-ship."

The thick column moved on down the river-road, Pausch riding beside Ahrens at the head of the Hesse-Hanau guns. As they reached the top of the rise where the Rhetz regiment had deployed earlier, a hot fury of small-arms fire broke out in the hidden west. Then field-pieces began to slam. Ahrens stared at the tree-shrouded heights. It was odd to think that while he rode safely along in the pleasant fall sunshine, hundreds of Englishmen a mile or so away were driving hard at some anonymous mass of rebels through woods and clearings, that hot lead was whistling and biting deep, that men were writhing on the ground, clutching ripped bellies, torn arms, or lying silent with shattered heads. He felt a sense of unreality, of detachment that made the roaring and slamming in the west an impersonal din like a hurricane, a thunderstorm, a blind force that had no direction, no feeling.

He looked ahead and saw that the road dipped and climbed another hill. The Rhetz companies, white facings sharp against the blue of their coats, were deploying along its crest, the solitary dragoon cantering up on their right to halt, immobile, on the sky-line. Hooves drummed under the trees arching over a dirt road that led off to the west. Pausch stood in his stirrups to stare at the galloping horseman. "Here's news! Geismar of the staff! Look! Riding up to the Baron!"

There was a wailing, "Ha-a-a-alt!" Ahrens threw up his hand. The column settled down for another wait.

The raging fire off in the woods mounted to new heights. Pausch and Ahrens dismounted, climbed onto a limber, craning their necks. In the faraway din twelve-pounders and six-pounders roared and slammed through the endless stinging rattle of musket and rifle. Pausch chuckled. "That'll do it, that'll do it!"

Ahrens shivered with suppressed excitement, his booted foot tapping on the lunette of the piece. The muskets raved on, but suddenly the artillery was silent. He gripped Pausch by the arm. "They've lost their guns, they've lost their guns! By God, this is Bennington all over!"

Pausch shook his head irritably. "Nonsense, nonsense! Driven the rebels back and now they're moving the guns up by hand."

Ahrens slapped his palms together. "Can't be that! The small-arms fire hasn't changed, except that it's spreading to the west. And if Burgoyne were advancing, we'd move." A twelve-pounder roared again. "Same place! I'm right. The rebels took 'em and now the British have recaptured them."

Pausch squinted. "By God, I believe you!" he said suddenly. "Rebels took 'em, but didn't have horses to drag 'em away or linstocks to fire 'em. Now they've been driven off. Listen! That proves it! Now the rebels have taken 'em again!" The guns were silent, the small-arms fire ebbed and grew fainter, then crashed out again.

Ahrens shifted his feet uneasily. "Nothing on our front?" He looked south. The Rhetz companies were still deployed evenly along the crest. The dragoon, carbine on thigh, sat his old horse like a statue. There was a sharp crack. The horse suddenly tossed his head violently. Then his front legs slowly folded under him. He

322

lurched, rolled on the ground, the dragoon stepping free of the stirrups, and facing to the southwest, carbine at ready. The Rhetz lines stiffened, all heads staring in the direction of the shot. Pausch snorted. "Hoped that might mean something for us. Just a skirmisher, though. See— the Rhetz men are settling down again and the dragoon's getting his saddle off. No target for 'em." He faced west again.

The sun began to dip in the sky. The long shadows of the column stretched gaunt and thin on the grass by the high banks of the Hudson. Two men of the 47th, white facings soiled, tramped north toward the piled stores by the Swords house. One of them looked at the waiting Brunswickers, sneered and called: "Bain't goin' to Bennin'ton, be you?" His companion snickered, then spat, shouted: "Dutch buggers!" in a deep North-country voice. The men in the column stared dully at them.

The firing died away again, then tore the still air in a mad crescendo. A twelve-pounder roared. "Got 'em back again," said Ahrens. "Hello, here's Geismar on another of his one-man races. Hi! What's happening?"

The head of the column boiled with activity. An aide rode up the crest, two of the Rhetz companies hastily formed into column, moved off down the wood-road at a smart pace. The Riedesel regiment swayed slowly forward, countermarched and swung off in their wake as the Baron himself galloped down the road toward the guns, yelling: "Captain Pausch! Captain Pausch! Two sixes to start at once! At once, I say! Pull 'em up ahead of my regiment. Keep close to the Rhetz companies!" He spun his horse about, whirled away after the vanishing blue and white coats of the Rhetz men.

Pausch gained his saddle in one leap. "Lieutenant Dufail! Stay here in command of the company!" He turned to Ahrens. "I'm going ahead with the Baron. You bring on the guns!" He spouted a torrent of oaths, beat his cocked hat about his horse's withers and pounded off down the road.

323

Ahrens' voice rattled down the column. "Lieutenant Dufail! I want a single-mount. What? I don't care where you get it. Dismount that blasted farrier. Corporal Rentner, take that horse! Stay by me! Attention!" He swept his arm in a great arc. Traces creaked, off down the wood-road, a long line of jerking, straining heads following him. Ahrens looked back, saw the two pieces, each trailed by an ammunition cart, bend round the corner, straighten out. He spurred his horse, jabbed the air above him with his hand. The gun-teams broke into a trot, jolted along the road past the slow-moving files of the Riedesel regiment where sweating men stared at the flashing barrels of the six-pounders.

At the foot of a steep hill Ahrens broke the gait to a walk, mounted the crest, swung into a trot again. Far ahead he could see the rear files of the Rhetz companies and, beyond them, high trees in whose branches heavy smoke eddied sluggishly over a hidden inferno of musket and cannon. A wild figure galloped down the infantry column thrashing the air with a heavy hat. "Sing, by God! Louder! Like an army! Make 'em think you're a hundred thousand!" The horse pivoted on nimble feet, raced back to the head. The Baron's great voice roared on: "You drummers! Beat those drums, flay 'em, stave the heads in! Beat 'em, beat 'em, beat 'em!" The banging and crashing swelled and swelled in some hidden spot in the west, but above it the driving beat of the hymn rolled back to the straining Hanau guners.

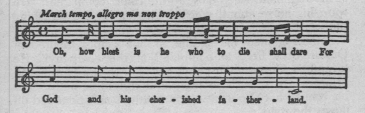

March tempo, allegro ma non troppo

Oh, how blest is he who to die shall dare For
God and his cher-ished fa-ther-land.

"Sing! Shout!" stormed the Baron. The voices roared on:

"All shall honor the man who was true unto death,
For God and his native land who fell;
Who a hero's blood for his freedom's good,
For God and for his country gave,
Sleepeth sweet in the grave."

The road fell away into a deep ravine, scattered sunshine glinting on its swampy bottom. The infantry slithered down the slope, toiled up the high bank. Ahrens reined in, seeing in his imagination guns mired to the hubs in the marshy bottom, exhausted horses floundering. To the right he saw a stumpy figure in blue and red waving a frantic arm by a rude bridge of logs. Ahrens turned in his saddle. "Corporal Rentner, take charge!" Then he galloped his sweating horse diagonally down the slope to the log bridge where Pausch roared and shouted.

"Can you bring the guns down here?" Pausch yelled. He was not six feet from Ahrens but the roaring in the west had swelled to a furious blast.

Ahrens looked back at the tracks his mount had made. The hoof-prints bit clean and sharp into the bank. Abruptly he nodded. "Got to. They'll mire beyond hope if we go straight down. It's our only chance."

His horse flew up the soft bank, clods flying from pounding hooves. "Unsling your drag-ropes! All hands on the first piece, all hands! Drivers! Down the slope, one piece at a time. Slant off along the slope toward the log bridge. Cannoneers, lash your drag-ropes to the nigh side and pull like hell! If a piece turns over we're lost and there's nothing but you and your ropes to keep 'em from turning. Smart, now!"

The lead horse of the first piece swung gingerly out from the road, pawing ahead with cautious feet like a cat in the snow. The cannoneers dug their feet into the soft ground, tugged and strained against the force of gravity that sought to tear the heavy gun away from them, sent it rolling down to the glimmering swamp at the bottom. Step by step the horses crawled along, drivers tense in the saddles. Once the off-wheel jarred on a rock, the piece teetered crazily, fighting the men, who lay back against the slope, crimson-faced, drag-ropes searing their tough palms. A blue and red figure raced past Ahrens, jammed its shoulder against the outer side of the lower wheel, feet digging into the ground, veins straining on a solid, sweating neck.

Ahrens yelled: "Get out of there, Rentner, get out! My God, if the piece rolls—" The heavy gun balanced, then its upmost wheel thudded into the ground. Rentner trotted away, wiping his face. Ahrens stared after him as the horses suddenly felt level ground under their feet, began to trot briskly. He heard Pausch yell: "Across the bridge! Pull up on the other side and wait. Bring on the others!"

One by one the other vehicles were eased along the scarred slope of the ravine to the log-bridge. Pausch danced among them. "Who was that madman who jumped under the wheel of the first piece? Who was he? I want his name. The Elector shall hear of him. By God, he's a soldier, he's—he's a gunner! Now—bring 'em on, Lieutenant!" Pausch's purple face appeared like a jack-in-the-box over his saddle, a booted leg swung and his horse shot up the slope. Over his shoulder he bellowed: "Hear that hell up ahead? They need us!"

Ahrens' shout cut through the din. "Drag-ropes again! Cannoneers on the wheels if you can't hook your ropes on. Every man! Oh—thank God!" Red coats flashed at the top of the slope, a boiling mass of British infantry poured on past the horses, laid shoulders against the piece, joined with the Hanauers in shoving, pulling, pushing. Officers and men were sweating together. A gray-haired captain of the 9th tugged at the end of Ott's

326

drag-rope, an ensign pushed at the broad axle with a private of the 20th.

Musketry crashed in a solid volley close by. Ahrens shouted: "That's Rhetz! They're in action. Get that first piece moving! Rentner! Gallop up ahead and take a look at the ground!"

The first piece started its heavy crawl, hooves digging frantically, blue jackets and red straining together. The ammunition cart followed, then the second piece. Ahrens' horse, heaving like a bellows, scrambled upward, raced out onto the level. The air was dim with smoke that bit pungently at eyes and nostrils, blurred the late sunshine filtering down through thinning trees. Somewhere up ahead Pausch was roaring: "Come on! Come on!"

A solid figure stepped from the shelter of a tree. "Best field of fire here, sir!" said Rentner hoarsely.

"Good lad, Rentner! Can we maneuver?"

"Any side, sir!"

Ahrens turned back toward the straining gun teams, cut his arm hard across his body, pointing up the ill-marked trail that led away through the trees. Farther down the road Pausch appeared. "You're to go between the 9th and the 21st, the 9th and the 21st." His voice rolled on ahead of his horse's hooves. "What the devil are you pulling off there for?"

Ahrens looked down at Rentner. The latter nodded. "That's what he told me, sir. There they are, yellow facings and blue facings." Ahrens faced the Captain. "We're right, sir. I've had this reconnoitered."

"But what field of fire, what range?"

"Field of fire excellent, sir. Range—pistol-shot."

"Pistol-shot, pistol-shot? How d'you know?"

Rentner held out his hat. There was a neat bullet-hole in the crown. "I've been to see, sir."

Pausch waved his arms. "Take 'em in, take 'em in!"

Walking in front of the lead horse through the trees was like walking in a dream, Ahrens thought. There was no sound in the whole world, not a footfall, the beat of a hoof or the rumble of a wheel—nothing but one gigantic, hellish din that sucked all other noises into itself, engulfed them, stifled them. Smoke drifted thicker and thicker and the westering sun shone with a sickly yellow tinge, unreal, a nightmare light. Something rapped hollowly against a tall tree, a severed branch hung low. The rapping was repeated, increased. The men plodding beside the guns looked up, unspoken questions in their eyes. Another bullet splashed against a rock, others sent clusters of leaves drifting down in lazy spirals.

Ahrens squinted through the smoke. The trees were thinning more and more. He caught a hint of vague shifting figures ahead. Then he suddenly stepped out into a broad clearing filled with ragged lines of men in red whose desperate, blackened faces were staring south as they fumbled in their cartridge boxes.

The clearing was a good four hundred yards across and more than that in length and its floor of trampled grass was littered with sprawling forms in red. In front of Ahrens the yellow facings of the 9th loomed through drifting smoke and beyond them to the right he could just make out the blue of the 21st, woefully thin companies who stood among their own dead and drove their rammers into their muskets with mechanical perfection. On either flank, close to the wooded edges, the 20th and the 62nd were dim figures, firing into a smoke cloud.

Ahrens wheeled about. "Unlimber! Advance by dragropes!" His feet were like lead, his legs light and purposeless and he ran forward into the gap between the two regiments, staring at the thick welter of bodies that sprawled uselessly. A lieutenant, wild-eyed and blackened like a fiend, sprang at him, tore off his shoulderknot. "It's suicide, it's suicide! I'm the last officer in my company. They climb the trees and shoot us." His voice was thin and reedy, his hand shook as he hurled the heavy knot into the smoke. Then he darted back to his men.

The first piece trundled into place, the second was wheeled up beside it. Ahrens roared: "Load with grape!" and found his voice echoing oddly in a sudden hush. His men leaped about the muzzles, rammers drove into the barrels with a slick, metallic sound, startling in the stillness.

Then a weird note gurgled among the distant trees, a liquid sound that gobbled and quavered. From a dozen different points, it was taken up, a senseless, idiot gibbering. Ahrens' eyes widened. "What the devil is that?" he muttered. On the flank of the 9th a thickset sergeant groaned, a sound that seemed to be wrenched out of him. "It's them bloody buckskins again. They've shot the Major and the Captain. Listen at it—God-damned sound, drives me fair mad. They won't close with us. Just fire and break and gobble and come on again. S'elp me God, I can't face 'em again!"

The smoke drifted away. Ahrens saw dark bunches high in the trees, bunches that flashed out a strange glitter as they moved in the sun. A rifle cracked. Ott dropped his linstock, staggered and fell across the trail. "Gone?" Ahrens could hardly realize that it was his voice, speaking so low and even. "Move him off, poor lad. Meusel, take the linstock. And hold your fire, both pieces, till you see my arm drop."

Again the woods filled with the unearthly gobbling, closer this time. A young voice, high with excitement, squealed: "It's Morgan again!" The voice rose still higher. "Here they come!" The distant woods vomited out low-running men in buckskin shirts and fur caps who trailed long rifles after them. Then the brown lines sank to the ground, welled out smoke in ripping crashes. The sergeant on the flank of the 9th tumbled heavily, clawing at a bright jet that gushed out over his yellow collar. The line of the 9th wavered, men staggering, falling. Ahrens turned to his gunners, folding his arms to keep his hands from shaking. The hot wind of a bullet had burned across his cheek. "Hold your fire till they

329

rush," he said. Then he thought how odd it was that his voice wouldn't rise beyond that low pitch. A tall man, stretched on the grass behind the flank company, rolled slowly from side to side, making a high thin noise, almost as though he were humming to himself, the sound singing out from shattered, bloody jaws.

The front of the 9th suddenly flamed and roared. Ahrens held up an arm, dropped it. His pieces crashed and he saw long rifles toss in the air through the smoke, saw fringed shirts whirl and fall. A new roaring burst forth on his left, and the Baron's voice soared above the musketry, shrieking: "Sing! Shout! Beat those drums!"

The woods spilled out thin lines of men in homespun, white cross-belts neat over open-throated shirts, men who moved at a quick, light trot to prolong the right of the buckskins. Ahrens' guns crashed again and again. Far away on his left he could see blue uniforms coming into the clearing, could hear pounding drums as the Baron brought on his fresh troops who began to lap around the flank of the men from the woods.

A hand fell on Ahrens' collar, swung him about. "There are two English guns off on the left." Pausch's face was wild and streaked with sweat, his stock rode high about his ears. "They're there by that little cabin and not a soul to man 'em. Take six men and get 'em going. The rebels are getting ready to rush the 20th. I'll stay here!" His heavy hand pounded down between Ahrens' shoulder-blades.

Rentner, Pach, Schmidt, Heisse and two others ran behind Ahrens over the slippery grass, bent over like men in a heavy rain. The air was full of sharp, hissing, whining noises and thick smoke drifted back from the crumbling regiments who fired, loaded and fired. The two pieces shone in the sun in front of the cabin on the right flank of the 20th, but their crews lay in heavy heaps of blue and red, red-spattered on the stump-studded ground. "Plenty of ammunition stacked here! Grape again! Here they are!"

The guns blazed at the swift-moving lines, which were blotted out in the drifting smoke. In the ranks of the 20th, men plunged and pitched. The survivors closed up silently, firing. A freshening wind tore the smoke-pall to shreds. Ahrens saw the rebel lines falling back to the shelter of the woods, brown-coated men who moved unhurriedly, companies halting in their retreat to turn and fire as their neighbors slipped away. Twice more Ahrens' guns blazed and grape-shot rattled harshly among the trees. "Cease fire! Swab out the bore! 'Count your rounds, Rentner, and be ready for the next rush."

A blue and red heap in the grass stirred, rolled over. A rich voice that seemed on the verge of breaking out in a chuckle said: "Glory be to God, and it's Lieutenant Ahrens! It's a fine battle we're having this day and ain't the Yankees darlin's? They fight near as good as if they were Irish, God keep 'em."

Ahrens knelt by the black-haired giant who smiled seraphically up at him. "You're not hit badly?"

"A devil of a man in a leather shirt climbed a tree and threw lead at me. Caught me below the knee, may hell roast him, and when I'm standing I'm falling down for the pain of it, so I try to crawl away and the same devil's spawn blows a hole in the skirt of my jacket. So I tells myself: 'Shawn, it's here he wants you to stay,' so I lie here and tell the boys what to do till there's none of 'em left to tell, may they rest in peace for brave gunners. None left but me and young Hadden and he's gone to find more men after tying a fine bandage on me that's given me a leg of fire. You'd not be having a drop of rum on you, Lieutenant?"

Ahrens gave him his flask. O'Callaghan drank deeply. "'Tis the breath of life flowin' back into my soul," he said. "Now you'll be keeping your eye out for Yankees. There's nothin' I can tell you to do, for the devils shoot better dead than we shoot livin' and there's a matter of forty of my lads lyin' stiff in the sun."

Ahrens nodded. "Just serve the pieces and take what they send you."

O'Callaghan turned, gritted his teeth. "This leg of fire! Yes, and a man's work it is. But they're slacking and I've not seen the little banshee, Arnold, whipping his men on. I'm thinking maybe he's hit and more's the pity. It's a grand little man. Hah! And will you be listening to that!"

The rifle-fire that had been incessant off on the right now swelled all along the line. Ahrens sprang to his feet. "Solid-shot among those trees! Land a few ricochets where they're thickest! Grape, if they rush us again!" The pieces slammed, the gunners serving them like dead-eyed sweating automata. Long-range bullets rapped against the wooden trails, dug various spurts in the ground.

Suddenly the melting right flank of the 20th wavered, sagged. A few men staggered out of line, heads shielded by bent arms. Then hooves drummed in the wood-road and out from the shadow of the trees rode Gentleman Johnny, flashing in scarlet and white, a cluster of white-faced officers close behind him. Burgoyne's carefully powdered head shone in the late sun as he swept off his hat, his rich voice boomed out: "Well done, the 20th! Lads, I'm proud of you!"

The ranks stiffened, incredulous eyes stared from blackened faces. Burgoyne rode on, reined in his horse by the shaken right flank and looked calmly across the torn field to the woods where brown masses of the Yankees were forming. A murmur ran through the 20th, swelled. A wild-eyed private dragged himself over the ground, a blood-drenched leg trailing stiffly through the grass. He croaked: " 'Ere, mate, give us a hand up. It's old Gentleman Johnny. 'Elp me back into line. It's Gentleman Johnny!" Wounded men staggered to their feet, shouting: "It's Gentleman Johnny himself! Good old Gentleman Johnny! *'E'll* see us through!"

Ahrens heard a scrambling behind him. O'Callaghan

heaved his vast bulk forward, clawed at the trail of the second piece, and levered himself upright, staring at the smiling man on the sleek horse, at the knot of riders behind him. The ensign threw up a heavy arm. "You 20th! You'll be waitin' for a gunner to cheer the man? Where's your voices?"

Gentleman Johnny bowed courteously at the spent men who suddenly found themselves yelling wildly, waving their hats. Ahrens' guns slammed in union, then a dead hush settled over the front of the 20th. In the stillness, Burgoyne gravely lifted his head. "Now then, lads, here they come." He looked over his shoulder, spoke quietly: "A touch of grape, gentlemen, if you please." Then he recognized Ahrens, waved a hand. "Glad to have you here, my boy. The 20th appreciates smart gunnery." He folded his hands on his pommel again, turned his fine eyes to the front.

"Grape! Grape!" shouted Ahrens. He wiped the sweat from his eyes with a moist hand. "A touch of grape, if you please!" he muttered. "Might have been asking me to deal a hand at loo!" He raised his voice. "Trail a bit to the left, Rentner, a bit to the left! Now!" He dropped his arm, the pieces crashed.

The men in brown were slowly working out from the edge of the woods, skilfully using what cover there was, firing with stinging effect. Ahrens saw Burgoyne's hat suddenly fly in the air, saw a jagged rent appear in the fullness of his jacket. The General only bent over, gentled his horse, shouted something to the infantry that Ahrens could not hear.

The guns crashed and stunned, the infantry fired in steadier volleys. Then among the trees on the left blue coats showed darkly, fresh muskets opened fire on the exposed right flank of the rebels. Gentleman Johnny nodded calmly, cried in his full voice: "The Riedesel regiment, and very prettily timed!" The line of brown men checked, halted, then fell back slowly and in good order, firing as they retreated to the shelter of the

333

woods. Burgoyne's voice rolled out again: "You see, gentlemen—there's a fine object lesson for us. The Yankees neglected to cover their right flank and our Brunswick friends had no trouble in crumpling it up." He gathered his horse, signaled his staff and galloped off down the wood-road.

Firing slowly died away in the darkening woods, which grew still except for an uneasy stirring and the occasional echoing, imbecile gobbling that Ahrens had heard in front of the 9th. He drew a damp cuff across his forehead and sank down on the broad float of the trail, feeling desperately weak and empty. His men sprawled on the ground or rested their backs against the high wheels of the pieces, legs stretched out before them. The red ranks of the 20th began to waver and one by one the infantrymen sank to the ground, panting. Ahrens watched them dully, saw some men, faces flushed an angry feathery red, lying quietly with out-flung limbs, while others, deadly white, heaved themselves up on trembling knees, gagging and vomiting. The hush was unearthly.

Then far away by the wreck of the 62nd a single voice lifted, quavering. "Water! Water, water!" The cry was taken up, spread like gun-fire along a front. "Water, water, water! Oh, God! Water!" An English gunner, his abdomen a tangle of bloody rags, slowly levered himself up on his elbows near the second piece. His eyes bulged vacantly, his mouth quivered like a fish's gills. Then a gush of black blood welled out from between his caked lips. His elbows gave way, he twitched and lay still. Ahrens shuddered, then struck his knees, sprang up. "On your feet, lads! Swab out the bores, restack the ammunition. Can't tell what'll happen now. May move after the rebels. When you're done, give a hand to some of these fellows lying about here, but if they're shot in the belly, for God's sake don't give 'em water no matter how much they may shout." The men scrambled stiffly to their feet, moved toward the muzzles of the guns.

Ahrens watched them. "Pursuit? With *these* troops? Chase the rebels in dark woods?" He looked across at the tangled bodies of the 20th, saw a surgeon and two surgeon's mates moving slowly among them. Behind him O'Callaghan's singing voice complained: "And if I come to lay my hands on that monkey of a Hadden, I'll be after windin' this bandage round his neck as tight as he twisted it on my knee."

Ahrens turned. A short fat man was kneeling by the huge ensign, adjusting a fresh bandage about the Irishman's thick calf. O'Callaghan went on: "May the patron saint of gunners, and that's Saint Barbara, bless you, Doctor. The leg's like a yearling colt's. And now you might be lookin' after my Hessian friends here. I doubt any of ours out there are needin' your offices. Hope is past over them. Now you'll be fetchin' me that musket over there, that has no owner." He struggled to his feet, wedged the musket under his arm like a crutch and waved his free hand at Ahrens. "This is the Hessian boy, though you'd not be thinkin' it, Doctor, who kept me alive for your knives and probes with a bit of rum. Now it's back to camp I go, and if I'm not up and about for the next scuffle with that little leprechaun of an Arnold, with my bare hands I work over your skull till it's soft as an overboiled Wexford potato!"

The doctor chuckled, reached up to pat the giant's thick shoulder. "If you move an eyelash before I look at the leg again, I'll bring Arnold in and let him stamp on your shin-bone—just over the bandage. Your men all right, Lieutenant?"

"Nothing that food and sleep won't heal, thanks," said Ahrens. Then he began to sniff. There was something in the air that brought vividly to his mind the memory of an intolerable agony in his wrist, of a red, sinewy neck straining against the slow pressure of his crooked arm and elbow. O'Callaghan gave a sharp howl. "Look at the red snakes! Spend five hours, they do, daubin' themselves with war-paint and then run home at the first shot. And now here they come that it's all over!"

Dark shapes, reptile, inhuman, were flitting stealthily past the line of battered regiments. In the half-light, Ahrens saw an Indian bend over, place a moccasined foot on the neck of a dark-clad body. Long fingers twined in the matted hair, wrenched the head around. Then metal gleamed dully, the Indian tugged, whooped hideously and held something high in air. Other whoops answered him. Skulking shapes glided far away by the edge of the woods, in the middle distance. A long file of men, shovels over their shoulders, moved past the guns at a trot. O'Callaghan waved a huge arm. "It's the glory of war you're seein'. Surgeons, burying-squads and scalpin'-knives."

Ahrens nodded. "The full flavor of romance. It's— What's the matter?"

O'Callaghan let out a whinnying cry that rose to a thin shriek. "The skulkin' red bastards! Look, look, look! And the poor devil still breathin'! Oh, you stinkin' spawn of hell! The good God and his saints give me my leg back and I'll be rippin' your dirty heart out with my own hands." He thumped the muzzle of his musket-crutch frantically on the ground, hopping about with blazing eyes.

The field swam before Ahrens' eyes, then rocked back to steadiness. In the dusk, by a broad stump, an Indian bent low over a body, one foot firm on the neck. Ahrens saw the naked, coppery arm slowly twist the head, fingers deep in damp hair. A knife glittered. Feebly an arm rose, wavered, clawed futilely at the red wrist.

Ahrens staggered. O'Callaghan's great hand whacked hard on his shoulder. "Alive, I tell you, and it's one of ours! God curse the tricky light! Alive! And it's this minute I'm seein' the yellow collar to the jacket." He roared and capered. "Oh, for a sound leg and I'd tear the head from his shoulders with my bare hands, rip out his stinkin' heart!"

336

Ahrens' long legs carried him to the neatly stacked carbines of his squad in one bound. He knelt by the first piece, heedless of the staring eyes of his men, brought his sights on the crouching figure. The Indian seemed to be annoyed by the fluttering hand that struck and struck at his wrist. He straightened his torso, drew a tomahawk from his belt with a swift, smooth gesture. Ahrens pulled the trigger of his carbine. Dirt spurted close by the Indian, who started, sprang back, then scuttered away through the chill dusk.

Ahrens pounded the butt of the carbine on the ground. "Missed him, missed him," he snarled at himself. "A child's shot." Wearily he rose, sent his men out to bring in the infantryman.

A tall, thin man, yellow facings on his jacket, trotted past. Ahrens flung out a long arm. "Where are you going? To your regiment? The 20th? Tell your commanding officer that he'd better search for his wounded. The Indians are scalping everyone they find, no matter what the uniform. Tell him he'd better send a runner to the other regiments to warn them."

The man stared at him, saluted and ran off through the clearing. Ahrens leaned against a gun-wheel, waiting for Captain Pausch and fresh orders. He thought that Judith must be well on toward Albany, lurching over her safe western road.

Ahrens shivered in the dank night air that filled the North Branch ravine and looked with little relish on his companion who huddled in a greasy blanket and moved a slow finger over the wavy lines of Ahrens' neat map. The shaven head was crowned with a scalp-lock, but the hair was a coarse brown. The face was painted and smeared, but the nose was a broad snub and the palm of the hand that hovered over the paper sheet by the guttering candle-end showed a dirty white.

"Well?" said Ahrens.

The man raised his head, wiped his grimy hands on

337

the shiny knees of his Indian leggings. "There ain't no other road beyond here. It's just like I said, here on the map. See? This trace runs past Freeman's Farm—that's the little cabin in the clearing near where the 20th was today—and heads northwest. Then it dies, like, off in the woods. And they ain't *no* road that runs south. Go west from the farm a hundred miles and you won't find no other."

Ahrens made an impatient gesture. "The road I heard of was west of the armies, and ran south to Albany."

The man shook his head. "They ain't no sich. I hunted the woods near thirty year, knew 'em before Old Freeman came and cut his big clearin'. A body comin' down from the north *might* hit into this little trace, but that would lead right plumb through Freeman's place, right where I was when you hollered at me, and on to the river-road."

Ahrens set his jaws. Judith's note had been explicit. "A road to the west of the armies." Now this masquerading Tory swore, and the map bore him out, that there was no road other than the one through Freeman's Farm. He sighed, handed the man a flat bottle, which was stowed away in some mysterious fold of the greasy blanket.

"Think the rebels will attack again?" he asked, staring at the incongruity of the brown scalp-lock.

"Might. They got that feller Arnold an' he's liable to do most anything. Got some good men—Glover an' Poore an' Cilley an' Morgan. Wasn't no one leadin' 'em at the end, though, else we'd all have our throats cut. Mostly Massachusetts men and God how I hate 'em! I'm a Johnson man from the Mohawk."

"Do many of you dress like that?"

"Most. There ain't a settler nowhere that ain't scared of an Indian, so we dress like 'em an' raid with 'em. Guess I got near as many scalps as that Wyandot chief that was killed this afternoon. Every rebel scalp I get, I feel that much easier. One less bastard."

Ahrens repressed a shudder. The man went on. "Won't

be so easy now. Gettin' near bigger towns. Little cabins and farms, lonely ones. That's where the scalps are. Guess most of my lot'll pull foot when you get near Albany!" He looked at Ahrens, then added, "*If* you get near Albany."

"Do many of the rebels dress like Indians?"

"They dasn't, they're so scared of a real Indian. I'm different. I'm a Johnson man. Brother was with Sillinger."

"With whom?"

"Sillinger, that one that tried to take Stanwix."

"Oh—St. Leger?"

"Call it how you like. That's the feller." The man rose in the little canvas shelter. "Thanks for the rum."

"Just a minute," said Ahrens. "Heard a damn noise in the clearing today—sort of a gobble. What was it?"

The Tory scratched his head. "Gobble? Oh. Guess that was Morgan. Big Pennsylvania Irishman. Best ranger in America and would be with us, only a lobster-back officer had him flogged when Morgan was drivin' mules with Braddock's expedition back in '55."

"Well, what about that noise?"

"Turkey-call. Made of birch-bark. Morgan uses it like Fraser'd use a drum. Rally his men, let 'em know where he is. They were the fellers in the buckskin that blasted the 62nd. Killed a sight of officers all over the field. Use Kentucky rifles an' they ain't a man that can't shoot the whiskers off a field-mouse at a hundred yards. That all you wanted?" He wound his blanket tighter about him, stepped out into the raw night.

Ahrens folded his map, slipped it carefully back into its case. Then he blew out his candle-stub and stretched out on his bed of pine-boughs. He was stunned by the Tory's confirmation of his Holster Atlas. He stared up at his damp canvas roof, property of some Brunswicker now stiffening in the ghastly clearing by Freeman's cabin. A road to the west of the armies. But there was no road to the west. Slowly he pieced together Judith's reasoning. "She wanted to skirt the armies and make for Albany. Oh, the devil! I see it now! She's never watched an army on the march. She thought of the whole lot of us moving in single file along that river-road. Then she must have set out down that very trace that runs through Freeman's place. She'd figure that would be four or five miles away from the river and safe for her. Oh, God Almighty! She might have driven right into that battle! How'll I ever—what's that?"

A high-pitched howling, full-throated almost musical, soared up from the west, mounted, swelled till it seemed that a hundred furry throats were joining in. Ahrens swore. "Blast this war! Nothing but noises! First the axes in the forest, then the muskets in the night, that damned gobble of Morgan's today and now every dog in camp gives tongue. Must be the cold air."

Masked in the heavy morning mist, Burgoyne's army formed in a thick line that stretched from the clearings west of Freeman's Farm to the edge of the bluffs close over the river. By the off-wheel of the first piece, Ahrens knelt in the grass, his gunners crouching in a dim circle about him. He scratched quick diagrams with a bit of twig on a bare patch of ground. "Is that clear? I think it will help if you take your posts that way when the guns are moved by hand. And another thing—we were a bit slow in loading yesterday. When we go into action to-day, space yourselves this way—" Again his stick scrabbled in the dirt. "You'll save a good deal of time, particularly in the handling of the cartridges." He dusted off his hands. "Blast this fog! Can't see a thing. As for today, we've a new assignment. The General saw your work by the Freeman cottage yesterday and liked it. We're independent of the rest of the guns and must expect to be thrown about where we're most needed. You take orders only from me, and I take them only from the General himself or from General Phillips. 9th is here on our right, the 21st on our left and beyond that all I know is that as soon as the fog lifts, Fraser will throw the advance corps against the rebel works—wherever they may be. Any questions? Good. Everyone will be watching us today—including the rebels."

The men fell back to their posts, moving briskly. Ahrens stared at the thick white wall ahead of him, an almost tangible opaque mass that swallowed up all the horses of the gun-team except the one closest to the limber. He cursed the fog again, but deep within himself he exulted. His guns had been picked by Burgoyne out of the whole army, detached for use wherever well-served guns might be needed in a hurry. No telling where such duties might lead. He walked up and down by the piece, slapping his hands, watching the dim bulk of the 9th, which showed faintly through the fog on the right, punctuated with a few scattered moments of real terror. He looked over at the 9th again, stared. "Where the devil has the 9th gone?" he muttered. He stared again, then shouted: "Rentner! Did you see the 9th move out?"

A shape blurred in the mist, a fog-muffled voice answered: "No, sir! Nor the 21st."

The veiled masses on the right and left had vanished. Then the fog wavered again, filled with moving shapes sifting vaguely toward him. "Hi! What's this?" he shouted. "Cannoneers! Posts!" The figures became clearer. He whistled with relief as he saw the familiar round skull-caps of the British infantry. Then he frowned. "What the devil are they doing, parading about in the fog? They moved up and then they counter-marched." Still the 9th came on, passed their original post, pressed on toward the rear. Ahrens ran up to a young lieutenant, a slim boy with a drawn, haggard face. "What's happening?"

The boy threw up his arms. "Don't ask me. Just had orders the whole attack is off. We're to return to camp." From the swinging files in the mist a hoarse voice muttered: "And a good thing, too. Yesterday was enough!" The tone was sullen, lifeless. Another voice muttered:

341

"Enough of that bloody gobble-gobble. Fair sours my grog on me."

Ahrens turned on his heel. "Might have passed the order on to us. We'd look pretty sitting here in the open if the fog lifted and showed those blasted brown-coats moving down on us. Damnation! My own command and a free hand." He walked heavily back to his guns, ordered a countermarch and plodded dully back to camp in the wake of the second piece.

The Redoubt

A RUNNER from the south slipped through the Yankee lines, brought word that down in New York Clinton was stirring, planning a move against the Highlands of the Hudson. Frantically Burgoyne entrenched, built a solid chain of works across the bluffs, across the meadows and on to the river's edge. There was a strong redoubt west of Freeman's Farm, manned by Brunswickers under Breymann. Another rose in front of the farm itself, commanded by the young Earl of Balcarres. A third, strongest of all, frowned over the Hudson where the bateaux swung and rocked in Wilbur's Basin.

The terrain in front of the works was a welter of broken ground, huge trees and scrubby undergrowth at which European eyes stared in vain. Small Yankee patrols burst on their outposts by day. By night the rustling gloom spat red.

South of the haunted belt of scrub and forest, Gates sat motionless, intriguing, quarreling, whispering against Arnold, against Lincoln, but ventured no move against the shaken invaders.

VIII

The Redoubt

OBLIVIOUS to the steady autumn drizzle, Ahrens sat on a rough chair in his canvas shelter, close by the permanent post of his pieces on the right flank of the 9th, and jabbed viciously at his boot with an awl from which waxed thread dangled. He screwed up his eyes, held his breath. The patch was just in place now, would cover that gaping split across his instep. Carefully he drew the thread tight, knotted it, then slipped the boot on his right foot, twisting his ankle from side to side to be sure that the patch would not chafe. There was a low chuckle outside, a voice drawled: "Charming scene of domesticity!"

Ahrens looked up, saw Charteris scrambling up the slippery path that led from the North Branch ravine. "Hello, Major! Thought you were off to Ticonderoga on some special mission."

Charteris eased his long frame under the sodden canvas, threw off his oilskin cape. "So did I. Blasted rebels had other ideas."

Ahrens slipped off his boot, worried at a loose end of thread. "Rebels? *North* of us? I didn't know there were any. There are too many in those woods to the south to suit me."

Charteris laughed. "Nor did I know—nor Gentleman Johnny. Not sure he quite believes me now. But there they are. Need a company to convoy one small letter as

345

far as Fort Edward. Country's alive with 'em. Lincoln's men, Warner's men, God knows whose men."

"What did the General say?"

Charteris smiled sourly. "Oh, asked our Tory friend Skene and the blasted fool said they were Loyalists, that I'd misunderstood their signs. What kind of a sign is it when a God-damned farmer shoots your hat off your head and another shoots it out of your hand when you try to pick it up?"

Ahrens reached into the dark recesses of his tent. "You need a bit of rum, Major." He rolled a small keg out onto the dirt floor.

"Rum! Now, where in the devil's name did you get that?" Charteris examined the rough staves. "No brand. Hence not from His Majesty's stores. Why, blast it, I had to pay a damned sutler more than a pound for most inferior gin—a pound for one bottle that hardly wet my throat." He took the mug that Ahrens held out, drank deeply. Then he exhaled noisily. "No water in that!" He wiped his eyes. "A keg of that and I'd go to Ticonderoga alone and then south all the way to New York. Where'd you get it?"

" 'Procured locally,' as the regulations euphemistically state. But look here, Major, what's happening here? We had a small collision with the rebels, then began to dig. We've been here ever since, eating up our last supplies and acting as an obliging target to rebel skirmishers. What's back of it?"

Charteris held out his mug. "Runner came through on the twenty-first—that was, let me see, two days after the fight in the clearing. Letter from Clinton. Most secret. Clinton, on his own word, is about to move up the Hudson. Gentleman Johnny thinks we'd best dig in here till Gates begins to feel Clinton's pressure. Gentleman Johnny was impressed by the rebels in the clearing."

"And you?" Ahrens looked at him quizzically.

Charteris settled his stock, coughed slightly. "Damned if I don't begin to think you were right. I mean about

Hubbardton and Bennington and so on. Look here. Those regiments of ours—same ones that fought at—"

Ahrens held up a hand. "I know. I can name their battle-honors and spell them all backwards."

Charteris laughed. "Didn't know I was so competent a teacher."

"Oh, you are," said Ahrens. "And you've had excellent abetting. As soon as a young sprig of an ensign finds out that I can speak. English and—more—march under the sacred aegis of Harrow, he unbends and begs leave to inform me that the Fighting Umpti-umphth, sir, had the honor to serve under His Gracious Highness, the Lord of Joshua at the siege of Jericho and hence disdains to employ such cowardly methods of fighting as taking cover, aiming shots and so on. But you were impressed?"

"Had to be. Know how many of the 62nd reported fit for duty after that battle? About fifty-five. Bad business, underrating the enemy. Why, that bolt of lightning they called Arnold only had infantry; not a single field-piece. Gad, I'd hate to be in Gentleman Johnny's shoes. His next move? What move *can* he make?"

"So meanwhile we sit here and eat up the last of our provisions and you have to pay a pound for a bottle of bad gin. Look at my jacket! Leather patches at the elbows. Look at that boot! And look at the men! Rotten food in the daytime. Most of 'em are seized for outpost duty at night and get no sleep, thanks to the Yankee skirmishers. When they do sleep, it doesn't rest 'em; nerves all on edge. Speak suddenly to a man and he'll jump a rod and then cover you with his musket."

Charteris nodded. "Five men hung this morning. Caught trying to desert. Twelve men of the 9th slipped away last night and gave themselves up to Gates. Twenty men from Specht's lot, the day before."

"And these blasted camp-dogs! They never let up. I tell you, Major, I'll begin to howl with them if they keep it up much longer."

"Shan't worry till I see you burying bones." Charteris

347

set down his mug. "However, Fraser's tending to the dogs. Ordered the provost to hang any dog who can't give the countersign or—"

"Or repeat the battle-honors of the 20th," suggested Ahrens.

"Exactly, exactly." Charteris nodded. "No—no more rum, thanks." He tapped his foot nervously, started to speak, changed his mind, then blurted out: "Look here—I'm sick of staff work and that damned piddling promotion-grabbing crowd at Headquarters."

Ahrens raised his eyebrows. "Sick of it? Why not apply for work with troops?"

"Did. Phillips won't have it. Says staff needs a trained gunner. Why, I don't know. No one wants a gunner's advice." His foot jiggled ceaselessly. "I say—caught a rumor that you'd been playing blind-man's-buff with the rebels out there in the woods."

Ahrens nodded. "I'm out nearly every night with some of my men who take to the work. Breymann is furious. There's nothing like it in regulations, he says."

"Heard about that, too. Exploded to the Baron. Wanted you hanged, drawn, quartered, then cashiered, deprived of all emoluments and finally shot."

Ahrens made a disgusted sound. "Damned slave-driver. He ought to serve with the Bashi-bazouks. What did the Baron say?"

"Think the Baron was disturbed. But before he could say anything, the Baroness trotted up and informed Breymann that your family was so old that it scorned the use of 'von' or 'zu.' Added that two of your cousins dine frequently at Potsdam. Breymann withdrew in the face of artillery heavier than his own. The Baroness was so sweet to him afterward that I thought he'd explode."

"I hope he stays quiet. He could make trouble, could old Breymann. Well, if you're really sick of staff, I'll add my prayers to yours that you get relieved. I don't guarantee their efficacy, though.'

348

Charteris studied his sleek blue sleeve. "Blast it, look here. Can't get away from staff. But what do you say—I mean how about—well, I'd like to go with you on your next prowl."

Ahrens' eyes widened. "Out there? Beyond our patrols? The rebels have damn well got the upper hand, you know."

"I know. Like to go, just the same."

"But—but my men and I have had special training. Shaky times out there, very often."

Charteris smoothed his red lapels. "Oh, quite, quite."

"Can't stop for anyone, you know. A sergeant of the 9th went with us last night. He didn't come back. Don't know what happened to him."

"Must expect risks, I suppose."

"You still want to come? Are you a good shot? How are you in broken country—and at night?"

"Shoot about average. Done a lot of deer-stalking in Scotland. Better let me come along. Our responsibility, of course. Realize the risks."

"Not thinking of *your* risks. A clumsy man can easily get the party wiped out. For instance—when we got that rum from a rebel outpost that wasn't too alert, I nearly choked holding back a sneezing fit. Pache dropped his carbine on a dead bough. Snapped like a pistol. Luckily there weren't any rebels around."

Charteris spoke almost meekly. "I see. But I'm sure I'll be deft enough."

Ahrens suddenly found his stomach muscles shaking with suppressed laughter. He turned away. "Oh, all right, Major. We start tonight. Ten o'clock. Assemble here. You'll have to get your own equipment. Leather overalls, shirt, skull-cap, carbine, and hatchet."

Charteris sprang to his feet. "Right! Ten o'clock, then. As for equipment, I'll see the Tory colonel, Peters. He's got some reserve trappings and judging by the rate his men are deserting, he'll have no use for a lot of it."

349

"This is the deepest we've been yet," whispered Ahrens.

Charteris' round cap nodded in the gloom by the big oak. "And still no sign of the rebel works. They certainly push their patrols out far enough. If they keep on, they'll be stealing Gentleman Johnny's champagne. Or Mrs. Lewis. We think we do well, if we patrol fifty yards beyond our redoubts."

"We've gone nearly a mile and seen nothing. Shows you how far *they* go. What's that noise?"

"Heisse scratching himself, sir." Rentner's muffled voice carried the hint of a grin. "Says American lice are worse than the Hanau kind."

Someone stifled a snicker in the dark. "Ought to know. He lived in Kahlstrasse."

"Quiet, there! We'll go back now. Cut over the same hill we took last night." The little party slipped north through the dark, Charteris close to Ahrens' elbow. "Sorry we couldn't show you better sport tonight, Major. Rebels seem peaceful. They've got a strong-point about fifty yards east of that oak where we halted. No good trying to get near it. Too alert."

Their way took them northwest, close to the fringe of the battle of the nineteenth. Ahrens silently pointed down into a rocky hollow, close on their left. Three bodies sprawled grotesquely on the sloping ground. "Passed them last night," Ahrens whispered. "Two rebels and a woman. Must have been hit by some stray burst of fire—Rhetz' lot, probably. Woman's hands are full of sodden cartridges."

Charteris stared. "*Woman?* Camp-follower?"

Ahrens shrugged. "Looked more like the sort of farm woman we saw in the cabins around Skenesboro."

"Don't like that—don't like that. We're not fighting an army. We're fighting a nation."

"Came to the same conclusion when I saw old men and boys in the Hubbardton woods. They—God Almighty! What's that!" He halted the patrol, listening to a hideous scream that echoed with knife-like sharpness through the trees ahead, a scream so high-pitched it was almost an hysterical laugh. Close behind him he could hear Charteris' breath hissing. Again the scream tore at their ears. Pache crouched by a great rock, trembling. "Don't go near it, don't go near it! It's a ghost from the battle!"

Shaken, Ahrens drew a deep breath. "Never seen a ghost. Come on! Let's have a look at it." He signaled, his men spread out. Cautiously the party worked its way among brush and rocks. Ahrens, leading, stared ahead. Then he gave a strangled cry, his men moving up on either side of him.

At the foot of a dead elm lay a man who propped himself feebly on one elbow and lashed futilely with a small hatchet at a swarm of vague, gray shapes that danced about him with slinking hindquarters and bushy tails trailing.

Charteris started to his feet, only to be dragged back by Ahrens' long arm. "This may draw rebels. Keep down."

"But that man! He's helpless and those blasted dogs after him!" He raised his carbine.

Ahrens knocked the muzzle down. "There are eight of us. No good getting ourselves killed. Wouldn't help him. If the dogs get our scent, it may frighten 'em off." He moistened a finger, held it in the air. "Damn it. Air almost dead and in the wrong direction, anyway." As he spoke, one of the slinking shapes, growling horribly, ducked nimbly past the wavering hatchet, muzzle pressed close to the man's throat. "Oh, Christ!" He seized a heavy, round stone, sprang to his feet. His arm swung in a wide arc. The stone flew hissing through the air. There was a sharp thud, the animal sprang back with a howl, spun in sharp circles and raced off into the undergrowth, one leg dragging. The others froze, pointed muzzles lifted, then scuttered off in the darkness.

351

"See to the man, Charteris." Ahrens clubbed his carbine and sprinted across the open space, past the tree and into the woods beyond, where something thrashed and flailed among dead branches. Charteris stared after him, open-mouthed. He heard Ahrens' footsteps grow faint, then halt suddenly. There were heavy, clotted sounds, a sharp crash, and then silence.

Charteris felt a tug at his sleeve. "I think he'll want us to go on, sir." Charteris pulled himself together, nodded.

The man under the tree moaned feebly. Charteris knelt by him, unslinging his own water-bottle. He felt a hand on his shoulder. Rentner was looking down at him, shaking his head, pointing to the welter of black blood that spread over the man's ragged waistcoat, stained the yellow facings of his jacket.

"He'd die in agony if he drank, sir," Rentner whispered. Then he pointed to the long gashes on the man's neck above his greasy stock. "Nothing to do, sir," he said.

Footsteps sounded behind them, a straining voice whispered: "Is he badly off?"

The little group looked up. Ahrens staggered under the heavy, furry burden that weighted down his shoulders. One knee showed bare and bloody through a fresh rent in his leather overalls. With a heave, he dumped the carcass on the ground. "There's your dog, Major. Fine a wolf-bitch as I ever saw. Nearly ripped my leg off with those rat-trap jaws. How's the man?" He knelt by Charteris. "H'm. It's Sergeant Baily. With us last night and wandered off."

The sergeant's eyes slowly opened. "Knew you'd come, sir." His voice was feeble, his breath hot and foul. "Got lost, I did. Rebel shot me with buckshot. In the belly. Two of 'em tried to help me to our lines, but someone fired on them, so they left me here." He drew a long quivering breath. "Oh-h-h-h! It do hurt cruel, sir. Can't you do something, sir?"

352

Ahrens' jaws tightened. "Rentner! Take the party along. I'll join you by the big rock over the crest."

In the shelter of the big rock, the party waited, the men stretched out on leaves and moss, Charteris erect and alert, leaning against a low ash. "Close to the lines, now, sir. No need to be so careful. Getting on toward sunrise, too. Agh! Listen to that." Far in the west a wolf lifted his voice, another answered. The hollow, musical howl seemed to fill the whole lightening sky. Charteris shuddered, thinking of the man in red and the gray shapes that circled and capered about him.

From the crest a voice called: "On your feet. March straight back to camp and don't forget to hail the picket of the 20th out beyond the first redoubt or they'll think you're rebels."

Charteris' eyes widened. In the dim light he could see Ahrens' heavy shoulders looming against the sky-line; his carbine jutted out before him, covering the two men who walked ahead. One of them was weighted down with the body of the wolf.

"What the devil have you been up to?" laughed Charteris.

"These gentlemen seem to prefer the cells of Chambly to Gates' barracks. Gave themselves up to me and I thought one of them might carry the wolf—a present for Fraser and the provost—after I've taken its skin for my bed. Push along, now. We'll talk to these men in my tent, then send 'em on to the provost."

The two prisoners, one tall and thin in his fringed buckskins and fur cap, the other medium in height but broad and dressed in a short blue jacket and white trousers, moved easily ahead among the men of the patrol, who stared at the dead wolf draped over the buckskin's shoulders.

Charteris fell in step with Ahrens. "What did you do for the sergeant?"

"He's all right. His belly was drilled like a sieve with that blasted buckshot."

"All right? What did you *do*?"

"We couldn't move him back to camp. He'd die on the way—and most unpleasantly."

"So you *left* him?"

Ahrens nodded. "There's a thick vein in the neck. His stock made it bulge. I don't think he even felt the prick of my knife. He thought he was going to sleep, and said he felt easier. I stayed with him till I couldn't feel his pulse. Then the two rebels came up, unarmed, and gave themselves up to me. I thought we might talk to 'em a bit. We might learn something."

Charteris marveled. "And to think that this is the young Hessian whom I lectured on discipline at Der Rosentrauch."

The man in buckskin balanced his coon cap on his knee, the furry tail at the back swinging as he held out his mug for more rum. Ahrens filled it. "So you and your friend thought you'd be better off with us? Did you think of taking service with us?"

The man's leathery face contorted, his eyes flashed. "Do I look like a God-damn turncoat? And this here soldier ain't my friend." He jerked a thick thumb at the man in blue. "He's Massachusetts. I'm Virginia. We don't like the blue-nosed bastards."

The other nodded approvingly. "And we ain't exactly partial to Virginians."

Charteris repressed a grin. "What are your regiments?"

The Virginan drank. "I'm from Captain Claiborne's company of Morgan's rifles. We shoots, mostly, and we don't like officers and we don't like Massachusetts men. This here soldier, he's from Vose's regiment, Glover's brigade."

"He ain't lyin'," said the other.

Ahrens leaned forward. "How many men has Gates got?"

354

The Virginian turned to his companion. "Now, ain't that the God-damnest question?" He fixed Ahrens with a hard eye. "Mister, I told you I ain't a turncoat. And if so I answers you, I'll be telling you a hundred thousand."

The man in blue nodded. "More," he said.

"Why did you come to us?" asked Charteris.

"Reckon that's our business," said the Virginian sourly. The other deserter added, "Personal."

"Rations low?" asked Ahrens.

"We're feedin' ample, powerful ample." The lean man held out his mug again.

"Too much flogging?" asked Charteris.

"Ain't nary a lash been laid to a man since we marched up from Trenton."

"Too many floggings, too little food—those are the usual reasons for desertion," observed Charteris. "I must say this puzzles me."

Ahrens leaned back, affected a yawn. "It appears to me, Major, that these men are just soft. Got tired of the life and thought they'd quit."

The Virginian leaped to his feet, dashed the cap with the trailing coon-tail to the ground. "Soft? Soft? Three years I've fit, and so's he. But God damn me, when that calf-livered, blinking, goggle-eyed old midwife of a Gates goes and breaks the only man in camp that's fit to lead Virginians, breaks him 'cause he knows we'll follow that man into the jaws of hell and come back with the teeth, takes his command away from him and gives it to a lot of damn snivelin' clerks that ain't never done nothin' but wear pens back of their ears and count stinkin' cod-fish in a God-damned office—" He paused for breath.

Glover's man nodded. "We ain't partial to Gates."

The rifleman went on. "Why, damn my soul to hell, that little catamount, he aint knee-high to a weasel, but he'll take raw militia and put the fear of God into 'em till, by God, they'll traipse up and tear the haslet out'n a ten-foot b'ar. He seen the lobster-backs in the blaze up

355

yonder and he begun to prance and chomp his teeth and spit live coals and then he says, 'Where's Morgan's men?' and then he bends over that big horse of his'n and the fust thing we knowed we were hangin' onto the horse's tail, the whole company of us, and the little man was rollin' into the redcoats like a dozen tornadoes. Didn't bother to shoot none, he didn't. Just flung his claws about and generals and colonels begun flyin' through the air and landin' in tree-tops and heads and arms and legs was tossin' about like twelve dogs in a b'ar-pit. An' what's he doin' now? Racin' up and down the camp, stompin' his feet like a gamecock and can't give an order to a corporal!" He flung out his arms. "Why, I'm a son of a bitch if he didn't even make the Massachusetts men fight like Virginians—almost."

Glover's man nodded. "He's talking about a New Englander."

Charteris drew a deep breath. "He seems to be something of a warrior, by our lean friend's account. Would it be violating a confidence to tell his name?"

The Virginian raised his long arms to the gray sky. "Why, God damn my soul, who the hell do you think I been talkin' about? Arnold, Benedict Arnold. There ain't nary a man in that camp that wouldn't storm God's own golden throne behind Benedict Arnold. But they ain't another in the camp that's fit to lead a Friends' meetin' in prayer. That's why we come out tonight."

The Massachusetts man looked at Ahrens, nodding gravely. "He's put it in a nutshell."

Ahrens controlled his features, said, "Thank you, gentlemen," with equal gravity. Then he rose. "Now, gentlemen, here comes the provost guard. Hope your trip to Chambly won't be too unpleasant."

"That's news." Charteris watched the pair marching off between files of red jackets. "Dissension in the camp and Arnold out of the picture. He was present up in the clearing. Then he vanished and the attack broke down, lost direction. Think I'll run along and pass the word on to Gentleman Johnny. Makes our chances look considerably brighter."

"If he'll act on it," commented Ahrens. "Hope you enjoyed your walk in the forest."

Charteris bowed ironically. "Charming. And let me know when you go out again."

Ahrens bowed to the little figure on the deep porch of the house by the Great Redoubt. "My compliments on the bonnets, Baroness. Never saw the girls look prettier."

Baroness Riedesel smiled down on the two furry heads beside her. "I think Gustava's is a little large. But then, I never tried to sew bits of fur together before. Rockel got the fur from an Indian. He *said* the Indian didn't need it any more." She sighed pleasantly. "It's a comfort to think that the savages, even nasty ones like ours, have got all the furs they need and more. Do you know what *I* did? When we left Fort Edward, I sent every last stitch of heavy clothing I owned back to Ticonderoga and haven't a thing but summery stuffs, and neither has Lady Acland or Mrs. Reynal or Mrs. Harnage. These nights!"

"If you'll allow me, Baroness, I've a fine wolf-skin that my men are curing most expertly. I'd be very glad to think that it was doing something to make up for the havoc our delay is playing with your wardrobe and your comfort."

She pursed up her red mouth, shook her head. "Oh, I couldn't allow it. No, no, really. You'll need it yourself, up there in the damp ravine. Oh—do you think there'd be enough for a cape for both the girls in it? Friedericka has been coughing so lately."

"I'll send it down," said Ahrens laughing.

The Baroness smiled, blue eyes shining. "That will be very nice, Lieutenant Ahrens. Is it a big wolf? Do you think I could get a cape for myself out of it, too?"

"It's colossal. My men suspect that it was a were-wolf. And if it isn't big enough, I'll find another for you."

"*Find* one? Where did you get this one?"

Ahrens looked at her solemnly. "Upon my honor, I threw a stone at it."

The little Baroness folded her hands, pursed up her lips. "There, Friedericka and Gustava, when you get back to Wolfenbüttel, you can tell the little Steinmetz girls that your pelisses are trimmed with the fur of a wolf that a Hessian officer killed with a stone."

Ahrens found two pairs of intensely blue eyes staring gravely up at him. Their mother nodded at him as though he and she shared a secret. He grinned wryly. She went on: "But what brings you way back here to our part of the world? I thought you spent all your time in the woods beyond the redoubts. I've heard *such* stories about you."

"I rode back to see about fodder for the gun-teams. The horses are skin and bone. There just doesn't seem to be any fodder."

"That's serious, isn't it?"

Ahrens coughed. "Well, I expect in a day or so we'll send men up the river to the meadows. They'll cut enough grass to feed the horses a lifetime."

The Baroness patted the little girls' heads with fine impartiality. "Isn't he nice? Coming back here and cheering up the women?" She laughed at Ahrens. "Don't forget I'm a soldier's daughter and a soldier's wife. I can see what's happening. I know that the rebels have worked up the east bank of the river. I know they've crossed it. There are lots of them, no more than five miles back there—just watching us. Fodder in the meadows! The whole army would have to go. And I'll tell you something else—it will be all over camp tomorrow and the General will hear of it the next day. That man—what's his name now?—oh, yes, the one at Bennington, Stark. Well, he captured the entire garrison at Fort Edward yesterday afternoon. It's true. Major Acland told Lady Acland and she told Mrs. Harnage and Mrs.

Harnage told Mrs. Reynal. Gustava overheard them and told me."

"Does the Baron know?"

"Not yet, but you're going to tell him when you go back. I've hardly seen him since the battle. He came in for dinner last night and told me he hadn't had his clothes off in five days. Never sleeps. The night before last he had to make five separate and distinct trips to the redoubts."

Ahrens nodded. "None of us get much sleep," he said. "Poor old Gentleman Johnny! Hate to be in his place."

The Baroness made a face. "Gentleman Johnny was here last night. Oh, so very, very gallant and bowing. 'And what does the little *Baroness* think *I* ought to do now? Ladies are wisest, eh, Baron?'" She mimicked the General's voice and gesture.

Ahrens snorted. "What did you tell him?"

"Oh, the little Baroness told him he ought to go and write another play!"

On the slope of the dark ravine a maple flamed like a dull torch among the gray rocks. Beyond it an ash glowed, a pale lemon-colored ball of crisping leaves, startling against the intense green-black of a towering pine. "Almost worth lice and rags and a playwright general who can't seem to stage a happy ending to his own drama," thought Ahrens. "Never dreamed there could be such colors. If I painted these river-banks and exhibited in Dresden, I'd be called drunk and a liar." He picked his way carefully along the greasy path at the bottom of North Branch ravine, then followed a crooked trail that climbed the steep, high banks between rocks and bushes.

The tents of Pausch's gunners clung close to the rocky lip, spread away easy and west in a blazing line. The man had hacked off sprays and branches of flaming leaves, wedged them over tent-doors, festooned them in graceful trails from the poles, fashioned crude holders

359

out of birch-bark and lined the company street with branches of crimson, russet, maroon, orange. In striking contrast, the streets of the 9th to the east and the 21st to the west were stark, naked-looking. As he entered Pausch's wide tent, Ahrens smiled to notice that even that tough old veteran had boughs and sprays tucked into every possible corner.

Pausch rustled papers in his scarred hands, waved Ahrens to a seat on an upturned keg. "We're going out again," he said.

"The whole army?" Ahrens' back stiffened.

"No, no. About fifteen hundred. Move tomorrow morning. Auxiliaries make a swing to the west. Main body moves in three columns—like this—" He picked up a flattened bullet, scribbled on a sheet of cartridge paper. "British light infantry and their 24th regiment on the right. Then in the center—here—is a strange and wonderful thing. It is the second column, which someone has seen fit to build out of scraps and tags from every one of our regiments."

"No single unit? You mean the Rhetz or the Riedesel regiments supported by odd companies from the others?"

"Oh, no indeed. I mean no such thing. *This* is the way the staff decrees it. Gaze upon it and wonder." Pausch spoke humbly, his mouth as straight and tight as a ruled line.

"But, for God's sake, why? There'll be no cohesion to it, no unity. Why?"

Pausch shook his grizzled head, scratched furtively at his shoulders. "Ah, why indeed! Beyond this second column is the third and last—composed entirely of British grenadiers of the advance corps."

"Well, I suppose the staff has a reason for that second column. First and third are fine. What do we do, having formed?"

"Having formed, we march south, tending to a few little matters like broken bridges over the brooks and ravines beyond the Freeman Farm clearing. Then the

360

columns deploy into a single long line which will be under the personal observation of Generals von Fraser, von Phillips, Riedesel—*and* von Burgoyne, who is said to have unpacked a brand-new uniform for the occasion."

Ahrens studied the Captain's scrawl. "I think I'd rather take my men and see if I can find more rum in the woods. I find this plan shocking both artistically and professionally. What are they doing about guns?"

"Twelve pieces. Four English sixes, two twelves and two howitzers. Then I'm to take two sixes. So are you. You go with the British grenadiers on the left, with the same freedom you had when we marched out in the fog and then marched back. I have an idea you'll not be idle."

Ahrens drummed his long fingers against the side of the keg. "To be used where there's trouble, eh? Flattering. Don't know about the men, though. The army's been on half-rations for five days now. And you've noticed the flour that's issued? Moldly, full of thin, six-inch worms and any number of white, legged things that poke out pale heads and leer at you. Oh, the men are willing enough. It's stamina I'm worrying about."

Pausch shrugged. "Can't be helped. I'm banking on the rum that von Burgoyne issued to the army."

"Don't think that rum helped or will help much," growled Ahrens.

Pausch stared. "Not help? This is an army, isn't it? Did you ever hear of any God-damn army that wasn't helped by rum? Battles, wars, have been won with rum and nothing else."

"Different in this case, sir. Our whole contingent got four barrels. That's good. *But*—the English got eight. The men have heard about it and their language is making the bark peel off the oak trees."

Pausch waved his hand. "They'll drink up and forget, drink up and forget." Then he scowled. "Good God, we've *got* to move somewhere. D'you know this night-and-day staring at woods full of rebels they can't see is

361

telling on the men? They're cracking, I tell you. Hospitals are full. And yesterday a man in the Specht regiment went mad and flew at his corporal with a bayonet. And they found three of Riedesel's men up beyond the Great Redoubt by the river, cooking, *cooking*, mind you, for a lot of Indian stragglers. Daft as hatters, every one of 'em and not a wound. Good men, too, on their past records. But no sleep, rotten food and being fired at twenty-four hours a day by a lot of farmers they can't see—it just broke 'em, that's all." He sighed. "Well, this move may be the best thing. Clear to you—your part?"

Ahrens nodded. "My part is. I just go along and wait until Phillips or someone trumpets at me. But how about the columns? You say they march south—then what happens? What's the objective?"

"Well, what do *you* think?"

"Can't make it out. We're too strong for a reconnaissance in force. We're too weak for a serious attack. What *is* the answer?"

"Very simple." Pausch spread out his hands. "There isn't any."

"*Isn't* any?"

"Not a ghost. Can't reason it out any other way. This von Burgoyne—he's at his wit's end. Likewise he's a gambler. He's desperate. He's just launching out into the country—it's fairly open there, by the way—and praying that something will happen to nullify the bad cards he holds."

Ahrens rubbed his chin, frowning. "What do you think will happen, Captain?"

Pausch stretched out his hand, crisscrossed with white scars. He ran his fingers delicately over a spray of maple that shone in his dim tent. "Ever see such colors?" he said.

It was very still in the wheatfield, very still and hot. Ahrens stood back of his shining six-pounders on the right of the long line of British grenadiers. He could

362

hear equipment rustle as the men shifted uneasily, leaning on their muskets and staring at the tangled woods that lay beyond the last spears of wheat. To the right rear the hunched roof of a small cabin jutted, its ridge stained with scarlet as a big man leaned against the mud-and-stick chimney and stared south through a long brass telescope.

Staccato conversation drifted to Ahrens from the blue and red ranks where two platoons of the Hesse-Hanau infantry linked up with the British. "What's the fat sheep's-head expect to see, poking that thing at the trees? Expect to see what Gates has for breakfast?" ... "What he had for dinner." There was a snicker. "Look. There's the Baron on the roof, now, and Geismar with him. Lord Jesus, my mouth's dry." ... "I'll let you lick the inside of my canteen. It's empty, same as yours." There was another snicker, a note of tense hysteria, meaningless.

From the rear, two British privates trotted past Ahrens. One of them unslung his haversack, dumped its contents into some bushes. His companion stared. "Your *rations?*"

"Haversack's too bloody heavy. Hell, I'll get more at the night's encampment. Gentleman Johnny won't let us starve." They ran on.

Ahrens watched his own men, kneeling quietly by the pieces. He wondered if they felt as empty, as futile as he did, if their eyes were flicking about the wheatfield as restlessly as his, if their ears picked up trivial sounds like the clink of a bridle ring back there where the gun-teams waited with the limbers. He saw the gun-squads looking at him. "All loaded and ready?" he asked, then fumed to himself: "Damn silly question. Been loaded these twenty minutes."

He watched the tall figure of Major Acland moving up and down in front of his grenadiers, hands clasped behind his back, eyes on the ground—an English gentleman out for an easy stroll, oblivious to all other living beings. Each time the Major reached the left of his line, he absently tapped the English six-pounders in position there with a light stick. Ahrens could hear the tiny sound, thin, metallic *flink-flink*. Suddenly the Major threw back his head, glared angrily down the slope at the extreme left, stiffened. Then he stepped quickly back, took his post on the flank of his men.

A long line of brown faces under battered cocked hats slowly rose into sight from the dead ground beyond, then broad shoulders in homespun, chests cut across with white belts. A strangled voice in the red line yelled: "Here they come!"

Ahrens raised his hand. "Hold your fire. You've no proper targets yet." The two gunners dropped their linstocks. Acland's roaring voice swept across the wheat. "Raise firelocks!" The hush was uncanny, the world empty of sound except for the dull drumming of hundreds of steady feet climbing the hill off there on the left. Then from the right there quavered up from distant trees a lunatic gibbering which swelled, gobbled in endless imbecility. Ahrens felt cold prickles along his spine.

The field about the grenadiers erupted in flaring, echoing white smoke. Above the din Acland's voice roared out: "Fix bayonets! Charge the damned rebels!" Then the smoke welled up the slope, red figures tossed and pitched. The wheatfield was blotted out from the rest of the world by a dense pall which echoed, roared, shrieked. Ahrens' guns slammed and slammed. Pache fell, and Heisse. Ahrens sprang forward, threw all his strength against a stubborn trail, snatched up a linstock, slapped it across the breech of a piece, which blasted smoke and flame at the touch. Off on the right the blue lines of the Germans were crumbling, melting; the grenadiers were falling back, slowly, then desperately. The uproar rose and rose. Then high over it all a single voice whinnied: "It's Arnold! Oh, Christ Almighty, it's Arnold!" Through the haze Ahrens saw a huge horse, a little man in prim blue and buff who raved and stormed and rose in his stirrups, sword high, and catapulted among the silver helmets of the Hesse-Hanau grenadiers.

A bullet scored the back of Ahrens' hand, another jarred between his heel and the ground. Bright wood showed in a dozen places on the dull wood of the trails, hissing things caromed and glanced from the shining barrels. Another gunner fell, coughing and choking, hands to a crimson stock. Ahrens yelled: "Who's that? Passau? Move him clear! Grape again, grape!" He seized the rammer of the first piece, drove the charge home. Through the smoke he saw Rentner's arm drop, saw the linstock, glowing, fall on the breech. The concussion jarred him. "Trail left! See 'em, see 'em? Good! Grape!" He ran blindly back through the smoke, helped a struggling man heave the trail of the second piece, darted back to the first. Hooves thudded past him and a horse, bared teeth ghastly white in a high-flung head, galloped between the guns. As he tore past, a long coil of bluish intestine slipped down from a bloody belly, dragged, flicked against flying hooves.

A hand tugged at Ahrens' shoulder, a wild, sweaty face stared into his. "From General Phillips! Move out the guns! Fall back, I say! God damn it, fall back!"

Ahrens' voice crashed out. "Drag-ropes. Pieces to the rear!" He turned. "Limbers!" But the ground where the limbers had halted was a tangle of horses, some still, some screaming through straining, arched throats. He sprang forward, unwound the drag-rope from Passau's stiffening shoulder, hooked the clamp by a trunion of the first piece, strained with his men. The second bumped along the ground behind them. "Who's on the trail there? Rentner and Stahl? Make for the road through the woods there!" Heads down, feet digging, the crews broke into a slow trot. Over his shoulder Ahrens saw the last of the grenadiers face about, fire a volley at the steadily advancing rebels, saw the two English pieces being swung about by brawny men in gray and brown,

365

heard a deep shout, "Come on, New Hampshire!" The captured guns bellowed, solid-shot ricocheted across the trampled wheat.

Ahrens set all his strength against the drag-rope, his eyes on the ground. The field flowed past him. He saw broken stalks, sprawling bodies in red and white, a rail fence where Major Acland lay, white breeches soaked with red, cursing his retreating men through pale lips. A tall grenadier halted to stare at the lumbering guns, swore, slung his musket over his back and snatched at Ahrens' drag-rope. "Best let me do this, sir!" He wound the rope about him, heaved with the Hanau men. Another grenadier found purchase just above the axle, added his weight. Ahrens stepped back, waited for the second piece. An Englishman strained at the hand-spike beside a stocky Hanauer, others pushed from behind. Back of them, the wheatfield was covered with broken companies falling away before brown lines, gray lines, blue lines of rebels. Far off in the west, Morgan's turkey-call gibbered and gobbled. By the wreck of two companies of Specht's regiment. Arnold's horse shot like a bolt, a screaming line of swift-moving men running at his heels.

The soft dirt road that rolled down into the valley toward the twin hills and their redoubts was choked with shattered, flying men, red coats and blue, skull-caps and silver helmets and bearskins hopelessly mixed. At the last high point of the road, where it slipped abruptly through the steep woods, Ahrens faced about, raised his carbine and fired at the oncoming rebels. Then he slung it across his shoulders, started down the hill after his guns. From the woods at his left a hidden trail flashed with scarlet and white, with the iridescent sheen of well-groomed horses. Gentleman Johnny galloped out on the crowded road, his jacket tattered, his hat pierced. He rose in his stirrups. "To the redoubts, lads! The camp must be held to the last man! D'you hear? *To the last man!*" From the beaten ruck ahead, haggard, drawn faces, powder-smeared, turned to stare. Then lack-luster eyes shone, sullen faces brightened. A roar swept up. "Ay, lads! It's good old Gentleman Johnny!" High and clear a cockney whine sang through the air. "We'll 'old, sir. Never you fear! We'll 'old for Gentleman Johnny!" Burgoyne rode on down the line. There were undisguised tears trickling down his full, ruddy cheeks.

Ahrens stumbled on after his piece, the broken road tripping and catching at his patched boots. He wiped his streaming forehead. "The man's a magician. Even the Rhetz lot are cheering him now."

Then a cracked voice hailed him, a shaking hand pawed at his arm. "Where's the sense to this, where's the sense? I showed you the plans, told you there was no God-damn sense to them." It was Captain Pausch, hatless, his uniform torn, a long cut on his face. He staggered slightly. Ahrens threw an arm over his shoulder, steadying him. The cracked voice went on. "The first guns I ever lost in forty years' service, the first guns. Forty years and never a gun lost till today. And twenty-two of my lads stiffening in the wheat up there, twenty-two of the best and all because that scarlet and white son of a bitch didn't know what to do. Thought he was playing one of his piddling little card games. Oh, my God! Have we any guns left? Have we *any*? And that hell-hound on horseback, Arnold, is rallying the rebels back there. Where are my guns? My guns and the gunners I trained myself?"

Ahrens tightened his arm over Pausch's old shoulders. "Lucky enough to bring mine off. They were close by the road. Never mind about yours, sir. We'll get 'em back. The British guns by the grenadiers didn't get a chance to fire once. The rebels clubbed the gunners and took their linstocks away. Turned the guns on us."

Pausch lifted his head. "Didn't even fire? By God, *we* did. Blew the rebels to hell, and spiked the guns before we had to fall back. Two of the rebels had me, but Pfeffer came up and helped me. Eh, there! Watch out!"

A Hanau grenadier bumped into Pausch, then staggered off down the road, head low, hand clutching at a dripping shoulder. "Poor lad," said Ahrens. "Hold up, Captain. Behind you." He dragged the veteran to the side of the road.

Drumming hooves brought on a straining line of twelve horses, a heavy twelve-pounder lurching and clanking behind them. The long, single hitch cut blindly through a mass of men ahead, lunged onto a clear stretch which was broken only by the reeling figure of the Hanau grenadier. As the horses stamped by, he lurched, cannoned into a bay shoulder, jumped stiffly, balanced, then staggered back against the next horse. A heavy foot struck against him, his knees gave way and he fell headlong under the iron hooves, his helmet spinning crazily into the grass by the roadside. His blue arms struck out, his white legs thrashed. Then the wheels of the limber of the piece jolted heavily. The grenadier lay quiet in the soft road.

Sick and dizzy, Ahrens stared at the limp body. Then it was trampled under foot by a knot of hurrying Jaegers and British grenadiers. The distant woods echoed to maniac gobbling. Ahrens seized Pausch by the arm, hurried him along. He looked over his shoulder and saw the last of Balcarres' light infantrymen retiring sullenly, in very fair order, holding back the press of the rebels. He broke into a trot, the Captain clumping beside him. They overtook a knot of three horsemen riding slowly toward the camp. The middle rider was supported by the two on either side. Ahrens stared in horror at Fraser's deathly white face, at the red-black smears on his trim waistcoat as the General swayed in the saddle, chin low on his breast. He shook his head, hurried Pausch along, caught up with his two guns. His men strained grimly on in good order. He heard Pausch give an approving grunt.

By a fallen oak, a tall man lounged, bridle over his blue arm. "Been looking all over the battle for you,

368

young fellow. You're to post your guns in Breymann's redoubt. That's the hill on the left, you know. Better hurry. Good many accidents happening this day. Nearly as bad as your blasted woods." Charteris vaulted into his saddle, then stared at Ahrens' companion. He recognized the veteran, his face softened. "Didn't know you at once, Captain. Bad light here." He dropped a hand on Pausch's shoulder. "Want you to know, General Phillips said yours were the best fought guns he'd ever seen. Said you were an honor to the service. Wanted to tell you." He nodded, galloped off.

Pausch straightened his old back. "Come on, come on, Lieutenant! Mustn't waste time. Let's get the guns to the damned redoubt!"

Ahrens stared through the echoing smoke that eddied from the crude embrasure of Breymann's redoubt. The ball from the first piece had ricocheted down the stump-studded slope and lost itself in the thick brush through which shadowy clouds of buckskin figures filtered and drifted to vanish with their long rifles in the broken ground. His own men, ragged and blackened, looked expectantly at him. Far down the hillside, rifles began to crack viciously. He shook his head. "Only waste ammunition. Load up with grape and wait till they try to rush the breast-works. Better give another half-turn to the elevating screw, Rentner. That does it. If they rush, they'll come like a blast out of hell. If a man's hit, drag him off. We can't afford any stumbling or fumbling."

The gun-crew heaved on the drag-ropes, ran the piece back from the embrasure. Ahrens dropped on one knee, running a grimy thumb over a rough spot on his chin which his hasty razor had missed that morning. With half his mind he watched his crew, with the other he dully cursed the Yankee who had shot the bottom out of his water-bottle back there in the clearing. A hand fell

369

on his shoulder, a heavy voice said: "Think they'll attack?"

"Ready for them if they do, Captain. You set the second piece in the angle of the redoubt over there?"

Pausch nodded. "We'll get a fine cross-fire with grape across the whole shoulder in front of this section with our two pieces. Don't believe we'll have the chance, though."

Ahrens scrambled to his feet. "You don't? Take a look down the slope. Must be three hundred of those devils in buckskin there. See—watch the smoke-puffs." Pausch joined him in the embrasure. "There's one by the rocks. One—two, three, say, five from those trees. Figure that as a fairly solid line and there are your three hundred." Pausch pursed his lips and nodded. "Say three hundred," Ahrens went on. Then, "Hi! Look. Short blue jackets and white breeches on the buckskins' left. They're—they're Glover's men, Massachusetts boatmen turned infantry."

Pausch rumbled in his throat. "Blast 'em! Looks bad! They're massing—no, they're taking cover like the others. Well, let 'em. They'll never take this redoubt by long-range rifle-fire. Let 'em blaze all they like."

Ahrens rubbed his hand over the smooth brass of the barrel.

"All very well, Captain. No one's leading 'em now. They've just blundered in here. But supposing Arnold or someone like that took 'em in hand and threw 'em at us? We've a breast-high redoubt, two field-pieces and a scratch lot of grenadiers and light infantry. Two hundred at the most. If it came to a retreat again, think of that mass of women and sutlers and sick back there in the tents by the north wall."

"Oh, yes, yes, yes," said Pausch testily. "*If* they had Arnold and *if* they weren't out of hand and *if* they could make the sun stand still for three or four hours. *But* they're leaderless, scattered and it's almost dusk. No, no. Whoever is running this for the Yankees has thrown his

370

whole force against the rest of our army over there at Balcarres' redoubt."

Ahrens looked east to the thudding smoke-pall that showed over the trees a half-mile away. "I hope you're right. Wonder what is happening over there? We might as well be in another world for all we know of things. Listen! It's thinning out, that row over there."

The pandemonium on distant Freeman's hill suddenly ebbed to a desultory chatter of small-arms fire. Pausch narrowed his eyes. "Maybe they've had enough. Look— they've stopped firing down there, too."

Ahrens looked out through the slow-settling gloom. "Not going, are they?" Then he gasped, pointed.

Among the stumps and fallen logs, round coonskin caps edged into view, men in hunting shirts rose to their knees staring eastward and pointing, pointing at something hidden from the men in the embrasure by a bulge of the hill. Then a gigantic man sprang to a stump, waved a long rifle over his head, raised something to his lips. Ahrens shuddered as the hollow gobble bubbled and gurgled through the glass-clear dusk. A bellowing voice lifted the hairs on the back of his neck. "General! General Arnold! Here we are. It's me, General, me, Dan Morgan!" Hooves drummed among the trees and the growing mutter down the slope swelled to a roar as the buckskins leaped to their feet shrieking: "Arnold! General Arnold!" A huge bay burst through the brush, rocked to a halt on digging hooves. Its little rider vaulted clear of the saddle, raced to the huge Morgan, flung an arm over the fringed shoulder, made stabbing motions toward the redoubt.

Ahrens swung round on his heel, seized a hurrying sergeant of Jaegers by the collar. "Find Colonel Breymann at once! Tell him it's Arnold—got the name? Arnold, the Yankee! Hurry!" He gave the man a push.

At his elbow a bitter voice snarled: "What the hell do I care which of the farmers is down there?" Ahrens turned to find himself looking into Breymann's heavy, brutal face. The snarl went on. "Let him attack!" Then he raised his voice: "Grenadiers! Light infantry! The first man to leave his loop-hole will answer to *me*!" He walked away flicking at the rough ground with his naked sword.

Ahrens swore under his breath and ran back to the embrasure. Far down the slope the buckskins were forming in three long waves. Arnold had scrambled back in the saddle and was riding up and down among them, waving his cocked hat and shouting. On the left the Massachusetts men were fanning out, dressing with a rough but effective precision.

Then a hush fell over the redoubt. From the northwest a keen wind swooped down, drove scattered leaves about the broad wheels of the piece. Far in the rear among the gray-white tents a horse whinnied and smacked a flat hoof on the ground. From the thin line of grenadiers on the left, Ahrens heard a strangled voice half-whisper: "Dear God! It's coming now!" The idiot gobble of Morgan's call clucked and gibbered and suddenly the slope was alive with lean figures moving cautiously, figures in buckskin, figures in blue, and behind them all a little man in blue and buff held in check a mincing horse that danced and capered by the rear rank.

Ahrens sprang back from the embrasure, glanced across at Pausch, erect by the second piece, at the grenadiers and light infantry huddled close to the horseshoe curve of the redoubt. The hush deepened, was broken by the muffled crunch-crunch-crunch of hundreds of feet that beat a broken rhythm over the rough slope outside. From the center of the horseshoe Breymann's voice bellowed, "Steady!" Then from among the tents in the rear a clear song floated, high and piercing:

"O Carillon, je te revois encore,
Non plus, hélas, comme en ces jours bénis—"

372

Out of the corner of his eye Ahrens caught a flash of a slim figure, black hair bound with flame, a figure that ran lightly over the rough ground, head back, eyes flashing. Sun-browned hands held up the corners of a tattered apron which bulged with a rustling load of paper cartridges.

> *"Oui, près, de toi, venant chercher ma tombe,*
> *Pour mon drapeau, je viens ici mourir!"*

The song died away and Ahrens saw her kneeling by a knot of grenadiers whose clumsy hands snatched at her cartridges.

Far along the breastwork a Jaeger fired, a single shot that echoed weirdly in the dying light. Then the world outside welled up into a great roar: "It's the mercenaries, the God-damned mercenaries!" Footsteps beat faster, halted, a hundred rifles cracked, the footsteps drummed on, faster, faster, while a high voice raved: "At 'em, at 'em, at 'em!"

Rentner looked back at Ahrens, caught his nod, clapped the linstock across the breech. The piece crashed its charge of grape down the slope. "Again, again!" Ahrens yelled. "Grape! Fast! Fast! Fast!" The piece roared again, but above its din Ahrens heard that high voice again, the voice that he had heard raving in the bitter stubble of the clearing: "To the sally-port! Drive it in! Crash it in! Let me at 'em! New Englanders! Virginians! Follow me!"

The brown lines in front of the pieces had sunk to the ground. Coonskin caps edged cautiously around ragged stumps, lean hands slowly poked long rifle barrels into sight, fired carefully at the brass muzzles, but the rush had broken in the deadly cross-fire of grape.

Far away to the right, Arnold's voice raved on and a great tidal-wave of fur caps and fringed shirts surged in a fighting, swearing storm up to the breastworks, over them, drove and beat at the big grenadiers and the wiry

373

Jaegers, who fell back slowly. Hot lead began to spatter about Ahrens' piece from the flank. A gunner staggered back against him, collapsed, his blood black and thick on the rammer-staff that he still clutched. Ahrens snatched up the rammer. Something twanged in the air and the dry wood of the staff splintered. A heavy hand seized him by the shoulder, Pausch's voice bellowed: "Get the guns away! Head for the east sally-port!"

Ahrens stared to his right. Three grenadiers lay in pools of blood by their loop-holes. The rest were drifting aimlessly toward thick groups of infantry who were falling back from the earthworks. He took a deep breath. "By God, they've let us down! Come on! Save the piece! Drag-ropes! To the rear!" He stooped, gripped the handspike. A blue-coated figure leaped beside him in the dusk. Rentner's voice was low but steady.

"Only three of us left, sir. They just got Ahlefeld through the head. We'll get it out."

Ahrens nodded, watched the heavy wheels stir, then roll slowly over the rough ground and plunge into the reeking murk of Breymann's redoubt. To the left he could see a thick line of grenadiers standing firm against the rushing waves of buckskins. Behind them a broken wrack of men ran heavily from the action. Somewhere in the dusk a woman's voice was shrieking: "Feu! Feu! Oh, les poltrons! Oh, les gueux! Feu! Feu!" Her voice soared higher:

> *"Réveillez-vous Apportant ma bannière,*
> *Sur vos tombeaux, je viens ici mourir!"*

Dimly Ahrens saw her flaming bandeau bobbing among the towering brass of the grenadiers, saw her hard little fists drumming at the broad chest of the fugitives, heard her scream again: "Oh, les poltrons! 'Cré nom de Dieu! Les poltrons!" Then voice and form were swallowed up in a fresh whirlwind of shouting and musketry.

The press grew thicker as the piece neared the east

374

sally-port and the tents that clustered about it. Grenadiers and Jaegers threw away their muskets, ran with lowered heads. Steel flashed among them, and Ahrens heard Breymann's voice, strangled with fury: "Cowardly swine! Back to your posts! You stinking cowards!" There was another flash. A man screamed and Ahrens saw Breymann standing with drawn sword before a cowering knot of infantry. One blue figure lay stretched at his feet, another writhed in agony, clawing at a bloody belly. "Back, I say, you gutter-scum! You would, would you!" He lunged and a Jaeger staggered back, a gash across his face. "Back! Back! Cowardly swine! Back! Oh, God Almighty! For once a gun when I need it! You, gunner!" Breymann, his heavy face crimson with rage, lurched through the mob, one hand pointing at Ahrens.

Ahrens spoke crisply. "Move, you men. Keep right on! Our men have bayonets and the rebels haven't. Plenty of time—plenty of time. Straight through the sally-port."

Breymann yelled again. "You, gunner! Don't you hear me? I want that gun slued round! I want grape, round-shot, anything, in that stinking mess there!" He waved a bloody sword toward the north.

Ahrens stiffened to attention. "Sorry, sir. Couldn't fire on the rebels now without hitting our own men."

"Rebels! Rebels! What the hell do I care about rebels! Cleve is still holding them at the west end. It's these cowardly swine that won't stand and fight. Fire on 'em, God damn it, fire on 'em!"

"Fire? On our own men?" Ahrens' eyes began to snap.

Breymann waved his sword. "You heard me! Fire there, there, there into the thick of 'em. By God, they'll turn and fight then! Give the order! Halt your men. Give the order or by God I'll spit you like those swine there!"

Ahrens spoke slowly, surprised to find his voice low. "You *order* me to do this, Colonel?"

"Blazing hell, do you think I'm *asking* you? Carry out the order!"

Ahrens looked through the dark at his crew, obediently trundling the piece along. There seemed to be only two men on the ropes now. He turned back to the Colonel. "With all due respect, sir, you may fry your orders in the hottest corner of hell. Further—I'll personally shoot any gunner of mine who tries to carry out your orders."

Breymann's sword made a quick arc. A carbine cracked by Ahrens' elbow. Breymann dropped his sword, stood staring before him with an expression of stupid incredulity. Slowly his knees sagged, he coughed once, sharply, then pitched forward. There was a low cheer, almost a moan of relief from the mob. A swarm of grenadiers pushed forward, their heavy boots thudding over Breymann's broad back. The rout flowed on, breasted a slight rise and strained on toward the sally-port.

The dark, swarming field whirled before Ahrens' eyes. He swayed, then steadied himself. His arm shot out and clutched a stocky shape that was quietly ducking its head back through the sling of its carbine. The shape moved, a low voice said: "That partly squares us, sir, for the gun-park at Hanau. Now I'd best get back to the piece." Rentner trotted away through the gloom.

Ahrens stepped clear of the jostling push, leaned against a tall stump, panting. With a frayed cuff he wiped the sweat from his forehead, then started as a burst of flames swept up from the farthest of the close-packed tents. He straightened up. "Plundering, by God! We'll get off lightly now." He glanced at the tangled mass of soldiers, women, sutler's carts that beat on through the dark toward the sally-port, then back at the last of the defenders, who were running heavily from the west wall, all but unnoticed by the buckskins and the bluecoats who rioted among the burning tents and the stores. Then a high voice rose, split the darkness: "There they go, there they go! The last of 'em. Follow me! By God, we'll roll 'em up, smash 'em, drive 'em into the Hudson! Virginia! Massachusetts! Dan Morgan!

We'll take Burgoyne in the rear! His whole God-damned camp is open now!" Ahrens could see a great horse rearing and plunging among scattered knots of Yankees, its rider beating the air with his hat and screaming: "Virginia! Massachusetts! Who's with me!"

The darkness rumbled. A great voice boomed: "It's the General! It's Arnold! Drop the loot!" Vague lines began to form about the capering horse and Morgan's ghastly call gobbled through the thin cold air. The great bay spun about, its feet drummed in a furious gallop, while Arnold raved: "At 'em! At 'em! At 'em!"

Beyond the pools of light from the burning tents, Ahrens saw a Jaeger kneel, saw his musket spurt flame. The bay screamed, reared, beat the air with its forefeet, then crashed to the ground.

Almost regretfully Ahrens shook his head. "Goodnight, General Arnold!" he muttered. Then he ran along in the wake of his piece, calling to the fugitives. "Easy, easy! There's be no pursuit now! Easy! Easy!" The dark stream of haggard women, silent white-faced children, stumbling infantry, closed about him.

A harsh, bitter wind howled through the blackness and drove stinging rain in long, slanting sheets down the valley of the Hudson. Ahrens, plashing along the miry road in his leaky boots, smeared a sopping cuff across his eyes in a useless gesture and stared through the water-soaked night. Ahead of him the brass muzzle of the first piece bobbed and ducked like a dim halo. He could just make out the blurred form of Rentner, plodding on, one hand resting on the broad trail. In the rear he could hear the lead-horse of the second piece squelching heavily along in a shower of liquid mud. The wet meadows on the left stirred with vague shapes, half seen, half heard. On the right the dull ruffle of the river glowed faintly, its stippled surface scarred with the blunt noses of the bateaux which struggled to keep abreast of the retreating column.

Through the hum of the wind and the pitiless hiss of the rain a steady beat of voices spouted out of the night. Close by the grinding gun-wheels a grenadier trotted heavily, crying tonelessly over and over like a man in a delirium: "Fritz! Fritz! Where are you, Fritz? Fritz!" An angry English voice cried: "Damn you for a lot of Dutch buggers! Can't you understand *anything?* The staff, the staff! Where's the staff?" Farther off heavy Frisian tones rumbled: "But I *saw* them, Captain. Thirty Riedesel grenadiers under a sergeant. They reserved their arms and marched back toward the Yankee lines. Thirty deserters, sir, and a sergeant!" Ahrens dashed the water from his shapeless hat, jammed it back on his soaking head. "Thirty deserters? And twenty sneaked away from Specht's regiment last night. Ho! Steady, there, steady!"

A man had cannoned into him, cursing. Then he growled: "Who the devil's that? Oh—Lieutenant Ahrens. My apologies. This storm and the darkness set my nerves on edge. I'm Lieutenant Gallwitz of the Specht regiment."

"Specht's? What are you doing back here?"

"Looking for my regiment. I suppose it's up ahead."

"Better walk with me." Ahrens drew him into the streaming mud of the road. "Very easy to walk into a horse or a set of wheels and get run down. Or else break your leg in a pot-hole. Just keep within arm's reach of the muzzle and you'll be pretty safe. God! What a night!"

Gallwitz shook himself like some great, sodden dog. "Damn that red and white madman, Burgoyne. No reason why we couldn't be thirty miles up the river now, and out of reach of those devils. They let us alone the night after the battle, and all today. We could have retreated twenty-four hours ago. But no! His cursed pride wouldn't let him."

"I heard his men didn't want to retreat, either. But then, our lot left camp hours ago. They may have changed."

Gallwitz shook his head. "The grenadiers are still howling to get at the rebels again. I've just come back from the camp-site and heard them. They claim the Yankees won't be able to fire in this weather, and that there'll be a chance to get in with the bayonet."

"That's like the English," grunted Ahrens. "You have to kill them to convince them that they're beaten and then they'll still argue. Our men don't seem to mind the retreat, though."

"Why should they? Or rather why should we? Nothing to us. This isn't our war. If Burgoyne wants us to advance, we'll advance. If it's retreat—why, that's all right, too. My complaint is that that sheep's-head playwright has given the Yankees time to pull themselves together. They were worse disorganized than we were. Now—" He shrugged wet shoulders.

"Any sign that they were stirring when you left camp?"

"Not much. Balcarres is still there with the rearguard. He's leaving all the camp-fires burning—if the rain doesn't put them out. But I *could* see the Yankee officers across that damned ravine, riding up and down with lanterns in their hands. God help us if they do attack us on this road, strung out as we are."

"Bad, damn bad," agreed Ahrens. "But they haven't many bayonets and they can't keep their powder dry in this weather, so I refuse to worry about them as long as the rain keeps up. Hello! What's that along the east bank? See? Those lights?"

A quarter of a mile away across the sullen flood, an irregular flaring chain moved parallel to the crawling column. Gallwitz cupped his thick hands about his eyes. "H'm. One, three, six lights. Say seventy-five men. Tory scouts and what's left of our Indians, probably. Patrolling the east bank."

Ahrens shook his head. "Tories? Indians? Not a chance! They're up in the advance guard, as far away from the rebels as they can get. *Those* must be—yes,

damn my soul, they're Yankees and they're shooting!
Shooting at the bateaux!"

Gallwitz stared. "Now, how the devil do they keep
their powder dry?"

Ahrens laughed grimly. "Probably with my oilskin. I
left it for them in Breymann's redoubt. The lights! Look,
they're scrambling down the east bank. God help us,
they've got boats!"

On the dark surface of the river muskets cracked.
There were hollow poundings, rain-drenched shouts.
Gallwitz gripped Ahrens by the arm. "The stores—the
last of our stores are in the bateaux! Bright angels of
God. They're towing three of them away. See the
lights—there by the point?"

"And a canoe riding in their wake! Listen—they're
shouting!"

Across the rain-swept stream a voice boomed: "Much
obliged, you God-damned mercenaries! We'll come back
for more!" There was a roar of laughter from the black
stream. "Tell Burgoyne we've sent all our *men* home.
We don't need 'em any more. Just keeping boys under
twelve." There were more shouts. Close under the river-
bank, a man began to sing.

> "When Burgoyne, the King's commander,
> Was going to his duty,
> Through all the crowd
> He smiled and bowed
> To every bloody beauty.
> The city rung with feats he'd done
> In Portugal and Flanders
> And all the town thought he'd be crowned
> The first of Alexanders."

Another bellow from the river: "Where's Burgoyne?
Tell him we want to hear him read his Putnam Creek
proclamation again! He forgot to put in some of his titles
the first time."

380

Uncomprehending, the column splashed on. Whistles and catcalls swept up in an endless shower from the river. "What's the matter? Didn't you like Albany? Why don't you answer? Are you *all* damned mercenaries?" Then a heavy voice shouted: "Quiet, there! You on the bank! Listen! Don't worry about your women. We captured a boat load of 'em. They've been put on one of your bateaux that we didn't want. They're safe and going on with you. Do you hear?" The column pushed along, voiceless. "Do you hear? Hell, guts and molasses! They're *all* mercenaries. Potteiger, tell 'em what I said!"

Deep German words boomed up from the river. The silence over the column thickened, then an incredulous snarl rippled down its length. A single yell of, "Stinking turncoat!" rapped out from the dark mass of infantry beyond Ahrens' piece. "Turncoat nothing!" The German on the river laughed. "I hold land on the Mohawk from my grandfather. Tell your half-wit dukes and electors that I wouldn't trade an inch of it for the whole valley of the Elbe." A thin voice whined: "Oh, for a dry priming. I'd drill that swine through the guts." There was another laugh. "Not unless you've learned to shoot better than you did in the clearing! We'll be back for more bateaux later!" Ahrens caught the faint swish of a paddle. The river was quiet again.

Gallwitz snorted. "Stupid swine! Bandying words with Yankee peasants! And, anyway, it's unfair—as I said, it's not our war."

Ahrens stepped knee-deep in a muddy pot-hole. He scrambled out cursing. "Too bad we can't convince the Yankees of that!"

"How long have we been halted, Rentner?"

A bulky form stirred in the thick fog, shivering. "Here's your watch, sir. One hour since you woke me. Did you sleep, sir?"

"As well as I could, propped up between the wheel and the barrel. While you dozed off, two men were run

381

over up ahead there. They slept in the grass off the road and a sutler's cart went over them." He thrust his hands deep in the clammy pockets of his breeches, hugged his elbows tight against his ribs. "Good thing our squad stayed on the road. One hour, eh? Then we've been sitting here in the fog and the rain for five blasted hours!"

"What do you think it means, sir?"

"Don't know. What do the men say?"

"Not much. They're too cold. The Rhetz men up ahead say that the English have slipped off in the fog and left us to face the rebels. They say the English are going by forced marches back to Fort Edward, reopen the lines to Ticonderoga. Then they'll refit and wait for another army to come north up the Hudson."

"An army coming north up the Hudson?" Ahrens laughed hoarsely. "Is that shave still going round? But about the English leaving us in the lurch—you don't believe that, do you?"

"I couldn't say, sir. They're funny. Sometimes they'll share their rations with us. Other times they treat us like strays. Tilley of Barner's speaks some English. He says an Englishmen told him we were like all native troops. We'd do quite well if we had white officers."

Ahrens grunted. "Insulting bastard! What did Tilley do?"

"Nothing, sir. The Baron forbade dueling. And, besides, the English don't fight fair. They strike with their hands. You know—like this." Rentner doubled up a knotty fist. "But they may have given us the slip, for all I know."

Ahrens frowned. "You tell the men that we're halted in a very strong defensive position. You know it's higher ground because the air's colder. Feel that wind? We've come off the river meadows onto the heights. And the British couldn't have slipped past without our knowing." Rentner nodded. "Now I'm going up to the head of the column and see what's happening. Light enough to move about safely. Have the men see if they can't grub

382

up a little dry wood for a fire. I may be able to do something about coffee."

Hands still deep in his pockets, he trotted awkwardly along the fog-bound column, teeth chattering as his gait brought his drenched uniform in contact with unexpected spots on his body. Beyond the lead horse of the first piece he saw the stacked arms of the Rhetz regiment, the men sprawled in the mud in their ragged uniforms. Some of them slept quietly, others snored heavily or moaned in their sleep. "Pomp and panoply of war," grunted Ahrens to himself. "Look at that thin man with his queue undone and his hair in the mud! Rhetz—that means Specht next and then Riedesel. Will any of them know anything?"

He splashed on, talking with haggard, mud-stained lieutenants, with tattered, hollow-eyed sergeants, but no one could say more than that a halt had been ordered and no command given since that time, five hours before. By a wasted company of the Riedesel regiment a tall captain gingerly stroked a filthy cloth bound about a bony wrist and squinted at the maddening fog. "It may be we're waiting for the barges to come up. Then we'll be able to issue rations." His eyes danced nervously about. "Curse this hell-begotten mist! I can't look at it without thinking that any minute it may flash out a volley of those rifles. I swear my men would jump into the river if they heard one gobble of that damned thing the Yankees were blowing."

"I'm not sure I'd not join them. You haven't seen a sutler's cart about here, have you?"

"Seen? I've not seen anything that was more than five feet off the road."

Ahrens nodded. "Think I'll take a run through the fields. I might stumble on one and I'll freeze if I don't keep moving."

The water-logged meadows were a great bowl of milky fog in which muffled sounds from the thousands on the road echoed hollowly. Ahrens trotted on, thinking, "Now if I don't break my neck over a rock or stumble into some buckskins, I ought to find a sutler. God knows they were thick enough up to last night."

Something blurred darkly in the fog before him. Close by he could hear the crump-crump of grazing horses. He quickened his pace, shouted: "Hi!" A few paces away stood a light cart, its shafts propped up by a rough slab of wood. The body of the cart was finished off like a deep calèche and the open front was covered with a wide sheet of waterproof cloth. He shouted again, then stopped abruptly.

Over the top of the waterproof popped a round face, deep blue eyes wide above cheeks that shone with moisture. The little mouth was puckered and an admonitory forefinger lay gently on the lips. Ahrens gasped. "My dear Baroness! I apologize. I've been looking for news and coffee. I had no idea I was disturbing you. The fog, you know. I thought this might be a sutler's cart. Where is the Baron?"

The Baroness' mouth pursed more tightly than ever. Then her eyes began to sparkle, the corners of her mouth twitched. An arm muffled in blue wool reached cautiously out over the waterproof, unhooked it, swept it back with a triumphant gesture. A big man in light blue and buff sprawled on the deep-cushioned seat beside the Baroness, his disheveled head resting on her shoulder one muddy boot dangling over the side of the calèche. In the crook of his right elbow, Ahrens could see Friedericka's blond head, while Gustava was a flattened blur beyond.

The Baroness screwed her head around, looked tenderly at her sleeping husband. "Poor boy. He was so tired. When we got the order to halt, I sent Rockel to look for him. The Baron thought we'd not wait longer than fifteen minutes, tucked his head on my shoulder and—here we are. I didn't have the heart to wake him."

The Baron's eyelids fluttered in his flushed face. Then his eyes opened wide, staring. He sat bold upright.

384

"Dear God! It's light! Fritschen! Have you let me sleep while the army went on? Fritschen, it's past dawn!" He rubbed his eyes, struggled against a yawn. "Oh, it's you, Ahrens. Has the rearguard passed us yet? Where's Rockel? He must harness up. Rockel!"

His wife patted his shoulder. "Now, now. The army hasn't moved a step. And as there wasn't room for Lena and you and me and the three girls in the calèche, I sent her back to the wagons with Rockel. I only hope her intentions were honorable. She was ogling Rockel and for an old soldier he's terribly sensitive."

"The Baroness is right, sir. No orders have come, and the men are sleeping in the mud."

Riedesel jumped heavily to the ground, groaning and rubbing his knees. "Why wasn't I told! No orders! Has that man crawled away to some warm corner with his bottle while my men stiffen in the mud? He gave the order to halt. I've got it in writing. By God, we should be ten, fifteen miles up the river!" He settled his sword belt about his ample waist. "Criminal, criminal. We're inviting Gates to snap us up. Where are my aides? Oh, under that tree? Rout 'em out, Ahrens. Tell 'em to follow me. By God, I'll start *something* moving!"

With the gaping toe of his boot, Ahrens stirred a cluster of wet forms that huddled in the pathetic defenselessness of sleep, saw them stagger to their feet, shivering and cursing, and totter on numb legs after the striding Baron. From the calèche an arm waved wildly, scaled something dark through the dripping fog. "Friederich Adolf von Riedesel! Your hat! Pull your cloak about you and *don't* splash through those puddles! You *know* how easily you take cold!"

On the broad seat Friedericka and Gustava stirred sleepily, rolled themselves into a tight knot under a blanket of gray fur. On the Baroness' lap the bundle that was Caroline showed a tight pink fist and one sternly closed eye. "They've been so good, Lieutenant. So long as they have your wolfskin, they're perfectly happy.

385

They won't look at a blanket, and as for *linen*—" she rolled up her eyes—"Heaven knows what I'll do with them when I get them back to dull old Wolfenbüttel."

Ahrens coughed dryly. "At our present rate of march, any worries about Wolfenbüttel are so far in the future that you may dismiss them. Why don't you think of the chances of betrothing the girls to some rising young Yankees?"

The Baroness nibbled daintily at a slim forefinger, looked at Ahrens through solemn blue eyes. "Mmmm. They'd have land, I suppose. I declare I'll speak to the Baron about it. He seemed very much taken with that Arnold and with a man called Dearborn. Do you suppose they have sons? We could always send a note through the lines to ask." She shifted the amorphous Caroline, settled the wolfskin about Friedericka and Gustava. "It's not raining so hard, now. And I do believe that the fog is lifting. Yes, I can see the ears of one of the horses—see them? Just the ears, wambling about in the fog all by themselves."

"Always fog down this valley in the morning, rain or shine. Yes, its lifting a little. The wind must have shifted." He looked off toward the river. Gray shapes moved in the cottony mass that covered land and water as the wretched column stirred in its muddy tracks.

"This is nice." The Baroness pulled a thick cape closer about her. "Now we can see those lovely leaves. We—" She stopped short, set her mouth in a tight line. "Five mortal hours we've sat in this calèche and all the time there was a cabin not fifty paces away. Look at that! And smoke coming out of the chimney!"

Beyond the tethered horses the ragged lines of a slab roof jutted through the thinning mist, rough bark gleaming dully in the rain. From the mud-and-stick chimney a woolly trickle of smoke oozed. As the wind freshened, the gray curtain rolled slowly away from meadow and river, leaving a world that was sharp, clear, under the slanting drizzle. The door of the cabin opened, a figure

386

in faded red and smeared white stared through bleary eyes at the wet morning. He yawned, flung a glittering cascade of empty bottles onto the rain-beaded grass. A harsh Scotch voice snarled behind him: "Wad ye now! Ye feckless fool! I' the back, mon, i' the back." The servant grumbled, stepped gingerly into the rain, gathered up the bottles and walked with short, high steps to the rear of the cabin.

"Bottles!" The Baroness sat bolt upright, eyes staring. "Bottles—after a night like this! Who could— Look at those carts in back! I've seen *them* before! And that lady's portmanteau! It *must* be—"

There was scarlet and white in the black oblong of the doorway. Gentleman Johnny Burgoyne, shaved and powdered, rubbed his hands and smiled at the scattering mists, called over his shoulder, laughing, to someone hidden in the cabin.

The waterproof apron of the calèche rustled as the Baroness' firm little hands flung it back. Her sharp heels smacked into the dripping turf. "You stay here and see that the girls don't roll off the seat." Ahrens had a fleeting glimpse of a tight-set chin, snapping eyes, as the Baroness, her very skirts bristling, raced over the humpy ground to the cabin.

Gentleman Johnny's smile flashed through the wet air. "Aha! My dear Baroness!" He bowed, covertly closing the door behind him. "Always fresh and always charming. I vow you're sweet as a rose on whose petals the morning dew glitters. Ha-ha! But your eyes, my dear Baroness, would dull any glitter, would shame the very sunshine on the broad ripples of the river!"

"Ripples! Roses!" The Baroness planted herself squarely in front of the General. "Those bottles! That smoke! General Burgoyne, I—I wish the Yankees had captured you! You hid away here with your fire and your bottles and—and—" Her eyes indicated the covered carts and the portmanteaux beyond the cabin. "With your bottles! Five hours and more and your men froze in

387

the mud! No orders! Just waited and froze, and if that Arnold had come down out of the fog, they would have been butchered in their tracks and you none the wiser. They're sleeping in the mud, English and Brunswickers and Hessians together, while you—you—"

Gentleman Johnny clapped his hand. "By George, Baroness, there speaks the soldier's wife and the soldier's daughter. Your father would have been proud to hear you, and so would the good Baron. Thinking of the men first, the men first. Gad, I honor you for that. And you'll be glad to hear that when the last of the bateaux come up, rations will be issued. Rations, madame, and damme if I won't order an extra tot of rum all around for the men to drink to the health of the lady whose pretty head was concerned on their account." He wagged a finger at her, bent over and went on in a confidential tone. "And then do you know what we'll do? We'll hold a review. Yes, a review of the whole force, and then—"

"A review! Hold a review!" The Baroness' voice was high with anger. She trembled, started to speak. Then she stamped her foot, whirled about and marched to the calèche. Ahrens could see that her eyes were blurred, her chin quivering.

The Siege

LIKE a sluggish river of muddied red and blue, Burgoyne's army inched painfully north. Gates dallied, fidgeted and at last set out in cautious pursuit.

North, south, east and west the Yankee lines slowly closed in. Crafty and noncommittal, Gates watched his opponent while sharp-eyed infantry filtered through woods and fields, drawing an ever tighter net about the battered regiments which huddled in their earthworks near the Marshall house. Rifles cracked and muskets slammed every hour of the day and night. Gates brought up artillery from his old works to the south of Freeman's Farm. For the first time in the campaign, cannon backed up the stinging menace of Yankee small-arms.

IX

The Siege

YANKEE drums rolled and slammed in the flat lands across the Fish Kill. Ahrens slowly opened his eyes, scowled at the river-mist that rolled sullenly over the earthworks, then slipped out of the sodden blanket that he shared with the battered Pausch. There was a rumble from across the river, something whistled and shrieked through the air, ended its flight in a distant crash of boards. Ahrens, crouching low over a bucket of muddy water, cursed. Pausch opened one bloodshot eye, nodded wisely. "Another through the Marshall house," he observed. He sat up on the blanket, listened, as a salvo yelled through the air. "Those are across the open space near the Rhetz regiment. What the devil are you splashing cold water about for?"

Ahrens grunted. "Call these swamp-scourings water? These ablutions, Captain, have nothing to do with cleanliness. Merely a ritual inspired by morbid family pride. Gad, what a racket those drums are kicking up over there!"

Pausch edged his feet into stiff boots, adjusted his stock. "There, my toilet's complete. Those drums? Oh, yes. Calling Gates to breakfast."

"Hope his is better than ours. Did you know that the Yankees snapped up the last of our bateaux last night? It was while I was on guard."

Pausch groaned. "No more rations, then, except what

391

we have in our wagons. No more clothes. No more powder and shot."

"Plenty of that left in the tumbrils. Were you at the south works yesterday while the Baron was inspecting?"

Pausch fumbled in a greasy haversack, pulled out a doleful-looking slab of bacon. "South works? No."

"Pretty sight there. Gentleman Johnny himself couldn't have imagined anything more dramatic. Everyone was staring off into the mist. By God, it rolled back like a curtain and there were heavy columns of Yankees within fifty paces of the works. Nixon's brigade, I heard later."

"Fifty *paces*! What happened?"

"Why, every one of us saw another Bunker Hill, with the Yankees as recipients this time. You could have heard a whisper. The gunners were blowing on their linstocks and the infantry were fingering their triggers. Then the next second—there weren't any Yankees—just a flood of brown coats going pell-mell down the hill. I saw an old sergeant of the 20th crying."

"Close thing. Proves that a rabble won't stand against regular troops. This bushwhacking around Freeman's Farm doesn't show anything."

"Rabble? You should have seen them. Tumbled down the slope like so many meal-sacks, and when they reached the bottom, there they were, in neat formation and marching off without a scratch, singing that song about—you know, I wrote out a translation for you—'I'm John Burgoyne and Burgoyne John, sir!' No, they weren't a rabble. They were just practical."

Pausch shook his head. "Bad soldiering, bad soldiering!"

Ahrens patted his streaming face with a sheet of cartridge paper. "Hasn't it occurred to you, Captain, that during a war, you don't have much time for soldiering? Take old Praetorius of Prinz Friederich's regiment. His norm is a review before a Grand Duke in perfect weather. But he's lost here, because Grand Dukes aren't present in these blasted forests in any overwhelming numbers and you can't plan on the weather."

"You'll end by turning us all into rangers. Here's your share of the bacon. It's all cooked. Shall we light a fire to warm it up? It's clammy as a fish's belly now."

Ahrens held out his hand. "Fish or no fish, I eat mine cold. I may be overtimid, but every time I strike flint and steel together here, I expect to see one of those damned Virginians hanging his long nose over the redoubt to see what we have for breakfast." He began gnawing at the greasy slab. "What orders for today?"

The Yankee guns opened in another fury of explosions and shrieking projectiles. Pausch shook his fist at the hissing air. "Big parley at Burgoyne's. Even I'm invited."

"Parley?"

"Don't know what for. I'm betting we attack. We can't sit here. The only safe places in camp are the big 'V' of this redoubt, the other side of the hill where Burgoyne's marquee is and the cellar of the Marshall house. Those damn rifles sweep every bit of ground that the cannon can't reach. We've all our horses hidden in that hollow beyond the marquee. There's no fodder where they are. They break away, trying to graze and then the Yankees shoot them. All the rolling ground behind the 9th is speckled with dead horses. God above, don't they stink!"

"Water, too," said Ahrens. "What you're drinking there out of my bottle was scooped up from a cluster of hoofprints, filtered through my last handkerchief and has stood just about long enough to have most of the sediment settle to the bottom. At least, I hope it has. Don't jar it."

Pausch snarled. "Two rivers almost flowing over our feet and no water!"

"Can't be helped. They've shot at least ten men who've tried to fill buckets. Well, here's the fog lifting. That means that Gates' gunners will be slamming at everything that moves!"

In the growing light, sullen men of the Riedesel regiment staggered to their feet, in the long, prow-shaped redoubt, scraped at the sticky mud that clung to their facings. Sentries, bluish-white with cold, stared over their shoulders, watched the hard-eyed sergeants routing out their reliefs. Somewhere in the thinning fog, a Yankee gun slammed heavily. A fresh rustle of drums broke out. Pausch looked up at the deepening blue of the sky. "Now if I can hug this parapet as far as the curve of that little hill, then duck behind those rocks, I'll be in a dead space and out of reach. Damnation!" A rifle-bullet sang wickedly through the air. "If I can get Burgoyne's ear—or the Baron's, damned if I won't plead for a chance to slip a few men through the lines, a few men who can rush north to Ticonderoga and bring down the men that are rotting up there."

Ahrens was absorbed in the priming of his pistol. "That's been tried, Captain."

"Tried? By whom? Our men?"

"No." Ahrens tightened the flint. "Not our men. Some Indians."

"Indians? Where did they go?"

"They didn't. They used every trick they knew of in the dark and in the broken country. Finally some Massachusetts men captured the whole lot."

"Indians? And *they* couldn't get through! Good God! Did the Yankees cut their throats?"

"Worse."

"Eh? Worse? You don't mean they tortured 'em!"

"Worse again. They painted 'em white—a color that's peculiarly offensive to this particular tribe for some reason or other—and sent 'em back with a note to Gentleman Johnny. Said they had no objection to feeding Englishmen or even mercenaries—meaning us—but as for Indians, no indeed."

Pausch stroked his bristly jaws. "If Indians couldn't slip through—" He tossed up his hands.

"Another thing." Ahrens glanced around, drew Pausch away from a knot of scowling Rhetz men who squatted to their cold bacon. "In your ear. You'll see the Baron? Tell him this. I heard last night—never mind how—that the Brunswick infantry and the Hanauers have taken a vow that if the rebels attack, they'll fire just one volley and then ground their arms."

Pausch's jaw sagged. "One volley? And then surrender?"

"Not an infantryman of ours will fire more than one round. Even that they'll fire in the air."

Pausch whispered: "That's treason! It's mutiny."

Ahrens shrugged. "It's worse than that. It's the truth. Our gunners are still sound. I happened to learn that two or three were wavering and—and had a short chat with them. They'll stand. But what good is that if all the infantry give up? I thought the Baron better know."

Pausch squared his shoulders, set his mouth in a thin line. "I'll see the Baron even—even, by God, if I have to violate military etiquette to do it." He smacked his fist into his open palm. "Yes, damned if I won't! Now what are you up to this morning?"

"Dufail's in charge of what's left of our guns. If the rebels let us alone, I'll run over to the Marshall house."

"*Marshall* house! Why, in God's name? No one there but the women and the wounded that the Baroness rounded up and hid in the cellars because *someone*"—his jaw set again—"someone in high authority forgot all about 'em. What do you want there?"

"Just occurred to me that some of the sick and wounded may make a miraculous recovery if I can have a word with 'em."

"Malingerers?" Pausch's eyebrows went up.

"I don't say. But I learned that a little Irishman named Donohoe had been taken with a severe case of flux as soon as the rebels opened their guns on us. He's there and there may be others."

Pausch snorted, barked, "Good luck!" and trotted stiffly off along the south edge of the redoubt, keeping close. Ahrens watched him break into the open as the

Yankee guns roared a crescendo, saw him spring for the shelter of a low hill, reappear, running hard, across a clear space. Nausea sprang in Ahrens throat as a thudding cloud of dust and rocks hid the stocky little figure. Then he gasped with relief as Pausch, mud-splashed, scrambled to his feet and dived behind a tumbled mass of rocks. He saw a glint of gilt buttons, a soiled red cuff waving, caught a dull gleam of yellow teeth. A faint voice shouted: "Fooled 'em, by God!" Pausch waved again and walked calmly off, out of reach of cannon or rifle.

By the gaping wooden walls and shattered windows of the Marshall house, Ahrens straightened up, beat clotted dirt from his coat and breeches. Three times in the mile that lay between the main army and the sagging farm, he had plunged headlong to shelter as the flat meadows on the east side of the Hudson flowered in echoing puffs of smoke and flame. Now he drew a deep breath and looked south over the rolling country that stood clear and sharp in the still autumn morning. The great intrenched camp with its moving points of red and blue jutted up from the plain at his right front. Beyond it he could see the sparkle of the Fish Kill as it swept down in a great "V" before joining the broad Hudson. The flat lands across the Hudson and south of the Fish Kill were quiet, but seethed with the subdued flash and twinkle of armed men in motion. The Yankee guns were silent for the moment. There was a thin hush, broken only by the stunning crash of a twenty-four-pounder off by the lines of the 21st, pitching solid-shot at one-minute intervals onto the throat of the river-road below the mouth of the Fish Kill. He rubbed his smooth-shaven chin, frowned at the road. "Looks hospitable, but if I walk south I'll run into Gates' men and if I follow it north, that long-legged Stark will have a chance to make up for missing me at Bennington. Bennington—if I cross the river and manage to slip past Fellows' men, I'll be at the mouth of the Batten Kill, and the road that would lead me back to Bennington. They say it's bad luck for a soldier to double on his tracks. I'm seeing too many places and people for the second time. Still, I'll be damn glad to see Ticonderoga again. Hope we don't take as long going back as we did coming down!"

He pushed open the heavy door and peered cautiously down the long stone steps into the rumbling twilight of the triple cellars of the Marshall house. Uncertain shapes passed back and forth in front of a guttering lamp which rolled out a pall of inky, stinking smoke; voices twittered and whined and croaked. Ahrens narrowed his eyes, started slowly down the stairs. A fresh, crisp voice rose to meet him: "Yes, it was on the way from Wolfenbüttel to Dortrecht, where we were to go on board. Just the children and Lena in the coach with me, and Rockel driving on the box. Pine woods, Mrs. Reynal, and so dark. Rockel was driving very slowly and all at once something soft and heavy hit me. Right through the carriage window! I was so frightened I grabbed it. Ugh! It was soft and woolly. I screamed so loud that Rockel heard me. Guess what it was! A man! Yes, a man. The police had hanged him to a tree by the road and there he was with his legs dangling right through the carriage window! Traveling is much pleasanter and safer in America.... Oh, here's Lieutenant Ahrens again."

Ahrens stared through the murk, saw the little Baroness sitting bolt upright on a pile of straw, her elder daughters close beside her. Caroline was nowhere to be seen. A pale English woman sat easily on another bundle of straw, hands calmly knitting while haunted eyes shot this way and that. In the darker recesses, vague forms stirred, shifted, rustled, whispered.

Ahrens bowed. "What may I do for you, Baroness?"

Hands folded primly in her lap she answered: "We are doing very nicely. Unless you could get some w-a-t-e-r. Certain people are very t-h-i-r-s-t-y." Her blue eyes flicked toward the blond heads beside her.

"I wish I might, Baroness. The Yankees don't want us to. They take drastic means of showing their disapproval—"

She clasped her hands suddenly. "Oh, oh, oh! They're calling again!"

Through the stone wall Ahrens heard faint groans, gabbling words, then high-pitched overtones that reminded him of wet fingers drawn over glass.

She shook her head. "Forty wounded men here and only the women to look after them. They're in the second cellar and beyond them are our women. The others here are English. We've no medicines and the surgeons don't like to come here. Have you seen the Baron?"

"Last night."

"Last night!" She sighed. "I envy you. None of us have set foot outside this cellar since the Yankee guns opened up three days ago. What a place this was! Seventy people had been crowded in here and none of them had gone out." She wrinkled her nose. "None of them. But I found that the quartermaster had lots of vinegar, so Mrs. Reynal and I and the rest of the women took brooms and vinegar and what water we could get and scrubbed these cellars. It's different now." She nodded vigorously and pursed her lips. "It's going to stay different. Oh, dear!" She started, huddled back against the wall. "They're beginning again!"

Far away in the outer sunlight there was a dull thud. Something yelled in the air, battered at the side of the house, crashed away in a series of deafening thuds. The Baroness put her hands to her cheeks. "The worst thing is to hear them bump-bump-bumping over the floors upstairs. Here's another!"

Ahrens felt sickening emptiness, a sagging of his knees. Being cannonaded in the open country was one thing. It was another to crouch in a blind hole, to hear a heavy-timbered house collapsing in a shattering roar directly over head. The pounding was incessant now. He noticed that the little Riedesels' eyes widened, lifted to

398

their mother with each crash. Otherwise they gave no sign, uttered no sound. She smiled down at them. "This is just like the Kobolds in the Hartz Mountains playing at nine-pins on stormy nights." The two little heads nodded solemnly, resumed their unwinking study of the heavy rafters above them.

Ahrens stared at the Baroness in awed admiration. She leaned forward, whispered: "I'm so frightened. I'm simply terrified. And if you ever tell the Baron I'll make him transfer you to the sappers. Ohhhhh! They've stopped. *Do* you think they're bombarding us on purpose?"

Ahrens shook his head. "There's a redoubt just below the house—what's left of the advance corps and some Hesse-Hanau grenadiers. It's a difficult target. This house catches the overs; the shorts plow up the road. Where's Caroline? I hope—"

The Baroness pointed. "She's in that basket." Ahrens saw a vague shape swinging from the ceiling. "It's attached to a rope that runs to the door to the second cellar. Caroline acts as a weight so the door closes of itself and when anyone goes in—the motion rocks her. Your corporal, Rentner, rigged that up. His wife is in the third cellar. He made her stay there and I promised to look after her."

The door to the outer world opened. A firm step rang on the treads. Ahrens looked up to see a tall girl edging carefully down, something heavy dangling from each hand. "Where does the Baroness wish me to put these?" asked Hedwig.

The Baroness gasped. "Hedwig Rentner! It's—it's *water!*"

Hedwig set two buckets down on the dirt floor. She straightened up, rubbed blistered hands together. "Yes, Baroness, water!"

"But—but, Hedwig—where—?"

"From the cold spring close by the river, Baroness."

Ahrens felt his throat tighten. "Hedwig! *You* went to the spring? Ten men have—"

Hedwig curtsied. "I didn't see the Lieutenant. Fifteen men now."

"And you went?"

"I did not think the rebels would shoot at a woman."

"Did they?"

"No, Lieutenant. They were hidden all along the opposite bank and when I came to the spring, one of them shouted something, then they all got up and waved their hats. They held their muskets upside down. The little girls, Baroness—I have a cup."

Mrs. Reynal looked up from her knitting. "Tell her she's a sportsman, whatever that may be in German." Her needles clicked on.

"One cup apiece for the girls—one only, Hedwig. I want the rest for the wounded. Will you help me, Lieutenant? Hedwig, I—I want to say, I want to tell you, but if I say anything I'm going to cry. Come with me, young man."

Ahrens, carrying both buckets, followed the Baroness. "I came here to see your patients. I think I may be able to cure one or two of them."

She looked over her shoulder at him, eyebrows raised." Cure? I don't see— Oh, you think there may be malingerers. Ye-e-es, there may be a few. But help me first. And there's an Englishman I want you to talk to. An ensign. He's from Rugby. They shot him through both legs. This house was a hospital until the Yankees began on it. This ensign was waiting his turn. His best friend was on the operating table—to have a leg off. The first ball came through the wall, killed the surgeon and shattered the boy's other leg. He died, of course. This ensign you're to talk to saw it all. It was his best friend—and he's only just sixteen."

With the heavy, sweetish reek of gangrene hanging in his throat and nostrils, Ahrens followed the Baroness from one damp truss of straw to the next, treading carefully through the dimness of the crowded cellar. Above them the old house rocked and shook from time to time and masses of iron crashed and bumped over the old timbers. At last the Baroness rose, smiled shakily at him through the dank stench and trotted away to the first cellar. Then Ahrens set his jaw, stood over a truss and began to speak in a low, level voice.

It was nearly noon when he left the splintered walls of the Marshall house and began his breakneck journey back to the redoubt. Through the bright fall sunshine, three red jackets and two blue followed him.

Ahrens stumbled down the redoubt through the thin night air. "God above, but I'm tired! Three hours staring across the river. The Yankees were quiet for once. Not a shot. That must mean that they're planning something especially hellish and I'll have that turkey-gobble rattling around in my head again. Wonder why they lit all those big fires along the Fish Kill." He began counting the loopholes that glimmered dully in the face of the redoubt. "Six, seven, eight—and here's Pausch, rolled up in our blanket like a sausage." He bent down, shook the Captain's shoulder. "Safe again, Captain. The Yankees didn't even try to blow my head off this time."

Pausch grunted, stirred. Ahrens kicked off his boots, loosened his stock and edged under the blanket. "What happened at the meeting at Burgoyne's?"

"Meeting? Meeting? Good God, let me sleep!"

"No orders? Nothing settled?"

Pausch growled: "Everything settled."

Ahrens sat up, eager. "Settled? What is it? Ticonderoga and a forced march? Or do we attack?"

"Blast your eyes! Do you want to freeze me? Lie down or else give me the rest of the blanket!" The veteran tugged at the flapping edge.

"That better?" Ahrens stretched his long legs beside the Captain. "But what is it? Attack or retreat? Albany or Ticonderoga?"

Pausch shook his shoulders impatiently. "Neither!"

Ahrens groaned. "Good God! Just sit here and wait till they lose their heads and attack us? Oh, blast it, that's too much. The army's rotting away fast enough as it is. Here—I've an idea. Let me pick my gun crew; we'll knock a gun to pieces; ferry it across the river at night; set it up below the bend in the Fish Kill; throw some red-hot shot among that mass of rebel powder wagons just back of the flat-topped hill. You know where they are. Blow up their whole blasted supply. How do you like that? By God, I'll do it and invite Charteris to come along." He shook the Captain. "Have I your permission? Won't that be better than sitting here, waiting for them to come across the river after us? Just a six-pounder and eight men! I'll bet the Yankees are getting slack enough so we can do it and not lose a man!"

Pausch lay silent in his half of the blanket. Ahrens shook him again. "Will you give permission?"

In the dark the old Captain shook his head angrily.

"It's bound to succeed," Ahrens urged. "And even if we lose the piece, lose the crew—isn't that better than sitting here, rotting, starving, dying of scurvy?"

Pausch stirred, turned his head slightly. "Did I say we were going to sit here?"

"Why—yes; yes, you did. We're not retreating. We're not attacking. What else?" Suddenly he clutched the veteran's hard shoulder. "God above, man! What the hell are you saying? Captain, Captain Pausch—why, you're telling me—Burgoyne, the Baron, our regiments—they wouldn't— Dear Christ, wake up!"

Pausch spoke sharply. "I'm awake. It's surrender!"

"Surrender! To the Yankees! *Our* troops! The Elector's troops! The men we've trained! Not surrender—" He lay back, shaken, weak. The word "surrender" beat like the Yankee artillery through his head, throbbed like the rustling, echoing drums that had called up the homespun men from pine-fringed farms and from rocky cities far away on the coast, from lush plantations by warm rivers

402

and from the peril-girt trails of the Western mountains. His brain whirled. He saw again the calm face of the old man in the fields beyond Hubbardton, the gray farmers who drifted like wind-blown spray through the woods by Bennington, the lean men in buckskin who rallied to Morgan's ghastly gobbling call, the body of the woman in the woods by Freeman's Farm, hands clutching sodden cartridges, the waves of hard-faced men who raced and yelled and cursed in the wake of the mad Arnold.

Surrender! His eyes felt hard and dry, the lids stiff as though they would never close again. Surrender! He saw Spangenberg, the tall gentle man who loved running water and the scent of pines, dead across the trail of his piece. Meister, whose dead face his men would not let him see; Heisse, stark in the grass by the heavy wheels of the piece; Pache, whirling round and round clasping his head in hands whose fingers spouted blood.

Surrender, surrender, surrender! To the men who had called their roll below him in the black woods, a roll of names that reeked of the New World, names of men who had come because they had voted in their town meeting that it was fitting they should. To the men he had seen shambling about the bald top of Mount Independence on a hot morning in July, to the men whose axes had beat a devil's tattoo in his brain and in the brain of the army through those hot, fly-plagued days at the head of Champlain. To men of Philadelphia, of New York, of Boston. Of Boston. To the men, perhaps, of Judith Hunnewell's family.

Judith! Where was she now? She had ridden into the battle, on the fringe where the Indians were. Had she turned back? Was the Conestoga wagon a charred wreck beside a bundle of sodden clothes in the wet woods? The woods were wet in the ravines near Freeman's Farm, wet, with leaves that blazed like dusty jewels. Ott, the tall man from Darnstadt had loved those leaves, had buried his dingy shelter in them, and now Ott was prey for the wolves in a clearing by a cabin. The cabin in the woods on the road to Hubbardton had smoldered and in the dooryard sprawled puppets in sticky-scarlet caps, scarlet like— He shook himself. Was his brain cracking?

He was suddenly aware that his skin was dry, burning, his bones aching with deep, stabbing twinges, his throat parched and stiff. Waves of heat swept over him, drying his eyeballs, cracking the skin on his hands. He thought, "Here's a go of fever!" then started as his thought echoed back from the dirt wall of the redoubt. He had spoken out loud, then found that he was shivering, his hands shaking so that he could not control them. He tried to fix his eyes on a bright star directly over him, but the star turned into a flickering light by a black river where long files of sullen men marched in the rain to thud up the gangplanks of squalid river-boats. His ears buzzed to their tread. The marching files wouldn't sing and that was a pity, because they were marching to surrender to a savage old man whose snow-white beard fanned out across a naked chest smeared with Indian paints.

Surrender! Surrender! The flood of heat raced back over him, drenching him in sweat. Surrendering and the men wouldn't sing and old La Corne St. Luc was sneering at them from his six and a half feet of bone and muscle. Judith would understand that Hanau men couldn't sing, surrendering like that. The poor men stolen from their farms and shops. If she could only help him onto his feet, he could make that so clear to St. Luc.

A hand slipped under his head. Pausch's voice, from an immense distance, said: "Here, boy, here. I've saved some rum for you."

Rum burned his throat, cleared away the fever-fog a little. A hard hand patted his shoulder, Pausch's voice went on: "Here, boy, here. You're young, and after all it's not our army and it's not our war." Ahrens drank again. With the returning fever, sleep swooped down on him like a deep, black deluge.

Hours later he waked, dry of mouth and light of head. Some question had been tormenting his mind through his fever-sleep. He rolled his eyes about. Pausch sat huddled on the fire-step of the redoubt, watching him. Faintly Ahrens whispered: "What's the name of this place?"

Pausch bent over him. "Name?"

"Yes, name of this place. Want to know."

"Go to sleep, boy, go to sleep."

"But I want to know."

Deft hands settled the blanket about his throat. "The map calls it Saratoga. Go to sleep."

A steady wind from the west brought a sickening reek of decay from the rolling meadows where the stiff legs of horses and oxen jutted grotesquely to the morning sun. Pausch shifted his feet nervously, ran quick fingers around his stock. "Well," he cleared his throat, "well, this is the day."

Ahrens, pale and drawn, nodded, his eyes on a pair of horsemen who cantered easily over the ford of the Fish Kill, reined in and dismounted at the foot of the redoubt of the 9th. "Who are they?" Hands behind him, he jerked a shoulder toward the figures in dark blue and buff.

Pausch stroked his lined jaws. "It's easy to see that you were flat on your back during the armistice and the negotiations. That's Wilkinson, Gates' aide, with *his* aide in tow. He spent more time here than in Gates' camp during the squabblings over terms. Everyone knows him by sight."

"Much squabbling and arguing?" asked Ahrens.

"Things came damn close to blowing up once or twice. This Wilkinson smoothed over the last row. He talked Gates into agreeing to Burgoyne's demand that the—the terms be called 'convention' and not 'capitulation.' The devil! What difference does it make!"

"'The Convention of Saratoga.' Yes. Gentleman

Johnny couldn't miss that. It would tickle his ear. Of course he'd want it. By the way—" Ahrens coughed—"by the way, what about—well, you know—Burgoyne?"

Pausch shook his head. "Still over there in that cabin. He's been locked away there ever since he signed. Not even Balcarres has seen him. People say—"

"I know." Ahrens frowned. "Drinking himself to death. Or else he's already blown his brains out. Or gone mad. Or all three." He stared at the distant cabin, whose cold chimney and shuttered windows denied any life within its slab walls. "Gad, I believe every man not on duty is watching that cabin!" Scattered over the green meadows, still lush in spite of the early fall, knots of men in bright red, in faded red, men in sleek uniforms, men in tatters, clustered, drifted, squatted, eying the silent cabin over their shoulders.

"H'm." Pausch ran an expert eye over the groups. "A lot there who *ought* to be on duty. Some of our men on the little hill by the Marshall house, too. Wonder—wonder what he'll do." Hands behind him, he rocked back and forth on his heels. "You all right now?"

Ahrens nodded. "Weak as spruce-beer, but sound otherwise. The surgeon you brought over cheerfully told me that I'd have recurrent attacks for a year or more—increasing in violence till they—or I—were worn out. Seems to be a favorite fever of this part of the world." He stared at the cabin again. "I wonder—look, there's a shutter open! No, just a shadow from the eaves. Damn it, he'll have to come out soon. There's Wilkinson waiting to take him over to Gates. *No* one seen him, you say?"

"Not a soul."

"Not even—"

Pausch eyed the profound blue of the fall sky. "No, not even—She slipped out of camp last night. Free passage back to Ticonderoga from Gates. You see, she had a standing order in writing from Burgoyne about her carts and things. The sentries didn't dare stop her when they

406

saw it. She must be beyond Fort Edward now. I wonder who had to tell *him* about it?"

"So the poor devil's all alone. Look, Captain, I swear the crowd's growing every minute. Let's get nearer." They walked along a slippery path that made a ribbon of sullen brown across the meadows. Two privates of the 24th, green facings livid against the faded red of their jackets, thumped past them at a heavy trot, fear-haunted eyes fixed on the bleak walls of the cabin. One of them panted: "You'll see! 'E'll not leave us, not 'im!" The other shook his head. "'O's seen 'im? I asks yer, 'o's seen 'im. I tell yer, 'e's in Boston at this minute. 'E went aw'y in the night!"

The flat land in front of the cabin hummed with a stifled, uneasy buzz. Ahrens looked curiously at the countless shifting groups of officers and enlisted men who seemed to have submerged rank in their anxious concern, who tried to keep their eyes casual and careless. "Odd," he said. "All the crowd is gathered at the front. No one at all at the sides or in the rear."

Pausch jerked his head. "And every man has his back turned toward the door. Damn, but it's hot!" He wiped his forehead with a trembling hand.

"Hot?" Ahrens stared. Then he realized that his own hands were damp and clammy. He found his feet tapping in time to the shrieking of Yankee fifes across the Fish Kill, fifes that rose and shrilled above the mutter of drums. "Lively," he said.

"Yankee music." Pausch's face was twitching slightly. "An Englishman told me. *Yankee Doodle*. It was written by an Englishman, making fun of the Yankees. Now it's their hymn." He ran his knotty fingers up and down the facings of his jacket. The music died away in a last triumphant banging of drums and raving of fifes. The air was deadly still. Wheels rumbled by the ford across the Hudson. Pausch swallowed, tilted his head toward the river. "Yankee rations. Gates—Gates is feeding our men."

Ahrens tore his eyes from the door, looked at Pausch.

"Gates? Oh, yes." Then he clamped his hands on Pausch's rigid arm. "My God—what, what—"

Around the end of the cabin tore a wild-eyed private, face crimson, jaws working hysterically. He ripped off his battered hat, smashed it on the ground. His voice screeched like a fife: " 'Ere 'e is! 'Ere 'e is! It's Gentleman Johnny and 'e's all prinked out like a bloody jibby-horse!"

There was a glint of a bay head, a flash and dazzle of scarlet and white. Close on the heels of the screaming man rode Gentleman Johnny Burgoyne, hair sleek and snowy with powder, coat gleaming with fresh gold lace, boots mirroring the shifting group that stood frozen in the bright grass. The air was dead, still, heavy, and the slow beat of the bay's hooves smacked sharp and clear. Then a tattered man of the 9th dropped on his knees, shielding his wet face with his arm, a trembling hand stretched out. A strangled voice croaked: "Up, the 47th! Three cheers for Gentleman Johnny!" The still air shivered, the flat meadow erupted in a pelting swarm of men in faded red who ran shouting after the mincing bay, engulfing the trim staff that rode behind. Ahrens found himself swept along with the rest, Pausch close beside him. A gray-haired English major jostled him, bumped into a private of the 20th. Gentleman Johnny's hat swept off, his fresh ruddy face was grave in the sunlight. Close by him ran a tall sergeant, alternately saluting and snatching off his hat. "It ain't true, sir! It ain't true! They say so, but it ain't true." His hand clawed at the General's stirrup. "It ain't true!"

Gentleman Johnny reined in. His voice was full, courteous, as he bent down to the panting sergeant. "What's not true, my lad?"

The sergeant gulped, saluted. "They say, sir, they say as how you're leavin' us. That the Yankees have a ship to take you back to England. An' leavin' us here!"

Back went the sleek powdered head. Gentleman Johnny's white teeth flashed, his full laugh rang out over the

408

meadows. "Leave you!" His voice was rich, deep. "Leave *you!* That be damned for a shave." He grew grave, stood in his stirrups. "Listen, lads! Where you go, I go, and, by God, the devil himself can't budge me from that! And wherever we are, I'll fight for the rights of the British soldier against Heaven and Hell. The rights of the British soldier and"—he bowed—"his allies!" His clenched fist shot out in a stabbing gesture. Then he saluted, touched his mare with his shining spurs and trotted quickly off toward the foot of the jutting redoubt, where the blue and buff figure of Wilkinson waited.

The steam from the camp-kettles was thick, fragrant. Ahrens sat on a grassy bank close by the river-road and sniffed luxuriously, watched chunks of Yankee beef, smooth slices of potatoes, round flanks of onions, well up to the smoking surface of the water, turn, sink in a slow train of bubbles. Across the pot peered the wrinkled foreheads of two officers of the Specht regiment, one a Swiss, the other a Florentine.

"I'd never trust my man to do this." The Swiss wagged his head, quivered his nostrils. He plunged a wooden ladle deep in the kettle, carefully brought it to the surface. "There, Crosetti, as one Brunswicker to another—" He held the ladle under the latter's nose.

Crosetti laughed. "It's so long since I've been near cooked beef that I'm no proper judge. But I *think*—" he crooked his swarthy forefinger—"I *think* a little garlic? Eh? What do you say?" He turned his bright eyes on Ahrens.

"The only thing it needs is speed," laughed Ahrens. "That damned fever has left me with the appetite of a ten-year-old. Isn't it about ready, Schoch?"

Schoch grinned. "In a moment. Then we shall fortify ourselves against the ordeal of the afternoon."

"The surrender." Ahrens bit his lip.

"You dread it? Why?" Crosetti peered through the steam. "*We* aren't surrendering. We just happen to be

409

with the army that is—an army that's lost its war." He reached out, patted the thick-set Swiss on the shoulder. "The good Schoch agrees?"

Schoch whirled the ladle about in the kettle. "We're better off. No more fighting. And our pay goes on just the same. In a year's time I'll be back in the Bâle looking for another billet that will be easy enough to get. You, Ahrens, better try the French service. They appreciate gunners. And Crosetti—what will you do?"

Crosetti winked. "I'll bury myself at the university, write a thesis on the difference between Indian women and half-breeds. They'll give me a doctorate and then I'll go and see what the Turkish service is like. If you talk well about women they'll make you a pasha at the very least. But I'm in no hurry. King George's gold makes an agreeable tinkle in my ears." He poked Ahrens in the ribs. "Why do you dread today? More money, less fighting, that's all it means to *us*."

Ahrens sighed. "I don't know. I hate the idea of marching those men up, making them stack their arms in front of all the Yankees. The Yankees won't be gentle, you know. They've a rough edge to their tongues. They've some songs about Burgoyne that would make a dragoon blush. Damn it, I wish it were over. Isn't that blasted stew about ready?"

A voice down the road hailed. Ahrens looked up, saw the tall form of Charteris beckoning through the clear air. Beside him stood a still taller man in blue and red. Ahrens groaned. "Save my share, you fellows." He scrambled to his feet, walked swiftly down the road. "Now, who the devil is that with Charteris and what does he want? Blue and red—that's all right. But good God! The cuffs are nearly up to his elbow, the lapels go halfway round his ribs!"

Worn, thin of face, but lazy-eyed and negligent as ever, Charteris waved airily. "Hello, young fellow! Heard you'd been low with a fever. Look here, this is Lieutenant Peabody of the Continental artillery."

410

Ahrens acknowledged Peabody's salute, noted the steady gray eyes, lean jaws, gaunt yet muscular limbs of the American.

Charteris went on: "Told Peabody about you. He's here to see about—you know, the guns and that sort of thing. We turn over everything that's Government property. Personal effects we keep, but the guns, the gunners' carbines, swords if they have 'em, limbers, horses. Everything. Leave him in your hands now."

"But how about Captain Pausch?" asked Ahrens.

"Oh, *you* speak English. Much easier. Besides—the old chap asked that you see to it. Taking it hard. I'm doing the same for our lot. Williams would have a stroke if he saw anyone touch his guns. Don't know just where I'll be for the next few hours. Keep in touch, though." He flourished a careless hand, walked away toward the Fish Kill ford.

Ahrens turned stiffly to the American gunner. "I suppose you want to get at this as soon as you can."

Peabody inclined his head gravely. "I should be pleased."

"What do you want? The usual thing? Double line, open ranks, carbines on the ground?" He felt a futile irritation stealing over him, an unreasonable urge to make things as difficult as possible for this tall man who wore blue and red so awkwardly.

The American hesitated, drew the back of his hand under his long chin. "Well—if you like. You see, this is the first time I've ever had to do with a—I mean, I don't know much about parade-ground things. I'm just a gunner. I—I just want to get this over with."

"H'm!" thought Ahrens. "Trying to hurry me through? No, you don't!" Aloud he said curtly: "The men are at mess now. Having the first hot meal in days. Of course, if you insist, I can have them drummed out."

Peabody spread out his hands. "Oh, no. No! Not for worlds!"

Ahrens went on: "When they've finished mess, then.

411

What is the plan? March them across the river with the others? Have them stack arms in the presence of your army?"

"In the presence of *our* army? No, no, no! You see, we thought it might be less—that is, it might be better if you did it here!"

"Here?" Ahrens' eyes widened. "General Gates plans to move his force *here*?"

"Why, no. That isn't it at all!" He shifted his feet uneasily. , "See here! Just before you come to the mouth of the Fish Kill, you'll see the ruins of an old fort. Baron Dieskau built it, I think, back in the fifties. If you'll march your men there at about three, they can stack their arms out of sight. I'm to look after the artillery and Morton of Nixon's brigade is to see to the infantry. But I assure you we shan't be about then. Now if you'll just look at this list that Major Charteris gave me and tell me if it tallies with yours—yes—just leave the guns in the park, march the gunners to the old fort and then start across the ford when you get the signal. Then you'll be on the Albany road. I understand that's your route."

Ahrens blinked. "Just a moment, Lieutenant! Do I understand that *I* am to march the gunners to the fort—that we stack arms out of sight of the—the American army, and then cross the river? There's no formal 'laying-down of arms'?"

Peabody shook his head violently. "Not at all, not at all. We thought this would be—the most acceptable way."

"This is most unusual." Ahrens felt a weight lifting from his spirit. "Most unusual. It is extremely thoughtful. I have never heard of such a thing. It's a true courtesy. The men will appreciate it. So shall I."

Peabody reddened, fumbled with the clumsy sword-hilt that swung so awkwardly from his belt. "Then after you've crossed the ford, your men will fall out to draw rations for their march. My friends and I will be glad if you will join us over a roast and a brace of duck. You'll

412

come? I'll look for you at the halting-place." He bowed stiffly. "Oh—one more thing. Will you allow me?" He fumbled in the pocket of his white breeches, drew out a bit of string. With frowning earnestness he measured the depth of Ahrens' cuff, knotted the string expertly, measured the facings, knotted again. Then he sighed and slipped the string back in his pocket. "You see, my wife made this uniform. We had no model—only the description in the Boston *Gazette*." He patted his pocket with a smile of satisfaction. "*Now* I can send her the proper proportions!"

Under a row of flaming maples that grew close to the grass-blurred ruins of Dieskau's old fort, the Hesse-Hanau artillery company stood in apathetic silence by its rows of stacked carbines. Sergeant Behr, left arm swathed in clumsy bandages, called the roll, which the ranks answered in a staccato mutter. Ahrens ran his eye along the thin lines where the newer uniforms of the few recruits who had joined the company after the passage of the Hudson stood out boldly against the monotonous background of faded, tattered blue and red. Among the older men he saw gaping seams, awkward patches, split elbows, cuffs worn to a fuzzy fringe, broken boots bound up with rags. One gunner in the rear rank huddled his bony shoulders under the fringed shirt of some captured Yankee rifleman, another stood forlornly in a dragoon's coat. Cocked hats were torn, battered, the cockades drooping or shorn away.

The roll-call ended. Behr spun about, saluted, droned: "Company present, sir," spun again and marched heavily to his post on the right flank. Ahrens stepped forward. The drab ranks stiffened. In his mind there sprang a sharp vignette of a staring cluster of wet peasants in the long, dim room of Der Rosenstrauch, a thick-necked colonel roaring at them while a sleepy-eyed Englishman lolled by the bright fire. "What the devil can I say to them?" he wondered. "Do they remember their welcome to the service? That fat fool in Hanau talked to them about the service of the Elector. Hell! They're here in this American meadow because the Elector sold them. What will he do with them when they drift down the Main again?" A deadening sense of depression flooded over him, took the color from the blaze of the maples, dimmed the thin, sun-drenched air. It was a depression that had nothing to do with the surrender, nothing to do with the slow, useless miles of toil behind them, nothing to do with the futile agony of the clearings or the rain-soaked woods near Bennington. "From the Main to the Hudson—because the Elector needed more money for his mistresses and couldn't get another groat through taxes. God above—to what will they return? Perhaps the men who stayed in the clearings are the lucky ones. Damned if I'll shrug it off because—'it's the way things are.' There is another way—must be another."

He was aware of patient eyes on him, some expectant, some sullen, some lifeless and inert. He set his firm jaw. "Sixty-odd gunners—and I saw more than a hundred swarming among the trees at Crown Point!" He took a deep breath, stretched his lungs as though he could crush the profound melancholy that seemed to stifle him. The sound of his voice was startling in the clear October air. "You know that a convention has been signed. There will be no more fighting. As soon as possible the army will march across the provinces to the port of Boston. There it will wait until a fleet has been assembled to take it back to Europe. Under the convention none of us, from the highest to the lowest, may bear arms against the Americans. *Our* American war is over. Your pay and rations will continue until such time as the Elector sees fit to discharge you after your return to Hanau, your return home."

He paused. There was no lifting of the dull cloud that hung over the Hanau men, no flicker of joy. He went on: "Captain Pausch has gone on with the Baron. Lieutenant Dufail is still ill. As the remaining officer I shall, in a few moments, march you across the ford to the Yankee lines. We shall have to pass through their army. There are many of them who have lived rough lives. It may be that your reception over there will be rough. But remember this—" his voice soared, his arm swept up— "remember this, you Hanau gunners: You have fought. You have fought well. It is no fault of your own that you march, unarmed, through the Yankee lines. No matter what that reception is, I want to know, as I lead you, that the Hanau gunners behind me are marching through the enemy lines with their heads and their hearts high! Sergeant Behr—the command is 'at ease.'"

He turned away, lips tight. He had felt no response from that streak of faded blue and red that was the company. Dejected, he stared at the long lines of ownerless muskets, stacked beyond the old ramparts by the infantry regiments, at the slow belt of brass and blue that splashed across the ford of the shallow Fish Kill. Then from behind him a ragged cheer rippled up from the right of the line, spread, thudded flatly across the sunny meadow. The field and the cheering men blurred before him as he turned and tugged at his shabby hat.

The last rank of the Rhetz regiment disappeared over the rise in a wave of broad blue backs, a clumsy bear-cub shuffling and waddling after it. Ahrens splashed through the shallows of the Fish Kill, stamped his feet on the hard, crumbly surface of the Albany road. Behind him the faded remnant of the company churned the muddy water, squelched in their leaky boots onto dry land. The three surviving drummers heading the column whirled their sticks mechanically, the drum-heads muttered and began to pick up a subdued rhythm which was drowned out at once by a sudden squealing and slamming of American field music hidden in the high ground ahead. "That blasted tune again!" thought Ahrens. "What did Pausch call it? Oh, yes. *Yankee*

415

Doodle! What a name!" But he found his head wagging in time to the half-heard notes.

Under a birch that was a glowing candle of yellow leaves, he halted to watch his men bend to the steep slope ahead of them. Their heads were drooped, their feet did not answer the low-throbbing Hanau drums, they merely pushed on in a heavy-gaited mass of dull jackets and streaked white breeches, their eyes on the crisp dirt which hissed under their feet. He frowned. Many of the men who plodded past were strangers to him, men who had served in the reserve park, with the heavier pieces. He couldn't count on them. He shook his head, then trotted rapidly toward the leading squads of the column, formed of his own men. His eyes sought out a broad-shouldered form, striding solidly along, steady of eye and tight of jaw. He found his man, gripped him by the arm and said in a low tone: "Rentner! I'm counting on you. Don't let the company slouch through the Yankees. Remember the retreat from Bennington!" The steady eyes shifted slightly, the tight jaws moved. Ahrens went on: "Watch my hand—when I drop it, do what you can." He took his place at the head of the company, the three drummers banging and thumping just in front of him.

The Yankee music died away in a last triumphant shriek and rattle. There was nothing in the world except the final steep stride of the road and the mutter of his own drums. A hidden voice roared: "Present arms!" Ahrens topped the rise, to the click of hundreds of heavy muskets being shifted. Then the urgent scream of *Yankee Doodle* beat on his ears again, sent little icicles drilling up and down his spine. By the side of the road a solid square of fifers and drummers in brown and red, blue and red, in homespun, in smocks, in fringed shirts, blasted the thin fall air, the fifers red-faced and squinting, the drummers nodding and rolling their shoulders as they crashed into the refrain, exultant, insistent, jubilant.

416

And beyond the field music stretched line on line of bristling muskets.

Ahrens' jaw dropped. There never were such soldiers, he told himself, the thing was a mad fantasy, a fever-warped vision. There were tall old men in the flank-companies, old men with clubbed gray hair, old men with grotesque wigs, with cocked hats, with round hats, old men who clutched muskets a century out of date, old men in neat breeches and woollen hose, old men in overalls, in Indian leggings. They were bearded, they were shaven. They stood strong and silent, these old men, silent and almost terrifying. Yet it seemed to Ahrens that they were dimmed, blotted out by the youth that exuded from the double line that hedged the road, by the strength that glowed in keen young faces, sunburned and clear-eyed. Muskets were held awkwardly, yet they were at home in the hands that held them, in hands that knew and talked to every inch of wood and iron.

In a hush broken only by the thud of its own feet, the Hesse-Hanau artillery company marched on through lines of men from the Berkshire Hills, through companies in trim blue and red of the Continental line, through incredibly tall men from the Alleghenies and the Blue Ridge in fringed shirts and round coonskin caps. With a start he realized that the fields behind these trimly aligned, silent ranks were swarming. It had seemed to him as though the entire world had narrowed to a rutted lane hedged in by an unending double line of tall, hawk-nosed men in homespun, in uniform, in buckskin. But now he saw that the sunshine beyond these leans faces was alive with country-people on foot, in wagons, astride fat-backed plow horses. By the flank of one company, a small boy, solemn in cocked hat and buckled shoes, edged silently closer and closer to the rear rank, timidly caught hold of the skirts of a rifleman's coat, stood staring with round, brown eyes at the passing aliens. Ahrens repressed a grin as the rifleman laid down his piece, caught up the boy, carried him to a fat, laughing woman, then trotted back, retrieved his piece and became a statue once more.

"This silence," thought Ahrens. "Not a jeer, not a cat-call! I wish I could feel sure that our people would behave as well with the roles reversed. The step's dragging again. By God, here's my chance."

The line of brown uniforms through which the company was marching ended in a cluster of wide tents about which he could see crisp blue and buff surrounding a full, scarlet and white figure in the shadow of a towering pine. He raised his hand, dropped it. From behind, a single voice, strong and resonant, sang:

"Oh, how blest is he who to die shall dare—"

Others joined in, uncertainly, then with growing strength.

"For God and his cherished fatherland.
All shall honor the man who was true unto death,
For God and his native land who fell;
Who a hero's blood for his freedom's good,
For God and for his country gave,
Sleepeth sweet in the grave."

The step became crisp and sure. He could almost feel the lift of sixty heads behind him, the straightening of sixty weary pairs of shoulders.

He had passed the last of the brown infantry. The sheen of scarlet and white was very close. Out of the corner of his eye he saw Gentleman Johnny's face flush, saw his head go back. A well-tended hand fell on the shoulder of the little spectacled man in blue and buff who stood beside him. The rich voice rolled out: "There, General Gates. You've been commenting on my allies. Let me tell you, sir, that I'd pit this handful of gunners from Hanau against any hundred you might choose from

418

Mr. Washington's armies. Gad, sir, see 'em step! Hear that singing! Not *our* sort of singing, eh, General? We like something more lively, eh? But does 'em credit, does 'em credit." He raised his voice: "Well done, young fellow! The Baron shall hear of this!"

The company swept on. Ahrens caught a low mutter from the stoop-shouldered Gates, then Burgoyne's rich voice: "Oh, yes, yes, yes. Speaks English. Old Harrow boy. Of course, *I'm* from Westminster!" Gates goggled his eyes, head wagging.

There were more brown jackets beyond the tents, files and files of lean men in homespun. The gunners sang on, marching at a firm parade step. In a grove ahead the blue coats of the Rhetz regiment halted, then filed off to the right, the bear-cub breaking into a rocking gallop as he tried to keep up with the maze of black-gaitered legs in front of him.

A din broke out in the sunny fields beyond the bristling Yankee muskets. Ahrens saw crowds of slovenly, loose-mouthed women, shifty-eyed, unpleasant-looking men. There was a shout of, "Here's more mercenaries!" A raw-boned woman, tousled hair slipping from a greasy mobcap, began thumping on a tin dish, howling: "Mercenaries, mercenaries!" The banging grew. A gangling man drank from a bottle, smeared the back of a grimy hand across his mouth and yelled: "Where's Jane M'Crae?" A mounted officer swung out from the stiff companies that lined the road, spurred his horse through the milling crowd, shouting angrily at them. The din died away. A rigid lieutenant, loose smock belted with a rusty old sword, parted his lips a fraction of an inch, called out to the marching gunners: "Don't mind them. They're only camp-followers, York Staters." Ahrens raised his hand slightly in acknowledgement.

Across the meadows to the left, a thin thread of red, splashed with green, flowed swiftly as companies of the 24th marched to some hidden destination. A sullen murmur, like the steady drone of a swarm of bees, seemed

419

to hang in the air over them. Ahrens raised his eyebrows, pursed his lips. "A little out of hand, eh?" he thought. A freshening wind brought angry shouts to him. "Y'd not stand to the bagnet, y' rebel scum!" ... "'Ide be'ind trees, like a mucky lot o' God-damn poachers!" ... "God help ye if so we ever catches yer in the open! Soldiers! Oh, my bleedin' Christ!" The homespun ranks stood motionless, silent. Off by the Fish Kill the massed fifes and drums squeaked and thudded away at the exultant flourishes of *Yankee Doodle*.

From a clump of scarlet and rust maples, stepped a tall, heavily built man, captain's epaulets clumsily stitched to a black coat that reeked of the pulpit. At his side was a still taller man in a beautifully tailored uniform of dark blue, faced with red. The captain gravely saluted Ahrens, indicated his tall lieutenant. "Livermore will show you your assembly place." Livermore grinned sheepishly, fell into step with the Hanau gunners. The captain adjusted a heavy wig, then turned off to the broad meadows. A loose-jointed private, trailing a heavy musket, raced across the road, galloped after him, yelling: "Joel! Joel! Just got a letter from Ma! Joel! She asks do you want to buy Ez Perkins' stand of black walnut t'other side Sorrow Hollow!" He flapped a sheet of paper, shambled on beside the black coat, waving long arms and talking animatedly. Ahrens stared.

Livermore coughed. "That's the Captain's brother." He strode along, trying desperately to match his step to the Hanau rhythm. He coughed again. "I'm afraid we don't—don't look much like soldiers to you."

There was a far-away shout: "Yankee bastards! Wouldn't stand up ter a man in a fair fight!" Ahrens sniffed. "Soldiers? Thank God, no!" Livermore's eyes widened.

There was a dull buzz of voices from the candle-lit depths of the ruined shed. Peabody slipped his arm under Ahrens', guided him through the half-charred doorframe. The buzz died abruptly, six heads looked up, squinting, from the rough trestle with its litter of wooden dishes and mugs. Peabody cleared his throat diffidently. "Here's our guest, gentlemen," he began. "Lieutenant Ahrens of—"

A rumbling voice broke in from the head of the long table. "He's known to us, Dick, but we ain't known to him. I've been duly elevated into this chair—which is a damned beef-keg—elevated by acclaim. You'll take your time from me."

Ahrens, blinking in the flicker of the dribbling candles, saw a huge man, broad face buried in a mass of gingery whiskers, pointing to an up-ended keg. The voice rumbled on. "Will you set yourself here, sir? Here, beside Mr. Conant. That's it, and Dick'll set himself beside you." The great beard reared back, sharp blue eyes glinted in the half-light. "Now we're settled. Dan'l, will you fill up a dish for our guest, while I name the company to him."

Ahrens straddled his keg, eyes watering with the unaccustomed reek and savor of the joints and fowl which were strewn about the board. The giant, erect over his keg, turned to him. "Sir, I welcome you in the name of our company. I'm Calvin Nickerson of Cape Cod and Marblehead, captain in Colonel Wigglesworth's regiment, Glover's brigade."

"No need to name *your* regiment to me, Captain," said Ahrens. "Your blue jacket and white breeches fairly shouted at me."

Bushy eyebrows jerked upward. "You know the uniform, sir?"

Ahrens laughed. "My first meeting with it was such that I'm very happy to see it at a friendly board rather than across those damned clearings at Freeman's Farm."

There was an approving mutter round the table. Nickerson rumbled in his throat, scratched awkwardly at his clubbed hair. "Yes, sir, we were there, we were there. H'm, h'm." He rumbled again, embarrassed. "Yes, yes.

421

H'm, now at your left, sir,—Mr. Jacob Conant of Salem—he's militia."

Ahrens found himself bowing to a prim-faced man of fifty in a beautifully tailored civilian's coat of bottle-green, a prim-faced man who murmured between thin, clean-shaven lips that he was honored. Nickerson boomed on, naming the company.

There was Daniel Shays in Continental brown and red, a tall man with heavy jaw-muscles, prominent cheek-bones and hot, fanatic's eyes who nodded grimly as he slashed and hacked at a great roast of beef. Beside Shays sat Nathan Howland, militia, a little, solid man with the down-drooping mouth and sad eyes of a patient, thwarted child. Howland never spoke, but kept turning his big head and mournful eyes toward each speaker in turn. Beyond Howland, Ahrens bowed to short, fattish Israel Trumbull of the Connecticut militia, then to a grave-faced, bearded giant at the foot of the table whom Nickerson hailed as Lem Carter.

"And that's all, sir, saving Dick Peabody, and him you know. Every man, sir, is happy to welcome you as I said and every man is hoping with me that you ain't too saddened about—about events because—well—" he shuffled his feet—"well, because we wish you well, sir." Nickerson flushed, drew a broad hand across his forehead.

Ahrens said gravely, "It is never pleasant to lose, Captain, but if lose we must, we couldn't ask for more generous captors. Everything has been exemplary. Believe me, it is appreciated."

Nickerson clawed at his stock, shuffled his feet again, staring wildly about the shed. "Eh—well, that's—I man—Oh, damn it, Dan'l, ain't you dished our guest's supper yet?" He frowned, collapsed heavily on his keg.

Shays reached a long arm across the table, handed Ahrens a broad wooden dish heaped with meat and vegetables. "There you are." His voice was sharp, rasping. "Beef, succotash, a bit of squash, and some punkin. Nathan, toss over a slab of that turkey and a hunch of bread. Not like what you feed off in your European palaces, but it's good, plain man's victuals."

Ahrens gratefully inhaled the steam that rose from his dish. "This is luxury. If you knew what our diet has been for weeks past! As for salt—" his forefinger tapped a birch-bark saucer heaped with rough grains—"salt was something we treasured as far back as August."

The prim-faced Conant ceremoniously handed him a horn spoon and an iron knife. "Now, when the Frenchman, the little Marquis de Lafayette, was welcomed at Newport," he said, "he was served a dish that I wish I might set before you now instead of this plain country fare. I was present, sir. This dish consisted of a dove, inserted in a partridge, the partridge in a guinea-fowl, the fowl in a duck, the duck in a capon, and that, sir, was inserted in a prime Buzzard's Bay turkey. The whole was then roasted and carved crosswise." He made sawing motions with his bottle-green arm.

Nickerson goggled his eyes. "Fit for a lord, Mr. Conant, fit for a lord! Dan'l—d'you know our guest's a lord? Yes, sir! Dick told me. A Hessian lord!" He beamed along the board. "What d'you think of me, settin' my legs under the same table as a real lord!" He threw back his head, rumbling and chuckling.

Ahrens frowned. "Now, where the devil did they get hold of that?" he wondered. "Charteris—he must have told Peabody." Aloud he said, "My father had a small title. But you must remember that lords in Europe are thick as—as Arnold's men in a clearing."

There was a chuckle round the table. Even the mournful Howland smiled faintly, his big eyes swinging slowly along the board. Carter shoveled food into his mouth. " 'Thick as Arnold's men!' " he repeated, his big beard bulging and shifting as he chewed. "That's spoken polite. Sir, you're a real man's well's a real lord." He nodded gravely, dug his spoon into his wooden dish.

A silence fell on the dim shed, a silence punctuated by the soft scrape of horn on wood, the muffled champing

423

of food and occasional half-grunted requests for beef, bread, succotash. At last Ahrens sighed, laid down his spoon and knife. He felt Shays' hot eyes on him. "'Tain't to your liking?"

"Very much to my liking. Especially the—what do you call it? Succotash? It's new to me. But—" he shook his head regretfully—"we've been on short rations so long that I seem to have lost the habit of eating. I assure you it's a matter of deep sorrow."

Trumbull peered down the table at him, then at Nickerson. "Cal, they ain't a law agin rum in this place? Rum always sets my victuals handsome. Maybe it'd do the same by our guest."

Nickerson reached to the floor, swung up a heavy jug and thudded its thick base on the table. "Only two mugs and they're wood," he observed sadly. "No matter. Send 'em up this end, Lem, and I'll pour the rum and start 'em on their way. There's water in that barrel just back of Nate Howland." The rum reeked and gurgled into the copper-bound mugs, water splashed in a shiny jet. "Now—one goes down this side, one down t'other. Drink hearty and keep 'em movin'."

A contented peace settled over the table. Ahrens took a mug from the correct Mr. Conant, let the stinging rum flood his throat, passed it on to Peabody. His mind seemed slowly to be wakening from the killing lethargy into which the weeks of virtual siege by the Hudson and the Fish Kill had plunged it. With new eyes he looked on the strange men who made him so casually welcome at their table. He had seen them and their kind shifting through deep woods, had seen them flood over the stubbly fields by Bennington and charge shouting through the smoke of British and Hessian guns in the ravaged clearings by the river. Was it possible? Out of the corner of his eye he watched Conant, so like a prosperous Rhenish merchant, with his careful voice and indulgent smile; the huge Nickerson with his tang of the sea; grave, awkward Carter and the silent Howland with

424

his slow-shifting eyes. They had come from scattered corners of the colonies to sit at this board with him just because a laughing man in scarlet and white had marched soldiers from English shires and from European duchies through a tangled wilderness and down a broad tidal river. What was the knot that bound the scholarly Conant and gently bred Peabody to the full-bodied uncouthness of Nickerson, the backwoods crudity of Shays and Carter, the provincialism of Trumbull?

He drank rum again, passed the mug to Peabody. He closed his eyes. Vividly he could recall the faces of the six hosts—snub-nosed, hook-nosed, lean-jawed, full-faced. Yet back of his lids he saw them all transformed by some subtle re-agent so that each kept its own likeness, yet assumed a common stamp—a leanness, a strong calm. They were all like that old man in the fields of Hubbardton. He opened his eyes, glanced along the table. Each was an individual and yet all were from the same mold. "Must be the rum," he thought. "Rum—or is that damn fever coming back?" He started. Trumbull was speaking to him.

"I was just sayin'—we were wonderin' what you did?"

Ahrens' eyes widened. "Did?" he repeated.

Carter wagged his thick beard. "That's it. What do you do?"

Elbows on the table, Shays rasped, "Yes—do. What's your trade?"

Ahrens laughed. "My trade?" He patted the facings of his jacket, faded to the shade of a dead leaf. "These used to be red. I'm carried on the rolls as a gunner."

Howland's eyes roved back and forth across the board. Shays shook his head. "No, no. We mean—what do you *do*?"

Conant coughed discreetly, smiled gently to himself. Nickerson leaned forward. "He means—well, he means what do you do. I'll allow I'm curious myself. What do you *do*? Now, Dan Shays works his land south of Worcester, Mr. Conant builds ships and sails 'em—or did till the King's ministers passed that God-damn Port Bill. I sailed ships myself and sailed clear 'round the world. Now, someday Dick Peabody will be a sawbones and Lem Carter's got a real nice smithy in Barre, and Iz Trumbull, now in *his* town, Stamford in Connecticut, Iz keeps the store. Nate Howland, why, he tends to the gristmill just south of Petersham."

For the first time Howland's drooping lips opened slightly. In a voice that seemed forced out of him he said,"I'm hog-reeve, too."

"And he's hog-reeve," Nickerson amended. "Now you, sir—?"

Ahrens blinked under the battery of level eyes that were turned on him, frankly searching. "You gentlemen must excuse my denseness," he said. "My only trade is gunnery."

Carter's eyes widened. "Sure, now! You ain't never mastered no other trade? You don't look to me like a man as *enjoyed* killin' folks."

Ahrens laughed. "I don't and the trade's not entirely my own choice." He was slightly disconcerted by the sadly shaking heads. It seemed to him that there was a gentle pity in Carter's grave eyes, as though the bearded man found himself looking on a social misfit. Ahrens read the same look all around the table, save for Conant, who smiled quietly to himself behind a long cherry-wood pipe, and Peabody, who frowned slightly, drumming slender fingers on the board. Trumbull stirred uneasily. "You're learned? There's a heap of surveyin' to be done hereabouts." Shays pushed at his awkwardly clubbed hair. "Maybe you could teach school. You ain't Papist? No? Well, schoolmasters is hard comeby here. Hi! Listen to that!" He held up a work-scarred hand.

Outside in the darkness Ahrens heard a subdued rustling and clumping, caught a sense of movement in the fall night. Conant deftly drew out a heavy gold watch. "Gone seven. That will be Poor's brigade moving out. I judge those to be Colonel Scammell's men. Cilley and Hale marched out an hour ago."

"Marched out?" Ahrens' eyes widened. "Where?"

Conant replaced his watch. "South, sir, to join General Washington. All the Continental line goes tonight."

"South? South?" Ahrens was puzzled.

Conant nodded. "South to New Jersey. The General is watching Lord Howe."

Ahrens nodded. "And the war goes on. I'd forgotten Odd, isn't it?"

"It goes on. You'll not misunderstand me if I say that I'm glad it doesn't go on for you? I've been watching you. I should be sorry to think of you mangled in a Jersey meadow. What lies ahead of you won't be easy. It will try you, but you'll survive."

"It's an awful thought—captivity till the transports come for us. And yet—and yet there's something that almost smothers bitterness, a deep curiosity. No, it's more than that. In a minor way, it's like being a witness at Creation." He inclined his head slightly toward the others at the table absorbed in a dozen discussions and arguments.

Conant turned quiet eyes on him. "You've already witnessed a miracle. You've seen men from Massachusetts and Virginia and New Hampshire and New York united for a common end. Oh, they've marched out before, but then it was always as subjects of the King. But now! We could so easily have split up, one colony snarling at another. To me the thought is staggering. Presently Nickerson will take the road with his company. He'll end up in New Jersey or Pennsylvania and be brigaded, like as not, with Virginians. Perhaps with Carolinians. It's—it's staggering, as I say. It's an *American* army. I wish my father were alive to see it. And the militia! Why, in his day the militia wouldn't turn out unless their own towns were threatened. Now we have New Hampshire militia, ten Broeck's men from Albany, Connecticut men like Trumbull. Now we militia men

427

will go home but," his prim lips tightened, "by God, sir, a precedent has been set, a precedent that will never die."

Ahrens nodded thoughtfully. He lowered his voice. "But this table! You're a man of substance, Nickerson a competent ship's master, Shays a farmer, a working farmer, and Trumbull a storekeeper! If I described this group in Dresden, they'd laugh me out of the garrison."

Conant laid well-tended fingers on Ahrens' ragged cuff. "You miss a point, my friend. *You* say that Trumbull is a storekeeper. But—" his forefinger tapped the back of Ahrens' hand—"but *Nickerson* said that in his town, *he keeps the store.*"

Ahrens narrowed his eyes. "I begin to understand—a little. *He* keeps the store, another may see to the posts, a third builds ships, a fourth is a—a surveyor and a fifth is the smith? Yes, I see, I think. There is a whole philosophy in your correction."

Conant smiled patiently. "We are poor in men here in America. Who will be hired when he may be master, even though he is master of a few rocky acres, or a village store or a smithy? In Salem I build ships. Folk are thicker there along the coast. I may hire my adze-men, my top-sawyers and my ship-masters. But were I, say, far up the Maine coast, then if I want to build, I must swing an adze myself and think myself none the smaller for the swinging. I may grow tired of Salem. Then what? There is nothing to bind me there. I can push on up the Maine coast. Or I may work west to the Great Lakes and set up my ways on their shores. So may Trumbull. He can set up his pitch west of the Alleghenies and cater to the people who are streaming beyond the mountains. Little Howland may sell his gristmill near Petersham and settle out on the Ohio. Trumbull will still keep the store and Howland will still see to the milling.

Ahrens passed his hand over his forehead. "This makes me a little dizzy. Let me ask this—Nickerson here

428

shouts to Iz Trumbull. But one and all they call you *Mr.* Conant."

"I see. I see. Put it down to my gray hairs and a little to the fact that I have some small power in things maritime. But—let me settle in Howland's Petersham; he'll still call me—if he ever speaks—Mr. Conant, but by God, sir, he'll fight me like a wildcat if I contrary him at the town meeting."

Ahrens looked at the rest of the company. Nickerson was leaning over Shays' shoulder, backing him in some argument against Carter. Trumbull was listening eagerly to Peabody, who described a possible canal system to bring central Massachusetts nearer the sea. Howland, sitting lower and lower on his keg, kept head and eyes turning slowly from group to group, the corners of his mouth drooping.

Voices rattled outside. A red-faced man, cocked hat sidewise on his head, suddenly appeared in the ruined doorway, swaying on his feet. He raised an unsteady hand, pointed at Nickerson. "There he is! M' cap'n. Goin' complain! They took my musket away, m' God-damn musket. Cap'n, they took it 'way just 'cause I swore I'd shoot that God-damn general. Christ, cap'n, ain't we all been tryin' to shoot 'm?"

Nickerson straightened up. His neck reddened and bulged with heavy muscles. "You, Graves! You're under arrest! You—" Another form, cool and steady, loomed in the darkness behind Graves. "Sergeant Kimball, sir. I'll look to him." A hand fell on Graves' shoulder, pushed him away on unsteady feet. Nickerson bellowed into the night: "We march at one o'clock! Make him carry Charley Worth's pack. Charley's ailin' some!" Then he bent over Shays' shoulder once more.

Ahrens looked up, eyes somber. "Look here, Mr. Conant—if the woods are full of drunken soldiers trying to get a pot-shot at a general—"

Conant smiled. "Too drunk to shoot. He'll cool off on the march." From across the table Trumbull nodded.

429

"Scare him a bit, maybe. Do him good, but he won't get shot."

Ahrens bit his lip. "Even so—to shoot at a general who is a prisoner—"

Conant sat bolt upright on his keg. Trumbull leaned across the board, his face red. Nickerson's voice rumbled out: "Who'd you think he was aimin' to shoot at? Burgoyne?" His voice was almost shrill. *"Burgoyne?* Not while there's a man of Glover's brigade on his feet. He's our guest. I'll choke with my bare hands anyone that so much as looks cross-eyed at him."

Ahrens was bewildered. "Then who—"

Shays' voice rasped sharply: "Why, that son of a bitch Schuyler!"

Conant looked quizzically at Ahrens. "Our guest seems puzzled that the man Graves should want to shoot one of our own generals," he said gently. "While I deprecate the idea, I suggest that Dan Shays explain why General Schuyler is not popular with New Englanders."

Shays' red, rough hands worked awkwardly, his hot eyes fixed themselves on Ahrens. "I'm just a farmer. But I'm a patriot. I was first out in '75 and I carried an espontoon at Bunker Hill. I was—"

Conant held up a hand. "Yes, yes, Dan, but about the General."

Shays frowned. "I was comin' to that. I'm a patriot. I'm an American. Americans declared themselves free and independent. I heard Isaiah Thomas read that declaration with my own ears. It was on the steps of the town hall at Worcester and it sounded like a hymn to me. It was good. It was true." He kneaded a rough fist against his open palm. "Now, sir, what follows? What follows is this." His jaws worked, his eyes narrowed to slits under knotted brows until Ahrens felt he could see the tumult of thought working, working through the man's brain. The others leaned forward on the table, eyes on Shays. It was deadly still, save for the unbroken

430

shuffling crunch in the night outside as long companies filed off to Albany and the south.

Shays slowly opened his eyes. "What follows, sir, is this. We're independent, but—we've got to govern ourselves. How are we going to govern ourselves? By a king? By a lot of lords?" His fist crashed on the table. Howland blinked slowly. "Never, by God! It's got to be by *my* voice and Calvin Nickerson's voice and Iz Trumbull's and Mr. Conant's and—and everybody's voice. Now, Schuyler—" his face flushed with anger—"now, Schuyler—there's folks as loves him, folks as wants to see him made a kind of king. But this Schuyler, he lives like a lord. He owns this ground we sit on here, owns more God-damned acres than the Angel Gabriel could fly over 'tween dawn and sunset. They're his and the towns on 'em are his, *his*. They's shops in them towns, factories and they all work for King Schuyler an' *he* says what a man gets for a load of beaver or a span of horses or a bushel of corn. Who gets the good of all this? Schuyler. For who does the little man work? Schuyler. If Schuyler don't like a man, off he goes and all his years of work are wasted. I'm a bad worker and I make toys for the Schuyler brats, toadyin'. Then Schuyler likes me. I'm a good man and keep myself to myself and don't truckle. Then Schuyler turns me out and puts in the stinkin' toady that made toys for the little princes but let his land run to waste. They say this Schuyler ain't a bad man, but there's been bad Schuylers afore him. There'll be bad ones after him. And before I see this country ruled by him and his friends, I'll shoot him like I'd shoot a mean Injun, so help me God." He paused. His face was sweat-dotted, working.

In a low tone Conant murmured to Ahrens: "You perceive there would be a slight difference between keeping the store in Trumbull's village along the Sound and keeping a store on the Schuyler estates? Schuyler's a good man, a fine man, but he's living in an old century. We hope to sail into a new one."

Shays went on: "I've nothing 'gainst Schuyler as a man. He's kind to the folk on his lands. But one man—it just ain't right that *one* man have all that power. And if Schuyler and his like rule this country we'll all be touchin' our forelocks to some God-damn lord that rides through the towns that used to be ours, and wonders how much more he can tax us." He snatched up a mug of rum and water, drained it at a gulp, sat staring at his hands.

Ahrens nodded slowly. "I begin to see. But, Lieutenant Shays, I've heard it said at headquarters that Mr.—excuse me, General Washington, is also a large landholder, owns huge tracts like Schuyler. Yet it seems to me you're well on the way to putting yourself in his hands."

A wave of dissent swept round the table. Howland raised sad eyes to Ahrens, spoke in his strangled voice. "He's a moderate man."

Conant smiled slowly. "Howland has given Washington the New Englander's highest tribute. He's right, too. That's why we in the East prefer Gates as a *commander* to Schuyler. We cannot separate command and politics. Hence we put up with Gates, who doesn't do too badly and whom we *know* our representatives in Philadelphia can dominate."

"In other words," said Ahrens, "even if you can beat the British armies—"

Conant's jaws snapped. "We shall!"

"Then, let us say when you have beaten the British, if you find yourself with a—a feudal government of your own, you will have lost your war."

Conant's face was grave. "We shall have lost our fight. Why are we fighting? Largely, *I* feel, because the King's ministers insisted on treating us as though we were living on a vast estate, which was contrary to our charters and to all justice. Let us start an industry—say, well," he turned up his eyes, "say hats!" He snatched off his own glossy beaver, threw it on the table. "Silly to go to war

432

over a hat, isn't it? But this hat covers a principle as well as my aged head. We have beaver skins in America. We have skilled workers. At Danbury in Connecticut this hat was turned out. You see it is fine work. It is not costly. In England they make beavers, too, as fine as this but much dearer. The English hatters bellow at Parliament. Presently there is an act which says no hats may be made in America and none may be imported save those made in England. Where are our hatters? Where is our trade? Then multiply that by a dozen other industries. So we go to war over a hat." He smiled dryly. "We bore the brunt in men and money to keep the French and the Indians from making the Hudson valley and New England a vast province for King Louis. We sent Massachusetts men to the Indies. Why? To make large profits for London? That is not our way. We are free men, not vassals. Shall we fight and be vassals of a Schuyler or a small group of Schuylers? What do you say, Carter?"

Carter's dark beard bristled. "I say to that, Mr. Conant, that we fight for a country, a free country builded, sir, on three p'ints." He hammered on the table. "Builded on the three p'ints that have held New England together—a free church, free schools and the town meetin'."

Ahrens turned to Conant. "Yes, I begin to see—not only about Schuyler. I see—well, a lot of things that have puzzled me since I first came down Champlain. I see why you are here, and—" he smiled wryly—"why I am."

Conant raised a cautious hand. "You must judge moderately, sir. Mind, a Virginian would put the case differently. So would a Pennsylvanian. But only differently on the surface. The verities remain. We must believe in them, no matter how we phrase them. Otherwise—we fight in vain."

Ahrens eyed the keen faces about him. "You should have little trouble safeguarding what you win," he said.

"What material for an army! Why, you could count on a standing army of fifty, seventy thousand. Good God! Men like these, better equipped, perhaps better trained—"

Shays' bitter rasp stabbed across the table. "No, you don't! We don't want no army, no—no—"

"Praetorian Guard?" suggested Conant.

"That's it! No Praetorian Guard to tempt an honest man into bein' a tyrant! No, sir! I'll serve long as they want—*in this war*! Then I go back to my farm, same's Cal Nickerson'll make for his ship, Carter for his smithy, an' General Knox for his bookshop in Boston. There's work to be done. Soldierin' ain't work."

Nickerson tilted the rum-jug again, sent the two mugs on their jerky course down the table. Ahrens turned to Conant. "What do you hear of General Arnold? I happened to see his—well, shall we say accident? I can assure you that he has the admiration of every man of our armies."

Conant dug the dottle out of his pipe, rapped the bowl gently on the table. "His accident won't be fatal. He was wounded again in the leg that he smashed at Quebec. But the doctors say he's a troublesome patient."

"I can imagine that. By the way, how did he happen to be on the field? We had information that he had been relieved of his command—that he was virtually a prisoner."

Conant blew through the stem of his pipe, looking at Ahrens with owlish eyes. "A mere technicality, and technicalities have never bothered Benedict Arnold. He heard the firing, became somewhat restive, so restive, in fact, that he had to ride out and see what was happening. You were witness to the rest."

"Against orders? I must say he seems to have carried matters with rather a high hand. Didn't General Gates try to stop him?"

"Why, yes. In fact, he sent an aide after him. The

434

aide didn't catch up with Arnold until he was wounded. Then he delivered his message."

Ahrens laughed. "Timely, to say the least. What was the message?"

"The message?" Conant stroked his chin. "Why, it was calm, brief and soldierly. 'General Gates begs that General Arnold will do nothing rash.' After delivering which, the aide rode away, conscious of a duty well done."

"Epic!" marveled Ahrens. "Ah, thanks." The mug of rum was handed him. He drank, and passed it on. "There is a strong rumor in our camp that as soon as he recovers, General Arnold is to succeed General Washington in command of all your armies."

Conant smiled indulgently. "I scarcely think so."

"But he's a magnificent leader. We took some hard knocks there at Freeman's Farm. And when you stop to think that our regiments are all veteran and that Arnold attacked them without a single field-piece, why—it's unparalleled. The Baron, Phillips, Hamilton, men who have served in the Low Countries, all say they never dreamed of anything like it. Shrewd use of troops, a genius for picking the weak spot in an enemy line, endless courage and such fire that I swear he could almost have drawn our own men along with him."

"Oh," said Conant, "no one will ever question Benedict Arnold's leadership, still less his courage. He was born to capture Olympus with forlorn hopes. We owe him a great debt, a heavy debt."

"Then why do you shake your head over my rumor?"

Conant gingerly tested the temperature of his pipe against his shaven cheek, sighed, put it away. "Why? Well, let's see what our friends about the table say. Lem Carter—Lem! Our guest brings an interesting rumor from his camp. They say there that Arnold is to take over command from George Washington."

Carter drank carefully, passed the mug on to Trum-

435

bull. He wiped his bearded lips on his sleeve, then rumbled. " 'Tain't so."

Ahrens leaned forward. "Why do you say that? I've been telling Mr. Conant how much our armies admire him."

Carter frowned heavily. "Just ain't so, that's all."

"Iz Trumbull," Conant called. "Put down that mug or give it to Nate Howland. What do you say to our friend's question? You're a Connecticut man. You used to live in New Haven." He said in a lower tone to Ahrens, "That's Arnold's town, New Haven."

Trumbull pushed his keg back from the table. "Why not Arnold? He's a gifted man, as you tell. So why not?" He drew in his lips, stared upward at the canvas roof of the old shed. "Look here. It's like this. Do you mind when you were just a little shaver and your ma'd set out a big crock of dough in the kitchen—baking day? And do you mind you'd sneak out there into the kitchen when she was busy with pots and pans and you'd see the dough, not quite riz? And you'd watch your ma. She might be turning a roast or making soft soap or what not. And then you'd stick your finger in the crock?" He leaned on the table. "Now you might have been to the pump and scrubbed your hands till they was pink, but just the same they'd be a little black mark in that dough where you'd stuck your finger." He blew out his cheeks, nodding. "Well, sir, that's like Arnold. He's all you say he is and more and I'll take oath on it. But—he leaves a little black mark on everything his fingers touch. I knowed him years ago. In trade, in politics and now in the army. They ain't nothing that Benedict Arnold touches that don't carry the black mark. Now, George Washington, he's a big landholder, he ain't a New Englander, but they's something mighty clean about George. He don't leave black marks."

"I think your question is answered, Lieutenant," murmured Conant. "Gold is the man's god. For gold he'd do anything."

436

Footsteps beat in the night outside. Two tall forms blurred in the doorway. "Lem Carter! Where's Lem Carter? Why, there's the God-damn old porcupine!" Ahrens looked up to see a lean man, flushed of face and unnaturally bright of eye, beating the bearded man between the shoulders, while a second shifted the straps of a heavy pack over a loose country coat and grinned vaguely at the company.

Nickerson flung up a heavy hand. "Come for Lem, have you? Better set a piece and take a nip of rum."

"Just what we come for—first rum, then Lem. We've been bibblin' a heap and knowed that Lem never gits intostecated. He'll start us over the road. We're seein' double now and that makes the road twicet as long. Hi-yi! We're Dana-bound!"

Grave and unruffled, Carter introduced the pair as the Farnum brothers. "They farm a mite in Dana. That's near Barre." The brothers balanced a board between Carter's keg and Trumbull's, perched precariously on it, and applied themselves to undiluted rum, eyes roving about the table.

The elder suddenly straightened. "Hi! By damn. There's Nate Howland!" The younger whooped, "Nate! By God, look at Nate a-settin' there, a-drinkin' of his rum!" He reached past Trumbull, slapped the silent Howland on the back. "Nate, you snappin'-turtle! How you feelin'?"

Howland's eyes turned slowly. His hand reached out, closed about the mug. He drank, then said painfully, "Tol'ble agile."

The brothers exchanged glances, nodding. "That's rum," said one. "Makes him downright talkative," the other agreed. "Hi, Nate, bet you'll hate to go back to Petersham after all this luxury!" He waved a hand at the charred walls of the shed, at the canvas laid over the rafters. "Ain't it true, Nate, that folks in Petersham still lives in wigwams and sod-huts? Huh, ain't it?"

437

Howland's eyes moved sadly toward the pair. He sighed, then murmured:

> *"Petersham for beauty, Barre for pride,*
> *If it hadn't been for salt-fish,*
> *Dana would 'a' died."*

He sighed again, drank.

Carter smiled somberly. "They sell a sight o' salt-fish in Dana," he explained to Ahens.

The brothers leaned eagerly on the table. "But look here, Lem, we ain't stayin' in Dana. Listen. Soon's things quiet a mite—there's all that land south the lake, Skene's land. We been talkin'." The flush died from his face. "Lem, Nate, all that land and by God we'll sink a canal that'll tie up old Champlain and the God-damn Hudson."

Shay's rasp cut the air. "Float goods from Canada to the sea? Who's goin'? You like that, Lem? By God, I'll bring twenty-thirty families from Worcester county and—"

"Canal? Canal? An' another linkin' Albany and the Lakes? What d'you think of that? It'll—" . . . "And a road runnin' slap back from Worcester through Rutland and Barre to the Hudson! No! *North* of the Old Bay Path. A road fit for a Conestoga wagon, fit for three of 'em abreast!" . . . "And from New Haven slap up through Connecticut, up to the Hampshire Grants, up to that prime farm country!" . . . "Why, by a tax on every township! It's easy! Open up the country, open up the west. By God, we c'n do it!"

The shed seemed to melt into a great uproar. Ahrens heard of rocky farms in the shadow of Chocorua or by the ledges of Monadnock, of the sandy lowlands along the Sound. Voices shouted of choosing a new sheriff or altering the course of a river, of fencing a pound, of chains of posts to stretch far west to the Mississippi and beyond. Nickerson's voice roared: "In twenty years!

Why, by God, in twenty years you won't know the country!"

"In twenty years!" thought Ahrens. "What won't they do in twenty untroubled years! And in twenty years—where shall *I* be?"

Voices stormed, pleaded, argued, orated. In the night outside Ahrens could hear the steady tramp of the men who were marching south under a harvest moon, marching south to join Washington.

The Convention Troops

THE GREAT POOL *of men which had slowly gathered by the Fish Kill and the Hudson brimmed, flowed away in three great streams and a score of rivulets.*

Gates' Continentals slipped off down the west bank of the Hudson, off to the south to join Washington. By companies and platoons the militia of twenty counties trudged along the old trails to hill villages, seaside towns and young, striving cities. In a stream of faded red the British rolled weaponless across the Hudson, nosed sullenly into the Berkshire Hills, headed through Williamstown and Northampton. To the south a sluggish belt of rusty blue crept across the great river at Stillwater, trailed on through Shaghticoke and Kinderhoek, dully breasted the low rampart of the Taconic Mountains, then spilled over into the rocky valleys of western Massachusetts. By the Housatonic the ragged bluecoats faced east, lumbered on, the few wagons and pack-horses allowed by the Convention lurching and pitching in their wake.

X

The Convention Troops

THE SKY was a belt of dull bronze over the eastern hills as the Hesse-Hanau artillery company wound along a rutted, frost-touched road. Thin-boled maples held huddles of sere leaves to the biting wind and the rough gray stones of the straggling walls in the fields were dusted with white. By the leading squad of the company, Ahrens swung on through the clear, sharp air, the battered Pausch stumping grimly at his elbow.

"What was the name of that town where we slept last night?" asked the veteran abruptly.

Ahrens swung a heavy stick about, trying to work the numbness from his hands and arms. "Last night? Great Barrington. We're well into Massachusetts now."

Pausch grunted. "These damn English names! Worse than the Indian ones. 'Great Barrington!' 'Massachusetts!' Don't see how you remember 'em."

Ahrens laughed. "Do you know the name of that river we crossed after we left the town?" He pointed his stick back along the plodding column of faded blue and red.

"River? No."

"The Housatonic."

Pausch's seamed face wrinkled. "Gaaah!" he said.

Ahrens tucked his stick under his arm, jammed his hands into his coat pockets. "Don't forget our names sound as weird to the Yankees as theirs do to us. My host last night thought I was making fun of him when I introduced von Schlagenteuffel."

"Ugh!" Pausch shook his head. "I believe you've turned half Yankee yourself! You can't compare names like that! Why, von Schlagenteuffel's a perfectly simple German name. But 'Great Barrington,' 'Housatonic!' ... Where did you sleep?"

"I was lucky. Had a room to myself and a big bed, the first proper bed I've slept in since—by God, since I was in Quebec! Had a good dinner, too. Dined with my host. He's a selectman, named Simeon Chase. You saw me with him just before sunrise."

Pausch nodded approvingly. *"That's* more like a name! What's a selectman?"

"Selectman? Oh, it means a—a chosen man. Something like a syndic."

Pausch shook his head sadly. "They take you in, my boy, they take you in badly. That man a syndic! Why a syndic's an important person. And I saw *that* one driving home his cows when we marched in last night."

"So's Chase an important man. Reads Greek and Latin, farms his own acres, runs a sawmill, owns a big herd and was colonel in the militia in the French wars."

Pausch stamped angrily along the whitened ruts. *"But* he drove home his own *cows!* He's a peasant, not a syndic. Gullible, gullible!"

Ahrens smiled. "We're in a far country, Captain, and a strange one."

Pausch sputtered. "Strange! After we—after we marched across the Fish Kill to the Yankee army—I don't know where *you* went, but some officers gave me dinner, Yankee officers. They were from Albany or somewhere near there. They talked a kind of German. I must say they were almighty polite. But dear Jesus! Captains and majors and colonels, and all they could talk about was land along the Mohawk or shops in the river-towns. They even offered me a farm if I'd come down there. *Me!* A gunner!"

444

Ahrens nodded. "I know. The lot that fed me were building bridges and laying out roads and electing sheriffs—when they weren't talking politics."

"And there was some of that for me," Pausch grunted. "*Officers!* Or so they called themselves. And they had a sentry at the door of the tent where we dined, a sentry in a big wig and lugging a musket that was so old that it must have been here when the country was discovered!" He raised knotty fists to the brightening sky. "That sentry! He'd lay down his musket and come in and help himself from the officers' table! Slapped *me* on the shoulder and wanted to drink rum with me!"

Ahrens repressed a grin. "Appalling, isn't it?"

Pausch made a wailing sound in his throat. "And that's not all! You know Ettlinger of Specht's? Fancies himself a scholar. Well, he quoted a Latin tag and damn my bones if that sentry didn't poke his God-damn head into the tent and correct him! The *sentry!* Said he had a tense wrong. The sentry, a private soldier, correcting a captain of Specht's! My God! There was a Yankee major who could hardly speak English or German so's anyone could understand him and then the God-damn sentry laughs at Ettlinger's Latin!" He picked up a stick, lashed viciously at a clump of milkweed. The pods shattered and feathery tufts of down floated through the glass-clear air. "And look at that!"

The road sloped gently past a broad field whose surface bristled with orderly rows of corn-shocks. Among silvery-brown husks the red gold of pumpkins glowed richly. Two tall men, fur-capped, moved easily among the shocks.

Pausch repeated. "Look at that! Can't let their land alone for a minute! And those are the men we're supposed to treat as *soldiers!*"

"You must admit, Captain, that they've done a good deal to earn the title, even if they are farmers!"

Pausch growled on. Ahrens nodded from time to time,

feigning attention. Actually he was listening to the comments of the patient men who plodded heavily behind their officers. "Look at those shocks! That's *farmin'* " ... "Too thick at the base." ... "Don't have to repair the stone-walls; if there's a hole, just rip another rock out of the land." ... "Now my woman an' me, we'd get twelve-fourteen bushels in that corner." A thick voice jeered: "Y' damn yokels! Can't think of nothin' but manure-spreadin'! I want to get loose in a *town!*"

Pausch's tones rose above the buzz of the ranks. "And damn Latin and damn Greek and damn their talk of freedom. Damn their poacher's ways and their stinking rifles. *I'll* never call 'em soldiers. Boors, that's what they are, a rabble of boors!"

"Aren't you a little hard, Captain?" Ahrens eyed the tough old face. "They fed our men there on the Fish Kill. They fed all the officers in their messes—not just *fed* us, either, we were guests. Now this is the twenty-fifth. We left the Fish Kill on the nineteenth. What do you think of the treatment we've had from the towns and villages? Think, now—we've passed through Stillwater and Kinderhoek and Nobletown and—oh, a dozen places."

Pausch's eye brightened. "Ah—Kinderhoek! That sounds like some of the towns in the Low Countries! Why—what about the towns?"

"Take Great Barrington. You and I had good rooms. We got the non-commissioned officers into rooms. The rest of the company and the women were stowed away in warm barns and sheds. The two companies of the Rhetz regiment that had lagged behind were in a tight warehouse."

"Ye-e-s," said Pausch. "Quarters were good."

"Better than good. The townsfolk had the right to turn us into the fields for the night. Then the wife of my host—Mrs. Chase—went to look at the women and the brats. Do you know what she did? She sent round to all the neighbors and made them bring pails of milk—milk for our women."

446

"Didn't hear that," growled Pausch.

"Then you remember the sawmill? Just below the falls? There's an old man who lives in the little hut by the mill—a sort of caretaker. Well, he's got two sick grenadiers from the advance corps in that hut. He says he'll send them on when they're fit. Now the advance corps—what's left of it—is two days' march ahead of us. That old man has kept them three days and will keep them a week longer probably and never a groat he'll get for it. And then do you remember Nobletown? When we marched through, the girls brought baskets of apples to the roadside and tossed them to the men. Oh, yes, I know they laughed, too, but if you were a Yankee girl wouldn't you laugh at a Rhetz grenadier wearing a nightcap and carrying a puppy in his helmet?"

Pausch wagged his head. "Yes, yes, I know all that. But you're young, you're gullible. Why, when I remember half the things you've told me on the march I swear I think you're more a Yankee than Gates or Arnold. You believe anything. When you're *my* age—" He tightened his lips. "No. *I'm* not fooled! There's something damn dirty and damn nasty back of all these smiles and charities. Some say we might be sold. Sold as slaves to Indians. I hear there are hundreds and thousands of Indians in this province, hundreds and thousands and they say they all want slaves. Why, God damn it, isn't the *name* of the province enough to give you the creeps?"

Ahrens nodded innocently. "Now if we were only in Pennsylvania, where there are towns called Wommelsdorf and Gnadenhütten—"

Pausch purred in his throat. "Ah—Gnadenhütten! Yes, I think I might be more trustful *there!*" He turned, walked backward a few steps, his hard old eye running up and down the column. Then he swung about, stumped on. "Where are our guards? When we left—left that place this morning, there were about twenty farmers with long squirrel guns tagging along at the rear of the company. And there's nothing behind us except half the Specht regiment and Barner's men and they're a day's march behind."

"The guards?" Ahrens laughed. "They're all militia. They drop off all along the road." He looked back. "There they are. Only a half-dozen left. See—there goes one of them up that trail through the beech grove. The others are waving to him."

The column marched on in silence, crossed an echoing plank bridge which spanned a boiling brook, then bent to a steep slope. At the crest Ahrens looked far ahead over a sheer valley to a sharp ridge beyond. A tattered blue snake crawled slowly up the scar of the road across the valley. "The Rhetz regiment," he thought, eyeing the dull, slack coils. He closed his eyes, remembering that same Rhetz regiment marching down to the beach at Crown Point, its white facings sharp against the blue of its trim coats, bayonets shining, cross-belts pipeclayed and cocked hats crisp and jaunty.

Feet scrunched on the crumbling ruts, a rather sharp voice drawled: "Thought I'd step 'long the road a piece with you."

Ahrens looked round at a lean, loose-jointed man of about twenty who ambled up past the head of the column, heavy musket slung across bony shoulders, wide-brimmed hat pushed back over untidy hair. The man turned prominent brown eyes on him.

"Heard tell you're the mercenary as talks English. I ain't talked with a mercenary before. I'm George March. My father's got land t'other side Chicopee Falls. It's good land. Abner, that's my brother, he don't like farmin'. He's set up a tan-yard, so Father's leavin' the farm to me. 'Course, there's my sister Deborah, but Will Hewlett over 'cross the pond, he's takin' her to wife, so that leaves the land to me. What did you say your trade was?"

"I'm a student," said Ahrens gravely. The question, so startling to him in the ruined shed by the Fish Kill had become commonplace since the column first plunged

448

away through the quiet towns east of the Hudson and he had found that the status of student quite satisfied the interminably curious country-people.

March nodded. "In a college. We got one. It's by Boston. There's another down there somewhere." He jerked his head toward the south. "Here, I ain't very sociable." He gave a loose-joined skip, edged in between Ahrens and the rigid Pausch. "I'm militia, Captain Hooker's comp'ny. Used to be Jed Thomas', but we didn't like him and 'lected Hooker. He's a moderate man."

"You are quite right," said Ahrens solemnly.

"We were," agreed March. They plodded on across the valley floor and up a sunny slope where late-ripen= ing apples were bright against somber, gnarled trunks. March shifted the sling of his musket. "Thomas was too strict. He'd get mad on the march if we let off at crows in the fields or woodchucks. We lay north of you." Suddenly he began to guffaw. "Haw, haw, haw! Say, if Burgoyne had moved spryer, you'd of walked right over us in the night! We was tired and forgot to mount guard. We was all asleep. Come mornin', there was Burgoyne down the river, not a mile away!"

Ahrens suddenly remembered a freezing, drenching night by the Hudson, a long, halted column and then, in the wet dawn, a figure in fresh scarlet and white smiling and bowing to a furious little woman. No sentries! His brain whirled. Why, if—if Burgoyne had moved only a little, they would all be free men, safe and well supplied at Fort Edward or Ticonderoga! The patient, ragged gunners behind them would be warmly dressed and free of the uncertain future toward which they marched so uncomplainingly. "Glad Pausch can't understand this— this and March's talk about electing captains!" He bit his lip, his mind full of somber thoughts. March ambled on, entirely content with himself and his company. Then he addressed himself to the glaring Pausch.

"Now, what was it you said *your* trade was?"

Ahrens broke in hurriedly. "The Captain doesn't speak much English. He's—he's a teacher."

March stared respectfully at Pausch. "Now, that's an honest trade. Up Chicopee way we need a teacher bad, but folks just won't pay proper. Ten pound a year and found ain't right." He waved a red fist. "I'm hurrin' back now so's I can speak at town meetin'. Fifteen pound a year and found ain't a mite too much. Mister—he turned to Ahrens—"if you ain't got schools, what have you got? Nothin'! I look to speak, as I say. My gran'ther, he's Moderator."

"And a moderate man, I trust," said Ahrens.

"He's a moderate man. He was ag'in turnin' from the King. Then Jared Combs stopped by from Monson and told about Burgoyne bringin' Injuns to turn loose ag'in the settlements. Gran'ther called Abner and me and just said: 'Boys, you will do what's fittin'.' So Abner and me, we went out with the militia. Now I'm spoilin' to get back for the town meetin'. An' there's a barn-raisin' at Ledyard's over Ludlow-way."

They topped the crest of the ridge and looked down a long, gentle slope. Far in the distance the dim line of the Rhetz regiment crawled on through a yellowing light. March squinted at the thickening sky. "Settin' in for bad weather. Goin' to be a hard winter. The geese are honkin' high and early this year. Hi! There's more mercenaries ahead and some militia followin' 'em. Springfield boys, I guess. I'll step out a mite and join 'em." His loose stride lengthened, he stepped easily away. Over his shoulder he called: "Well, goodby, both."

Pausch's voice ripped hoarsely from his congested throat. "A God-damn common soldier, walking with *us*, with *me*! Why did you let him? I'd have sent that dumb-head on his way, if I could only handle English."

Ahrens glanced at the seamed old face that bobbed along beside him. "At least you were spared Master March's news," he thought.

"Being friendly, you'd call it," growled Pausch. "Well,

450

I don't trust 'em. There's something bad afoot. It's not natural. Well, about time for a halt. Give the command, will you?"

The men sprawled on the soft bank by the side of the road. Pausch leaned against a thick oak, studying the march-orders that had reached him at Great Barrington. Ahrens sat on a stone-wall, studying a white village that sat snugly by the bend of a swift river in the valley below them. He looked up as wheels crunched in the dirt. A country cart was crawling slowly toward them, the driver sitting very erect on the seat. Ahrens watched it idly. Then as it came nearer, he swore under his breath. He tapped Pausch on the shoulder. "Captain—look at this rig!"

Pausch glanced approvingly at the well-groomed chunky horses that clumped easily along the road. Then his mouth tightened.

"Sergeant Elberfeld! Out of that wagon! Here—Ahrens! Call your men. He's a deserter!"

The man on the seat saluted, grinning sheepishly. "My duty to you, Captain. But I'm no deserter."

"No deserter! You recognize him, Ahrens! Elberfeld, sergeant to Captain O'Connell of the dragoons! You don't deny it? Then out of that wagon!"

"I was took prisoner, Captain. Took in the woods near Bennington. Now I'm on parole. So was Captain O'Connell. He's in residence at Westminster."

"Prisoner? Parole?" A trace of pity crept into Pausch's lined face. "Damn it! That's bad! Look here, Sergeant, just—just leave your team here. Fall in with the company. I'll send you ahead to the Baron tomorrow."

Ahrens watched the sergeant's thick fingers plucking nervously at the whiplash. "Don't you want to come with us, Sergeant?"

The man settled the thick lapels of his homespun coat and shot a grateful glance at Ahrens. Then he looked dubiously at Pausch. "That's kind, sir. But—" he pushed back his country-made hat, grinned again—"but I

451

think—I like it where I am. I help work a sawmill near a town called Hadley. The folk are good to me. They needed a man badly who knew metals at that mill. No, I think I'll stay in Hadley. With all due respect to you, sir," he added hastily.

"Don't—don't you *want* to come with us?" Pausch's jaw dropped.

The Sergeant shifted uneasily on the broad seat. "No, sir, and besides, there's my parole. But there are a lot of the dragoons and some grenadiers in these parts, mostly in the north. They heard of your coming this way, and there's some that'll slip into ranks. But as for me—thanking you again sir, no!"

He saluted, clucked to his team and rolled on, shouting to the men who sprawled by the roadside. Pausch glared after him. "There you are, young man. I told you there's something bad afoot."

A tearing wind drove sheets of rain over the bowl-like hills into the black valley. The trees along the road were vague, tossing shapes and across the wet field at the right a mad stream flashed white in the storm. Ahrens hugged his tattered cape close, hunched his shoulders about his ears, shivering. Pausch's voice sounded strained above the relentless hissing of the rain: "Can't be more than five miles to that town—what is it?"

"Palmer," said Ahrens. "Damn those people in Springfield. Why couldn't they have found room for us?"

There was a cold chuckle by his side. "Ha! Told you there was something bad brewing. Turned us out like a lot of thieves. And I wanted to have a look at the arsenal there."

Ahrens brightened. "Did you see those guns ranged out in front of the main building?"

Pausch grunted. "Light carriages. Ought to handle easily."

"Looked too heavy in the breech, though. Now, the cascable on the three-pounders—big as a cabbage!"

452

"Like to have seen more." Pausch's voice was sad. "Oh, damn those people! Add ten-fifteen miles to our march and God knows what sort of houses we'll find. There were good houses, big ones in Springfield. How many guns do you think that arsenal could turn out in a year?"

"Hard to say." The wind howled louder. The pines on the round black hills hummed and droned like a great organ. "When did this rain start? When we were in Westfield, wasn't it? Three days ago. And those New Englanders bragged about their climate!"

"Worse than Canada. If you'd been here last year—! Any sign of those five men?"

"No, they've deserted. There's work to be had in all these towns. People are glad to take 'em in."

They splashed on in silence, the feet of the little company squelching in the mud behind them. Ahrens tugged at his cloak, bent his head against the gale. "Captain, I'm beginning to believe that doctor of yours," he said suddenly.

"What doctor?"

"Siemann, the surgeon from the Riedesel regiment. You brought him over when I had that bout of fever at Saratoga. He told me then that I'd have recurrent attacks. I was freezing a minute ago. Now I'm on fire and someone is pounding the back of my neck with a mallet."

Pausch's hard hand gripped his arm. "Here, boy, you're staggering. You fall out with me, right here." He dragged Ahrens to the side of the road, signaled the company to go on. Ahrens, through mounting waves of heat, saw the men plod heavily past, saw the half-dozen women of the company, shawled and loaded with heavy bundles, flounder on in their wake. Then a great bulk blurred in the dark. He heard Pausch's voice shouting against the storm: "You, Hummel! Halt that wagon. Yes—here. Let the pack horses go past. Now stow this officer inside and don't let him out till I give the word."

Ahrens heard his own voice protesting feebly, felt himself being tugged and pushed. Then he realized dimly that he was lying on something soft, with a dry cape about him. Through a whirling mist he heard Pausch's aggrieved voice crying: "Lord Jesus! On a night like this he yells for water! Hummel, your water-bottle." Then the fever took him solidly, plunged him into a stream that was now freezing, now boiling, that tossed and battered his aching body.

Strong light pried at Ahrens' lids, slowly and painfully forced them open. He blinked, moved his head slightly, then stared hard. He lay in a wide bed in a little room whose walls were broad smooth boards of pine, broken by a casement window through which a bright sun poured and by a small fireplace of mellow red brick. He blinked again, stared at the rag rug that lay on the solid planks of the floor, at the Betty-lamp that hung by the shallow mantel, at the slat-back chair which held his uniform. He tried to sit up, but sank back on the pillow exhausted. Then he grinned feebly. "What would Pausch say to this? Something bad afoot. Good God, but I'm weak. How long— Where am I, anyway? Palmer—that was the halt. Palmer! About six when the fever hit me. Certainly got rid of it quickly. Lord! The company'll have marched by now. Wonder how I'll—" He dozed again.

Later he wakened to the sound of wagon-wheels grinding under his casement. He sat up, feeling weak but much steadier. "They'll be miles down the road!" He swung his feet to the floor, stared at the loose nightshirt of coarse linen that fell about his knees, then padded across the room to the chair by the fire. "Hello, hello!" he muttered. "Uniform's dry as a chip. And mended! My boots greased." He dressed hurriedly, slipped the iron latch of the pine door and started shakily down a steep, dark staircase, fumbled with the latch of a second door at the bottom.

A crisp voice said: "Heard you stirrin' above. Thought

454

you might relish a bit of broth." Bewildered, Ahrens bowed to the calm-faced elderly woman who stirred a small iron pot swinging from a crane in the deep-throated fireplace. He was sure he had never seen her before and this big, clean, sun-lit kitchen was strange to him.

The woman bustled about, set a thick, crockery bowl on a well-scrubbed table, poured steaming broth from the kettle. "There!" she said. "Set yourself."

Ahrens still stared. "You are very good. I'm—I'm very much in your debt."

The woman flounced her wide black skirts. "Oh, hush, hush. Set yourself and eat that broth. You were ailin' bad when they left you here."

Ahrens sat down, eyes on the woman. "*Left* me here?" he repeated stupidly.

"Well, you didn't walk here, I'll answer for that. Now eat that broth. It's prime chicken. Eat it and don't ask questions."

The broth was rich, creamy, with great lumps of chicken and bits of crust floating in it. He ate slowly, conscious of a great emptiness. He felt absurdly weak, nervously weak as though he might shout if someone spoke to him suddenly. He shook his head angrily, centered his attention on the rows of vegetables drying on hooks sunk in the ceiling, on the great oak settle by the fire, on the heavy musket and carved powder-horn that hung over the mantel. The woman, arms folded over her ample stomach, watched him. When the bowl was empty, she silently filled it again. Strength flowed back into him, he felt warmth creep into his unshaven cheeks.

The woman nodded. "That's better!" Then she pursed her lips. "Young man, you been starin' at me and at the kitchen so's a body'd think you'd never laid eyes on me or it before."

Ahrens laid down his spoon. "I hope I wasn't rude. You've been very good. Honestly, it is the first time that I remember seeing you or this room."

She raised her hands. "Land o' Goshen! You come here the second; this is the fifth. An' the first night you slep' on that settle. An' every night since Joel or I set up with you. Hope you slep' warm. We sent most of our blankets to the army."

Ahrens shook his head, looked out through the leaded casement. The sun was bright on the crisp grass of a broad common that sloped away to the east, edged by a solid brown road. Through bare-branched elms he could see a line of white houses, neatly fenced, a thin-spired church. "This is like a new world to me. I've never seen that common before. Good Lord! November fifth! Why—why, on the fifth we were supposed to be in Worcester, no, Marlboro. Four days! I could have sworn it was last night that Pausch stowed me into the wagon."

The woman swept the spotless hearth with a turkey-wing. "The night of the second," she said. "First the Britainers went through, then the mercenaries. Seems like I never saw so many men. 'Twas like Babel. Britainers an' mercenaries, all marchin' east in the rain, poor souls. Then Parson Allison—he's head of the Committee of Safety—he came in the night an' knocked on the door an' told Joel there was a sick mercenary. An old man with a face like a door-knocker brought you. Him, an' a young man with a nut-cracker mouth an' a pretty woman lookin' over his shoulder in the rain. They grieved about you. So we put you here on the settle an' the next day you still ailed bad, so we bedded you in Caleb's room. He was taken by the Britainers down on Long Island an' never a word we hear. There's a comfortin' prayer that Parson Allison says for all prisoners an' captives. We thought your folks'd feel easier could they ever know you were in Caleb's room. An' we felt easier 'bout Caleb, somehow."

Ahrens turned to the window again. "It's the damned fever," he told himself, as the bright common blurred and the old elms seemed to quiver and dance before him. Then he said slowly: "When I rejoin the army—I

456

think that General Burgoyne holds me in some favor—I shall be very glad to make what inquiries I can. There are bureaus, offices, that could help. A word from the General—he's really a very humane man—"

She inclined her head gravely. "That would be kindly in you. He's Caleb Gifford, sergeant in Jonathan Ward's regiment. It's the 21st Massachusetts. You'll write it down?"

Ahrens bent over his notebook, scribbled away with a flattened bullet. The heavy door that led to the sun-lit world outside shook, swung open. A tall, gray-haired man stepped gravely into the room, caped greatcoat billowing about him.

"Your servant, sir," he said with a slow nod. "I'm happy to see you better." He crossed to a cupboard by the wide fireplace, opened it. "I judged it better to put your money-belt here." He laid its clinking length on the table. "You'll know better than I what's in it, sir."

"If it were a hundred times its weight, it couldn't equal my debt to your house, sir," said Ahrens.

Mrs. Gifford whisked the turkey broom about. "That's a pretty speech, young man. Guess you mean it."

"Wouldn't surprise me a mite," said Gifford. He hung his heavy coat by the fire, drew up a chair by the table. "Now, sir, I have made inquiries among all the neighbors." He shook his head. "There's no one in these parts named Hunnewell."

Ahrens started. "Hunnewell? Did you say Hunnewell?"

Mrs. Gifford's thin eyebrows went up. "Who else? Why, from the first night you hollered that you had to find a girl named Hunnewell. You hollered a lot. Most in a heathen tongue that Joel—he's scholar'd—says is German, but a lot in the King's English. Didn't he, Joel?"

"Fever takes folks that way. Yes, sir, but you were tolerable persistent. Last night you asked me to go look for her. You seemed so sure you'd find her here that I hitched up and drove down the road a piece."

457

"And—and because of my ravings, you drove through the country, asking for a name I mentioned!"

The man looked soberly at him. "When a brother calls so urgently, it is not right to sit idle. Besides, folks are scattered some, these days. Yes, sir, scattered. There's twelve strange families in town. But not a soul in Cherry Valley or Leicester ever heard the name."

Ahrens blinked. "Did you say *Leicester*? You drove so far!"

Mrs. Gifford stirred the fire with a bright brass poker. "Far? Leicester ain't far. It's here."

"But this is Palmer!" protested Ahrens. "The map showed it."

Gifford narrowed his eyes. "Young man, you *were* ailing. You've rode across two counties since Palmer and never the wiser."

"Then the company's only at Marlboro. I must get on!" He sprang to his feet, only to sink back again, the room swimming about him.

Mrs. Gifford looked at him sadly. "The army ain't goin' anywhere particular. You'd best lie by one more day."

Her husband nodded. "Young Ichabod Prentiss is driving a load of meal to Worcester in the morning. You'd best tarry and ride down with him."

"Hear that, young man?" she said. "Joel—he's goin' to write the King about Caleb."

Gifford scrubbed at the bright steel buttons on his waistcoat. "Caleb? Yes. I'd take that kindly." He cleared his throat. "I feel a mite empty, Mother. Why don't you bring out a bit of gingerbread and a jug of new cider. Our friend looks a mite peaked, too."

A fresh loaf smoked on the table, clear cider shone in pewter mugs. Gifford bent his head reverently.

"God save the free and independent States of America!"

"Yeh," said Ichabod Prentiss. "I marched out ag'in Burgoyne."

Ahrens drew the bearskin robe over his knees, eyed the gangling muffled man who slouched on the seat beside him. "And came back safely, I hope," he said.

Prentiss nodded. "Didn't get to fight. Time was up."

"What d'you mean, 'time was up'?"

"'Listed for thirty days. Got to the Hudson on the twenty-ninth day. Marched home on the thirtieth. Time was up."

"You reached the Hudson, turned around and marched home again?"

"Yeh." He slapped the reins across the broad backs of his horses. "C'd see you fellers fine. We was on the east bank. Heard a sight o' shootin' over there. But our time was up." He clucked to the horses, fell silent.

The wagon rolled steadily down an interminable hill through cultivated fields and scattered farms. An occasional big house loomed proud and aloof on the slopes. Ahrens shivered, climbed off the seat and stretched himself on the meal-sacks. "So I called for Judith," he thought. "Seems that I can't keep her out of my mind. Lord, what *could* have happened to her? She *must* have driven that crazy old wagon into the middle of the fight. Or did she start early enough to get through to Albany? Or delay and get caught in the backwash of the retreat? Hope it was Albany. What was left of our Indians got thoroughly out of hand those last days. It couldn't have been that. I'd have had word somehow. I paid that Tory a pound to scour the woods to the west and promised another pound if he found anything. It must have been Albany. Well, I'll never see her again. Pretty figure I'd cut. The Ragged Prisoner and the Rebel Maid—good title for Gentleman Johnny. Oh—she *must* have heard the firing, taken another road. But there wasn't another road." He began to doze to the soft jolting under him.

He woke with a start. Prentiss was prodding him with his whip-handle. "Comin' into Worcester. Main Street."

Ahrens propped himself up on his elbow, stared at a street of low, straggling houses, snug and tight-looking under the leaden sky. A smart gig swung out of a side lane, pulled up before the clinking forge of a blacksmith's shop. A very pretty girl minced across the road on high pattens. From a deep hollow to the right came the whining screech of a sawmill. Ahrens scrambled back onto the seat. "You're stopping here?"

"Not yet. This is just the beginnin'. I'll set you by the Exchange Hotel. That's way down by Court Hill."

They rolled on under bare, arching elms. To the west and north, sheer ridges rose in sweeping bastions, spilling down into the valley of the town in a series of low rounded hills. The houses were bigger now, more pretentious, but with a severe purity of line that Ahrens found pleasing. Prentiss pointed with his whip again. On a gentle slope a half-dozen mansions raised fanlighted doors, primly spaced windows, above carefully tended grounds. Prentiss grunted.

"Nobil'ty Hill. Tories, mostly. That's why the doors are nailed up. That's the Chandler place. You've heard of Chandler? Why, he owned more land 'round here. Big man in these parts. Guess the Committee'll take his land, though. He's a King's man."

"Not big enough to beat the Committee?"

"Ain't no one big enough for that. Jailed two men, respect'ble men, last week. Why? 'Cause they was insolent to the Committee, that's why."

In a broad, sanded room of the Exchange Hotel, Ahrens ate cold beef, drank rum, while Prentiss talked earnestly with a fat man who warmed himself by the copper-sheathed bar. In a smaller room close by, wigged men shouted and laughed. Scraps of conversation drifted through the smoke-laden air. "It was when the Britonians came through. They halted by the common, close to the Town Hall. George, here, he yelled to Toby Blake. Toby was inside the hall. George yelled: 'Come out,

460

Toby. The Britonians have got a lord with 'em!' And Toby opened that little window by the door and hollered: 'Tell the General the only Lord I ever want to see is the Lord God Jehovah!'" ... "Wonder what happened when they marched past General Ward's house on the Shrewsbury road." ... "Know what happened when Washington went by? Artemas Ward ain't partial to Washington and when he rode by, there was old Artemas standing by the window. What'd Artemas do? Why, he turned around, flipped up his coat-tails and presented his fat arse for that bone-faced Virginian to admire. Haw, haw, haw. The Artemas salute!"

Prentiss clumped heavily over to Ahrens' table. "That fat feller, he's Timothy Churchill. He'll take you far's Marlboro. That's fifteen mile along. Mebbe you can find a cart to Sudbury. But there's a good inn at Marlboro. No, no, I ain't takin' no money off you. Comin' to town anyways."

"I'm piling up a terrific debt to citizens of the Col—of the Free States of America. At least, let me thank you."

"Oh, that's all right." Prentiss waved expansively. "I b'lieve in helpin' a feller that's down on his luck. How'd you feed while I was gone?"

"Magnificently." Ahrens slapped his lean stomach. "Tell me one thing—what do they call the custard that they brought me?"

Prentiss peered at the smeared dishes. "Custard? Why, that's a punkin pie!" He wagged his head. "You didn't know? Folks must fare awful bad in Europe."

The wheels of Churchill's cart rumbled over the floating bridge that spanned the wooded throat of Lake Quinsigamond, then grated slowly up the stony slope that led to the village of Shrewsbury. Ahrens huddled sacking about his shoulders and listened to the steady beat of the rain on the canvas cover overhead. Churchill sat hunched on the box, his fat, petulant face screwed up against the fine spray that blew in on him. He turned a round glistening cheek toward the inside of the cart. "What was that letter you writ, back there in the Exchange?"

Ahrens snorted impatiently. "Do these people never stop asking questions?" he thought angrily. He checked his rising temper. "Just a line to the Giffords in Leicester. They were very kind to me."

Churchill nodded. "Guess so. But they're cantankerous folk."

"Cantankerous? You mean crabbed? Look here, they—"

"They're New Englanders. All New Englanders is cantankerous."

"Where do you come from, that you're so glib about them?"

"I'm a New Englander. That's how I know. They're grievin' bad 'bout that snaggle-toothed Caleb of theirs. Don't do to fret. He'll come traipsin' home soon's we've beat the Britainers."

"You expect to beat Lord Howe, with all his trained troops?"

Churchill turned round on the seat, looked solemnly back at Ahrens. "Well, *you* ain't exactly militia."

"I deserved that," thought Ahrens. Then he said: "We have to admit, Mr. Churchill, that your raw troops did very well."

"All we want. No reg'lar army after the war, neither. Now, some of the big-wigs in Philadelphia—no, they're in York now—they set up a squall that we was to hire foreign troops, Hessians and Spaniards and Portygees and such, to fight for us."

"*Hessians?*" Ahrens' head jerked back. "To fight along with—with Washington?"

" 'Twas argued in Congress. But Sam Adams, he riz up directly."

"What did he say?" asked Ahrens.

"He said 'No.' " Churchill flicked the wet flanks of the horses with a long whip.

The cart rolled on past Shrewsbury common with its

462

fringe of white houses, green-shuttered, and its towering elms. From a hidden road a lumbering Conestoga wagon crunched out onto the main highway. In its wake a boy drove three patient-eyed cows. Churchill waved his whip, shouted. Over his shoulder he explained: "Settlers. From Framingham. Goin' out to the Ohio country."

The rain redoubled in intensity. Ahrens shivered, buried his feet in the straw that covered the bottom of the cart. Through the open end of the canvas he could see an apparently endless succession of deep valleys and rolling, wooded ridges. There were graceful white church-spires among the leafless trees, solid houses, some shingled, some clapboarded, in straggling groups along the road, tucked away in valleys or bold on the hill-tops.

"What's the end?" he thought. "*Our* accounts are settled, but then there's Howe with the main army in New Jersey, a big, solid force operating in good country. Howe's got cavalry, too. Then there's the British fleet. *And*—there's precedent. These Yankees look sane and yet what a crazy world they're trying to build. Town meetings! Free schools! An elected Congress to steer things! Soldiers electing their officers! Build new roads. Tax the towns for them because the townspeople vote to pay the costs! Yet—I understand this a lot better from Judith's story. Her father was the quintessence of all these people I've talked to. And having talked with them, I can understand him. Crazy ideas and his was the craziest. Wonderful—*if* they could be carried out. But it's contrary to all reason—to all precedent. Things *aren't* like that! Mrs. Gifford sent nearly all her blankets to the army. Why? No one made her. Her son marched off with the 21st Massachusetts. Why? Because it was 'fittin'.' It's hopeless. It *must* be. Lord! They beat us—but what an army!"

Water began to drip from the canvas top. Churchill was a silent huddle of wet cloth on the seat. Ahrens shifted his cloak, moved his valise out of range of a growing trickle of water, rearranged the sacking.

463

"The officers! Wait a minute. I'm thinking with the mind of some of those fellows on staff—or Baum or Breymann. Nickerson was better educated than—well, a dozen regimental officers, British, Brunswick or Hessian, that I could name. Conant was a match for Burgoyne in sauvity and manner, his superior in breadth. The private who corrected Ettlinger's Latin! How poor old Pausch suffered over that! And that Carter! I doubt if he could do much more than write his own name. But he had power. What was his credo? 'Free church, free schools and the town meetin'.' Damn it—he spoke for all those men there. Clever man, that Conant—chose Carter to formulate the creed. Now, the Earl of Balcarres would sneer—very politely, because he's a gentleman—at Carter." His jaw set, he pounded fist into palm, unknowing. "Balcarres, Burgoyne, Pausch, the Baron, Phillips—the whole lot of us—we're living desperately in the—the fifteenth century. *These* men are trying—God, how they're trying!—to grow into the nineteenth. They're staggering, they're blundering, they're floundering, but they're *trying.*"

The steaming horses strained and tugged as they breasted a long, winding hill. Churchill shouted hoarsely at them. The rain drummed and boomed on the canvas. "Will they do it? They fight against awful odds. Two years and more and what have they done? Gage flummoxed himself out of Boston. Arnold nearly took Quebec, but lost his army up there in Canada. Carlton drove him from Champlain. Then Burgoyne drove St. Clair out of Ticonderoga. Fort Anne fell and Fort Edward. Lake George became a British lake. The Indians were loosed on the country. That must have been discouraging news. Yet—yet there seems to be a tough kernel. No matter how we shatter their armies, they always drift away just before the coup de grâce—then they're back at us like a pack of madmen. And all the time they talk of opening up the west, building canals, electing sheriffs and fencing a pound on a town common. Nickerson shouting: 'In twenty years you won't know this country!' Canals, sheriffs, pounds around a mess-table!" Slowly he nodded. "By God, I believe they will! I believe they will. I'd like to see it. I'd like to be a part of it."

That night he stayed at a farmhouse ten miles beyond Marlboro, where a solemn-eyed girl of eight sat by a roaring fire and carefully whittled at a birch stick which was to become a broom. As he greedily put away a great bowl of what the farmer's wife called hasty pudding the girl asked him if it were true that Hessians ate people. In a rain-swept morning, another cart took him on past Weston. By evening he had to be helped from the cart, chills and fever shaking him again, an agony of pain behind his eyes. The next day he insisted on taking the road again, shivering miserably in the cart of a passing farmer. He must get to Cambridge! Once in Cambridge—in warm barracks or a snug house, then he could coddle himself till the transports came. He kept calling to the farmer: "I must get there! You won't forget in case I sleep? Captain Pausch, at the barracks of the Hesse-Hanau artillery company. You won't forget? I *must* get there. Be all right in good, warm barracks!"

"I'll git you there," said the farmer.

A heavy gale from the northwest whipped clouds of sharp-fingered sleet around the barracks that huddled on the crest and slopes of Winter Hill. In the murk of the officers' room, Number 4 Barrack, Captain Pausch wrapped his tattered cloak more tightly about his hard, old shoulders, burrowed his broken boots into the moldy straw that covered the dirt floor and watched a tangled heap of blankets in the dim corner farthest from the door. By his side, four scarecrow lieutenants of the Rhetz regiment squatted over a card-game, wrangling endlessly.

The heap stirred, a ragged blue arm, red-cuffed, tossed itself clear of the blankets. Pausch leaned forward, his rickety chair rocking and creaking. "So you've decided to wake? Siemann was here an hour ago, forced some kind of foul brew down your throat and told me you'd be looking up presently. Feel better?"

Ahrens passed shaky hands over his eyes. "Same as always. The fever breaks and leaves me weak as a kitten. Am I going to have this in my bones all my life?"

A blast of wind tore at the old sacking nailed across the gaping window-hole and a trickle of water zigzagged crazily down the flimsy wall. Pausch shrugged. "We'd given you up for all time. The last we saw of you was when we rolled you up on a settle in that little hilltown back there. For all we knew, you might have joined up with your Yankee friends. Then that carter from—from—"

"Watertown—I remember that much, anyway," said Ahrens.

"Well, from that place, then. The carter brought you in last night. You'd been in his house five days, and then tried to walk the rest of the way by yourself. You got about ten feet, and then he threw you in his cart and drove here."

"Five days!" Ahrens stared. "Well, nothing surprises me now. This may be 1780, for all I know. I felt fine in Worcester and thought I was free of this damned fever for good." He raised his head, looked around. "Dear God, don't tell me these are our quarters! Why—the floor's dirt! There are holes in the roof! In the walls! Here—does the General know this? According to the Convention, we're to be quartered in lodgings suitable to our rank. We—"

Pausch broke in. "Well, I warned you, I warned you." He scuffed his feet in the straw. "The Yankees had *some* reason for all that hypocritical kindness along the road. Now look at us!" He snorted through his beak-like nose. "Don't say I didn't warn you! Six officers in this room, twelve feet by twelve. Eighty-two men and nine women and a flock of brats in the main barracks. No firewood, freezing weather and the God-damnedest, surliest guards that ever—well, they'd disgrace even an Italian prison."

Ahrens drew the back of his hand across the stubble of his chin. "And I had pictured brick buildings, deep fireplaces, beds! And if these are *our* quarters, what's happening to the men?"

"You'll see soon enough. This kennel of ours, well, it's just a cubicle built into the corner of the barracks. The men have the rest of it."

"But, for God's sake, how long?" protested Ahrens.

"Until the damned place falls to pieces." Pausch looked up as the gale howled louder and louder about the eaves. "And I should say that would be no more than forty-eight hours if this wind keeps up." He drew his cape tighter about his throat. "Then, I presume, we'll be graciously permitted to build ourselves little hutches out of the wreckage."

Ahrens laughed. "If you only knew how I'd dreamed of those warm barracks that waited for us at the end of the march!"

"If I only knew!" Pausch cackled. "You kept us awake all last night talking about them—that is, when you weren't roaring in English. Talking about your Yankee pets, I suppose." He smiled grimly. "You'll be singing a different tune in a day or so."

Water dripped hollowly from the roof. The Rhetz men flapped their cards and argued in dull, mechanical tones. Pausch went on. "Yet things have improved, though you'd find it hard to believe. You should have been with us when we marched into this damned town. Pouring rain, no orders, nothing ready. Men wandering about in the mud and never a roof to cover them. Von Burgoyne and von Phillips jammed into a little, dirty room in a tavern off the square by the college. The Riedesels, girls and all, crowded into another foul den. All the baggage dumped in the middle of the common opposite the church and no sign of a guard. Then we were marched off to these barracks, and let me tell you that this one,

Number 4, is the cream of the lot. You ought to see where Barner's men and Specht's are quartered. And if we complain we're told it damned well serves us right and we ought to be singing hymns of thanksgiving that we're not pitched into the Maine forests."

"But—but the Yankees won't let this go on," protested Ahrens, bewildered.

Pausch chuckled heavily. "Won't they? This is November fourteenth. We've been here since the seventh. The only change I look for is for the Yankees to turn us out of these barracks and let us shift for ourselves in the open fields."

Ahrens shook his head impatiently. "They'll do *some-thing*. Gentleman Johnny won't stand for treatment like this. And, anyway, the transports will come for us in a few weeks, a month. God, this place stinks like a stoat's den."

"You get used to that," said Pausch, philosophically. "We've all our gunners under this roof and a platoon or two of Rhetz men. They moored a bear and two raccoons just by our door. I made them move in a hurry. It's not quite so thick now." He tweaked the point of his nose. "Lord Jesus, how that bear did stink!"

A heavy whiff of cold, fetid air swept into the little room as the door quivered on its hinges, swung shakily open. A tall, stoop-shouldered man stood in the gap, blowing on raw, chapped hands. The four card players looked up. "Any hope?" one of them asked.

The newcomer shook his head. "Same as yesterday."

Pausch slowly freed a foot from its nest of damp straw and prodded Ahrens gently in the ribs. "Listen, my Yankee friend," he chuckled.

The tall man stamped about on the dank floor, his feet shapeless lumps of burlap. "There's not a God-damned ray of hope, I tell you," he rasped angrily. "I've been at the Baron's. He's still in that sewer and all his brats with him. The ink froze on his pen when he tried to write an order. He lit a candle and the wind blew so strong through the cracks in the wall that the flame gave one flicker and died. Lena, the maid, had washed the baby's diapers. Well, they were frozen stiff, hanging by the hole in the wall that the Yankees call a fireplace."

One of the players coughed. "No worse off than we are, Falkendorf. At least, we've no brats."

"No worse off! We shouldn't be *badly* off! Look, I walked out what they call Brattle Street. Houses? By God, they're mansions. Big houses, fine houses!" He squatted by the players. Pausch watched Ahrens out of the corner of his eye. Falkendorf carefully unwound layer after layer of sacking from his feet, draped the coarse cloth over a wooden peg sunk in the wall. He went on. "Mansions, that's what they are. Fine as houses in Europe! Fine, big doorways with carving over them! Broad windows, chimneys that'd warm a battalion! But try and get in! If they're not empty, then they're rented for a thaler a month to some blue-nosed bastard of a Yankee patriot. You see? All Loyalist houses. Will the patriot move?" He spat on the dirt floor. Pausch chuckled hoarsely.

A Rhetz man drearily riffled the cards. "How about those big buildings we saw? Those by—by Harvard Square, they call it?"

"The college? Harvard College? By God, there's room there for every officer. Tight roofs, wide chimneys. But—" He threw up gaunt hands.

Ahrens hitched his blankets over his shoulder. "Well, you can't blame them for keeping us out of the college. Do you expect they're going to turn out the faculty and students just to make us comfortable?"

Falendorf looked up sourly. "So *you're* awake, are you? Hope you keep your damn mouth shut tonight. Well, I don't expect the Yankees to do *anything* to make us comfortable. As for the colleges, the Baron tells me that most of the people live in the town. Just a few in the college buildings. And, then, vacation time is coming, some Yankee saint's day they call Thanksgiving.

Well, they've all but nailed the doors up, for fear we'll get in. Christ, above, are we lepers?"

"This is beyond me," said Ahrens wearily. "The Yankees aren't like this. As soon as the people of Cambridge see what's going on, they'll change things. This *is* Cambridge, I suppose?"

Pausch shook his head impatiently. "Damned if I'll truckle to the Yankee swine by learning their heathenish names. This may be on the moon for all of me."

One of the card players looked up. "The college is in Cambridge. The map shows this place, Winter Hill, is in Charlestown. So is Prospect Hill where the British are."

Another voice growled, "Doesn't matter what the names are. It's the damnedest, bleakest country I ever saw. Worse than the Polish marshes and the people are worse swine than the Poles. What have you got there, Falkendorf?"

The tall man was bending over a bundle. "Something I brought in under my cape. Look!" He held up three solid chunks of wood. "You know that sentry-box by the main road up Winter Hill? The sentry was away, so I ripped up the little seat inside."

Pausch's eyes shone. "This is heaven. We'll toast our feet, by God! We'll toast our feet!"

"See, Lieutenant! They have given us good beef, good vegetables!" Hedwig knelt by Ahrens' blankets, a wooden bowl in her hard, capable hands. Ahrens sat up eagerly, sniffing the rich steam.

"A stew, Hedwig?" He took the bowl, stirred the iron spoon about. "There is plenty for the men?"

She smiled. "A whole ox, sir, and sacks of onions and potatoes! Ah, it's good to see the Lieutenant eat!"

Ahrens wagged his head. "I told that sawbones he was crazy. I could get up today and march to the Hudson and back. And with this stew!" He buried the spoon in the reeking bowl. "Where are Captain Pausch and the others, Hedwig?"

470

"They are walking up and down outside the barracks. There was only just enough wood for cooking, so the gentlemen warm themselves by walking in the rain. It is the only way."

Ahrens eyed her. "But how do you do, you and the corporal? Your cheeks are red and your eyes as bright as they were in Hanau."

"The folk were good to us on the march, Lieutenant. Often I slept in a bed and one woman gave me shoes, another a warm cape. Then my man mended a cart for a widow—it was when we halted in the rain by the big river. The Lieutenant remembers?"

Ahrens nodded. "The Connecticut. That was just before the fever began to come back."

"I do not remember the name. But the widow gave me stockings and we slept by a big fire in her kitchen. I would like to have stayed. She was good to us."

"What do the men say about the people here in Cambridge, Hedwig?"

"They are very bitter, sir."

Ahrens set down the empty bowl. "And you agree, Hedwig?"

She shook her head. "It is hard to blame the folk here. They are tired of war. There have been many soldiers and the town is small."

"Many soldiers? How do you know that?"

"These barracks, Lieutenant. They are not new, nor are we the first to live in them. It was always hard at home when troops were quartered on the town. War is not kind to poor folk." She picked up the bowl, smiling. "It was good to see you eat, sir." She stood up, her swelling figure neat and trim in her patched and mended clothes. "The Lieutenant is to rest, now, or the Captain will be angry." Ahrens saw her move easily out the door, then heard her gasp.

In the dim vastness of the barracks, Ahrens saw a gleam of scarlet and white. A full, firm voice rolled and echoed.

471

"Sir, I have completed my inspection of the barracks. I am in honor and duty, and with the fullest conviction, compelled to join my voice with the other officers and assert, sir, that the quarters allotted the troops would not be held fit for horned cattle in any part of the world. I've seen many jails preferable. I repeat, Mr. Crane, that the article of the Convention respecting quarters *must* be properly fulfilled before any parole whatever shall be signed. That, sir, is a resolution that no man of my command will depart from." Feet scraped on the dirt floor outside the little room. The voice came nearer. "Look at the room for officers, Mr. Crane, and you, General Heath!"

Into the murky room stepped Gentleman Johnny Burgoyne, crisp and bright. At his elbow Ahrens saw a lean-faced man in drab civilian's clothes, a ruddy sad-looking officer in Continental blue and buff, and in the background Generals Phillips and Hamilton, the former scowling, the latter disdainful. Gentleman Johnny's arm shot out. "This room, General Heath! Hello, hello. There's some one in here." He peered. "Why—it's young Ahrens! No, no, no! Don't get up! Don't think of it! There, Mr. Crane! A sick officer! A fine, brave soldier, a first-rate gunner, and here he lies in this sty while all those high-ceiled halls along your Brattle Street are idle. Let me tell you, sir, the world shall hear of this! By God, the world shall learn of Cambridge and its people! You boast that your little college here is a century and a half old." His scarlet arm shot out. "I pledge my word as a British officer and as a gentleman that Harvard's elder sisters in the old world shall look upon her with scorn, with disdain. The humanities! What can you teach, Mr. Crane, that will live down the example you set here? They shall hear, sir, all of them. Oxford, Cambridge, Heidelberg, Bonn and Jena! Look at this officer here! Look at those shivering men outside in the filthy sheds. Look at the women and the half-naked babies. They freeze while the walls of

Cambridge and the walls of Harvard turn away in indifference!"

The lean-faced man looked coldly at Burgoyne. "You were not bidden here, sir. You were not bidden to America. Common soldiers, common officers—they must accept what the fortunes of war bring them."

The American officer looked away, eyes heavy and sad. Burgoyne threw back his head. "There is not a *common* soldier nor a *common* officer in the armies that followed me, Mr. Crane. I shall ever be ready to testify that it is through no fault of theirs that they find themselves captives. They strove and endured beyond mortal comprehension—and in silence. They are still silent, but, by God, their general will *not* be silent. The Convention was duly signed by General Gates and in that Convention there was stipulation for suitable quarters. Look about you, Mr. Crane!"

Crane folded his hands across the head of his silver-topped stick. "I am not aware that Mr. Gates had plenary powers to effect a Convention in the name of the United States of America. Nor am I aware that Congress, having duly met and deliberated, has ratified that Convention. Mr. Gates exceeded his powers."

Gentleman Johnny's eyes flashed. His lips tightened. "So the men suffer, Mr. Crane! The officers suffer. I assure you, sir, that my own quarters are no better than this kennel."

Crane looked at the blue and buff officer. "The Committee authorized General Heath some time ago to offer you the choice of the Inman estate, close by Central Square or the Apthorp house across from the college. Fine, commodious houses, both of them. General Health, did you fail to transmit the wishes of the Committee?"

Heath flushed, started to speak. Burgoyne quickly put out his hand. "General Heath—I beg of you. Permit me—" He bowed courteously to the American. "The Committee's offer was promptly and faithfully forwarded to me by General Heath. I find it hard to believe that the

473

Committee is unaware of my reply. I give myself the pleasure of repeating the gist of it, Mr. Crane, for your information. I wrote General Heath that until the infringements of the Convention are redressed, in regard to the quartering of the troops, officers and men alike, I cannot, I *will* not accept personally any other accommodations than those which it is my present misfortune to occupy. That, sir, is my answer. And permit me to add that we are all convinced that we should have no cause for complaint if powers of redress were vested in General Heath, who has shown himself in every way to be a gentleman, a man of honor and a credit to his uniform."

Crane nodded dryly. "But allow me to point out to you, General, that such matters lie entirely outside of his province. This whole matter concerns itself with the supreme powers of the State."

Burgoyne looked steadily at Crane. "But when such powers are unable or unwilling to enforce their authority and the inhabitants of this town lack the—the common civilization to assist us without it—" he raised his chin, eyes bright and steady—"then, sir, the public faith is broke and these poor men are the immediate sufferers!"

Heath gasped. Crane stared coldly at Burgoyne. "Are you aware, General Burgoyne, of the implications of what you say? Would you care to commit them to writing?"

"Implications be damned, Mr. Crane. And if it concerns the welfare of my men, then I'll write the truth in letters of fire under the nose of the Devil himself. I believe, sir, our tour of inspection is at an end?" He bent over, patted Ahrens on the shoulder. "Get well fast, my lad. I'll send my own physician over to have a look at you. We'll get you on your feet by sunrise tomorrow, damned if we won't." Then without a glance at the cold-eyed Crane, Gentleman Johnny slipped his arm under the stout Heath's, walked out of the room. From the outer gloom Ahrens heard the full voice rolling on: "Oh, my dear Heath, you must know him. He'll be useful. Old Harrow boy. Of course, *I* was Westminster."

Among his blankets Ahrens grinned to himself. Then he began to turn over in his mind the scene he had just witnessed. "Now, what the devil was it that Gentleman Johnny said?" he thought. " 'Faith'? Oh—'the public faith is broke.' Why the devil did the most unpleasant Mr. Crane warn him about that? It's true enough. The Yankees haven't fulfilled their part of the Convention; we have. They've broken faith. Why—why did Crane jump so?"

Pausch leaned back in his crazy chair, stretched his legs out before him and wiggled his feet ecstatically. "Boots, real boots!" he chuckled, running his fingers lovingly over the smooth leather that reached from knee to heel. "Look at 'em, Ahrens! Boots!" He rose, stumped up and down the little room, grinning. "And these!" He stooped over, picked up the wrecked leather that had carried him down the Hudson and across Massachusetts. "Heels gone, soles gone, uppers gone, toes gone. Now, they're *all* gone!" He pitched the dilapidated pair into the darkest corner of the room.

Ahrens grinned at the veteran. "Where did you get them, Captain?" he said. "I'm out and about now. I could do with a pair."

Pausch shook his head. "I could take you there. It's near the college. But these damn Yankee names! *I* won't learn 'em."

Ahrens picked up the stiff paper in which the boots had arrived, read "Independence Bootery, Louis Archambault, Proprietor." He smothered a laugh. "You'll *take* me there, though?" he asked.

Pausch tramped about, smiling happily. "Glad to, glad to. Only don't ask me to learn Yankee names. So you really feel stronger now?"

"Gentleman Johnny's physician says I'm fit as a fiddle and doubts if I'll have any more of these attacks now

475

that cold weather is setting in. He won't answer, though, if I go where it's warm and damp. What do you think of my turning the gunners out and drilling a bit?"

"*Drilling?* For God's sake, what for?"

"It'll give them something to do. They'll rot like sheep if they just sit about these dark barracks and mope. Why, there hasn't been a fight in a week and it's three days since the Yankees complained of stolen firewood. And look here. The first time I go over to Cambridge, I'll buy a set of tenpins."

Pausch groaned. "Oh God, they're grown men. Don't coddle 'em so much. Tenpins!" He snorted. "Tenpins! Well, I'll pay half. Where are you going?"

"Out in the sun—while it lasts," said Ahrens. "There's a warm spot by the east wall of the barracks. I've been cooped up so long that just sitting in the open is a treat."

In the half-light of the shed-like building, ragged men huddled over cards, women squabbled dully about kettles and bedding, filthy children in fantastic clothes played on the dirt floor. By the far door an apathetic bear rocked slowly to and fro, crooning to itself. Ahrens picked his way among the tumbling brats, gingerly patted the bear and freed a raccoon cub that had hopelessly entangled itself in its cord. Then he pushed at the shaky door and stepped into a flood of clear, cold sunshine.

Down the slope of Winter Hill, some twenty tottering barracks straggled to a flat meadow, bristling with black, ugly stumps. In the distance a cold blue river wound through frozen marshes. Ahrens sat on a sunwarmed rock and watched a slow procession of country carts creak up the hill, rumble along the crest and move jerkily down the other slope toward a faraway huddle of houses by a crossroads. Wherever he looked the stumpy plain was broken by low hills or cut by sluggish streams. Off to the east a graciously proportioned house seemed to bask calmly in broad, well-laid-out grounds.

"Wish I knew more about this," thought Ahrens.

476

"Now, that smear of red brick across the basin to the east—that must be Boston. That's Medford, north by the crossroads. The Mystic River in front of me and the Charles east and south. Wish I had a map. Lord, look at those stumps! What a waste of wood! This road that cuts up over Winter Hill comes from—from Charlestown and splits three ways on the crest—Medford this way, Arlington straight ahead and the fork I can't see leads to Cambridge. Or at least, that's what Falkendorf says. Wonder what's going on under all those roofs down there in the meadows—and in that big house on the point. I wonder—now in Cambridge her family would be remembered, at least. Her father was something in the college. Greek, wasn't it? As soon as I can walk—"

The big barrack door rattled, a lazy voice said. "Run you to earth at last. Sunning yourself on a rock like a snake. Tell me you've been ailing, young fellow." Immaculate in a glossy new uniform, Charteris smiled from the doorway, a real concern in his eyes that vanished as soon as Ahrens' gaze met his.

"Come and join me, Major. Sit down here and tell me the gossip of the army."

Charteris shook his head. "Can't. You're to join me and become part of the gossip. I'm to take you away. Got a mansion for you."

"Take me away?" Ahrens shook his head. "Look here, Major, I can't loll in a staff palace while the men freeze here."

"No choice. Gentleman Johnny's orders. Matter of fact, we need you badly. Someone to speak for Brunswickers and Hessians, you know. Hardly a man on the Baron's staff can handle a word of English. Anyway, we're getting lodgings in town for quite a few of the officers. Stop worrying about Pausch. You'll be in a good position to use undue influence in getting him snug quarters. Oh, and you're to bring an orderly with you. Suggest that corporal—you know, the Rosenstrauch one with the pretty wife. Oh, yes, she can come. We've a big house, I tell you. I'll send a note to Pausch."

Arm in arm they turned the corner of the barracks. Ahrens stopped abruptly, staring at the smart, shining chaise that stood on the road leading to the west valley and Cambridge. Its paint was glossy, its harness bright and the horse stepped about impatiently on well-blackened hooves. A grinning negro boy in a trim livery stood by the animal's head.

"Good God, Major, am I dreaming? That chaise? That horse? This might be London. Ahrens spread out his worn blue cloak. "Here, you'd better take that black imp into the chaise with you. I'll trudge behind in the mud."

Charteris laughed. "Into the chaise with you. It's the fruit again of undue influence. You, Nero, hop into the rumble as soon as I take the lines and don't get tangled up with the wheels."

Charteris seized the reins, squared his elbows. "Now then, Nero!" He flourished his whip. The chaise rocketed off, took a sharp corner on one wheel and catapulted down the steep slope. Charteris skilfully checked the mad rush of the horse. "Appreciate a beast like this! Life! Spirit!" he shouted cheerfully above the rumble of the wheels. "Ha! Listen to Nero praying back there in the rumble!"

"That's not Nero," said Ahrens feebly. Charteris shouted with laughter.

The chaise rolled smoothly along the level meadows past the foot of Prospect Hill, which was littered with shaky barracks and sheds, red figures moving about over the frosty paths. "Coming into Charleston Lane," said Charteris. "See that low house by the crossroads? Piper's Tavern. First-rate rum and gin there, and a pipe or two of really fine Madeira. Gad! Do enjoy driving this horse. Bolted with me twice this morning and kicked Nero across the stable last night. Call her Blitzen. Not my idea. The Baroness christened him."

Ahrens eyed Blitzen's sleek flanks approvingly,

watched the smooth, effortless action of the glossy haunches. He sighed. "I'm in a new world. An hour ago I was breathing the reek of a Rhetz bear and marveling over Pausch's new boots. Now you turn up in this rig, looking as though you'd stepped off the Horse Guards' Parade and tell me about the Madeira at Piper's Tavern. Have you left the army and turned New England squire?"

Charteris' jaw tightened. "Not likely. These blasted Yankees. Pig-headed. Stupid. Can't seem to understand that they're rebels. Why, back in Northampton, I think it was, I lodged in a parson's house. Know what he told me? Said *we* were rebels. 'Pon my honor he did. Rebelling against the will of a free people! Gad!"

He drove on in silence. Suddenly he pointed with his whip. "See that chimney? Off there to the northwest? Snow's Tavern. Good man, Snow. For five shillings he'll smuggle you into Boston. Went there last night with Kingston and Vallancey—you know, the assistant quartermaster-general. Went to a place called the Bell-in-Hand. Lord knows where, after that. Each place we went the tone was lower and the price higher. Introduce you to Snow."

The chaise rattled over a solid wooden bridge, then danced along a level stretch as Charteris gave Blitzen her head. The road was smooth, well-paved. Occasional trim houses raised their chimneys among bare-branched elms and oaks. Far ahead, warm brick shone gently in an open meadow. Charteris waved his whip. "Coming to the college. By God, if ever I plant my guns on Prospect Hill. I'll drop the heaviest shot in my tumbrils through those damned roofs. Room for us all. Blasted stiff-necked bastards. Won't give us a corner. The Overseers, the Corporation, the Faculty! We'll damage the buildings, we'll corrupt the students, we'll turn Papist, we'll settle there for life, it's too big for us, it's too small! Christ! The Faculty will agree to give us one building if the Corporation sees fit. The Corporation will consider the matter, if agreeable to the wishes of the Overseers. The Overseers advise caution, as they do not wish to offend the Faculty, and all the time the three sets of pompous yokels are laughing up their sleeves, nudging one another in the ribs. Look—here comes one of them now, an Overseer! Called on him with Gentleman Johnny and Heath!"

A neatly turned-out chaise rattled easily over the road toward them, driven by an elderly man in sober black. Charteris raised his whip in stiff salute. The Overseer turned a solemn, long-chinned face, inclined his head gravely. Charteris flicked Blitzen lightly. "Gad, did you see him? Spine so stiff I could hear his neck creak when he bowed. So God-damned conscious of his own righteousness. Every time he drives out he sits up there like a poker, thinking that every soul he passes bows humbly and says, 'There goes an Overseer of Harvard!' What that man needs is a drink and a wench, Ahrens, a drink and a wench."

Ahrens nodded. "A stern man, but a just. That's how he sees himself. And you've doubtless hit his needs perfectly. Still, I can't blame the college when I look at it from its point of view. They turn the students out, give us all the buildings. That's fine—for us. But who can say how they'll be able to start things off once we're gone?"

"Doesn't matter, that I can see. Little college. Only a hundred and fifty years old. No—not quite that, I think. It's of no importance. The important thing is that we, an army on parole, have to live in kennels while those buildings could house us."

"A century and a half! God above, Major, if it were much older, why—why, the first Overseers and Faculty would have been Indians. And then—this place didn't spring out of a wigwam, anyway. It was founded by Englishmen bred up in your own universities, carried on by them."

Charteris snorted. "Tell you what, young Ahrens. In any country there's something rotten about a group of men that are always concerned with the minds of young boys. Oh, mean well, of course. But they never grow up themselves. Lower their minds to the seventeens and eighteens. Never fails. Now, take a case in point. This green we're coming to. Call it the college yard around here. Smooth, level. Wanted it badly, myself. See now—what a perfect cricket pitch! Would they listen to me? By God, so far as *they're* concerned I may lay out my cricket pitch in the marshes down by the Charles. Why—what are you laughing at?"

Ahrens coughed. "Oh—just your—your description of the needs of that stiff old Overseer."

Charteris grinned, highly pleased, "Oh, that. Here's the college now, on our left." He reined in. "That three-story affair is Hollis Hall, the one beyond it with the white cupola is Harvard, Massachusetts Hall beyond it—the one with the chimneys at either end and the white balustrade running along the roof."

Ahrens sat up, interested. In those very buildings, Judith's father had taught, had probably stood in the sun on the high sandstone porch of Harvard Hall and talked of his ideal state with students, with townsfolk, with faculty members. "It's out of the soil, it's out of the people," said Ahrens. "See how that rose brick, the white paint, those roof-lines belong to the landscape just as much as those elms yonder by the wooden buildings. And that little chapel. It's severe and yet there's grace to it. No spire, but look at the sweep to those high-arched windows. What do you call the chapel?"

"You get the God-damnedest ideas," snorted Charteris. "They'd not house cooks in buildings like those at Oxford, now. If you really want to know, that little dog-house is Holden Chapel. Swear if I hadn't seen you tweaking a wolf's nose I'd think you were a dominie at heart. Cambridge Common on your right, containing five barracks that go way back to 1775, three cows and two moldy cannon. Christ Church, mostly Tory so I can't tell you much about it."

481

He swung Blitzen round the west side of the Common, flicked her into a brisk trot down a wide, elm-lined street. Ahrens caught a hint of terraced grounds, of high-fronted houses. "You told me you had a mansion for me, Major? Don't say it's on *this* street! In my rags, and tatters! I couldn't live up to it."

Charteris nodded. "This is the street. Most of the staff are bedded down in the Vassall house and I've got a small room all earmarked for you. Fine house, till the Yankees let it run to pot. The Vassals were Tories, so their trim grounds look as though Riedesel's dragoons had marched and countermarched across them. Lot of the windows are minus glass and some of the doors won't close. Roof leaks in spots. Not a stick of furniture. Changing all that, though. About your clothes. Found a first-rate tailor just off Harvard Square and a boot-maker who's at least passable. Don't worry about cost. Long's you've a Brattle Street address, you'll get credit." He stretched out a long arm. "Look at the fit of that sleeve! Perfect! Wish I could say as much for the bootmaker. Here we are."

He turned the chaise up a curving, graveled drive, pulled in before a wide-doored façade through whose windows open fires twinkled and snapped in the noon light. Charteris jumped out, tossed the reins to Nero, who had scrambled around somehow from the rumble. "This way, young fellow," said the Major.

A trim, powdered orderly swung open the heavy door with its gleaming brass knocker. Ahrens followed Charteris into a great, white-paneled hall, his spurs ringing on the polished floor. Before him a wide shallow staircase mounted gracefully, its mahogany bannister gleaming. Two English privates stirred thick brushes in paint-pots, shook their heads over the deep gouges and nicks in the treads.

Charteris nodded to them. "How goes it, lads?"

The nearer man straightened up, raised a paint-smeared hand to his forehead. "Poorly, sir. It do hurt me

482

cruel to see what the Yankees done to fine wood. Them bannisters, now. They shine, as you might say, sir. But they won't never again show the prime grain that's in 'em."

Ahrens ran his finger down a deep scrape. "Pity, isn't it? You seem to know your trade, though."

The man nodded. "I was a joiner afore I 'listed for a sojer, sir. In Glossop, in Derbyshire." He stared mournfully at the scrape. "'Tain't Christian, sir, to treat wood like this."

"That's good work," said Charteris. "Tell the orderly-sergeant that you're to have a ration of beer when you're through, you and your mate. Now, young fellow, come into the orderly room. I'll show you a map so you won't have a Yankee running a bayonet into you for breaking bounds."

Bright sun poured through the three tall windows of the bare orderly room, whose parquetry floor was dinted and scarred by careless feet. The fine broad mirror that hung over the crackling fireplace was mildewed and broken. "Get the men busy in here, next," said Charteris. "Now this map."

On the east wall of the room a huge map was tacked over torn, ragged paper. Ahrens fingered a dangling streamer.

"Fine paper as ever came out of Canton. Look—it's the garden pattern. Some lout has drawn mustaches on the face of the little mandarin here."

Charteris coughed. "Oh—that. Afraid that happened the other night. Emptied a few bottles here and young Townshend insisted the mandarin looked like Cleve of Specht's. Put the mustache on to prove his point. But the map. See this red line? Our limits."

Ahrens ran a finger over the spidery lines. "The Charles, the Mystic—yes, here's Winter Hill."

Charteris picked up a broken quill pen from the rude table by the fire. "Start here. Charlestown Neck. Swan's shop. Follow the road to Cambridge along to this

483

crossroads and Fort Number Three. Big house here, marked Mr. Codman's. Swing down to Inman's house by Central Square, then straight along the Charles to the Cambridge Bridge. That's just behind us and quite close to the college. Leads to Brighton and Alston. Then we go along the north bank of the Charles. Prime shooting, there, by the way. Out with Hamilton the other day. Fine bag. We'll go out, you and I. Well, the north bank till we come to Watertown Bridge. Cross that on the Boston road as far as Angier's Corner. Swing back again to Remington's house and Learned's Tavern—fine punch there and a fish chowder that's fit for the gods. Now we're back on the Cambridge road again. Here's Richardson's Tavern, the Burying Ground on your right. Clear?"

Ahrens nodded. "This leads us right into Brattle Street again and on past the Common to Massachusetts Avenue."

"Right. Follow that and you'll come to the inn of the invaluable Mr. Snow. But you can keep on going to Cooper's Tavern. Gives us the east shore of Menotomy Pond, but none of the Fresh Pond. Now we turn again and follow this road on past Mystic Pond to Medford and the house of Peter Tufts. Then south, skimming the edge of your Winter Hill and back to Swam's again."

"Precious little territory for an active man," said Ahrens.

Charteris grunted. "Should have seen the first limits they wanted to give us. Just a strip of land about the two hills, Prospect and Winter. Not so bad. There's cockfighting at Richardson's Tavern. Natural amphitheater for it just outside the building. Laying out a race course—foot-races only—through the town. Good fowling in the marshes and I'll get a cricket pitch somehow. Take you to your room now. Your man Rentner and his wife will be in that outbuilding."

Together they edged up the stairs past the Glossop man and his mate. "You've had your ears open in Cambridge," said Ahrens. "Did you ever hear of a family named Hunnewell? No? Well, I—I just wondered."

Ahrens stepped across the broad threshold of the Sewall house, handed his sleek blue cape and cocked hat to the bowing dragoon orderly by the door. Then he stopped, blinking. From sconces and mantels, dozens of candles flared, turned the polished floors of the great front rooms into dull lakes of fire, glowed on masses of evergreen and holly, danced in a wavering pattern on the sky-blue silk of the Baroness' low-cut dress as she stood by a tall mirror, chatting with Gentleman Johnny. Close by her side, in miniature replicas of their mother's costume, Friedericka and Gustava turned solemn eyes on the four musicians—three Riedesel dragoons and a Hesse-Hanau grenadier—who sat in a hemlock-smothered alcove under the wide staircase, fingering their violins. Blue, green, red uniforms moved slowly and easily about, or sat around card-tables in a deep, square room beyond the stairs.

Rockel, magnificent in Jaeger green and red, stalked up to Ahrens, bowed like a major-domo, then led the way to the little woman in sky-blue, trumpeting: "Lieutenant Kurt Ahrens of the Hesse-Hanau artillery company, Baroness!"

Gentleman Johnny moved away in a blaze of scarlet and white. Ahrens bowed over his hostess' little hand. "My compliments, Baroness."

She inclined her head gravely, then broke into a smile. "If you could have seen this house! Rats! Mice! Doors falling off their hinges. Not a stick of furniture but an old table and a broken trammel."

"You have brought Wolfenbüttel to Cambridge. But I meant the blue silk. It—"

The Baroness touched the curly heads beside her. "*Don't* they look nice?" She bent over. "Lieutenant Ahrens was admiring your dresses, girls."

485

The girls rolled grave blue eyes up at Ahrens, essayed wabbling curtsies, to which he bowed profoundly.

Their mother steadied them. "There, that was very nice." She turned her attention back to Ahrens. "The Cambridge and Boston guests are very late. We sent cards to fifty families. I hope—" She broke off suddenly, fixed him with a blue stare. "Kurt Ahrens! *What* have you been doing to yourself! Why—you've powdered your hair!"

Ahrens laughed. "The first time since Quebec, Baroness, and in honor of your ball and the Duke's birthday."

She shook her head. "Powder! And you've silk stockings and slippers!"

"And don't forget the satin knee-breeches. Charteris' tailor sent to Boston for the material. When I came downstairs at the Vassall house tonight, Rentner didn't know me, and I'm sure that Hedwig didn't approve at all."

The Baroness pursed her lips, her eyes dancing. "I think it would be wise if I sent the girls to bed now. They're at an impressionable age. But I suppose I must keep my promise to let them sit up until the guests come —that is, the Yankee guests. Now, do run along and be sure that your captain has plenty of punch. He won't dance when the time comes and he doesn't play cards and that little snip of a Captain Graves was dreadfully rude to him. And then you might take the Baron's hand when the Yankees come—he's playing with Geismar and the Earl of Balcarres and General Phillips. Oh, and when you pass the musicians, do tell Kirschener—he's the one who looks something like a moose—not to forget that his first minuet is to be Handel—the one from the overture to *Samson*."

Ahrens bowed, moved off toward the back of the house, his feet feeling oddly light in stockings and slippers after months of clumsy boots. In a corner of the card-room he found Pausch, staring moodily at a glass of punch. He turned sad eyes on Ahrens. "I'd give anything to be back in that first room they gave us on Winter Hill. Yes—and a snowstorm blowing up from the river." He shuddered. "My feet hurt and this punch is going to give me a headache. Make no mistake about that. A headache that'll shake my teeth loose. I'm sleepy. And every soul who can speak German is either crouching over a mess of sticky cards or talking about fiddles and minuets."

Ahrens took him by the arm. "Let's sit over here. So. Now I'll send a dragoon after rum. The Baroness said you were to have whatever you wanted." He pulled out his watch. "Hello. It *is* late! Past ten and not a Yankee in sight. Wonder—"

Rockel's harsh voice echoed: "Mrs. Carter and Miss Schuyler!"

Pausch jigged at Ahrens' elbow. "The rum can wait! I want to have a look at the rebels."

Ahrens peered over the Captain's shoulder, saw a tall handsome woman in flowered silk, a slim, kitten-faced girl in green and silver curtsying to the Baroness. The Baron, who had hurried from the card-table at Rockel's call, was beaming on them.

Pausch sniffed. "Don't they look funny! What's the matter with 'em?"

Ahrens raised his eyebrows. "Damn fine-looking girls. Oh—their dresses. They still cling to the Watteau style. That was dead in Dresden ten years ago. Wonder who they are? Carter? Schuyler? Nice shoulders on the little one. What do you say, Captain?"

Pausch teetered on aching toes. "Wish I could see! They've a crowd around 'em now. Von Burgoyne, Geismar, Seydlitz, the Earl, Middendorf, von Hamilton."

Ahrens settled the facings of his jacket. "Come on, Captain. I'll have the Baroness present us!"

Pausch hung back, clawing at his stock. "Better wait! Better wait! There's too—too many people and the Baron has backed the younger one into a corner by the low

487

sofa. There's von Charteris with him. Oh, better—better wait!"

"Nonsense!" Ahrens tugged at his sleeve. "We'll—Hi! What's that?"

A dull glow rose out of the blackness beyond the windows, deepened to a sullen red. Pausch grinned like a schoolboy.

"See? See? Red fire in honor of the Duke. Look, look! There go the flares! A squib! Our gunners made 'em! There's more red fire."

A file of servants and orderlies tramped past from the rear of the house, gingerly balancing sparkling trays of bright glasses. The Baron's hearty voice rolled out: "General Burgoyne, may I ask you to propose the toast?"

Ahrens seized Pausch by the elbow, dragged him into the great crowded room. Gentleman Johnny, ruddy face glowing, powdered head thrown back, stood glass in hand beside the Baron.

"Baron von Riedesel—Baroness—" he bowed—"our fair guests and brother-officers. I am most happy to propose this toast on the occasion of the birthday of His Highness, the Duke of Brunswick!" He bowed again, thrust a hand into the bosom of his gleaming white waistcoat. "I am peculiarly happy that there are to drink this toast with us, these fair guests who are more than guests, who are tokens of—"

Rough voices shouted outside the great door, fists pounded against its solid frame. Gentleman Johnny paused, eyebrows raised, as Rockel, with face like a mask, seized the latch and opened it a crack. It was flung back in his face; a heavy-featured man, frayed baldrick over civilian's clothes, pushed past him, stared at the brilliant rooms. Behind him Ahrens saw a dull twinkle of rusty bayonets, a huddle of shabby cocked hats. Beyond the bayonets a vague crowd moved and shifted in the leaping glow of the red fire. A high voice yelled: "It's the mercenaries again! They're up to no good!"

Calm and suave the Baron stepped forward. The Baroness gathered the girls to her, lips compressed and eyes flashing.

In careful English the Baron asked: "To what do I owe this honor?"

The officer tapped nervously on the worn leather scabbard of his old sword. He swallowed hard, then said: "The people want to know what this means. What are you up to?"

The Baron looked around helplessly, caught Ahrens' eye. Ahrens stepped quickly up to the florid man in blue and buff. "The Baron directs me to tell you that this is a private gathering to celebrate the birthday of His Highness, the Duke of Brunswick. There is no intent to alarm or disturb the people of Cambridge."

The officer turned sour eyes on him. "Dukes and Highnesses don't mean nothin' here. If you're up to no trouble, what d'you burn signals for?"

Ahrens raised a soothing hand. "No signals, I assure you. Just an illumination. It's an old custom, like—like your Thanksgiving. We always do it on the Duke's birthday."

"Thanksgiving, Thanksgiving! Where'd *you* hear tell of Thanksgiving?" The officer shifted his feet uneasily. "Well, guess it's all right. Only don't—" His eye caught the two guests, who stood close by the Baroness. He strode noisily across the floor, halted before the taller, who looked at him with evident repugnance. "At least *you've* got to account to me!"

Mrs. Carter threw back her head. "To General Heath if he likes. Surely not to you."

The officer laughed hoarsely, snapped his fingers. "I don't care that for General Heath. I'm militia. I'm only answerable to the Committee of Safety. You know what the orders was about this?"

Mrs. Carter's chin lifted itself higher. "My father happens to be General Phillip Schuyler of the Continental

489

Army. This is my sister." She trailed a slim hand toward the younger girl.

"Schuyler don't count none 'round here."

"My husband, Mr. Carter, is a member of the Boston Committee of Safety. He could not attend himself, but approved my coming." Hands lightly clasped before her, she looked coldly at the man. "It will give me great pleasure to speak to him about you—great pleasure."

The man looked sullen. "Orders was that no one in Boston nor Cambridge was to come here tonight."

The younger girl stepped up, linked her arm with her sister, smiling brightly. "Wouldn't it be simplest for you to put us under arrest? Then in the morning you could explain why the wife of a Committee-man *and* his sister-in-law were lodged in a Cambridge jail."

"Don't want to make trouble." His eyes jumped shiftily around the silent ring of guests. "Don't want no trouble at all. I—"

Ahrens whispered to the Baron, who frowned, then suddenly grinned boyishly, nodding. Ahrens tapped the man on the shoulder. "The Baron wishes me to tell you, Captain—"

There was a low growl. "Lieutenant Wheelwright, Medford Militia."

"Lieutenant Wheelwright, then. The Baron admires your devotion to duty and will be glad to report to the Cambridge Committee that you carried out its wishes in an able and soldierly way. He would be very glad if you would join him—if your duties permit—in drinking the health of General Washington."

Wheelwright rubbed his unshaven chin. "They could see me through the windows. And there's the men."

Ahrens took him by the arm. "Come with me, then. You see, the Baron may not leave his guests, but—just you and I, eh? And send the men round to the back of the house. They'll get a bit of rum punch. This way, Lieutenant."

Ahrens stood by Wheelwright in the light snow and watched the militiamen shuffle out from the back-door of the Sewall house. Two of them were round-faced boys, several were decrepit old men, one a negro and another an obvious Indian. Ahrens raised his eyebrows.

"An emergency guard, Lieutenant?"

Wheelwright shook his head. "Same's usual. Half ain't militia at all. The reg'lar guards get sick o' turnin' out, so they hire anyone that wants a shilling. That fat boy, now, he's Widder Blake's boy, turned fourteen. The old feller with the beard, he's Bud Hinckley. Bud ain't just right in the head. The nigger used to be a slave on the Royall place, and the Indian come down from Maine on a barque loaded with lumber. That foreign feller in there—he'll write the Committee?"

"I'll write the letter for him," said Ahrens gravely.

"That ought to hold Boston, too, in case them high-nosed Schuyler bitches starts talkin'." He worried at his long chin. "You'll say I done it like a soldier? That'll be fine." He turned to his shivering men. "G'wan home, boys." The detail shambled off across the ruins of the Sewall garden, clumping heavily through a shattered hedge, scuffing their way up an embankment. Wheelwright put out his hand. "You ain't a bad feller for a mercenary. You live at Vassall's? I'll look by and take a drink from you." He waved, tucked his clumsy sword under his arm and trudged on after his men.

Ahrens watched him plod away through the feathery flakes, then turned back to the house. Rockel swung open the door for him and Ahrens heard the Baroness' clear voice crying: "Now we'll have our minuet just as if there were a hundred people here. Kirshener!" Softly, gently, the violins broke into the *Samson* minuet, swelled gracefully into the main theme. From the doorway Ahrens could see Kirschener's long heavy face bent over his instrument. The man's eyes were far away, lost, pleading, as the delicate pathos of the air flowed on. The rough fabric of his cuff scraped gently across the mellow wood, his clumsy boot stirred. Beyond him, the Hesse-Hanau man, tears welling from his eyes, broke into an obbligato, his thoughts on some echoing room along the Main, perhaps the great gilded hall at Phillipsruhe. The notes quavered in inexpressible pathos, the man's face twitched and quivered. The sad gaiety of the theme went on.

"Poor devil!" thought Ahrens. Then his face broke into a grin. Gentleman Johnny was leading the first minuet with Friedericka; Charteris behind him bent far down as Gustava clung to a long finger. Then came the Baron and Mrs. Carter, the Baroness and the Earl of Balcarres, Geismar and the Schuyler girl. The dance went on, coupee, high step, balance. The couples swayed, bowed, curtsied, while Rockel, from the door, watched with grim approval.

Ahrens passed on into the card-room, stood back of General Hamilton as he cautiously staked a hand against Phillips and Spiegel of the Rhetz regiment. Pausch looked up, yawning, from a stiff chair. "What did that dumb-head want?" he growled. "Do you know I haven't had my rum yet? You were going to get it for me." He looked sleepy and fretful. Ahrens called a servant and in a moment the old captain was purring over a glass.

The minuet came to an end. Gentleman Johnny's voice cried: "The girls were charming, Baroness, charming. I vow I was beartbroken when changes in partners took 'em away from me."

The Baroness laughed. "Now curtsy to General Burgoyne, girls, and run away and find Lena. It's twice your bedtime."

Ahrens heard little feet pattering off across the shiny floors. Then Gentleman Johnny's voice boomed again: "My dear Miss Schuyler, you really must commend me to your father when next you write. He was most hospitable to me in Albany at a—ah—a rather trying time. And"—Ahrens could almost hear him bow—"to the Baron and the charming Baroness as well."

Again the violins wailed out. "Haydn this time," thought Ahrens. His foot tapped the floor. "Like to tread a measure myself. Damn it, why didn't the others come?" He settled into his chair, concentrated on Hamilton's play, which was excellent. Outside, the violins sang sadly, piercingly on, the three couples in the big room threaded gravely through the mazes of the minuet.

The games went on. Cards riffled and fluttered, markers clicked dryly. The violins swung from Haydn to Bach. Pausch alternately sipped and yawned, looked covertly at his watch. In a lull in the music Ahrens looked up, saw Rockel standing silently by his shoulder, eyebrows raised.

He got up quietly, followed the green shoulders out into the hall by the violins, where the Baroness stood, calm but white-faced.

"How may I help you, Baroness?" he asked.

"Come away from the musicians. There. Now tell me. Have you seen the girls?"

"Girls? Friedericka and Gustava? I heard you send them to find Lena."

"But didn't you see them? Well, they didn't find Lena. And they're not in their beds and not in their room."

"Caroline?"

"Sound asleep, but no sign of the others."

"You've looked everywhere, of course. Does the Baron know?"

"Not yet." Her face suddenly puckered. "Oh, where *can* they be! You don't suppose—those men, tonight—"

Ahrens shook his head. "They were ill-conditioned, but I don't think vicious. They went away quietly. Let's think, now. Walk along with me. The girls, looking for Lena, would have gone up the stairs? Good. First, they might have looked into this room—just servants and glasses. Then—this way up the stairs." He slowly climbed the broad shallow staircase, the Baroness close at his elbow. "They'd come here to this first landing, then—"

He felt a sudden chill as his eye rested on low, open windows.

He felt a tug at his elbow, heard a whisper. "No—no. I looked there—at once."

He halted on the landing, chin in hand. "To this landing. Then—" He looked at the smooth white panels. "Then—I think—" He pointed. The Baroness stared at him, then at the panels. At the base of the wide boards on the landing, a wisp of sky-blue showed. Ahrens laughed. "There you are—playing hide-and-seek from Lena." He bent down, swung open the hidden door.

In the black gap, golden hair shone, sky-blue glittered in a shaft of light. The two girls were curled up in each other's arms, sound asleep. Ahrens bent down, gently lifted Friedericka. Her bright head rolled on her little shoulders. Her face was flushed and she breathed heavily. He stared at her. "Here, Baroness—you'd better take Gustava. Where is their room?"

He walked lightly down the long hall to the open door where Lena, white-faced and mob-cap awry, hovered. He laid Friedericka on the wide bed. She lay still, flushed face startling against the white pillow. The Baroness gently put Gustava beside her.

Ahrens frowned, watching them. "They were well tonight?"

"Lively as kittens, both of them. You don't—don't think—Why, they're just asleep, that's all."

"Don't like to alarm you, Baroness. That flush, the breathing. The fever took me that way. Have you a doctor among the guests? I didn't notice everyone in the card-room."

She looked at him, wide-eyed. "Doctor? Oh, it *is* just sleep! Gustava!" She shook her gently by the shoulder. The golden head rolled on the pillow. Lena wavered about the bed, her eyes haunted.

The Baroness straightened up. "I think—I should be very glad if you would call the Baron, quietly."

Ahrens nodded, bent once more over the bed. Suddenly he sniffed, frowned, sniffed again, his face close to Friedericka's button of a nose. Then he looked up at Lena. "Have you had any punch, any wine tonight?"

Lena gasped, shook her head.

"Then notice her breath. I'm sure of it."

Lena wiped her eyes, put her head close to the pillow. She stared. "God help me! It's rum!" She backed away, staring.

The Baroness sniffed. "Are you sure? I can't smell a thing!"

Ahrens glanced at Lena. "Sure, isn't it? You see, Baroness, I don't dare drink just yet, after that fever of mine. You had wine at dinner, punch afterward, and then you drank healths while I was with the charming Wheelwright. Look—her eyes are open!"

Friedericka was staring vacantly at the ceiling. Her mother crossed quickly to her. "What is it, dear?"

The girl passed a hot hand across her forehead. She licked her lips a little, then said in a thin voice: "Funny."

"What's funny, dear?"

"Me."

"What did you do? Tell Mama."

"Downstairs. You and Papa said it was good to drink to the Duke." She spoke slowly through stiff lips. "Brown stuff in a glass in the little room where Rockel was. So Gustava and I drank to the Duke. Then we went to find Lena. It's funny. Sleepy." Her eyes closed again.

Ahrens stifled a laugh. The Baroness held up a finger.

"Her father's own daughter!" She pursed her lips. "Well, Lena and I know *just* what to do. Down you go, young man and don't you dare tell the Baron." She looked down at the sky-blue mites. "Staggered up the stairs, opened that little cupboard and just fell in."

"May I take my leave now, Baroness? And thank you for a charming evening?"

"It wasn't dull, was it? No guests, Yankee soldiers and my lost lambs here." She smiled, eyes sparkling. "You

495

know, that's what I like about being in America. *Something is always happening!*"

Ahrens picked his way down the broad walk that led to Brattle Street, where Nero waited in Charteris' chaise. By the broken gate a muffled figure lolled, clinging to a towering musket. Ahrens stopped. "I thought that Lieutenant Wheelwright sent all of you home."

The figure turned its head, showing a long thin face under a battered hat. "Sent me back to watch for more signals. Jed Fisher should've come, but he give me a shilling, so I come." He pulled his heavy greatcoat about him.

"Cambridge man?" asked Ahrens.

"Me or Fisher?"

"You."

"We both are. Why?"

"Did you ever know of a Hunnewell family in Cambridge?"

"Hunnewell? There's a Hunnewell house out Charlestown way. Near Winter Hill."

"That's not the one," said Ahrens. "I asked."

The man scratched his head. "Hunnewell. Don't mean the folk that lived over there?" He pointed diagonally across the street to a dim bulk that loomed through the light snow, a bulk whose hip-roof sloped gracefully to meet far-reaching elm-boughs.

"That house? I thought that was the Carver house."

"Thad Carver, he bought it from Hunnewell, near ten year ago, maybe more."

"Was that Hunnewell a tutor at the college?"

The man spat. "Maybe. I used to bring 'em wood. God-damnedest old wind-bag. Picked up ten year ago and took his family. Never heerd on since. Nice-lookin' gals he had. No, they never come back. Old Carver, he was a Tory, so they ain't a shred o' glass left in the windows. Chucked a good half-ton of rock in there myself."

Ahrens stared at the rambling, solid frame that contrived to throw out an air of mellow comfort even in the desolate snowy night. The man beside him coughed and shuffled his feet. From the chaise Nero fidgeted and fretted with the whip. Ahrens roused himself, climbed into the seat.

In the high-roofed carriage shed of the Vassall house, Rentner knelt by Charteris' chaise, ran skilled fingers along the felloes of the off-wheel, shook the axle gently. Nero crouched beside him, watching with bulging eyes. On the floor by the harness room, a new blue and red jacket lay across a gaudy livery. Ahrens, entering quietly, watched the pair. Nero chattered in oddly-accented English to which Rentner occasionally replied in terse Rhenish monosyllables as he carefully turned a spanner. He dropped the spanner, reached for the wrench that Nero fingered with restless hands. Then he rose abruptly.

"Sorry, sir. Didn't see you."

Nero remained squatting by the wheel, showing white teeth in a broad grin.

"That's all right, Corporal. How's the chaise?"

Rentner scratched his head, tilting his cocked hat over his eyes. "Hard to say, sir. The work is sound. If only the Major wouldn't go 'round corners on one wheel. It strains here and here." He touched the glossy wood.

"It will take an act of God to make the Major change his ways." Ahrens shook his head. "You went to Winter Hill yesterday? Did you get that list?"

Rentner picked up his coat, drew a folded paper out of the pocket. "Signed by Sergeant Behr, sir. It tells where all the men are."

Ahrens opened the sheet. "H'm. A lot of them. Let's see. Here's Schwartz, tinsmith, gone to Methuen. Vogel, butcher, to Acton. Pfister, gilder, to Boston. Leistenschneider, fuller, to Concord. Hofer, silversmith, to Waban. Schecker, Naumann, Niehoff and so on. Doesn't leave many for the drills. How do the men like going about the country?"

497

"They like it, sir. Wages are high."

"It is hard getting about? The language, I mean."

Rentner shook his head. "Places are written on a slip of paper and the names of the folk who want work done. Then the soldiers take the slip to the guard-house on the Common and the guard sets them on the road. Usually they find a cart going that way, like Vogel when he went to Acton."

"The Yankees all right?"

"Just as they were on the march, sir. Some surly ones, of course. But they all like good work and they'll pay for it."

"Have you had a chance to go?"

"You give me one free day in four. I repaired a coach over in Lexington two days ago, and fixed a spinning-wheel down this street yesterday."

"Glad to be off the Hill?"

Rentner gathered up his tools. "It's not so bad there now, sir. Of course, the guards are surly, but in our old barracks they've mended the roof with the wood you sent out. And since you spoke to the Baron, all the regiments are drilling, using poles instead of muskets. The men grumble a lot but they like it better than being idle. The Baron's having a review tomorrow, just like old times."

"And the new breeches came up from Newport this morning. You'd heard that?"

"No, sir. The men will be glad. They're Yankee breeches?"

"No; the British hold Newport, down in Rhode Island. The Yankees let a few wagons come up from there. Shoes, too. Have you finished with the chaise? Well, then, I've some papers to go to the Baron and to Captain Pausch. You know where they live now?"

"Not if they've moved, sir."

"Well, the Baron and his family are in the Sewall house. That's down Brattle Street about half a mile. It's on the other side of the street close by the Vassall Lane.

When you get there, ask Rockel or Lena where the Captain is. He's taken the house the Baron used to have, the Judah Monis place. Sergeant Crummit in the orderly room will give you the papers. He expects you. If anyone asks for me, say that I'm off to see General Burgoyne at the Apthorp house, just across from the college."

Ahrens crunched down the gravel walk of the Vassall house, walked rapidly along Brattle Street, turned toward the Common with its cluster of ragged barracks where militiamen leaned drearily on old muskets, passed the squat tower of Christ Church and picked his way across the muddy expanse of Harvard Square. A light coach whirred past him behind quick-stepping horses, a farmer's cart, piled high with red-gold pumpkins, creaked stolidly down the road to the Cambridge Bridge and Alston. A pair of girls hurried across from the college yard, with its mellow brick buildings, eying the tall Hessian over fox-muffs while a glum-faced civilian in rusty black stared sourly at them.

There was a mass of color by the trees at the rear of the Apthorp house, a moving pool of red and blue. Ahrens saw other uniformed figures hurrying along by the low fence that shut in the yard from the outer world, turning out of side streets by twos and threes. He quickened his pace. "Wonder what's happening at the General's?" he thought. "What's all that shouting? Nothing wrong, I hope. Lord, a mutiny would just about finish things."

The crowd was thick, swelling every moment. Ahrens elbowed his way through a knot of privates of the 9th, wedged past a silent group of Specht's men. A hoarse voice shouted: "Five to three on Jemmy Sproule against the field! Five to three, five to three!" Over a mass of shabby bearskin caps a red fist shot up, waved a clinking bag. "Five to three on Jemmy Sproule against the field, Jemmy Sproule of the 21st!" A grenadier sergeant shouted: "Even money on Tom Kirk of the 9th, Tom Kirk!"

"Why did I worry?" growled Ahrens. "These English!"

A dozen shirt-sleeved men knelt easily by a mark, regimental colors wound through their waistbands as the crowd about them boiled and shifted, screaming odds, yelling for takers, officers and men pushing, shoving at each other. Suddenly the shouting swelled to a voiceless roar. "Eeeeyah! It's Gentleman Johnny!"

From the second-floor balcony Burgoyne smiled, held up a white hand. "Major Charteris has asked me to start this, the first, I hope, of many races." He beamed on the men. "Now, lads, I told the Major that I'd be honored, but—" he looked gravely down—"but I thought it best to refuse. Because—I'm not worthy. Why, lads, when I was at Westminster, there wasn't a boy in the school who couldn't give me ten yards and beat me!" He threw back his head, chuckling. "Now if it were cricket! But I look down there and I see Jem Sproule and Tom Kirk and Evan Evans and Dick Morgan and all the rest. *I* start *them*? Nonsense. So *I've* asked Major the Earl of Balcarres, a *real* runner, to give you the word, and he says he'll be honored. Now, lads, you know the course. Up Harvard Square, Massachusetts Avenue to Linnaean Street, down Garden Street and back. Two miles of Yankee ground and good English legs covering 'em. You're Britons, you're sportsmen. You'll run a fair race and I know I'll be as proud of you—" he threw back his fine head—"as proud of you, by Gad, as I've been of you every minute it's been my honor to command you. And I'm offering five pounds and a keg of beer to the company of the man that wins. May that be the best man. Now, Balcarres!"

Ahrens trotted along the path to the front of the house, with its sweeping view of the Charles, a roaring cheer for Gentleman Johnny echoing in his ears. He shook his head. "He's a wonder! If he gave the word now, those men would beat their way to Canada with their bare fists."

He looked up at the pilastered front of the great house

with its pedimented doorway. "You've sheltered worse men than Gentleman Johnny. Maybe you've never sheltered better, even if the Reverend East Apthorp did build you."

The afternoon sun streamed through the windows of the Apthorp house, picked out the gold embroidery on Gentleman Johnny's coat and paled the fire that snapped on the broad hearth. Ahrens sat back in a low wing-chair and sipped appreciatively at a glass of Madeira. What *is* our status, then?" he asked.

Burgoyne leaned over his table wearily. "I'm damned if *I* know. I know what it ought to be. But that bloody Congress says something different every time the clock ticks. The Convention said expressly that we were to be assured safe passage across to Boston, there to await the transports to take us back to Europe. Well, here we are, but Congress is making difficulties about the transports. Afraid we'll put in at New York or something. In the meantime, are we prisoners? Obviously not, because our officers command our troops. Our officers wear side-arms. Again, if we were prisoners the Yankees would be forced to subsist us, pay the officers and men. As it is, we pay for every crumb of bread, every stick of fire-wood, when we can get it. We disburse from the army chest every penny of pay." He shook his head. "I tell you, we've got to be very careful or else we'll be interned until Howe finally beats Washington to his knees. Good God, we ought to be on the high seas this very moment." He looked gravely at Ahrens.

Ahrens nodded. "The men are betting from week to week. It's hard to know what to tell them."

Gentleman Johnny sighed. "Dashed hard. Tell 'em it's the Yankees' fault and there'll be brawls all over Cambridge. Tell 'em Heath is the villain and they'll mob the guards. Now, that is one thing that *mustn't* happen. Sporadic rows we can't help. But any mass demonstration!" He shook his head. "I shudder to think of what the rebel

501

Congress might do; truly, I shudder." He turned his fine eyes on Ahrens. "Now, I may talk all I please. But I'm merely the Commanding Officer, I speak only officially. But, if we're to live here, live without heads being broken, yes, and throats cut—I mean that—throats cut— something *must* slake down the embers on our side, *something* must temper the Cambridge bitterness toward us. I can issue proclamations telling the Cantabrigians that we love 'em, yearn over 'em. What is that? An official statement that the first glower or curt word on the part of one of our officers or men will cancel. Heath can say in orders that every article of the Convention will be strictly adhered to, that we shall be dealt with fairly. And that? *He* means it, but an exhibition like that at the Baron's the other night—by the way, wasn't she magnificent?—will have us all cursing and storming." He rose, walked slowly to the windows that looked down to the Charles. Softly he hummed *Over the Hills and Far Away*. Then he turned suddenly. "Know General Heath?"

"I saw him that day you came to the Winter Hill Barracks with that genial man Crane."

"General Heath, sir, is a gentleman. That Roxbury farmer has more natural breeding in his fingertips than half that park at White's or Almack's with whom I used to drink and gamble. I have a real affection for him. When this rebellion is over, there will be, I fear, many hangings, many." He strode back to his chair, thumped his hand on the table, "I shall exert, sir, every ounce of influence, every shred of eloquence that is at my disposal, to save the neck of that man from Roxbury. Now, I have watched you for a long time. You have my confidence. I want you to go to General Heath."

Ahrens' eyes widened. "You want *me* to go to him?"

Burgoyne nodded. "He expects someone from me. These papers will be a pretext. Talk to him. Tell him what the men say. Listen, listen well to what *he* says. No—I don't know what that will be, but I *do* know

502

Heath. Then let it be known among the officers, British and your lot too, that you've talked to him, that I have and that the Baron has. Let 'em know we're doing all we can and that Heath is. You see? You're such a good link, speaking both languages and with good friends in both armies. It may help tide us over a rough time. Then, too, Heath may find that you can help him."

Ahrens looked surprised. "Help? The opinion of a junior officer, just gossiping about?"

Burgoyne pursed his lips. My dear fellow, in Parliament we know very well that the right whisper in the galleries is worth ten speeches on the floor. What Heath may think of for you, I don't know. For us, it is enormously important that our people feel that at heart the Yankees are honest, even if they are—"

Ahrens smiled at his Madeira. "New Englanders is cantankerous," he murmured.

Burgoyne threw back his head. "Now, who the devil told you that?"

"A New Englander."

General Heath spread out thick, work-roughened hands. "You see the situation? *I* don't like to think of all those big houses in Cambridge, the college buildings vacant while your men freeze on Winter Hill. *I* don't like to think of the rents—well, between you and me they're terrible—that your officers have to pay here while over in Medford and in Watertown there'd be plenty of space if only the Committees there would open the towns. But the military, sir, are not supreme in Massachusetts nor in any of the States. I, as a General of the Continental Armies, can't send a sergeant to Mr. Wigglesworth's house, or to Mr. Hastings' or to Dr. Moore's, with a message to clear out. I can't fix the rent they charge if they *do* turn out. I can't order the Corporation of Harvard to open Massachusetts Hall or even Holden Chapel to your people."

Ahrens nodded. "That, of course, is what many of us

find it hard to understand. Many of us see treasures beyond our reach and look to you, as commanding officer, to push them toward us. Now in Europe, the Baron could clear out a dozen convents, requisition space, supplies and so on. You see, a lot of us think in those terms."

Heath rubbed the dome of his large bald head. "Your Baron couldn't clear out convents here. There ain't any. And *some* kinds of supplies—well, he could requisition till he was blue in the face. Take firewood. See any large forests about Cambridge? 'Course not. They were all hacked away a century ago."

"And not replanted? That's amazing."

"Replant? Why? The country's big and it's full of trees. Still, I admit it might have been wise. Here in Cambridge they've always been hard put to it for firewood, always. Even with the small population. Most of what they burn—and in Boston, too—has to be brought down from Maine by water. Some winters are hard. That's one reason, perhaps, why the folk about here don't open their arms to five thousand additional bodies to be kept warm and bellies to be cooked for. Why, sir, I doubt if a Continental Army would fare much better here than you do. Then those lawyers down there in Congress!" He puffed out his ruddy cheeks, rubbed his head again. "The orders they send me! Make 'em do this.' 'Don't let 'em do that.'" He grinned suddenly. "Hell, ain't it?"

Ahrens began to feel a glow of liking for this heavy man in blue and buff, for the boyish smile that sprang so startlingly from the hundreds of tiny lines of his weather-beaten face.

"It seems to me, General, that as time goes on, you, as commanding officer, will inevitably take over all power. You'll be able—you'll have to be able—to make the civilians toe the mark."

Heath folded thick hands on the table. "Now, young man, you meant that kindly. But it's something that

504

I'd never wish for, not even when I'm damning and blazing at the Committees and town meetings. Turn the country over to a military government? Why, why what'd happen to the Massachusetts Assembly? To the town meetings? Would some damn colonel or adjutant from Jersey or Pennsylvania come up here and take *my* farm for the army? Or Joey Gifford's? Come and tell *me* to quit planting corn and put the land under beans?" His pale eyebrows went up, his eyes widened. "Why, young man, what d'you think we've been fighting for? No, sir! I'll look to the rights of the Convention Troops to the best of my ability, but I'll tell you right now I'd feed 'em all to the fish in Boston Harbor rather than see a loblolly of a colonel or a general taking away the powers from the rightful authorities. And the rightful authorities *are* the people, even when they're pig-headed and mean and cantankerous. General Heath, sir, is only their servant."

Ahrens looked gravely at the broad, earnest, puzzled face. "You've a difficult job here, General. You'll find yourself unpopular with many people, but you'll never lose respect."

Heath inclined his heavy head. "That's kind of you, sir. It *is* difficult. It's important. In time, honest men may suffer for what's done here. Misunderstanding's as thick as a fog off Monomoy. The Convention soldier looks on the Boston and Cambridge folk as a pack of cold-blooded, rowdy cheats. But how does the Bostonian, the Cambridge man look on that soldier? Why, to him the Britisher is only the cruel tool of a set of tyrants. The Brunswickers, the Hessians, are nothing but hired bullies. You see? Of course, it's all wrong, all wrong," he went on hastily. "But that won't keep honest men from suffering, as I said. Your general, for whom I have the greatest respect, is one who may suffer. Gates is another. Then there are folk about Cambridge whose actions may be misunderstood." He looked almost sheepishly at Ahrens. "I'm—I'm writing my memoirs." He clasped and unclasped his big hands. "Not that the memoirs of William Heath, the Roxbury farmer, are important. No, no, I don't think that. But—" he thumped his fist on the table— "but in 'em will be the truth as I know it, the truth of what happened to the Convention Troops after their march across our State." He pushed back his chair, burrowed in a shallow drawer. "Here's a few sheets. Like to see 'em?"

"Your memoirs? You're showing *me*, one of the Conventioners, what you're writing?"

Heath's eyebrows went up. "Why not? It's about you, and what happened to you." He examined his thick fingers as though he had never seen them before, shaking his head sadly. "My hands are better suited to the plow than to the pen or sword."

Ahrens stared at the crabbed, strong script. " 'Our General,' " he read, " 'was awoke, called from his bed and informed that a detachment of the British Army were out.' This is about General Washington—this bit, I mean?"

Heath pulled a pair of iron-rimmed spectacles from his pocket, slid them down toward the tip of his nose and walked around the table to Ahrens' chair. "General Washington? Where? Don't recall that I said much about George. Where d'you see it?"

"Here," said Ahrens. "Under the date of April 19, 1775. It says, 'Our General was awoke' and so on."

Heath put away his glasses, walked heavily back to his seat. " 'Our General,' Why, that means *me*. I use it everywhere instead of 'I.' 'I' don't look—well, it don't look modest. It ain't—"

Ahrens looked at the stout general with something like affection. "You mean it doesn't look moderate, sir?"

Heath's broad face broke into a grin. "Let's have some rum, young man!" He rose, wheezing slightly, produced a squat bottle and two glasses from a cupboard built into the wall by the fireplace. "Good Medford. We'll not spoil it with water. Your health!" He pursed his lips, looking quizzically at Ahrens. "Now, why did your General send *you* to me? A sergeant could have brought those papers. By God, he knew you'd get 'round me with your meaching ways. Well, you have. Here I've gabbled all afternoon when I should have been—oh, Lord! Repairs at Fort Number Three, a courtmartial, a complaint that you are corrupting the students, another that the students are corrupting you. Then a Boston parson bellows because you've set up a billiard-table at the Blue Anchor just off Harvard Square. He can hear the rustle of the devil's scaly wings. Oh, Jehosophat!" He rumpled up the tufts of hair that sprouted over his ears and stared mournfully at Ahrens.

"I ought to have taken my leave, sir. As a matter of fact—well, I must admit that I lost sight of the time. I've learned a lot, General. I've felt very bitter about our men up there—about the way we've been fleeced for the privilege of occupying hencoops. At least, I know now that a lot of what we curse about is unmeant. It—it just happens and—"

Heath leaned forward earnestly. "It would help so much, sir, if others of you knew that. If they knew that *all* Yankees aren't devils, that we're a mixture of lazy men and stupid men and indifferent men and honest men and downright mean men. Guess we're like any other lot of folk. We're new and we're trying to do new things. Perhaps we're not very clever and we blunder and stumble and sometimes people suffer. We're living in a new house and we don't know our way around in the dark very well yet. Now, into the Cambridge room of the new house, you are suddenly pitchforked, pitchforked in among folk who are still groping in the dark. Perhaps the house is badly built. But it's the best we know and in time we'll level the sills and open a window or two and deepen the fireplaces and make the doors wider. But all that must be hard for a European to know."

Ahrens sipped his rum, coughed a little. "It wouldn't

507

surprise me, General, if a good many of the Conventioners *did* know that before long."

Heath leaned back in his chair, stared at the beamed
ceiling. "Well, it wouldn't startle me one mite if they
did. Not a mite." He smiled benignly. "Don't you think
that all the gain's on your side either. You've told me a
lot. I've talked with your General and your Baron. But
we've got to be official before we can be friendly. It
hampers. Now—here's me, Billy Heath from Roxbury,
just sitting over a drink with—with Kurt Ahrens from
Dresden. Yes, you've told me things, things you can't
write down 'cause they won't stay writ, but I can say a
word here and there in Cambridge and Boston, a word I
couldn't have said before 'cause I didn't know." He
plucked at his full, double chin. "Now, will you do something for me? For me and the Conventioners? Good. I
happen to know that Dr. John Winthrop will be at home
tonight. He's a member of the Corporation of Harvard.
He lives on Love Lane—no, they call it Linnaean Street
now. Go call on him. Tell him you came from me and
ask him—oh, anything about the colleges. Winthrop's a
hard man, a cold man. He's like one of those icebergs that
drift down the Maine coast. But you're not afraid of
new ideas and you're not afraid of telling your own.
Listen to him. Think over what he says. And make no
mistake—he'll think over what *you* say. Then we may be
able to sow a few more seeds of peace where they'll
sprout best."

Ahrens set down his glass. "You think he'll talk with
me—a gunner lieutenant?"

Heath nodded. "Yes—yes." He spoke slowly. "You see,
you're a moderate man."

Ahrens walked out of the Wadsworth house feeling a
little dizzy.

Under the high roof of the Vassall house Ahrens ran a
critical eye over the boots that his English orderly had
polished, picked his white waistcoat from a chair and

breathed on its gilt buttons. Somewhere in the depths of the great house a young English voice shouted: "Ahrens! Kurt Ahrens!"

He kicked the door of his little room open, shouted down the stairs: "Who is it? Stillman?"

"Who'd you think? Washington? Yes, it's Stillman. Look here, Ahrens. Having a paper-chase tonight. There'll be a moon. Stevens is the fox and we've got a rare pack. Penhallow of the 9th is seeing to the scent. We're counting on you. Right? Start an hour after dinner. Hounds that get tired can lie up at Richardson's Tavern. And we'll steal a few Yankee door-knockers on the way back."

Ahrens grinned, then deepened his voice. "See here, Ensign Stillman, are you giving *orders* to a full lieutenant?"

The fresh voice whooped: "Oh, blast you for a bloody Dutchman! Say you'll come."

"Love to, but I'm on duty. The General's given me a special job. He wants me to show Cambridge my new uniform. The town hasn't seen it by moonlight yet." He picked a loose thread from the gold braid on his cuff. "Tell the pack I'll give a pound of salt-pork to the hound that finishes first."

He closed the door on a burst of profanity from below and slipped on his jacket, working his wide shoulders back and forth. "Oh, Lord—more ruffians!"

Running feet thudded on the narrow staircase outside, the door shivered on its hinges. Ahrens stared. "Good God, Charteris! What the devil's the matter?"

Charteris, his usually languid eyes bright with excitement, laid a finger on his lips and closed the door. Then he seized Ahrens by the shoulders and whirled him about, kicking up his heels in a wild jig.

Ahrens freed himself, laughing, as Charteris collapsed on a chair, panting. "What the *devil* has got into you?"

The tall major sprang to his feet, opened the door quickly, then closed it again. "Don't tell a soul, not a soul!" His voice was a hoarse whisper. He bent double, slapped his white breeches.

"Tell what, for God's sake?"

Charteris' jaw worked, then he said in a strangled voice: "The transports!"

Ahrens shook him by his heavy epaulette. "What? What? Transports? Where?" His eyes were suddenly bright.

Charteris nodded. "On my honor! Sighted off Boston this afternoon! His Majesty's ships! His Majesty's transports!"

Ahrens sat down suddenly on his narrow bed. "Transports!" he repeated. "Major! You're sure? Transports! Then we'll be—"

Charteris sprang to his feet. "Be going *home*! Home! Understand, you thick-headed Dutchman? Home, home, home! Deckspace for every bloody man!"

Ahrens jumped up, beat Charteris between his broad shoulders. "Home! We'll be going home! We! And the men! And—"

"And Gentleman Johnny and every God-damn bear and raccoon and squirrel." Charteris flicked out a fine lawn handkerchief and wiped his streaming face. "Lord! Can't really believe it yet. Swear I haven't been so excited since I made a century, not out!" He collapsed onto the chair again.

"Gentleman Johnny knows? And the Baron?" asked Ahrens, panting.

Charteris waved a blue arm at him. "No! No! Not a soul. Probably Heath doesn't know. I—I slipped over to Charlestown—just a little way out of bounds. The ferryman who took me into Boston the last time saw the sails from Beacon Hill. There's no mistake. Supposed to be a dead secret; no one in Boston is talking about it, he says."

Ahrens started for the door. "I'm going to tell—"

Charteris' hand fell on his shoulder. "No, no, no. Not a soul. Look—there's a paper-chase tonight. Every man Jack in the house'll be out. I've brought in a keg of rum, bottles and bottles of wine. Surprise the lads when they get back. They'll come stragglin' in and find the table all set and liquor enough to float the transports. Announce it to 'em then! Let 'em whoop, let 'em sing, let 'em drink! Not a word in the meantime. Count on you." He slapped Ahrens on the shoulder, ran down the stairs.

Ahrens sat down on his bed. "Home! Back to—" He stared at the bare wall. "But this is damned silly!" The wild, contagious elation of Charteris began to ebb away. "It's damned foolishness! Going home! Of *course* I want to. Did that bloody fever sour my brains? Transports off Boston. He said there was no mistake." Mechanically he picked up one of his new boots, freshly polished for the evening. "No use seeing Dr. Winthrop now, I suppose. Might as well join the pack. Or see what Charteris is up to. Help him get ready for the celebration. Hell! I've put the damn boot on." Suddenly he found himself wrestling with the other. He flung open the door. "Oh, Charteris!" he shouted. "May Nero drive me out tonight? Got to see a Yankee over on Linnaean Street. Business for Gentleman Johnny!"

Tall and spare, Dr. Winthrop hopped suddenly from his high-backed chair, trotted to the hearth with quick, bent-kneed steps, prodded the fire viciously with a brass-handled poker. He glared at the trail of bright sparks that whisked up the chimney, then turned to Ahrens. "I may assure you, sir, that anyone who attempts to reopen the subject will find himself most—most unpopular." He dropped the poker into its brass holder with a dry rattle, thrust his hands under his long coat-tails and trotted up and down before the hearth. "Most unpopular." His faded eyes under bushy brows fastened themselves on Ahrens. "The Overseers of the college, the Corporation, the Faculty—" he gave his coat-tails a flip as he mentioned each body—"are unanimous. I can't see—I can't see how Mr. Heath took it upon himself to

511

hold out any hope, any hope to you that the buildings would be thrown open."

Ahrens sat forward in his chair. "But, Dr. Winthrop, General Heath gave me no encouragement. The idea—I hope I've not been importunate—was my own. You see, the Baron speaks very little English, so I made a reconnaissance party of one. It is hard on the men, of course, but we can only sympathize with your wish not to break up the student-body. However, learning an indefinite vacation had suddenly been ordered for it—you see how it struck me—how it will strike everyone—those buildings idle and our men so wretchedly housed. Many of the officers, too. Captain Cleve, for example, can see the street outside through the walls of his room."

Dr. Winthrop trotted and shuffled back and forth on his little beat. "I must confess that I am unmoved. Come, now, come! What, pray, have the Overseers, the Corporation and the Faculty to do with the housing of Mr. Cleve?" He wheeled about, faced Ahrens, his coat-tails jerking and tossing.

Ahrens threw out his hands. "In the name of common humanity, sir. How can your college, which teaches the humanities, neglect to practice them? What will the world's judgment be?"

Dr. Winthrop set off again, shuffling up and down in the clear lamp-light which mellowed the walls of the book-lined study, blended the soft hues of the Oriental rug on the polished floor. "Judgment? Judgment?" he said. "I may inform you that this is not our first experience with the military. We've had Mr. Ward and Mr. Putnam here. The military have stamped upon us and spat upon us and tried to spend our last dollar. In '75, Cambridge pullulated with troops. Our hands were forced. In Massachusetts Hall, six hundred and forty soldiers were crammed like cranberries; the same number in Hollis. Each building accommodates sixty-four students. The Yard was covered with tents. Over one hundred men festered in Holden Chapel."

"There would be no need—" Ahrens began.

"And Harvard Hall," Winthrop went on. "It was burned in 1762. We were at some pains to rebuild it, some pains. We purchased lead, to make a suitable roof. The military filled the hall with stores, stripped the lead from the roof for bullets. Now, come come! What is the Corporation, pray? Among other things, it is the body in which the property of the college is vested, vested. We are answerable for such property. And the purpose of such property? To educate young minds. You spoke of the world's judgment. Now—now such judgment may be harsh. But—" he swung about, pointed a dry old finger at Ahrens—"what would that judgment be if we, as a Corporation, were forced to say a year, two years hence: 'We closed the college to shelter foreign troops. Now our buildings are wrecked, the students, the faculty scattered in a dozen States. The Continental Armies will not relinquish Hollis Hall. Mr. Washington wants Massachusetts Hall for five years more.' Tell me—tell me, what would the judgment of the world be on such trustees?"

"But the men, sir. The buildings are idle *now*, while the men—and the officers, too—suffer because the Convention has not been fulfilled."

Winthrop waved a lean hand. "Your men. Yes. You must think of them. But you look to one generation only. We as Trustees must look to ten, to a hundred. We must keep the college unencumbered." He flipped his coattails, trotted off on his endless sentry-go. "The country needs the college, will need it more than ever in the next half-century. If we snap the thread now, snap the thread now, who, pray, may say when we may mend it? I cannot expect that you, as a European, will comprehend how great will be our peculiar need of such a source of potential leaders."

"Have I your permission, sir, to repeat what you have told me to the Baron?"

"Why—why should a European be interested in the convictions of a member of the Corporation of Harvard

513

College? But tell him, tell him. And Mr. Burgoyne, too, if it pleases you. Their men shout at me in my own Cambridge streets, chalk offensive inscriptions on the college buildings, on the particular doorsteps of the Corporation. But Mr. Burgoyne knows that such evidences of disfavor will not swerve us, not warp our consciences, our consciences. I have the honor, sir, to wish you a very good evening."

Ahrens rose, bowed stiffly. "It was good of you, Dr. Winthrop, to receive me." He bowed again, walked to the door.

Footsteps shuffled on the thick rug behind him. Dr. Winthrop trotted past his elbow, opened the door with a creaky bow, made a quick little stab and shook Ahrens' hand. "Come and dine with me, dine with me. I'll send a note, very shortly."

Ahrens looked into the faded old eyes, startled. "I'll be honored, sir."

There was another bobbing bow. "A note. Very shortly. Ah—ah—" He hesitated, laid a wrinkled hand on Ahrens' red cuff. "Pray step back into the room for a moment. There is something I feel it would be well to impart to you."

Ahrens pushed past the orderly by the heavy door of the Vasall house. "Where's Major Charteris?" he snapped.

"In the dinin'-room sir. Beggin' yer pardon, sir, the Major—'e's a bit above 'imself, if yer tykes my meanin', sir."

"Above himself?" Ahrens paused on the threshold. From the high-ceiled room at the back of the house a gay, strong voice sang:

"As I was going to Derby—'twas on a market day—
I met the fattest ram, sir, that ever was fed on hay.
This ram was fat behind, sir, this ram was fat before
This ram was ten yards—

514

"Stole away, sir! It's Ahrens! 'Pon my soul, it's Kurt Ahrens!"

The Major stood by the low mantel, swaying slightly, a tumbler of rum in his hand. "Look upon my work. Look an'—an' marvel!"

Ahrens crossed the floor, took Charteris' glass from him. "For God's sake, Major, hold hard!"

Charteris laughed. "Greedy—tha's what you are. Listen. Make an epigram. Hear me say it? Epigram. 'Cambridge, a city in America, noteworthy for its polished floors and its unpolished inhabitants.' Gi' me that glass."

Ahrens set the glass on the mantel. "Major, I'm serious. Pull up. Tell me—have the hounds come back yet?" He shook him by the arm. "*Have* they come back?"

Charteris shook his head solemnly. "Not a bloody hound. Serious. Look at that!" He waved a hand at the long, rough table that stood incongruously on the shining floor. "Waitin' for 'em!" Twenty glasses and twenty bottles, neatly ranged on the board, shone in the flickering candle-light. By each was a sheet of thick paper. "M'own idea. Look. No, no, don't be pawin' at me. Know it's serious." He walked unsteadily to the table, snatched up a paper. "Look—passage to England. One for each man in the mess. Name 'n' rank. In due form. See. B' God, I swear Lloyds' would underwrite these passages. Made 'em just like real ones. See—this yours. Entitles Kurt Ahrens to one passage to Hanau on His Majesty's God-damn ship *Turkey*. That's for Morgan's turkey-call. Remembered you liked it. Y' see, I couldn't find out real names, so I made 'em up, see? Own idea. Now you're pullin' at me again. All right, I'll sit down."

Ahrens shook him again. "God above, Major, listen to me! Those transports. They—"

Charteris waved an uncertain arm. "*I* know. Off Boston. They'll wait—"

"Listen, will you! The transports! Who knows about 'em? You've told no one?"

515

"Not even m' better self. Jus' you. Waitin' for hounds. Tell 'em then. Celebrate! Drinks!"

"Thank God for that! Major, this is bad news. The transports *aren't* for us! They've put out to sea again."

"Rubbish, m'lad. Past Deer Island this mornin'."

"Get this through your head! They've put to sea again. The Yankees wouldn't let 'em land."

Charteris picked up his glass, began to drink. Then he blinked, fell back in his chair, staring at Ahrens. "What? What? Not for us? Gone away? Away? Oh, my bleedin' Jesus!" He pried himself to his feet, staring blearily at Ahrens. "You're jokin'. Yankee saw 'em. In the harbor. You're jokin'." He caught Ahrens by the sleeve. "Look at me. You're—you're—" He staggered, caught himself on the mantel. His voice dropped. "No. No, by God, you're not! You're not!" His voice soared to a shriek. "The swine! The filthy bastards! They did turn 'em back. Wanted us here till last penny's spent!" He started for the door. "Nero! Nero! I want Blitzen. 'N a hurry. Oh, by God, the blue-nosed bastards! Nero!"

Ahrens darted across the floor, caught Charteris by the collar. "Major, Major! Where are you going?"

"Let go, damn you! I'm goin' t' take Blitzen. Goin' to Prospect Hill n' tell those freezin' men there that the transports were here and the Yankees turned 'em back. 'N if a guard gets in my way, s' help me, I'll break his God-damn Yankee neck. Yell it to 'em, howl it to 'em. By God, there won't be a stick left standin' in Cambridge tomorrow, or a live Yankee. By God, I'll turn 'em loose. They'll follow me, they'll follow me. The God-damn college, the stinkin' little church, the smug houses! 'N I'll tell all the poor German bastards on Winter Hill and they'll come. Seize the arms! Muskets, bayonets! Oh, by God, when I get through with this Christ-crazy town, by God, they'll crawl to us on their hands and knees beggin' us to go an leave 'em in peace. Nero, Nero! God damn it, get Blitzen! Ahrens, you stay here and tell the others. Join me by Piper's Tavern." Ahrens caught at his arm again. Charteris flailed out, swept him against the wall. "Out of my way!"

Like a flash Ahrens side-stepped, pinned Charteris' arm in a paralyzing lock. "For God's sake, Major, *listen* to me!"

Charteris swayed and struggled, his breath hissing through clenched teeth. "God damn you, let go. Let go! By God, you'll fight me for this! Let me go. Goin' to Prospect Hill!"

Ahrens suddenly loosed his hold. "All right, Major. Go ahead. Go to the Hill. Then see Gentleman Johnny trying to explain to Germaine *why* his troops mutinied. Won't Germaine be merciful? *You* know him. Gentleman Johnny's troops mutinied. He couldn't control 'em. And *who* led 'em on?"

Charteris reeled against the wall, drawing a shaking hand across his wet forehead. "What's that? Gentleman Johnny? Mutiny?" He blinked. "God! What was I goin' to do!" He steadied himself, crossed to the mantel. "I want that rum." He snatched up the glass, gulped down the drink. "Feel better, now." White of face he stared at Ahrens. "That's true, then?"

Ahrens nodded. "I learned it just a few moments ago from a member of the college Corporation who also sits on the Committee of Safety. Gentleman Johnny made a horrible mistake. I heard him use a phrase, days ago on Winter Hill, to a Mr. Crane. Now he has put it into a letter to Gates and Gates has sent it on to Congress. The words are, 'The public faith is broke.' So Congress reasons that we'll consider ourselves free of the Convention, free to join Howe if we can. They also claim we've violated it in one or two points, so they've declared the whole document suspended till further notice. Hence the transports were turned back."

Charteris sat dully on a chair. "Congress turned 'em back. Not Cambridge's fault at all. See that right enough." He passed his hand over his eyes. "God, the men mustn't know, though. Wouldn't understand."

"That's up to you." Ahrens spoke crisply. "They'll hear of it in time perhaps, but will they believe it? Only you and I *know*. Now let's get rid of your passage papers. Here. I'll burn 'em. No, no. Let me. You go get cold water on your face. Hurry now. I'll meet the hounds when they come in. I'll have a story for 'em."

Charteris looked fixedly at him. "You're a good chap, Ahrens. Won't forget this." His step was steady as he went through the door.

Ahrens swept up an armful of Charteris' pitiful scraps of paper, pitched them into the fire, jammed the last white shred into the heart of the coals. In the night outside a voice whooped: "What a run! See Stensrood take that scunner on the sharp turn by the Burying Ground?" Feet tramped in the broad hall. Stillman's flushed face appeared at the door. "Hello, Ahrens! Missed a damn good run. Hi! Why the candles? Why the bottles? Bad habit, drinkin' by yourself, bad habit!" He shouted into the hall. "Come on, you chaps! Kurt Ahrens is playing boniface!"

An untidy horde of flushed, laughing men poured into the room, pushing, shouting. Ahrens jumped on a chair. "The Major and I had to miss the run, but we decided not to let you have all the fun. So we set out a little liquor for ourselves and we're going to let you watch us—for the first drink. After that it's every man for himself."

The room exploded in a great shout, the officers rushed to the tables. A lazy voice cried, "No you don't, Digby. Ahrens and I first." Charteris, languid of eye, neat of hair and stock, stood in the doorway. "Give me that glass. Got yours, Ahrens? There. Now the rest of you—on your marks! Get set! Go!"

Corks popped and glasses clinked in a babel of good-natured brawling. Charteris shouted again: "Quiet, you young whelps! We've put a prize up. A prize of a magnum of champagne for the man who tells the best shave!"

A roar of laughter went up. A fresh-faced boy elbowed his way to the front. "I've got it! Heard it at the Apthorp house today. We assemble secretly at night, march to Newport. Then we take ship, land at Philadelphia and take Washington prisoner!" There was a howl, a dozen voices shouted at once. "But this is true! Overland to Canada and then—".... "Each officer gets a lump sum of twenty pounds for every week he's in America after the—".... "Boston has broken away from Washington. We're going to fight for the Bostonians against him and—"

Charteris listened with lazy eyes. He shook his head. "Amateurs, the lot of you. Got the best myself. Listen. Transports came into Boston today. Yankees sent 'em home and now—"

A whoop drowned him out. Feet stamped on the floor. A shrill voice yelled: "But a man can't win his own prize, damn it!"

Over the swaying heads, Ahrens' eyes met Charteris'.

Deftly balancing four cups of negus on an inadequate tray, Ahrens edged and threaded his way through the crowded, smoky card-room of the Sewall house. From a dim corner Pausch loomed suddenly, held out a gnarled hand. "Give me two of those, two of those at once. I nearly froze coming here. Dear God! January is on us with a vengeance. Come on—have you no pity on me?"

Aherns held up a restraining hand. "Sorry, Captain. These are for Miss Schuyler and the Ticknor girls. Too mild for you, anyway. And I heard Rockel bawling to Kleinschmidt to bring up hot rum. It could only have been for you."

"Hot rum?" Pausch looked appeased. "Yes, it must be for me. Don't know what soldiers are coming to. Look at that little Englishman in the corner. Do you know what he's drinking? Tea! I saw it, tea!" He rumbled in his throat. "And the rest of you—wine or that hot muck

519

you've got in the cup. Look—here's Balcarres stalking you."

Ahrens saw the Earl's handsome face peering from the doorway. "Oh—there you are! Whose are these? I'll take 'em."

Ahrens shook his head. "No, you won't. Many thanks, all the same."

"Oh, yes, I will. Got to. Gentleman Johnny's looking for you. He's ornamenting the fireplace in the west room, talking to our hostess. Now the cups. Miss Schuyler and—oh, yes, those pretty blond sisters. Now you hurry along and find the General. The next minuet 'll start in a few minutes."

Ahrens wound his way through a press of bright uniforms, soft-hued evening gowns, civilians' coats of plum, cherry, snuff and sleek black. In the west room the Baroness stood on tiptoe, waved a hand to him.

"Isn't this worse than the woods by Fort Anne? Do you know how many couples are here tonight? Sixty-two and I haven't dared count the card-players." Her blue eyes swept over the packed rooms. "I've not seen the Baron in an hour—not since I put the girls to bed. I did it myself, this time." She turned to Burgoyne. "Do you know that all but ten of the townsfolk I sent cards to are here? And those ten sent most prompt and polite regrets. I believed nearly all of them."

Gentleman Johnny smiled on Ahrens. "What did I tell you about a whisper in the galleries, young man? I particularly wanted you to know that a friend of yours, a Dr. Winthrop, shuffled up to me not ten minutes ago, presented himself and informed me that quite by accident he had spoken to the Committee at Watertown. We're to have twelve houses there. Then he did the same thing—oh, quite by accident—at Medford. Eight houses there, young man, eight. Ended by saying that you were most agreeable, that under no circumstances would he vote to throw open the college to us and shuffled off. Seen my friend General Heath?"

"He's in the card-room, sir, playing with General Hamilton and a Judge Minot of Boston. Hamilton has met his match, to judge from his expression. No news from Congress, sir?"

Burgoyne shook his powdered head. "Not a hint. I hear they're trying to deal directly with London. Say that Gates had no power to sign such a pact and doubt if I did. No, no. Things are exasperating as ever. Our army, sir, is a giant, being stung to death by a swarm of gnats. Gulliver and the Lilliputians! Can't see what they're up to."

Ahrens adjusted his sword-knot. "It occurred to me, sir, that we'd be a pretty valuable pawn in case anything disastrous happened to Washington and his lot. I've heard whispers that he's none too comfortable in his winter quarters down in Pennsylvania. What's the name of the place? Oh, yes. Valley Forge."

Gentleman Johnny pinched his lips. "H'm. A pawn. By Gad, I'd not thought of that! Swear Heath hasn't either. The damned sharpies! Oh, well, something'll happen to Washington very soon. Just as soon as Billy Howe moves out of Philadelphia. A pity. I hear Washington's an agreeable chap, real gentleman. Poor old Billy. He thought the war would end when he took the capital. Now he'll have to go trailing out in the snow for the coup de grâce."

Hidden violins wailed out in a Bach minuet. Gentleman Johnny bowed to the Baroness. "We begin this number, I believe?" She smiled, slipped her arm through his and trailed off through the crowd, her powdered head bobbing by Burgoyne's scarlet elbow.

Ahrens held his hands to the blaze, watched the dancers over his shoulder. Charteris was stepping elegantly with a plump laughing girl from Medford whom Ahrens had had as partner for a few turns earlier in the evening. The Baron, for all his stoutness, bowed gracefully to a gray-haired woman, wife of a Boston merchant. In a corner by a punch-bowl, the Ticknor girls were making Geismar pronounce "Massachusetts" over and over, while Cleve shouted with laughter at his accent.

Shuffling footsteps drew near the fire. Ahrens turned to find Dr. Winthrop stabbing a jerky hand at him. "It occurred to me, young man, when I called on our kind hostess the other day, that she might find these quarters a little cramped, a little cramped." He sidled up to the fire, slipped his hands under his sleek black coat-tails. "Look at this. Disgraceful. She wants bigger rooms."

Ahrens smiled dryly. "This is a palace. When the Baroness first came here, she was mewed up in a foul den off the square. You know—Bradish's Inn. Then she moved to the old Monis house. I'm sure you don't know the people who held the house—they were boors. The man was all right, but the woman—she was straight out of a Fielding novel and behaved like a fishwife to the Baroness."

Winthrop coughed explosively. "Did she! Did she!" He shifted before the fire. "H'm, h'm. But of course, that was in the earlier days, earlier days." He turned to Ahrens, coat-tails flipping. "No, sir, it won't do. She wants a bigger house."

Ahrens laughed. "I've hunted the limits allowed us. This is the best there is."

Winthrop shook his head. "Not at all. Not at all. Now, I took the opportunity of writing a note before I came here tonight." He dove into his tail-pockets, drew out a paper. "Do you know Judge Hemingway's house? On Brattle Street?"

"The Hemingway house?" Ahrens frowned. "Yes—on the other side of the street and out toward Watertown. It's a beautiful place."

"That is the opinion of many. Now, Judge Hemingway is an acquaintance of mine. I happen to know that he contemplates moving his residence to Marblehead, to Marblehead, where he has another house, larger than this. I have ventured to write the Judge, suggesting that his house be made available to the Baroness and her family." He dabbed at Ahrens with the paper. "Now, you may present this note with the utmost confidence to the Judge. I have informed him that the Riedesels are most respectable people, most respectable, and that you, the bearer, have dined at my house. Mind, I've said nothing to our hostess. But—but you go to the Judge, the Judge. Then come back and tell me what he says."

Ahrens took the note. "This is most kind of you, Dr. Winthrop. I shall be—"

Winthrop waved an impatient hand. "I don't like crowded rooms! Now I want my carriage, my carriage."

A hard afternoon sun slanted down across the marshes of the Charles, shimmered on the snowy meadows, lighting up white-fringed boughs of the Brattle Street elms. Ahrens pulled his blue cape closer about his throat, turned in the saddle of his country-bred roan and looked back at Rentner, who sat ruddy and solid on a shambling bay. "How are things on Winter Hill these days?" His breath steamed in the still, cold air.

"About the same, sir. I was there yesterday. The barracks are better, though, and firewood seems easier to get. Corporal Zimmer has taught his bear-cub to carry a musket. Keisler lost his squirrels in the snowstorm last week and found them again in Lieutenant Asche's coat pocket. Schornstein's wife had twins. Two men from the Specht—"

Ahrens threw up his hand, laughing. "It's all the same, I see. What do you hear about the British?"

Rentner shook his head. "They're too surly, sir. They act as though they still owned the country. It doesn't sit well with the Yankees. And they fight with anyone who comes near them. They make bad prisoners."

"How about our men—the ones who have been working in the Yankee villages?"

"They get about, sir. But it's harder, now the snow's fallen, so they live in the villages where they work.

523

The Committee allows it. Then the ones who are left skate a lot on the little ponds at the foot of the hill. Hoogezeele of the Jaegers—he's from Zandaam, sir—he knows how to make skates out of wood. They're fine till they get wet."

Ahrens nodded. "Sounds better than the first weeks we were there. What was Hedwig doing on that ladder this morning?"

"She's made curtains for our windows. Did a bit of sewing for a Yankee woman and got paid in cloth. Then she found that the window-frame leaked and she was plugging it."

"Ought to be careful, climbing about on ladders like that."

Rentner shrugged his caped shoulders, tilted his cocked hat. "So I told her, sir. She's getting close to her time."

"I thought so. I told Siemann to stand by for a call."

"Thank you, sir. But Major Charteris—he says he'll send for a doctor he knows in Boston."

"Good for the Major. I don't like army doctors, either." He straightened in his saddle, watched the twin wreaths of steam that jetted from the roan's nostrils, then began to count the scattered houses. "Sewall—Carver—the little one with the roof falling in—Weld—ah—there it is!"

Off in the meadows on the left rose the graceful hip-roof and square chimneys of the Hemingway house. The sun touched a dozen windows, flamed them into molten gold, made a silver plume of the smoke that curled lazily up into the thin blue air. He pricked his horse into a trot, turned in the wide drive and reined up before the block. He tossed the reins to Rentner. "I shan't be long. Trot the beasts up and down if you get cold."

The prim-faced maid, eyes severe under her mob-cap, took the letter gingerly, then showed him into a small room off the hall. Ahrens stood before the little fire, warming his hands and looking about him. There was a small mahogany table standing on spindly, fluted legs, a tall secretary behind whose glass door old bindings were mellow and rich. The round mirror in its gilt frame reflected the portrait of a stern-faced man whose lace collar fell over a gleaming cuirass. He shook his head. "And this room is not more than two miles from those rat-ridden barracks on Winter Hill. Damn—hope that didn't tear!" He bent over to disentangle his long spur from the edge of a wide hooked-rug. Guiltily he scuffed his foot over the spot, turned to admire a pair of Dresden figurines on the mantel. Then he stared at the painting of a Flemish tavern scene that hung above them. "I'll bet a year's pay that's a Teniers! Teniers! I'd like to bring Anburey here. He'd know in a second."

He laid his hat and cape over a frail chair, then sat on a low, carved settee by the south window, looking at the picture. There was a light step in the hall, a smothered exclamation. A low voice stammered: "Kurt! Kurt Ahrens!"

He sprang to his feet as though a musket-ball had grazed him. From the narrow doorway, Judith Hunnewell stared at him, hands pressed to her cheeks. "Kurt!" she cried again. "They told me you were dead, dead on the Old Bay Path. They *all* told me!"

He darted to her, hands outstretched. "Judith, Judith! Where did you go? There *was* no road to the west."

Still staring, she laid trembling fingers in his. "Oh, Kurt, why did they tell me that?"

"Tell you what? Who told you?" His eyes were bright on hers.

"That you were dead. They all told me. Kurt—I'm a little dizzy." She crossed to the settee, sank down on it, her wide skirts of blue lute-string billowing about her.

He laughed happily. "But I'm not dead, Judith. I never was." He sat by her. "But you—I'm a little dizzy myself. You—in *this* house of all houses in Cambridge! I—I can't believe it. *Where* did you go, that first day of fighting? There was no road. I had rangers hunting for you and the old wagon, but never a word did I hear from you after the note that your old Indian brought me in the early morning by the river." His face suddenly darkened. "Judith—we've been here months. You couldn't have helped knowing that Burgoyne's army was in Cambridge. Surely, the least inquiry on your part would have told you I was here."

She looked up at him, eyes grave on his. "But I told you I thought you were dead. So many people told me. I only came to Cambridge last night. Had I known—I should have come at once, weeks ago. Do I need to tell you?"

He took her hand. It lay quietly in his. "I know, Judith. But—those weeks? Where were you? I'd—I'd given you up. But I did ask about you. I've seen your old house."

She sighed, then began to speak in a low voice. "It's a long story, Kurt. I did set out along that west road. It was early, but I saw a lot of your soldiers and English. They let me go by. I drove on through the woods and some men in fur caps stopped me. They were very rude and made me drive on to a big camp with trenches and cannon—lots of cannon. They called me a Tory spy."

Ahrens sat up. "You—a spy? Why, the—"

"Then I was sent to General Gates. I knew people who knew him, but he wouldn't believe me. I was sent back to Albany. They put me in jail."

Ahrens smothered an oath. "In jail?"

Eyes on the smooth floor she nodded. He noticed that the cheeks that had been so softly curved and sun-browned were thin and pale, that a splash of white swept up from her forehead across the high-piled masses of black hair. "In jail," she said again. "Oh, don't be sorry for me, Kurt. Things happen to people in war-time. I never saw anyone from Boston—only men from Pennsylvania and Virginia. They'd been told I was a spy, so of course to them I was. They weren't to blame. But—oh, those other women in the jail!" She shuddered.

526

He stroked her hand gently. "That's all over, Judith. How—but perhaps you'd rather not talk."

She shook her head. "I was being taken one day to Gates for more questioning. Ugh! Such a nasty, leering little man. But on the way I saw General Learned, a Massachusetts man. I called, almost screamed to him. Then I was taken back to jail, but the next day they released me. Gates wrote a most groveling apology and some of the officers' wives called on me at my inn. They were kind. Many of the officers called too. Colonel Morgan came. He wanted to apologize. It seems his men arrested me. His apology was such a contrast to Gates'. Did you ever hear of Colonel Morgan?"

Ahrens groaned. "Hear of him! Did he have that—that blasted turkey-call with him? It nearly drove us crazy! Then from Albany?"

"I joined a party of people Boston-bound. On the road we met stragglers, men in brass helmets, men in green coats. I asked them about you, but they couldn't tell me anything. Poor things—they were so dazed. Then we crossed the Connecticut and met more stragglers and at Worcester an artilleryman told me you'd—you'd died of fever on the road. I didn't believe him, but another man in Marlboro said the same thing and that a friend of his had seen you buried in a town called Palmer. Then I heard again from a farmer near Weston that a gunner officer had died in a neighbor's house. He described you perfectly. Oh—that road! From Worcester on I felt as though I were carrying a stone in my heart. I'd only seen you three times, Kurt, and I kept telling myself I was silly, but then I'd remember how I shot at you when you were so lost, and how you brought your men out into the woods at night when you thought the Indians were about and then how you saved me when those Wyandots attacked the wagon. I learned that the troops had gone to Cambridge, but I didn't care then. I went on to Marblehead to my uncle's; I was very sick, there. The doctor thought it was a flux of the lungs. I'd been wet and chilled on the road." She turned to him suddenly, buried her head against his shoulder. "Oh, Kurt, I *did* think you were dead. I can't quite believe yet that we're both here!"

He gave a low laugh, drew her close. "I wanted your head just there the moment I saw you in the doorway. I knew from the first that I loved you, my Judith, but I knew it all the more when I thought I'd lost you. Look at me, Judith, and say that you love me."

She slipped an arm about his neck, turned moist eyes up to his. "I told you in the hollow by the wagon, Kurt. I haven't changed. I love you."

He tightened his arm and she nestled into his shoulder. He said: "I did have a fever on me during the march, and they left me behind. At a town called Leicester an old man and his wife took care of me. He heard me calling your name in my fever and drove all over the country asking for a family of Hunnewell. They were good people. Pausch and Rentner left me there."

She raised her head. "Rentner? I was afraid to ask. In Albany I heard dreadful stories of the battles."

Ahrens laughed. "You're answered—he's—" He sat up, pulled out his watch. "Good God, I've left the poor devil walking the horses up and down in the cold. She sprang to her feet. "Kurt Ahrens! You didn't! Where is he?"

"At your very door, doubtless cursing me thoroughly. Here, I'll tell him to take the horses back to the Vassall house."

"You'll do no such thing! Our stable-man will take the horses and Rentner will sit by the kitchen fire." She slipped out into the broad hall, picked up a wrap from a carved chest and opened the heavy door. Ahrens, watching from the window, saw Rentner stiffen in the saddle, gape, then grin his tight grin as he touched his hat. Presently he dismounted and was lost to sight behind one of the pillars of the door. Ahrens fidgeted in the warm room. "Got enough to talk about," he grumbled. "Ah—there he goes." He heard the door slam,

528

then Judith's voice calling: "Huldah! Huldah! Please have tea ready in the kitchen!"

He stepped back to the fireplace, leaned on the mantel and stared at the leaping flames. "Lord above, I'm going daft with all this. Here she was with her head on my shoulder. But—maybe it's the shock of seeing me suddenly—that and gratitude for the time with the Wyandots."

High heels clicked on the smooth floor. Ahrens looked up, suddenly felt his lips dry, his hands moist. "Judith—" he began. She came to him, eyes bright and hands seeking his.

"Yes, Kurt."

"Why—Judith, you—I suppose you know you're going to marry me."

She laughed softly, flicking at a gilt button on his waistcoat. Then she looked up. "I suppose I am, Kurt." The smile faded from her lips. Gently she drew his head down, kissed him, slipped her arms about his wide shoulders.

In a wild burst of exultation he swept her up in his arms. "You are, Judith, you are! Say that again! You are!" He picked her up bodily, carried her to the settee. "Now, sit so. Put your head back where it was." He bent over her. The room grew very still.

The fire snapped and crackled on the hearth. A short log burned through, thudded softly into feathery ashes, then snapped like a pistol and drove a spark into the hem of Judith's dress. Ahrens leaned over, flicked it away. "You know, Judith," he went on, "it won't be an easy life—for a while. You're joining the Convention Troops. No one knows what is in store for them. We may be held as prisoners until the end of the war; we may be sent off anywhere."

She reached up, laid soft fingers on his cheek. "Nothing will be hard, Kurt. Once—long ago, I was bold enough to think of a scene like this. Just you and me and a fire and planning. And then the thought of giving

529

up America, burying myself in Europe—even with you—just seemed impossible."

He shook her gently by the shoulder. "Europe? Europe? Who said anything about Europe? Judith, my own, I'm never going back to Europe. Let the debts eat up the estates—they're no good to me. I've had good schools and good tutors, but my education never began till I crossed the Atlantic. You've started me, you. and Mr. Conant and Carter and General Heath and Dr. Winthrop and a hundred others that I'll tell you about some day." He kissed her. "Europe? Never!"

She ran her fingers through his hair. "I'd go if you wanted it, Kurt. I don't care where you are or how we live. I'd go. But oh—" her arms tightened about his neck—"I'm so happy that it's to be America. Kurt, you're right. You're ready to live here. Most people aren't—they aren't fit to, yet. It demands a lot, but it will give more. When I came down the stairs this afternoon and saw you there in your blue and red—"

Ahrens laid a hand over her lips. "Do you know, I forgot to ask my very first question? How did you come to be in this house?"

She opened her eyes wide. "Why, Kurt, I did tell you. It's my uncle's. I stayed in his other house in Marblehead. He's poorly and wants to go there to live, so I came down to get him, to save my aunt the trip. Kurt—shall we live in Cambridge or Marblehead?"

"Cambridge or Marblehead? Neither. Do you know what we're going to do?" He took her face in his hands. "We're going back to the round hill beyond Fort Anne. We're going to bring life to it again."

Her eyes sparkled. "Kurt—you don't mean it! The round hill! Oh, there are dozens of people ready to go as soon as things are quiet and we'll need dozens more." She gripped his red lapel. "Oh, what we'll do there! Kurt!" She threw her arms about him.

"Do that again," he laughed quietly. "Yes, the round hill and, Judith, we'll take Rentner and Hedwig and the
530

little Rentner-to-be. And a lot of the men want to stay in America and we'll pick the best. Can you imagine what a life like that will mean to them?"

She nodded. "And we'll not break up over the way things are. We'll try to live as people ought to live. But we—we won't try to defy the elements."

"Free men on free lands! What a place we'll make of that! You and I and the others. But just you and I at first. Kiss me, Judith. I'm a very, very lucky man."

The fire snapped and crackled away, the room grew dimmer and dimmer. Gently he raised her round chin, looked into her eyes. "You've grown very silent, my Judith."

She gave a low laugh. "I was just thinking. We'll build our cabin on that level spot on the south slope. Then we'll have a road down to Wood Creek, and a reservoir on the summit by the big rocks and lots of cattle on the low lands, and then we'll turn the cabin into a house and the house into a mansion. And we'll get a printing-press from Albany and looms and build a bindery. And we'll have streets like Brattle Street all over the hill and then the second year—"

He smiled down at her. "And then—? The second year? Aren't you going a bit fast?"

She wrinkled her nose at him. "Oh, you've no imagination, no fancy. First a cabin, then a village, then a town—"

He drew her to him, kissed her gently. "But, my own, you must go a little slowly for me. You see, I'm a moderate man."

NOVEMBER, 1778. For the second time, weary columns of red and blue crept across Massachusetts. Now they headed west, following the old trails that led down to New York, across New Jersey, Pennsylvania to a desolate waste near Charlottesville in Virginia. As the theater of war shifted to the south, the Charlottesville cantonments were broken up and blue jackets and red scattered to Winchester in the Shenandoah, to Frederick in Maryland and to Lancaster in Pennsylvania. "The public faith was broke" and the Convention Troops were doomed to rot, in defiance of the Convention, until the thudding guns about Yorktown were stilled. In England, Gentleman Johnny Burgoyne, on parole, sought audience with the King, but was turned away. He demanded a trial, which was refused him, and Germaine shrugged away his demands that something be done for the men who had faced Yankee bullets in the echoing clearings about Freeman's Farm.

Pinnacle Books proudly presents

A BICENTENNIAL CLASSICS SERIES

Starting with four great American historical novels by Bruce Lancaster, one of America's most distinguished historians.

———TRUMPET TO ARMS An exceptionally crafted romance spun beautifully amidst the fury of the American Revolution. (PB-887, 1.75)
"Explosive in style . . . *Trumpet to Arms* is always easy to read and strikes a note as stirring as a call to battle."
—*The Boston Globe*

———THE SECRET ROAD A fascinating, yet little known account of the exploits of Washington's Secret Service. A gripping story of America's first espionage unit. (PB-889, 1.75)
"A veteran craftsman at the top of his form."
—*The New York Times*

———PHANTOM FORTRESS A masterful treatment of the career of General Francis Marion, known to history as "The Swamp Fox." (PB-905, 1.75)
"History that is good and galloping, for competent scholarship underlies the romantic story."
—*New York Herald Tribune*

———BLIND JOURNEY An absorbing tale of romance and adventure that moves from 18th-century France and its grandeur to the carnage of revolutionary America. A story no one should miss. (PB-915, 1.75)
"Romance, adventure . . . full pulsing life. Bruce Lancaster's best."
—*The Boston Herald*

Check which books you want. If you can't find any of these books at your local bookstore, simply send the cover price plus 25¢ per book for postage and handling to us and we'll mail you your book(s).

PINNACLE BOOKS
275 Madison Avenue, New York, New York 10016